Typewriter Pub, an imprint of Blvnp Incorporated
A Nevada Corporation
1887 Whitney Mesa DR #2002
Henderson, NV 89014
www.typewriterpub.com/info@typewriterpub.com

ISBN: **978-1-64434-127-8**

DISCLAIMER
This book is a work of fiction. The characters, incidents, and dialogue
are drawn from the author's imagination and are not to be construed as
real. While references might be made to actual historical events or
existing locations, the names, characters, places, and incidents are either
products of the author's imagination or are used fictitiously, and any
resemblance to actual persons living or dead, business establishments,
events or locales is entirely coincidental.

LUPUS DEUS

SOPHIA MOORE

My mother, my best friend and the readers
for making me the writer that I am.

PROLOGUE

The gods anxiously looked down at their creation—who had lost control of himself for decades, and now that he had changed, he was becoming nothing but trouble. He was no longer known as the "Messenger of the gods" but a god, and had won the title fair and square. He showed those who stood against him that he was not one to shy away from bloodshed for those accused of disloyalty.

He was vicious. The gods watched him as he slaughtered his victims who were nothing to him but a bunch of toys to play with, making sure to leave a horrible mess even for those foul enough to appreciate a killing spree.

He was seductive. His appearance far from ugly, as was expected in light of his reputation, equaled those of the male gods in the room. And he knew it so well.

He was ruthless. As they kept watching him, they became horrified at the rate his power grew each day, so much so that his power was becoming too much even for the gods to handle. They feared he would use it against them.

It wasn't a secret that they couldn't have been more neglectful and devious to him as a boy. They took him from his home when they saw he was useful, and turned him into what he had become. The gods sat in silence around the glass-like table with distant eyes. Finally, one spoke—Alstha, the goddess of war and knowledge.

"Something must be done immediately! He is murdering hundreds of innocent lives by the minute!" she exclaimed outraged.

"We cannot do a thing. We made sure of that when we made him indestructible," Eccasto, the god of intelligence and instinct, spoke regretfully.

"And whose bright idea was that?! We've all seen what the boy can do. I swear, something terrible will happen to us if we do not find a way to stop him," Fate spoke.

The gods froze as the latter rarely spoke. His words were like the law and if he was threatened for their future, then this could mean far worse than they thought.

The boy trained with Alstha for war and knowledge; Eccasto, for discernment; Fate, for intelligence and preparedness.

He had been trained by the gods, except for one who they thought he would not need in his missions—Luna, or as people called her, Mother Luna. All eyes turned to her as she cocked her brow in question.

"What?" Her melodic voice echoed through the vast room.

"You're the only one with powers he wasn't trained with," Fate spoke with caution yet mirth.

"And?" she questioned. The gods looked at Fate curiously.

"Mother Luna, what is the one thing you give your children that none of us can give?" he asked, standing from his chair and making his way to her.

"A mate," she answered proudly.

The other gods gasped in surprise at what Fate was planning of. Fate tsk-tsked, took her hand, and kissed it softly.

"I can give a lover and take one away," Fate said.

She snatched her hand back forcefully and her beautiful features were marred by an animalistic expression. Her lips parted, her teeth bared, and her angry eyes narrowed in warning.

"Be calm, Mother Moon. I will not harm any of your . . . innocent children." She calmed herself slowly, but the wild look in her eyes remained.

"Hope. You give your children hope. Hope for having someone to cherish, to trust, and to love."

"Yes I do. But what of it?" She sounded exasperated, echoing the thoughts of every other god in the room.

"The boy has nobody to love. No family and no one to call his own. Look at him. He comes and goes as he pleases. He's free, too free."

It finally dawned on them and they agreed, but they didn't fully grasp the end game yet.

"Send him a warrior! She will tame his heart!" Alstha yelled with glee.

"No, send him a heartless girl. He will pin for her affection, and his instincts will let him do nothing more dangerous!" Eccasto said.

The other gods yelled out their thoughts and opinions about who she should be and why, but Fate raised his hand and shut them up.

"No." The gods looked on at him flabbergasted, not comprehending how Fate could not see the brilliance of their ideas.

"So, who shall I mate him to, Fate?" Luna asked with excitement in her eyes. Everyone knew she loved matching couples together, even the most impossible pairs.

2

"She will be gentle like the autumn breeze, catching him off guard. This will fuel his desire to know her," Fate said, giving Eccasto a pointed look.

"But, she will also be stubborn and defend herself against him with bravery unlike anything he has ever known. She will get him off his high horse and let his feet touch ground once more to teach him humility." Fate looked at Alstha.

"She will be be beautiful, of course, but not the kind of beauty he's accustomed himself with. This will open his eyes to see people for who they are and not for how they look. She will bring him peace and joy. He will hope for things he thought he would never want. She will tame his whole being: power, spirit, soul, and heart."

The room was silent until one of them spoke.

"Will she be his undoing?"

"Can you do it, Mother Luna?" Fate asked, challenging her.

She replied with a smirk. She lifted her hands from the table. Mist surrounded them. The sun suddenly set, and the moon rose to the clouds. Luna chanted under her breath like usual, but this time everyone watched closely, knowing that their future was ironically at stake. For once, Luna did something different.

She brought her wrist to her mouth and bit it, allowing the blood to flow and drop generously before the wound sealed. Fate's eyes narrowed.

The blood slowly began to take solid form, then blue blood appeared, making the others hiss out.

"It's the boy's blood!"

"What are you doing?!" Fate shouted, alarmed by the gleam in her wild eyes.

Luna continued to chant, ignoring the other gods. Both of their blood began to merge. Luna's blood took on a purple hint right before touching the boy's. The drops of blood clashed for a moment before becoming one and vanishing into thin air. Luna tilted her head to the side before blinking.

The gods glared at her.

"What did you do?" Repeated Fate, an edge to his tone .

Luna gave him a wide smile and said, "Behold! The birth of Vivian Grey."

CHAPTER I

"He's looking at us."

"I know."

"I don't like him looking at us." I snorted at my wolf.

"And what do you want me to do about it?"

"Claw his eyes out."

I rolled my eyes at my wolf. My hands gripped the armrests tightly as we passed another turbulence., and my fingers were pale from exerting too much force. I had no problem flying but since my wolf hated being off the ground, it was extremely easy to piss her off. Being connected to each other meant that I was well in tune with her. She'd been eyeing passengers in the plane ever since we got on and hadn't stopped trying to convince me to claw at anyone's face.

Calm down, we've only got a few minutes left before we can get out of this plane. I'm not going to claw his eyes out just because he's looking at us.

I could feel her mirth and excitement at the concept of solid ground. She settled down without another word. I opened the blinds from the window next to me, and tried to make something out of the view, but we were still too high off ground. My thoughts went back to the reason behind my trip.

A few years back, werewolf territories were being trespassed by wolves from an unknown pack. It wasn't until these wolves began attacking and taking members when the alphas realized that the invasion wasn't random. Packs were being hunted down and scavenged one at a time, starting from one side of the world to the other. Whoever led the attack was mysterious. At first, fingers were pointed at one another for someone to be blamed, but soon it was discerned that no one was safe.

The wolves moved faster than light and were stronger than alphas. They would linger and wait for an order before attacking. The packs prepared as much as they could, but they would always end up defeated. What was the reason behind these assaults? That was the million-dollar question.

These wolves appeared out of nowhere and disappear as they pleased. They took everything they wanted, and attacked like a trained hunting pack, yet they seemed to be just ordinary members. Who was in charge of them? We suspected that no one wanted to lay their cards on the table, and risk their heads if he heard.

My pack seemed to be next on the hit list. My parents decided to send me over to my cousin Lily, who was from the Cusco pack. A lot of members in the pack had done the same to their daughters, perceiving that most of those who were taken were young women. Surprisingly, some of those who had been abducted returned unharmed and were unaware of their whereabouts.

My parents were supposed to be with me but my mom got sick. Dad, being the overprotective mate that he is, locked her in the room after cleaning the house excessively one day, and said he wasn't going to risk her getting worse, even though she was barely sniffing. She bared her teeth at him for that. Dad wasn't worried that they would try to take Mom. She was mated after all, and older than the girls who were usually taken.

Being away from my parents made me anxious, but I knew that they could take care of themselves. When this whole mess was over, I would be reunited with them back home in no time. Who was I anyway? I'd probably just get returned. One thing is certain: whoever was behind this mayhem wasn't joking around.They wanted something, and by the way things were leading up, they seem to be getting it.

~ • ~

A brown-haired woman was running at me with open arms. I wasn't the type to avoid physical contact, but when you were in a plane sitting for such long hours, you would tend to feel gross and unhygienic. Which was me at the moment.

"Hey Lily," I said as I hugged her, aware that I was somewhat trying to keep distance but because she was squeezing me so hard, it was unavoidable.

"Wow, you've gotten big since I've seen you," she exclaimed, surprised. *Because that's something every girl would want to hear.* I rolled my eyes at the thought. Lily was nine years older than me. She had manageable long brown locks that fell in soft waves around her oval-shaped face. Her sharp high brows gave off the impression that she was easily surprised, and her small lashes framed her dark brown eyes. Additionally, the crinkled lines on the corner of her eyes made her look younger, but her filled-in cheeks were not helping. At five foot five, she was an energetic person for someone at the age of twenty-seven.

"Gee, thanks. And yes I'm fine after having to endure such a long flight," I responded sarcastically. She shot me an apologetic look before grabbing one of my bags.

"You know what I mean Vivian. I wasn't calling you fat. I was just saying that you seem to have grown taller. No need to rip my throat out," she said defensively, placing her free hand in front of her throat as if to protect it. I rolled my eyes at her theatrics. We exited the airport and made our way to her car where we placed my bags in. Lily got in the car and began to drive us towards our destination.

"You got your pack papers, right kid?" I nodded in response as she hummed and continued to drive in calm silence. She glanced over at me many times throughout the ride until she finally said what was on her mind.

"Now, don't be alarmed but there's a bit more security around Cusco's pack land. I'm not allowed to say the reason why, but don't worry about it, just listen and stick to the rules." This was new but not that alarming. I looked at her, but didn't ask. I was doubtful that this was their way of staying on guard for the attacks.

Every wolf knew better than to try to get information about a different pack; it was seen as suspicious, and could start more problems than it was worth. When on another pack's land, the foreign visitor had to bring their ID, show their pack birthmark, and a signed document from someone of high rank allowing the visit, not to mention obey any rules and regulations given. Alphas took trespassing and security seriously nowadays.

Lily drove into a path in the forest that was easy to navigate only for those who were familiar with the way. The deeper we got into the forest, the calmer my wolf became. The scenery was different, but similar to what she knew. Around ten minutes after, we passed a sign that read in big bold letters:

Private Property. Do Not Pass. Will Be Shot on Sight.

To any human, that would have been sufficient enough to stop them, but most wolves knew that it was just a warning to humans. Werewolves, if they chose to pass, would be stopped before they were even a mile close to official pack grounds. As if to show me I was correct, two large men with weapons stepped out of nowhere a few feet away before the car.

Lily slowed down to a stop before them and rolled down the windows. One walked slowly to the car while the other stood in front with eyes steady on me and hand positioned to pull his gun out in case I were to make one wrong move, which was startling given that I have visited in the past.

"Lillian Grey, born on Cusco soil and still a member," Lily stated seriously. The man next to her window looked at us before taking a deep breath and inhaling to take in our scents. Lily had the scent of the lands, while I probably reeked of humans.

6

"What about her?" he asked with a gruff and cautious voice. I took that as my cue.

"Vivian Grey, born on Defluo soil and still a member. Granted permission for a visit regarding family matters. Documents in check," I said as professionally as I could with my heart beating loudly in my chest and hands shaking a little. I had been doing this many times but it was still a bit nerve-wracking.

"Papers, mark, and ID."

Nodding, I took my papers out from my bag, fished for my wallet, and took out my ID. I gave them to him. He read them over and then looked back and forth between the ID and me as if I had changed in the last two years I took it. He handed them back to me. I still had brown eyes with a bit of baby fat on me and brown hair cut to the shoulders.

"Mark?" he asked. I reached for the zipper of my hood, and unzipped it, pulling the left collar of my shirt down to show my mark. My pack's mark was just like the others: three slashes of claws but a line going through the middle of it, and two perfect circles underneath. I pulled my collar back up, but left the hood unzipped.

His expression turned blank for a moment and then he nodded at the guy in front, giving us the clear. Lily began to move forward as soon as the other man moved from in front of us. This happened two times more before we were allowed to get in and pass a big gate that protected the pack. Lily was right. The security was undeniably tedious.

While most believed that werewolves guarded pack land in wolf form, they only do that inside the gate's perimeter. A pack's main concern was being seen by humans, thus, armed werewolves in human form.

"Okay, now we can start the fun!" Lily exclaimed, breaking me out of my thoughts.

"Can I shower, and . . . I don't know, maybe . . . eat?" I asked her in an over exasperated tone, and she rolled her eyes.

"Okay, okay. I'll go feed you before you call your mom and tell her I have not been taking care of you for the first few hours. She'd skin me alive," she said jokingly, I think.

When we pulled up to her house and she got me settled in, I took a much-needed shower and felt the results immediately. I was no longer ill-tempered. I took in my appearance before I went down. My short straight cut auburn hair fell right below my collarbone. My pale skin was slightly flushed from the heated water, and my large brown doe-like eyes framed my face with high arched eyebrows that made it seem as if I was a know-it-all.

My small pointed nose made my chubby cheeks look childish on a square face. I wasn't fat or fit, but I was okay with that. My lips unconsciously turned up at the corners. I skipped down the stairs and into the kitchen with a smile on my face. Lily looked at me suspiciously, but I just smile back at her.

"What did you break?" She accused, putting down the sandwich she was making to cross her arms over her chest. I dropped my jaw and widened my eyes pretending to be hurt.

"What? I'm offended, Lily. I would never break anything in your house," I said, putting a hand over my heart. I knew it was utter bullshit because a few years back, I had broken her living room chair after sitting on it. To this day, I still say it was because it was an old chair, and not that I was heavy at all. The corners of her lips twitched letting me know that she was probably thinking about that too. She just shook her head at me and placed a plate in front of me before taking a chair and settling on it herself.

"So how have you been, kid?" she asked.

"We're all good. A bit worried, but good. How about you?" I answered, picking up the sandwich and took a bite out of it while she talked to me.

"I've been good here. Staying out of trouble. But between you and me," she whispered as if someone was listening, "I sneak out every Friday to head to the library."

I choked on my sandwich.

"B-but you live alone, there's no need to sneak out." I looked at her incredulously.

"I know." She smirked at me. It took me a while to figure out she was joking.

"I like to live wild." She exaggerated, moving her arms up. I shook my head at my crazy cousin. She was an odd one.

We spent the whole two hours catching up, but after awhile, I began to feel the exhaustion creeping in and was itching to have some quiet time.

"I'm gonna go to bed. The earlier I go to sleep, the more time we'll have tomorrow," I blurted out quickly, already making my way out of the chair and up the stairs.

"All right. We'll go for a run tomorrow if you want." She waved me off, standing, and stretching her arms over her head.

"Yes! My wolf needs it. Good night, Lily." I smiled at her.

"Night."

I hated jet lag but thankfully, I finally fell asleep two hours after. My eyes closed slowly as darkness crept in, taking me to dreamland.

8

That, however, didn't last long because a loud screeching sound suddenly blasted in the air, startling me from my sleep. A few seconds later, screaming followed. I wiped my eyes furiously, trying to wake myself up. At first I thought I was seeing things, but then I noticed a red light flashing outside the house along with a blaring noise. Loud stomps made their way to my room scaring me, and my wolf began to growl in my head anxiously.

When my door busted open, I stopped mid-scream realizing it was Lily, panting and pale. Her brown hair was frizzy on one side, her eyes were bright and wild with fear and panic. I leaped out of bed and moved towards her. When I got closer, she suddenly came forward and gripped my shoulders, trying to open her mouth to say something. At the same time, a booming voice was heard from a megaphone.

"Code Red: All women and children, make your way to the safe bunker. We are under attack. I repeat, go to the bunker. We are under attack."

It took us a while to realize what was said.

"We have to go now!" she said.

I looked at Lily, who was trembling with fear. Why was the pack under attack? Could it be . . . And why did it have to be when I was sleeping?!

She grabbed my hand and pulled me down the stairs. She pulled the door open and peeked out. My heart was beating like a hummingbird's wings. My breath was loud. A thin layer of cold sweat had begun to form at the back of my neck. We looked around and saw people in sweatpants and baggy shirts running around in fear in different directions.

"Let's go," Lily said before taking off. I run after her, not wanting to be left behind. I sped up when I heard bullets going off in the distance and loud snarls. My blood pumped faster in my veins, and my body was heating up with the sudden workout that I had to remind myself to keep my cool.

Keep calm. People do stupid mistakes when they panic, and trip.

"What's going on Lily? What—" I stopped, crashing into her back. She turned to look at me as if words were rushing out of her mouth.

"Your parents didn't know this because if they had, they wouldn't have sent you here. Shit! If we make it, they're gonna kill me. I'm sorry, I shouldn't have let you come. My pack got a warning that we were next, but it was out of their pattern so we didn't believe it could be true. Oh man, this is messed up!" She looked around nervously as she spoke. The alarm had stopped, but the flashing red light and gunshots were still dying out.

9

"Warning, what? When?!" I shouted at her. I felt like I couldn't breathe no matter how many times I tried. It seemed like the air wouldn't make its way into my lungs. I was too young to have a panic attack!

"I'll explain later, but we have to go to the bunker. Come on, stay close!" We ran into the part of the forest everyone else seemed to be headed towards. I didn't like this, not a bit, and I felt like I was running around blindly. This wasn't my pack. I didn't know much about this land, and if I did, I would have chosen to get away from danger, and would not draw myself closer to it. I scowled into the darkness we were headed towards.

As we ran away, the sound of fighting and shots faded, letting me know we were safe, but I felt uneasy knowing people were still in danger. When a large building came into view, I could see women and children pushing their way into the property—everyone was trying to get in. When Lily and I tried to get in, we were shoved around and got separated.

"Lily?" I said loudly when I couldn't see her. Everyone was crying and talking at the same time. "*Lily?!*" I cried out louder. I may not have been as close to Lily, but she was family and the only person I have. I felt someone grasp onto my left hand and I spun around relieved, seeing Lily next to me.

"Oh, thank fuck!" I exclaimed.

"Sorry, I was swept away at the door." She hurriedly walked us over to a wall and slid down. I followed suit despite my hurting legs. My mind had been demanding for an answer, and my wolf agreed with me.

"What's going on, Lily?" She looked up at me, holding back a sob. My jaw clenched as tears fell down my cheeks. I chose to suppress my feelings and put my hand on her shoulder, hoping to calm her though I wasn't sure I was helping. She took a deep breath for a moment and then closed her eyes, squeezing them shut.

"Tell me what's going on? What kind of warning did your pack get? Who's attacking?" *And why the fuck did you let me come here if your pack is in danger?* I didn't say the last one out loud, but my wolf's annoyance was very much fueling my own. She took in a shaky breath, but didn't open her eyes.

"I can't tell you everything because I'm bound by my alpha, but what I can tell you is that *he* wants something, someone. I don't know! My alpha got a letter a few months ago saying we were next but it didn't fit the pattern so he paid it no mind; he said we would be safe. But *he* got offended. *He* didn't like it. We affronted *him*, insulted *him*, we were tactless. And now we're going to pay. Alpha thought *he* was a myth, a fraud. Alpha was cocky. Alpha was wrong," she whispered, seemingly more to herself than to me. It scared me to see Lily act this way, her

10

speech pattern almost childlike and choppy. But that wasn't what concerned me.

"Who is it, Lily? Who did . . . Alpha disrespect?" I asked, not knowing how to phrase my question better. She looked up at me with her blank large brown eyes.

"Lupus Deus."

CHAPTER 2

Nightmares. Bad dreams. Fear. It doesn't matter what it was called; everyone had one. Sometimes it was something that would slither its way into your life like an undeniable desire.

Inevitable. Unauthorized. Unwanted.

It was that lingering thought of negativity that would follow you from reality into your dreams. It would sink its teeth into your hopes and poison all the goodness in your life until you realize that it was all a lie or a myth. Sometimes ignorance is bliss.

As children of the moon, we were surrounded by humans who believed we were evil, but we ignored them. We were born different, and we couldn't change based on their opinions.

However, even monsters had fears of imaginary creatures in the closet or under the bed—Lupus Deus was at the top of that list.

A myth, legend, or a haunting; whatever you call it. A story; that's what he would always be.

He's who kids were told to look out for, lurking in the woods at night.

He's who women were warned to stay away from.

He's the enemy men go to battle against.

He's the feared shadow looming over your house.

He's the god who roams, darkness and evil monsters following in his wake.

He's the savage that reminds us to be in control of our wolves.

The alpha of all alphas—The wolf god.

As I looked at Lily, I felt an icy chill cover my arms, giving me goosebumps—which shouldn't have been possible with all of the warm bodies crowded together in the bunker. My chest suddenly felt hollow and cold, and my body felt numb.

Women were clutching on to their children, whispering words into their ears to calm them, yet their eyes looked horrified. Others were on their knees praying for forgiveness and for the lives of those in and outside the building. Older women were huddled together gazing at the entrance with hope on their faces.

The Lupus Deus, I repeated in my head. My wolf was silent, but I could still feel her presence, prepared.

The Lupus Deus.

The god controlled by hatred, whose thirst for violence and blood was likened to the human body's need for oxygen. The god who was sent once every hundred of years as a warning from the gods above. The god who wasn't born a god, but a man clothed with mystery and a threat to everyone—who even at the mere mention of his name, every pack avoided like the plague, whose presence made wolves fall to their knees in submission instilling in their minds that no one was above him—he was the law.

He was always lurking in the shadows, watching for those who disobeyed his rules. He came and went like a ghost, ready to kill anyone who stood in his way. The merciless punisher; anyone who opposed him faced a vicious animal.

He was compared to Voldemort in Harry Potter—*he who shall not be named* or whatever. We all knew it was him behind the attacks, but we could only hope that it wasn't. After all, hadn't we convinced ourselves that fear was just a product of our creative minds?

I looked over at Lily, who was rocking back and forth. Could she be wrong and misinformed? *I pray she is wrong!*

I felt relieved at the thought of my cousin acting weird. I had accepted that she might have been given the wrong information. Lily was so wrapped up in her thoughts that she didn't even look up. I walked up to an older looking woman with gray hair and dark brown eyes. She seemed a little out of it, but other than that, she looked fine and responsive.

"Excuse me?" I asked, making her jump in fright, and I felt guilty.

"O-oh y-yes?" She stuttered, intertwining her hands nervously.

"Do you know what's going on?" I asked softly, trying to put her at ease with talking to a stranger.

"Oh, it's horrible! I was just sitting there watching the TV series Supernatural and then the alarms went off! It's so bad, I thought Alpha Klein said we had a month to prepare before an attack. "

"Now what—" I interrupted.

"Who's attacking?" I asked as naturally as I could.

She paled at the question, and took in a deep breath. Her eyes flicked to the side twice before whispering in a small voice, "Lupus Deus."

"I'm sorry, what was that?" I asked through clenched teeth. I could feel fear starting to creep into my veins.

"Lup—" Her mouth hung open and her eyes went wide as if seeing a ghost. I looked at her in confusion. What was she doing?

13

She's being summoned through a mind-link, my wolf said. She hated being clueless as much as I did.

The woman turned her head over to the left, looking at something. I noticed how quiet it had become. Suddenly, in the direction everyone was looking at, a door—which wasn't the entrance—opened, releasing a sliver of white light. Something was happening because they all shuffled out the door. Was it over? Were we allowed to leave? If we were, why couldn't we use the same door we came in through?

Lily appeared out of nowhere, eyes wide and full of cautious. I opened my mouth to ask her what was going on, but she shook her head violently from side to side. She lifted her finger to her lips to hush me and then tapped her ears. Hearing. . . shushing. . . door opening and people leaving quietly.

Oh my god. Something was happening. Something bad. And whoever or whatever was going on was just around the territory. This must be an escape panel. We were fleeing.

I probably looked like a ghost as my face turned pale. I was hesitant to leave, but Lily grabbed my arm and we shuffled over to the exit doors. We entered a sort of an underground tunnel with smooth wide walls, as darkness surrounded us from all angles. Calling on my wolf's eyesight didn't even help; my eyes were desperately looking for light. Although we were trying to be as discreet as possible, our footsteps against the concrete floors could still be heard as well as our pounding hearts, and the tears falling out of fear rose into the air. I wanted to push us forward to the front where the luna was leading us, and be the first to get out of this dark hell of never-ending turns and walls, but I could barely make out the back of people's heads.

I could feel Lily next to me and was focused on not losing her. It was unclear where we were heading to. We were just following the crowd blindly, hoping to find our way out. The journey seemed to go on forever until we finally came to a halt when a cluster in front of us stopped moving forward, and the strong but silvery voice of a woman spoke out. From the sound of her commanding voice, it had to be the luna.

"I will be dividing you into groups. I'm going to open the door, and as soon as I tell you to go, I want you to run into the woods as fast as you can, shift, and make your way into the Zauks pack." Everyone was surprised and murmurs could be heard.

"Yes I know," she said before taking a shuddering breath, though I couldn't see her face. "I have to stay here. This is a direct command from your luna. Get out of here, and do not look back if you get the chance."

The women and children were silent at the luna's command. Her voice was more powerful than an alpha's in extreme situations.

14

I felt Lily's iron grip on my arm. I held my breath as they all responded in unison, anguish lacing their voices.

"Yes, Luna Emma," they answered solemnly.

"Take care. Are you ready?" Her loud voice echoed through the tunnels, making most of us wince, and then we covered our eyes as light slowly seeped through.

I watched as large groups of women and their children were ushered off into the night, waiting until we saw them make it to what seemed like the borders of the territory. I wonder if this was a backup plan for them—to seek another pack for security. Who was to say they wouldn't be attacked?

When the group before us made it to the edge, our group was pushed forward with Lily and me in the middle. We could barely see the direction we were heading, but that didn't mean we couldn't run as fast as those ahead of us. A woman next to me clutched on to her children and by the look in her eyes, was determined to do whatever it took to save her children. I caught a glimpse of the sight waiting outside and was frightened, but my fearless wolf took over.

At the end of the tunnel was a large and peaceful green meadow in the coldness of the night. We had to pass by it to get into a forest I presumed led to Zauks Pack. I didn't realize why it took so long for the she-wolves to get to the border until I realized we were basically like sheep in an open, vacant land waiting for the wolves to pounce. We were open targets and that wasn't a comforting thought.

"One." I snapped my head over to the golden-haired woman who was counting. She must be the luna.

"Two." All the women adjusted themselves for the run, getting ready. I allowed my wolf to push forward.

My stance went from slumped to prepared and confident. My wolf raised our body to stand on the tips of our toes to run. Our abdominal muscles were clenching with slow breathing as adrenaline pumped through my body at an alarming rate.

"Three." Everybody took off running into the clearing.

We shot off like a bullet, running for our lives. Although agility was a wolf's nature, knowing that our lives were in danger doubled our speed. I smiled sensing victory as we got closer to the edge of the forest—but I was wrong.

Suddenly, large wolves of all shapes and sizes shot into the clearing, forming a large wall in front of us, snarling and snapping. I dug my heels into the ground and skidded to a stop, almost falling over my feet at the sudden jerk. My eyes widened at the sight before me.

Whimpers and shrieks could be heard at the sight of the army before us. There could have been twenty-five of them. I heard the sound

15

of a loud click behind me. I glanced quickly behind my shoulder to see that the door was closed.

The luna had closed the door to the tunnel.

My wolf snarled out loud at the betrayal and situation we were put in. My head turned back to face the threat before us. Anger filled me to the core, pushing the fear of uncertainty away. I would rather die fighting before they could take me. I was angered by the coward who called himself "a god" but could not show his face.

The she-wolves began to retreat together, huddling with their whimpering pups. Our eyes were fixed solely on the wolves who stood between us and our freedom. It was evident that we were outnumbered, but we were not going to surrender. We growled when four large wolves stepped forward breaking the wall they had in front of us. They would surely regret it if they got any closer.

The wolves in front of us were larger than normal werewolves, including the warriors. They were covered in blood. Others had a few chunks of meat torn off of them, but they didn't seem to mind it. One thing was certain: they all had the same color in their eyes. No matter what the stories said, wolf's color eyes wouldn't change once turned, no. Eyes stayed the same color as the human eyes, but these wolves all had the same eye color.

Silver. Every single pair of eyes trained on us were the same cool shade of silver; it was unnerving. I could feel my wolf pushing for release, urging me to do something, anything but stand still. It was deathly still in the meadow. The she-wolves not knowing how to react other than growling in warning and the enemy wolves staying still but not allowing us to move forward. What are they waiting for?

Questions just kept ringing through my head. I snapped out of my thoughts when the silhouette of a tall muscular man showed up, and as he stepped away from the shadow of the trees, his face became clearer. He had matted, curly dark hair. Defined features rested on his oval face. He had bushy eyebrows furrowed above a pair of catlike green eyes and naturally dark lips, giving off a smirk. The man was perfectly handsome, if it wasn't for his threatening expression.

The wolves in front of us made way for the man to pass. His hands were behind his back; his stride was long and quick. He paused for a moment, making us shift from foot to foot with unease. He scanned everyone of us with his alert green eyes. I could see how strong he looked. Was he the leader? I didn't feel the tremendous power that was spoken of so he couldn't be the wolf god, could he? He lifted his head a little higher and pushed his chest forward before booming out, "Most of you won't remember this, but I'll humor you. No, we won't kill your children. They're of no use to us." The she-wolves released a sigh of relief.

16

"We would rather do this quickly, so if you please." He motioned for us to come forward.

Does this crazy bitch really think we will obey them?

The she-wolves decided on their own. Some took a step backwards. Some made a run for it, only to be pursued by some of our captors. A handful of us were left in the same spot. I grabbed Lily before she could run. Wolves liked to chase and if we were caught, who knew what those monsters would do to us? I looked around for a clue on what to do. Run or fight? I clenched my fists and shifted back and forth between feet. As I looked at the man, his eyes were on me, and my body froze under the scrutiny of those narrowed green slits. He looked at Lily, then to me alternately with a sly and mischievous expression on his face that alarmed me.

"You two, come here," he demanded. Lily and I tensed up, then looked at each other.

"Fuck you," we responded at the same time. I wanted to add *bitch,* but I wasn't going to add fuel to the fire. His expression didn't change, but the wolves behind him snarled at us. I growled back but apparently the remaining she-wolves didn't appreciate our tone either because they backed up, leaving Lily and me in front.

"Two brave little pups, aren't you?" he said in a flat tone right before he adjusted his posture; it looked like something was going to happen. Lily must have sensed it too because we took off running to the right as fast as we could, but it wasn't fast enough because I heard Lily let out a shriek, followed by a thump.

"Run!" Lily screamed.

I quickly glanced behind me to see her being tackled by a large reddish-looking wolf, but then suddenly, the large green-eyed man sprinted at me with amazing speed, closing in on me with every step he took. His black boots didn't seem to touch the ground. I pushed myself to run faster, but each step I took wobbled. Why is it that when you need something, you yourself manage to fuck it up? Where was that supposed werewolf gracefulness?

I was tackled from behind before I could make it to the edge of the forest. He wrapped his hands around my body and all of a sudden, I felt an electric zap go through me. He grunted before we went flipping mid-fall and landed on the ground with me on top.

I struggled to get out of his hold, placing one foot on the ground, straddling him. His large hands clamped on my wrists like chains but not enough to bruise me. I was horrified that I would be taken by this brute.

"Let me go! Let me go!" I shouted, trying to claw at his hands, but that didn't work. I reached for his expressionless face, but he managed to stop me. I huffed as my muscles were tired and my body had started to weaken, but I couldn't give up.

I leaned forward to bite his face with my canines. My wolf was growling in my mind, but I could feel something familiar in my chest that I couldn't fathom. I was suddenly in an upright position, standing in front of the dark-haired man with his hands still holding me like a prisoner. He crossed my arms in front of me to avoid any more attacks, but I was able to kick him. He ignored it, blocking me when I tried to kick his "friend" down there.

With one hand, he clasped both of mine while his other hand reached for my chin. I leaned back, trying to pull my arms. *He was going to snap my neck!* I doubled my efforts in panic.

I turned my head violently, but he grabbed me roughly by the chin and tilted my head to meet his ecstatic expression before it went blank. His glazed eyes were focused on me; he must have been mind linking with whoever bastard was behind this. I used all of my energy to break free, but just as my chance came, his green eyes flickered to black, then to silver until it slowly transformed into a mesmerizing shade of blue that had me frozen in my spot.

Everything faded at that moment except those vivid, hypnotizing blue eyes. Something seemed to change in that instant, pulling me from deep within—a force stronger than will, stronger than life, searching for the missing link. Subsequently, his hold became gentle and he loosened his grip. From the corner of my eye, I saw his pointer finger linger and make its way down to the corner of my lips where it hovered over, then slid to the other side.

The trail left a burning path to my core, scorching my body. My wolf purred and went weak at his touch. As much as it pulled me in and made me feel alive, I knew something was wrong, but I couldn't figure what it was. I tried to close my eyes to regain control but every time I did, it just dissolved into nothingness, and my thoughts would go back to those lovely blue eyes.

His blue eyes blinked at me as if taking me in, before he nodded once at me. His blue eyes flickered back to black, then to a cat-like green as if the spell was broken.

It seemed like the man was regaining some sort of control over himself with his grasp still on me. I freed myself from his hold, and turned away running for my life.

"Release all other she-wolves! Mission complete. A1-2 has been found," he yelled.

I thought about saving Lily as I ran towards the edge of the forest, but as soon as I was close to freedom, somebody grabbed my shoulders with its fingers around my neck and pushed me down firmly. I felt like I was about to faint. I was seeing dots, my body suddenly weighing a ton, causing me to fall back against the body behind me. Before passing out, I heard one last thing from my captor:

"We found A1-2, everyone. We found our little luna."

CHAPTER 3

My neck hurt so bad when I woke up, but felt comfortable being covered by something heavy. It provided a lot of heat like fire, but I would gladly burn myself in it for its comfort.

Strange. Whatever kind of fire it was, it didn't hurt me. Instead, it surrounded me like a layer of skin keeping me warm and made me feel all fuzzy on the inside as my heart beat slowly and calmly. I could feel it travelling all over my body up to my face. I suddenly felt a shiver when a trail of heat made its way slowly from the corner of my right eye to the corner of my lips . . . *wait, what?* My brows furrowed. Whatever pattern it was making seemed familiar but stronger this time. Then I remembered everything before my unplanned sleep attack. The visit, Lily, the pack, the green-eyed kidnapper, and then darkness.

I snapped my eyes open. The first thing I saw were the man's blue eyes meeting mine as his body hovered over mine. Our proximity allowed me to see him clearly.

He was gorgeous in every sense of the word. He could be a god. His thick raven-colored hair was slicked back with a few loose strands falling over his forehead. His black trimmed eyebrows arched at the corners and long thick black eyelashes casted a shadow over deepset piercing blue eyes. His looks left me shaking to my core; his eyes were fixed on me, and I didn't quite know why but it left me dazzled and intimidated. My gaze trailed down to his long upturned nose above his perfectly shaped lips. He had an oblong face with angular cheekbones and a strong sharp jawline.

Who was he? Where did he come from? I took in a breath, inhaling his raw aromatic scent—when a good-looking guy passes you by, and the strong scent he's wearing grabs your attention, wouldn't you be stunned for a moment? That's exactly how I felt about this man. He had a mouth-watering smell, tempting the darkest side of me to make an appearance.

Just then I realized he was lying on top of me.

His bulging biceps were on either side of my face while his body was firmly pressed on mine. He had one of his hands in my hair while the other was tracing my face with his pointer finger. He looked calm and comfortable. I was freaking out on the inside, and I was sure that my eyes were wide out of fright. My breathing was coming out quick and uneven. My hands were gripping onto what felt like silk blankets. Why were we on a bed? I tried to feel my clothes and was relieved I wasn't naked. *Good.*

My wolf was purring in my head, but didn't say a thing. *Why are you purring mutt! You should be clawing at him. He could be a rapist!*

The blue-eyed man narrowed his eyes at me and scowled. It took me by surprise when he dipped his head and rested it on my left shoulder. His pale smooth skin was touching my cheek, and I heard him inhale deeply. He let out an aggressive growl, making me whimper out of fear, before looking back at me.

"W-what are you doing? Who the hell are you? Get off of me!" I exclaimed. I liked hot guys as much as the other girls, but I would not let a random guy, who I barely knew, lie on top of me.

The man said nothing. He just kept staring with those watchful eyes, radiating with power and dominance.

Mate. I pushed my head back into a fluffy pillow; my eyes felt like they were about to pop out. For a second, everything was still but he was silent.

Mate. No, my wolf would have been the first to speak, but that would mean that this hunk would be mine. I looked back at him; he was too good-looking to be mine.

"No way," I whispered, and saw his blue eyes gaze at me with anger, darkening almost immediately.

His pupils constricted, turning his beautiful blue eyes black, as the latter expanded completely over his eyeballs. His lip curled over his lip like a wolf would when baring teeth. I could feel evil and darkness behind those eyes, making me shriek in fear and begin to thrash underneath him. I've never seen those kind of wolf eyes before!

I moved my body as much as I could, but I couldn't get away from him. I lifted my arms towards his chest and tried to shove him, ignoring the warmth spreading through my palms. I lifted my legs and hips trying to buck him off, but it was as if his body suddenly weighed a ton. I called upon my wolf's strength but that didn't help me either. His eyes went back to blue, but that didn't stop me from trying to slip from under him.

His lips parted, giving me a glimpse of a pair of impressive white filed teeth with long sharp-looking canines. A part of me wondered if he used Crescent Crisp and Clear toothpaste. Stupid, I know.

"*Stop,*" he said in a deep, husky, and thick voice with an unknown accent.

21

Suprisingly, I involuntarily stopped thrashing underneath him. While what he said made sense in my mind, my ears could not comprehend the noises his lips made. I had never taken any language class in school besides Spanish, and I'm pretty sure I shouldn't have been able to understand what he said, but I did.

My body just froze as I looked up dazzled by the man on top of me. How was this happening? My limbs locked and tightened into place involuntarily, and my heart was beating frantically in my chest. He tilted his head with a gaze that made me want to squirm, but I couldn't. I wanted to open my mouth to yell, to shout, and get this hot weirdo off of me. My wolf was silent. I could feel she was uneasy but majority of her emotions were happiness and excitement. Out of all the wolves, mine must have been the most carefree in the worst of times.

"*Now, why would the gods send me a mate? Is this luna card a peace offering? Well played Fate, well played,*" the blue-eyed god muttered lowly under his breath with a cross look on his face.

Although his tone was scornful, I sensed he wasn't asking me; he just seemed curious. What surprised me was how fast my brain seemed to understand whatever language he was speaking. Did he have anything to do with this?

Did he say "an offering"? Oh, hell no. I am not a sacrifice! Who was this guy talking about? Luna? What was going on? This guy couldn't be my mate, could he? Why was I here? Where was "here" anyway? Gods? I had a shitload of questions, but I would gladly stay quiet if it meant this intimidating man was far, far away from me with his bewitching eyes and beautiful hair that I wanted to run my fingers—No, no, no. I needed to focus on the situation at hand.

Great. I got to finally meet my mate who turned out to be in a crazy cult; not even a pack, but a cult that kills the innocent and I'm next. Just my luck too.

The man suddenly leaned his head closer until he was inches away from my lips and eyes, making me hold my breath. He looked calmly into my eyes before closing his. His nose was touching mine, skimming over my left cheek while breathing in my scent. If I were weak, I would have swooned. He then whispered his next words in a chillingly flat tone with his breath fanning over my shoulder.

"*Although you enthrall me, I do not believe those ass-kissers. I do not trust you. You are so . . . cute. It's a shame.*"

Whatever hold he had on me was suddenly broken and unlocked my muscles. I was consumed by fear at his threat, and my mind was telling me he would kill me any minute. My wolf disagreed and would't believe me, but the human part of me knew by the calculating look in his eyes and the vicious way his lips were pulled back baring his teeth that I was right.

22

I was surprised to hear the thickness of his words. This time, he spoke in english, and it scared me more than him speaking his odd-sounding language.

"Now, what shall I do with you?" His voice was smooth but provocative. He looked like he was enjoying our position. His english pronunciation was clear but with an edge to it, as if he hadn't used it in a while.

I couldn't think of a better answer than the one I gave, and had I died then and there I think I would have been embarrassed that those were my last words.

"Let me go," I answered and saw his face was devoid of any emotion. I could sense he was suprised as if he expected me to either not answer or beg for my life, which I would if it was the only choice.

"No," he stated, his tone matching his expression.

'No?" I began to babble. *He had to let me go right? I mean, mate or not he couldn't keep me here, wherever that was, against my will. I chose not to mention the mate thing; maybe he'd ignore it like I would.* My wolf growled at me for thinking we would be able to ignore this fine-looking specimen.

"Look, I don't know your name and that's fine; let's keep it at that. I won't need to tell anyone about this whole misunderstanding. You're clearly looking for someone else and I'm not her. You know, mistakes happen and it's not that people get kidnapped at random, but who knows, wrong place, wrong time right?" I said.

He blinked at me.

I continued, but the more I talked, the more he seemed to realize I was a nutcase. Mom did say that if I would ever be kidnapped, my abductors would release me, realizing that it would cost them more to keep me because you know, hostages gotta eat, and I love food and talking.

"You know, while we're agreeing about releasing me," His eyes narrowed, "you might as well get off of me. Personal space is something everyone has a right to, and you're not following the rules, buddy. You're in my bubble, *my* bubble. Now if I had a choice, I wouldn't be all up in your bubble, so you should get out of mine. It's time for me to go, so I'm just gonna be on my way now, but you kind of have to get off of me first. I'm not calling you fat or anything but you weigh like—"

"Stop talking, woman!" he said.

My mouth shut at his command. I narrowed my eyes at him bravely, knowing it was him controlling me.

"I will not release you, so you might just as well accept that now and move on because it's likely that you will never leave here. At least alive, that is." Dread welled up in my chest while tears pricked at the corner of my eyes. He spoke with empty words, as if he didn't just threaten me. And since he *had* just done it, I guess what really hurt was that he said so as if he didn't just call me his mate.

One of his hands fisted my hair and pulled me closer to his face. I closed my eyes out of fright at the emotions coursing through my body. Fear, excitement, happiness, anger, and confusion. I was overwhelmed and didn't know what was going on at the moment. He took in a deep breath and then groaned deeply from the back of his throat, the sound he made made me shift my legs under him.

"As much as I'm sure I would enjoy the perks of a mating bond and this is probably what they want, I won't kill you. I don't know who I am to you and you to me, but I have no doubt those bastards were behind this. I won't fall into their hands to mark or mate you. Who knows? You might be on their side and kill me in my sleep." Every single one of his words felt like a stab to my heart.

My wolf snarled at the accusations thrown at us by our mate, but I could tell it was pretense to hide her pain. We wanted to whimper and plead for him to take back his words. A hollow feeling penetrated my chest, as my heart clenched in pain.

"I don't know what this is all about, but please just let me go if you don't . . . don't want me." I forced the words to come out of my mouth. They came out a whisper of pain.

Mates are chosen for a reason. Both destined for each other. Rejecting your other half is taboo, and a weak mate wouldn't last a chance once the other walked away. One mate will always be stronger, and when the mating bond is completed, there would be equality between the two. Based on the power radiating from him, I knew he would be fine without me while I would probably crawl into the forest and yell my pain out for death to claim me. His tone was darker when he spoke, forcing my eyes to open. I caught his eyes gazing intently down at me with a strange expression.

"Whether you work for them or not, we were made for each other. If you do, then I will be happy showing you whose side to choose," His eyes held a dark sensual promise in them that made my heart start pounding all over again, "but if you don't, I'm sure I can still change your mind. But you are not leaving. Ever."

The blood pumping in my veins was hot like molten lava, and my nerves came back to life. In my mind, I was angered by the way he treated me: so casual one second and then threatening me the next. He ended up confusing me by claiming and not claiming me at the same time. My body, to put it short, found his words a turn on. The way he seductively spoke with confidence as if he knew exactly what he wanted and was just giving a warning. But what did he want?

"Why?" I asked.

I had absolutely no idea what he was talking about. Who did he think I work for? What did he mean when he spoke of our bond? Why would he not claim me but keep me here if he didn't want me? All these questions were stuck in my head.

He didn't answer. He just looked at me with those wild-like blue eyes, and I could see he wasn't going to answer so I went for an easier question.

"What's your name?" I asked seriously with my brows arched.

"I'll humor you." His face darkened for a moment, but he gave me a smirk. He leaned down to whisper, "You all call me the *Lupus Deus.*"

I momentarily froze from where I was standing, immediately raised my arms, and pushed his shoulders. He allowed me to shove him which was surprising. He rolled over me to lie beside where I had been. I scrambled off of the large silver bed and tumbled a little, before I was able to turn in search of the door. Tremendous fear surged in me, causing me to stumble as I hurriedly made my steps forward.

"Oh my god, oh my god. Shit. Fucking fuck! This cannot be happening to me!"

My wolf was quite a traitor. I put my mental barrier up so she couldn't force her ways to control me. It was risky but I had to. For all I knew, she would submit to him with no hesitation.

I was so stupid. How did I not realize it when everything was just right before my eyes? I should have known when I opened my eyes, but his looks distracted me.

Stupid! Stupid!Stupid!

The room was large with the bed close to the wall. At the center, the floor was lifted up, and as I looked around the black-painted walls, I saw the furniture being pushed back. I finally saw a door and ran to it, but it was locked. I turned to look at the god on the bed, crossing his arms under his head, and following me with his eyes. I looked past him and saw a door that looked like the exit. I looked back at him and saw that he sat up. His face said it all—I dare you. I looked down at my feet and realized I was barefoot. *What?* I ignored it and without looking at him, I took off across the room towards the large black door. As my hand reached for the handle, a large shadow loomed over me, and I felt his presence behind me before my body was slammed against the door I was aiming for.

"No!" I wheezed out.

Before I could move, my hands were suddenly grabbed by the wrist, and were forcefully pinned above my head. I felt his legs part behind me and pelvis push against my back. How tall was this guy? He pushed my stomach harder into the door, limiting my movement. His legs slipped in between mine, parting my legs. I was sure he'd put me in a starfish position, and had I not been afraid of him, I would have found it slightly more . . . pleasing.

I felt him move around a little before he lowered his head next to my ear. I felt a little victorious at the thought of him having to make himself shorter to reach me. My skin pricked at his grip. I clenched my hands into fists and pulled at his hold. He tsk-tsked behind me.

"How foolish of you, Vivian." I held still when I heard my name come out of his mouth. My eyes widened for three reasons:

First, he obviously knew my name.

Second, his other arm made its way down to my waist. I held my breath as this was a little too intimate for me. I couldn't help but be watchful as to where our bodies touched, and how his fingers felt against my shirt.

Third, I wasn't facing the door anymore but his chest.

He brought me back to the bed faster than I thought possible. I looked up and gulped. While we were lying down with him on top, I didn't realize how huge he was. He had a strong and lean figure yet he was broad and firm that my head barely made it to his chest. A black T-shirt stretched over his pecs, the shirt clinging to him for dear life. Lucky shirt. I didn't look up from his chest. Every second that passed made me shift from under his hold.

"While I admire your drive, that isn't the door you're looking for. Stay away from it. Both doors in fact," he said coarsely with a hint of smugness in his tone.

"Look Mr. Lupus god. Yeah, nice meeting you. Heard a lot about you. But now that I know who you are, I'm 129.1 percent sure that this is a whole misunderstanding. Whoever brought me was most definitely high. We probably aren't even mates to begin with," I sort of flinched at my words. "Once again, I think I should go. You wouldn't want to waste your time on someone as insignificant as me. You know, you probably have people to kill, torture, kidnap, . . . release . . ." I tried once more to hint out my freedom.

He ignored my words and leaned his head down to nuzzle the top of my head. His chest got closer to my face, and I had to fight the urge to nuzzle him back, not knowing how he would react.

"I'm going to let go of you now," he said. I sighed in relief. "Physically, I mean. I'll be back soon. You are not to leave this room without me." I clenched my teeth. I suddenly felt my feet being pushed into the ground.

He made his way to a door that I had missed. Damn! Not trusting myself, I didn't move from my position. I didn't know whether I would try pushing past him or collapse onto the floor with everything that had gone on lately. I still didn't look at his face while he walked back, not even looking in his direction when he talked. I glared at a plug in the wall by me.

"Just to let you know, if you do work for them, if you try to send a message to them, it won't work. And if you do somehow, I'll know. And believe me when I tell you that it won't end good for you if I find out," he stated harshly, delivering the threat loud and clear. Out of the corner of my eye I saw him turn his back to me. Who the hell did he mean by *them*?

I heard the door open and before he walked out I chose to look up, making eye contact with him. We stared at each other for what seemed like forever. His multicolored blue met my chocolate-brown. His face was expressionless and mine probably pale with sudden tiredness. It looked like he was thinking something over in his head; whatever it was, he made a choice.

"You can call me, Zaliver," he said flatly and shut the door.

"Zaliver," I repeated in a dazed whisper that seemed to echo through the quiet room. His name rolled off of my tongue perfectly. Zaliver, the Lupus Deus.

My mate.

CHAPTER 4

I managed to make it to the edge of the bed before my legs buckled from exhaustion.

Me? A god's mate? What kind of joke was this? A cruel one, most definitely.

There must be some sort of mistake. I was a simple wolf and there was nothing special about me at all—shifted at fifteen, an ordinary pack member, who never went out to party or dated because I preferred to wait for my mate. A lot of wolves didn't find me attractive, but I like to think I was single by choice.

Who would want a socially awkward mate like me? Remembering those piercing blue eyes gazing back at me with a dark promise and those plump red lips made me question life. I shivered, and I hadn't even thought of that god-like body. Oh but wait, he's a god. Silly me.

I sighed, put my face in my hands, and took a deep breath. I wasn't going to break. I couldn't break. Not now. I needed to be strong to return to my family. But if I did manage to escape, he would look for my pack first. Maybe he would even take my parents hostage until I gave myself up. I closed my eyes.

Why do you want to escape?

Because my mate is a crazy savage who goes around kidnapping, killing, and taking people.

I could feel my wolf pushing at my barrier so I let it down.

But how do you know that? Give him a chance, she argued.

Did you not see the way he acted? One second he was threatening me, saying he's not going to claim us but we weren't allowed to leave.

He can't keep telling us how to use our body too! I don't want that type of mate.

As much as it pained me to speak ill of my own mate, I wasn't blind to things I didn't like. No one, no matter how bad the situation, should delude themselves into a better idea of life. Everyone was responsible for their own lives and well-being, and I wasn't going to neglect mine for a moment of bliss. What kind of life would I have with my mate if I did? Would he mark me or keep me trapped in here? Would I be stuck forever by his side without actually being acknowledged as his mate?

I didn't deserve that. No one did. I wanted my romance, my prince even if he wasn't perfect. I knew I shouldn't judge my mate but come on! Guilty until proven innocent? The only reason I met the guy was because he had his pack kidnap me. He wouldn't even get a trial. Not from me.

What about Lily and the rest of the women? Were they alright? I shot off the bed and made my way to the door. Or, I thought I did.

"Fuck you, you sexy god wolf," I mumbled under my breath.

Everytime I tried to get to the door, something heavy pulled me back. It seemed like there was an invisible wall in front of me. Is this how uninvited vampires felt from the Vampire Diaries when they weren't allowed into a home? What pain!

How could he just tell me to stay and follow his orders? It made me seem like a dog. The next thing I know, he'll be telling me to go and fetch.

It looked like he didn't notice me understanding his words when he switched to that weird language. But how did I even know what he was saying? Was it his doing or mine?

After a while, I just gave up and began to look around the large room. I ignored the door that I had thought was the exit after staring at it for a while. Yah, no. There was only one window from what I could tell. It was covered by long silky silver curtains. After moving the curtains, I cursed at my mate, Zaliver.

The room had metal blinds. Like literally, metal blinds that were closed and bolted to the frame so I wouldn't try to jump out, I guess. It kind of reminded me of Iron Man, but I somehow doubted that the wolf god had time to sit around and watch Tony Stark be a billionaire, playboy—whatever. I tilted my head at the strong shield-like blinds. Were these already here even before I got in?

The room had a black couch, some cabinets, a few large hanging mirrors here and there, a white furry rug (which I avoided), some random paintings, lamps, and a desk. There actually weren't any objects in the room to personalize it. The room was practically empty when it came down to personal belongings, no pictures or knickknacks that could have clued me as to what type of things he liked; it was as it wasn't his. Maybe he stayed in another room with a woman. Maybe the only reason he didn't seem to want me as a mate was because he already had a preference for another. My wolf snarled.

I'm going to cut his balls off in his sleep, if he does sleep.

29

She was jealous if it wasn't clear and so was I but at a calmer level.

Oh, who am I lying to?

My hands clenched at the thought of any female touching my mate's toned arms and abs and running her fingers through his pitch black hair. Even if I didn't like him, he was still mine.

I shook off my thoughts and went back to lie on the bed, not bothering to go to his clothes to sniff at them. I'd be the only girl with bad luck to end up getting caught checking my mate's underwear. I raised my legs to look at my bare feet. I wonder where my shoes were? How long has it been since I was captured? Hours? Days? Where am I?

Let's make a list, I told my wolf and felt her amusement.

And what shall it be called, topic as well? she asked, following along.

"How about . . . shit! I should have done this to save my life."

She snorted but agreed.

"First, I don't know where I am.

Second, I don't know why I'm here.

Third, I don't know how I got here.

Fourth, I don't know where my family is.

Fifth, I don't know why a sexy ass-god became my mate when I'm just an ordinary wolf.

Sixth, I don't know what day it is.

Seventh, I don't know what's going to happen to me.

Eighth, I don't know what my intimidating, sexy giant mate is thinking.

Ninth, I don't know what my sexy, intimidating giant mate keeps rambling on about."

My stomach rumbled.

"Tenth, I don't know when these people are going to fucking feed me!"

Personally, I think the last one was the most important.

Oh how I loved my wolf. She was like my best friend. I was never alone ever. Okay, that sounded creepy.

I thought I would wait for hours and maybe even days before anyone would bother to give me attention; you could just imagine my surprise when my mate barged into the room with a green-eyed man who was probably one of my captors. I immediately stood up with eyes narrowed at both of them.

"You." I looked at the man standing beside my mate. His height was close to my towering mate's who was scowling at me for whatever reason with his arms behind his back. The man smiled widely at me with distrustful eyes.

My eyes switched over to Zaliver. I felt uncomfortable with the way he was looking at me.

"My name is Albericus. I'm the—"

"That kinda sounds like . . . like Algebraic–us, Algebraic. Like *algebra . . . math*," I said.

The man seemed to be disgusted. My face scrunched at what came out of my mouth. How stupid of me!

"No. Not like algebra, little girl," he growled. I tilted my head to the side, giving him a look.

I don't give a fuck what he says, his name reminds me of math. I don't know how, but it does. I hate math.

"Are you sure . . ." I kept going.

"If you end up—" he grumbled under his breath.

"Enough, already." An authoritative tone rang in the room. Algebra and I shut our mouths like kids getting a scolding. Zaliver looked down at me and then turned to the door.

"Follow."

Without a thought, my feet followed where he went, passing the door, and going into the dark halls. Algebra was walking behind me in a stuffy kind of silence.

"Where are we going?" I asked.

Silence.

"Where are you guys taking me?"

Silence.

I sighed, thinking they had no intention of answering me.

I looked around as we headed down, then up and then down once more, making confusing turns. Wherever we were headed to was in the deepest end of this place with our footsteps echoing around the concrete walls. I couldn't sense anyone else in the building, but I could be wrong.

Where could they be taking me? Are they going to let me go now? I felt a quick sense of relief along with sadness. I didn't want to part with Zaliver so soon. No, he wouldn't be letting me go soon.

I turned to look behind me catching the glaring green eyes of Algebra. I looked back to Zaliver whose arms were flexed and hands were clasped behind, striding gracefully. If he wasn't going to let me go and if he wasn't going to see me as his mate then what did he plan to do with me? I didn't think I wanted to hear the answer. I needed a plan to escape; my wolf thoroughly disliked my idea, but I didn't really care what she liked at the moment.

We stopped beside the first gray door. The hall extended to a never-ending passage but a large chest covered in black blocked my view. I looked up at Zaliver's expectant face while the large metal door had been pushed opened and it seemed like I was the first to enter. The

31

walls in the room were painted white but the floor was bare. I saw a chair backed against a wall with lots of straps attached to its feet and armrests. I didn't have to guess why I was to be placed in here.

"Oh, hell no. No, no, no, no." I shook my head back and forth, taking steps backwards, my pulse racing. Fear and panic ran through my veins. I tried to push away from the door but hit a chest instead. A comforting warmth surrounded me, and I knew who it was but I didn't want to believe he would do such a thing to me.

"Go to the chair and sit still."

Of course, just like the other times, my body followed his command. I fought for control. I was screaming both in my head and out of my mouth. I bet I was a sight. A pale brown-haired girl in sweats screaming while she casually walked over and sat in a chair. Tears were streaming down my face. I was just as angry as I was scared. How dare he!

I didn't want to get tortured, much less die! He couldn't do this! Was this the god they spoke of? Would he show me the monster everyone feared?

"Please! You can't do this! I've done nothing wrong!"

Zaliver walked over to me, his frame towering above me with blank eyes. His beautiful face subconsciously sparked hope and fear in my heart, the type only a mate could. He wouldn't hurt me, right? He was so hauntingly beautiful, and the fact that I didn't know a thing about this god known for his cruelty didn't help.

"Shh," he said.

I tried to be quiet and took in shaky breaths. I wanted to wipe my sweaty face but was not able to.

Algebra was at the door with a somber look on his face. Zaliver said he wouldn't hurt me if I was innocent of not working for whoever *they* were. I didn't even have a job yet. I don't even work for a *them*. I calmed down just a little at the thought. He hadn't used the restraints on me so I was fine, just paralyzed in a sense.

"I'm not going to hurt you so there's no sense in crying. This isn't a normal interrogation, Vivian," Zaliver spoke, agitated. "This is just a quick and efficient way to get what I want. And what I want is to figure out what you know. I can't have you near me without doing this and I need to know what your role is in this little plan of theirs."

"This won't hurt, but it will drain you. I sincerely hope . . ." His face softened a bit towards the end, but he quickly bounced back to his distant expression and didn't finish whatever he was going to say. I was shaking on the inside, pushing against the invisible force holding me down to this chair but it was too strong. What was he going to say?

I sincerely hope, you die?

I sincerely hope, you're not a traitor?

32

I sincerely hope . . .

Zaliver lifted his hands to my face. His fingers hovered for a second before they made contact. They could hear my breath hitch, his fingertips lingered on my cheek where tears were streaming and travelled up to my temples. His fingers began to feel warmer and then hot in a flash, I could feel my pulse at his fingertips. He then touched my forehead and felt force pushing against my mental barrier. The force weakened as it pushed forward like a ghost through a wall. I was prepared to push back and fight for my mental block to stay up but he just slipped through. I wasn't ready for this. He was right. There was no pain, but there was discomfort—the feeling of being violated in an intimate manner.

I couldn't feel his fingers anymore, but I knew they were there. I didn't know what he was doing, but I could feel him in my mind. I felt him go through my thoughts, secrets, and memories which was a total invasion of privacy. Each memory and thought he passed through clung to him and floated on their own. My energy was leaving me while my head felt overwhelmed by his presence in my mind. My wolf was whimpering as her mind was searched as well. Pack life, trees, and wilderness. Insecurities and wishes. All of me was laid bare.

Images flashed through my head like a slideshow, but they were too fast to focus on, and I was getting exhausted. I looked at his face, changing expression from caution to bewilderment, surprise, and then awe. It morphed to horror as my eyes began to flutter close.

He snatched his hands back quickly from my face. Whatever hold that glued me to the chair was gone, making my head fall forward along with my body. Maybe I'd get lucky and sink right through the ground, into a portal, and fall into my bed back home and then realize this was all some crazy dream.

I felt strong arms wrap around me, and my head made to rest on a shoulder. Zaliver quickly picked me up with his arms sweeping under me and grabbing hold of my legs. I wanted him to hold me, but I didn't, but then I wanted him to hold me but then again I didn't. I was going mad with my desire and anger.

"No. Put me down," I growled. It might have sounded weak because he didn't answer me.

He held me to his chest as he walked over to the door. I wanted to push him away, but I was weak. I closed my eyes but didn't surrender my will to the darkness. I just needed to regain my mental energy to regain control of my limbs.

I've had enough of this jerk telling me what to do with my body and then going through my head without permission. He invaded my privacy, my thoughts, my memories and all because he could. He

33

didn't even bother to ask me. He could have asked me. Not like I had anything to hide.

Algebra must have opened the door when Zaliver was walking with me in his arms without moving me an inch; it then closed quickly. Algebra spoke cautiously.

"So?" I heard him ask.

I waited for Zaliver's answer. What was the point of all of this?

"Clear. She doesn't know a thing," he whispered in a hoarse voice, then cleared his throat. I wanted to open my eyes to see his face, but I didn't even have enough energy for that.

"Really?" he said while opening the doors for Zaliver to get through.

Where is he taking me now?

"Yes. She's clueless, but she seems to understand me when I speak in Latin," he stated. Something in his tone made me want to move around in his arms. Latin? That's the language then.

"Isn't that right?"

When I was finally able to open my eyes, Zaliver gazed at me with his head tilted and lips parted as if he didn't understand something. If only I could move my arms, I would take a swing at his face. God or not, he deserved to be punched.

I said nothing as I looked at him. I was too tired to speak. What good was a body if the mind couldn't use it for its purpose? Well, this jerk didn't seem to have any problem apparently.

"What? That's . . . I've been with you for a long time, but I still don't even understand you at times. Why do you think is that? That she understands, I mean," Algebra asked but Zaliver didn't answer.

I looked over at him and saw him peer down at me. He really was good-looking when he wasn't scowling.

His arms tightened around me with his eyes still on me, but I tried to avoid it. What now? His blue eyes had gone cold again, a dark expression shadowing over him. I felt "jackhammers" in my stomach, and this wasn't the way I pictured myself being carried by my mate for the first time.

Zaliver was still walking with me in his arms along another hallway. The walls were soft blue with brown framed paintings hanging on the walls, and tables with flowers on top. We turned a corner, and I saw multiple doors leading elsewhere, hearing chatters and . . . laughter?

I saw Algebra slip into one of those doorways and enter a spacious place where I spotted toys and shoes on the floor. Who lived here?

At the end of the hall was a spiral staircase and floors made of glass, leading to another floor and more hallways. Could this be his pack house? If Zaliver was the Lupus Deus, then why would he have a pack? If you're a wolf god, why would you have a pack? Wouldn't every pack be considered his pack?

We then entered a huge living room decorated with black couches and wide windows with clear curtains, which allowed sunshine to filter through. I could still hear laughter in the air as we walked in to a large kitchen with a table in the middle of the room. He put me down on a chair and began to pull things out. What was he doing? Was he making food?

The laughter of two guys and three ladies died down when they noticed Zaliver carrying me in his arms. They bowed their heads and looked at me, while he paid them no heed.

Both of the guys had cream blonde hair that was combed back, large dark brown eyes, and baby faces. I could tell they were twins. The only difference was that the one on the left had higher cheekbones and the one on the right had a more pronounced jawline. They both wore light wash jeans, but the former had on a green button-down shirt while the latter wore blue. The three girls were each completely different from each other. The closest one to me was a dark-skinned girl with short hair. She had hazel eyes with a hint of green in them, her face was well-rounded with a rounded nose and thin lips; she was the tallest girl in the group. The girl next to her was the cutest thing I had ever seen— standing at five foot one, dark red hair, and dark green eyes with a heart-shaped baby face. The girl next to her had caramel-colored skin, black hair, brown eyes, full lips, and looked around my height and age.

All of them were looking at me while I looked back at them awkwardly.

They all had curious and nervous looks on their faces, I looked towards Zaliver who was busy putting something together. I couldn't see over his large figure what exactly he was doing with his hands, but I could smell food. He moved swiftly and gracefully. I watched his muscles flex and tense with his movement down to his strong legs covered in fit pants.

Snap out of it, woman! Do not check him out. He is the enemy! Remember! He just scrambled your brains with his fingers alone. I reminded myself.

I'd like him to scramble those fingers next but my perverted wolf purred in my head, of course, not bothering to be angry with him.

Ignoring her words, my thoughts took on a different course. Now this guy knows everything about me while I know next to nothing about him. I looked back at the people who were still by the door. This time their eyes were switching between me and Zaliver. I tried not to blush but since he didn't even bother to notice the awkward situation, I cleared my throat.

"Uh . . . hi!" Wow. Can I be any cooler?

Don't answer that.

The tall dark-skinned girl smiled brightly at me and waved from her spot while the others gave a weary smile back.

"Hello! I'm Amber, this is Leslie, Angela, those two are Drake and Blake." She pointed to each of her friends. So the red-haired girl was Leslie, the caramel-colored girl was Angela, and the blue shirted twin was Drake and the other Blake. Or was it the other way around? Shit.

I returned their smiles; at least they were friendly.

"I'm Vivian. Nice to meet you all." They nodded and finally entered the kitchen.

The boys walked to one of the large refrigerators and pulled out four bottles of Coke and water. They handed the girls the soda while one of the twins kept the bottle of water. Leslie and Angela just leaned against the counter top and looked at me. Amber was boldly making her way to me to pull out a chair, when Zaliver who hadn't said a thing or glanced at them let out a threatening growl that had Amber halting midstep. *What the hell?*

All of us stood rooted to the ground and the air was suddenly thick with fear. I'm sure all of us were wide-eyed, looking at Zaliver's direction. He had his back to us, but his head turned to our direction with a glare directed at Amber. While I'm sure it looked threatening to the others with his height and bulging muscles, to me it painted a completely different picture. The light coming from the window shined down on him perfectly; his black hair shined like a dark halo, a black strand of hair falling over those icy blue orbs.

Amber took a few steps backwards with her head lowered until she hit the wall. What the heck was that about? Her friends threw each other the same look before discretely talking to each other while looking at us.

Zaliver turned quickly with a plate in his hands and strolled over to the table, ignoring everyone in the room, and placed the plate in front of me. I looked up at him, disregarding the plate. He was looking at me with a blank face and pursed lips, then crossed his arms over his large chest. I looked down at my plate. There were five large pancakes on my plate, already cut up and with syrup. How fast is this guy? He can cook? I looked back up at him.

"Eat," he demanded. I was hungry but that was just plain rude.

I glared back at him, still angry about the invasion of my privacy. Now that I was seated down properly and the scare of thinking I was going to be tortured was gone, I felt calmer and braver while regaining my energy.

"I understand that we're wolves, but I do eat civilized at the table. Can I have a fork, please?" I said sarcastically.

The people in the kitchen had a mixture of shock and horrified expressions on their faces as if they were given homework for summer. Looking back at Zaliver, I saw the frosty look on his face and his clenched jaw. He surprised me when he didn't say a thing and walked over to a cabinet, pulling out a fork.

He walked over and handed it to me. He crossed his arms over his chest again and sat beside me. I shifted a little in my chair at his proximity. Too close! Too close!

I began to eat the pancakes quickly, serving my hunger—my number one priority. Fuck everyone else in the room, I was hungry. When I finally finished, I realized how hungry I was when the plate was empty. Zaliver had a pleased expression on his face, his eyes not moving from my face. Without looking over his shoulder, he ordered, "Get her a bottle of water."

One of the twins quickly opened the refrigerator and walked over to the table, water in hand. I took it gratefully and saw his slightly nervous expression.

"Thank you."

"No problem."

Even though I was basically ordered to do it, he was probably thinking.

I drank from the bottle and put it down. Now what?

"So . . ." I said, not knowing where to start.

"What?" Zaliver asked, leaning forward. It was ridiculous how tall this man was. Even when seated he was still taller than me.

"Can I go now? I think you got what you wanted," I said bitterly towards him. I knew the others were listening but I didn't care.

I needed to go home. I wanted to go home.

After his little interrogation made it clear to me that my own mate didn't trust me. He chose to go through my mind and invade my privacy, instead of trusting my word. I would have answered anything he asked honestly.

"I already told you Vivian. The answer is no, and I will not repeat myself, so drop it," he said harshly. I flinched at his words, but then my anger resurfaced.

I stood from the table without a word and walked out of the kitchen. I heard a chair scraping loudly followed by footsteps. A rough hand yanked me and turned me around.

"Where the hell do you think you're going?" Zaliver growled out with his blue eyes growing stormy. I tried to yank my hand out of his grasp but it was too strong. Fine. He obviously wins in strength, so it was time for a different course.

37

"Let go," I said evenly.

"No. Now answer me," he demanded. I lifted my head and looked him squarely in the eyes.

"I'm looking for the door." His eyes widened for a moment. His pupils dilated and was changing from blue to black. I held my ground even though I was alarmed and felt the chill in my arms.

"I said you couldn't leave," he said slowly. This made me take a slight step back. He was radiating with anger and power but was speaking calmly; not a good combination.

"I-I'm done asking for your permission. I was trying to be polite but you've got no reason to keep me here. You got what you wanted, now let me go," I said softly, pulling my arm. He was breathing deeply, his nostrils flaring.

"No reason, huh?" he asked sarcastically and smiled.

The room began to feel cold. I held my breath as he pulled me closer, releasing my hand and wrapping it around my waist. His nose was touching mine before he closed his eyes, and let his nose trail down to my cheek and then back to my nose. I felt my legs weaken a bit and. I took in a shaky breath .

"So you being mine isn't reason enough?" He smirked mockingly. He didn't know how I felt about him, and the fact that this was probably all a game to him made me angry. I tried to push at him.

"Let me go, you jackass! I'm going home and you can't stop me. I can't believe you! I know you don't want me so I'll do us both a favor and rej—" All of a sudden, he put me over his shoulder faster than I could realize, knocking the air out of me. Zaliver was moving fast, too fast that it couldn't even be called running. Everything around me was a blur of color, and every sound was mixed together. My hair moved around me as if a tornado was in the room.

We came to a stop and before I could gasp for air, I was thrown into the air and landed on something soft that made me bounce. I squealed in shock and realized it was a bed. The room we were in was dark with little light passing through the curtains, giving the room an ominous feeling. Zaliver's shadow was at the door. I quickly crawled back with wide eyes. My instincts flared, and everything was telling me that I was in tiny quarters with a gigantic predator.

Zaliver looked down at me with smoldering eyes and parted lips that showed his lengthened canines. His head was cocked to the side showing more of his neck. He took slow deliberate steps towards me, his head was tilted down, making his lashes cast a shadow over his stormy intense eyes. Pure and utter seduction was what he was doing. He had an alluring air around him that had my eyes glued to his every move, but even then at the back of my head, I noted the coldness on his face.

As he neared the bed, I glanced at the door and then back at him, and he smiled. He tsk-tsked at me and surprised me by reaching for the bottom of his black V-neck top and pulling it over his large frame. My eyes widened at this animalistic side to him. My wolf was howling like it were a full moon.

He was lean and muscular in all the right places—his broad shoulders, a solid chest, smooth-looking skin that I itched to touch with my fingertips, and his toned and firm stomach. His pants were held up with a black belt. As I trailed my eyes back to him, I could feel him igniting a spark within me that was becoming brighter and brighter .

"Am I to your liking?" he asked, taking another step towards the bed.

I was breathing so quickly that it was hard to swallow. I've never been in a situation like this before. No guy had ever thrown me on his bed and then took his shirt off. He was beyond hot and that did not help. This shit was better than imagination.

I wasn't going to give him the pleasure of knowing that though. I fixed my dazed expression, and looked him straight in the eye with a serious expression.

"You're a solid ass eight out of ten."

I thought he would laugh at my pathetic joke or even growl at it. I didn't think he would lunge at me with an enraged look on his face.

I screamed and quickly rolled over, barely missing the hands that were reaching for me. I kept rolling until I hit the ground where I scrambled to get up. A hand reached for my wrist, pulling me into a bare chest. He wrapped his arms around me and let us fall back. When we hit the bed, he quickly rolled us over, straddling me and pinned my arms above my head. My hair was a mess, and I was panting like crazy but in an odd sense, I felt happy. I could almost pretend this was play.

He leaned down and began to nuzzle my neck with his nose tickling me. I moved my hands, itching to touch his smooth-skinned torso as he tightened his hold.

"You were going to reject me, weren't you? Even though I said you were mine. Such a naughty girl. Girls like you need to be punished," he purred in my ear. My eyes widened at his words. I shook my head back and forth.

"No! I wasn't. I was just angry. I swear, I wasn't." It was true, blame it on the heat of the moment. He hummed against my throat, taking a deep breath.

"You smell so good. Maybe I will mark you. Who knows, it might keep you in your place." I froze. I was sure I wanted him to mark me, but now? No way. My anger came flaring back.

"Umm, let's not push it. I mean we don't even know each—forget that. I don't know you, you rude ass bitch. You went through my

39

memories and thoughts to get something you could have just asked me. Get the fuck off of me!" I thrashed under his hold. He pulled back baring his teeth at me as his eyes turned black. I bared my own and snarled, refusing to be intimidated when I knew he was wrong. His messy but sexy hair fanned over his eyes.

He opened his mouth to speak only to close it and sigh. He got up and pulled his shirt back on, his eyes returning to blue, leaving me in the same position. He made his way to the door and yanked it open. Algebra stood with his hands ready to knock. Zaliver heard him before he knocked?

"Sorry man, we've got a situation that needs handling," Algebra said, not even glancing past Zaliver, who nodded at him.

Zaliver turned to look at me intensely with his eyes smoldering again. I sat up to look at him with a flushed face.

"Use the room as you please. I'll be back later to finish what I started," he said in a deep voice before leaving me without another word like a fish out of water.

I sat for a moment and realized something. He didn't command me to stay here. He didn't say I couldn't leave; I was free!

I leapt off the bed and was heading for the door when I thought he was probably still around. If I left then, there was a chance that I would bump into him. There was no time to waste. Zaliver was a god, and it was difficult to remember that when he was shirtless and pissing me off. Whatever situation was going on, it could have been a tough one. He would probably take a while at least, I hoped.

I didn't bother looking around as I would be leaving soon, but I thought of taking advantage of the situation. I walked over to the bathroom and opened it slightly. Making sure there was an extra towel, I went back to the room and looked for something to wear. I opened a drawer and was surprised to see clothing already there—men's clothes—Zaliver's to be exact. They all carried his scent, not to mention there were no other colors except black. Was I in his room? Was this actually his room and not the one where I first woke up in?

There were other things and random articles of clothing on the floor. His bed was covered with dark blue sheets. There were more things in here than the last room, almost decorated in the same sense. I pulled out the smallest shirt I could find along with the smallest sweats, and took a pair of his briefs which made me snicker a bit.

I headed back into the bathroom. It was elegant in a combination of black and silver—dark but soothing. The floor tiles in the shower were pitch black while the rest were melted silver. I stripped and entered his shower, and fell in love with it as soon as I figured out how to use it. Instead of the usual crappy showers where there's only one water hose, there were two on each wall and on the ceiling. It was heaven. I used his rich-smelling shampoo and conditioner—the reason behind the minty freshness that wafts off from him sometimes. I showered quickly and didn't bother looking in the mirror. I still had brown eyes, short hair, and a chubby face. I doubted that would change just because I met my mate.

I quickly changed into the clothes I picked, having to adjust them a lot so they wouldn't slip off from me. The shirt was more like a dress and the shorts were like pants, which was ridiculous. I ran my fingers through my short hair, and pushed it away from my face. I took in a deep breath and was making my way to the door when I heard a distinctive sound.

It stopped me in my tracks and made me turn around with wide eyes. Could I be this lucky? My eyes scanned the room and landed on the black device with a flashing green dot. I quickly ran to the phone praying he didn't have a password on it. Yes! What type of idiot doesn't lock their phone in this century?

Our idiot. I agreed with my wolf.

I waited for the call from a guy called "Freden" to end and then quickly went to the call button. I typed my dad's number knowing that if I called my mom she wouldn't pick up. My finger hovered over the green button.

Come on! Do it! What's stopping you?

What *was* stopping me?

I thought it over that this could be my only and last chance to call them; but what if Zaliver had his phone tracked and realized I called my parents? I couldn't do that to them no matter how worried they probably were now. I erased the number and put the phone down.

I groaned as I couldn't call 911 either. I could hear the conversation now.

"911 what's your emergency?"

"I've been kidnapped by my mate who's a god. He won't mark me or let me leave, this does count as kidnapping right?"

Yeah, the only thing I would get was probably a scolding over the phone by some stranger, then an idea hit me.

I grabbed his phone to track his location, and turned it on. While waiting, I smiled at my little victory, I would soon know exactly where I was and how to get out of here.

My smile disappeared as I read the screen.

• The Bermuda Triangle.

"What. The. Actual. Fuck?"

The Bermuda Triangle?

I thought this place was prohibited for anyone, even more so to live in it. It was said that technology wouldn't work here, and that things around it ended up going missing because of some strange time

41

lapse or some shit. I tried to recall all of my geography lessons, but only managed to remember my teacher saying something about the island being declared off limits for anyone to fly near it (such as planes) for the last eighty years due to some sort of freak storm accident.

"How the fuck am I supposed to get out of the Bermuda Triangle?"

The door opened. Zaliver stood and leaned against the door with a collected look on his face. I clenched his phone in my hands. He was back too soon.

"That's the thing. You're not," he said.

I could feel my heart sinking. I was indeed trapped in here.

CHAPTER 5

"You see, Vivian, even if you somehow escaped this house and passed all the guards, patrols, and cameras, there's no way in hell you'd get off this island without me knowing." Zaliver walked towards me as he spoke.

When he got near me, he gently took his phone out of my hands and glanced at it, then back at me, but all I could do was look past him as if I didn't see anything.

There really was no escaping here, was there? I was trapped in here forever. *Forever?* No. There had to be a way out. I looked at Zaliver, who is typing something on his phone with displeasure on his face. He looked over at me and cocked his brow.

I stayed silent, looked at him, and began to think deeply. If there were water, household tools, and a pack, then that must mean that this was a living environment for people. Last time I heard, the BT was just a large island ignored by the world for being unlucky. If you lived here and went around kidnapping girls from around the world, wouldn't you need to leave and come back constantly?

Not only that. If his phone worked enough to locate where we were, wouldn't that mean he would have to get technology to work first?

I pursed my lips at Zaliver. He was still looking at me cautiously.

"You've built a living society on an island ignored by the human government," I stated without hesitation. He blinked at me in surprise. There was a reason I was at the top of my class in high school. Also, never underestimate a woman, especially the confident chubby ones.

"My, my, you're a smart one, aren't you? And here I thought I'd have to explain things to you," he said in a sardonic tone. I wished he was not as good-looking as he was. Even when being rude, my wolf wouldn't get mad at him. I clenched my jaw. It's not like I could do anything as well; he was stronger than me in all senses.

"So you have a pack, and you're like the alpha? How does living in the Bermuda Triangle exactly works? How did I get from

Washington DC to here?" I asked, looking for a way to wrap my head around everything.

He stared at me for a long time and spoke the best choice of words with pride. He walked around the room, picking up things and setting them in places. When I began to walk over to the bed, he stopped to look at me until I sat down.

"Indeed, I do have a pack. Even though I definitely have a higher rank than alphas, I work like one. My pack, just like every other pack and alpha, is ran by me." He sneered the words out. "I truly am the alpha of all alphas," he said proudly.

I couldn't help the pride that welled up in my chest. I found it very hot that he could dominate everyone, but it also made me nervous. There had to be a reason or a sacrifice for someone to have such power and control. What price did he pay for all of this?

Walking over to one of the large couches, he continued talking and sat down with his hands set on his thighs.

"After a few meaningless years, I wanted a pack of my own while still running other packs from afar. Why not here? Getting a force field wasn't even a problem." He lifted his hands. A few meaningless years? I cocked my head anxiously. How old could Zaliver be? He looked like he was in his mid to late twenties, maybe twenty-five? Though I knew that couldn't be true as the rumors of the famous Lupus Deus weren't just around for a few years. They've been around for a few centuries.

"H-How old are you exactly, Zaliver?" I interrupted, earning a glare from him.

"Does it matter?"

I shook my head hesitantly at him. To be honest, it didn't, but I felt like it was important. Werewolves weren't immortal creatures like everyone believed. We just aged slowly, so for him to be talking so casually about years was concerning. Was his life span longer than mine? If I were to die first, would he miss me? Would he move on without me?

My heart clenched at the thought. He sighed and ran his hand through his hair, pushing back the strands that always fell over his face. I bit the inside of my cheek as he looked like a petulant child. Well . . . a childish man.

"I'm not going to tell you my birth date because I truly don't know when or where I was born. My first few years of existence are a blur." He turned to look at something on the wall. I had a feeling he was lying to me; there was a slimy feeling in my chest. I curled my tongue in my mouth and kept silent.

"I'm old but not that old, around 600 years old," he grumbled out. With widened eyes, I stood up on my feet and pointed a finger at him.

44

"You pedo-bear! Get away from me, you creep!" I yelled out. Zaliver stood from his spot and marched over to me, snatching my hand and putting it on his abdomen.

"Does this feel like a beer belly to you?" he growled angrily at me. I shook my head without moving my hand. If I did, I was sure he would reconsider seeing me as a mate and not the girl who basically felt him up. He let go of my hand and stepped back, glaring at me. Well, someone was a little sensitive when it comes to age.

"Sorry," I said, realizing how childish I had acted.

"Questions are over. Now, do you want to stay here all day, or do you want to see your new home?" he asked, adding smugness in his voice. I scowled at him. He knew I was trapped; hell, it was obvious.

"Fine," I mumbled, following him out of the door and trying hard not to stare at that black-jean-covered ass. While in the middle of the hallway, I contemplated whether to ask him or not, then chose to do it anyway.

"Hey, what exactly do you plan with me being here? I do want to go to college you know, and I have no plans on being stuck here for long." He stopped and turned to look at me with annoyance.

"I know, I know. I get the whole 'You're not leaving blah blah blah blah blah.' Doesn't mean I agree though." I made air quotation marks with my fingers and saw his amused face.

"How old are you?"

"Definitely younger than you. Eighteen. Why?" I asked defensively, not liking the way his face fell slightly. I'm an adult as well.

"You're young. You're not going to college," he stated like it was obvious. He turned to walk away from me, but I shot off in front of him.

"Wait! Wait! Wait! Hold up! What do you mean I'm not going to college? Last time I checked, I wasn't asking your permission. Legally speaking, being eighteen makes me an adult," I said. Who was he to tell me what I could do with my future?

The man we want in our future. My wolf chose to comment at the worst of times. Shit.

Go back to your cave, mutt.

"We have colleges here, but since there are men, you aren't going. Besides, you need not work for anything," he said. He tried to walk past me, but I blocked him.

"Why does it matter if there are guys going to college here? I'm not going to live here forever by the way, and FYI, I do need to work. Do you just expect me to stay by your side and do nothing everyday?"

I was not going to lie, that sounded nice. It was almost like having everything handed to you on a silver platter, but as nice as it sounded, I knew it came at a huge price—my freedom and pride. There was nothing wrong with being housewives, but I couldn't cook my whole life.

"Look. I don't know how you see this whole mate situation working out, but let me tell you what I know. I know you don't plan on marking me like a normal mate would because you said it yourself. It was clearly a rejection. I don't plan on living with someone who doesn't want me," I said sourly. I ignored my clenched heart and fisted my hands. It really was no use being with him if he wouldn't want me. I'd be torturing myself just by being around him everyday.

He lifted his head to the ceiling and sighed roughly. I stared at his throat, distracted by his smooth skin that suddenly made my gums ache. I rubbed my tongue over my teeth as if to calm the teeth that wanted to come out to mark our mate.

It was just the two of us in our heated gaze, blue against brown. My skin began to feel as if it was being caressed; my face, my arms, and my back. The touch was gentle yet rough at the same time. I didn't know how to describe the warmth and pleasure I felt. I shivered as the touch became light like a feather over my face.

My eyes widened as I looked up at Zaliver with a shocked and half-lidded look. I knew it was him even if he was just standing in front of me, not physically touching me. He looked at me with hooded eyes, but he had a coy look on his face. He leaned into me slightly while his face was looming over me. I felt like whatever touch was holding me tilted my head to his. My breathing was heavy while his breath fanned over my face.

"Let me clear something for you Vivian. You. Are. Mine. With or without mark." He smirked.

"They sent you to me as a bargaining chip, hoping to stop me. They were sadly mistaken. In reality, I just gained something out of their stupidity. It also helps that you aren't tainted by this world, and I plan on keeping it like that. So my dear Vivian, you were made for this god, and this god will be damned if he let anyone take you from him, including yourself," he said with dark humor.

As soon as he leaned back, all the touching sensation stopped. I was left feeling tipsy and slack-jawed. With or without mark, I was his? Before I could think more about his words, he pulled me by the hand down a corridor and stopped at a living room that looked more like a game room.

When we entered the lighted living room, I was surprised to see people. They were mostly large men with fit build and women dressed in black clothing. They were people of all colors and shapes. They all stopped what they were doing as soon as we entered, and stood up to bow their heads.

46

"Alpha Lupus," they chorused before looking at me.

I wanted to step behind Zaliver but remained where I was. I tried to pull my hand out of his before it started to sweat, but he just squeezed it, making everyone looked to our hands. Their heads tilted back up and then their eyes widened in mixed emotions. Zaliver spoke loudly in an authoritative voice.

"This is Vivian, my mate." They were surprised to hear Zaliver's words. I felt something warm in my chest at the acceptance from the people I just met—the more so for Zaliver to have said it out loud, claiming me in front of everyone. My wolf howled in my head and her tail wagged.

"She isn't safe to wander around the island yet, so I'll be assigning guards here while I prepare for tonight's meeting. Johnson, Courtney, Luke, and Mila, step forward," Zaliver stated. This jackass really likes leaving me in the dark. It isn't safe to wander around my ass. It was more like, it isn't free to wander.

"I—" I closed my mouth as his hand squeezed mine a bit painfully. JACKASS!

Four wolves, two men and two women, stepped forward. Without question, they surpassed my height; one was even taller than Zaliver. It was amusing to see a large grown male bowing to Zaliver, who was a few inches shorter than him.

Both fit, brown-eyed women had their hair pulled back in ponytails. One woman had pale skin and a scar that went down her right eyebrow; the other was tan and had a serious expression on her face. The men had the same build. The taller one had curly blond hair that was pulled back with a few loose strands falling on the sides. He had lovely big blue eyes with a mischievous look in them. The one next to him had red hair and green eyes, reminding me of the girl I met before. What was her name? Lana? I think that was it.

As the four got closer, they knelt down on their knees. Zaliver let go of my hand and made his way to them. I watched in wonder as Zaliver walked towards them. He paused every once in a while, making the room tense. He then slightly nodded and spoke.

"Will you protect her with your life?"

He gave me four guards! That was more than enough! There was no need for that.

"Yes Alpha," they answered in unison. My breath got stuck in my throat.

Have you ever had someone who promised to protect you with their life? If you had, imagine that, times four.

"Because if you fail, you will pay with your life."

As serious as his threat was, I felt moved at his actions.

See? He does care. My wolf said.

47

Right. Maybe I was being too hard on him.

"Yes Alpha," they repeated.

"Come," Zaliver said as he walked over to me.

He grabbed my hand and pulled me. I heard shuffling and presumed the four had followed. Trying not to be rude, I glanced behind me and saw the others a few feet behind us as if giving us privacy. They stopped gazing at us when I looked at them, so I turned back in embarrassment.

"Why do they bow their heads?" I asked. It wasn't the first question I wanted to ask, but it was the first to come out.

Zaliver opened a glass door and led me to who-knows-where. I shivered a bit.

"Because I am a god, and you are my mate. To not bow to me would mean to challenge me. Other alphas are under me, so they do not get one," he stated. I guess that made sense.

"Why did you give me guards?" I asked displeased. "I would have appreciated a warning even if it came out like, 'Oh hey, I'm going to have you followed. You don't mind, right?'" He glanced at me from his side and looked back forward.

"This is no ordinary pack, Vivian. Your . . . existence, for a better word, hasn't been explained yet, which means the pack isn't aware of who you are. You could be mistaken as an intruder," he explained.

I arched my brows and chuckled a bit. He looked at me with suspicion, so I explained myself quickly.

"You said intruder as if I would purposely swim my ass across the ocean to come here. Do you know what's in the water? Sharks! Nuh uh, I'mma stay my ass on land," I muttered the last part to myself. I was so distracted by my short banter that I hadn't noticed Zaliver smiling behind me.

He shook his head and kept walking to the living where we first were.

"Man, that was a workout. What floor are we at?" I pulled my arm across my chest like I was stretching. Zaliver pulled out his phone from his back pocket and began tapping on it.

"Fifth floor," he said.

"Damn. You need an elevator. If I'm staying here, I demand a room on the first floor. I'm not climbing all those stairs," I said, dreading the walk.

"We do and no," he said, lifting his head to look at me.

"You do? Wait, you have an elevator? Then why the heck did we take the stairs? And what do you mean no?" I almost shouted, peeved at him. That was mean. I hope he stubbed his toe on a corner wall, but it would probably hurt the wall more.

48

"I said no because you're staying in my room with me," he said, pulling out a wallet from his back pocket. He then pulled out a sleek black card and handed it to me.

"Wait—"

"I have to go. I'll see you later. Explore. Don't leave her side for anything. I expect for her day to be nothing less than perfect," he said quickly. He pulled me into his arms and inhaled my scent, then he was gone.

Puff like smoke, moving faster than I could comprehend and leaving me dumbfounded. I held out his black card and looked around with an open mouth.

"What?" Where would he go?

I turned again. I was surprised to see the four guards appear out of nowhere. The tall blond male stepped forward. He had an ecstatic expression on his face.

"I'm Johnson, the fun one. The redhead is Luke, party pooper. The one with the scar is Courtney, enough said. And the other one is Mila, secretly wants to—" Mila quickly walked over to Johnson and began to beat him with her arms.

"The hell is wrong with you!" She was jumping up and down to hit his face, but because he was so tall, it became impossible. Johnson just laughed it off. Luke stepped forward and pulled the pair behind him with an apologetic look on his face.

"I'm so sorry about that Luna. Johnson can be a bit . . . strange." His voice was soft and yet ear-catching. Courtney stood in between the two adults who were now looking down at the floor.

"Uhhh," I muttered.

The black card began to heat up in my hands, so I switched it over to my other hand. Money really does burn out easier when it's not ours to spend. The four guards looked at me patiently. They all looked older than me, but I got a calming sensation coming from them. Usually my wolf was tense with new wolves, but with everyone here, she was . . . elevated. I snapped out of my thinking and looked at them sheepishly. They must think I'm a total airhead.

"Sorry, sorry. It's just that I woke up a few hours ago, and to be honest, I still don't know what's going on. He just gave me his card and left," I said. I felt myself flush under their amused stares.

"It's alright, Luna. Alpha Lupus mind linked us to take you shopping for the day, so you feel more comfortable here. He said not to worry about the cost and to spend until you tire." Courtney said happily.

I huffed and looked down at the black card in my hand.

"Oh, that jackass doesn't tell me anything," I said dryly.

I looked up and saw Johnson grabbing his neck as he choked. The others were looking at me in shock, even Luke was gazing at me with astonishment.

"What?" I asked.

"S-Sorry. We just aren't used to hearing someone talk about Alpha in such a way," Mila spoke and looked at Johnson who was patting his chest.

"Damn. I almost wished he was here to hear that but then again, I think I like our Luna with her head on her shoulders," Johnson said. I think I would have been scared with his comment, but I remembered calling him a jackass before, so it wasn't that scary at all.

Good. You're trusting him now. My wolf said.

It's not trust. It's me knowing I can get away with calling a god a jackass.

"Umm . . . Would you like to go shopping now, Luna?" Courtney asked politely.

I looked down at the card. A devious expression made its way to my face.

"Awww, I recognize that look on her face. My little sister gets that when she takes my card and shops as revenge," Johnson said painfully.

I looked up at the guards in front of me, not at all ashamed or embarrassed at the creepy smile on my face.

"I usually don't like spending people's money, but who am I to deny something that was given to me?" I said.

"Why do I sense we're going to die today?" Mila whispered.

"Because we probably are," Johnson replied dryly.

I laughed. Zaliver had made a mistake.

He just placed my freedom in my hands.

~•~

"When Alpha said shopping, I don't think he meant this kind of shopping. Please don't buy a boat," Luke pleaded for the hundredth time.

I just hushed him with a wave of a hand. He began to tug on his hair and mumble something.

Zaliver wouldn't really kill them. I thought.

"It's the best in stock, little woman. Nothing can get you to your destination swifter and faster than this beauty right here," the kind old man said happily.

I know I was being stupid, but what did I have to lose? Who knows, maybe Zaliver was wrong, and I could get off the island faster than he could catch me. The boat in front of me was fairly small and

50

enough for at least two people. It was light red with dark yellow lettering on the side that read "Freedom." Could be a sign from above.

After telling the guards I wanted to go to the docks, they quickly agreed, not knowing my motives. When we left the house, I was surprised to see the island not looking anything like I thought it would. There were streets, houses, stores, and people walking around like normal. There were wolves once and a while though. It was just like being in the states but full of wolves. When we finally made our way to the large dock, I asked to see the smallest boats. They quickly realized I wasn't there to just gaze at them. Luke became a bit panicky while Courtney and Mila watched from afar, looking around for any signs of danger. Johnson, well, he had disappeared.

"So how much?" I asked, trying to be confident. How much did Zaliver have in his card? Would it max out?

"Well, for a pretty smile like yours, I'll sell it at 15,000. How about it?" he asked. I wasn't a boat person, so I wasn't sure if he was ripping me off. I also had to consider how much Zaliver had in his card. Six hundred years was extremely long to build up and save money.

"Deal," I said.

Luke began to let out whining noises behind me and walked back and forth.

"Luna, I'm sorry but I can't allow you to buy the boat because I'm sure I can guess what it's for. Alpha should know," Luke said with a somber look.

I quickly tried to redirect him before he could mind link Zaliver.

"It's not, I pro—" Luke and the old man in front of me suddenly blinked, then their eyes turned silver.

"Vivian," they said in unison

My eyes widened. It shocked me and, at the same time, piqued my wolf's interest. I didn't know what was going on, but I knew who was behind it.

"Zaliver," I whispered.

"What do you think you're doing?" I gulped air. Even though he wasn't here physically, he still found a way to intimidate me. I tucked my hair behind my ear.

"I-I uh, well I was—"

"Not thinking. That's what you were doing. Did you honestly think I had only given you four guards and then expect you not to do something stupid? I have you watched. Careful, mate," they interrupted me. My eyes flickered between both of them, not entirely sure whom to look.

He had me watched? I looked around me but couldn't find anyone suspicious. I clenched my jaw, and clamped my teeth tightly.

51

"Don't you have work to do?" I asked annoyingly.

It made perfect sense for me to try to leave but to be watched was stupid. He had already given me four guards, what exactly did he think I would carry out besides an escape plan?

"Yes I do, but you keep distracting me. I'd like to get everything done for tonight's meeting, so please do me a favor and just shop without trouble. I don't want to be mind linked that my mate is trying to purchase a boat from Old Kenny while I'm in a meeting. Do I make myself clear?" I nodded, feeling scolded.

Luke and the old man blinked as the color in their eyes changed back to their normal.

"Wow, I've never had him do that to me. I've only heard about it," Luke said with awe.

The old man began to shake and put a hand on his chest. I reached out to touch him, but he stepped back quickly.

"I'm so sorry, Luna. I had no idea who you were. I'm so sorry if I was disrespectful. I'm so sorry, but Alpha will not allow me to sell the boat. I'm so sorry. I'm so—" he said shaking. I could see he was scared for his life as if I would accuse him of kicking me in the face. I thought I would feel uneasy being called Luna, but it felt as if they were simply calling me by my first name.

"It's all right, really. I'm sorry for any trouble I have caused. I- I'm just going to go now. Have a nice day," I said, slowly walking backwards with Luke by my side.

I made my way out of the docks with a scowl on my face. Mila, Courtney, and Johnson waited at the corner of a sidewalk for us. When I got to them, they all looked down at the ground. I sighed.

"Where did you go?" I asked Johnson with a raised brow. He smiled widely at me.

"My sister needed a hand. She was around this area. Sorry for not asking direct permission," he said sincerely.

"So, what's there to do in the Bermuda Triangle?" I asked. They all looked at each other before looking at me.

"Follow us, Luna," Mila said, a devious expression made its way to her face. Maybe I shouldn't have asked.

~•~

"Beat her, ass man!"

"Come on, bitch! Show me what you got!"

"Do you even got booty? Cuz if you do, you ain't movin' it!"

"Mine is bigger than yours, Court! I'd shut that trap of yours!

"

"I'm gonna winnn!"

52

"You gonna win these nuts!"

Shake it by Metro Station was playing while Johnson and I battled out an intense game of Wii. We had been dancing against each other for a good hour, bonding with the group after a few words slipped out. Turned out, Johnson and I are pretty competitive when it came to dancing, and foul language was normal. Mila, Court, and Luke were cheering at us from the side.

They had taken me to an arcade called "Gamers Brawl" and we haven't left since. I could happily say now that we were bonding, the tension felt lesser around us. We had attracted a small crowd with our yelling or maybe everyone in the store, not much of a difference.

Winner flashed in front of my TV screen. Johnson fell to his knees, yelling out curses. Mila and Court bounced up and down and then laughed at Johnson. Luke patted him on the back with an amused smile on his face.

"Good game, Viv, even though I still think you cheated," Johnson said, dusting off his knees. He patted me on the head and walked over to Mila with a flirtatious look on his face.

"Hey Milaaa."

I rolled my eyes. Turned out, those two had an on-and-off kind of relationship. No wonder with all that teasing.

"That was awesome. I haven't seen anyone beat him in weeks. This ought to knock some sense into his thick head," Court said as she handed me a water bottle while I wiped my damp forehead.

"Thanks. I didn't really care if I won. I just couldn't miss the chance to see Johnny The Giant dance." I snickered. We both looked over and saw Luke shaking his head as he too was looking at Mila. He tried to get Johnson to leave her alone but failed as the latter walked beside her.

"So your brother, he . . ." I trailed off. They looked at each other with a blank expression in their faces.

"What? What is it?" I asked, hoping one of them would answer me.

Luke walked over to me with the others behind him, pushing me gently to the door.

"Alpha is ready for you. The meeting starts when you get there," he said. The playful Luke was gone. The others had taunting expressions. I could feel the tension coming off from them, but why?

"What's this meeting everyone keeps talking about? Are we going there now?" I questioned them.

"We're taking you to the Lupus temple grounds. We're having a meeting, so you can meet the pack." Johnson answered, pulling his blond curls, which was probably his habit.

53

I reluctantly followed as everyone made their way out and began moving farther and farther towards a forest.

"W-Wait! As in now, *now*?" I asked.

I wasn't ready to meet the pack. Not at all. I wasn't even wearing my own clothes. Damn it. Why didn't I go shopping like Zaliver suggested? Now I'm going to meet everyone in this raggedy version of me.

"Yup. All of the pack. Alpha is going to introduce you to everyone," Johnson replied.

I could feel my heart pump in my chest at the thought of meeting all of those people. It seemed like being Zaliver's mate finally hit me. The shock almost made me stumble. .

Holy shit! I was the mate of a god. A god! I was meant for a god and him for me. Who the fuck did I save in my past life to have this happen to me? Was I really good enough for him? Weren't there more qualified and prettier women in the world than me?

"Do not put yourself down! We are the way we are for a reason!" they said.

"I agree. Sorry, but I still didn't want to. What if they don't like me? I couldn't—"

"We're here."

"Ah shit."

What was in front of me left me speechless.

CHAPTER 6

When I was in middle school, we had a school trip where I was lucky enough to be one of the few to head over to the temples of Cambodia. Those structures were no joke. They seemed to go on forever in all directions with its halls chipped and covered in vines of roots that had grown over them. They stood tall and gave a peaceful effect.

The temples in front of me reminded me of those, and I did say temples, as in more than one.

They were positioned like the Egyptian pyramids but built like nothing I've ever seen in my life. From where I stood, they looked like a mixture of different architecture; tall towers at every edge and arcs connecting each building like bridges but in a puzzling way. Some parts of the temples were open to the outside; they didn't have walls as if they were knocked down. From what I could tell, there also weren't any roof, but I could see a glimpse of what I thought were stairs. The outside seemed to be made up of rocks and bright materials. I squinted my eyes at the colorful spots—exotic jewels—that stood out.

This was some Hogwarts shit right here.

"Breathtaking, isn't it?" Court said, standing next to me. I nodded, not wanting to take my eyes off the temples.

The setting sun gave it a calming look, but I wasn't fooled. Supernatural temples usually had dark stories behind them. They were intended for the ones who had the highest of ranks but never without a price. I bit the inside of my cheek. Zaliver had three temples. How dark was his past? Even the temples, the gods, Fate and Mother Luna paled to these.

Zaliver, what have you done? How strong are you? I wondered.

Luke cleared his throat, making me look at him.

"A few members of the pack will be waiting around. I'm warning you, Luna. Our traditions are a bit different from ordinary packs. Alpha asked me to tell you to stick by his side for the rest of the night. I can't say why, but be cautious. Those who are able to get into this pack . . . well, you'll see over time."

55

The hell was that supposed to mean? When Luke finished speaking, his eyes slowly leaked into silver. Before I could ask, a hypnotizing, dark cry pierced the air and a howl with gripping power made everyone enter the beautiful temple. By the eagerness of my wolf, I knew it was Zaliver calling for us, but it still did nothing to calm me down at what was waiting for me. If only I was able to question Luke on his vague warning.

I stared in wonder as we passed the large temples, then I saw them. I didn't have to make eye contact with them to see their glowing silver eyes in the darkness of the night. All heads turned to look at me as if I had worn white to an all-black funeral. They were all standing around, looking at me with a mixture of suspicion and confusion. Their eyes glowed in liquid silver while mine remained brown. I could understand why they were staring at me, but their watchful eyes gave me goosebumps. There was something dark in those gazes. For once, I wondered if they were even wolves.

I felt like the looks on their faces were the same one Dean Winchester had when he looked at food or, to be more specific, pie.

Head up. Don't let them intimidate you. We are the luna of this pack—Zaliver's mate.

I did a mental nod in appreciation and marched on as if I knew where or why I was here. The wolves in their wolf form weren't actually many like I initially thought. Most were in their human form. They were not speaking to each other. Perhaps, they actually were but through mind link. They just stared at one another and, once in a while, would strangely tilt their head.

In the temples, wolves usually meditate in their wolf form, you could say, to be at peace or to speak and pray to the god of choice, but Luke's warning rang in my ears. If the customs of this pack were different, then what were these temples exactly for? Being Zaliver as the only known god, how did this whole situation work?

My guards led me to what must have been the front of the meeting space. We walked around wolves who were wondering who I was. New member? A caught trespasser? Criminal?

It was odd because of the position we had behind the temples. The large structure casted a shadow on us, keeping the rising moon light away. I looked around and found us surrounded by large boulders, rocks, and trees. I made sure not to make eye contact with anyone as I glanced. My guards began to spread around me but kept close enough to reach me easily.

I shifted foot to foot, feeling uneasy.

Maybe I was way over my head here. I was beginning to see the different side of the pack, and I was left confused. My wolf peered around and took in her surroundings, trying to gather clues about what

56

could happen next. Even my guards around me seemed a little on edge; they were shifting side to side as if waiting for something.

Where was Zaliver? I wanted to see the only person who I felt safe-ish around to give me comfort. I looked up to see if I could see him hiding.

I was so busy looking for my mate that I didn't feel him appear beside me. When I cranked my head to turn once more, I had to take a step back out of fright over the large frame that leaned over me and the broad chest close to my face. It seemed like any tension would disappear when I looked into his eyes and messy hair.

"Damn! You scared me!" I exclaimed, placing a hand on my chest. I felt my heart racing.

He looked at me with a raised brow. I felt like I was getting better at reading his expressions. Even though he wasn't smiling at me, the slight twitch of his lip and tightness of his eyes made me believe he was amused at my reaction. I peeked around him and saw everyone looking at me. Johnson had a smirk on his face but other than him, the others around us looked at me with intrigue.

"Did I now?" he asked, leaning his head closer to mine. I held my breath for a moment before squaring my shoulders.

"You know you did. So what's going on?" I demanded, aware I was speaking to someone of high authority. My wolf liked that we seemed to be bolder around our mate and so did I.

He looked at me for a moment before facing the pack members. The youngest ones seemed to be around early teens. Court and Mila both winked at me as if to send me a message, but I had no idea what they meant.

Zaliver spoke and everyone paid attention to him. It was mesmerizing to watch Zaliver speak, but I finally got a piece of this confusing puzzle.

"You are all aware of the recent raids our pack have done. I'm here to confirm its suspension. Eighteen years ago, I received a note that a baby girl would be born. The child would grow and would be destined to be mine. Of course, I didn't believe it until a few years ago happened. I'm here to say it is true." My eyes widened at each word that left his mouth.

Someone predicted I was meant for Zaliver? The raids were meant to find me? I was unsure on how to feel about what I heard.

"I present to you my mate, Vivian Grey, your luna." Zaliver took a step to the side, presenting me to the surprised crowd. I knew what they saw: a brown-haired and tired girl who was still in her sweats. Man, I was a sight.

I forced myself to smile. I tried not to look into their silver eyes and avoided reading their minds because they still freaked me out. I wasn't sure how I felt about the luna role yet. Zaliver might be distant, but it made me happy to see that he at least saw me as his pack's luna even if I wasn't a good choice.

I and power wouldn't mix well, just like me and kids. I was a horrible leader. It was the reason no one liked working with me in school projects. I either ended up doing all the work and bossing them around or doing none of the work and still bossing them around.

Zaliver took a step closer to me. His height made me look pathetic next to him. This must be what normal people felt when taking pictures with Kobe. The pack's scary expressions turned pleasant. However, there was that one bitch in the crowd whose glare didn't fade.

"As a celebration, the pack is allowed to hunt all together tonight." All eyes lit up like fire as it wasn't allowed for a pack to hunt together. I mean it could be possible in small groups, but hunting all together was banned. It meant violent, hungry, wild wolves on the loose causing problems. If the humans—oh but wait, it was silly of me to forget.

Zaliver had a whole freaked island that was the size of a state for himself. They had nothing to worry about.

"That is all you need to know, and this changes nothing. Our plans remain the same. Spread the word. Enjoy." He snapped me out of my thoughts. I took in a breath as Zaliver pulled me into him just as his pack members dashed into the forest while a few of them remained, casting their eyes on me. Zaliver growled, making them take off to the forest without hesitation.

He released his hold of my arm and stepped back. He narrowed his eyes into the forest lands as if he was looking at something.

Or someone. My wolf snarled. Fiesty one, this one was.

Unlike most alphas, Zaliver didn't seem to use his voice so the others would obey him. It seemed like whatever he said would be taken as a command. It might be because he was beyond an alpha's rank. Questioning him would be crazy. It was impressive to see how loyal his members were.

"Zaliver, can we talk?" I was surprised when he snapped to me, his blue eyes seemed to darken.

"About what?" he asked in deeper and huskier voice.

"Uh . . . well . . . uh" I mumbled, unsure why his tone affected me in such way that left me stupid. I cleared my throat and took a breath.

"About all of this. I don't know what is going to happen, but I'm not okay with following your lead blindly. I'm in the dark here, and I'm confused with what you told them," I said.

He reached out to clasp his hand on my arm and pulled me to him. He wrapped his arms around me, making me place my hands on his

58

chest. My heart was thrashing wildly. This was too much for me to handle. Holy cow, he was firm!

"Hold your breath," he said.

"What?"

"Hold your breath," he stated once more. I looked at him suspiciously but did as told. Whatever he was planning, he'd better do it fast or else I would faint from loss of breath and anxiety of being too close to a being of perfection.

"Good."

The wind was suddenly whipping around me; my hair was flying all over the place; and my hands fisted into Zaliver's shirt as I pushed myself into him. I felt his chest rumbled, but I couldn't tell if it was a chuckle or a purr. I wanted to hear both.

"Breathe."

Could I breathe attractively?

I sounded like those people who just learned Zayn was leaving One Direction. I heard it earlier today when I was playing with Mila. Everyone gaped, sucking for air. When I finally was able to take control, Zaliver seemed pleased and released me. I looked around to see us standing in the middle of the living room.

"What? But . . . we were just outside! How?" I asked. He walked to the couch and sat down with his long legs stretching out in front of him. I walked over to him and just stood in front of him, waiting for an answer.

"I ran to get here. Some of the pack members were trying to listen in," he said. He lifted his arm and placed it over his head. I unknowingly watched his biceps.

"So, are you gonna answer my questions?" I asked, trying to play it off as if I hadn't been checking him out. He sighed out loud.

"Fine. The way I see it, you are mine, so you stay with me. I'm not going to let you leave unless I'm with you. I hope you settle in fast because your new life is here on this island with me. I'm not going to sugarcoat things for you. I don't know what the goal was for sending me a mate, but I'm stronger than them—"

"Than *them*? Who the hell are you talking about?" I shook with rage. I wanted answers, not riddles that leave me with more questions. I was so sick of being treated as a price of a bargain or whatever. I had feelings and damn them if they didn't see that.

"They," he snarled and closed his eyes, "are known to you as Fate and Mother Luna. That is all I will tell you because you only know of those two."

Those two? Had it not been Zaliver, I'm sure I would have grilled him on speaking of the gods so praised by wolves.

I was beginning to realize I had to prepare myself if I was to be around Zaliver. His experiences were different from mine. He knew things I didn't know about this world or probably even about myself. I pursed my lips at him but didn't push it.

"What about the 'mate' thing? How is that going to work between us? Are we just going to go our own ways on this island? You stay on your side, and I stay on mine?" I asked sarcastically, putting my hands on my hips.

I was distracted by the smile that graced his face. I and my wolf were deciding wether to respond to his smile or not.

"Technically, they're both mine since I own this island, but if you wish to see it that way, no, you will stay on whatever side I'm on. I won't deny we are mates, but our bond is a puzzle. The big bad wolf god and an eighteen-year-old pup. What a unique pair," he said in a wistful, curious tone and closed his eyes.

I felt like I was getting to see a new side of Zaliver, but I wasn't sure if he knew how he was acting. Something told me he was letting his guard down a little.

"So, is that a good thing or a bad thing? Because I'll tell you now, I'm no Juliet. I will go find my next Romeo if you won't take me as I am because of something you won't explain," I said.

Suddenly, Zaliver opened his eyes in pitch black before standing in front of me. I yelped in surprised, then gasped as he pushed me back until I felt something hit the back of my knees. It must have been a couch. Then, he leaned over.

"Let this be the last time you mention any involvement either romantically or physically with another male because I do not share, little one. I will rip apart the man who thinks he is brave enough to take what is rightfully mine right in front of you, so you will learn who the real man is." He leaned in closer as his black pupils retracted and changed to smoldering blue eyes.

"And then I will punish you for thinking about touching another male when you should only be thinking about touching me," he whispered.

Oh. My. God. I think my insides just exploded.

I was slightly relieved when he pulled back and walked back to the couch because it gave me enough time to close my eyes and remove the lustful look on my face. Sadly, my body was all like, "Take me! Make me yours!" I wasn't scared like I should have been at his threat. If I would be lost, it would be pleasing to know he didn't want me away from him. My wolf liked his possessiveness over us.

"Now that we have all of that taken cared of—"

"Wait! What the heck am I supposed to do here? And what about my family?" I asked.

His face became empty. Did that mean I would never see my family again? I don't think I would be able to handle this.

"Tomorrow you can . . . spend the day with me, I guess. As for your family, I'll think about it. Anything else?" he asked, standing up and walking to me once more.

"What about Lily and those other girls that this pack had taken? What happened to them?" I asked, taking his hand and allowing him to pull me up. We began to walk slowly to what I presumed to be my room, but I was bothered because I clearly remembered stating that I would not be sleeping in the same bed with him. It wasn't that I was afraid he would get all handsy at night. It was more like I was afraid for him. I had no doubt I would be the one getting touchy-feely. I was just trying to save myself from humiliation, but from what I understood, I don't think he would mind.

It seemed he had been touching me a lot since the last few hours we've been apart.

"Those girls were returned to their pack once I realized there was no connection formed, but every once in a while, a member would find a mate. I would grant them permission to keep them on the island. As for your cousin, I was informed she's fine in her pack or as well as an alpha-less pack can get," he said with dark humor.

"What do you mean by alpha-less?" I asked though I had an idea what his words meant. Zaliver just looked forward as we walked, the halls were quiet but someone snoring could be heard occasionally.

Lily's words entered my mind: "Alpha disrespected him."

"Oh," I grasped.

Imagine if an alpha hated being disrespected, then how would an alpha of all alphas react? He wouldn't be forgiving. As sick as it was, I was just glad to hear Lily was fine. It would have bothered me not knowing what happened to her after I passed out. When Zaliver stopped before a familiar door, I stopped and glared at him as his hands held my hips.

"No way," I said.

"And why not? You're my mate. You belong with me, so you're sleeping with me." He opened the door and roughly shoved me in.

"Rude," I mumbled at him. I walked over to the bed, and as I sat on it, I felt a slight pitch and remembered the black credit card. I took it out and handed it to him.

"Here." He took the card while kicking off his black boots.

"Ah yes, your 'little boat' stunt today. Don't try it again if you don't want to end up like Rapunzel," he said, walking over to a bedside table and putting it down. He emptied his pants' pockets and took out his phone, keys, and a thick wallet.

61

"You mean free and with my family," I joked.

"No, locked up with a pet as company," he said dryly before walking into the bathroom, leaving the door wide open. Well someone's confident.

I quickly moved the covers off of one side and grabbed as many pillows from the couch in the room, creating a little wall to block him from me. This probably wouldn't work, eh? I chose the side by the door to sleep on. If he had a problem, he could sleep elsewhere. When Zaliver got out of the bathroom, he was shirtless and his hair was slightly damp. Trying not to stare and seem like an idiot, I turned around and began to fluff the pillows before getting in. The bed was designed for Zaliver's frame, so my form probably looked like a child's in a parent's bed. It was pitiful.

"Well, isn't that cute?"

I heard him move around the room for a bit before the lights turned off. I grabbed my pillow and turned my back towards him, facing the door. I knew he could hear my heavy breaths and probably the rushing of my blood. I wiggled my toes with all the energy that was still in my system. Even though it had been a long day and I was dead on my feet, I still couldn't believe everything. My brain was overthinking and underthinking and everything in between.

I held my breath, and as Zaliver got into the bed, he shifted around for a bit before settling down. I looked around the dark room, looking from the door to the painting beside it. I was freaking out.

"I can hear your eyes moving around the room."

Not creepy at all.

"And?" I asked.

"Go to sleep. Tomorrow will be a busy day," he said.

I tried to do as he said. It did calm me down after a while, but I had one last question for the day.

"Hey, Zaliver?"

He groaned deeply, "What?"

"What did you mean when you told your pack that you didn't believe it when someone told you you had a mate?" It had bugged me for a while now.

There was silence for a few minutes, but it felt like hours to me.

"Because people as twisted as me don't get mates. Now go to sleep before I make you," he threatened.

"Night then," I said, disturbed by his answer.

I must have dozed off, but I was half awake when Zaliver began to remove the pillows between us. He pulled me into his arms and rolled us, making him closer to the door. Even in my sleepy state, I still

62

managed to mumble a few words, "I should have known." I felt his chest move up and down from silent chuckles.

I wasn't too sure, but I think he ran his nose over my face before setting his head above mine on the pillow, resting his chin on me.

"Indeed. What's mine belongs in my arms. You, my sweet, belong to this wolf god."

CHAPTER 7

"I'm sorry, what?" I asked Zaliver after having our breakfast. I woke up and found him just staring at me that morning. After showering, I wore one of his clothes to his great pleasure for some reason and headed for breakfast. He said the first thing we needed to do was to visit the doctor.

Zaliver stared at me blankly as if not telling me I was going to get tested like some animal. I mean, I know I was part wolf but still.

"Um, I'm sorry. I think I heard you wrong. Could you repeat yourself, please?" I asked politely though my eyes were warning him to choose his words wisely.

"Fine. We're going to the doctor to get your blood tested."

"For what?" I asked.

Did he think I had an STD or something? My wolf growled, offended. He cleared his throat and looked out the window. There were are a lot of people moving around the house, but they paid us no attention. I had a feeling it wasn't by choice. As they passed by, their movements would slow down as if it was a command.

"I just want to check on your health and some other things," he stated as my forehead creased in confusion.

He wanted to check on my health? For what? I smiled inwardly but then frowned and narrowed my eyes at him.

"Are you saying there's something wrong with my health?" I asked him. He looked at me with his blue eyes, startling me for a moment by their vividness. I was uncertain if I'd ever get used to seeing them. It wouldn't get him out of this mess because what I was really asked was something completely different. In other words, are you calling me fat?

"Oh no. I've seen females lay this trap out on their mates. I'm not falling for this. Come on, get up," he said with an edge in his voice. I let out a little laughter but stood up, ignoring his response. He wouldn't go down this path no matter what came out of my mouth. I knew that for a fact.

"Alright, fine." I said begrudgingly, still not sure what to make by this. I was about to pick up my plate when Zaliver put the plates in the sink and was back in a blink of an eye.

"Umm, thanks." He nodded.

I followed him to the back of the house and was surprised after realizing it wasn't a house at all. It was a large mansion that had underground floors. It was a white-colored mansion with other colors added to it. Parts of the walls seemed to be made of wood and brick, blended into a smooth-looking material.

"Where are you going?" I asked. I saw a large flat building with two wide doors. We must be going to a garage then.

"I could get us to the doctor faster, but I figured you'd like to see the way rather than just appear at his door," he spoke without facing me.

I watched him walk in front of me. Every step he took made his scrumptious rump looked even more grabbable. I had to fist my hands and cross them over my chest. I recalled him walking around in his sexy legs after his shower this morning, his towel barely wrapping his hips. Drops of water were dripping slowly to his abdomen, then he suddenly disappeared behind that darn towel.

I couldn't help daydreaming about it. I looked back up and saw a wicked smirk on his face, flaming me up. Today, he was wearing all black like always, but this time, he added a black leather jacket to his "Damon Salvatore" look. It made him look like the badass he was, making me think in a different perspective.

I couldn't see the future, but I could already see a problem. Zaliver was a god of many stories, and in each and every one of those, he was a cold-hearted killer. While the real emotions I had seen from him were of caution, coldness, amusement, and obvious possessiveness, I hadn't seen him as an angry and violent wolf god. Other than the strange Latin words here and there, he seemed like a normal or a really strong alpha with that scary speed, but then again, what did I know about him?

"Hey Zaliver, can I ask you some questions?" I asked, but he didn't answer me. Color me surprised!

We finally got to the garage where he grabbed the handle of the bottom door and pulled up. It immediately went up and hit the roof with a bang, making me flinch at the loud sound. He turned back to look at me, but I didn't bother to look at him.

In front of me was a dark red Chevrolet Camaro with a black stripe down its middle. I stared in awe at the car of my dreams.

I need to touch the car. I need to get in the car, I said to myself, not caring what Zaliver thought at the moment.

I took slow steps to the car as if not to scare it away. With my hand outstretched in front of me, I held my breath for a moment as soon as my finger made contact with the smooth hood. I think my eyes even watered a little as I ran my hand back and forth.

"I think you like the car," Zaliver's amused voice snapped me out of my little trance. I pulled my hand back immediately and turned to look at him with a sheepish look. It took me a second to feel the slight shift in my being, but I had a sense of pride that wasn't coming from me. I ignored the weird sensation that came over me and nodded at him.

"Quite the car. What's not to like? So, we're taking this one, right?" I asked hopeful, even though I didn't see any other car around us in this very large garage. He lifted a black key in between his fingers and waved it back and forth. I squealed in delight and went to open the door.

Like always, Zaliver somehow beat me to the car door. He was behind me with his hand covering mine on the door handle, then he leaned into me.

"Let me get that for you," he said softly.

I let out a shaky breath and nodded before stepping to the side to let him open the door. Leave it to him to distract me when I'm finally about to get into my dream car.

I know something else he can get for us, my perverted wolf said in my head.

I let out a little cough, surprised at her sudden choice of words.

I climbed into the car and curiously looked around. I was surprised at the smell. Zaliver's scent was faint, and it was overpowered by the smell of a new car. Maybe it was new by the looks of it. He closed the door and came in on the other side.

He started the car and sat on the seat.

"What is it? Are you waiting for something?" I asked, looking around. He shook his head and just looked at me, making me realize how awkward he seemed in this car. He pushed the seat back, but with his large frame, the seat was too little for him. I somehow felt bad for the guy, but he was the one who bought the car.

"Put your seatbelt on."

I did as told and watched him begin to drive. He pulled out the car and drove smoothly.

"Hey, what about you?"

He shook his head at me and said, "The island's streets are safer than anywhere else, but I prefer you wearing the seatbelt. I don't need it."

"Fine. Fly out of the window if you want to. Don't complain when you do though." I huffed at him before looking out the window.

Although I meant what I said, the other part of me couldn't help but think it might actually happen.

After a few minutes of silence and watching people going about their business, he spoke, "Sure."

I looked at him from the corner of my eyes. *What?*

"What?" I voiced out my question. He stopped at a red light and turned to look at me with a weary but serious look on his face.

"You wanted to ask me some questions. Now's your chance," he said. I thought he had ignored me, but I guessed not. I'd better not waste my chance then.

"Okay. Um . . . so, why do wolves' eyes in your pack turn silver? No other pack has done that before," I asked, motioning my hand to my eyes. I turned my full attention to him, not wanting to miss any indication or clue. He clenched his jaw before he relaxed completely. He shifted his expression to his usual cold look as if he was bored.

"Because no other pack is led by a god. My wolves call upon my strength when in battle, on a mission, or just to show their spiritual respect to me," he answered.

"They call upon your strength? But won't that make you weaker, especially if everyone use it at the same time? Is that why no one have seen you in years to centuries because you have grown weak?" I asked him.

"No. If anything, it makes me even stronger. While they borrow my strength, I still retain it. I actually feed off—" he stopped and pursed his lips. I tilted my head at him, wanting to know what he was going to say.

I didn't need to be told twice when to drop something, so I asked another question. I would ask him again later, but for now, I had to get information from him while he was willing to give. Who knew when the next chance would come?

"Okay. So what about your whole Latin command thing? How does that work? Why do I understand it?" He glanced at me and then answered in Latin as if testing me once more.

"It's a direct command from me to your wolf. Stronger than sacred alpha word binding. Whatever I say to your wolf in Latin becomes the only important thing to your wolf—the direct command."

Alpha word binding was basically calling on the voice and spirit of his wolf to control a crowd of wolves in any type of situations. Whatever came out of his mouth would be hard to ignore. You could try to resist, but it would always be a failure. It's scary to imagine that there could be something more powerful than that.

"Direct command?" I whispered under my breath, contemplating it over. He nodded at me.

"How it works is too long of a story. How you understand . .
." He narrowed his eyes and clenched his hands on the steering wheel
even tighter until his knuckles turned white. For a second, I thought he
would break it. He must have used a lot of restraint since I didn't hear it
give way even a bit.

"I'm not completely sure," he added.

So he didn't know either then.

"What about that mind thing you did to me? By the way, still
not cool," I said with a hint of displeasure ringing out strong in my tone.
He let out a chuckle.

"I'm sorry. Happy now? It was needed. I had to know what
you knew and see if you could be trusted," he stated before he lifted a
hand off the wheel, letting it rest on the car door. I leaped at the chance
to ask this one next, "To see if I knew what?"

"Next question," he demanded.

I bit my lip and thought over. Zaliver wasn't going to answer
all of my questions, and while I'd like to think he was being honest with
me, there was no way to prove it. After all, he didn't become the
strongest person possibly in the entire world by telling all of his secrets. I
had the feeling he would tell me eventually. Now wasn't the time since it
was the second day since we met. I guess I shouldn't have expected him
to reveal everything to me. We weren't like most mates, so I chose to
bring my questions down a notch.

"Back home, you're sort of a myth because no one has actually
seen you. We've only heard of places your pack raided to do things in
your name. Why is that no one has ever seen you? I mean," I simplified
my question when I saw his confused expression, which cleared up after
I explained.

"Because I see no need for me to leave my home to go deal
with small problems when my men can do it for me. I actually used to,
but when I was living in their human land, I got tired of the
overconfident wolves who thought they could challenge my position.
They would come seek me out after hearing how long I've been around.
Their surprised expressions and walkouts no longer interest me. Like,
what? Thought they were going to kick an old man's ass? Think again."
He scoffed.

I let out a laugh as I could picture it myself. Huge men yelled
out curses and threats, expecting a balding and hunched man with a cane
but then a handsome, muscular man would come out in a strong stance.

"So what about the island? How do you get things in and out
of here without getting the humans' attention?" I was genuinely curious
and wasn't aiming to escape anymore. Might have been due to that nice
sleep I had last night.

Zaliver lifted up his brow and looked at me from head to toe, thinking if I was aiming for information to escape, but he either believed it wasn't a problem or he was overly confident I couldn't get away.

"I've been around for a long time, long enough to make friends. After finding this place, I decided to make it my new home even though I didn't have any idea about the pack yet. I didn't want the humans to sink or destroy the land with all the pollution and sickness, so I had a witch put a repelling border around the island to keep all humans and supernatural beings that don't have my permission out."

"But I've seen maps of this place. The only thing you can see is water and a few islands on the edge. How is it that this big-ass island doesn't show up?" I asked now intrigued with the mystery. If a witch had put a border around the land, she must have been incredibly strong. Zaliver found this place before the humans did.

"Because that's what I want you to see. To keep everyone away from the border, we made the island invisible or almost submerged. The lands are actually a lot bigger than you think, perhaps as big as Texas. That's why when planes, boats, or anything else related tries to get close, they're either met ahead by a storm, sinkhole, tidal waves, or even lightning. It's the border keeping everyone away," he said his amazing idea proudly.

"Wow. That explains why this is the only place that the human government and explorers avoided to be around. It's the border that keeps them away, but that doesn't explain how you get things exported in and out of here," I said, still impressed by the clever thinking of my mate.

"That's for me to know and you to dot, dot, dot," he joked. I pursed my lips, wanting to know the answer to the mystery. I sighed when he kept silent. I looked forward and realized we had been driving for a while now. We were in a much more packed place with buildings looking tall and dominant. It almost gave off the same air as a hospital which reminded me of why we were in this car in the first place.

"So why are we going to the doctor? I can assure you that I'm perfectly fine," I said.

"You'll see in a few minutes." He pulled up in front of a white building with four floors and lots of windows. There was a sign in front that read "Laboratory of Experimental Research." My eyes widened in alarm at the word *experimental*. Turning the car off, Zaliver was about to get out when I spoke.

"Uhh, I thought we were going to the doctor. That does *not* look like a hospital to me," I stated with suspicion and narrowed my eyes on him. He rolled his blue eyes at me and got out of the car. He slammed the door and walked around to my side. I wasn't going to get out unless he explained, but he opened the door on my side and waited.

"Come on, get out. We are going to see a doctor. He's just a bit different, but he's still a doctor."

I undid my seatbelt and got out. I pointed a finger at him, ignoring the angry look he threw at me for a little show of disrespect.

"If I get poked even once, I'm out. I swear, I will swim my ass off this island and disappear without a trace. You'll be looking for me for so long that it will make you "Finding Nemo" and look like a kid waiting for his dad around the block," I stated. Without looking back at him, I walked off to what must have been the entrance.

After a thundering growl, a loud crash and stomping of feet over glass followed. As soon as I got to the door, Zaliver calmly held it open for me as if nothing happened. I walked past him with a quick "thanks."

Zaliver walked in front of me, passing the receptionist who stared gaping at us or mostly at Zaliver. It seemed he knew where he was going and which codes to punch in to pass through tightly-locked doors. We went down a flight of stairs before stopping in front of a bright blue door. A dark-skinned man in a white lab coat was standing at the doorway. He had an excited smile on his wrinkled face, which made me calm down a little.

When we entered the room, I was relieved to see that it really did look like a doctor's room. He pointed at the only chair in the room—which I found odd—for me to sit on. Zaliver greeted the man, shook his hands, and patted his shoulder. He leaned against the wall beside me and crossed his arms over his chest.

"Hello Vivian, my name is Doctor Mickelson, but you can call me Dr. Mick. I'm not sure if you know why you're here." He saw Zaliver shaking his head and nodded. "Okay, so when Zaliver informed me about you, he said he wanted to conduct a research. Note why you aren't marked like normal mates yet?" I glared at the doctor for the reminder. He flinched a little and glanced to Zaliver, who must have had a scary expression on his face because he immediately apologized.

"Sorry! That came out wrong. Well, the reason for that was he wants to know how both of you will   react to a mating bite and bond. It's the first we've ever heard of such—a bond between a wolf and a wolf god," Dr. Mick explained quickly with his light brown eyes lighting up in wonder. What he said made me took a deep breath. I guess it was the constant question of why he wouldn't explain the reason for not marking me.

At first I thought it was just because he didn't like me or because he was just doing it to be a jackass. I turned to look at him. He was glaring at the doctor before he looked at me.

"Why didn't you just say that instead of avoiding the question?" I asked, peeved at all the worrying that he caused me. He shrugged and turned back to the doctor. I was not sure whether I was annoyed or not with my mate.

"So what types of tests do you need to do? What do you need from me?" I asked, wanting to know the outcome as well. Dr. Mick walked to his desk where he picked up a clipboard and walked back to me.

"Does this mean you'll agree to helping out?" he asked.

"At this point, I don't really have another choice. I'm curious as well," I stated honestly and lifted my hand to tuck a strand of hair behind my ear.

"Okay. First, we're going to do all the basics like temperature, height, weight, allergies, etc., then we'll go on from that," he said while writing a list.

"Are we both going to do it or just me?" I asked.

"Just you. We did this a long time ago, but because my body," Zaliver paused for second, "no, just you." I looked at him with a frown on my face, but he ignored it. What was he going to say about his body?

"Okay, let's get started."

After checking my eyes, ears, and all that breath-in-and-breath-out stuff, he had me stand by the wall to check my height. I was nervous because I knew he would be checking my weight in front of Zaliver after this. He had been watching us like a hawk the whole time. Have you ever had your weight said out loud? No? Well, good for you. This almost reminded me of middle school when the P.E. teacher had us weighed in front of each other. The other kids always commented on my weight.

Unlike werewolf stories, we were not born fit just because we had wolves within us. I mean, we sure ate like we were starved, but ours were like human bodies. While in human form, our wolves were dormant or in a state of sleep. That's why whenever we needed to use something from our wolves, we had to call on that specific ability. The same goes for our metabolic system. Some wolves were born lucky enough not to call on that quick food-breaking wolf system while others, like me, processed out food in human speed. Only when in wolf form would it speed up, which helped us stay fit enough that it wasn't a worry. I wasn't fat, but I guess you could say what I had was baby fat that hadn't left me from my younger years. I wasn't really comfortable with scales or numbers.

"Step up on the scale." I stepped reluctantly, knowing my good-looking, fit, and god of a mate was watching.

Man, what an embarrassment! I just hoped Dr. Mick kept his mouth shut in order for this to pass.

My luck, Dr. Mick noted it down and didn't look up to ask me.

71

"You're a bit above your height and weight. Have you always weighed this much?" Shit.

"Yes," I said thickly, wanting to pound in his face with each words.

"Is your metabolism like a wolf or close to a human's?

"Humans," I answered quietly. I didn't want to look at Zaliver as if I was swallowed by a whale right now.

"Is it just you or do your other family members have the same system?" Fuck.

"Just me." I had decided I didn't like Dr. Mick anymore.

I bit the bottom of my lip, wanting this humiliation to be over. I would go on a diet after this.

"Do you plan to diet?"

We both jumped at the infuriated growl that came behind me. Zaliver growled at Dr. Mick, who dropped to his knees in front of me, bearing his neck. I was surprised that I could feel the amount of power he was radiating in anger.

"She is perfect the way she is. You are making her uncomfortable. Do not forget your place, pup! Wrap this up immediately." He boomed at the quivering doctor.

I think I felt my heart lighten at his words. A small smile was slipping on my face. My embarrassment disappeared immediately and was replaced by a warm feeling of sunshine.

"I'm truly sorry. I meant no disrespect Vi—Luna Vivian. I apologize for my stupidity. Please forgive me," Dr. Mick said from his uncomfortable position. I could smell his unbearable fear. I sighed just wanting things to be over and get out of here.

"Sure," I said though it sounded forced even in my ears. I couldn't help it that even my wolf felt pissed at the doctor. She had half a mind to say "no" just to see how Zaliver would handle it.

After that, he got a blood sample from me and gave another apology when we left. Once back in the car, I turned to look at Zaliver. His anger was no longer visible, but I could faintly feel it.

"Thanks," I said, knowing I didn't have to explain myself. He turned to look at me with his blue eyes piercing mine.

"That will never happen again. I promise you that," he said with a serious look in his handsome face. Without another word, we drove off.

While a large part of me was overjoyed at his words, a small part of me feared that dark look on his face.

~•~

We pulled up into a clearing. In wolf or human form, there were like a hundred men and women working out, sparring and training

72

seriously. They were all in workout clothings. We drove right off the road and on the grass. Because the car windows were tinted, some peered in curiously.

I immediately recognized Algebra as he made his way to the car. He was wearing black sweatpants and a white t-shirt that showed off his hard-earned muscles. His brown hair seemed almost lighter in the sun, and his green eyes were focused on the car.

"I want you to know that you're safe on this island. We can show you how tough our security team is," Zaliver said, turning off the car and smirking at me before getting out and opening the front door for me. All eyes were glued at me as soon as I got out, but even the eyes of all these wolves, who no doubt could kick my ass, could make me as nervous as when Zaliver looked at me.

After walking closer to us, Algebra whistled while staring at the car. I rolled my eyes when Zaliver and him did a fist bump followed by the shoulders.

"I haven't seen you drive a car besides the "Black Beauty" in what could be years. Is this new?" he asked Zaliver, who just nodded at him. Algebra turned to me with a playful look on his face. His eyes were secretive as if he knew something I didn't.

"Hello, Luna Vivian. How do you do this fine morning?" he said gleefully. I couldn't help myself from responding.

"Hello, Algebra. I'm doing fine. How about you?" His amused expression immediately turned dry, and by looking at his green eyes, he seemed annoyed.

"Just peachy," he replied sourly.

Zaliver cleared his throat and turned to look at the crowd that had slowly and secretly moved closer to us. They all bowed their heads to Zaliver but looked at me with curiousity.

"Continue your training. Your Luna will be watching, so don't fool around." With a wave of his hand, they continued their training with more enthusiasm and fierceness.

Zaliver turned towards me and put his hand on my shoulder while gazing at me with an unusual expression. I couldn't tell if he was worried, angry, distracted, or cautious, but whatever it was made me worry.

"I want you to look at the movement and technique they use. Be my look out for slackers," he said sarcastically. He looked at me for a second more and then nodded to himself slowly.

"Go, sit on that bench. I'll be back in a few seconds. I have to talk to Albericus," he said, pointing to a bench big enough to hold an entire football team a few feet away. I nodded at him, watching him and Algebra walk away from the clearing. I guess they were mind linking because of the various changes in their facial expression.

I would have to pass by a few fighting partners before reaching the bench. Unless they weren't going away from the group in quick movements, they wouldn't get near me. Besides, I was going to pass by quickly. I didn't wish to be hit. That shit would hurt, even for a werewolf.

I was so close to the bench when one of the pairs came out of nowhere. My feet were both swept from underneath me, causing me to fall forward and hit the ground. My palms took most of the hit, and my face was slightly stinging from the little rocks. The wind was knocked out of me. All the grunting, hitting, and fighting suddenly stopped. The clearing went dead silent.

Suddenly, a shadow loomed over. I lifted my head, ignoring the sting on my palms in protest. A pretty pale brown-eyed girl with her long black hair moving in the wind stared down at me. She looked at me with a false look of surprise, and the corners of her lips turned up a little. I could spot a lying bitch a mile away, and this one was just inches away.

"Oh no, did that hurt?" she whispered as if there weren't werewolves all around us with sensitive hearing. I narrowed my eyes at her.

"Well, it wouldn't have hurt if you were our alpha's real mate you little lyi—"

Zaliver appeared behind the girl. His expression was a livid one, and his eyes were the deadly black that would suck you into his darkness. The air around him was frightening. His hair had fallen over most of his face, masking his true expression. Whatever it was, it was horrific, and I just knew. He made eye contact with me. I don't know how, but I just had the feeling his eyes scanned over me before narrowing.

His hands shot up quicker than light, wrapped themselves around the girl's head, and twisted it around to a gruesome angle. He was so fast that her expression froze on her last words. Her eyes were opened, glaring right at me.

He tossed her body across the clearing like a rock. I was frozen. I didn't know if it was shock, fear, disbelief, or what. But there I was, wide-eyed on the ground, in the silent clearing that held more than fifty witnesses. I couldn't feel anything. I couldn't think.

With the same infuriated expression, Zaliver reached down for me with the same hands that ended the life of that girl. I was conflicted but didn't know why. He scooped me into his arms and held me close to his chest, bridal style. I didn't protest or move. I just looked at him with a glazed look in my eyes. I didn't know how long we stood there just looking into each other's eyes, but when it ended, his face had become doleful. He began walking past everyone, but I didn't care about them. He looked down at me one last time.

74

"Close your eyes and sleep. Dream only of pleasant things. When you wake up . . . I will be nothing more than a nightmare."

CHAPTER 8

I felt like I had rested for a few years when I woke up, but it was probably just hours. I didn't need to open my eyes to remember. I wanted to get the image of that girl's head snapping so close to me out of my head. It was even scarier when complete darkness seemed to surround Zaliver with his black eyes and angry expression.

I squeezed my eyes even tighter, making the little white spots appear behind my lids, and sighed out loud.

I wasn't sure how I felt at the moment and how I should feel towards Zaliver. Hate him? Fear him? My mind and wolf were at war against each other. While the human side of me knew what Zaliver did was wrong and cold, my wolf was telling me it was the nature of wolves and life in general. Zaliver just protected and acted on instinct when it came to us; his anger was more than what regular alphas would have done when their mate would be put in the same situation.

A part of me was convinced to label him a monster, but the other accepted it as justified.

Was I in real danger? No, I wasn't sure she tripped over me on purpose, but I doubted she planned on pummeling to death, at least not with a witness. It wasn't like I was going to let her lay a hand on me without a fight. I wasn't a warrior like she probably was, but I would put up a pretty damn decent fight. Why couldn't he have just asked her what her problem was? There was no need to kill her for tripping over me.

While thinking about it logically, I felt like freaking out by how calm I was watching my first death at close range, which was also done by my mate. I mean I killed a bunny or four in my life but that had been for meals. Then again, I think I must have unconsciously prepared myself for this. Earlier today, I was thinking about the stories about Zaliver being a cold killer. I guess I had expected him to do something like this one day but just not so soon.

I opened my eyes, and my sight adjusted to the dark room. I looked towards the dark curtains, not at all surprised to see darkness past them. It was nighttime. I slept the entire day. This island seemed to be bad for my health. If only I didn't get tested or loaded with information,

I wouldn't have knocked out. We'll, it was better than getting knocked up. I joked, trying to distract myself.

I pulled myself into a sitting position, immediately feeling the coldness and heaviness on my wrists. I closed my eyes as annoyance hit me and took in a deep breath.

"He didn't," I said to myself out loud.

"I did," a familiar monotone voice said.

Opening my eyes, I saw Zaliver sitting on a couch facing the bed. He sat with his legs parted and arms crossed over his chest. His face was fixed on a blank expression, and his black hair covered his blue eyes. The room was so dark he almost seemed like a shadow. Seeing him now made me feel . . . I don't know.

I reflected on his expression, unsure of how to act. How would you bring up a murder? *So, about that chick you killed today . . .* I don't think so. I breathed in deeply.

"Why?" I asked, lifting my left hand in chains. He dared to chain both of my wrists up to the bed. I glared at him, but he didn't even appeared bothered by what he had done. Of course, if he didn't feel guilty about snapping someone's neck, why would he feel guilty about chaining me up?

"Do I need a reason?" he questioned me. The nerve of this man.

"Yes! Yes, you actually do!" I snapped at him.

"Can you guess why I chained you up after killing someone in front of you?" He turned his head away from mine and looked to the window as if looking out through closed curtains. I realized he had a point.

I stood up and pulled the chains. I was surprised when it just kept on coming. I walked towards the bathroom and was even more bewildered when I made it to the shower. I looked at Zaliver suspiciously.

"Why are the chains so long?" I asked him.

"I had them made for you," he said casually.

"I don't know which bothers me more. Is it the length of these chains that makes me roam freely in the room or the fact that you had these made for me?" I said dryly, tugging at the chains until I felt resistance. They were stronger than I expected, even my wolf's strength didn't denture anything.

I turned to look at Zaliver and clasped my hands together before walking towards him. I stopped in front of him, noting how tense he looked. My wolf, who would always take his side in any given situation, pushed me to comfort our mate.

"Okay, look, I'm not going to lie. Seeing you kill that girl did freak me out, but I kinda expected you to do something like that." He

77

tilted his head at me. "No offense. I just figured that your years on this planet as a wolf god bounded you to kill someone. Let's not pretend wolves don't go around slaughtering rogues by every chance they get. I just didn't expect it to happen so fast, so close, and totally unjustified!" I explained.

While I spoke, his face changed from blank to surprised, followed by a portion of relief and then to anger. He made me take a step back in surprise when he stood and loomed over me. I tilted my head to look at him. His black hair hung away from his dark blue eyes. I gasped and blinked repeatedly at the black veins that seemed to move slowly under his eyes. They were pulsing black underneath his skin. It was frightening and then of course, he had to open his mouth and show me those sharp long pearly whites.

"Unjustified?! You call what she did unjustified?" he spat out his words. His chest distractingly lifted up and down with the large breaths he was taking. I answered in a small voice. I really need to learn when to shut my mouth.

"She tripped over me. I really don't think killing her was the right choice." I said, looking at his chest.

"You're right." I looked up quickly, unable to believe he agreed with me so quickly. Does that mean he regretted killing her? I thought I needed to know the girl's name to pay my respects.

"Really? That's great."

"I should have tortured her first, then maybe I'd be calmer," he said, pissed.

My face fell.

"Of course," I said mostly to myself. I wasn't surprised by his answer, but I was still disappointed to hear how serious he was. I walked away from him and went to sit on the bed, walking over the annoying chains.

"Can you get this shit off of me! If I didn't feel like a prisoner before, I do now." I moved my arms widely in motion.

He crossed his arms over his chest, making his muscles bulge. I moved my eyes from his chest to avoid staring at his face. I was happy to see the veins gone, and that he was back in his gorgeous self again.

He studied me sitting there for a long time while I just looked back at him flatly.

"I had expected you to be uncontrollable, emotionally unstable, and scared out of your mind . . . of me. I thought you'd hate me for sure," he said before peering at me with curiosity on his face. His voice was tight yet controlled, and for a second, I thought I heard it waver.

I just shrugged at him and began fiddling the shiny chains on me, trying to find a way out of them.

78

"Warning. It'll catch up to me eventually," I said absent-mindedly, but I was completely being honest. It would be because I was a winger, always going with the flow but trying not to be ignorant of the things around me. Most of the time, whatever I choose to ignore and not give much attention would always come back to bite me in the ass.

"So you're not going to do anything crazy or try to runaway?" he asked me with a hint of disbelief. I couldn't blame him, almost.

"Yup, no crazy escape." I snorted. "Besides, it's more like swimming than running here." He cracked a little smile.

"Now that we understand each other, sort of, you'll let me out of these chains, right?" I asked him confidently.

"No." My head snapped up to look at him, bewildered.

"Why not?" I yelled at him.

Ignoring my tone, he cocked a brow on his sly face. It was just pissing me off.

"While I appreciate the honesty and warning, I'm not a man who take chances. Until your little breakdown happens, you're not leaving this room. If you want anything, just ask me," he said smartly.

For the first time, I snarled at him with a wet "I'm thinking of serious damage" kind that had his eyes narrowing and darkening at me. He did nothing but stood there while I snarled viciously at him. I wasn't a huge threat. Hell, I wasn't a threat to him at all, but I was pissed off and hadn't shifted in close to three days. I could feel it building up.

"You can't do that to me! I haven't shifted in three days, so unless you want an angry, crazy, and violent female wolf possibly stabbing you now or clawing your face off in your sleep, remove these chains," I spoke through gritted teeth.

His eyes widened in anger. His own growl erupted from his throat, vibrating through me and shaking the room, causing the chains to clank. My wolf tried to get me to submit to him, flattening her ears to her head but I refused. If I did, then it would always be like this—him forcing me to submit to him whenever he didn't agree with what I had in mind. If I wanted to at least have a somewhat equal ground with him, I had to stand up for myself.

"You idiot! Do you know how dangerous it is for your kind to hold in a shift? I can't believe you would endanger yourself like this. This just proves how much you need me to take care of you!" He scowled at me.

Huh! I looked at him slack-jawed.

What? Out of everything, all he heard was the shifting part. How the hell did this become about me depending on him all of a sudden? Where the hell did this come from?

"Wow, hold up there. First of all, it's not my fault that I haven't shifted in three days. I was on a plane, got kidnapped and knocked out by two and then knocked out again by three. So if there is anyone to blame here, it's you. I was planning to go for a run when Algebra freaking took me. One day! I'd like one day where I'm not getting put to sleep!" I exclaimed.

"Come on. We're going for a run and then you're going straight to bed after." He walked up to me and pulled out a key from his pocket. I held my hands out for him to unlock the chains, but he stopped in front of me. Looking at me straight in the eyes, he growled out.

"Behave." I rolled my eyes at him, just wanting to get these things off of me and shift into my wolf who was a getting more and more excited. She wanted to show off.

Behave, mutt.

Yeah, yeah. My wolf replied.

He searched my face for any clues that I might try to do something stupid. He then sighed and released me from my chains that fell to the floor with a sharp bang. I waved my hands, free from the cold and heavy chains.

"Come on."

~•~

Zaliver had me walked into the forest behind the house. I was excited to be surrounded by familiar scents. While the island was mostly forest, I hadn't actually entered one yet. We walked into it until Zaliver felt we were far away from the island.

Unlike most werewolf stories, our clothes wouldn't shred while shifting. I mean, think about it. When shifting, our bones would break and reform, and fur would sprout. We would be dead if we had to shift for a fight, especially if we were caught off guard. The first time our bones did break and our clothes tore off was when we had our earliest transitioning from human to wolf. After that, every shift was almost like a satisfying yawn. In human form, our wolf would be inside of us, and while we were in wolf form, our human body would be kept inside. It was just a switch of control. Our clothes would no longer shred, preventing us to go around naked. Over the centuries, it seemed wolves figured out how to keep clothes in order to keep our race a secret from humans.

I tried to ignore Zaliver's eyes on me as I closed my own to push forward my wolf. Shifting wasn't about how fast you could shift your body to defend yourself. It was about releasing yourself and taking control. If you were in danger, all you would have to do was trust your wolf. They would do the rest. When my wolf accepted me, I went into her mind and felt a tingle of warmth spreading from my heart to my body. When I opened my eyes, everything was clearer.

80

I looked at Zaliver who was raking his eyes over my wolf form. I knew what he saw. A dark caramel wolf whose fur went from light to dark, coloring my tail the darkest shade of black. I also had a patch of black fur on the tip of my left ear. Werewolves were a lot bigger than normal wolves, but not bigger than horses like some stories had told. I had a good height for a female werewolf. My wolf walked over to Zaliver who reached out to touch the top of our head. My wolf nudged at his leg with her snout.

"So soft," he murmured, running his hand through my fur and stopping to pull gently at my left ear.

No! I said.

Too late. My wolf purred loudly as my left ear was its soft spot. Zaliver froze wide-eyed in shock at the sudden noise. My wolf took this chance and began to rub our body on his legs.

Stop it, Dummy! We're wolves, not cats!

No, I want him to wear our scent. My wolf said.

He has. We've been with him all day and night.

Zaliver seemed to regain something and looked down at me with a playful glint in his eyes.

"You're quite the flirt, aren't you?" he said with his husky voice.

My wolf winked at him. I groaned inwardly.

Yeah, go ahead and flirt with him! It's not like I'm the one who's going to have to face him after we're done here. I told my wolf.

Wanting to get chased by her mate, my wolf suddenly turned and took off, leaving Zaliver behind. It seemed Zaliver himself didn't like her leaving him behind because he appeared beside us a second later still in human form, keeping up with us.

We were just running side by side next to each other until my wolf felt like she had her fill. Without warning, I slid mid stride with my back, causing me to shriek as I prepared myself for the impact. Zaliver wrapped his arms around my body and flipped us over mid-air with his back hitting the ground and me landing on top of him. These were the moments when I was glad our clothes appeared back on me.

Damn you, Wolf! I know what you're trying to do!

She snickered.

Bitch.

Helpful bitch. She corrected.

I froze for a second on top of Zaliver, who hadn't removed his arms around me. I slowly looked up and saw him already looking at me. His eyes were slowly darkening as I looked into them. It had always been him on top of me and not me on top of him. I could feel his heart beating under my hand, strong and fast. As we looked into the each other's eyes, I felt myself get pulled into the vast ocean of blue his eyes

81

held. Surrounded by his scent and feeling him underneath me, my body heated.

"Are you alright, Vivian?" he asked with his voice coming out provocative. I watched his plump red lips pronounce my name slowly and sensually.

I'm dead. I think my ovaries exploded with how hot that one sentence came out.

No, no, I'm not fine because my sexy-as-fuck mate is currently under me with his arms wrapped around me. We hadn't even kissed yet, and I already felt like dying on the inside.

"Uh yeah, s-sorry. I don't know what came over my wolf."

"She seems to be quite mischievous and playful." Without removing his hands, he rolled us over, making me under him this time. He placed his forearm on either side of me, putting his face real close to mine.

"It makes me wonder if you'll be like this in bed," he whispered. The intensity of his blue eyes was making me shake.

I made a strange sound from the back of my throat, unsure how to breathe or respond. I would like to take back what I said earlier; I'm dead now. Then, my sass came back to tease him, and his reactions were funny.

"Why do you say that like you have a chance?" I asked jokingly, hoping to lighten up the atmosphere. I wasn't into losing my virginity on day two on the forest floor with my mate.

He narrowed his eyes on me while a growl was slowly building up from his chest. I could feel it with how close he was to me. His lip slightly curled up to bare his teeth at me. I felt both his legs shift on either side of me, and his hips were pushing to my lower half, officially pinning it. Quicker than I could protest, he had my hands pinned above me.

I looked at him wide-eyed. *Did I over do it now?*

"Why must you push me to my limits? I recommend you watch your tongue. I've never let rude remarks slip in the span of forty-five hours. I will not let another remark about you and a male slip. Now let's go, you must be hungry." He suddenly had us both upright and held my hand. He led us through the forest with me stumbling like an idiot behind him.

Holy cow, that was intense. I had never been really close to the male population except for my dad and a few cousins. I was pretty sure it wasn't normal for male wolves to be so possessive. It took a few seconds for my heart to beat normally and take a stupid man's last words. I was hungry, really hungry. I stared down at our hands as we walked; his were big and felt soft yet rough. They covered my whole hand. It left me thinking about the strength these hands had.

"What was her name?" I asked quietly, the slight tightening of his hand let me know he knew who I was asking about.

"Martha, and I don't want to talk about her anymore. Whatever problem she had with you is no longer a problem," he said coldly with his shoulders rolling back.

I pursed my lips but didn't push it. Rest in peace, Martha, I guess. Hope you wouldn't haunt me in your afterlife for getting you killed.

"Why didn't you shift?" I asked him, changing the subject.

He glanced at me and gave a weary smile. Great, another question to avoid. I was getting really tired of this.

"Next question?" I asked irritated and he nodded.

"What's your favorite color?"

He snorted at me and shook his head.

"Really? Black." Expected.

I was going to start with small questions and build up, trying to see which topics he avoided.

"Song?"

"None." I gave him a disbelieving look to which he shrugged.

"Movie?"

"None."

"TV show?"

"None."

"Sport?"

"They're pointless." At least they weren't repetitive answer.

"Favorite book

"None."

"The heck is wrong with you?" I asked, exasperated.

"What?" he asked, amused. I think he was playing with me or he liked to annoy me. I huffed at him as he knew what he was doing.

"So, are you not going to ask me?" I asked after silence had fallen over us. I could see the pack house' porch lights from a distance.

"I don't need to. I already know." I blinked at him. He smirked down at me cockily.

"You like the color violet. Your favorite song at the moment is Often by The Weeknd. Your favorite show is The Vampire Diaries. You don't have a favorite sport, but your favorite book is 50 Shades of Grey. Kinky." He listed them, making me feel mortified at the last one. His amused expression then turned dry.

"You also favor that Christian guy." He scowled at the ground. For a moment, I thanked the Lord that he was just a character because I had no doubt that Zaliver would have killed him if he was real. Hashtag Team Grey. Sorry Zaliver.

Why was it that the tables always turned on me?

"I'll make you something to eat and then off to bed," he said as he opened the front door and walked us straight to the kitchen. He pulled out a chair for me and then pushed me in. While he pulled things out for me to eat, I looked at the clock and it read 11:57. It wasn't so late.

Zaliver kept acting like he wasn't giving anything about himself away or did anything romantic like how normal mates should, but I felt that this might be his own way of showing me he cared. I wished I knew more about him, yet the chance of him opening up to me seemed impossible. Could it have something to do with the other gods he spoke of? He mentioned not wanting to mark me because of them and then took me to get checked as if to see if I had something that could hurt him.

Could that be it? I shuddered at the thought of hurting Zaliver. I didn't want to darken my thoughts even further so I pushed it to the back of my mind.

Zaliver ended up making soup for both of us. I thought we wouldn't be full. Whatever he put on it filled me up to the top.

"Now, bed."

"But I'm not tired." I whined. He rolled his eyes at me before we went to our room.

Oh god, I even began calling it our room. Man, I had to figure out what my position here was because without the mating mark, I couldn't really count myself as luna. If anything, I was just an intruder the alpha didn't want to let go.

"Give me your hands," he said, picking up the chains. I shook my head back and forth.

"Nuh uh, I'm not putting those things on. There's no need." I let out a relieved sigh when he dropped them to the ground.

"Fine, but you'll be wearing them tomorrow when I leave." My ears perked at his words.

"We'll see about that. What are you doing?" I asked.

Turning around, he walked to his drawer and pulled out bottoms and a pair of pj's, handing them to me.

"Business," he said, walking into the bathroom and turning on the lights.

I contemplated it would give me free time away from him, which was much-needed.

When he walked, I changed quickly while sitting on the couch. I ran my fingers through my hair.

"If I am going to live here, I guess I will go job searching tomorrow. I don't have my papers here though," I murmured. Maybe Zaliver could pull some strings.

"You don't need them because you won't be working. If you want something just tell me," he said in a brusque manner. He came and sat next to me, putting his hand around the back of the couch, almost around me.

I thought he could hook me up with a job.

"If I'm going to be living here, I need a job, Zaliver," I stressed out the word *job*.

"And why do you think you need a job?" he asked rudely, leaning closer to me.

"Oh, I don't know. Maybe to buy clothing because I can't keep wearing your clothes for the rest of my life or however long I'm going to be here. I have other necessities and future needs too," I tried to explain myself.

He tsked.

"If you want some—"

"I'm not just going to ask you when I want something. That's called being a gold digger," I said, looking at him with faint amusement. He rolled his eyes at me.

"I remember when that word first came out. Believe me when I tell you that you're using it in the wrong context. But it's not gold digging when your mate, me, is here to give you anything you ask for," he said.

"I don't care. I'm not living off of you."

His mood suddenly darkened. I got the sense of anger coming from him.

"Why does it sound like you're planning to find a job to pay off rent?" He snarled at me, making me blink at him. Sometimes when he talked, it was hard for me to follow. The man came up with the oddest conclusions.

"Is that what it sounds like to you?" He nodded at me.

"That's not it—"

"Then what is it?" He demanded.

"I-I just want to . . . Well, I'm not sure what type of relationship this is, if you can even call it that. Moreover, I have no idea how to handle the sudden change that comes with you. I wasn't ready for a mate but then you came along or you kidnapped me. Then, you turned out to be a god, so that was shocking. I guess a job can me help me find some stability of some sort," I explained, looking at nothing in particular. I felt my chest lighten after getting my thoughts out. Minutes passed, Zaliver was still saying nothing, so I turned and found him looking straight at me with a blank face.

I bit my lip, unsure if I annoyed him with my babbling. He let out a soft chuckle and ran his fingers through his thick black hair.

"What?" I asked anxiously. I felt like I showed him a portion of my self.

"I initially thought their plan of sending you was to use the bond at their advantage, that you'd be a little seductive doll to play me into their trap. But now I realize that it's the opposite." His tone was ironic.

"What?" I asked, confused at his rambling.

Is he saying we can't be seductive? That fucker. My wolf grumbled.

He suddenly let out a booming laugh, throwing his head back with his hands going to his stomach. I had never heard Zaliver laughed so hard in all the times I've been here. His laughter, although unexpected, warmed my heart. But just how sudden it came, it also disappeared quickly. I suddenly found myself under him.

He smirked with his hand coming up to trace the corner of my eye and down to the corner of my lip and then over it. I slowly looked down from his eyes to his lips with a fiery trail following his finger.

"Oh my luck. You truly aren't tainted by the horrors of this world. You're just . . . you. And now that I see that, I plan to enjoy every second." He smiled down at me with a coy look, his blue eyes dazzling me.

"What are you going on about?" I asked him softly.

"Hush," he said playfully and then he kissed me.

CHAPTER 9

It took me a moment to realize what he had done and what we were doing. My eyes were closing a second too late. Immediately, it felt like my senses were on overdrive. I could feel everything; I could feel him. His body was adding warmth to my body, and his heartbeat was strong and loud.

His lips, firmly pressed onto mine, were as soft as silk. After a few seconds, his lips began to pull on my bottom lip. The sensual movement was making me shake a little. I was slightly frozen, not knowing what to do or think. This was my first kiss. What the fuck was I supposed to do? As if fearing I would pull away, his hand cupped my face, keeping my face still; the other supported him so as not to crush me, not that I would mind though.

I went on instinct and moved my lips to do the same. I lifted my hands and placed them on his back. He tensed at first and then he relaxed. As he began to make patterns on my lips, I slid my hands down his back and gripped his firm waist. His kiss became rougher as his teeth pulled the bottom of my lip. I parted my lips, getting the demand. Blood pumped fast in my body, and my skin felt sensitive against the rough clothing. My body was surrounded and engulfed by scorching flames, but Zaliver controlled them.

Our bond that had grown weak due to us not doing what normal mates should do suddenly exploded like a fireworks show. Hitting us full fledge, we both let out soft groans at the feeling of our bond connecting and intertwining again like two golden strings.

As soon as the tip of his tongue traced over my bottom lip, it was like I became possessed at the little taste of him. His taste was like a drug, and I was becoming addicted to it. There was nothing in this world like him. I wanted more. I think I surprised him when I responded just as aggressively to his kiss. I tugged his waist down as his tongue explored the inside of my mouth, taking the lead tentatively. I let my tongue push against his.

He pulled back and growled lowly at me. For once, his blue eyes were not black but a vibrant blue that almost seemed to glow. We were both breathing heavily, and every time I took in a breath, he would breath out, making our chest slightly rub against each other. Slightly dazed and bewildered, I looked up at him with a surprised yet happy smile on my face. My wolf was somewhere passed out in my head from the feeling he gave us. When I felt I could breathe properly, I spoke with my voice sounding breathless.

"Not that I'm complaining, but where did that come from?" I asked. He was a sight above me. His black hair was hanging over his face. His blue eyes were intense with carnal desires burning in them. His red lips were slightly swollen.

I felt proud knowing what I made him. I became possessive, wanting to be the only one to see him like this. Unconsciously, my hands that were still on his waist pulled him down closer, if that was even possible. He gave me a little smirk as if sensing my thoughts; he probably could now.

"What? Can't I just kiss my adorable little mate?" he asked in fake innocence. I rolled my eyes at him and shook my head.

"You took me to the doctor to see if you could keep your so-called adorable little mate," I pointed out.

He pushed himself off of me and stood up. I slowly sat up, watching him raise his arms and stretch. His shirt lifted a bit, showing off the beginnings of his "V".

"I was going to keep you no matter what. I just wanted to know . . . if I have to expect any surprises. You never know what to expect when it comes to the mating bond. The bond is meant to bring two beings together, becoming each other's strength; however, a mate also becomes a weakness. When people have a weakness, they are easily manipulated and blinded by what they think will lead to their own happiness," he said. His mood became serious, sobering me up.

That one sentence made me feel like there was an undertone to his words. Like this was something I shouldn't forget. Had he been hurt? Was . . . there someone before me? Of course there was. My chest felt like a heavy weight was dumped on it, but I tried to think around this pain. We were mates; our bond was stronger than anything. It had to be.

"Now come on and go to bed." His serious expression turned devious, brows lifting suggestively at me. "Unless you have other activities in mind—" I shot off the couch and bounced onto the bed faster than light, rolling onto my side and wrapped the blanket around me like a burrito until it covered my head.

"Good night!" He chuckled.

~•~

"I'm giving you my card again. Buy something this time." I nodded at Zaliver.

"I'm serious. I expect you to buy thirty of everything: shirts, pants, skirts, earrings," his voice lowered a little," bras, and underwears, as well as lingerie." My eyes widened and my face heated up.

"Are you serious? Thirty? I don't, I mean, isn't that a little going overboard? And why the hell do I need lingerie? I already told you, I don't want to live off you."

"Yes, yes, no, and for me. Let me explain to you why living off of me shouldn't bother you since you clearly won't just take my word for it. If you spend five million today and another tomorrow, the only thing you do to my bank will be removing ten pennies . . . in my first bank account out of the many. So think of it as a favor that you're doing for me. I have no problem letting all that money sit there, but if you spend it, you'll be contributing to the stores, which will make the owners very happy, knowing their luna is buying from them," he said casually.

I bit my lip and thought of his words. Ten pennies? Five million? How rich was this guy? If he saw it as a favor and help to store owners, then I shouldn't feel bad about it, right? I'd be helping him and myself.

An amused smile formed on my face. "You are very slick with your words, I'll give you that. Fine, you win. Just don't come complaining to me when you end up broke," I joked, partly serious. I reached up to grab the black card out of his hand, but he grabbed and pulled me to him.

"Stick to your guards. If you need me, just ask Luke," he said. I was startled when he leaned down and pecked me on the lips, lingering for a second. Just like the first time, he gave me his card and vanished.

I slumped a little, looking at the floor. I took in a much-needed breath and ran my hand over my face. That man . . . was something, but I was partly glad he wasn't around me now. It would give me free time to evaluate my new life. I wasn't going to try to leave like last time. He said I could call and maybe leave to see my parents if I behaved appropriately. I wasn't going to mess that up. Zaliver didn't have to do anything for me, but he did. I wasn't blind to see that much.

As I made my way to the living room, I passed by the guards' break room. I didn't pay much attention until four bodies walked out in a single file line and walked with me. Mila, Courtney, Johnson, and Luke were silent as snakes. If it hadn't been for Johnson smacking Mila on the butt, I wouldn't have heard them. I turned around in time to watch her pulling her fist back and Luke grabbing it.

"Why is it that you can never behave in front of our luna?" He snapped at them. I smiled at each of them, glad to see familiar people. They were wearing their signature black uniforms I suppose, but this time, each had earpieces.

"Hey, how are you guys?" I asked as we made our way down and into the living room. I had already eaten earlier today with Zaliver, but I didn't want to stay cooped up.

"We're good, Luna. Is there anywhere you like to go today?" Court asked politely. I took out the black card from the shorts I was wearing and waved it in front of them. Luke's green eyes tightened a little as if remembering I was trying to buy a boat last time. I put him out of his misery and said, "Don't worry. I'm not going boat shopping today. There will be no attempt to break out this time." He nodded but the expression remained the same—tight and tense. I blew out a breath and shrugged. There was no point in trying to convince him; I better just show him.

"That's great! You'll love the stores here. Our malls are nothing like the humans have," Mila exclaimed, snatching her hand out of Luke's and walking up to me.

"How so?" I asked.

"Well for one, you don't have to worry about someone suddenly shifting or the big secret being out since everyone here are wolves . . . or the majority at least are," she added. My eyes widened at the news of humans living among wolves.

"There are humans here?" I asked lowly with the surprise still on my face. Mila nodded but it was Luke who explained.

"Just those mated to wolves here, but other than that, just wolves." I exhaled the breath I didn't know I was holding, relieved and slightly confused.

"So . . . any malls in mind?" I asked after a moment of silence.

~•~

I was officially annoyed and felt slightly rejected by the pack.

After being escorted to the largest mall on this side of the island, I came to realize fairly and quickly how fast pack news would spread, especially when it involved the alpha snapping someone's neck for his mate. I was treated with respect in every store I entered. It would have been fine if the wolves hadn't been: A, shaking; B, stuttering and apologizing for nothing; and C, avoiding me like I was that one weirdo you see in the streets late at night, thinking I was going to rob you so you pick up your pace and look the other way. I wanted to meet new people and mingle with the pack and get as much information as possible, but with the way things were going, I'd have better luck getting information from Zaliver. We all knew how much he loved to talk.

"It's fine, Luna. They're just not sure how to handle you yet. That's all. The pack never really expected to have a female alpha," Court comforted me as I looked through some shirts. I guess my sulking showed as much as I felt it. I shrugged, not wanting to talk about it. They had a point though. I wouldn't want to hang around with the girl who got a pack member killed, no matter what her rank was.

After picking out thirty shirts, Court helped me carry some of them. Mila and the others made sure everything was fine. They switched places every few minutes to keep me company as well as to get to know each other better. As we walked to the register, I noted the girl who was there looked like she was about to faint at the sight of me. Her eyes were wide in fright and curiosity, and her already pale skin was a shade paler. I put on my best smile and walked to her.

"Hello!" I put down the shirts in front of her while Court followed silently.

"H-Hello. I-I hope you're pleased with our s-store, L-Luna," she greeted with her eyes remained low. Her hand was shaking while quickly scanning the tags.

"The store is very nice. Good work." I praised her with a forced smile on my face. I got the hint that I wasn't wanted around. It hurt both me and my wolf to see pack members avoiding us. After all, we were supposed to be their luna even if the idea itself seemed beyond a dream to me.

After she packed the bags, we left. I was surprised after learning that all of my bags would be sent to the pack house immediately. All I really had to do was pick and pay.

Mila, Johnson, and Luke were already waiting for us outside when we walked out. We had only been shopping for about two hours, and none of them mentioned about being hungry, so I figured we were alright for another hour or so. We sort of just drifted from store to store, walking around, and one of them would point something out to me. It wasn't until Johnson's phone rang when my day really began.

"Sorry," he said sheepishly. I just shrugged at him, still a bit under the weather.

"Warning: If I end up getting fired, I'll set you on fire. What do you want?" he asked with annoyance in his tone, or something else like, exasperation. I didn't want to be rude, so I tried not to listen but failed.

"Oh come on, bro! You know you love me. Besides if you get fired, I'll give you a job here; plus, Mark says that if you even get anywhere near me with a lighter, he'll kill you. Thanks babe. Anywho, I'll need you for like two minutes—" Johnson interrupted the feminine voice. Must be his sister, I guess.

91

"No way! You already pulled me out the other day. I'm lucky I didn't get caught ditching the job on the first day," he growled onto the phone. Mila, who was beside me, sort of snickered discreetly.

"I know, but this is important. It will also be the last time. I swear, I really need your help," the woman pleaded on the phone.

"Why can't Mark help you? I thought that was what mates are for, to help each other," Johnson asked. His eyes narrowed at nothing in particular.

"Because he's busy. I'm sorry I'm such a bother to you during work. I just . . . I thought I'd always have my big brother around to help me when I need him the most, even with the small things." The woman's voice became smaller and more emotional that Johnson's eyes became softer, making me smile.

"Like when we were little and I couldn't reach Mom's cookies because she would always put them on the top shelf. You always reached them for me, so I'd give you half. I knew then you'd always have my back, but it's all right. I know we've grown into adults, and I understand if you no longer care about me. I guess I'll just do it myself," she ended in a sad tone.

Johnson looked to me, and before he could open his mouth, I nodded at him. He mouthed a "thank you" and sighed into the phone.

"Fine. I'll be there in a few," he said softly into the phone, tugging his blond curls that fell out of his band. A squeal blasted on the other side of the phone.

"Good. Your spot is already open. I knew you'd fall for that," the women mocked. Johnson's eyes narrowed again.

"You manipulative little witch!" he yelled into the phone, catching a few eyes. I let out a small laugh.

"You say that like it's a bad thing. Love you bro, see you in a few," she hung up before he could say anything else.

"I can't believe I fell for that again," Johnson mumbled to himself, putting his phone into his pocket and yanking harshly on his curls again.

The girls and I looked at each other before letting out loud laughter at the tall wall of muscles with curls sulking because he just got played by his little sister. Luke shook his head and patted Johnson on the shoulder.

"You are laughing because you have no idea what it is like to be an older brother having a little sister who knows all your weaknesses and later becomes one. It's like a never-ending curse," he said somberly.

"Ahhh man! Sorry, Luna. I'll be back in a few," Johnson said, but before he could turn and leave, I spoke.

"Do you mind if I come?" I asked shyly, not wanting to intrude. I just did not want to spend another second in the mall with a pack that didn't really want me around. His eyes became wide before he smiled at me.

"No problem, Luna. I'm sure my sister will be delighted to meet you," he said with real excitement in his voice. The thought of meeting someone who might actually like me, who might give me a chance to win her over thrilled me. We followed Johnson out of the mall and into the car we came in—a large BMW. As we piled in, I finally asked some questions.

"So, do you know what your sister wants you to do?" He shrugged at me and shook his head.

"She always makes me do odd jobs at the store, so I don't know what it is exactly."

"What type of store does she own?" I was taken aback by the sudden flush of his cheeks and the redness of his ears. I couldn't help but think of some really odd stores.

After a pause, he answered, "Victoria's Secret."

I wasn't sure what made him flush when that wasn't so bad.

"Wait, what type of *odd* jobs do you get at a store like that?" I asked with horror. My imagination was running wild.

Johnson didn't answer. All he did was groan. He somehow managed to tuck and curl his large frame, ducking his head under his arms. Mila and Luke laughed in the front seat.

"Aw, man, I still have the pictures when she made you model a new set of lin—" A loud and choked-out growl erupted from Johnson, followed by a mixture of mortification, embarrassment, anger, and annoyance in his face.

"You said you deleted those!" He scowled at the front seat. Mila turned around in her seat, her eyes slightly dazed from laughing.

"And you said you deleted my pics in that red bikini when we were in freshman year. I saw your Facebook post!" she said, her eyes narrowed in slight anger.

Johnson's face went from angry to false innocence. He looked up, blinking his large blue eyes at her.

"I don't know what you're talking about. It must have been some other Johnson. It's a common name you know," he pointed out. His hands were locked on his lap, but his fingers twitched, making me think he wanted to pull on his curls again.

"Liar! Your Facebook name is Johnson WiggleWiggleWiggle. I threw a look of disbelief at him. What type of name was Johnson WiggleWiggleWiggle?

"You got something against my last name?" he said in false offense. She rolled her eyes at him.

93

I looked at Court beside me and mouthed, "WiggleWiggleWiggle." She shook her head and mouthed, "Jason Derulo." I nodded.

"As a matter of fact, I do. First, it's stupid. Second, delete the picture. Third, the last time I checked, you don't have anything to wiggle." I wanted to say "burn" and make a sizzling noise, but that would be immature to do, right?

Johnson, ignoring the obvious "burn," smirked at her and leaned forward. His large frame made him a lot more closer to her than if I had done so, and I'm technically closer than he is.

"Baby, the last time you checked, we were both drunk. But if you want to check my wiggle, let me see yours first," he said. Her eyes widened before her whole face turned red. Smooth!

Well, that escalated quickly. "Johnson, calm the heck down, man. We're here. You too, Mila, behave. Both of you!" Luke scolded, but he couldn't hide his amusement. I felt like he was somehow the mother of the group.

When we arrived, they climbed out of the car to check if the area was clear before letting me out. The building in front was large and very fashionable-looking. In fact, it looked like the same Victoria's Secret store from outside the island.

Suddenly, Zaliver's words came to my mind. *Bras, underwear . . . lingerie.*

My face turned into a rosy color. I didn't get to buy any of those because of how odd everyone was around me, but I couldn't just not buy it. Now, I had to, not for Zaliver but because I was not about to go around like captain commando.

We entered the store immediately. Johnson walked away for a moment and came back a second later with a petite feminine blonde who has blue eyes that looked similar to him. She seemed to be a few years older than me, dressed in a light purple dress. I smiled and was surprised to see her large baby bump. Her eyes immediately sought out mine. I held my breath preparing myself for her to react like the others, but I was happy to see her smile back at me without fear in her eyes. She extended her hand, and I shook it politely.

"Hello, I'm Johnson's sister, Hannah. You must be Luna Vivian. A pleasure to meet you," she said sincerely. I could tell she meant it. She looked at me in the eyes, but my wolf didn't feel like she was challenging us or anything like that. She was showing us a different level of respect and approval which was oddly pleasant.

"Call me Vivian." It would be nice to make a friend who wasn't guarding me.

"Will do. Let me know if there's anything I can do to help. And as for you my *dear* brother," her friendly smile towards me turned somewhat evil on her brother, "I have a job for you." They then walked to the other side of the store.

"I'll be outside, Luna, patrolling and yeah." Luke seemed uncomfortable in the store. He didn't even wait and just bolted for the door. What was it about these types of stores that made men uncomfortable when they wouldn't hesitate taking the product off their partners?

"Well, this looks like a good time for you to do your thing. I'm sure you don't want us around for this. It'll probably make you feel uncomfortable," Court said. Both her and Mila had mischievous looks on their faces. I blushed and looked anywhere to avoid them.

"You can leave. I'm curious to know what our Luna is going to seduce the alpha with. Perhaps this nice red thong with matching lacy—" I snatched the thong out of her hands which she held up for everyone to practically see and threw it back in the box where she got it from.

"I'm not going to seduce him. I'm just here to shop. Now if you'll excuse me." I walked off with as much confidence as I could; knowing no matter what I would say, everyone here would probably judge my undergarment choice on whether it would attract Zaliver's attention as if this was for him.

It is, though. My wolf argued.

Shut up. No, it's not. I said.

Get the red thong!

I said shut up!

Fine . . . the black one then.

I blocked her out after that. I was halfway done picking all of my undergarments when the funniest thing I have ever seen passed by me: Johnson in a costume—women's undergarments.

I think I might have snorted at some point but so did every other woman in the store. I knew it was wrong, but it was too funny to hold it in. He was red-faced and scowling down at a smiling Hannah. It was just wrong. His obviously masculine face was sticking out with his curls pulled down. His lean muscles were bulging out of the sides. The measurements weren't even good. The man had half boob on his side!

"You are the best brother ever," she said.

He went outside and stood. Aside from catching Luke's attention, he also caught the attention of the people entering the store. They talked to him and made hand gestures. At least, the costume was working. I'm guessing this was for advertisement. Hannah stopped next to me and looked at her brother through the window.

"Haha, can't believe he fell for this." She laughed.

"What do you mean?"

"I told him sales are low, and we need an eye-catching strategy. I will have to wear a costume and stand outside to gain attention. Being the doting older brother that he is, he volunteered because I am pregnant. Of course, I didn't mention there's actually someone more masculine and that never in a hundred years would I stand outside because sales are doing fine," she said with an amused expression on her face.

I looked at her warily. I think I now understand what Luke was talking about when it comes to little sisters. She must have been able to read my expressions because she quickly explained.

"He called me *fat* during my second month. No one should ever call a pregnant woman *fat*. It's just not something a woman could forget." We both looked at each other before bursting out laughing.

"I think you just became my best friend," I said. She threw her hand over my shoulder, which was odd because she was a few inches shorter than me.

"I knew there is something I will like about you." I smiled at her.

She looked down at my stack of undergarments and gave me that same evil smile she gave her brother before he came out dressed like a woman. Oh no. I narrowed my eyes at her.

"So . . . how do you feel about see-through lingeries?

~•~

It was safe to say I had become best friends with a psychotic, evil pregnant woman who enjoyed watching people squirm. Hannah did not let me leave the store until I tried on every provocative piece she shoved at me. Some of those pieces made me want to get on my knees and pray for forgiveness. I had drawn the line on the see-through ones. I mean really, what was the point?

After that, she left the store to one of her workers and spent the rest of the day with me, giving me a tour of a lifetime. While Johnson was funny and childishly playful, Hannah was brutally honest, straightforward, and not shy at all. While on tour, she noticed the distance people keep from me. She also called out a waiter who kept apologizing to me after accidentally spilling my drink before it got to the table. Her words did not only snap the waiter of whatever fear he had on me but also seemed to calm the people eating at the restaurant.

"Yo, we got your sorry the first and fiftieth time. I think she gets it. Chill, dude. No blood, no foul." The air went silent. Even though Hannah was the one who spoke, all eyes were on me as if expecting me to yell or something.

96

"I-I'm . . ." The poor guy didn't even know what to say anymore. He just stood there with his hands wringing out his apron and eyes looking misty as if he was about to cry. I felt distressed at seeing this and acted on instinct.

Ignoring the prying eyes, I rose from the table and put a hand on the guy's shoulder, not minding his slight jump and whimper. Luke and the others were close by, refusing to eat with us but sticking close enough to keep me safe if something went wrong.

"Hey, can you look at me? I kinda feel like I'm talking to myself." I joked, making my tone soft and soothing.

He looked up hesitantly. His light brown hair had the same shade as his eyes. I smiled at him, but he still had a slightly panicked and frightened look on his face.

"What's your name?" I asked.

"J-Jedadiah," he whispered as if he had condemned himself.

"Well Jedadiah, I want you to know that it's totally cool that you dropped the drinks. Just like my friend had said, "No blood, no foul." Besides I'm sure if there was blood, it would be obvious because I bit my lip from hunger than you dropping something on me." I could tell my words calmed him, enough to make him realize his life wasn't on the line. I wanted him completely and utterly relaxed in my presence, call it me wanting to at least get someone's trust.

He nodded and gave me a small smile. I sat back down, pleased to have eased him somehow.

"What would you like to order?" he asked, his tone was a bit confident this time.

"Finally, man, I thought I was gonna die here. Let me get another lemonade, a cheeseburger with bacon, no mayo or mustard, lots of fries or onion rings, garlic bread, a slice of pizza, and salad. Come back when I'm done. I might want a banana split or chocolate cake . . . maybe both?" Hannah said and later found us looking at her in bewilderment and incredulity.

"What?" She snapped at both of us with her right eye twitching.

Jedediah and I looked at each other and then at her.

"Nothing," we said in unison.

"That's what I thought. You might be Luna, but I've got no problem letting you stand outside my store in a costume. The same goes for you, pup."

"Oookay. I'll have two grilled cheese sandwiches with tomato sauce, garlic bread, and a bottle of Sprite. Try not to drop it this time," I said with a wink. His mouth dropped, and the poor kid's cheeks blushed. He nodded eagerly and took off with a smile. After that, the tenson in the restaurant was gone.

After dinner, we dropped Hannah off and then came back to the pack house. I was tempted to say *home* but something held me back. We came in pretty late. Most, if not all, the lights were off and snoring could be heard.

After saying goodnight to the others, I made my way to my or Zaliver's room. I was surprised to realize that I managed a whole day without any real drama with the man. Maybe things were finally calming down. I really need to stop jinxing myself.

When I opened the bedroom door, I was disappointed at the darkness of the room, thinking Zaliver might be coming in late. I shut the door behind me and was feeling the wall for the switch when my hand made contact with a familiar warmth. My hand rested above Zaliver's shoulder. He was tense and rigid.

"Zaliver?" I whispered into the dark. My heart was pounding into my chest. Why the hell would he stand in the dark?

Like always, his movement was faster than possibly normal. He roughly wrapped his hands around mine. He began pulling me to what I presumed was the bed. This was becoming his normal habit.

"Zaliver?" I asked again. This time, my voice shook with worry, fear, and excitement. Excitement? For what?

He suddenly stopped and shoved me down, making me lose my footing and fall onto the bed face first. I shouted a little and then shrieked when I was suddenly flipped on my back. I squinted at Zaliver's form in the dark. It didn't matter that I was a werewolf. His room was dark as heck. He was dressed in black, not to mention the cold aura he was giving off.

What was his deal? I looked at him and dared not to move, pushing some imaginary line. I was right.

"What's wrong? What are you—" He cut me off with a low growl that progressively turned into a loud snarl.

He lowered himself onto me, slowly getting on his hands and knees on top of me until his face hovered dangerously close. His blue eyes seemed to glow in the dark. Mixed emotions swam in those eyes— anger, betrayal, confusion, desire, and a darkness so deep that I had to fight the natural instinct to crawl away from him.

Why was he feeling all those emotions? Why do I always find myself pinned under this man?

"What's wrong, my dear sweet mate"—he purred out the words into my face. His voice was seducing my body to believe. His words were the gentlest of touches, but my mind heard the anger and iciness in his tone—"is you touching another male. You flirted with him and then you dared to wink at him!"

He slid one hand down my arm, around waist, and under my back, spreading his fingers over me and pushing me against him. I

98

instinctively curved my back to be closer to him, his intoxicating scent buzzed my senses. His other hand gently grabbed at my hair, enough to keep my head close to him. He shifted his weight to his elbow.

"I don't know what you're talking about," I whispered. He then let out a humorless laugh.

"You're telling me you don't remember that pup from the restaurant, Jedadiah," he snarled out the name. My eyes widened in recognition. So that's what this was about. He thought I was flirting with the waiter Jedadiah? I shook my head.

"No. I wasn't flirting. The poor kid was just—" He pulled his head back and snarled viciously at me, making me attempt to shrink back.

"I don't care! You touched him. You flirted with him. You winked at him. Do you not remember what I told you?" His words were hard as stone, but he whispered the words as if he read poetry to me. I was shaking in my bones, even my wolf didn't know what to do with the situation. She was intrigued at this side of him while I was frightened.

"Don't hurt him! Please!" His wild eyes narrowed at me.

"What? You've got feelings for the boy? Tell me!" Although his voice was rough and angry, I felt a sense of . . . panic through our bond.

"Zaliver, listen to yourself. You're blowing this out of proportion! I don't even know the kid," I pointed out, trying to reason with him. He was being crazy!

"Because he's just a kid. He can't take care of you the way I can. No. I can do so much more than what that boy can. You said it yourself, he's just as kid, but I, I'm a man. I can take care of your needs the way no other man in this whole planet can," he said, lowering his face, and skimmed his nose lightly over mine and then down my cheek. Then, I got it.

Was Zaliver . . . jealous? Was he jealous that I was concerned with another male? But why? Before I could finish my thoughts he planted his lips to mine. His lips were rough and frantic but were driving me crazy that I responded with the same intensity. This wasn't like the first kiss we grew up with. This one was like a dam had been opened and a flood of raw feeling and need surrounded us, drowned us. This kiss was almost punishing.

His lips would draw away from me in each time I pushed myself up to be closer to him. He pulled away, leaving our lips barely connecting. Because of his hold on my hair, I couldn't reach them, even with my back arched to meet his lips. I moaned with want, needing to feel him pressed against me completely. Where was this side of me coming from? Something in me pulled under my navel and a torturous heat spread in me. He sucked on my bottom lip and then bit it roughly

99

without breaking the skin, but enough for it to sting. He cooled it with his tongue, immediately healing it, putting that part of me out of misery. My mind was in a daze, no longer caring what we had talked about. Just when I thought Zaliver was going to firmly kiss me, he pulled back and gazed at me with a blank face. I looked at him through dazzled eyes, breathing heavily.

"I will get the test results on how our bodies will take each other tomorrow. I don't know what the results will be, but I do know one thing," he said seriously. I sobered up at his words and gazed up at him worried.

"What?" I almost didn't want to ask, afraid of what his words would be.

"That before tomorrow night, you'll have some sort of mark that represents you're mine. Until then . . ." *Clank*.

My eyes widened in disbelief at him. No! Not this again! He slowly pulled up off of me and stood at the end of the bed, looking down at me roguishly.

"I can't believe you chained me again!" I yelled at him, not bothering to move other than to sit up. The weight of the chains was adding to my anger. I was not an animal he could chain up and take a stroll with whenever he wants!

He just shrugged at me and walked to the door. He knew damn well that if he tried to sleep anywhere near me, I'd kill him.

"I'll kick your ass for this!" I yelled out.

I grabbed a pillow out of anger and flung it at him with all my might. I fumed even more when he let it hit him and lifted a brow at me.

"And at that point, you'll already be marked as mine." He turned his back.

"Son of bitch!" I yelled out one last time, not willing to let him have the last word.

"Never said I wasn't. Night, my sweet." He walked out and closed the door. I stared at the door for a few moments and longer, trying to will him to walk back in, so I could keep yelling insults at him. When he didn't, I let out an aggravated sigh. What did he mean by "some sort of mark?" I thought anxiously.

That night, my imagination didn't let me sleep with all of the possibilities.

CHAPTER 10

ZALIVER AZRALA

I shut the door and stood behind it. I heard her movements on the bed and my name that was cursed out in anger. Staring blankly at the wall, my mind was racing with hundreds of thoughts.

Who knew such a small brown-haired beauty could drive me crazy? While I did feel a bit wretched, I mainly felt an odd sense of ease knowing she was trapped in my room. It was wrong, no doubt, but it felt so right. She made me chain her to the bed. I wasn't blind to her lustful gazes and wandering hands when we slept. I never brought them up because I enjoyed them too much and avoided making her feel self-conscious about it.

I made my way to my office, which was located far away from the room, in less than a few seconds. I slammed the door with much force, creating a loud bang that shook the room. I walked towards my chair and sat on it with a sigh. I spun around to look at the window behind me and watched the moon high in the sky, illuminating the dark and cold room.

The beast within me wanted to be released and return to the little brown-haired vixen on my bed. Sitting on my chair, my pants suddenly felt tight around my manhood. With all the naughty images in my head, a dark smile made its way to my face. We both wanted to march back up there to show her who she belonged to. We wanted to dominate her and sink our teeth into her silky smooth skin over and over to claim her, firing away the doubts that she might have.

A mate—someone who I had never even dreamed of having in my entire existence. I had been around longer than the mating bond. Anyone would think I would be the first one to have a mate, which was ironic. I watched wolves meet their destined loved ones and then drift away into blissful oblivion over the years. They had the privilege to find that one person to be with them, but I knew that even before wolves began mating, I had no one for me—that I would walk the world alone for all eternity.

Then, I got a word from a reliable source that a mate was created for me; that Moon Goddess was nice enough to grant me one. I rolled my eyes, for those bastards didn't have nice bones in their bodies. I learned that from experience. They were pulling out their big guns to distract and soften me up as if that would ever happen after the betrayal and shit they pulled on me.

I didn't believe it, but I didn't underestimate its possibility either. There was a small part of me that wondered what it would be like to actually have a mate; to not be trapped in a never-ending world of one-night stands and loneliness that seemed to grow and pierce my chest. I sent men to look discreetly into packs for women who seemed to have even the slightest bit of oddity among all other wolves, but they would always come back empty-handed. No she-wolf with beyond normal wolf strength, speed, or sight stood out.

As the years passed, I began to think she was just a myth to distract me, or worse, a lowly male wolf mated and bonded with the mate intended for me and used his scent to hide her. Even though I expected her to only bring deceptions and false promises to seduce me into forgetting my plans, I couldn't deny myself the curiosity of knowing what the great Moon Goddess believed would fit me best. I had never spent more than a few minutes in the same room with her, but the way I saw it, she gave me the impression of a mischievous woman who loved to play but could also endanger me if she wanted to. She was the only one whom I did not hold a grudge against though I didn't particularly like her.

I realized that if I were to create something the enemy wanted, I would drag it out by keeping it low, visible to the eye but surrounded by distractions. Instead of sending men to search around, I sent them to bring all women in all ages at first, but I thought logically and managed to narrow down their ages in descending order.

I met petrified young women who feared for their lives every single time. They had no idea what was going on or what was going to happen to them. I knew enough that even if I were a mile apart from my mate, I would feel something strange. However, every single woman didn't even spark my interest, so I had their memories erased and had them returned to their packs.

And then it happened.

On the last mission that Albericus went on, I saw something odd in his wolf. I had always been attuned to the wolves, so I didn't think much of it. But something stirred the beast inside me, and in a moment of distraction, he overpowered me. It was shocking. Never in history had he ever shown interests on using the powers we were gifted with. He only cared for the brutal strength and in causing destruction wherever he went.

102

As he tuned in with Albericus, I understood the interest. A girl smaller than him was in his arms. His eyes were locked in her chocolate-brown ones as his emotions shifted from surprise to bewilderment, but what made it off-the-wall was the need to protect her and bring her to me.

Then, I knew she was the one.

I shook my head and focused on the problem, or rather, my problem at hand. Tapping my fingers to a soothing rhythm on my leg, I watched a cloud floated over the moon, covering it and making the sky looked mysterious. The moon's glow was still visible around the edges of the cloud. At that moment, I felt like I was the moon and Vivian was my cloud, except she wasn't blocking me and I wasn't hidden. I was holding her close to me, so she wouldn't float away. I wouldn't let her.

"My little cloud," I mused to myself.

Who would have thought the big bad Lupus Deus would be sappy over a five-four brown-eyed she-wolf, who was now chained to my bed probably contemplating of murder. She could contemplate all she wanted. It's not like she could kill me.

Speaking of kill, my light humor vanished and the darkness that I always kept locked within me slowly seeped out. The already cold room went below zero with darkness filling its every corner. I could feel my eyes glow in the dark with the staggering energy welled up in me. While a huge part of me wanted to kill Jedadiah Calbes for being touched by Vivian, I knew I had to acknowledge that nothing harmful happened with that simple contact. I couldn't help it. Just the thought of her with another male or giving what was meant for me to another sent me into a path of jealousy, but the jealousy was nothing compared to what the mere thought of a male touching her could do to me. A volcanic anger grew in me. My canines protruded from my mouth. My chest lifted up and down, heaving with anger and hatred to whoever would dare touch her. The beast fueled the fire by showing me images of tearing bodies apart, ripping the flesh from their bones, and doing unimaginable things.

A humorless chuckle escaped me. Just how did Vivian, the innocent little thing, perfectly match my savaged self? She intrigued me immensely. I knew I frightened her at some point, but she was good at hiding her feelings. At times, I caught a whiff of her fear whenever I did something rash, which began to be a constant thing with her; but it disappeared just as fast as it came. Even that seemed to give me a strange emotion. Did I enjoy her fears? Did I thrive off of it? What exactly did I want from her?

A disturbing feeling grew in my chest. I didn't know what to do with it, but while experiencing goosebumps, I could feel that

103

something was wrong as tension and calmness took over me simultaneously.

The beast roared and began fighting for control, thrashing, and pushing against my mental blocks, sending me pain with all its strength. I clenched my hand and spun the chair around back to the desk, pulling a drawer open. Even in the dark, I managed to find the syringe filled with dark purple liquid. I reached in and pulled it out.

At the sight of the syringe, he fought harder for control and brought physical pain inside my chest using his slashing claws, causing me to release a hiss. I didn't stop as blood seeped into my veins. My black shirt was torn, exposing the wounds that quickly healed, while the beast continued its mayhem.

I plunged the needle into my right arm, ignoring the slight sting, and exhaled as the burning liquid rushed through my veins and silenced the beast. It left him weak and gave me peace. Slowly, darkness crept back to me until the dangerous tint left the cold office. He wasn't always a pain, but in moments of extreme uneasiness, the beast would try to force himself out, which always led to unnecessary bloodshed. After a few years, I grew tired and created a stronger sedative.

I rose to my feet and went out to the forest. I needed to feel nature close to me, but it no longer had the same calming effect as before. The beast wanted something, or rather, someone else to calm him.

I was nothing like the wolves who gave me the ridiculous name *Lupus Deus*. I was not a wolf, and I didn't act like one. I was higher than them. I could understand why they would believe it. I was animalistic. Although I did the same things an ordinary wolf would do— such as, growling, snarling, howling at the moon, and using my heightened senses—at the end of the day, I was much more than a wolf.

Legends, stories, and aging memories could also be at fault as well because I hadn't shifted in front of wolves in more than a hundred years. I had done it once and paid the price. No one had seen my true form since that dark day, but it did leave legends of a certain monster.

It wasn't difficult to rein the beast inside like how I initially believed. With the power I had on the wolves, I could command them to stay far away whenever I chose to transform. The only downside to this was the constant shots I had to get to tame him. If it weren't for those, I had no doubt that I would have to fight him tooth and nail to get a decent amount of control. I was bloodthirsty, but sometimes, his atrocities curled my stomach.

As the clouds moved slowly away from the moon, I faintly wondered what Vivian would think of my true nature. Would she look at me as an abomination? A monster? Would she be disgusted at the mere sight of me whenever our paths crossed? I ignored the disturbing feeling because even so, I would still keep her.

I felt his familiar spark before I heard him, so I waited for him at where I was. Albericus, my loyal companion for many years, lived longer than a normal wolf could—another doing on my part. If I would be immortal and mateless, I didn't see why I couldn't let my best friend live a little longer. It wasn't as if he minded though. Time was what he needed as well.

His shadow came closer to me. I could see his green eyes narrowed down on my slightly torn shirt. I heard him sniff, catching the faint blood on my shirt. One downside of having a best friend who had been with you for very long time was that they don't take warnings seriously, not until you're at your worst, Moreover, they believed they're trying to help. Albericus believed I should tone down on Vivian for a bit, so she wouldn't become a target as our plans progressed. But he didn't have the knowledge or experience as I did, and she did become a target as soon as the idea of making her my mate became a fact. Nothing I did or acted upon would change that. So, why should I hold myself back more than I already had? The thought was ridiculous.

"You've taken your shot," he noted. I nodded, not needing to say anything. He understood me most of the times without the need to voice myself out.

He crossed his arms over his chest, looking at me like a scolding parent.

"That's already the fourth since she's been here." I clenched my jaw and said nothing. I just looked at the sky and wondered if there would be more clouds passing by the moon soon. The weather could be so unpredictable.

"You never had to take a lot of these before. She's already cha—" I snarled at him, not liking his tone. I restrained the darkness that wanted to escape from me and turn my friend into my prey.

"She isn't changing anything. I'm not dying nor weakened in her presence. Moreover, I haven't forgotten our plans. The only thing happening is that the beast is pushing me to mark her before they decide to change their minds about letting me have a mate." The thought left me a bit panicked. I didn't want to lose her before I got the chance to figure what I could have, what we could have.

He snorted at me and shook his head. After a moment, I tried to lighten the mood, but I could feel his wolf's anxiousness.

"So, either they knew you'd be suspicious of her to the point of withholding the mate bond, thus cockblocking you, or their plan is to knock you out with meds." I threw him a side glare at his stupidity and walked off, but of course, he followed behind.

"You know I have a point. Besides, even if she isn't anything bad now, it doesn't mean she won't be later." I stopped midstride and faced him. He cringed back a bit but looked into my black eyes.

Albericus didn't have anything against Vivian. He was just protective of me, and while I appreciated it, I wished he could drop the matter or I would be forced to drop him.

"You think I haven't thought of that? I thought of each and every way they can manipulate the only good thing that has ever happened to me by having her be the reason for my downfall."

There was a dangerous edge in my voice, which I had never used on him before. He quickly realized he was pushing me too far.

He held his head down but tilted to bare his neck to me, but I ignored his gesture of submission. I walked over to a tree and grew out my claws, swiping them down and up the tree as chunks of wood flew into the air. I punched the tree repeatedly, completely distorting and reshaping it until it gave a loud croak, broke down, and fell over.

The tree had it the worst. For all my body knew, I could have just punched a wall. I knew I shouldn't have acted out on Albericus when he was just doing his job and pointing out the obvious, but I seemed reflexive to defend Vivian from even the truest words. How strange.

Exhaling my anger and frustration, I looked in the direction of the pack house. We were far enough that normal wolves wouldn't be able to see it, but I wasn't normal. I could see through the trees and the branches as if the pack house was a few feet away rather than miles. I focused my hearing to the house. My hearing and awareness of everything around me was so amplified that when I tuned into something, it was almost as if I were a ghost, as if I were actually there.

Hearing past the TV's, music, fighting and happy couples, the sleeping and chatting wolves, I moved my hearing to the section where I knew my room was located and listened in on what Vivian was doing. She was already in bed. Her heartbeat was a soft lullaby. She would change her position every once in a while, dragging the chains along the silk covers, then she would fall asleep only to toss and turn again. It gave me a twisted pleasure to know she couldn't sleep comfortably without me.

Knowing she was already in bed, I pulled my hearing back and focused on my silent beta and friend.

"Do you know what the worst part about this whole mate situation is?" I asked him quietly.

He didn't respond.

"The fact that they sent her to me." I turned around to look at him. His eyes took in my serious expression.

106

"I thought you'd be pleased to have a mate. You always looked at mated couples with longing. Why would them giving you a mate be such a bad thing, besides the obvious?" he said slowly, picking his words carefully.

"Because they can take her from me," I answered blankly, not showing him how deeply that simple statement tormented me.

I cleared my throat. I shifted my entire self from a pathetic man that I was becoming to the military man that I was much more comfortable being.

"How are the preparations going? Anything I need to step into?" I demanded, looking him straight in the eyes and taking control of the situation once more.

"Everything is going according to plan. There's nothing you need to go over that needs checking in this department," he too answered seriously, showing no indication of his thoughts on the previous subject.

"Tell Hogan to report in the morning. I need to go to New Orléans and New York in a week. I want to make sure he knows what to do while I'm gone as well as Luke and Sawyer. Have the results of the test they did on Vivian and my blood delivered and dropped off at my desk as soon as possible. No one is to read it." I began walking in the direction of the pack house; my feet seemed to have a mind of their own.

"Sure thing. Anything else?" he asked, preparing to follow the orders.

I looked over my shoulder.

"How's the search for Aurora going?"

His expression darkened as he clenched his fists. While I needed her for certain things, Albericus had some unfinished business with the witch. He could do what he wanted with her after I got what I needed, but even I had no idea or inkling of how things between the two would end. They had much to discuss.

"She's a slippery little witch, but I'll get her next time. We've already narrowed down her location. She can't possibly go far with the covens banishing her. She's running out of ways to escape. We just have to figure out how to outstand her spells." I nodded in understanding and walked off.

"Bring her to me in no less than two weeks. Time is something you shouldn't waste for an upcoming war." I knew the command was a cruel one, but I needed her now. I didn't wait to hear his response.

As I made my way back to the pack house, I passed by a multitude of wolves. Some bowed their heads as a sign of respect while others came over to talk to me. When I got to my floor, I moved faster than light and reached the room in an instant. The door did not make a sound as if it hadn't been opened. I walked over to Vivian in slow and quiet steps. I could already see her wearing the new pajamas she bought. Her scent smelled more mouth-watering than usual. While it pleased me that she had her own things now, I was met with faint disappointment that she no longer had to wear my clothes and use my things. It seemed she had slipped the chains through the armholes. It shouldn't have been amusing, but I just couldn't resist to smile. She was right. I was a jackass.

Looming over, I studied her features and the way her brows naturally arched as if she was lifting them in a mocking way. She had a small button-like nose and her long black lashes framing her heavy eyes gave her a sultry look with her head tilted at the right angle when I kissed her. My eyes trailed down to those plump soft red lips, wanting to run the tip of my tongue over them. Her soft porcelain skin made me want to touch her constantly.

She was small and barely made it to my chest, but she was curvy and generously gifted in the places that counted. I should know. I had that body pinned under mine the first time she opened her eyes. Just remembering the feel of her soft body under mine had me hardening to the point of discomfort. She was a mixture of innocence tainted by every man's erotic dream.

She was sensual, desirable, and provocative in the smallest of gestures. She could turn me and probably every other male in the room into the red-blooded creatures that we were—the reason why I had to keep her close and locked up because she was just too tempting. I reached down, forming a lock of her silky hair in between my fingers and feeling its softness.

I froze as she shifted closer to me at the edge of the bed. When she got closer, she let out a sigh and seemed a little restful that I hadn't noticed her stress lines disappearing. I did't need as much sleep as wolves or humans did. Hell, I didn't need sleep at all, but ever since she came, my body had a hard time not following her to bed. It was like a magnetic pull that I wanted to feel her under me, next to me as she slept. It might sound creepy, but I liked watching her sleep. Her heartbeat was soothing. It put me to sleep, which was incredibly hard to do with all the voices and thoughts running in my head.

What had this girl done to me? The feeling of warmth and joy were new to me and all these new emotions were damn near frightening. My pleasures usually involved in conquering lands, jewels, prizes, killings, violence, and sexual activities (which Vivian and I have done). Why the hell did I feel like I was basking in warmth when she's near me?

I shook my head and gazed upon her neck where my mark should be.

Ignoring the dark thoughts and all the troubles, I focused on my little mate who didn't seem to grasp the complete darkness within me. My entire being demanded to possess her in every way until she forgets what life without me is; until she knew and cared for nothing else but me. I wanted her sole attention, to know her inside and out, and to know what would frighten or make her happy. I had been into her mind, so I knew her more than anyone else, yet the questions in my mind remained unanswered. I didn't just want to know. I needed to know.

I wanted her and others to know that she was mine, but with the constant uncertainty of our bond, I was left with scanty choices. I had to stake a claim to her now before anyone else did; not that they would dare, but it was always a possibility. A possibility I wouldn't take. I once lived in a world where possibilities were a blessing. Look where that got me. A million little ideas on ways to mark her as mine came to mind, but only one sparked my amusement.

"I wonder how she feels about tattoos?"

The files on your desk. Albericus voice entered my head, but I didn't respond.

I looked at Vivian one last time and left the room, making my way to my office where Albericus was waiting for me. I took the green file and opened it, scanning Vivian's basic work.

"Spread the word: Kiwi is banned on the island. Stop all ports with the fruit and have the pack either eat them or throw them away. If they have any problem with it, they can talk it up with me," I said, not looking up to meet his questioning face.

"And may I ask why?" I briefly lifted my eyes to meet his amused smile.

"She's allergic," I said. He hummed in response.

"So what does it say?" He was impatient like me, but I had to be careful and read it all. I couldn't miss a thing; I couldn't afford to.

"It says that after twenty-four hours, my blood came back normal even after being in contact with hers. No changes, no sudden cell diminishes, everything seems—" I stopped and reread the last few lines.

"Interesting, very interesting," I said.

"What's interesting? What? What does it say?" Albericus was anxious and eager to know.

"While my blood work came back to normal, hers however did not." I handed him the file. He scanned it with surprise and bewilderment before becoming speechless.

"You're right. This is interesting. Um . . . wow, that's. . . something." I nodded.

"Indeed."

Suddenly, my little cloud of confusion became a storm.

109

CHAPTER 11

I hadn't seen Zaliver since he chained me last night. It was a good thing that I was in the mood of strangling him. Perhaps with his own chains too. The idea didn't seem half bad to me.

My wolf was just as annoyed as I was, which made me glad she wouldn't allow him to get away with everything. His reasons were way off for his childish behavior. He knew it well like I did deep down in my heart. He must know deep, deep, *deep* down. I hoped.

I only placed my hand on the young man's shoulder! As if it was some sort of betrayal. I shook my head. I tried everything to get the chains off—like, hitting it, chewing on it (bad idea), trying to get my hands out, breaking it, and pulling at the chain. Nothing worked. I barely dented the thing.

The alarm clock read eight fifty in the morning, making me sigh out loud in both frustration and exhaustion. Although at some point, I did fall asleep last night, but it quickly went away. I just wasn't comfortable at all. I missed the warmth of Zaliver's body—his strong arms wrapped around me, holding me close to him. I wanted to hug him and feel his lips on mine. How was it possible that I managed to sleep without needing anyone to cuddle for almost eighteen years but could no longer stand the thought of sleeping alone after spending a night or two with my mate?

I groaned and threw my head back on the bed. I was so flimsy when it came to him. One moment, I was angry, wanting to crack his bones; however, I would surprisingly feel sad later on while longing for his presence. Was this what people meant by relationships being a rollercoaster of emotions? It oddly wasn't that bad if I had to go through it with Zaliver, but I wondered if he felt anything the way I did. To what extent could his emotions be for me besides the obvious possessiveness and protectiveness?

Last night, I had the privilege of having the room for myself to think about everything so far. I was mainly curious and worried about what Zaliver meant about marking me. Would he finally mark me? A shot of joy and happiness hit me as well as fear and distress.

Distress because I wasn't sure what to do here for the rest of my life. How would I be useful to the man who ruled and controlled all of those around him?

Fear for two different reasons: Firstly, the actual process of marking. Marking a mate is extremely intimate and pleasurable, not to mention giving a push to the process of mating each other. Secondly, I had no doubt Zaliver's possessiveness and overprotectiveness would reach an extreme level that would make me feel like a caged animal, by just thinking about it. Not to mention I didn't exactly think his heart was on the act of marking itself. It seemed like he would only be doing it out of possessiveness more than anything else. The thought gave a disappointed pang to my chest. How possessive could the guy ever get?

A knock at the door had my ears perking at the hope of him coming to unlock me. When the door opened to reveal a baby bump, I immediately knew who it was.

"Hey, Hannah," I said, waving casually at her as if I weren't chained to my bed. I wonder how it looked like to her. Alpha and Luna doing kinky things? Kidnapped mate? Both of those didn't fit me well.

She entered the room carrying a tray of food and giggled after seeing my position. She then placed the tray on the bedside table. It had french toast, orange juice, and a fruit salad. My stomach grumbled at the sight.

"Alpha sent me up here to keep you company. He didn't say why, but I think I understand now. So, what would you do?" she asked, sitting down on the couch. I reached for the food and glared at her while she blinked at me with an innocent look in those big baby blue eyes.

"And why do you assume I'm in the wrong disposition? Why can't he be wrong and be chained up while I go out and do god-knows-what!" I stabbed a strawberry with my fork and put it in my mouth, chewing it hard and fast that I accidentally bit my lip.

"Owww! It hurts!" I whined, cupping my jaw. My lip slowly healed, and the coppery taste in my mouth quickly disappeared.

Hannah rolled her eyes and rubbed her stomach.

"I'm sure you like to chain our alpha up, but I don't think he's into that. Well, who knows? And as for what he's doing, you do realize there is a thing called *phone* in this world. It's wonderful. It let's you communicate from a distance, record your brother's stupid moments, take pictures of your mate, and reminds you when it's time to go to the doctor for a check up. They're really great, and yes, I know I sound like the tiger from the cereal."

I smiled at her and ate as we talked. She seemed capable of managing my mood.

"And no, you're still in the wrong," she added a second later.

"What? How?" I asked, reaching for the orange juice.

111

"Well, you're unmarked, unmated, and absolutely pretty. That's like waving a piece of chicken in The Hunger Games," she explained. My brows furrowed at her and then I laughed.

"What?" she asked slowly.

"Have you actually watched The Hunger Games? I asked her.

"No, why?" Her face held a confused expression, so I explained.

"It's not what you think. Matter of fact, it's not even about food. It's more like survival of the fittest. They pick people and leave them in the forest where they kill each other until only one remains alive and come out as the winner."

Her face was horrified and annoyed at the true story of the movie. When she mentioned chicken and The Hunger Games, I kinda figured she hadn't actually watched it because that's what I thought when I first heard of it.

"Then why is it called The Hunger Games if it's not about food?"

I shrugged in response. I wasn't crazy about movies, so I didn't really know. After a moment of silence, she said, "Humans are odd."

"I agree. How come you haven't watched it yet though?" I asked curiously.

She got a wicked glint in her eyes and pointed to her stomach.

"One word, girl, honeymoon. This baby didn't just make itself. That would have been cool though, but I'm pretty sure I'm not a virgin." She joked while I made a face at her.

"TMI, girl. I'm glad to hear you've got some though." We laughed.

After talking about random things and me finishing my food, her phone rang. I tried not to listen, but I was chained and she was my only entertainment at the moment.

"This is your wife speaking." I lifted a brow at how she answered the phone, but she just smiled at me. What if it hadn't been her mate on the other line? How awkward would that have been.

"Well I'm glad to hear that, honey. How are you? Do you need anything? The baby?" A male's somewhat frantic and yet calm voice said over the line.

"I'm fine, Mark. Baby's fine," she said softly. Her eyes had a loving glint in them, which surprised me. Even though she was talking to someone invisible, I could still see how she loved him dearly.

"Good. You call me if you need anything," he said. Hannah rolled her eyes.

"You called me, remember? Besides the check up, what else do you need?" she asked.

112

I looked around the room and played with my hands to appear discreet, but I'm pretty sure she knew I was listening.

"Oh right, sorry. Um, what was it . . . oh yeah, Johnson is at home rearranging the baby's room. Something about having the right to pimp up the room as an uncle—" Before he was done, Hannah got up from her seat.

"Sorry, Viv. Gotta go! That idiot is not allowed to touch anything! How could you let him in the house, Mark?" With a quick wave and an apologetic look on her face, she was out of the room. I laughed at her, knowing she was pregnant but had the will of forty-five men. I found myself scared for one of my bodyguards even though Johnson was the tallest.

I was left alone, thinking about what Hannah said. I guess I could call Zaliver. For some reason, he hasn't contacted me via link, which meant calling him in an old-fashioned way. I thought of searching for a phone after taking a shower.

I stood from the bed and popped some of my joints. I walked into the bathroom with the chains dragged behind me. I had to leave the door slightly open to leave room for the chains, which I didn't like. Everyone knows you're not supposed to shower with the door open; that's how creeps get in. I stripped and entered the shower, relaxing my body in the hot water. I was slightly annoyed at each clink that the chains made as they hit each other while I was washing my hair, but I couldn't exactly remove them. It felt good to shower using feminine products. My shampoo had the smell of fruit blends and lavender.

When I finished, I wrapped a towel around my body and stepped out. I was slightly surprised to see that the door was fully opened, but I guess it was expected after all the tugging. I was walking to the closet when I saw something on the bed. Nearing it, I found a note on top of a computer and picked it up, then my heart's beating went fast. The note had extremely neat yet rough handwriting which said:

Vivian,

I'm very much aware of your lack of entertainment, so here you go. It works fine, but do not log in to any social media sites just yet. I'm trusting you on this. I will see you at nine. You will be marked.

Ps. Lock the damn door next time you shower. Had I not prohibited anyone from coming up here—I need not to finish. You have a beautiful figure, my dear.

You are mine, Zaliver.

I wasn't sure what expression I had on my face, but it probably was a mixture of surprise, annoyance, anger, relief, amusement, mortification, happiness and then mortification again. He was here while I was in the shower and had seen my figure? He peeked! My whole face felt hot. I shut my eyes tightly and took a deep breath. I guess I should lock the outside door when I shower, but back home, I never needed to do so. I guess old habits die hard. I was amused at the signature he ended it with; I giggled a bit. Zaliver was going to try to mark me at some point at nine.

Not try. He's going to mark us. My wolf said. I could feel her giddiness.

Not to mark. It could have been something else if the paperwork says so, but I had no idea what . . .

I went to the closet and pulled out a sleeveless dress I bought yesterday. While I felt comfortable in Zaliver's clothes, I preferred my own. I picked out a matching set of undergarments. I guess I should count myself lucky to have bought it yesterday, or else, I couldn't imagine how I would have managed with the chains. The bra was becoming a problem. It was uncomfortable, so I wore it without using the straps. I slipped on some socks and went over to the bed and checked the computer out.

I knew how to use the computer, and that was all I cared about. Zaliver already hooked up the computer to the internet. I stared at the background for a bit. I was pretty sure it was a chosen background since computers were either usually black or had the company's logo or some random nice photographic scenes, but this one didn't quiet . . .

The background was a night sky, highlighting the moon and clouds floating peacefully in front. I tilted my head, thinking Zaliver probably liked this kind of atmosphere.

I did as I was told and didn't log in to Facebook or my Gmail accounts even though I badly wanted to do so. I had no doubt he would somehow find out, and right now, I wasn't trying to piss the man off. I was tempted to—very much. Since I didn't feel like playing any games and didn't have anything else to do, I went on YouTube, knowing it would be the perfect thing to pass the time with. Throughout the day, I had several knocks on the door from an elderly woman named Delva. She told me the first time that she was to check up on me and make sure that anything I wanted was given to me.

I was embarrassed she had seen me chained up, but she told me it wasn't unusual. Every once in a while, a male would chain his mate up if he felt his position was at risk, which confused me a bit. This was normal? The idea made me snort. She probably just said that to lessen my embarrassment, but if she didn't, then wouldn't that mean Zaliver felt threatened? Delva brought me snacks and drinks as well as lunch. I spent most of the day in bed, eating while watching random videos. If Zaliver's plan was to make me fat, then it would work.

I would admit I get bored with watching videos. At some point, I walked away from the computer and looked around the room, mainly at Zaliver's things. I went into his drawer and opened it. I knew if

I touched his things, he would be able to smell it; but, I concluded that if he was going to lock me in his room and think I wasn't going to explore, he was sadly mistaken. I was mainly curious about his choice of clothing. He was mainly into dark colors. I wanted to see that he, at least, had one white shirt. I pulled out one of the shirts, and surprise, it was black. I unfolded it and brought it closer to me, inhaling his scent that brought calmness over me. I hugged the shirt to my chest, surprised by the depth of my emotions. I really missed him.

I knew a part of me was still angry at him, but the larger part of me missed him immensely. I knew we didn't talk a lot about ourselves or about him and that we were either arguing, making jokes, or getting stuck in a sexual tension. I folded his shirt and closed the drawer, and just threw myself on the bed.

I knew that I liked the monster everyone thought Zaliver was because even though I didn't understand him completely, I felt like everything he did had a reason. Then there were those brief moments where he'd say something that showed me he cared a lot about me, when I thought he wouldn't notice. I guess the saying "actions speak louder than words" referred to him. I took in a shaky breath, realizing that I was falling for my mate which was scary. I had never felt this strong about another person in my life before. To know that we were meant for each other almost felt like a dream.

When the clock read eight fifty in the afternoon, I began pacing the room, glancing at the door after a few seconds. It felt like I had a football game going on in my stomach. I brought my fingers to my mouth. I didn't bite my nails since I hated the feeling, but I was tempted to.

What will Zaliver do as soon as he walks in? How can he mark me if he won't actually mark me? Does that even make sense? As soon as the clock read eight fifty-nine, I stopped my pacing and looked at the door, waiting. When the eight turned into a nine right on the dot, the door swung open to show my tall and dark mate. I held my breath as he entered and closed the door with his electric blue eyes on me. We didn't speak or move. He looked at me as I looked at him.

Like always, he wore all black and his hair was pushed back. I could see his fingers went through it. He looked as beautiful as ever and even though I could sense darkness surrounding him, I still wasn't afraid of him. His eyes scanned over me, making me want to move around, but I held still. He took slow deliberate steps towards me as if we were going to spring on him at any moment, which I would have done earlier. I was too anxious to muster any physical annoyance towards him.

When he stood in front of me, I looked up at him while he gazed down at me. All of my emotions started to seep in, and I couldn't help but smile softly at him. His eyes trailed down to my lips and then back to me. He scanned my face and then slowly smiled back at me. It was dumb, but it almost felt like we were in on a little secret.

I was feeling extremely brave for some reason and slowly lifted my arms and wrapped them around Zaliver's waist. His eyes widened a bit and he froze, but he didn't push me away so I didn't stop what I was doing. I trailed my hands from his waist to his back slowly, feeling his firm muscles and the warmth his body gave off. I looked into his eyes as I tugged him closer. I knew he wanted me to move him closer to my body because his steps seemed robotic and stiff. I could feel his chest heaving and his breaths coming out laboring. I laid my head on his trunk, listening to each soothing thump his heartbeat made. It took awhile but he slowly, very slowly, raised his arms and wrapped them around me. I smiled into his shirt.

"I missed you," I confessed. He made an odd noise in the back of his throat that sounded like a mixture between acknowledgment and choking. His arms tightened around me, pulling me closer.

"I thought you'd be angry at me," he said with his voice coming out deep and hoarse.

"Oh I am."

"But . . ."

"Eh."

"Eh?" He pulled back to look at me with amusement on his face, but I could also see a deeper emotion brewing under his eyes.

"I missed you; that's all. Now, can you take these off of me. I've been cooped up all day, and I refused to be so any longer," I said stubbornly, raising a hand to shake the chains. He smirked down at me, showing a wicked glint in his eyes that had my abdominal muscles tightening up.

"Ah yes, the chains. So you want them off, do you?" he asked. I nodded eagerly at him. His expression became dark; not a dangerous though, but a carnal darkness that in its own way was dangerous.

"The chains can go, but first, " He lifted one of his hands and swept my hair behind my ear and to the side, leaving my left shoulder fully exposed to his hungry gaze.

"W-What are you doing?" I stuttered out. My breathing was speeding up.

"I received the papers. I can mark you, but for now I'm going to give you a different type of mark," he said with a twisted smile. For a second, his face became serious but quickly changed back. I became curious but was buying time concurrently.

"What were the results? Is everything okay?" I asked, trying to divert his eyes my shoulder.

"Perfect. Everything's perfect." I studied him closely, not being able to tell whether he was telling the truth or not.

116

"Really? Then can I see—"

"Shhh," he said, leaning down to plant his lips on my mine silencing me.

Our lips moved against each other perfectly in sync, not too rough nor too soft—Just perfect.

When we pulled back, he kept going and trailing kisses down my face to my neck where he began to suck softly. I shut my eyes as an unexpected moan came from me which made him push me against his body. He growled out and continued his path. I raised my hands to his thick mane and began combing my fingers through the silky strands. His lips were fast and hot on my neck. Working on instinct, I hitched up one of my legs around him. He easily lifted it up higher and picked up the other, making me hitch my legs around his waist.

I didn't open my eyes as he began to walk. He didn't stop kissing my neck. Every now and then, I would feel his canines scrape my skin making me shake and feel like a mess. When my back touched the bed covers, Zaliver laid on top of me. I could feel his member every time he or I shifted. Feminine pride swelled up in me and my wolf at the knowledge that we could work up our mate. He slowly trailed back up to capture my lips once more. When I ran out of air, we both pulled back, breathing heavily. He looked down at me with lust and desire. His eyes were intense and made me feel like he wanted to devour me entirely.

Holy shit! Talking about hot and heavy. He rolled off of me and stretched his arms out. With a hand, he pulled out a key from his pocket and undid the chains. I picked the chains up and pushed them off the bed. My neck felt sensitive, and I had no doubt I either had one large ass hickey or multiple hickeys. After a moment in silence, he spoke,

"Well, that was fun. We should do this again sometime." I scoffed at his neutral tone.

"As long as it doesn't involve me chained up and locked in all day," I said, turning my head to glare at him playfully. He looked at me with a grin on his face. I've never seen him this relaxed or happy; it suited him well.

"I'm going on a business trip next week, just to . . . uh . . . tell you," he said slowly. A frown made its way to my face at the news. I didn't want him to leave.

"Can I go?" His face softened up a bit.

"Not yet. Maybe one day," he promised. My frown deepened but I nodded at him. It was better than a flat *no*. I wanted to know what he could have been doing when we weren't together. Trying to make the situation better, he spoke again, "I'll bring you souvenirs. Lots of them." I smiled at him and nodded.

"I want to get to know you," I said. He grinned back at me.

"Me too."

"How long are you going to be gone for?" I asked.

"A week." Before I could feel sad, he added, "But when I come back, we can spend more time together. Deal?" he asked.

I like the sound of that. "Deal."

CHAPTER 12

"I miss him," I complained. Hannah shook her head and continued to check the stock. We were in the back of her store where they kept all the goodies that couldn't go in the front.

"I would be surprised if you didn't. Don't worry, he said he'd call as soon as he'd land and then every two hours. In the meantime, relax." She comforted me as she checked something on the clipboard and moved to the next box.

"I know, I know, but that doesn't seem to matter at my wolf. She's just adding on by painting pictures in my head. What if there's a storm and their plane crashes? I don't even know if he can swim! Oh my god, I'm horrible. I didn't even check his suitcase. What if he runs out of something? He can't go nude. . . I'd kill him," I mumbled that last part to myself.

I'd never been worried about someone traveling far away from me. As soon as I had seen him disappear into the plane, I felt a sense of panic and despair to have him back. I knew it was ridiculous and that the man could take care of himself . . . and me . . . and everyone on the plane. I just couldn't seem to accept the truth even if I knew I was over reacting.

"Ahh, women! Calm the heck down before you die on my watch, mind you. I'd like Alpha not to return because his mate had a panic attack. He may not have marked you, but he can still feel you. So breath, in and out or die quietly for me to have enough time to get Mark and me out before they find your body in the store," she whispered at me. Her face was red with annoyance but still had an understanding look.

"Die quietly? Gee, thanks. Feeling your love," I muttered sarcastically. As she insisted, I took a deep breath and closed my eyes. It helped my wolf a little but she settled down.

"Good. Now sit there and wait for me to finish so we can go." She happily patted my head as she walked by me, I slumped in my chair and closed my eyes, leaning my head on a box next to my chair.

119

My hand reached up to where I knew the hickeys would be even if I couldn't necessarily feel the rise of them. I smiled as the memory of first seeing them resurfaced.

~•~

"Zaliver!"

He stood behind me in a flash with an expectant look on his face with his hands in his pockets. As usual, he was dressed head to toe in black but looked stunning in his clothes.

"Yes?" he asked casually, too calm for my liking.

"Do you see this? I thought you'd give me one or two. How the hell did you manage to get my whole neck?!" I held my hair up and turned my neck side to side, trying to get a good angle.

He'd somehow managed to not only get one side last night but also the other side. How did he even manage that he only kissed one side? I dropped my hair and turned to him with an accusing look directed to his smug face. His blue eyes were bright and lively even though his expression had minimal amusement. This was not funny! It was embarrassing and weird.

"Well?" I asked again putting my hands on my hips and turning to fully look at him, looking up at him with a scowl on my face. He smiled and crossed his arms over his shoulder, leaning on the door frame. That made his muscles seemed to push his black shirt out making me realize that I was not intimidating, at least not to him.

"Well . . . You seemed quite happy with me doing it last night," he murmured under his breath.

"What's that supposed to mean?" I asked, wondering at what point this did happen last night. We talked and then went to sleep, and maybe kissed here and there, but there's no way he managed to kiss my neck without me knowing . . . right? He smirked at me as if he was reading my mind, and leaned into me.

"You can get a bit distracted when pleasures involved, it seems." I looked at him gaping.

"No way!"

"Can't wait to prove you wrong." He walked out with a dark smile.

I shivered at the thought.

~•~

"Alrighty then. I'm all done here so let's go," Hannah's voice pulled me out of my memory. I stood up and followed her out.

After Zaliver left this morning, I decided to spend as much time with people, a.k.a. Hannah and the guards since everyone else didn't seem to know how to act around me. They were weary and quiet but were over all polite, yet I could sense that they didn't truly believe or know if I was Zaliver's mate or if he even had one for the matter. Both I and my wolf didn't like that they doubted our bond, no matter how impossible it could be.

It had been a few days since Zaliver chained me and then gave me several hickeys, I had spent most of my time looking around the island, shopping, browsing, and spending time with Hannah and the others, but since I've never directly met Mark (her mate), they invited all of us to a dinner at their house. Zaliver had left earlier and I was already feeling down. Was it normal to miss a person so much?

Luke held the back door open for me and Hannah. Courtney and Mila were in a car behind us. I was grateful that everyone was giving me time to sort my thoughts and didn't call me out on my silence. Hannah chatted with her brother, and Luke drove silently. He'd glance at the mirror to check on me every now and then.

I watched the scenery pass by like a blur as I was not really seeing it; my thoughts were elsewhere.

~•~

I watched from the couch as Zaliver went back and forth from the closet to the black suit case in the bed and sighed.

"I can smell and sense your displeasure." I didn't say anything as I was not sure what to answer to that. I was bothered by a few things though. He put down whatever he was holding and turned to look at me with his brows pulled down.

"You're . . . upset on me leaving." His voice was uncertain, and I couldn't put my finger on.

"I've never actually considered this." I cocked my head, wanting to hear more.

He lifted a hand and held his chin; a sign that he was pondering over something and let out a sudden chuckle.

"You know, I've never really had to explain myself to anyone in the last three hundred years. I think I owe you an apology for not being considerate of your thoughts regarding my trip. I cannot cancel this one, but in the future, I promise to inform you of anything." I looked at him, duped. Talk about hitting the nail on the head.

"Apology accepted," I said quickly and realized how weird I looked like, staring at him like a moron.

He took a deep breath twice and exhaled quickly with a smirk on his handsome face.

"You're pleased now, good," he said randomly and continued to pack.

"Weirdo," I mumbled under my breath.

121

"I heard that."

"No you didn't." He hummed.

"Must be old age," I said. He looked at me over his shoulder and growled lowly; I lifted my hands up in surrender.

"While I'm gone, stay away from unmated males—"

"No arguments here. I enjoyed my freedom and knowing that I didn't have some poor guy slaughtered."

"Good, we're on the same page. I'll call as soon as I land in New York and will call every two hours. You will stay in our room every night while I'm gone, if you wish to stay at Hannah's, have Johnson call me." I nodded, even though I doubted that the thought didn't seem so bad. It could be like a sleep over . . . If you ignore that there would probably be wolves lurking outside the house guarding.

I'd long ago figured that he'd increased security on me if he was gone, I wasn't going to call him out on it, not yet at least. If we were going to get to know each other when he got back, then I wanted to show him that I trusted his judgement no matter how crazy and childish it could be at times—that's a step in trust.

"Okay. So, what exactly are you going for? Business trip?" I asked. He froze and unfroze, but I had already seen the change.

"Yes, business."

"So, about my gifts?" I smiled at him cheerily.

He looked at me before lunging with a fake roar, making me squeal while he grinned at me.

*

"And here we are, Luna. Welcome to my sister's humble—" Johnson's voice snapped me out of my thoughts, pointing out to a house we'd just pulled into.

"Humble? Fuck you. Your house is a humble shack, my house is fabulous. Well, come on in Vivian. Mark should be home by now." Hannah opened the door and went straight into the house.

Hannah's house was indeed fabulous. It was a two-story light blue house with a stoned walkway and a black car parked outside. Luke was laughing when Courtney and Mila pulled up. Johnson was grumbling to himself, storming into the house behind his sister.

"What's up with him?" Mila asked looking towards Johnson's direction.

"Hannah called his house a "humble shack" in comparison to her fabulous home," Luke explained, making the girls laughed while I cracked a smile.

Looking at the house, I wondered if Zaliver had ever considered maybe living in a house. Probably not but I wanted a house ever since I was little. I was good in decorating living spaces or decorating in general. I wondered what type of house he liked.

122

"Luna?" Luke asked anxiously. I turned to look at him while the girls were looking at me with the same look on their faces.

"Sorry, I was just admiring the house. Shall we?" They nodded slowly at me, but not before looking at each other. I could have sworn I saw a flash of silver in their eyes but I blinked and it was gone. I must have clung to whatever I could to think of Zaliver. I decided then and there that I wouldn't think about him here. I was going to meet Hannah's husband and a fellow pack member. I wanted him to like me and to show that I wasn't whatever the people here thought about me.

I took in a deep breath, shook my head and body, and walked to the front door with a nervous but excited smile. As soon as I entered the house, I was hit with the smell of lasagna and garlic bread. Heaven.

Hannah was standing next to a tall man with a normal built and height. From the back I could see he had a clean-cut and was wearing loose khaki shorts with a deep red shirt. I almost wanted to ask if it was actually Jake from State Farm but then he turned around.

Jake from State Farm most definitely did not have an eyebrow piercing, snake bites, and green eyes. I couldn't help being surprised so when he turned, he began laughing, Hannah shook her head with a smile on her face. Mark was handsome, no doubt, but what you saw in the back you didn't expect to get in the front. Note to self, do not judge a book from its cover, or back in this occasion.

"Takes them by surprise every time, never gets old. I'm Mark, but you probably already knew that. Hannah's been talking about you, Luna. It's a pleasure. Welcome to our . . . fabulous home," he said, sneaking a glance at Hannah who narrowed her eyes in warning but then smiled.

He extended his hand so I shook it quickly, silently sending a prayer that Zaliver wouldn't over act when he heard, he somehow always heard.

"Lunch will be done in a few, why don't you all go sit at the table. It's already set up. I'll be there." He pushed us out of the kitchen and into the living room.

"He cooks, he sets the table and he checks up on you. I approve." I joked to Hannah, she smiled at me with a secretive smile.

After Mark had brought the food in and everyone had settled down and began eating, I learned a lot about Mark. He worked as one of the pack's trackers and took care of Hannah and her pregnancy, but every once in the while he'd take a job, mid meal Zaliver showed up.

Luke was talking to Courtney when his eyes suddenly flashed silver and then stayed that way completely. He growled out loudly catching everyone's attention. I noted a little shift in Mark's body. He moved closer to Hannah just in case, but when he saw Luke's silver eyes, his head bowed down, and everyone else followed.

"Having a nice lunch, Vivian?" Zaliver asked using Luke's body.

I looked into his eyes and felt the connection, but it wasn't the same as having him around and looking into his blue eyes. I looked around everyone who were quiet and in a submissive position.

"Umm, Yeah. So . . . What's. . . ?" I trailed off not really knowing what to ask. Here I was missing him all day and when I finally get the chance to talk to him, I've got nothing to say.

"Just wanted to tell you that I've landed and wanted to know what you were up to," he said, looking around the table and at everyone.

"And you couldn't call?" I asked, lifting a brow in amusement. I was bit worried Luke would get mad at being used.

He smiled. "This is me calling."

I rolled my eyes. "Well thank you for the notice, as you can see everything is fine so please give Luke his body back," I said.

His eyes narrowed on me. For a moment I thought he'd do as he usually did and lunge for me, but he must have hated the thought of another male body other than his touching me because he gave a short growl.

"Fine. I'll call later." Then the silver flash in his eyes went gone.

Everyone let out a sigh and relaxed, looking amazed.

I picked up the fork I was eating with and began poking at what was left of my meal.

"Nice! Second time this happens." Luke was blinking rapidly.

"Sorry, I'll tell him to stop," I said sheepishly, hoping he wasn't too mad.

"No!No! It's totally fine. He can take body *any time* he wants! *Wherever* he wants! I don't mind!" Everyone looked at Luke.

There was utter silence until Johnson started laughing and making everyone lose control. Luke's face was flaming red by the time he understood why we were laughing.

"Dude, really? '*He can take my body when he wants wherever he wants?*' Man," Mark quoted.

"Wow, Luke I wasn't aware of the fact that you were pimping your body or else I would have rented you out a long time ago. Does your family know? How much?" Courtney joked across from him.

"I'm just gonna go to the bathroom now," Luke said hastily. I don't think he was mad; more like embarrassed.

"So Vivian, how does it feel to be mated to the scariest wolf on the planet?" Mark asked once the laughter died down. I smiled at him and shrugged as I still didn't know.

We all spent a long time a lot Hannah and Mark's house. I promised to drop by tomorrow; not that I had anything to do, but at some point I asked Luke to drop me off at the pack house.

Up in Zaliver's room, I laid down on the bed and looked at his side of the be. Knowing that he wouldn't be here for a whole week depressed me a lot. I got up and changed into one of his shirts; it was barely three in the afternoon but I was feeling a bit drained and a nap wouldn't kill time. As I laid in bed, I recalled the last time I saw Zaliver.

~•~

"Plane is here," he said.

I looked up at him with a raised brow as I couldn't hear it. Before I could open my mouth, he pointed south and my eyes widened as a small speck grew closer to us until I heard a faint rumble.

"Wow, that's cool." I said, still looking up at the distance. When the plane landed, men piled in with bags and boxes of different sizes all covered by a red cloth. Zaliver grabbed my chin and turned my gaze onto him.

"Hey, while I'm gone I want you to take care of yourself, do you hear me?" I nodded, his eyes were focused entirely on me. Eat everyday. Shift at least twice this week. Lock the damn door when you shower. Don't go anywhere alone, and don't forget to tell the guards if you want anything, if you—"

"Basically, don't die while you're gone, got it. I think I got this, seeing how I managed to live eighteen years without you." I smiled proudly at him, but he didn't smile.

He raised his hand to my head and tucked a strand a hair behind my ear. He trailed his pointer finger from the corner of my eye down to my lips over, then and back.

"But you don't have to anymore," he whispered before leaning down to kiss me.

Most of our kisses were rough and hot, but this one was soft and equally as passionate, stealing my breath away. He pulled back slowly. I felt something within me stir and cry out for him.

When he was the last one to get on, he said "good-bye."

"Take care, Vivian. Be a good cloud and don't cause too much trouble, okay?" I nodded and with one last kiss.

Walking back to the car, his words came back to me.

Cloud?

~•~

I was about to drift off when I heard something vibrating somewhere on the bed. I quickly sat up and began moving the covers around until I found an iPhone under Zaliver's pillow. Did he forget his

125

phone? I checked the caller ID and was surprised to see his name flashing on the screen. He couldn't call his phone from his phone, so I'm guessing this wasn't his. Did someone come into the room? There were no strange scents so I was left with one answer—the phone was for me. I quickly answered it.

"So, you can call via phone?" I said, leaning back down. His deep voice came through the other line.

"Of course I can. I just prefer a much clearer image as to what my mate is doing when I'm gone. How do you like your phone?" he asked, hearing papers shuffling on the other line.

"It's awesome, thanks. Anything interesting happened?" I asked, wanting to hear about his day—even if it had been a few-ish hours. He laughed.

"Nope, nothing that would interest you. But I did find the first of your gifts. I think you'll like it," he said.

"First of many?" I asked a smile on my face.

"Yes, first of many. You didn't just think—"

I really did want to know what he was going to say, but at that moment something in me brought immense pain into my stomach. I dropped the phone and curled myself into a ball as if to protect myself from an outside attack, but it was from the inside. I knew Zaliver was yelling into the phone, but I couldn't reach it.

I ran to the bathroom when I felt the need to vomit arise. When I got there, I immediately released everything. When I thought I was done, tears were streaming down myself face. My stomach was still in pain, and I felt hot and cold; I was shaking. I was wiping tears when I realized what were on my hands. I looked into the toilet to see what I had vomited—Blood.

And then I fainted on the cold bathroom floor with Zaliver shouting my name on the other line.

CHAPTER 13

Darkness.

A constant beeping sound could be heard in the room, and I was pretty sure there was something in my arm.

My body felt light and my head was a bit fuzzy, but the only thing that hurt the most was my upper stomach; a softer one though. You know that feeling when someone socked you and even after the hit, the pain would still sting and throb—yup, that's what it felt like.

I took in a deep breath through my nose, inhaling something that smelled like chemicals all over the place, including Zaliver's scent. I felt fine wherever I was, knowing his presence would make me feel secured. The room was cold and I felt like I was on a small bed, but not the bed Zaliver or I slept in. Thinking of him made me recall something, but just as fast as it came, my thoughts were gone . . . Now, what was it?

I tried to remember the last time I saw him, but all I could remember was hearing his voice. What was he saying? Something about . . . a gift? Why would he buy me a gift when it wasn't my birthday? I didn't do something extraordinary either. I was pretty sure I hadn't saved someone's life 2so what was the gift for? Where was he any way? Wait, traveling. Oh yeah, but if he was traveling, then why was his scent here? I decided it was time to open my eyes. Easier said than done, it took me what felt like forever to lift my eyelids that I had to force them to keep them open until drowsiness was gone.

I was met by soothing colors like soft lavender and jade painted on the walls. I didn't know why I was here though.

I sat up slowly, wincing a bit. I looked at my hands and had a flashback of them being covered in blood. My blood. Then I realized why I was here as well as Zaliver. He must have heard me vomiting while we were talking on the phone before I fell on the floor, and when I stopped responding, he came back. I felt a bit guilty for making him return.

I looked down at my arm and scowled at the needle, slowly pulling it out and removed it myself. My throat was dry. I felt tired but in a different way. Zaliver's scent was strong, but he wasn't here, then I suddenly had a craving for something sweet.

Getting on my feet was painful, but I was able to walk out slowly but stumbling mostly into the empty hall. The robe on me was thin, but it covered my body well. I wondered what time it was and where Zaliver was, but I was a bit more concerned with jacking the first snack machine I saw. It had plenty of sugar in there for me to consume.

When I made it to the machine, I looked at all the bars and other choices while my stomach growled in anticipation. I could hear the blaring sound, but it didn't hurt as it usually did. The flashing red light didn't blind me temporarily. My senses were all but smell.

I was thinking of taking all of them out when the alarm and a red flashing light went off. I felt like it was all happening through a thick glass wall.

"I wonder what happened?" I ignored the confusion and stared back at the vending machine. I thought of breaking the glass wall.

Loud and fast footsteps made their way down the hall towards my direction, and a large shadow loomed over me, but I ignored it.

Maybe if I ram the machine to the side, it would crack it. But if my senses were numbed, so was my strength. I turned to look for help and recognized who was behind me.

"Zaliver!" I exclaimed happily, surprised to see him. I had an odd urge to do something the moment I saw him, but I couldn't get a good sense of what.

He had bags under his eyes. His black hair was all over the place like he had just rolled out of bed. His hands were limp, and his face looked angry, worried, drained, and melancholic; I guessed.

"Viv—"

" Do you have a dollar?" I asked.

He must have been taken by surprise by my question because his face became bewildered. I walked up to him and poked him when he didn't answer. I ignored how good he smelled; it could be a new cologne.

"Hey. You got a dollar?"

"W-What?" His voice cracked at the beginning.

"*Do you have a dollar?*" He nodded slowly while his eyes were scanning over my body, and I did the same to him. He was wearing the same outfit from yesterday. Today? Tomorrow? Eh, they all looked the same.

"Why?" he asked, pulling out his wallet and taking out a wad of cash. Oh my god!

"Because I want those fruit snacks and those barbecue chips and sprite and that snickers bar and a sandwich, but they don't have a sandwich so I want that granola bar. Hey, you got *five* dollars?" I blinked up at him with an innocent look on my face.

128

He eyed me, the money and the snack machine. He pulled out another bill with a hesitant sigh.

"How about you pick one for the moment and if the doctor says *it's okay*, I'll get you all the candy you want later?" I thought about it. That meant more candy for later.

I snatched the dollar out of his hand before he could change his mind, and punched in the number for the fruit snacks. When I opened the bag and began eating, I stopped and frowned. I looked at the bag, then to Zaliver who was staring strangely at me.

"Want some?" I asked. He'd better say no.

He glanced at the bag, and pulled me into his arms, wrapping them around me. My arms bunched up in front of me, and I awkwardly ate out of the bag. Zaliver backed up into the wall next to the snack machine, and buried himself into my hair and neck, breathing in my scent.

I liked the warmth he gave off as it helped warming me up. I was too focused on how good he felt and smelled that I wanted to close eyes right then and there, to melt up against him, but I focused on the taste of the candy.

He began purring softly at first, but as time passed he got louder. I felt something in me move, but it all felt foggy. I tugged my arms down until they were on my sides and then wrapped them around Zaliver and patted him.

"There, there." He pulled away a bit to look at me and then went back purring. I felt a bit tired so I told him, "Can we go back home?" He took me by surprise when he picked me up bridal style and began walking down the hall.

"Why did you leave the room Vivian? You could have gotten hurt or worse! You are not in the conditions to be alone without me," he said menacingly. His voice was soft but, had I not been high on drugs, I would have noted the small things he was doing.

Like how often he would squeeze me closer to his body and how his thumbs rubbed the back or my thighs, which I didn't notice because of the drugs in my system. I was running my fingers through his hair.

"I wanted food, or something sweet, I think," I said.

"You should have hit the call button instead of disappearing," he said while taking me back to the room.

"Hello Luna Vivian. I am Dr. Leonard. How do you feel? Any pain?" The young man asked. He had blond hair and hazel. I wonder what happened to Dr.Mick? I sat down on the bed with Zaliver standing next to me. His hand was on my shoulder, and I took comfort at the gesture.

"Tired, and my body feels sore. So, what exactly happened to me? I remember throwing up blood and then passing out," I stated. I wondered how Zaliver got his hair so silky?

"I came back immediately when you didn't answer me. I had you moved to a hospital where Dr. Leonard took care of you," he answered.

"Thank you doctor. She's fine, right?" I looked up at Zaliver. His eyes turned to look seriously at the doctor who smiled at me and nodded after a brief pause.

"Completely. At the moment, you might not be yourself because the medication had numbed you from feeling any pain, but sleep and lots of water should be good as well as being around—" he suddenly cut himself off and coughed.

"Being around what?" I asked.

"Oh um . . ." He swallowed visibly and flickered his eyes beside me to a tensing Zaliver.

"Nature. He probably means *nature* since you are a wolf, and nature is a peaceful environment. Isn't that right, Doc?" There was an edge to the way Zaliver asked Dr.Leonard, but the doctor just smiled at me and nodded. I narrowed my eyes at them. I felt like I was missing something, but I didn't know what it was; I had a bad feeling.

"But what was wrong with me in the first place?" They looked at each other before Dr. Leonard and Zaliver walked to the corner of the room and whispered to each other. What the heck? Patient confidentiality? Am I not the freaking patient?

A nurse suddenly walked in and began fussing over me. She checked my eyes and ears as well as my pulse, before giving me a strained smile. Why do I have the feeling I was missing something big? I strained my hearing to try to hear what they were whispering about but I couldn't. My head began to hurt in the back.

Zaliver's eyes met mine as he talked to the doctor; his face was serious and determined. I looked back at him, hoping my expression would tell him that I wanted to know what was going on, but he looked away. I sighed and kicked my feet. Why wouldn't they tell me what was wrong? I'd been fine in the morning when he was here and as soon as he left I just . . . Fell into a funk, but I was fine.

Hearing his voice had made me extremely happy and then all of a sudden, it felt like I was getting torn apart from the inside. Maybe he was right—I needed to shift more, but I've never heard of anything like this. I needed to talk to my wolf, but for that to happen, the drugs had to be out my system first. I didn't realize Zaliver was in front of me until I looked up, too distracted because of my thoughts.

I stared up into his secretive blue eyes, and he looked back at me as well. I noticed that the doctor and the nurse were trying to leave so I hopped off the bed and attempted to stop them, but my feet wobbled. Zaliver's arm wrapped around my waist and held me close to his body.

"Wow." I put my hands on his shoulders to support myself.

"Careful there, Luna. Your body has been asleep for a few days, you really shouldn't . . . Uh . . . You're free to go now. Have a good evening." Dr. Leonard's face went from concerned to frightened in a flash. His eyes were looking over me to Zaliver, who was behind me. The fake mask of happy smiles and ease was slipping off the doctor's face instantaneously. He opened the door quickly and left with the nurse in tow, but I managed to see him hold his head and wince in pain before the door shut completely.

Days? I've been asleep for day? Aw man, that meant a sponge bath. Now I knew something was definitely wrong here. Every time the Doctor tried to tell me something, he'd look at Zaliver and would stop.

"What's going on Zaliver? Why didn't Dr.Leonard tell me what's happening? What did he tell you? What did you do to him just now? Tell me damn it!" I yelled frustrated. He held my arms and crossed them over my chest, limiting my movement. I felt his nose skim the side of my neck and shivered. He was breathing heavily, and his chest was rising and rubbing against my back.

I was drugged, but he could still get a reaction from me because I tilted my head to the side and let out a small moan, not caring what I sounded like at the moment. He growled and pushed himself closer to me. His mouth opened, feeling his canines grazing my skin, and my legs shook.

He suddenly pulled back and began pacing back and forth, running his hands through his hair. I took a shaky breath and sat back on the bed, then closed my eyes and took a deep breath. As the drugs wore off, I more alert, and my thoughts were becoming clearer until I could almost feel my wolf.

"I need to get you home," Zaliver spoke. His voice was gruff. I looked at him and pursed my lips. No more playing nice, Vivian.

"Not until you tell me what just happened and why it appears that no one is going to tell me and what's wrong with me. I have a right to know." I crossed my arms over my chest and looked at him squarely in the eyes. He glared back at me angrily with his chest lifting and dropping rapidly. I had no doubt that I was probably the first person to defy him in a long time. Lucky me.

"I'm trying to help you Vivian. Don't make this harder than it has to be. I need you home. I will explain things there." He was talking through clenched teeth with his hands fisted at his side.

"I am calm," I responded. He gave me a twisted smirk that made something drop in my stomach as I held in a shiver.

131

"I wasn't talking about you."

"Oh," I said.

Zaliver never spoke much of his wolf. Zaliver was more of an animal than a man though he was hiding it. It seemed odd because a human and his wolf were always equal, but not him. He acted on instinct and he had proven it. He was primal and undoubtedly lethal. He hadn't shifted ever since I met him, and that worries me. He would be much of an effort if his wolf was in control.

"Fine. But I want answers or—"

"Or what?" He snarled out, taking steps forward in front of me.

I lifted my chin at him, looking bravely into his livid blue eyes that seemed to warn me.

"Or you'll find yourself rejected and mateless." I was bluffing, but he didn't know that.

I really should have taken the warning in his eyes seriously.

Zaliver stood frozen. I took a step away from him and saw his eyes following me. He didn't lash out at me, or throw me over his shoulder like I thought he would. Instead, he looked at me with piercing eyes, and his face went blank. I was beginning to beat myself over my stupidity and thought of telling him it was a joke, but the damage was already done.

"Go to the bathroom and change your clothing there. Come out when your done."

He didn't even blink when he spoke. My eyes widened, and I was compelled to obey his command. I made my way to the bathroom where clothings were prepared for me. Shit! He was using direct command. He knew I wouldn't be able to do anything unless that it was what he wanted me to do. I have messed up big time if he was using it on me. Once I changed into loose sweatpants, baggy t-shirt, and hoodie, I walked out unable to look into the mirror, and see if I looked like crap which I think I did. He hadn't moved a muscle, and as soon as I stood in front of him, he took a grip of my elbow and began dragging me to the door. His hold wasn't soft or painful but was harsh and would leave a slight mark on my skin.

"Where are we going? Where are you taking me?" I asked scared. Zaliver looked cold and distant. Even more so than the first time I met him.

He let out a humorless laugh that echoed in the silent hall and stopped in front of an elevator where he hit the *down* button, then I heard a crunch. Looking at me from the side, he said, "I wanted to give you time, but you just threatened my position in your life. You wanted answers? Now you're going to get them and so much more."

132

The doors slid open. He roughly pushed me in, making me stumble. He stepped in and looked at me with a smirk that made him appear maniacal. What have I done?

"You might not enjoy this, but I most certainly will."

The doors closed.

CHAPTER 14

I was running.

I was running for my life.

I was running for my freedom.

I was running for my very own nature.

I was running from the last person I'd thought I'd run from in my life.

I was running from my mate.

I was running from Zaliver.

I couldn't hear him because of the pounding in my ears. The sound of my heart was like a hummingbird's wings. The twigs and dead leaves echoed in the silent forest.

But I knew. I knew he was close by, and that made me push myself harder, my hair whipped around my face as I looked around for anything to gain leverage. I couldn't run forever, and my body couldn't handle it. But he could.

Because he wasn't like me. He wasn't like any of us. I felt tears of fear and panic stream down my face, and my muscles ached for a break, but I couldn't. I wouldn't. My vision blurred because of the tears making it hard to see my direction. My emotions were all over the place with confusion, disbelief, fear, betrayal, anger, and hatred. Yes, hatred for my own mate. He was doing this against my will because he couldn't stand the thought of another man taking me.

In a way, I brought this on myself. I must have pushed him to his limits. I underestimated just how much Zaliver disbelieved the bond. Now he was going to prove it to me.

I looked behind me every time I thought I heard him. When I saw nothing but darkness, it just added to my fear because when I looked back, I swear I could feel his warmth and breathing on my neck—his cold and rough breathing.

I used to laugh about girls in horror movies who would run and look back and then trip. Now I realized that when you get chased, running with fear for your life, you would want to make sure putting much distance between you and your could-be killer.

I'd run to a certain direction for too long and he'd speed past me; so fast that it felt like a strong gust of wind was about to knock me out. I'd skid to a fall and stumble, but I would always back up on my feet again and run in another direction. I had scrapes and scratches, but I couldn't feel them with the adrenaline pumping through my veins. Even with my night vision, I couldn't see past the trees and vines, but I knew it must have already been sundown.

This was why he took us far away from everyone. He knew I'd run; he wanted a chase.

Suddenly, I fell and rolled all the way to a tree, roughly hitting my back. I was gasping for air, but I stood up and ran again with shaky legs.

I didn't know where I was going. I didn't know if I could get far away from him to call for help. But how? He had every wolf under his command; how could I ever escape from his island?

This wasn't going to end well for me and he knew that. I knew that.

This was all a sick game to him. Release and Catch. I guess he wanted me to feel like putting up a good fight, but he'd always win, and I would never fall for it.

The air was cold, but I was still running and wouldn't stop. I couldn't, eventhough I was already tired. I didn't know how long the chasing had been, and body was deeply exhausted. I was surprised how I survived.

On the spur of the moment, I felt my chest burning. My wolf howled, not knowing what to do as she was taken by surprise as well. It seemed like Zaliver would show himself out of nowhere and lunge for my throat.

Just then, I fell on the ground with a thud and let out a shriek. My hands were dug into the ground as I tried to stand up, but my body could no longer bear the enervation. I crawled as quickly as I could to the large tree a few feet away from me. My hands were shaking as they dug into the roots, grass, and rocks, ignoring the cuts and wounds on my skin. Once there, I forced myself to get up and wearily sat under the tree with my back against it. I crouched down, bringing my legs in closer to my trembling body, then I saw him at a distance. My body was struck with terror.

~•~

Minutes before

He parked the car in the middle of nowhere, and opened the front door. Without closing it, he yanked me out and began dragging me into the forest. I was usually be happy going into the forest with him, but now I was petrified. I had no idea what was running in his head. He was pulling me deeper and deeper into the forest. The tree branches and vines were getting thicker and thicker, blocking out the little sunlight in the sky. The further we went in, the more frightened I became.

"Zaliver?" I whispered, but he didn't answer.

I looked around at the darkening forest. I was anticipating that the drugs had worn off and that my wolf was finally be back.

Turned out that whatever drug they gave me knocked both my wolf and my human form out, but thankfully she wasn't unconscious.

What did you do to anger him?! My wolf said furiously.

I lied and said that I'd reject— I said.

You fool! You don't know what you've done. Why? You're such an idot!

I thought if he'd believe it, he'd tell me what was going on.

Well he definitely believed you. If we end up mateless tonight, I will never forgive you.

I don't think he'll leave us.

He better not.

She was still tired but settled down in the back of my head; her fear was strong.

I gave it a few more minutes before I yanked my hand out of his hold, stopping both him and me. I bit my lip when I saw his hands clench and unclench.

"Zaliver?"

"I thought they were taking you from me. I've never felt as panic-stricken as I did when you didn't answer me. All I could do was listen to you groaning in pain as you fell on the floor. Uselessness is a horrible feeling, Vivian." He turned around to face me.

I said nothing hoping that I would finally get the answers to my questions.

"*They,* being the gods above—like, Alstha, god of war and knowledge; Eccasto, god of intelligence; and the others. But your kind know only two among all of them: Fate and Luna, known as Mother Luna," he said, taking a step towards me. I remained rigid, letting him play with a strand of hair.

There were more gods? How had we not heard of them? But how did Zaliver know them? Surely he was a god, but as a wolf god, what could he do that Mother Luna couldn't? I began to ponder on what the difference between Zaliver and Mother Luna was.

"They made me what I am today, you know? I was their killing machine; a warning to any supernatural psychopath that didn't take them seriously. They didn't want to get their hands dirty at that time. I was their prized warrior. In a way, I am thankful to them. I mean, look at me. I'm at the top of the food chain. I have all the control an alpha could wish for—immortality, an army, and power beyond anyone's knowledge," he said.

A killing machine? Zaliver . . . My mind went blank.

"I have all this power and control, but for what?" He suddenly gave a humorless laugh and backed away from me, shaking his head side to side. I watched him carefully as he gave off an odd vibe.

"We were all humans chosen and trained for them, but I didn't know what we were trained for. They had such tremendous mind control back then. We were all like family with the soldiers, but we rarely saw the all mighty gods. We weren't allowed to interfere with them unless called upon. We used to worship them. I did worship them. I don't remember much of my past life, but I do remember one person— my brother." My head snapped back in surprise.

"Brother?" I asked. He nodded.

"Yeah, I had a brother and they slaughtered him." My eyes widened in disbelief. It was horrible and I had a feeling it wasn't even the worse.

"Okay, *technically*, I slaughtered him." I thought my heart had stopped for a moment.

"They demanded for the loyalty that we had as brothers, and commanded to show it to all of them, which we followed. I was always the better fighter; Joshula didn't stand a chance. I didn't even get to bury his body; they took him too." He looked down at his palms for a moment in silence. His voice had lowered to a whisper towards the end, and didn't bother to hide the anguish in his voice. I let out a breath I was holding.

I felt sad for Zaliver. He was forced to kill the only family he had. I could imagine the scars he carried with him. Scars which his immortal body didn't have, but his immortal soul did. He suddenly looked up with a crazed smile on his face; his eyes was gleaming with maliciousness.

"So I trained harder than ever until I was the best of all. I mean if one could fight hundreds, then why did they need thousands? So I slaughtered all my competitors. I gained the bastards' trusts. I became more than a soldier to them. I became family. Ironic, huh?"

I was now beginning to understand why Zaliver didn't speak much to me and acted mostly on instinct. He was fucking crazy.

"My plan was to get to the top, gain their trust, and slowly poison them against each other. Make them destroy themselves piece by piece like they made me destroy my brother. But then something interesting happened. Luna, or as your kind referred to as Mother Luna, joined the ranks to which Fate decided to play around a little. He was

137

curious about how the wolves worked so he sent me down to watch and report which I did like a good soldier, but Fate, being the competitive asshole that he is, couldn't stand the thought of Luna having the upper hand with a new species that could one day grow out of control. So what did he do? He moved me up a higher rank.

But no human could be a god; they're too easily killed. He wanted a god for the wolves—something similar, but nothing close to the same species—a genius plan. I'll give him that, but it would have worked so much better if he hadn't trained, transformed, and gave power to the only person in the world who hated all of them," he said calmly with his misty eyes as if recalling something.

I looked at him with narrowed eyes. What was he trying to tell me? What the hell was he then? I was getting a bad feeling; a feeling that reminded me of the fight or flight instinct, and I didn't like it one bit. He suddenly shook his head and crossed his arms over his chest. His eyes were focused on me. Zaliver was such a puzzle.

"But you? You were the curve ball, Vivian Grey." He began walking around me in circles like he was expecting me to do something extraordinary.

"When they discovered what my true motives were, they had already given me the power to destroy them. And what did they do? They sent down a peace-offering. I honestly believed when I first heard of you that you'd be some seductive little player of theirs to gain my trust and later stab me in the back after a good fuck. Imagine my surprise when I got this sexy, feisty little mate, radiating with innocence.

Of course, I didn't trust you. It wasn't until you started rambling that one night when I penetrated into your head effortlessly. You accidentally dropped your barriers and projected exactly what you were thinking. Your thoughts were so pure, so innocent that I realized I was looking at the wrong angle. Instead of thinking about murdering me, you were thinking about what I was thinking about you. You were thinking about us." .

I felt sick, but I wasn't sure on which part. In a way, Zaliver had the right to be angry about what had been done to him and his brother, but the actions he made, the way he said it, seemed so . . . unlike him. And then there was the "good fuck" part and me being a pawn in this game.

Was this bond even real? Hell, was I even real?

"And so I decided to take the one good thing that came out from all of this disaster—my beautiful little cloud. Catching my attention whose little things have made me going crazy, you know that? I'm always wondering what you're doing when I'm not with you. If you need anything, if you've eaten enough, or if you're ever bored." He sighed. I didn't want to melt into his words, but it was hard not to.

138

"But I couldn't mark you like I wanted to. I had to make sure that while your mind and heart were innocent, so should your body . . . no, not in that sense," he added, looking at me glaring at him.

"I just wanted to make sure that your blood is not a poison. The test results turned out clear, and was very much interesting. Very Interesting," he said, leaning down to me. I didn't move a muscle even though I wanted to punch him in his gorgeous face and run.

"Would you like to know what was so interesting about the test results?"

I nodded at him a bit frightened about what he would say.

"Okay, but first, you wanted to know about why you woke up in the hospital correct?" I gave a frustrated sigh but nodded. He was dodging but I didn't know why.

He looked down at me with a sad look on his face, but I ignored the pull that wanted me to hug him, comfort him.

"While we aren't the only couple of mates who haven't marked each other, we are the only ones with special conditions."

"What do you mean?" What conditions? A crazy mate and a kidnapee?

"All in do time Vivian," he said. "Because of that we didn't feel what was happening,we were spending almost all day and all night together so the bond was fine. But when I left to go on my trip, the growing distance made the bond strain and with no mark it had consequences. I apologize for that, I should have seen this. Since my body is different from yours, only you felt the pain. I went through a different reaction."

I listened carefully to his explanation, but the more he spoke the less sense isn't made to me. Sure mates weren't meant to be apart for long, but they could still be apart without pain. Zaliver hadn't even been gone for a full day and I almost died because we had been apart. Why did I feel it and not him? Did this have to do with whatever he was hinting at?

"I didn't want the doctor to say anything because it would just bring more questions but as always you pay too much attention to the things this others wouldn't." I snorted at him.

"I wouldn't call it paying attention, but I think anyone would be curious why the doctor wasn't telling the patient what was wrong." He smiled at me, but I didn't smile back.

"True, true. But then you threatened on rejecting me and I don't plan on letting that happen so we're back to your interesting test results." His face became dark and cold.

I'm beginning to get sick of that word. Interesting.

"I was bluffing. I wasn't going to really reject you," I confessed, and he eyed me with an empty face.

"Bluffing or not, I don't take chances. Especially when it comes to you. To us. You should have known this when you said it," he said critically

"While my results were normal, yours didn't. When my saliva made contact with your blood, your cells began to change," he said with a pleased tone. If he enjoyed that for some reason, I did not.

"Change how, Zaliver?" I asked slowly, preparing myself for the worst.

"Your cells changed completely. They morphed into new ones. It appears that whatever my saliva did, was triggering something that's already been dormant in you all along. Your new cells were homogeneous, " his tone was jovial; it would have made me happy if I was in a different situation.

"What?" I asked. Homogeneous?

"Compatible. Identical. Undifferentiated."

Compatible . . . but how? What's been dormant in me? I clenched my hands to stop them from shaking.

"What are you exactly?" I asked, for once staring at him in a new way.

Supernatural beings existed like fairies, witches,wizards, mermaids, vampires, and werewolves, but what the hell was he? He smiled softly, scanning my face.

"Zaliver, answer the damn question!" His chin lifted up. His jaw clenched, and his fierce blue eyes looked directly into mine.

"Lycan," he said forthright.

My neck tilted to the side. Was this a joke? Lycans were a myth.

"I'm serious, Zaliver," I said with my lips pursing at him.

"So am I." I shook my head at him not believing him.

"Think about it. A species similar to werewolves but are way too different from them—stronger, faster, and better than wolves. I command all wolves. Come on, Vivian," he said.

"That can't be true! I-I mean, it's a myth humans came up with to make werewolves look monstrous!" I didn't realize I was shaking until I spoke. Part of me accepted it, but it couldn't be true. Was I not a living proof that Lycans were a lie?

"And don't all myths start with the truth? I shifted in front of a human once and let them live. Next thing I know, "a two-legged beast howling at the moon" roams around. Tell me, Vivian. How many have seen the color of my wolf? None, because I have no wolf; I have a beast. Wouldn't the god of all wolves have to be the most evil? And what does that tell you? You know this, Vivian," he said earnestly.

He was telling the truth. He was telling the truth. Oh my god, he was telling the truth! How had no one ever noticed? He was stronger

140

than an alpha, for god's sake! He had never shifted in front of me or anyone for the matter; He was never around wolves outside of his pack. Did they know? A king is usually the best among his people. Zaliver was the only one of his kind. But how does this—wait.

"Zaliver?" I whispered with the eyes on the ground.

"You said my cells were . . . identical. Identical to what?" He leaned down next to my ear. I held my breath with fear for the unknown.

"Identical to me," he whispered. He quickly pecked the side of my face, snapping me out of my shock.

I instantly took a step back. He narrowed his eyes and took a few steps backwards as well. I watched him closely, trying to focus on something.

Zaliver began to remove his shirt, pulling it over his head, and threw it on the ground.

"What are you doing?" I gasped, watching as he unfastened his belt and unbuttoned his pants, pulling his zipper down. I looked away but looked back into his electric blue eyes.

"Unlike werewolves, my clothes don't shift back with me. I would be completely naked. Lucky you, huh." He stopped moving and smiled charmingly at me.

"You're going to . . . change? Why?" I asked. My voice was shaking with fear. I wasn't ready to see his. . . . other form. I just freaking found out that . . . Zaliver isn't like me and I just—Ahh, my head was spinning.

"Well, you did threaten to reject and leave me mateless."

"I was bluffing. You'll find that I do that a lot when I'm not in the right state of mind."

"Bluffing or not, you can only reject your mate if you're not marked. And I plan on marking you." He smiled darkly at me, making me gasp.

"But if you plan to mark me, then wouldn't I change if your saliva enters my system? And why do you need to anyway?! Com'on, let's end this," I said a bit hysterically. I didn't want to change into whatever he was; I was fine a wolf.

"Yes you will. And I'm doing it in my other form. The deeper the bite, the stronger the claim—the stronger our bond is—and no other will be able to take my place. Besides, If you transform, you'll become immortal and I don't have to worry about your death," he explained.

Which point in "I didn't want to change" wasn't clear to him?

"Look, we can find another way to mark me. We can do the hickey thing! I don't want to change. Really, I'm fine the way I am now," I pleaded with him, and his eyes hardened.

141

"No, those won't warn off others. You're free to be marked and be mated, and I can't let someone else have you. And no, you're not fine unclaimed. I'm sorry, Vivian. I can't lose the one good thing that's happened in my existence of pain and misery," he said solemnly. I shook my head back and forth, not believing.

"Why do you keep thinking someone's trying to take me from you!? No one likes me Zaliver. Everyone in your pack has stayed away from me out of fear of having you snap their necks. You have no reason to be like this; it makes no sense! I'm surprised you even like me!" I yelled at him, trying to make him see his mistakes.

"No, they've stayed away from you because I ordered them to. I knew that once they realized how kind and beautiful you are inside and out, they'd want to become friends with you and that would take your time away from me. Honestly woman, you underestimate how much I crave your whole being. I want you; all of you—your time, thoughts, desires and wishes, your body, pleasure, I want all of you," he confessed, motioning with his hands.

I really *did* underestimate him. While it was sweet, it was also bothersome that it led me to believe Zaliver had more issues than he was letting on. Issues that I wasn't sure I could help him with.

"Okay, but that doesn't mean they're going to take me from you, or that I'd willingly leave you Zaliver. You're my mate. My sick, twisted, and deranged mate who needed some serious love and care, and maybe a long and very expensive therapy treatment."

"I appreciate that, but you're getting marked whether you're willing or not. Remember what I said earlier: 'Something you won't enjoy, but I will.' Well this is it." He snapped.

"I won't forgive you if you do this," I said, hoping he'd somehow change his mind, but he shrugged indifferently at me.

"I don't mind earning your forgiveness for the rest of our lives because by then, I'll know that you're officially mine. Any ideas on how to win you over? I was thinking of bringing your parents over for a starter. Would you like that or how about—"

The fact that he would bring my parents made me both happy and mad. Happy because I was longing to see them. Mad because by the time they were here, he'd had already marked me and changed me.

"You can't do this to me! You can't mark me against my will. I don't want to change. Zaliver, please! What will happen to my wolf?" I yelled. Fear and dread were building up in me as my situation finally hit me. He slipped his pants off, standing in black underwear.

"I can and I will. I'm sorry if you don't want to change, but it's really not that bad. Think of the perks. You get to spend immortality with me by your side and giving you anything you want. As for your wolf, I doubt you'll lose each other. You won't change immediately. I'll give you a week or two at most. Now let me concentrate; it's been a while." His body crouched down to the ground.

"No! No! No! Please no!" I tried one last time but he didn't acknowledge my cry of despair. My wolf whined inside of me, hinting that for once, running from our mate wasn't such a bad idea.

His body began to shake. A thick black fur started to gro out of his skin at an alarming rate. His muscles seemed to move and grow under his skin. His built became bigger, taller, and leaner. His legs elongated, and his feet turned into long paws while his hands grew into claws. His beautiful face twisted and protruded, enlarging out into a snout. His thick black hair was thinning as dark hair spread over his face with two pointy ears forming. I heard cracks as his ribs broke and spread to make his form grow and narrow in certain places.

It was a brutal but beautiful transformation than a werewolf's. It seemed to be almost complete as the creature began rising up to its full height. Even from afar I could tell it would tower over me by more than Zaliver's height.

As the transformation was about to it end, I looked into the creature's eye, and gasped. His familiar blue eyes looked back at me— Zaliver's eyes. I shook my head, but it . . . I couldn't. The creature's eyes began darkening like when the moon was in transition, slowly disappearing as black took over. With one last look, I bolted.

I heard a loud growl vibrating the ground. My knees wanted to buckle from under me as a wave of power was transmitted from the growl reached me.

Do not run, mate. I'll be chasing you.

I screamed when a harsh and guttural version of Zaliver's voice drifted into my head. I didn't stop running to the direction where I thought the car was. Damn him! Where was the damn car he had left the door open and the keys in? I wanted to slow down and see if he was running behind me, but that would be stupid. When I heard and saw nothing, I began to curse at my horrible sense of direction. I think I somehow varied off whatever trail we took.

Fine, run. This will be fun.

I looked around me to see where he was, but saw nothing but darkness. His fur was black, and for all I knew he could be blending in and watching me.

I jumped over a log and ducked under a branch, almost hitting it. My eyes scanned everywhere with my ears strained to hear him.

You're fast. But I'm faster.

A blur of wind suddenly gusted me back, showing a large shape in the form of a giant beast. I yelped and spun on my heels, running in another direction. Oh god!

143

Just imagine how fast you'll be when you transform. We'll be able to run together at the same pace. Just give in, Vivian. The voice was soft and alluring, trying to persuade me to stop.

"No!" I shouted out loud.

I ran behind a tree and hid behind it, trying to catch my breath. The forest went silent and so was my head. But then the sound of claws scraping the back of the tree where I was at was horrible. I took off again, looking over my shoulder to see a large figure on two legs with a clawed hand and two sparkling black eyes gleaming back at me.

~ • ~

His large form was crouched, blending in the dark. I could only see its two shiny black eyes that reflected the little light that the night gave off. I could see a white cloud forming as he exhaled out. My chest dropped that I held my breath, hoping he would do nothing.

Slowly, he straightened his body to his towering height. His right foot slid over the ground in my direction followed by the other. It felt like I was on my way to my coffin with each step he took. I wanted to close my eyes and wake up to somewhere else. I wanted to run but I couldn't. My body was frozen in exhaustion and shock. I couldn't even feel my legs.

He was right. He was faster, stronger, and better than a werewolf. No werewolf would be able to run through the forest without making a sound, appearing behind me without even me sensing him. He was the ultimate wolf race. He was powerful.

The closer he got, the faster my heartbeat went. I couldn't breath. He was too much to handle. I was overwhelmed and felt like fainting.

"Stop. Please," I whimpered, wanting to look away from him but not being able to because no matter how monstrous, dangerous, and frightening he was, he was still equally beautiful and breathtaking. I could still see him even in his monstrous sight.

He did stop, but didn't move away from me.

I don't want you to hate me Vivian, but I'm going to mark you now.

As he began taking steps towards me, I closed my eyes and shook. Fear paralyzed me to my spot. I backed away when I felt heat hitting my face. I was about to open my eyes when I got an image of what he looked like and sobbed.

Vivian.

"W-Wait!" I croaked out, squeezing my eyes shut.

When nothing happened I continued.

"I-If you're going to do it, c-change b-back. Please, I-I can't. I can't do it like this. Not in this form. Please, it's too much. I can't handle it," I wept out.

My eyes weren't even looking at the beast I knew was in front of me, but just thinking about its larger than normal snout, opening to reveal sharp and large canines that were going to sink into my flesh, almost brought a whole new round of hysteria.

It was silent for what felt like a lifetime until the sound of bones snapping and movement met my ears. I exhaled and gulped a much-needed air into my lungs.

When I felt something reaching my face, I screamed and tried to get away by throwing myself on the ground. Suddenly, Zaliver lunged towards me, moving faster than light. He flipped me over, making me sat on his lap, straddling him.

He wrapped a hand around me while the other held the back of my head, making both of our eyes met.

"I'm sorry. He's a bit harder to control than I remember. After marking you, all of your cuts and scrapes should heal faster. Our bond will be so much stronger now." He might have been talking to me but his eyes were trained on my neck, his lips were parted to show elongated canines.

I knew I had lost just like he knew I would. It was now hitting me that I was mated to the strongest man of two species. He controlled one and made up the other. Nothing he wanted would escape. He had the means and the power, and if not, his own raw speed, strength, and senses was all he needed. His power had no limits, and I was trapped with him forever. No matter where I went, where I hid, he would still be there.

"No man should have this much power," I whispered to him both horrified and amazed. His blue eyes lingered on my neck and smiled devilishly at me.

"You're right."

He leaned down to my neck with his hand pushing my hair back and gripped my head, tilting it to the side. My heart pounded in my chest knowing what was about to happen. Claiming as his through his mark would drastically change my life, and I would be glued to his side for all eternity. He kissed the spot he must have deemed perfect and then skimmed his nose up to whisper complacently in my ear.

"But I get to share all this power with you." And with that, he threw his head back and bit into me, making me scream.

I could feel the blood flowing out of me and into his mouth as he sank his canines deeper into my skin. I cried out and tried to push him off, but he tightened his hold on me, pushing my neck closer to him.

Give in to it, feel me. His voice floated into my head soothingly.

I didn't want to but I gave in, tired of all the pain. I tried to relax, and only then did I realize what he meant.

We had been cautious around each other, but we still joked around. The true bond was us; two individual beings coming together, and losing ourselves in each other—wholly trusting that the other would be there; not to catch us when we fell, but to be ready to fall together.

Zaliver was there with me. I could feel what he felt; the power and raw electric sparks that flowed through his veins, I was so lost in him that I didn't know where to begin.

I was addicted to this arousing feeling that arose my temperature. I hadn't realized I had been unconsciously grinding my lower half on Zaliver until we both groaned. He pulled his mouth off of me, licking at his freshly made mark. I gasped at the unspeakable feeling and sensitivity.

My mind finally went back, well, to a lot of things; but the first one was the naked Zaliver.

I remembered the chase and the beast hiding within his body. Faster than I could blink, he scooped me up in his arms and walked. I glared up at him, but my body was in no position to move, knowing how far the distance was to where the car was parked.

"You do realize you're naked right?" He grinned down at me with his eyes lighting up. He seemed calmer and somehow peaceful.

"Yup." I pursed my lips and looked forward, fighting the urge to fall asleep.

He sighed.

"You're not happy with me, I know," he said matter-of-factly. I glanced at him. "No I am not. I don't even want to look at you, let alone be in your arms."

He threw his head back and let out a booming laugh that shook him while carrying me.

"Well that's my cue."

"Cue to what?" I asked.

"Let my wooing begin." He looked at me with a soft smile.

He kissed my forehead, ignoring me flinch and continued to walk.

CHAPTER 15

I groaned at the constant itch on my nose that made me lift my hand and scratch it, but it would always come back forcing me awake.

I blinked my eyes open and squinted at the fluffy white thing blocking my eyesight. My brows furrowed in confusion. I heard a deep chuckle, so I looked around the feather that was being held by the culprit—Zaliver. He was kneeling next to my side of the bed with an amused smile on his face. I immediately wanted to smile at him, but the memories from last night resurfaced.

I pursed my lips at him, not saying anything. His smile fell a little, and he didn't say anything about it. My stomach then growled at the scent of fresh streaming food close by. Pulling the large feather away from my face, he revealed one of those small bed tables with breakfast on it, as well as a single red rose. I glanced at Zaliver.

"Good morning, beautiful. Breakfast in bed to start your morning," he murmured softly, his eyes with excitement and joy gazing at me. I might be angry, but I wasn't rude.

"Thanks," I said without looking at him in the eyes and picked up the fork to begin eating. I wasn't really hungry because I just woke up and then there was the fact that Zaliver's stare was unnerving. I hated when people stared at me when I ate. Almost as if hearing my thoughts, he lifted his eyes from my face and reached for a strand of hair, which seemed to captivate his attention. By the moment I was full, he had figured out how to properly braid after many failed attempts. I didn't even ask why he was trying to braid.

"Is that all you're going to eat?" he asked, concerned. I nodded. He looked at me for a long time before sighing. He sat by my legs and moved the food to the floor.

We sat there in a few moments of silence. I knew I was mad over his actions and I was boiling at how and what he did, but I didn't feel mad.

"I'm sorry," he said sincerely. He laid his hand on the top of my thigh.

"I know." It was true his emotions shadowed mine in a sense, but his was a different type. He didn't regret his actions. He was just sorry. I didn't like it.

I really needed time to sort my thoughts and figure out what would happen, but I wanted to do it by myself. I pushed the covers off of me and stood. Zaliver followed my lead and looked at me with watchful eyes as I moved around the room. I went into the bathroom and changed into black jeans and a long-sleeved shirt.

"What are you doing?" he asked, nearing to stand behind me when I bent to tie my shoes. When I finished, I stood and backed away from him. I needed space to clear my head before his scent would completely overcome my senses, then the bond might push me to stay.

"I'm going for a walk." I pulled my hair into a ponytail and noticed how fast it was growing.

"I'll go with you," he said, looking for his shoes.

"No. I want to go alone," I said, turning to face him. He stopped. His face hardened at me but he slowly nodded.

"I'll call your guards—"

"Alone." I shook my head at him and crossed my arms over my chest.

He narrowed his eyes at me, his teeth grinding against each other. He opened his mouth to argue but then chose to shut it with clenched fists. Eyeing him, I couldn't help but be glad he wasn't putting up an argument like I thought he would, but I wouldn't put it past him to do something about the situation until he had the last word.

"But you have to take your phone."

See what I mean? I just nodded since it wasn't a ridiculous demand. He walked around the bed and to his side drawer, pulling it out. He handed the phone to me with his fingers trailing over mine. After lingering a little too long, his soft warm skin sent shivers down my spine.

"Call me if anything happens and if you want me to pick you up or get you something, okay?" He looked at me anxiously.

"Okay," I murmured, turning around and walking out without another word. I decided to head close to the forest but not head into it.

I waved or smiled to the people who smiled at me. The breeze cooled my face, and the calm air brought tranquility to my surroundings.

It was the perfect time to ponder everything that happened and to come into terms of what was going on. For once, I felt a bit lost, not knowing what to focus on. I sat down under a nice-looking tree and looked out to the quiet houses and stores. I probably sat there for a good hour until I had my thoughts in order and my emotions in check.

I was surprised Zaliver hadn't sent a S.W.A.T. team or came after me himself. I guessed this was his way of showing me he was capable of giving me space.

I closed my eyes for a moment and thought about my home and my family. Although I had Zaliver and my other new friends, I terribly missed my parents. I wondered what Zaliver had said about bringing them here. How would they react? Would they like Zaliver? I felt hope and joy at the possibility of having them here. I wanted to ask my mom so many questions. How would she feel about my relationship with Zaliver? Would we be happy together? How about the future?

And then there was Joshula, Zaliver's brother.

I honestly couldn't imagine him having a brother. Who could be the younger brother? Or older? How was their relationship? Why were they picked for their mysterious training? What were the gods up there up to? What was the purpose for all of this? For me? I felt like a bargain chip—a used and played pawn. I didn't like it.

I didn't like how Zaliver marked me without even knowing if I wanted to be marked by him. After being told and shown what I would become afterwards, I hesitated but he didn't. Now, I didn't know what would happen to me. If I couldn't handle Zaliver's true form, what the hell made him think turning me into one of his own would solve that? If anything, I was now afraid of myself.

What would I be like? Would the transformation be painful? Of course it would be. It looked painful. He said I wouldn't lose my wolf, but what about my thoughts? Physically, I knew I would be able to handle it but mentally? I was sure I would break.

I was angry at him for putting me in this position.

I suddenly heard a snap. I turned my head to the direction of the sound. Then, I heard a shuffling noise and a continuous thumping sound. I stood up for a few minutes before realizing what I was hearing—a wolf running with a pounding heart. But the thing was miles away. Far enough to strain a werewolf's hearing.

I blinked in surprise. Sure, I could hear everything else around me, but the things I had heard before were in sight and close by.

I sighed. I was already changing, and it hadn't even been twenty-four hours since I was bitten. Did I really have one to two weeks, as what Zaliver guessed I would have, before the change? Or was he wrong?

By now, the wolf had gotten closer and was about to burst through the forest in a few seconds.

A brown-coated wolf ran out of the forest. It hadn't noticed me yet, but when it did, I could tell it was taken by surprise because it tripped the moment it lifted its head in my direction. Its front legs froze but its back legs continued moving. I knew I shouldn't have laughed but I did.

It shook his head, huffed and then shifted back. I looked at it, curious as to who it could be. The wolf had a nice build, so I knew it wasn't a child.

A guy with light brown hair and dark brown eyes walked over to me, embarrassed. I smiled at him sheepishly, then stood as he neared. He looked vaguely familiar.

"You okay there?" I asked, trying to hide the laughter in my voice. His cheeks reddened but he nodded at me, bringing one of his hands up to scratch the back of his head as he looked down at the ground.

"Yeah. Man, this is embarrassing! Out of everyone, I tripped in front of the luna!" he scowled at the ground. I laughed a bit at him and then asked.

"How did you know I'm Luna?" I didn't tell him but then I remembered the little get-together Zaliver had with the pack. I was about to open my mouth and tell him to forget it, but he spoke.

"Oh well, I can feel it or more so my wolf," he explained with a confused look on his face as if he wasn't sure what he was saying.

"How?" I asked, tilting my head to look at him better.

He felt that I was Luna? How?

"Well, my wolf recognized you immediately and told me to stop, but I was confused as to why until it saw you. He could feel your wolf's presence," he said. I was a bit confused, but I would ask Zaliver later . . . when I was done giving him the cold shoulder. I gave out a forced laugh as my wolf was just as confused as me.

He smiled at me and extended a hand, which I shook.

"You may not remember me, but my name's Bl—"

"Blake, and your brother is Drake. Yes, I remember you now. Hi, how are you?" I asked, finally recalling where I had seen him. It was the twin with the high cheek bones. His brother, Drake, had the sharp jawline.

I met him and his brother. I think there were three girls in the kitchen after Zaliver interrogated me.

He nodded at me, looking a bit surprised.

"Yeah, uh . . . I'm good. You're good too . . . at distinguishing the difference. I mean . . . not all people can tell the difference between me and my brother." He gave out an awkward chuckle. I looked at him amused. He was so adorably awkward. It was funny.

"I'm sorry. I'm usually not this weird," he said. His eyes couldn't look straight at me. I waved a hand at him dismissively, not wanting him to feel uncomfortable.

"It's fine. I get it. He's just . . . uh . . ." I looked for another word, not wanting to outright call him strange or awkward.

"Awkward? Nah, he's an asshole . . . I-I mean . . . uhh . . . mean person? Yeah! He's a mean person!" he said with wide eyes.

"So, if your brother is an asshole . . . mean person I mean, then why aren't you two hanging out now?" I asked smiling. He sighed, relieved to see I was joking around with him.

He looked up excitedly and began moving his arms around in demonstration.

"So, Drake invited Leslie to a get together. You actually met her and Amber, as well as Angela when you met me and my brother. We were playing the non-alcoholic version of truth and dare because Leslie's brother, Luke, came and wherever Luke is, Johnson follows. His pregnant sister was with him and said if she couldn't have alcohol, none of us could. And so we were playing when Amber dared me to—"

"I'm sorry. Did you say Luke and Johnson? And Johnson's pregnant sister happens to have the name Hannah?" I cut off his rambling, not believing how the world worked. He nodded hesitantly, not sure where I was going with it.

"Oh, wow." It was a small world or island after all.

"Is there something wrong?" he asked with a panicked voice.

"Oh no, I was marveling over how small the world is. It's just that I know Luke, Johnson, and Hannah." He exhaled, then a happy smile made its way to his face.

"That's good to know, Luna. Some of the pack was worried you wouldn't like it here," he admitted. The tip of his foot was tapping the ground a few times as he looked down.

"Well, that's very considerate of them." I smiled happily at him, surprised to hear what he said.

"I'm sorry I interrupted you earlier. What was your dare?" I asked, wondering what the dare was. He laughed loudly, throwing his head back.

"Well, it's not half as exciting as bumping into the luna of all wolves." I tried not to think about the name. "All I had to do was run from our house to this side of the forest while Drake held his breath," he explained casually.

My eyes widened at him in horror.

"You mean to tell me that while we are talking, your brother has been holding his breath the whole time?" He nodded before his face scrunched up and then his eyes widened in realization.

"Oh my god! I've *killed* my *brother*! My *mom's* gonna *kill me*!" he exclaimed, frightened.

He began running back to the direction where he came from. I followed without a thought, wanting to make sure his brother was okay and that he wouldn't be charged with attempted murder.

Mid run, my phone rang. Without checking or stopping, I answered the call, making sure to keep my eyes on Blake who was faster than he looked.

"Hello?" I panted into the phone. There was a brief pause before Zaliver spoke.

"Vivian? Why are you running? Are you alright? What's going on?" he asked worried. I wasn't surprised he could hear me running even through the phone.

"Look, can't talk right now. I'm trying to prevent murder and if not, murder charges! Call you later." I hung up right before he began yelling my name. His emotions flared up.

I immediately realized I probably shouldn't have said that last part.

~ • ~

Blake bursted through a door with me behind him. There was a small group surrounding a guy who looked just like Blake, but he was red and almost purple in the face. He must be Drake.

"Breathe, you idiot. It's not worth dying!" Hannah screamed at him.

"Breathe! I'm back!" Before Blake could even finish his sentence, Drake inhaled loudly, gasping to get as much air as possible.

"Jesus Christ! Took you long enough! A few more seconds and I'd have to explain to Mark why Hannah and I weren't going to be home for dinner because we were behind bars for being bystanders to murder!" Johnson yelled, tugging on his curls that for once were out their usual ponytail.

"Haha, he looks like a tomato! We should take a picture!" an amused girl commented.

"It's a shame," another girl said, sounding displeased.

"Are you okay, Drake?" a small voice asked. The question came from a red-haired girl with green eyes, which were similar features to Luke. His sister, Leslie, was leaning over Drake who held a finger up to convey he needed a moment.

Hannah sat down on a couch. Next to her was a dark-skinned girl with short brown hair and light brown eyes. She had a smug smile on her face as she munched on some popcorn. I could tell she had a broadened sense of humor. Next to her with a blank look was who I presume was Angela: dark hair and eyes with caramel skin. She didn't seem to be very happy at the moment.

"Were you trying to kill me you lil' shit? As soon as I get my energy back, I'm gonna fuckin' cut you up into little pieces and . . . man,

152

I'm tired," Drake said with a huff, sort of getting off the ground to stand. Thanks to Leslie and Luke's help.

"Sorry, bro. I was running and then I bumped into—" Blake began to explain. I was standing behind him. All of their attention was fully on Drake that they hadn't noticed me yet.

"If you say a chick, I will tell Mom you purposely tried to murder your twin." Drake's face lightened up considerably. He stood and pointed a finger in his brother's direction with a scowl on his face.

"No! No! Well . . . yeah actually, it was—"

All of a sudden, a warrior's yell was heard before a thumping of feet heading into our direction or more so towards Blake.

"You dick!" Drake ran for Blake with his intention to tackle him, but he moved at the last minute.

"No! Luna!" Luke made eye contact with me as Blake moved.

"What?" Drake said, horrified. He tried to stop, but he was moving so fast it was impossible for him to halt.

It was like time slowed down as if each step Drake took was as slow as a snail's pace. I looked around and saw everyone's horrified expression. Luke was reaching for Drake as if to yank him back while the girls on the couch were slowly standing up. Johnson looked like he was in mid lunge. I guess to tackle Drake sideways before he reached me just in case Luke couldn't stop him.

I walked around Drake as he continued to move. I frowned at him and looked forward. His head would hit the wall if Johnson wouldn't manage to tackle him. I walked over to the couch where Leslie was. Her hands were slowly raising to cover her mouth in surprise. I picked up a fluffy looking pillow and placed it on the floor where I thought Drake would most likely hit.

"Good," I said, pleased with my work. I stood beside Blake whose eyes were slowly widening.

My eyes flashed.

As if the play button was pushed, time sped up as Johnson tackled Drake who hit the pillow just as I expected while the girls shrieked. Not even checking on Drake, Johnson jumped off of him and turned to look at the spot where I stood with a worried look on his face that slowly became confused. Everyone froze, prepared to help me up, but I wasn't hurt.

"What the fuck?" someone mumbled.

"Well . . . that was interesting," I said jokingly.

Blake gasped. His head snapped back, and everyone else in the room turned towards me with a mixture of surprise, disbelief, and relief.

"Luna, are you alright?" Luke asked, not missing a beat.

"Oh yeah, I'm fine. How about you, Drake? Did the pillow cushioned your head?" I asked, worried it had not.

He nodded up and down slowly. His expression was a mixture of confusion and bewilderment. Johnson turned his body to look at me with his blond curls bouncing.

"Damn, you're fast. You were holding back on me, weren't you? When we ran here, I mean," Blake said suspiciously. I gave him a tight-lipped smile, not sure what had happened myself. Was it odd I wasn't freaking out? I think I had an idea about what just happened.

"Viv? You sure you're alright? Come here and sit," Hannah said. She walked over to me and put her arm over my shoulder, steering me to the couch. The girls parted the way, making room for me.

"No, really, I'm fine. It's Drake that I'm worried—"

"I'm fine. I'm sorry, Luna. I didn't see you. I apologize for putting you in harm's way. I will gladly follow through whatever punishment you deem fit," Drake said, standing up and walking over to me with his neck bared. My eyes widened.

"Me too, Luna. Had I not moved, you wouldn't have been put in danger." Blake walked over and stood next to his brother and did the same thing.

"Wow, Wow. Calm down, boys. Take it easy. It was just an accident, and accidents happen all the time. Besides, nobody got hurt. Well, maybe Drake but we're all fine. Why don't we just put this behind us and move on?" I suggested, not wanting them to make this a big deal.

"I'm sorry, Luna, but they're right. They should be punished for endangering your safety," Luke said. Both he and Johnson walked up behind the boys with their serious faces, making the twins shrink.

"But it's fine," I tried to explain.

"Luna, as your guards, we have to make sure you're safe at all times, and these two—" Johnson tried saying.

"It's your day off. You're not working. This never happened." I was growing frustrated.

"But Luna, the alpha should know what happened."

Were they trying to get the twins killed?

"Guys." My voice came out sharper than intended, having immediate effect. Both bowed their head and held silence, so did the others.

I didn't know what it was, but usually when a disagreement went on, I would be the peacemaker. It was just that something about having my wishes on dropping this ignored had irked me. Subconsciously, I lifted my chin and narrowed my eyes. I wasn't sure, but I had a feeling I was emitting something off in waves.

"Really. No one got seriously hurt, so this little accident didn't happen. Just forget about this and go back to playing. Oh, and let's just keep this between us. Zaliver doesn't have to know." Whatever I was doing had an effect because they all nodded together, and with one look at each other, they calmed down.

"Thank you, Luna. You're very kind," Drake said, much more relaxed than before. Hannah and Leslie went on to chat softly in a corner while Amber was still munching on popcorn. I hadn't talked much to the girl but could already feel we would have great conversations. Angela was standing by Blake, looking at him. Hmm . . .

I spent a few minutes with them and then left, politely declining their arguments to stay and play but promised to do so next time. I didn't feel like being around people at the moment. I walked down the street, not really meeting the curious stares.

I sighed not being able to stall any longer.

I pulled out my phone and dialed Zaliver to make sure he didn't do anything drastic. He picked up on the first ring.

"Vivian, what the hell—" His voice was rough.

"I'm okay. Nothing to worry about," I said quickly, knowing he was mostly just worried if I was okay.

"What happened? Where are you?" I looked around, not seeing anything that marked where I was.

"Not sure. I'll be back,"

"No, stay there. I'll be there in a few."

"But you don't even know where I am." My brows furrowed in confusion.

"Stay there." He hung up.

The air shifted around me. I suddenly felt my head lighten a bit like I wasn't walking, but I knew I was. I frowned and noticed how quiet the streets went. Looking around, I met silver eyes. Everyone close by froze. Teens, adults, and children around were all staring at me. I was slightly freaked out. After their eyes flashed, they continued with what they were doing. That was seriously creepy on a large scale.

I barely even heard the soft thumping that was nearing me at lightning speed, and when I did, Zaliver was already beside me. Before I could say anything, he scooped me into his arms and continued running.

I closed my eyes and clutched at him with all my strength as he moved at frightening speed. My stomach felt like dropping. We suddenly stopped in front of our room. He let go of me, sliding my body down his, and leaned over me to open the door. I took the chance and entered.

"What happened? Are you hurt?" he asked, fussing over me. He took a step closer to me, but I held up a hand.

"Vivian." He tried taking a step again, but I backed up.

"I'm fine. No need to check me. I just bumped into a new friend, and there was a . . . uhh, complication, but everything is alright." His blue eyes narrowed suspiciously at me.

155

"What new friend? And you mentioned murder?" I chuckled at the last part.

"Just a friend, and yeah I did, but no one's dead. Everything is fine. You really didn't have to come and get me, but thanks." I bit my bottom lip and looked at Zaliver, suddenly wanting to be back in his arms.

No. I had to fight it or it would make him think he's gotten away with marking me, then he'll try to do something like this again.

His eyes dropped to my lips. I held my breath, making his blue eyes darken. His chest began lifting with his harsh breaths. His nostrils were flaring. He began taking large steps towards me. Each step made me take a step back nervously. I looked back. Seeing I was about to fall back into the desk, I sidestepped, foolishly believing he would stop there. He stepped back in front of me and lifted both arms on either side of me. He lowered his head, making his dark locks fall over his heated eyes.

"Vivian," he breathed out my name softly and groaned softly in my ear.

My lips parted as I gasped in shock at the reaction of my body. He skimmed his nose down my face and to my neck. I could feel my mark heating up as he neared it. One of his hands wrapped around my waist and pulled me closer to him while his other hand grabbed the back of my head to tilt it. I began breathing quickly. My body wanted whatever was going on to continue, but my mind was blank. He planted a soft kiss right above the mark, getting a little sound of pleasure from me. He skimmed his lips around the tender skin tortuously slow but never kissing the actual mark that seemed to pulse. My hands slowly worked their way up his shirt, clutching his toned waist.

"I want you so fucking bad that it hurts. Don't you want me too?" He purred softly in my ear.

I closed my eyes as he kissed back down and up my neck. He was raising my body temperature to a dangerous peak that my lower muscles were clenching.

"W-what . . ." My voice was deep and thick with desire.

"Let me take care of you."

He finally kissed my mark, planting his lips firmly on my heated skin. The amount of pleasure that came from that small action drove me crazy. A thick and murky fog of dark carnal desire for Zaliver was blocking all rational thoughts. I pushed myself closer to his as the blood in my veins boiled and gave out a pleasurable moan.

He quickly moved to my lips, meeting his fervent ones with my eager ones. He immediately took the dominant lead, deciding on a fast and rough and almost desperate kiss that I returned.

The hand that had gripped my waist slid down and cupped my butt. He picked up my leg and wrapped it around his waist, which gave him the perfect angle to push his hardness into me. I let out a soft purr. He

pushed me further into the wall, mostly pinning me with his hips. When I needed to breathe, he moved back down my neck and began nibbling lightly on the mark, making me grind my lower half on him. In the back of my mind, a red bell was going off.

Panting, I opened my eyes while he kissed my neck as if the fog was swarming deliberately in my head. I lifted one of my hands to run it through his hair, but when I did, I snapped out of whatever spell that was trapping me under this lust. My nails became sharp-looking claws that seemed to be out of control, growing and shortening as if indecisive. I realized I had been gripping Zaliver with these nails and pushed him off of me.

He growled annoyed, but I was too horrified at what I had done to tell him to shut up. His black shirt had four small punctured holes. I could see a little amount of blood on his skin. Even my own fingertips had a bit of blood. I felt like someone had punched a hole into my heart or I had been stabbed, but that wasn't as painful as knowing I had hurt Zaliver. I looked up at him with watery eyes. His annoyed expression dropped and concern filled it.

"I-I'm s-sorry! I-I didn't know. I'm sorry!" I choked out, guilt and shame filled me to the core. He stepped closer to me, lifting his hands to hold my head. His thumbs were wiping the tears that threatened to fall from my eyes. He looked like he was in an agonizing pain that just added to my guilt.

"Hey, shh, shh. What are you going on about? What's wrong, my little cloud?" he asked.

"Doesn't it hurt?" I asked. Perhaps he was in shock.

"Doesn't hurt what?" He smiled at me, but his eyes were confused.

I pushed him away softly and pointed to his torn shirt. He looked down and then backed up at me with understanding and adoration on his face, which just confused me more.

"Oh, little cloud. I'm fine, Vivian. Don't worry," he said, laughing a little while my brows furrowed at him. He was definitely in shock.

"Look." He pulled his shirt up and turned his torso to me. I leaned closer to inspect. The blood just sat on his smooth unpunctured skin. I blinked up at him, wondering if I was the crazy one.

"But I-I . . ." I trailed off not knowing what to say. He dropped his shirt and picked up my bloodied hand, cleaning my fingers with his black shirt.

157

"I heal fast. Besides, I didn't even feel it until you showed me. Don't worry about me." I nodded, unfocused.

"That shouldn't have happened," I said, referring to the little make out session we had.

Now that I had my head somewhat clear, I regretted not running for the door as soon as he began heading towards me in the first place.

"Why not? We're mates. That and much more will happen." His expression darkened and his eyes narrowed into slits. I sighed.

"You know why," I mumbled, trying to walk around him to get to the door before anything else would happen. His hand shot out and gripped my arm, pulling me back. I tugged my arm out of his hold and didn't move, noting the challenge in his eyes.

"No I don't. Is this because you're still angry about last night? Because I get it—"

"No you do not!" I hissed out at him with my fists clenching.

"Enlighten me then." He hissed back

Fine. He asked for it.

"You messed up on so many levels, Zaliver, that you should be happy I'm even talking to you. Let me explain to you what I'm feeling right now. Yes, you did tell me you would mark me at some point. However, you seemed to have forgotten to inform me of how you would do so. I'm also sure the fact that you were going to bind me to you forever without mentioning you were a Lycan, which I and everyone else thought was fake,

had slipped your mind. And let's not forget about you chasing me through the forest in your scary ass from when you planned to sink your larger-than-life teeth into my neck. Zaliver, you might as well have chased me with a goddamn knife! And if you think I'm only mad at you for that, then you're wrong.

I'm more than just mad. I'm furious at the fact you forced the mark on me after saying that once marked, I would become the very thing that made me run away in the first place. I'm livid at how you expected me to just follow along whatever you told me to do, keeping me in the dark and expecting me not to say or want to know what my own mate was up to. I'm boiling at the thought of being a pawn in a game I want nothing to do with. Being a peace offering to you doesn't sit well with me. I'm pissed at myself for not paying closer attention to your actions and then basically pushing your god damn red button. Most of all, I'm disappointed.

I'm disappointed at the fact that something so meaningful, beautiful, and intimate as marking your significant other was a letdown for us. Zaliver, we all grow up with expectations of how certain moments of our lives are going to happen and how they're going to play out, and yeah! Of course, they don't happen exactly like we planned them to, and no, they aren't perfect, but a marking? A marking is so much more, and I guess I'm just . . . upset on how we'll never have that semi-perfect moment between us and that point in time where we commence a new chapter for us. There. Are you happy now? I've gotten it off my chest."

While I was ranting, his face morphed into pain. He winced every time I mentioned wrongdoing on his part. He looked haunted by my response that I wanted to take the words back immediately, but I couldn't. Maybe I was being too harsh? I felt like a total bitch. I usually wouldn't rub people's mistakes in their faces. Holding on to this anger was bad for me, but it wouldn't just disappear like that.

His head was downcast, and his dark locks were concealing his expression from me. I searched within me for his emotions, but I felt like he had blocked me out. I felt even worse now. How did it go from me being angry at him to me feeling angry at myself?

"Zaliver—"

"No," he said gruffly, lifting his head slowly. His expression was clear and bleak, not showing me what he was truly feeling or thinking. His blue eyes stared into mine, swimming in their own sorrow.

"I should know how you feel. Even if you do hate me, I still want to know." His words pulled at my heartstrings.

"I don't hate you, Zaliver. To be frank, I don't think I could ever hate you, but I don't trust you right now. I'm sure we'll move past this." I confessed. If me giving him the cold shoulder would put him on edge and saying all of this would convince him that I hated him, then so be it. Honesty hurts but he needed to hear it.

It seemed like Zaliver had put up a front to everyone, but deep down, he had always cared or had wanted to care about something important to him after his brother. He just wanted to protect, provide, and take care of me. But would that excuse the way he acted? That was the big question, and I was leaning towards a big *no*.

He smiled painfully at me, leaning down to kiss my forehead softly for a while. I inhaled his scent. He pulled away a moment later and pulled out his phone and pushed some buttons. His blue eyes stared down seriously at me.

"Well, if we are to move on and for my wooing to truly work, I think I know what I have to do first." I looked at him, worried.

Who was he calling?

He surprised me when he handed me his phone as soon as the person on the other line picked up. I took it from him cautiously.

"Hello?" the other line asked. The voice was hoarse and thin but very familiar.

It should be. I grew up hearing that voice for the past eighteen years of my life.

My eyes widened at Zaliver with surprise. He nodded at me. "Mom?"

CHAPTER 16

"Mom?"

I held my breath as the other line went silent and then a choking sob escaped the phone.

"V-Vivian? Is that you?" My mom's voice trembled. My heart clenched painfully.

"Yeah, Mom, it's me," I whispered into the phone, having a hard time not to cry out of happiness. Her voice alone sent a wave of homesickness that had me wanting to be wrapped in her arms. It's not like I didn't miss her, but it hit me hard so much as soon as I heard her voice.

"Oh my god, my baby girl! I'm sure you probably don't have too much time, so I'll let you speak. Where are you? Who took you?" My brows furrowed at her words, but I quickly understood. She must be thinking how hard it was for me to somehow manage to call her despite being "kidnapped." I tried not to dwell on that and chose to enjoy her voice.

"No, Mom. It's fine. I can talk to you all I want." I looked up at Zaliver, forgetting he was there but wanting to let him know that I would fight him if he dared to take the phone from me. Thankfully, he just stared back with curiosity in his eyes. "Mom, I should probably explain some things," I said softly.

"Are they making you say this? If I go to the store, what do you think will be the first thing I will see? Skittles, Snickers, or a Hershey?" Her voice became strained as she tried to make it calm.

I took a shaky breath and gave a small chuckle into the phone. When I was little, I was a pretty weird child who didn't really take anything seriously but always claimed others were after me. So, I made plans if something were ever to happen; all written down in crayons, of course. One day, after school, I stormed into the house telling my mom that we needed to make a code in case I was kidnapped and somehow managed to send a message:

Skittles: Out of State or Country
Snickers: I know or recognize the kidnapper
Hershey: I'm being forced to say something

161

My mom shook her head, saying it wasn't something to joke about, but after throwing a tantrum, she agreed.

"I'm really fine, Mom. I can't believe you remembered that. It was such a long time ago," I said, surprised and filled with a strong emotion.

"Y-you're really okay? No Hershey?"

"No candy, Mom. I'm really alright and unharmed." I forced myself not to look at Zaliver whose gaze was set on me.

"B-but then where are you? Why haven't you came home? Are you in some sort of danger? If you are, we can protect you here, honey. Come home. Everyone's worried about you. We've all been looking for you. Your father tried to convince the alpha to send out a search party, but for some reason, the alpha said he can no longer feel your pack link yet still feels you." I felt guilty hearing every word she said. Even though Zaliver was behind my abduction, I hadn't really thought of how my parents took my sudden disappearance along with the other girls who went missing.

"I'm so sorry you and Dad worried about me, but I'm really fine. It's a long complicated story, Mom. One that I don't know how to begin with," I tried telling her. My body was overwhelmed with the sudden happiness, sadness, guilt, and worry. I felt my eyes stinging and tears slowly growing, so I blinked repeatedly.

I sat on the edge of the bed, aware of the fact that Zaliver was still silently observing me. I couldn't decide if it was because he didn't want me to say certain things or because he was genuinely concerned about me. The deeper part of me argued that no matter what, he would always care about my emotional and mental state as much as he did for me physically. The cold and angry part of me was saying he just didn't want everyone to know about me and that if he really cared, he wouldn't have done the things in the first place.

"I'm so confused, Vivian. What's going on, honey? You can come home, baby. Whatever is going on, we can deal with it together." Her words knocked down my composure. Tears streamed down my face and my breathing hitched. I clenched my fists as my eyesight became blurry.

"M-Mom, I missed you and Dad so much. I-I just don't know . . . it's um . . . I'm not . . ." I didn't know what to tell her.

So many things came to mind. I wanted to tell her I was kidnapped and I was going to go home. A part of me wanted to tell her about Zaliver, who would now become a part of my life whether I was upset with him or not. Telling her he kidnapped me would seem like nothing compared to telling her who I was mated to and what that really meant. Zaliver's reputation spoke of him to everyone. I was hesitant to say when most feared and hated him or believed he did not exist at all. What would my parents think of this?

I jumped when I felt him sit next to me on the bed. I looked up at him, confused and pained, with my eyes asking him for help in dealing with the situation. He willingly wrapped one arm around me to pull me in closer to him while the other gently pried the phone from my death grip and put the phone on speaker. I didn't realize, but through the bond, I had yelled out for his embrace, wanting to feel comforted in my moment of weakness.

"Mrs. Gray," he said into the phone. His voice was strong and clear, a replica of his facial expression. No hesitation. No worry. No confusion. I held my breath.

"W-who are you? Where's my daughter? Vivian! Vivian!" I bit my lip at her panicked tone.

"I'm right here, Mom. You're on speaker." My voice cracked a bit.

"What's going on? Vivian, tell me!"

"Mrs. Gray, you can calm down. Your daughter is well taken cared of and anything she wants is given to her. She is absolutely in no danger," Zaliver said.

Bet.

"Who the *hell* are *you*?" Her voice became sharp and harsh but still had a slight edge to it. Zaliver tensed slightly beside me probably because of her tone, but he remained calm.

"My name is Zaliver Azrala, your daughter's mate." The phone went dead for a couple of minutes before a large wail was heard. I leaned in, worried.

"Mom? Mom? Mom, are you alright?!"

She sniffed. "Oh, Vivian! Why didn't you just say you're with your mate? You're safe! Oh, thank you, Mr. Azrala. You've calmed my heart down now knowing my daughter is in the hands of her mate." I looked at the phone as if it were my mother with a look of bewilderment and confusion.

"Uhh, Mom it's not that easy—" I tried to explain. I didn't want her to know what really happened and what was happening now but still, even I knew it wasn't that easy.

"And why didn't you just call to let us know instead of worrying everyone, Vivian? Oh, poor Lily. After her alpha's death, she was in such a state of shock that she fainted. She doesn't even remember picking you up from the airport. The poor girl feels guilty for losing you in the chaos and has been looking for you nonstop." My guilt just got bigger and bigger. While I was here laughing and making new friends, my family had been looking for me. But why did Lily not—

Something came back to my mind.

163

When Algebra took us, he told someone to erase memories as if they were never there.

"Mom, you have to know—"

"That I've arranged for you and your husband to be brought to our location as soon as tomorrow." My head snapped over to look at Zaliver.

What? What was he doing?

We stared at each other. He was serious. I was confused, but my mom talking to me made me hold my questionings.

"Oh, that's wonderful, but how? And why can't you two come here?" There was happiness in my mom's voice. I guess now hearing I was not in danger and I was with my mate who she always believed would take care of me calmed her down considerably.

"For many reasons, Mrs. Gray. Won't you like to see where your daughter now lives?" His voice became persuasive and pleasant. If I was in my mom's shoes, even I would be curious to know.

"Uh, yes, I guess. So, you two are living together? I don't know how I and your father feel about that, Vivian. You two just met. Maybe Vivian should come home and both of you can—" His arm suddenly tightened around me. His hold was no longer comforting but possessive as he pulled me closer as if my mom would somehow reach in through the phone and pull me out of his arms.

"I'm not so sure about that. We have much to discuss that is why I'm having you both sent here, Mrs. Gray. We can all get to know each other. Will you not like that, Vivian?" He turned his dark eyes on me. His voice became tighter. His eyes were narrowed and fierce, daring me to oppose him. His emotions were shadowed. He was angered at the thought of my parents wanting to separate us even if it was just a suggestion.

"Uhh, yeah. We should meet up here, Mom. It'll be great," I said weakly, not being able to look away from him or oppose his wishes. In a sense, I was on his side as well. I didn't want to be away from him. I also didn't believe I could.

"Well, I'll discuss it with your father, sweetheart. Oh, my heart feels much lighter. Thank you for taking care of my daughter, Mr. Azrala." My mother's open nature was a gift, but right now, she was thanking my kidnapper-mate who she had no idea was the feared Lupus Deus.

"It's a pleasure. She's such a lovely person. I'm honored to have *forever* with her by my side," Zaliver said politely. His eyes were on me while a heated pool of desire slipped through the bond as well as dark mockery. I looked away.

164

"Oh, how adorable. I can't wait to meet you." While hearing my mother's glee, my stomach felt a bit sick. My mother actually believed he was joking about the *forever* part.

"Mom, I think you should know about—" Zaliver interrupted me once more.

"Your flight details will be sent to you shortly. I hate to do this, but we must end the call. You should be here in two days." I opened my mouth to protest and ask him why he wouldn't let me finish my goddamn sentences.

"Where are you two exactly?"

"Oh, why don't we make that a surprise? It adds on the excitement, Mrs. Gray, but do pack as if you're going to Hawaii." My mom squealed into the phone much to my surprise.

"Oh, thank the Lord for this miracle. You're safe and sound. We're going to see you in two days. We're going to Hawaii! Oh, I'm so happy."

"Mom—" My disbelief was painted on my face more than my tone of voice.

"We shall be in touch very soon, Mrs. Gray. See you soon," Zaliver said in an easy tone as if he wasn't deceiving my mother.

"Bye, Mr. Azrala. Bye, sweetheart! Oh, your father will be so happy to hear the news."

"Mom—"

CLICK.

I spun around to look at Zaliver who stood and turned his back. I heard constant clicks that meant he was texting. The conversation didn't go as I had thought, and while I was glad to hear my parents were now coming, I didn't know why we couldn't go and see them. I tried to tell my mom how we met or what was really happening, but he would interrupt me from doing so by sweet-talking with my mother.

"What the hell, Zaliver? Why didn't you let me tell her what is going on? And why are they coming here instead of the other way around?" I yelled at him angrily. He spun around and lifted a brow at me, putting his phone in his back pocket.

"For many reasons, Vivian. I don't think the conversation you wanted to have is appropriate over the phone, especially without your father. Besides, I have more explaining to do than you do. As for me bringing them here, it will be obvious. If they are here, they can see how well you are and will be in my care. If we are to leave the island, it will be catastrophic. You will become a target once the news about you being my mate gets out. Here, on the island, I can protect you without any trouble."

165

I pursed my lips but said nothing more after seeing his point. As much as I hated it, I would rather have my parents safe even if I wouldn't be home. He saw my resolve and calmed down a notch.

"Thanks for . . ." He nodded at me with understanding. My words faded off. I was really grateful to him for letting me speak to my mom even if it was brief and I was cut off many times. I now felt calmer after knowing how she was and telling her I was safe. I still had a few questions in my mind though.

"Why did she say the alpha cannot feel my pack link but can still feel me? And what about Lily not even remembering picking me up from the airport?" I asked him.

"Well, you're now a marked mate. Every wolf can feel a separate bond to us. There's the pack link that any member can feel, the mate bond between mates, the alpha link that lets alphas know who's in control, and the semi-complete link to us," he explained, crossing his arms over his chest.

"Semi-complete?" I asked. His eyes did that freaky glow thing but then went back to normal.

"You still have to transform into your other form," he said smoothly. I briefly paused. I didn't want to think about that just yet.

"What about Lily?" He nodded at me. I was not sure if it was about me not saying anything or him remembering something.

"I had Albericus erase memories of bringing you here. It was just a safety process."

"Okay. How about my parents? What are we going to do?" I turned from him and began walking back and forth with excitement and worry throughout the conversation. I pushed it out of my head and looked at the bright side of this mess.

"Don't worry. I have everything under control. I'm going to have them picked up tomorrow. They will be brought here and will be staying with us where you can explain to them how happy you are and will be here." I paused walking and glanced at him and continued walking.

He said it as if he knew for sure.

"So, they will be staying here with us?"

"No." I turned to look at him, confused.

"What do you mean? Where are they staying?" He looked at me for a long moment before answering.

"Come on."

He walked out of the room, grabbing his car keys. I followed him, concerned with where he was taking me. What did he mean by no? He better not be planning to put my parents in a hotel on the island.

He drove down the pack house road and made a left behind the house. We drove deeper and deeper into the forest behind the

166

house. I was beginning to think he would let my parents stay at a prison. I was about to yell at him when he pulled into a smooth trail.

There was a huge house coming into sight that made me wonder if this was meant to be the pack house. It had a similar build to the pack house but a more medieval and castle feeling to it with the smooth grey stone walls, balcony, and grand boulders outside on each side of the house. Zaliver pulled in front of the house and close to the low white steps. The house was beautiful and perfect in my eyes actually.

"Wow," I said, looking out the window.

"Here. They'll be staying here." There was something in the way Zaliver spoke that made me frown and turn to look at him.

Looking at him, I realized how tensed he was. Something else was there like an edge. His hands gripped the steering wheel tightly, his shoulders pushed back, and his blue eyes flickered from me to the house. He then stared out of the window after every second. His body language threw me off. It was strong and yet not so much. I tilted my head and searched through the bond. With wide eyes, I realized why he looked so odd. Zaliver was nervous.

I looked towards the house and stared a little longer. It was beautiful and didn't seem unkempt, but it gave off a lonely feeling. The one who lived here managed to make Zaliver, the big bad wolf god, nervous. Who could it be?

"Zaliver, who owns the house?" I asked, turning back to look at him. He looked at me before he cleared his throat, running his hands through his thick black mane before finally answering me with a sigh.

"We do."

Shock rang through my body as it wasn't the answer I expected to hear.

"W-what? You mean your house? Right?" I asked him. He bit his bottom lip. Desire burned through my body as I wanted to bite his lip as well, but I pushed it aside. He shook his head at me.

"No, our house. I-I had a house built for us." My eyes widened even more. I wasn't sure if it was because I had never heard him stutter out of nerves or because he had a house built for us.

"When?" I asked, having a hard time to swallow and turning to study the house. It looked new but also looked like no one lived in it.

"I-I . . . umm . . ." He gave a frustrated growl and covered his face with his hand.

My mouth parted at the sudden display he was giving—not the strong and confident god that everyone feared but a nervous and somewhat embarrassed man. A small smile made its way across my face. For him to struggle in saying something meant he was opening up to me, which I could guess was extremely hard for him. He was trying.

167

I took his hand that was covering his face and held it to my face. I kissed his knuckles before intertwining our fingers, giving him an encouraging smile. He looked at me with his blue eyes peering at me from under his thick black lashes while strands of hair fell forward. He was far from looking innocent, but at the moment, he looked like a compassionate man about to confess something he had kept to himself.

"I had it built as soon . . . as soon as I heard," he said slowly. His eyes were intense.

"Heard what?" I asked softly.

"About you. About them giving me a mate," he said.

What? That made no sense to me because that would have been a long time ago. He made it clear the first time we met that he didn't trust me. Why build a house for a mate he couldn't trust? Seeing my confused expression, he explained more.

"As time passed, I realized it could be a rumor or if I did find you, it would be impossible. So, I moved into the pack house and forgot about the house. It's furnished and everything."

"But why?" I still didn't understand. He smiled softly at me and reached over with his hand, pushing a strand of hair behind my ear. He softly creased my face before pulling away.

"Because I guess deep down, even monsters want families to love." With a squeeze, he let go of my hand and got out of the car.

My eyes teared up upon hearing him call himself a monster. I felt as if I just peaked at a Zaliver buried under layers of danger, anger, revenge, power, and darkness. A moment of clarity hit me during the few seconds it took him to open my door. Zaliver was a complex being who, even in the craziest of moments, reacted and acted off on emotion. Him marking me was a reaction to an action I took. He was still a jackass, but there was a new side to him.

He opened the door and held a hand out for me, which I quickly took. We stood side by side, looking up at the grand house—our house.

"Do you like it?" he asked me quietly, pulling out a key from his pocket. I smiled at him.

"I love it. It's perfect." Whatever insecurities he was carrying left him at that moment. He grinned excitedly at me, flashing his pearly whites.

He swept me off the ground, making me shriek in surprise and then laugh as he began spinning around. I continued to laugh as he stopped and began taking the steps up.

"What are you doing?" I giggled.

"Carrying you over the threshold," he said happily.

"That only works if we're married," I pointed out.

"I wouldn't be too sure about that." I shook my head at him with a smile. He began unlocking the door with one hand.

"So, how's my wooing going so far?" he asked, looking down at me with joy.

I lifted a brow at him, trying not to smile and failing miserably.

"I'll take that as a good sign." He was about to take a step in but stopped to look down at me seriously. His expression made me worry.

"I have to warn you, Vivian," he said seriously.

"What?" I asked, not sure what was going on.

"Most of my wooing will take place here as well as other things." He smirked at me with mischievous eyes. "In the living room, the floor, the bedrooms, the walls . . ."

"Zaliver!" I yelled at him but wasn't able to hide the laughter in my voice. I was shocked after finally getting his implications.

"The shower and tub, the stairs, the gym, pool—"

"We have a pool?" I asked excitedly as we entered the house.

"Yeah, wanna do it now? How about on the trampoline? We could really get it on—"

"Zaliver!" I flushed at his words. His booming laugh echoed.

He shut the door with his foot.

Right there and then, a big chunk of anger and resentment I had towards Zaliver flew away and made way for a new emotion.

A better but dangerous emotion.

CHAPTER 17

Two days passed a lot faster than I thought, especially when those two days were spent learning about our new house with my mate popping up every few hours with gifts and flowers and a dazzling smile with heart-stopping blue eyes.

I fixed up the house and added things from my shopping sprees with Hannah, who had way more fun decorating my house than I did. I kept looking for something to fix since my parents were coming in a few hours. I really needed to do something other than to shop. I was sure even Zaliver's card had its limits. *I think.*

At the moment, I was looking over my house-greeting outfit much to my dismay. I felt like one of those housewives inviting her parents into her new home with her husband to show we were living the grand life. I curled my hair a little and wore a silver chain around my neck and the diamond drop earrings Zaliver brought me yesterday to match my soft peach dress. I guess me dressing up all nice was a way to show my parents I was being very well cared for. I hadn't seen Zaliver since this morning. He said he was going to be running around the island to make sure everything was alright and in order before my parents' arrival.

I had a feeling he wanted everything to go perfectly, like he actually wanted my parents to like him. I thought it was cute yet very odd because I knew, at the end of the day, he was older and stronger than them, not to mention his word was final. Very odd indeed. In the first two days we—or more specifically, I—decided we needed a master plan to go along with. Zaliver listened carefully, but I could see the amusement in his eyes as he watched me pace the room.

~•~

I was walking back and forth in front of him in my pj's. My hair was tied up in a loose bun. Zaliver was sitting on the bed with his legs extended and crossed at the ankles, and his arms crossed over his chest.

"We should come up with a plan for my parents' coming. We should . . . Yes, we should," I muttered that last part mostly for myself as my nerves rattled in me.

I wasn't just nervous because they were coming. I actually wanted them to like Zaliver because according to him, my family was now his family—literally, his family. Zaliver, as far as he and I knew, had no family.

"And what do you have in mind?" he asked me.

I looked at him suspiciously because I was pretty sure he already had a plan or else he wouldn't have invited them. Zaliver was very . . . cunning if I must say so. I was beginning to see the man wouldn't do anything without a reason. It was a good yet very scary trait.

"Well, I'm not sure yet, but I know you must have some plan, right?" I turned to look at him.

"Indeed, I do. Your parents will be escorted here where you can greet them, but I will not be around for the first few minutes for two reasons. First is to obviously give you time with them," he explained.

"And the second?" I asked. He lifted a brow at me with a face of seriousness and playfulness.

"The other reason I don't leave the island is because of the effect my presence alone does to other wolves. Everyone here has already gotten used to the massive amount of power I radiate, more so than an alpha. What do you think your parents' reactions will be if I open the door? I'd really rather not make your parents drop to their knees when we first meet. I heard it's a bad impression," he said matter-of-factly.

It was true. I was guessing he had much more power than he let on because through the bond, I could feel an odd sensation of a strong destructive force behind a wall like he had a tight lid on a bottle of soda he had just shaken up. Every once in a while, he'd give off a wave of power. It was almost barely noticeable but still enough to catch attention. Even I struggled not to want to cower and that was just from him walking in, imagining an angry Zaliver . . . nope.

I guess it would give my parents a room to breathe with him being away, but I had no doubt they would feel his presence on the island. In a state full of millions of people, they would barely feel him, but on an island? Definitely. They would probably think it to be a presence of multiple alphas, but I wondered what they would think if it came from one man? Would their minds immediately go to the deadly god known as the Lupus Deus?

"Anddd . . . I also want you to try to butter them up for me. I mean, a little good talk wouldn't hurt." He smirked at me deviously. I shook my head at him, a small smile on my face.

"So, you're going to give me a few minutes alone with them to get them warmed up before you come in?" He nodded.

I bit my lip and pondered over the plan. It wasn't bad, but was there any proper way to show your parents your mate? There should have been a how-to-

171

introduce-your-powerful-and-deadly-mate-to-your-family guide. That would have been nice.

"I don't know . . ." I trailed off with uncertainty.

"Don't worry, Vivian. Everything is going to go fine. I really don't want you stressing out about this. Breathe." Zaliver stood up and walked towards me, putting his hands on my shoulders to keep me still. I looked up at him. His tone let off that he was hiding something.

"Why do you say that as if you already know how this is going to go down?" I asked with narrowed eyes. He looked down at me with a wry look in his face.

"Because I've been around long enough to learn things, to evaluate situations, and to find all types of possible outcomes." I looked at him with curiosity, wondering how that worked.

"Like what?" I asked. He took a strand of hair in between his fingers and stared at it.

"Well, one outcome is your parents are easy-going people with open minds who will have no problem with me because they're just happy you found your mate, no matter who I am. Another is they might freak out after realizing who I am. Out of fear or nerves, they will try to run with you before you get a word out to which I will react to not so nicely." His eyes flickered and darkened. "Let's not forget about the idea where one parent, usually males, may believe I kidnapped you to enjoy in a sick, twisted way. He will try to hurt or kill me to get you." I flinched at the thought of him getting hurt, let alone from my father.

"Those are a lot of possibilities," I said quietly, feeling the blood drain from my face. This didn't sound like a good idea, but what was there to do?

"Which is why I don't want you to worry." I gave him a look. "What I mean is you shouldn't stress over this because I'm not, am I? No, because whatever happens, we can handle it," he said sweetly, which I understood based on his feeling in the bond.

Whatever happens, I'll handle it. You'll stay by my side no matter what.

I smiled tensely at him, hoping everything would go smoothly.

~•~

I looked into the mirror one last time before deciding that this was as good as I could get without trying too hard. I was actually a bit more nervous over the fact that it would be the first time Zaliver saw me in a nice dress.

Made out of silk and cotton, the dress was a soft peach that made my slightly pale skin look rosy. It had a flowy skirt, a belt around my waist, and a large bow in the back. I liked that the top of the dress was long-sleeved but hanged from my wrists. I found it while shopping with Hannah. She had mentioned it looked good for the occasion and

172

said I should buy it because she also wanted to borrow it after she had the baby.

I had to agree with her, plus, it made my legs look great. I didn't want to wear heels, so I just put on some brown warrior sandals on. In total, I thought my outfit rocked. My wolf agreed too. I was glad to see that even after the marking, she was still with me without any problem. If anything, she seemed more animated and excited. I took that as a good sign.

What I did not know what to make of, however, was how I had heat flashes in the most random of moments. One second I was brushing my teeth, and the next thing I know, the brush snapped in half. My body would tense as what felt like a giant shiver racked my body, but instead of feeling cold, I would feel as if I was wrapped around too many blankets only for the feeling to pass.

Pushing the weirdness aside, I climbed down the stairs, down the hall, and into the kitchen. The house was just as grand as it looked. What I liked about it was that the front looked as if it was the entrance of a simple home. Zaliver said it looked more like a luxurious mansion towards the back. It had a homey feeling with soft browns and auburn wood, decorated with plush and comfortable couches. I loved it. Truth be told, I liked it so much I hadn't even left the front part of the house to look at the rest of it. I was sure the tour Zaliver would give my parents would be for me too.

I went into the kitchen for a glass of water, needing the cool refreshing water to calm myself down. The trick was finding a cup in the damn kitchen, and since I wasn't good at remembering things, I just pulled things open until I found them. Once I was done, I went into the living room to just sit in silence and reflect. I had been doing it a lot, I noticed.

I realized I hadn't mind linked Zaliver through the mating bond. He did it once but not through the bond. He used his alpha link to me. I closed my eyes and concentrated on finding the link. I pictured Zaliver in my mind. His image was easy to conjure up. As soon as his face popped up in my mind, I let the thread that connected us both come to life, letting the magic of the bond consume me. I let myself melt into the vibrant and warm golden red thread.

Zaliver's emotions were numbed a bit since we weren't close by, but since I concentrated on the bond, I could feel them as if they were my own even without actually feeling them myself. He was annoyed and a bit cold, not in the temperature sense, but he was filled with . . . I didn't want to say darkness, but that's the closest thing I could relate it to. Besides the annoyance, he felt nothing more. There was just a sense of nothingness, coldness, and emptiness. My face scrunched up in worry.

173

Without a thought, I let myself brush his mind, and the effect was both shocking and mesmerizing. As soon as he felt me, his whole being seemed to free and then he lit up. The darkness and annoyance in him seemed to have disappeared in a flash as if he was never feeling them. A sense of warmth and fluffy emotions were pouring from him, which left me awed. The thread thickened after the first time we connected together through mind link. He suddenly felt very much more connected to me.

"*Zaliver?*"

"*Vivian? Is everything alright?*"

His worry shined through both the link and his voice while a small sense of panic colored the thread from its vibrant golden red to a streak of blues.

"*Yeah, I . . . uh, I just wanted to talk to you.*" Great. Even in mind linking, I managed to sound like a dork, but I was still a bit confused about what had just happened.

"*Are you sure? I could be there in a few—*"

"*No, no. I'm fine really. No need to worry.*"

"*Are you sure?*"

"*Yup. Ummm . . . What are you doing now?*" I didn't want to ask or at least, not right away as it sounded awkward, but I was curious as to what made the sudden mood change.

"*I was just going over some files and reports from my third-in-command, Hogan Langer. Why?*"

"*I was just wondering why you were annoyed. That's all.*"

"*Annoyed. Oh.*"

There was a sudden shift coming from his end, from surprise to an emotion that could be felt strongly when someone was being sneaky.

"*Oh?*"

"*It's nothing. Your parents will be here soon.*"

I knew he was changing the conversation, but I wasn't very worried. For all I knew, he could be planning a surprise. Zaliver, after all, was a man of many surprises. I went along with it.

"*So, how much longer?*" I asked.

"*About an hour left. You nervous?*" he answered.

"*Yeah, you?*"

Amusement shone through the bond. I also noticed how his emotions were slightly less strong compared to how they were the first time. Maybe it was the distance?

"*No, not really. After all, I still get you to myself at the end of the day.*"

"*You make it seem as if you're about to meet my parents and not the other way around.*"

I laughed out loud at him.

174

"When will you stop by?"
"Give me forty-five minutes?"
"Okay. See you later."

We both lingered for a moment before pulling back.

I reached for my phone that I left earlier in the morning and began playing random games to take my mind off of things. Even then, I still couldn't. Pushing my parents' arrival to the farthest part of my mind, I began to think over some things. At first, I had thought what bothered me was the fact that I felt totally useless—just shopping and hanging around with Hannah—when I could and probably should be doing more. Soon, I came up with a plan to get Zaliver to give me something helpful to do. I then began to wonder what sort of job Zaliver had. I mean being the Lupus Deus was certainly different from being an alpha, especially when you had to run alphas who ran packs. How did that man manage to spend time with me?

I felt him coming before I heard him. The thread that connected us became shorter and shorter until it was gone and the normal bond feeling came back. His lighting speed made light sounds on the ground with each step. When I moved to stand up, he was already behind me inside the house.

"You know? You are wickedly fast. I'd hate to race," I told him, moving around the couch to go to him. His eyes trailed down from my face to look at my body. His blue eyes darkened until they turned pitch black. He looked back up with a hungry look on his face.

"You." I slowed down before I was actually in front of him. The look on his face was stopping me short.

My heart pounded in my chest, and my face flushed at the intense attention I was getting from him. He seemed to be taking in deep breaths. His black shirt stretched over his chest. I looked down at his firm abdomen. Well shit. If he's gonna check me out, then I would check him out too.

"You look beyond beautiful. The sun is the dullest star in the sky compared to your beauty," he said while taking slow steps towards me. "I wish I have more words to describe you, but you've outdone every single definition known to man. I'm speechless." He stood in front of me, looking down with heated eyes. The blue part in his eyes was returning slowly added on to whatever he was doing to me.

My lips parted at his words. The way he was gazing down at me made me feel like I was the most beautiful woman in the world. His words helped too. What was one to say to that? I was really impressed with him. I had thought he would say something like sexy or cute like guys usually do, but by saying beautiful . . . I don't know. It made me feel better somehow.

175

He took hold of my hand and brought it up to his lips where he gave me light kisses while looking up with those big blue eyes.

"I've taken it you've dabbled in poetry?" I joked lightly, not sure how to act. He smiled at me with a pound look in his eyes, staring at my slightly flustered and embarrassed self.

"A bit." He joked, walking around me and heading upstairs. I followed after him.

Entering the room, he went into the walk-in closet we were sharing, and I sat on the bed.

"Are you going to shower?" I asked him, fixing my skirt. Ugh, I liked dresses, but I had the mindset that I was always wearing pants, so it was really hard not to sit with my legs open sometimes.

"Yeah," he responded.

"Ooh, are you going to change into your fancy outfit that will probably consist of a black shirt, jeans, and combat boots?" I joked, blinking innocently at him after he poked his head out the closet and narrowed his eyes at me.

"Maybe I will. I'm not sure yet. There are so many black shirts I can wear, right?" he said sarcastically. I giggled and nodded at him. He rolled his eyes and went back in.

He walked out shoeless and entered the bathroom, not even bothering to close the door as he began to strip. Tossing his shirt on the ground and unbuckling his pants, he threw me a smirk. I scowled at him and looked away, secretly wanting to glance back but not having enough courage to do so.

When I heard the water run, I looked back. I was glad the shower was out of sight. I mean, I was glad Zaliver was out of sight. I was surprised at how comfortable I felt with the whole situation. This was sort of intimate—a little too intimate in this situation in fact.

"Hey, Zaliver?" I said in a normal tone, knowing he would be able to hear me through the shower.

"Yeah?"

"I'm thinking that while my parents are staying here, I should stay in a different room—" His infuriated growl cut me off.

"No! Don't be absurd. You're staying with me." There was a small bang that sounded like he slammed something.

I rolled my eyes and continued. A part of me was praying that he wouldn't make this into a bigger problem than it was. I didn't think it would help if my parents got here mid fight.

"Just until they're here. I mean, they don't know you. I'm pretty sure they aren't going to be happy knowing their daughter is in bed with her mate while they are sleeping under the same roof even if we haven't done anything. I just think it'll make them more

176

appreciative." I flushed a bit but not as bad as I would have with him in front of me.

"They will be *appreciating* me if I let them sleep in the *same* room because guess what, Vivian? If you and I were to sleep in different rooms, so will *they*," he growled from the bathroom angrily.

"You are being unbelievable!" I yelled at him, hoping to get him to see reason. That was just ridiculous. He couldn't really do that . . . never mind.

"Unbelievable? Unbelievable! I'll get out of the shower right now and show you what's unbelievable! I'm telling you now, you're staying with me." He snapped. My eyes widened at the direction his voice was coming from.

That innuendo though.

"Oh my god," I mumbled under my breath. To keep my virgin eyes pure, I said nothing more about the moving-to-another-room subject much to my wolf's displeasure.

"Fine, whatever. On a whole different topic, I want to ask and tell you as well that I don't want to just stay here all day or go shopping when I'm bored. I want something to do. I'm wondering if you have anything for me to do?" It went silent for a while. I could make out grumbles of displeasure coming from him.

After a while, I heard the water turn off. Zaliver stepped out of the bathroom with a white towel wrapped loosely around his waist, emphasizing how much skin he was showing as well as his huge build. Water droplets fell from his damp, toned skin. He began to walk to me with an irritated look on his face that slowly dissipated as he stopped before me.

His skin looked sun-kissed in contrast with the white towel. Each confident step that he took towards me made my lower region tighten pleasurably that I unconsciously bit my lip while trying to take in as much of his raw masculinity. I wanted to reach out and follow the trail of water drops in their passage down his abdomen and into the towel.

"Vivian?"

"Huh?" I responded, absent-minded.

My eyes were making their way down his chest to the light trail of hair that were hidden behind the towel.

I bet it's still going, my wolf whispered, making my body tingle.

"Vivian." I looked up because of the way my name came out of his lips. He looked back at me with an odd look—a mixture of surprise and coyness. Those very kissable lips.

"Why are you looking at me like you're about to—"

I didn't know where it came from, but I lunged to him with a strong yearning burning in me. A yearning for him. I had that feeling

177

you would get when you realized something too good to be true was a once-in-a-lifetime deal, like I would die if I didn't kiss him then and there. His reflexes being much quicker than mine allowed him to brace the impact and position himself, so we wouldn't fall back.

I threw my arms around him, forcefully tilting his head to the side and bringing my lips to his in one go. His response wasn't to freeze up from my sudden attack but to groan low in his chest and bring his strong arms around me. I squeaked in surprise as his hands traveled down my back to cup my butt and then quickly gripped me by the back of the thighs, making me wrap them around him and get lifted off the floor. I ignored how my dress clung to his wet body and how he was slowly walking forward to the bed as our lips passionately worked on each other, melting and working at a frantic pace as if we couldn't get enough of each other.

The more time we spent kissing, the hotter I burned. My body was urging me to push myself closer to Zaliver, which he returned just as much. My hands worked in his thick wet hair. I loved how every time I pulled on his locks, he would return the favor with a nip on the lips with his teeth, driving me insane. Just as he was laying me on the bed and climbing on top of me, he froze and slowly pulled back or at least tried to. He ended up pulling back and then pecking me on the lips until he finally jumped back.

He looked down at me with a strained look as if he didn't want to stop. So why did he? I looked up at him, pushing myself up on my elbows to look at him with a dopey look on my face. I felt at ease and almost as if I had entered a calm state. The yearning and desire in me was not gone, but I was satisfied.

"I'd love to continue this, but your parents are about to enter the front gate." In a snap, I was awake and very much aware of what was going on around me.

I sprang from the bed and fixed my dress, trying to compose myself while Zaliver was watching amused. Blood rushed to my cheeks as I recalled the way I jumped on him like a hungry animal. That and the tent poking up in his towel. I tried not to let my eyes linger much, but he stood there bravely, not trying to hide his arousal from me. I began patting down and rearranging the bottom of my dress, pulling my hand back only to realize it was slightly damp. Looking down, I saw I had water droplets on my dress.

"Awww, you got me all wet!" I grumbled, displeased at him even though it was technically me who attacked him. Zaliver made a choking sound that made me look at him worriedly.

"What? What's wrong?" He shook his head back and forth, laughing. After a while, he answered.

"Well, I'm glad," he said cheekily.

178

My face scrunched up in confusion.

Why would he be glad he got my dress—

And then I thought back on what I said and my eyes widened in horror and mortification. He grinned at me.

"Wait! Wait! Wait! No! No! No! That's not what I meant," I said quickly, shaking my head from side to side.

"Sure, it's not." He winked at me and whistled his way to the closet in a happy stride.

I took a step in his direction when the doorbell rang. I knew my parents were waiting, but I froze and bit my lip. I was fifty-fifty in wanting to run down the stairs and into my parents arms because the other fifty made me want to convince Zaliver. Deciding quickly, I turned with a huff and went to get the door.

"Don't take too long," I told him before leaving.

"I won't," he yelled out with humor in his voice.

Great! Words could't describe my humiliation.

Why? Why? Of all times to think innocently, why did it have to be now? Oh why?

I took a deep breath once I was on the lowest step, hoping my parents would just think the redness on my face was just heat. I hurriedly made my way to the door, excitement flooding my body. I was going to finally see my parents after such a long time! Before the door was even half-open, I had arms around me. My sobbing mother was in my arms while Dad hugged us both. I didn't waste a second and hugged them both back, wrapping one arm around my mom and the other to my dad.

My mom pulled back. Her brown eyes were red and filled with so much emotions. She looked at me. I gave her a small smile as tears welled up in my eyes, which just made her hug me again and slightly sob again. I looked at Mom and Dad who were both sniffing.

"Hey, Mom. Hey, Dad. Long time no see, huh?" I said softly.

They both pulled off me slowly and stepped back. My dad kept his arm around my mom's shoulder. Looking at them, I felt memories of my childhood flood my mind, making me love the people in front of me a lot more.

I actually looked a lot like both of my parents; I got a mixture of both. Both had brown eyes and hair. My dad would have a red tint on his skin when he spent too much time under the sun. My mother's small built matched her small delicate features. I got my upturned nose from her. My father's build wasn't huge, but he was still a large man, especially next to my mother. I most definitely inherited his height even if not by much. It's the inches that would count in the long run. I had his attitude as well, but it was rare for us to butt heads. Very rare. After hugging and kissing and a whole lot of comforted whispering to each other, I got them to come in and sit down.

179

"We've missed you so much, Vivian. We almost went crazy looking for you," my dad said. His voice was gruff but filled with emotion. He sat with my mother in the love seat while I sat on a lone chair.

"I've missed you too and to think I was supposed to move out and go to college. I kinda thought the moving out part would go a lot smoother." I joked lightly. I was glad to see my mom crack a smile through watery eyes.

After a short conversation of checking on me and asking me if I was alright, the tricky part came next. I realized it when my dad narrowed his eyes, and for the first time, he began to look around with a tensed frame. I thought he was beginning to notice a stronger presence in the house, but Mom was too distracted. While my mom was the outgoing and talkative one, my dad was quiet and watchful. But when my dad had to talk or was angry, he could be the most intimidating man ever. I couldn't tell how he and Zaliver would do in the same room. The last thought made me uneasy.

"So . . . your mother told me you've been with your mate the whole time. Is that true?" my dad asked after my mom, and I had finished. I panicked a little knowing it was about to get a whole lot more difficult to answer without Zaliver with me. It also didn't help that the way he asked me didn't seem very happy.

"Yeah."

His face studied me, not getting much from my short answer. I held still, not daring to move a muscle, and looked into the familiar brown eyes that often times could tell when something with me was off.

"Why didn't you call us as soon as you could? Young lady, while I'm glad you're safe, it still doesn't excuse that you left Lily's pack with your mate—who I dislike already—while her pack was under attack, not to mention you didn't even call afterwards. You made your mother and I worry. We took the risk of getting on a plane to god-knows-where in hopes to find out that you are truly safe. Now, tell me why we shouldn't take you home and lock you in until you're fifty? Mate or no mate," my dad said seriously. My mother looked shocked at his words but with understanding.

I hadn't realized it, but I had been tuned into the bond, picking up Zaliver's emotions. I realized he was listening and was very, very angry. Hoping to calm him down a bit and give me time, I sent a wave of calmness over to him. I felt some of his anger disappear, not much though. The rational part of me knew this was more of a dominate wolf thing than a child trying to disrespect her parents.

My anger, however, did not. It was an odd feeling. I knew I was angry, but at the same time, I wasn't. No, something inside me was angered by the tone of voice, the unwavering eye contact, and the disrespect my dad had just given me. Taking a slow deep breath, my shoulders squared and my chin tilted up. I calmly looked at my parents with a raised brow, staring at them for a few seconds. I could almost feel the atmosphere change with my mood as it dropped to a body freezing temperature.

I knew this cold. It was the authoritative side of me—the luna side that Zaliver's mark had brought out. Having done this once at the twin's house when I had to tell Luke and Johnson to stand down as I felt they were questioning my choice. My change didn't go unnoticed. My mother quickly looked away from me from instinct even though she had a confused look on her face. My father began to unconsciously tilt his head at me about to bear his neck with a dazed look on his face.

"Look—" I stopped and cleared my throat when I realized how cold I sounded, not the right tone.

I took in another breath and forcefully relaxed myself, knowing that parents had every right to be worried. But I also couldn't help the defensiveness that tried to creep over me.

"I know you're angry, but you two have to know there's more to this than you can ever possibly imagine. Even I can't control everything, Dad. I just know that these last few days haven't exactly been a walk in the park for me either, and, yes, I should have called but I couldn't," I tried to explain to them. After I cleared my throat, it seemed like they both snapped out of whatever trance they had been in. And now my mother listened carefully to everything I said while my father looked upset, very upset.

"Sweetheart, you can't just disappear after an attack, especially to a pack you visited. Our alpha was questioned because the luna of the pack was informed of your arrival as custom. With the death of the alpha and everyone not remembering seeing you, even Lily, your disappearance was too suspicious. You didn't even contact anyone and then suddenly called. You had us picked up by a luxurious car and a plane. We even had to leave our phones and not tell anyone where we're going to. For heaven's sake, we were even blindfolded to get here! Vivian, if you have anything to tell us, just tell us. What's happening?" my mother spoke softly. I listened with shock. My mouth dropped in surprise at her words.

"W-what?" I asked, stumped by the news.

Did they think I have something to do with their pack getting attacked? Well, I guess security was better than I thought. They picked up on one girl who visited and suddenly disappeared on the same day their pack was attacked and their alpha was killed. Great. I was probably seen as a fugitive. Wait. Did Zaliver know about this? My mom looked at my father.

"So, you didn't know?" my mom asked. Being too stupid to answer, I shook my head without looking at them. I was just staring at nothing in particular with wide eyes. I could tell by how I felt that I probably looked wan.

"Oh, but how did you avoid other guard wolves? Not everyone is looking for you for some reason. You're somewhat a suspect, but by order of someone of power, you're are considered not." *Grrr*, that jackass of a mate did know. "But enough wolves are looking for you; enough to notice if you crossed lands." My dad leaned forward explaining, obviously displeased himself with this.

My mom began to look around nervously as if sensing something while my dad spoke. I was still too shocked and bothered by what I was hearing. I was upset more than I thought to hear that people thought I was involved. Somehow, I was but not in the sense most thought. Had I not been upset, my emotions wouldn't have overpower my attention on Zaliver through the bond.

"Look, Vivian. We obviously don't believe any of that crap but not anymore. What's going on? Is this your mate's doing? Did he have something to do with the attack and your lost? Are you even mates?" I brought my shocked expression onto him, not believing his words or at least not entirely wanting to.

"No . . . well. No, No. He is my mate!" I defended with emotion, not liking how he doubted my bond with Zaliver. *He is my mate. He is mine.*

Just having my dad doubt the bond had me feeling on edge of something strong. Was this what Zaliver would feel when he went on his rants? Possessive and defensive?

My dad stood up to look down at me with a tight expression. My mom did as well but a bit slower as if cautious, but I paid her no attention. The room felt heavy as if a bomb was about to go off as my father and I both looked at each other.

"I haven't even met him. I can tell he's a bad influence on you. Look what's happening! You're said to be involved with the attacks! I can't believe what's happening. When we sent you to Lily's pack, it was to get you away from danger and not to run to it," my dad yelled, raising his arms. My face flushed with anger at his words.

Step.

Step.

"Chace," my mom whispered nervously, reaching out to tug on the bottom of his sweater. We both ignored her as we bickered.

Step.

Step.

"I can't believe you! You're right! You haven't met my mate yet, and you're already judging him." Shaking my head, I held my hand out at him. He took a step forward and latched onto my arm.

Step.

Step.

"Chace," my mom whispered more urgently to my dad. Her face looked frightened as the mood in the room dropped along with the temperature.

Step.

Step.

"Because he's given nothing good to like. I'm glad you're safe, but you're coming home with us immediately. You've been here for god knows how long and haven't even contacted us. Don't think I ignored how even where we are has been kept a secret from us. This is your mate's doing, isn't it?" He boomed, tugging me closer to him.

Step.

Step.

"Let go! You can't make me go anywhere I don't want to be. I'm a legal adult, Dad. You haven't even let me explain!" I shouted out and panicked for a moment, actually believing he could grab me and we would disappear out of sight as if he could teleport us off the island.

Thud.

"And where is this so-called mate?!" He scowled down at me angrily.

"Behind you," a chilled voice answered.

We all froze at the menacing voice that came, which was indeed behind my dad. He released my arm to spin around and look at who spoke. I heard his sharp intake of breath as he finally felt my mate's presence. Their eyes couldn't believe what they were seeing. I had that same feeling when I first laid eyes on Zaliver. He looked like what he was known to be—a god. I let my eyes skim his body from bottom to top.

Instead of his normal rough combat boots, he had on shiny black dress shoes. His long legs were wrapped around black slacks that fit him perfectly. They weren't his normal dress pants that were usually loose. They weren't as tight either, but from the look on the front, I just knew that if he turned around, I'd find a nice view from the back. His top half was covered in a tailored sky black that matched his hair color. I knew it was tailored because besides the fine material, it clung to his muscular body perfectly with no extra space. I could tell he had a white shirt underneath that was unbuttoned three buttons down. I knew his blue eyes would pop out even more than they ever could.

And just like I knew they would, they did. I was surprised to see his dark black silky strands slicked back. It just added to the

183

dominating dark aura he was giving off. Even with his cold expression, the disturbing way the corner of his lips twisted up to cruelly smile at my dad, and the casual way he stood—with his legs apart, both hands in his pocket, and clenched jaw—I still found him breathtaking.

While I and my father was bickering back and forth, I didn't realized Zaliver was listening to the conversation and to the way I was reacting through the bond. It seemed my poor mother was the only one who went uneasy with Zaliver radiating so much hostility and anger. Quickly thinking over the yelling that happened, I knew what Zaliver had gathered from it. I didn't know how he would react to it or at least I didn't want to imagine.

Out of instinct, my mom backed away with a terrified expression towards Zaliver, trying to get away from the large stranger who was radiating so much power. At the same time, she had both arms stretched out towards me and my father as if she was about to pull us out of danger. I couldn't see my dad's expression because he had his back at me, but I could tell from the way he was leaning away from Zaliver and the way his shoulders were slowly coming up higher and higher as if to shrink away that he was intimated immensely.

Without looking at me, Zaliver walked around my father and stopped by my side. My father's self preservation instinct kicked in. He stepped away and out of line, placing himself in front of my mother. I looked at him. He looked horrified while looking at Zaliver as if he couldn't believe what he was seeing. He knew Zaliver wasn't an alpha. He knew he was more.

Zaliver took his hands out of his pocket and reached for my hand that my father had grabbed. He took it gently from his hands and looked at it over with alert eyes. My father didn't grab it rough enough to leave a mark on my skin. I looked at Zaliver. His blue eyes flashed black and his top lip lifted up as if to snarl but he didn't. Spinning around quickly, he startled my parents with a large unjustified grin. I stood frozen on the spot, watching him, not sure what to do or how to even move.

"Hello. I'm Vivian's mate, Zaliver Azrala. But then that wouldn't matter, would it, Mr. Grey? I mean, you've made your opinion of me very clearly. You don't approve, do you? Hmmm." Zaliver walked towards them slowly with both hands behind his back, speaking casually. My parents began walking backwards towards the door. My mother looked at me. She was trying to send me a message through her eyes, but I wasn't thinking straight. I couldn't understand. My heart pounded in my chest. My hands and knees shook.

"Who the hell are you?" my father asked uneasily, keeping his eyes on Zaliver. It looked like he was forcing himself to focus, but everytime he did, he would look at his face painfully. He and my mother were making a sort of U-turn around the living room to get to the door. The lack of space between them and Zaliver was too uncomfortable.

Zaliver got a mocking look on his face as he danced with my parents like it was a game. My parents and I flinched. Zaliver didn't have good reactions.

"What? I'm the bad influence, remember?"

My dad glanced at me with panic and fear on his face, but I knew why he looked at me. I knew what he was asking. Was this your mate? But I didn't nod. I didn't breath. I didn't move. Through the bond, that same cold emptiness was coming from Zaliver.

"You know, that might be the first name that isn't insulting. I've been called much worse—monster, killer, an abomination, and many more. Those are just the ones on the top of my head, but I have to say that's the one that's stuck," he spoke with a large smile on his face, making his words all the worse.

"Zal—" I began to interrupt him, finding my voice but then losing it once his icy blue orbs flickered at me. His smile fell. We looked at each other for a few seconds. Through the bond, the darkness cleared a bit, but when my parents—who had used those few seconds to quickly back away to the door—took hold of my wrist and began to pull me out of the doorway that they managed to open, his eyes turned pitch black.

My mother yanked on my wrist and began dragging me from the deadly growl that came out of the house. I shook my head back and forth, digging my heels on the floor and sliding on the gravel.

"Stop! You're just going to make him an—" I tried to say, but my dad interrupted me.

"I'm so sorry, sweetheart. I should have seen this before! You'd never run away even if it was with your mate. I knew you got kidnapped!" he yelled out, looking around frantically for something. A car, I'm guessing.

I yanked my hand out of my mother's and yelled at them to stop, not wanting to worsen the situation. Things couldn't possibly get worse than this.

"STOP! You don't know what you're doing. We have to go back before this gets out of hand! Just let me talk to—"

A loud snarl was heard coming towards us as Zaliver walked over slowly like a predator hunting his prey. We hadn't made it far from the house. Realizing there was nothing around to get us out, my dad stepped in front of me and my mom was in a crouched, defensive position.

Oh no.

Stalking over, Zaliver stopped gracefully a few feet from us and undid his blazer, tossing it to the floor and rolling up his sleeves.

Oh god no.

185

"I was going to give you space and let you adjust to everything. I was going to respect anything you would say about me but then you upset, yelled, and hurt Vivian. That is something I cannot let go unpunished, father or not," he said vindictively.

My father took brave steps forward.

"I-I won't let you keep my daughter as your prisoner any longer even if it kills me," he said bravely, bringing his hands up to fight.

Zaliver smirked at my father. His eyes were gleaming wickedly. "A fight to death then."

My dad didn't know what he had said, but his body did as he began heading towards Zaliver.

Oh god, please no. Out of all my fears, why did it have to be this one?

I knew as soon as those two got close enough, it would be a total destruction. My father was, by no means, a warrior; but in our pack, every male was expected to learn to fight until they were of age to decide what they wanted to be. My dad was the best in his time. Zaliver, without a doubt, was a killing machine.

My mother's hands latched onto my shoulder as they began circling each other. Both were keeping distance. My breaths came short.

"Fucking hell," I swore.

My mother let out a small scream as my father transformed into his wolf to attack Zaliver who didn't shift much to my relief, but instead picked up my father as if he weighed nothing more than a basketball and tossed him to the ground. I was also relieved to see that he wasn't using his full strength. At least, he was restraining himself for now.

I took that last part back when I saw his claws grow out and saw him position himself to swipe at my father who had miraculously gotten back up. I had a feeling Zaliver was a ripping-out-hearts type of guy because that's what he would do if he were to kill my father.

This was all a huge misunderstanding. I just had to get them both to realize that.

I shrugged my mother's hands off and then avoided her attempts to restrain me as I ran full speed to the fight. As Zaliver's hand began to make its way to my father's wolf, who at that same moment was leaping to Zaliver, I realized I wouldn't make it in time.

My eyes flashed, and just like before, I was faster than light.

Time continued just as I got to them, and I did something I had never done before—I lunged between the two.

186

CHAPTER 18

My lunging was just in time. With adrenaline pumping in my body, I ducked Zaliver's swiping claws and lifted my foot out, kicking him straight on the crotch. His angered face morphed into one of pain and surprise, but I didn't care. I turned around quickly and dropped to my knees. I ignored the sting and wrapped my arms around my snarling father's wolf form and with surprising strength, pushed his body a few feet away.

I was ready for anything. I stood up and faced both of them. My chest was heaving. My claws were extended. I snarled at both of them for their actions. I was livid and wasn't the only one. Something strong and beastly inside me was fueling my anger and strength. My wolf was even upset.

How dare Zaliver think it was okay to just fight my dad to death? I was getting tired of following him left and right. My anger flared back up, making me realize he could calm me down with a few words and kisses, but not this time. He had crossed a line.

As for my dad, I understood his thinking and all, but he should have just let me explain instead of assuming. I was just annoyed at him mostly.

Zaliver was on the ground, cupping his crotch with a pained yet angered expression as if he couldn't believe I did that. I didn't even feel guilty. He was going to get that and more. My dad was getting back up and charging towards Zaliver again who was doing nothing but glaring up at me through his narrowed blue eyes.

Quickly calculating my dad was still under Zaliver's direct command to "fight until death" and was either unwillingly following it or not, I didn't care. I was Zaliver's mate. I was his equal. It was time I began accepting that as well as showing it.

Instead of fighting or pushing the pulsing energy that coursed through my body, I chose to embrace it.

"Sit and stay." Turning to my dad, my eyes flashed again. I calmly ordered my dad in a cold voice. I didn't have to yell the order or say it in Latin for him to suddenly stop mid run to Zaliver. He froze on command and shifted back, my command overcoming Zaliver's.

My mom ran to my dad and checked him over. Just by looking at him, I could see he had a few bruised ribs from being thrown, but he would heal in a few hours. Looking back at Zaliver, I saw him gritted his teeth and stood, clenching his hands into fists. He tried to take a step towards me, but I held up a finger at him.

"Stop. I've had enough of your macho shit. I will not take it anymore. This is enough, Zaliver. You can't keep doing this," I snarled out at him.

"Vivian—" His expression turned bitter.

"No! I'm serious. I'm done making excuses every time you fuck up. What is it? Why do you act like this?" I yelled out at him with my walls crumbling as I finally gave out and let go.

"You don't understand—"

"Of course I don't! You don't bloody open up to me! This won't work if you won't tell me what's going on!" I cried out with frustration eating me. I was jumpy. My body was ready to move around.

He snarled at me and I snarled back, not backing down. Something dark and wild was stirring in me, hoping this wouldn't turn into a bigger fight. His blue eyes glinted dangerously and flickered over to my parents who were both watching quietly. I took a step to my side, covering them from his view. He shook his head at me as if disappointed.

"So, you are choosing them over me? Over your own mate?" he asked coldly. His face was cleared of all emotions. I threw my arms up in annoyance and anger, not believing what he was saying.

"No one's choosing anyone, Zaliver! Don't you see that? They are my parents. You are my mate. I can't just have all of you in my life? Zaliver, you just told my father to fight you till death because you thought he'd take me away. What the hell, man! What were you thinking? How do you think that would have ended? Do you think I would be happy with you if you killed him?" I took a step in his direction.

I could see Zaliver's head turning. For once, someone stood up to him to make him see his faults, but I wasn't done.

"Every single time you do something, you know there's a consequence. But tell me Zaliver Azrala, Mr. Lupus Deus. After your victory and your grand winning final game, have you ever honestly thought about the destruction, the pain and grief you left behind?" With each word, I took a step to him until I stood in front of him, not fearing him or maybe just not caring. I reached up and took his chin roughly in my hand, making him look down at me.

I wasn't just referring to all of his past actions and winnings, which were now horrible stories of how he won and how many lives he destroyed. I was asking him why he had to involve death and violence to

188

get what he wanted and why he had to crush others even if at the end of the day, his prize was in his arms.

His blue eyes stared down at me. His emotions were flashing and changing. We were both breathing hard, refusing to look away from each other. I felt like this would be a changing moment for the both of us, but I couldn't tell if it were for better or worse. After a pause, he finally answered me.

"Yes," he said honestly. But I knew there was more to it than a one-worded answer. I reached up with my hand and cupped his face, being more gentle with my actions. I softly caressed his cheeks with my thumbs. I looked at him seriously.

"So why? Why do it if you knew that at the end of the day, you would win? Why act savagely towards others to get your goal? Why?" I whispered.

He closed his eyes and pushed his cheeks into my hands, staying silent for a moment. Through our bond, conflicting emotions were raging through him. For a moment, I thought I sensed anxiousness, maybe even regret, coming from him before they were all suddenly cut off as if his emotions had never even been there in the first place. When he opened his eyes, they were cold and unsympathetic. My breath hitched.

"Because I don't care what has to be done or who I have to destroy as long as at the end of the day, I get what I want." He stepped out of my hands and looked down at me with a raised brow. My hands dropped slowly as I looked at him, feeling as if something in me broke at his answer.

"My mistake, Vivian, was not showing you who I'm known to be. My mistake was trying to be someone who you'd be happy to spend the rest of your life with. I've been playing in pretense while dealing with danger on the sidelines. I've let you walk on the blind side, showing you the kind and caring Zaliver. But the truth is, once a monster, always a monster. I'm like a loaded gun made for destruction and pain. I am nobody's hero," he spoke frankly.

"I'm a repulsive creature of the night that was created to stalk, hunt, seduce, and kill my prey for the fun of it and you know this. Even our bond," he leaned in behind me and moved my hair to the side, "cannot make you blind to that. You've felt it as well, haven't you? The darkness that surrounds and clings to me like a second skin," he whispered into my ear.

I looked forward with my hands clenched into fists. I'd rather feel angry now than to feel the brutal honesty of his words, disappointment, and heartbreak. Everything he was saying was true. The darkness that came from Zaliver's side of the bond seemed to disappear when I was with him, like it was no longer there.

How had I not noticed? Easy. I always painted an image as to what a mate should be like. I failed to realize that as soon as Zaliver invaded my mind, his whole attitude changed. He was suddenly much more aware and mate-like. He played into the role I had set for him in my mind. Could that be it?

"But were your feelings a lie?" I asked slowly, not wanting to let the emotions leak through my voice.

I heard him sigh behind me and then he walked back in front of me.

"No, of course not. That my dear is honest to the core. I've honestly never thought of having a mate, so you are truly a blessing. Fate believed you will be enough to convince me to stop," Zaliver spoke casually, something I had never really heard from him. He suddenly seemed many, many years older than me with the way he acted and spoke.

His words felt like little cuts to the heart.

His once attractive attire didn't help. It made me feel like I was looking and talking to a stranger and not the Zaliver I was comfortable with, the one who wore black shirt and dark jeans and rough combat boots.

I felt like I was beginning to see a side of him that I hadn't met or had ignored.

People had different sides in them. The side the public could see, the one the family had always known, the side given to their partner, and the deepest, darkest part of themselves. It seemed I had only been living with the third one—the prince charming. I had let the bond manipulate my mind, forgetting and overlooking the fact that, mate or not, Zaliver was known to be ruthless and beastly even if he was just known to be myth.

He was the Lupus Deus, and I had forgotten that.

"Stop what?" I asked. He looked away from my eyes.

"War for the skies," he said somberly.

"You're . . . you're going to attack them? This is what this is all about? Why I was made to be your mate? To stop your revenge for your brother's death?" I said, outraged, suddenly feeling very much toyed and used.

There was so much more here than I had thought. Somehow, I was blind to it all. Romance really did make people blind.

"Don't be so surprised, Vivian. I've killed for much less." He threw me a pointed look. Martha, the girl in the clearing, came to mind.

"Besides, it's not I like don't have an army or the means to kill a fellow god, Vivian," he said matter-of-factly with his back towards me.

I suddenly heard multiple footsteps approaching the house and spun around when I heard my parents cry out in distress. A group of men and women surrounded us in a circle. Two of the men held my parents while another two injected them with something. They stopped struggling and fell unconscious.

I spun back.

"What the hell are you doing, Zaliver?" I asked. My voice was shaking with fear as to why he had us surrounded by so many people.

I looked around and was surprised to recognize Luke, Johnson, Mila, and Courtney in the crowd of large figures. They all looked serious, but I could see sadness in their eyes. I felt betrayal bloom in my chest from the people I trusted.

"I'm afraid I have pressing matters to attend to. I must cut this short. Vivian, it's been a pleasure." I didn't recognize the Zaliver before me. This one was serious, formal, and cold.

With his behaviour, my heart felt like it was shattering into a billion pieces. The power that was coursing through me was long gone instead iciness replaced it. He turned back to me. His blue eyes were brighter than I had ever seen them. His expression was unreadable, but he almost looked pained.

Something was wrong. I seemed to have missed something.

"What—" Out of instinct, I began taking steps backwards. Something was twisting in my stomach.

"Sleep. Grieve. Forget," he said softly.

The last thing I saw was Zaliver giving me a sad smile before darkness overcame my senses.

~ • ~

ZALIVER AZRALA

"Sleep. Grieve. Forget," I whispered to her.

I sent her a small smile before her eyes closed. I flashed to her side before her body dropped to the ground. Cradling her gently in my arms, I looked down at my little mate.

The pain of what I was doing began hitting me harder and harder every second that I looked down at her. Her face looked calm and peaceful; an expression that wasn't there while I was behaving like how I had been for so many years before meeting her—cold, uncaring, brusque, and an ass.

I brought her closer to my chest and cherished the seconds I had her in my arms, not caring of those pack members watching. I inhaled her scent, letting it register in my soul and body. I squeezed my eyes tightly as I kissed her forehead, her cheeks and then her lips that had driven me crazy earlier.

I heard Albericus neared me and put his hand on my shoulder. I didn't move for another few seconds. Standing up with her in my arms, I motioned for her personal guards to step forward. They knew what to do. With great restraint, I passed her over to Johnson. Looking them in the eyes, I spoke with a deadly seriousness, which I hadn't used in a long time.

"Guard her with your life." They all nodded and slowly retracted. The other guards around us were following them. I swallowed as I watched her being carried further and further away from me.

Once they were out of sight, I let the mask come back on and released the well of darkness that came from the beast within. I began walking into the forest, knowing Albericus would be behind me.

"I'm sorry. Had I known what was going on, I wouldn't have mind linked you. At least then, you wouldn't have had to make a bad impression or lie to her—" Albericus began. I could feel his guilt grow. I snarled at him to shut it.

I was in a fowl mood and in no position to comfort my beta, but it wasn't his fault either.

"It's not your fault. It's mine for not seeing something like this coming. Better a hard break than a clean one. It'll let the magic lock up her memories rather than drive her insane at the feeling that something died," I spoke empathetically. Inside, I could feel the distance between Vivian and me growing as well as the beast's anger and bloodthirst.

"Yeah, but still," he tried again. I sent him a look.

"Now, take me to Aurora. That witch has some serious explaining to do as to why I just had to send my mate and her parents away for their safety," I snarled out. My mood was darkening with each step through the forest.

Everything had been going fine. Even when Vivian's dad was ranting about taking her from me, I had been calm. But when Albericus mind linked me with some new information the witch had given, I knew what I had to do. I shouldn't have doubts about protecting my mate on our island, but the chance . . . I couldn't . . . wouldn't risk it.

Even if I ruined the chance of winning her parents over and eventually lost her, I preferred Vivian's hatred than the thought of her in danger from the unknown. I could only prepare with so much information, but even I didn't know what was headed towards us in the storm that came with war.

"She could have been lying you know. This could have all been a part of her plan," Albericus spoke with his words hinting on how mischievous his little witch mate was.

"You and I both know that while she may be an evil genius, Aurora Pattsen does not lie and is never wrong when she gets a premonition. I'd be a fool to ignore a warning from her, lie or not," I said, thinking over how much I hated the truth of my words. Albericus said no more, letting me wallow in my sadness and anger of having to separate myself from my mate in such a horrid way. Damn Fate. Damn me.

I was proud of the way she stood up against me and her father, taking us both stupidly but bravely. I truly wasn't going to kill her father, but I didn't expect the kick to the balls. I heard her and thought she was going to jump on me. Her foot came as a surprise.

My mood dropped again when I saw the building we were holding Aurora in. As we neared it, the words from her premonition came to me."

"What you hold close to the heart will not survive. For war is a field of no rules and morality, something you know of. But the last cards are in place as you have not changed the course of your path. In war, there are no rules but one unspoken yet agreed upon. Attack the heart. And what does an immortal man hold close to his heart that he couldn't hold before? His mate, Vivian."

Walking past the patrolling guards, we went into the building and straight into the holding rooms where she waited. She was strapped to a chair. Her eyes were covered with a thick black cloth to block her eyesight because we had realized Aurora was much better at magic and could think more quickly when she could see her targets. She wasn't a fan of the darkness. The type of magic she did was much more focused and specific than spiritual. That private information came from her angry mate himself.

Aurora was every bit as beautiful as she was forty years ago when I last saw her running from Albericus. Her long black hair curtained her sharp and attractive features. Under the cloth, I knew her black large eyes would be just as alert and watchful as always. She was just as tall as her mate with a long slender build.

Truth be told, my beta and her looked like a strange couple when they stood next to each other; but somehow in the small amount of time they spent with each other, I noticed how well they balanced each other out . . . until that awful day when everything went wrong for them.

Now it was plain sexual tension, arguments, anger, and much more between the two in the small room, but I ignored it with a grim face.

"Aurora," I said calmly. Her head snapped in my direction with a wicked small smile gracing her face.

"Zaliver, how nice to see you. Oh wait, I meant hear you since . . . you know? Judging by the blindfold, my dear mate must have told you my dislike for the dark. Honey? You there?" she said sarcastically, leaning back into her chair and crossing one leg over the other. They might have been apart for a while but the bond never diminished, so she could most definitely sense him beside me with his arms crossed over his chest.

Albericus grunted at her. His green eyes darkened as he looked at his mate up close for a very long time. After getting what I wanted from her, he could do as he pleased. My only purpose was to get more information as to what her message meant.

"Huh! I thought your mutt ass would be happy to see me. Guess not," she joked, trying to get a reaction from him. All he did was narrow his eyes at her.

"Aurora, I need—" I began but she interrupted me. I swear, forty years had passed and she still hadn't stopped doing that.

"To know what I meant blah blah blah. Still as direct as always huh, Zaliver? But I'm curious, what do you hold close to the heart?" She sat up in her chair with her head tilting to the side.

My teeth snapped together, knowing this would go a lot faster if I could just torture the information out of her, but Albericus would never let me.

I looked at him and nodded. He began walking towards her with canines extended. I might not be able to torture her, but he surely could. Just not the same way I had in mind.

Feeling him near, Aurora tried pushing herself further into her chair. He reached forward and moved her hair from the side of her neck and leaned in, hovering an inch away from her skin.

I had to give it to Albericus. He had much more restraint than I did. Had that been Vivian—

My body felt as if a shock went through it. I immediately stopped all thoughts of her, knowing I wouldn't be able to focus if I tuned in onto her.

As expected, Aurora began to yell out.

"Okay! Okay! I'll give what you want! Just get him and his teeth away from me!" With an angry expression, Albericus pulled back from her. I could read the hurt in his face.

Being the type of witch Aurora had become, she valued her freedom and her own mate more than anything. It was sad because that made threatening her all the more easy.

"Explain to me exactly what you know of the premonition," I said calmly, taking a chair and sitting in front of her.

After taking in a few deep breaths and pursing her lips, she let me know she was glaring under the cloth and began to speak.

"Well . . ."

CHAPTER 19

ZALIVER AZRALA

I rubbed my eyes, not caring about how my small amount of sleep was making me more and more dangerous for others to be around due to my slight shift of control. It was not like I wouldn't be able to heal anything I tore apart . . . except maybe death. I didn't need much sleep before, but ever since I was with *her,* I started to crave for rest.

Having my mind split into so many different tasks while functioning on little food and sleep and no mate's comfort was suddenly taking its toll on me. I wasn't one to struggle with mental tasks, but mind linking different members, going through their minds for anything that stuck out, keeping track on loose rogues around the world, listening in on alpha conversations, having wolves use my excessive energy for missions, sending out directions at every direction, and dealing with heightened senses, not to mention having my own thoughts to deal with as well as struggling not to use the only link I really wanted to use were struggles to the max.

It didn't help that I was overworking to catch the little snitch in the pack who was unfortunately good at being both discrete and slick with its ways. It had been a pain getting information day by day instead of having all of them on the spot like it usually did. The faster I solved this, the faster Vivian could come back.

Ever since Vivian left—or to correctly say—I made her leave forcefully four days ago, you could say I wasn't the safest person to be around. Before she came, I could work without sleep and even without the drug that kept my beast at bay from ripping everyone apart out of suspicion. I almost ripped my best friend's ex-ish mate's head off with my teeth for being so damn uninformative besides the vague warnings here and there. I most definitely didn't sit for an hour with Vivian's pillow in my arms like some fool.

Alright, maybe I did, but I couldn't help it. I missed her sweet and strangely puzzling scent that left me wanting more. The way her short brown silky locks always covered her face made me want to push it back. I missed the way her eyes would light up at the simplest of things and explaining them in a way that would make them seem truly profound. I craved to hold her soft and curvy body; to see her walking around with the cutest of outfits, covering what was so beautiful underneath; to hear her strong melodic voice drift through the room that would catch everyone's attention and even her snappish voice when yelling some rude comments.

I guess this was my punishment for my stupidity.

I sighed and leaned back in my chair, staring out of the window and waiting to hear back from Albericus regarding the little rat in the pack. I pushed my hair back roughly with my hand as it agitated me even more. I closed my eyes for a moment and took a breath, not moving from my spot.

After Aurora's vague description and some digging around of my own, I had to do more than just force myself not to tear every single member of my pack apart. Apparently, while I was with Vivian, someone took advantage and managed to get information about her out to someone—a sale out in my own pack. I was disappointed at the member who I selectively picked to live in a society of trust and loyalty and more disappointed with myself for not paying closer attention and letting this slip.

While I didn't regret spending time with Vivian, I did regret not making sure the island was safe for her. Bringing her here made me more worried about everyone, myself included; being safe from her and not the other way around. It was a rookie move.

One I hadn't made in a very, very, very long time to which I was paying now as consequence. I had a few suspects; by that, I meant too many. My usually calculating mind wasn't working. I hate to admit what the problem was—my consciousness.

I had no doubt that as soon as Vivian saw me, she would beat my ass. Sadly enough, I was okay with that. It was the least I deserved with all the crap I pulled on her but sometimes, I really just couldn't help behaving like an ass—a controlling, cold ass to be precise. It was more than just a bad habit to me. Before she came, I could think things through without a thought and enter a battle field without caring about the number of deaths. I ran from place to place, went wherever I please, took what I wanted, and mostly destroyed it in the end for fun. Thinking back on my behavior, I frowned.

And now . . . I couldn't focus on one thing without linking it to her. I couldn't use the link because it would undo the direct command. Using it on her was risky enough, now that she was changing. I wasn't stupid. I knew her changes meant the direct command would no longer work on her. If anything, it would be nothing more than a really strong request and the effect would still be strong but not as I thought.

196

While I couldn't use the link to her, which meant blocking my emotional and physical bond from her, she was subconsciously sending me her emotions—something she didn't have any idea about. I was thankful in a way that I could keep track of her without actually doing it. I knew the direct command didn't work as planned because she first woke up with confusion, longing, and a hint of anger. Even so, she couldn't feel its effect through the bond.

The only other way I knew she wasn't aware of what was going on was she hadn't discovered my mark on her. While she was asleep, I sent another witch to perform a spell similar to what was around the island—a spell to hide my bite mark on her but still have the same keep-unmated-males-away trait. To her, nothing would seem strange if she were to gaze at her neck. She wouldn't even notice that the mark of her pack, which identified each wolf of every pack, had faded as soon as my mark took place. I had to do a lot of mind changing and string pulling to get her back into the pack along with her parents without anyone questioning about her disappearance. As far as they knew, she went to her cousin's pack and came back a few days after the attack. Nothing more, nothing less.

The only problem was Vivian's two weeks were almost over, which meant the direct command would begin to fade slowly as her new side would emerge. Any little reminder of anything could spark a memory on her.

Having her was a huge risk to take, so I gave her guards to spend most of their time with her without me; at least, in a way that they would be a comfort to her. Selfishly enough, I secretly hoped she would see them fuck up, sparking her memory. It was bad, I know, but it was just a small part of me. The larger part was to let her stay away while I dealt with things and would later face her wrath.

I sensed two wolves nearing my office. My mood was darkening as I was forced to pause all thoughts of Vivian. Albericus and my third-in-command, Hogan, walked in. I met Hogan around twenty years ago. The brown-haired and brown-eyed man seemed good for the position. He was neat and organized, and he kept track of everything except for how the message got out. Hogan, as always, was dressed to impress. He wore a black dress slacks, a purple shirt, and a black tie. It was no secret he swung for the other team. I had no problem with that. I did, however, have a problem when people didn't do their jobs correctly, especially at the cost of what was currently happening.

Albericus closed the door and stood beside Hogan who had his arms over his chest while looking down at his black dress shoes. I looked at him and narrowed my eyes, then looked over to Albericus for him to proceed. Clearing his throat, he began.

"I interrogated everyone like you asked, but it seemed like no one contacted anyone outside of the pack. While checking over some files with Hogan, we learned one person did fill in a request to leave the island in the last two weeks," he spoke seriously. My leg began to bounce in agitation. Every once in a while, someone would want to leave, but I had left the small matters to either of these two. I had much more in my mind than to deal with "moving" problems.

"Leave permanently or just leave to come back later?" I asked, annoyed with their lack of straightforward answers.

"Permanently," Hogan spoke in his gruff voice. I could hear his nerves as he stood there like a statue. He should have been nervous. I turned my eyes to him, making him flinch back at my unchanging expression.

"And are you telling me you authorized this without checking for reasons or motives of leaving?" I said in a deadly quiet voice.

"No, I checked but . . ." His voice trailed off hesitantly.

"But what?" I asked through clenched teeth and claws digging into my chair. Albericus eyed my hands and took a step away from Hogan.

"Well, it's really not that simple. I mean I didn't have to check for reason. It was, well . . ." he said slowly, not explaining himself at all. He just admitted not doing his job completely.

I shot out of my seat and had my hand around his throat, lifting him off the ground all in a second.

Hogan thrashed as my hand tightened on his throat. I knew he was using his wolf strength to try to get me to let go, but it felt like nothing was challenging my grip. I brought his face closer to mine, setting his feet to the ground once more while his face began to turn purple like his shirt.

"I'm running out of patience, Hogan. When you speak to me, you will speak with reason and clarity. No evasions. I don't want moments of hesitation because I don't have the time nor the will for them. Now speak." I let him go and walked back to my chair, ignoring him gasping and panting.

"He had a mate! He . . . he had a mate and said he didn't want to live on the island with his mate's killer, no matter who you were. His reason to leave made sense. Everyone around knew," he said quickly, clutching his throat.

"Who?" Albericus asked, turning to look at Hogan who was eyeing the floor. This was why he was third-in-command and not beta. Lack of fight or courage. That and his need for order when it came to filing was helpful.

"Martha," I said, putting the clues together. It's not like I killed anyone besides her in the last few days. I brought my hand to my face and shook my head. This whole time I had been thinking of a larger group of people to point the blame at, but it seemed one little she-wolf was causing me a whole lot more trouble even if she was already dead. The beast growled at the irony in this.

Albericus turned to me with a frown on his face.

"Wait, you mean that girl who tripped Vivian in the training field? I thought you said she wasn't mated?"

I nodded. As soon as I snapped her neck, her spark went out because she was mated, half of it remained—her other half.

"She wasn't. The guy said he just found her earlier that day. They wanted to get to know each other because she wasn't sure he was good enough," Hogan said, standing up and looking blankly at the wall over my head.

"So, you're telling me you let the mate of a girl I killed go because of sympathy? Did it not occur to you that he would want revenge and that finding my mate would be the perfect thing to dish out to anyone with a grudge against me?" I yelled at him, raising back to my feet slowly while he paled.

Albericus grunted something under his breath and sighed before turning to face Hogan who right now seemed like the perfect stress toy my beast would like to take some anger out on. My beast grew his claws out, enlarging mine.

"What was his name? What's the name of the girl's mate?" he asked, pulling out his phone.

Hogan swallowed and shook his head. My brow twitched.

"That's the thing. I might have felt sympathy for the kid, but I didn't grant him permission to leave." Albericus and I froze and looked at each other.

"What do you mean?"

Breath, Zaliver. Third-in-command who didn't fuck up most of the time would be hard to find.

Hogan wiped his forehead with his hand and looked at the both of us with a worried expression.

"On the same day he requested to leave, you had me prepare documents on the pack's progress here and outfield, so I had to tell him to wait for a week for an answer as a protocol," he explained.

"Are you telling me the rat is still *here?*" My voice went dark as I thought of getting my hands on the slimeball. My mouth went dry with the thought of fresh blood. It had been a long time since I had a good kill. I felt excitement creep in on me.

Hogan nodded, seeming relieved at not being at the end of my anger.

"Name. Now!" I growled.

"Jack Ruston."

199

Repeating the name in my head, I let magic do its thing and saw one glowed the brightest out of the million of sparks. After focusing and directing myself to the glow, I reached for it and immediately knew where he was and where he was going. Knowing he wouldn't move gave me time as he would hide in the island, hiding out until he could make it out.

He wouldn't.

Going back into my own mind and body, I grinned at the boys, not caring how they both tensed and the worry and fright that wafted off of them. I nodded at Albericus. He quickly focused on me, understanding that the next few hours were about to get a whole lot more productive.

Any tiredness in my body vanished. My body straightened up and my shoulders rolled back. I tilted my head side to side, cracking the joints. I didn't even care that my hair was hanging over my eyes anymore. If anything, I knew it made the look on my face a whole lot more chilling. I pointed a finger at my beta and good friend.

"Put Jack Ruston into a room under the cells. You'll find him hiding four blocks away from where his mate lived. It is a rundown hotel that goes by the name Legrove at room 42. If he hears you, he'll hide out on the roof. Bring him to me. Now go." Without another word, Albericus shouted in the room, yelling orders into his phone to assemble a team with fierce green eyes and go back to their crazed feline-looking ways.

I swung my hand at Hogan, pointing to him and stayed silent.

"You . . . you are so damn lucky. By sticking to protocol, you saved your ass from being mauled by me and then fed to the sharks piece by piece while you watched too. Now go and look for who Jack Ruston had contacted in the last three months. I want nothing unturned." Hogan didn't need another word from me to leave the office. I could have sworn his shiny black shoes even left burn marks on my Egyptian carpet.

I didn't care if he did, I had my snitch. I just needed to know who he gave information to.

And when I find the one responsible for this whole mess, even Satan would reconsider the methods of torture they probably use in hell.

After all, one didn't just live centuries in a war zone without perfecting torture.

I smiled to myself.

I would let the beast out to play for this one.

~•~

200

Waking up to the smell of food, I gazed at the empty side of my bed. I bit my lip and furrowed my brows together. I had been doing this every morning, and I still didn't know why. Staring at the side of the bed, I stretched my arms out, feeling nothing.

I sighed and got up, cracking and stretching my body as I made my way down the stairs. I entered the kitchen where my dad was eating bacon awkwardly and my mom was leaning on the refrigerator with her professional black pants and button down blue shirt glaring, or better word, mugging my dad. A chuckle escaped my mouth at the sight of the two, not like I was about to walk into a possible war field. No not at all. Both of them looked at me. Dad looked a little relieved. I sat down at the other end of the table where my plate sat waiting and steaming.

I couldn't even properly enjoy my food with the awkward tension in the air. My mom looked like she wanted me to ask anyway with the way she kept throwing looks at me with a raised brow. You know? That look your mom got when she had a gossip about someone, but she wanted you to ask, so she didn't seem too nosy. Sighing, I gave in.

"So, how was your date last night?" I asked my mom. I found it really cute how they still had dates twenty years later.

I wished I would be like that with my mate. A sudden pang in my chest caught me off guard.

Ummm, ow.

My dad groaned, distracting me. He sent me a glare for asking to which I just shrugged. He put his head on the table in defeat. My mother huffed.

"Oh, don't get me started. You will not believe what your father did last night," she began, annoyed.

"Honey! How many times do I have to tell you I was not flirting with that woman? I have set my eyes only for you," Dad said, not lifting his head from the table. I watched, amused.

"What happened?" I asked Mom, now really interested while her eyes glared daggers at my poor dad.

"This man here, the man who I decided to have a family with despite his many mistakes while dating, was flirting with the waitr—"

"Was not! And why you gotta bring my mistakes into this? I'm sorry I set your hair on fire! It grew back," Dad said, annoyed, lifting his head to stare at my mom with a puppy face while working those large brown eyes I inherited.

"Shut your face, Chace, before I shut it for you!" Dad put his head back down with an unintelligible mumble.

201

I laughed at him.

"As I was saying, we were ordering when all of a sudden he learned that the restaurant we were at gave organic food. 'I have set my eyes only for you.' Really? 'What's your name? How long have you been working here? Has it always been like this?'" she growled out, stomping her foot and giving me a sour look.

My dad lifted his head and shot me a disbelieving look. I lifted a brow at her.

"Mom, you do realize that Dad is a food critic, right?" She rolled her eyes.

"Excuses. You should be on your mother's side. I gave birth to you after twenty hours of contractions!" She pointed a finger at me.

I raised my hands in the air and stood, clearing my plate away. Warning bells!

"I'm not on anybody's side." I paused for a moment. "Scratch that! I'm on the side that feeds me or wins. Good luck, Dad." I left the kitchen and went into the living room to watch TV.

"Gee, thanks, sweetheart. I'm feeling the love in this family!" Dad yelled while I responded with a laughter.

My mom could be so dramatic, but I thought that's what my dad loved about her. I tried to tune out their bickering, which was harder than usual. My hearing got a little more sensitive over the last few days.

I sat on the couch that was facing the TV and turned it on. Without anything in mind to watch, I flickered through the channels. I shifted around the couch to get comfortable—something I hadn't felt in days. My skin was so sensitive nowadays.

"How could you—."

"Buy this in—"

"Delivered to your—"

"Squat ladies! Your—"

"Tu quien piensas—"

". . . not the father—"

"Damon, this is serious!" Elena screamed.

I swear the amount of times someone screamed that at him.

I stopped clicking and let the Vampire Diaries play. As soon as Damon came on, my breath hitched. It wasn't because of his hotness. Looking at him made me go blank. I blinked multiple times and made a face. I squinted at the screen when a sense of déjà vu hit me. Black and blue. I shrugged and kept flickering through the TV.

"Somebody saaave meee!—"

"I got in one lil fight, and my mom got scared—"

"Next up, Hannah Mon—"

"I'm not your dad—" I went back.

". . . tana." My brows furrowed in confusion.

Staring at the screen, I frowned.

"Hannah. Hannah. Hannah?" The name rolled off my tongue without thought. Something about that name. Eh, I was too old to watch this.

Slap "Whore!"

"Oookay," I mumbled to myself, quickly changing the channel.

"What are you wearing Jake from State Farm?" My head tilted to the side.

"Uhh . . . khakis."

"She sounds hideous."

I turned the TV off. Why did I get the feeling like I had compared someone to Jake from State Farm before? Man, it had been a weird couple of days.

Ever since I woke up last Tuesday, I had been getting a lot of déjà vu along with weird feelings that were not even mine, just from other wolves. Man, I needed a run if I was beginning to think I could sense what others were feeling. Hold it. Maybe I was becoming psychic. Nah, I didn't have crystal balls or any type of balls matter of fact.

"Sweety, I'm going to work. If you need anything, ask your father because he isn't leaving until later. Bye." I nodded at her and with a kiss to the cheek, my mom walked out.

I sighed. I had nothing to do but to hang around the house. I heard Dad walk up to the couch before sitting next to me. He ran a hand down his face. I turned to look at him.

"So . . ." I began. He narrowed his eyes at me.

"I know, I know," he muttered.

"Where are you taking her tonight?" I asked, crossing my arms over my chest.

If Dad wouldn't take Mom out again, she would bring it up and basically complain on how bad the date was unless Dad replaced the memory. Mom worked like that. The funny thing was sometimes she wouldn't say anything, but just by looking at her face, you could tell she was talking smack inside her head. She just had this look.

"Forget about a restaurant. I'm going to make food for a picnic. Just the two of us. No one around. Yeah . . . she can't say squat if it's just the two of us." Dad's face lit up around his plan. I patted him on the back.

"Nice . . . unless she catches you eyeing a female duck. She might bring it home for dinner." I joked. Dad laughed, throwing his head back.

"True. So, are you just gonna laze around the house all week or do you plan to actually do something? Not that watching TV, listening to music, and surfing the web aren't productive," he asked. I

203

frowned not because I was offended at his words, but I was feeling a bit lost. What was I supposed to do here? Here? *Here* . . . Ugh, why was I questioning everything?

"Nah, I think I'll go to the park or something. Maybe I'll even drop by at some friends' houses," I said, figuring out it was a pretty nice plan. Dad nodded at me.

"Well if you go, just tell me. I'll give you a ride if you want," he said, standing up. I stood with him. It was the best time to get some fresh air anyway.

"Okay." I took two stairs at a time to my room after picking an outfit up and changed.

I went into the bathroom and began combing my hair. It had grown faster than I thought. How did I not notice how it had grown so fast in such a short time? Where had my head been? Tying it in a ponytail, I checked my outfit. Black jeans and a jumper, not like I was gonna meet anyone important today . . . or ever. I snorted at my small joke.

After putting my brush down, I was ready to go, but I kept looking at myself in the mirror, not to check myself or anything. My confused large brown eyes stared back at me. I looked a little paler than usual, but that wasn't too worrying. I tilted my head to the side and watched as my reflection did the same, but I felt like I was missing something in my reflection. Like if I didn't look hard enough, I would skipped over something. I felt like I was supposed to be doing something or had forgotten to do something important or just forgotten in general.

I squinted at the mirror, tilting my head back. Leaning into the mirror, I stared into my eyes. All I saw were big brown—

I gasped and moved back. I took a breath and leaned back in when nothing happened again. Staring deep into my eyes, I told myself not to move.

There!

My eyes remained the same, but something in my head stirred. It felt like my wolf was moving around, but it couldn't be her because I could sense her in the back of my head. She had been quiet in the last few days.

It was a small shift, but I could almost feel another life force. Impossible! Great, I was going crazy out of boredom. Maybe I did need fresh air. With one last look into the mirror, I left my room and grabbed my phone and keys.

Reaching my dad's office, I knocked on his door. He looked up from his computer.

"You want a ride?" he asked. I shook my head at him.

204

"Nah, we, chubby girls, gotta get a good work out once in a while or we will all disappear. We won't want that, will we?" I joked, entering his office. My dad shook his head at me with a small smile.

"You aren't fat."

"I said chubby!"

"You aren't chubby."

"Fine. Fluffy."

"You aren't—"

"The next one might be 'Damn!' Stop while you can," I said, pointing a finger at him.

"Ugh, what is it with the women of this family putting me in these positions? Why didn't we have a boy?" Dad said to himself, looking up at the ceiling as if it held all the answers.

"Because Mom said she'd castrate you if she had to push another baby out," I said dryly to him, sitting on the small two-seater couch. He tilted his head at me.

"Oh yeah."

Moms. You gotta love them.

"Hey, Dad . . ." I began. I guess my tone caught his attention because he frowned.

"What's up?" he said, leaning onto the desk and turning his body to face in my direction with concerned eyes. I groaned and threw my head back, taking a deep breath. I thought for a second before speaking to him.

"Do you—I don't know—ever get the feeling like you've forgotten something really important?" I asked. He nodded at me, clasping his hands in front of him.

"Plenty of times. Just the other day, I forgot to tell your mother I—" I shook my head at him.

"No, like you shouldn't be doing what you're doing even though it makes perfect sense as if you're supposed to be somewhere else doing something else?" I swung my legs over and sat up, placing a hand on both knees. Dad looked at me for a moment before an understanding look crossed his face. For a moment, I thought he understood me.

"Is this about you not being in college yet? Because it's okay to take a year off—" I stood and threw my hands up in frustration, walking back and forth in front of his desk and bringing a hand to my face.

"No! You're not getting me. I-I just keep getting this feeling like . . . I don't know." I sighed and stopped. I hated feeling confused. I was usually a quick thinker with clear thoughts but lately, everything had been a blur. I had moments when my mind was blank.

205

A sense in me pulsed, eyeing my dad. I could have sworn I almost felt his worry, confusion, and surprisingly enough, a bit of fear. Why would he be scared for me?

"Vivian, are you feeling alright? Maybe you should stay in?" Dad said, beginning to stand up. I lifted my hands and backed up to the door.

"No, sorry about that. I'll call you when I get back from the park." Without another word, I walked out and left the house.

Sometimes I was glad to be in a gated pack community. There were other times that I didn't feel like it that much. For one, it was a bit odd to know so many people you lived with were wolves. While many people lived together, yet you couldn't keep track of them all.

The park was a bit far from my house. It was one of the oldest parks nearby that was situated deeper into the forest and farther away from the houses. I learned about it in a project in middle school, and after being curious enough, I came with a few friends to see if it was still there. Technically, when I told my dad I would go to the park, I didn't lie. It was a park. At least, it used to be back in the days.

Passing a few familiar faces, I made just short talks after noticing how everyone I bumped into seemed to shift uncomfortably in front of me. I always got a sense of almost confused paranoia from them. Maybe I was giving off a weird vibe. Ha! Maybe I was weird.

The further away from the houses and buildings, the calmer my senses felt. They weren't being assaulted by constant noise and smell. Stepping over a broken tree branch and walking around a large puddle, I turned at the familiar medium foot-shaped boulder. Counting twenty large steps, I now stood in front of an old, rusty, and abandoned small park.

By no means was I ever going to actually get on. I always sat on the long rock bench. I was glad it wasn't made of wood. It would have rotted over time. Sitting there, I closed my eyes and breathed in the fresh untainted air and let my body relaxed. The walk got me tired more than I thought, more than it should have actually. I drifted asleep for a short while. I wasn't worried because no one really came around here. It was also pack land, not like anyone would just prance around.

You know that feeling when you're sleeping in your room and you could sense someone outside your room was planning to wake you up? An almost out-of-body seventh sleeping sense of sort? Yeah? Well, that's what I was about to go through.

The sound of slow deliberate footsteps made my ears twitch, but I didn't wake up. My body, though asleep, was somehow alert and my mind was half awake.

The next sound I caught were four loud thumps. No, not thumps but heartbeats. Odd. I shouldn't be able to hear heartbeats while in human form. I mused half awake. With my next shallow slow breath, I inhaled for the scents without thinking.

The word *familiar* floated around my head, but I quickly forgot them. Of course, they would be. I grew up in this pack, and I could have crossed them at some point.

The travelers got closer slowly, almost cautious. My ears listened to their words.

"We shouldn't be this close. It's a risk," a hushed male's voice said.

"Yeah, but she's asleep. We can't let her stay out here. You heard his orders," a female said. My half-awake self wondered what they were talking about.

"Trick is getting her awake, out, and home without getting caught at the same time," the same male said. There was a curse.

"Maybe if we throw something at her, she'll wake up and get scared enough to go home," a new male voice said, sounding hopeful. There was silence before a smack and then hushes.

"Quiet! And no, you idiot! As a wolf, she will more likely look into it, then get away from it. Shhh, stop. I think we've gotten close enough. Her senses are like his. He said to be extra cautious around her," a new voice spoke. This time a female.

What were they talking about? Me? Could it be me?

"Why do we get the hard jobs? I heard the other guys are having a great time kicking every ass trying to get in here," one of the women said. My brows furrowed.

Wait. Here? Who was trying to get in now?

My parents told me the random kidnappings had stopped sometime last week when I was away with . . . who was I away with again? My cousin . . . Lily, yeah, her. My mind went foggy for a moment.

"Because he trusts us with her more than the others," the first guy spoke. I realized they could be guards.

What were they doing at the park though? Where was their charge?

"So, how are we going to do this?" There was a long pause. By this time, my brain was slowly starting to wake up, but curiosity over what the group was doing won out, so I didn't move.

As they began bickering back and forth amongst themselves, I peeked, quickly taking in how the sun was still in the sky, which meant I must have been asleep for at least twenty or thirty minutes. Without moving a muscle, my eyes flickered over to the direction of the conversation that was slowly growing louder.

Squinting my eyes and looking past trees, branches, leaves, and more, I realized just how far they were.

How could I see them so clearly? I wasn't even borrowing my wolf's sight.

I frowned and stared at the figures that were huddled together. With curiosity eating me as to what they were doing, I decided to listen to the noisy side—something I inherited from my mom. It felt like something was telling me to do so.

Hoping it worked, I tensed my body to prepare myself. My plan was to stand either slow enough or quick enough to not get noticed, depending on how much my body helped me. I called upon my wolf's strength. Counting to three, I stood.

I was surprised after realizing I was already standing by the time I even thought of three. Cool.

"We're not about to launch pebbles at her—"

I turned to their direction. As fast and sneaky as possible, I made my way to a tree, then the same thing happened. I was there as soon as the thought passed my mind.

"We're also not going to set her front yard on fire in hopes her parents will call her."

I looked at the next tree and hopped from tree to tree as quickly and quietly as possible.

"What if we set a tree on fire—"

"And watch her try to control it? Yeah . . . no."

Their backs were turned from the direction I came from. Thinking of getting a clearer view of them, I moved around and away from where I came from. I felt like I was zooming past the trees and using them as cover. It felt cool.

"Well, I don't see you giving ideas!" A female snapped.

"Uh . . . guys—" the hopeful guy said.

"Fine. Let's send an animal, like a rabbit or something, close to her."

"That involves us catching a rabbit, which means running around."

I noticed the tallest of the group kept shifting around. His light-colored curls were bouncing a bit. Every time I tried to get a good view of them, I had to duck behind a tree.

"Uh, you guys—"

"That's stupid. Besides, how are we gonna get the thing go directly to her?"

I was surprised I had gotten this close without them even noticing me. Was I that good? Maybe I should become a spy.

"You guys—"

"Fine. Why don't we just call her? We all have her new number, haven't we?" There was a pause.

"Oh yeah!" They all began petting their pockets as if looking for their phones. I noticed they all wore black, not at all shifty.

"Hey!"

"What?" They all snapped at the tallest guy, but he didn't seem to care.

"She's gone."

"Told ya," the same hopeful guy said.

There was another pause before a choking sound was heard. The group shuffled, and instead of getting a clear view of their faces, the wall shuffled to look at something, turning their backs to me. I huffed in annoyance.

"Shit! Call her. Her location will be sent to us when she picks up. Just say it's a wrong number."

From what I could see, a red-haired man pulled out a phone and punched in numbers.

Getting tired of hiding behind the trees, I walked out quietly until I was a few feet behind them. I was guessing they didn't hear me because they were so busy listening to the dial.

Maybe I could help. I had been around here and hadn't heard or seen anyone. Also, I was brought up to be helpful to my fellow pack members. It sounded better than doing nothing at home anyway.

"Who did you lose?" I asked loudly.

They all froze where they were. I waited for them to turn around, but they stood still like statues.

My phone began to ring. I slowly looked down at my pocket and then back up to the frozen figures with wide eyes.

The tallest one with curly blond hair smacked his forehead with his palm.

"Bruh."

CHAPTER 20

The four strangers didn't turn to face me; they just stood still. My phone stopped ringing.

"Maybe if we don't move," the tall blond man began to whisper.

"Shut up!" the short red-haired guy whisper-shouted, interrupting the other.

"I can't believe this," a tall woman with her dark hair pulled back muttered. Her pony tail moved side to side as she shook her head.

"We are so dead," another with a similar hairdo said.

I wasn't sure what to do. They were all muttering stuff under their breath and not turning around to face me, but that thing with the phone was weird. They couldn't have called me, right? That would mean that they had been talking about me the whole time. I shook my head mentally. There was no way they were here for me; it must have just been some crazy coincidence.

I knew that any other person would have stayed away from them, but something told me they weren't dangerous. Well I mean, they looked like they were ready for action, but personally, I felt like they wouldn't hurt me. Something dark lurking inside me made me feel like if our judgment was wrong, we would take them. All of them.

"Hey!" I said, trying to get their attention. Since they weren't going to turn around to face me, I decided to try and walk around them to their fronts.

Keyword: Try.

Every time I took a step, they moved all together and sort of huddled in the opposite direction, making sure their backs were facing me. I felt confusion and suspicion build in me at their odd behavior.

"Hey, why won't you turn around?" I asked, trying again to go around them with no avail.

"Well—" The blond's head lifted a bit.

"Don't speak to her, stupid!" one of the women whisper-shouted at him and smacked him on the head, making him grumble.

"Why not? Hey, turn around, will you," I said a bit too forcefully, feeling frustrated and a bit offended at the same time.

They all began turning around robotically, their hands fisting up.

"Resist!"

"I can't!"

I frowned as they all turned around slowly. These four were odd. Very odd.

"What are you all—" I stopped as they faced me fully.

Red hair, green eyes.

Blond curls, blue eyes.

Black hair, brown eyes with a scar.

Black hair, brown eyes.

I felt the strongest sense of déjà vu hit me. I felt like a wave of blurry memories came crashing on me as if blank spots in my head were being filled, but I couldn't reach them. The feeling was so intense I stumbled back. As soon as they turned around, I knew they weren't from the pack, but I also knew they weren't here for trouble. Maybe they were visiting or something?

The people in front of me all took a hesitant step to me with their arms outstretched as if to catch me if I fell.

" Luke . . . Johnson . . . Mila . . . Courtney . . ." I mumbled without a thought. Their eyes widened with something that looked like both fear and panic.

"I'm sorry. D-do I know you all from somewhere? Have we all met before?" I asked, looking up at them wide-eyed, realizing how weird I was being and feeling. They all looked at each other and then at me. Their faces were grave and serious. The tall blond guy spoke with his eyes flickering all over my face.

"Do we look familiar?" The others inched closer a bit as if wanting to hear anxiously for my answer.

"Are those your names?" I said. I wanted to tell myself that I was just really good in answering guessing names, but the longer I looked at them, the more I felt I had seen them from somewhere.

It was the red-haired man with green eyes that spoke. While looking at him, I got a flash of someone else with the same eyes and hair but shorter and bit more feminine. Weird. My eyes flickered to the blog guy and got the same thing, but her face was a bit clearer in my mind. Friendly.

"Y-yes," he stammered after a moment of hesitation.

I gaped at them. So I did guess their names right, but how?

"So, we have met?" I asked again. He nodded. I wanted to pull at my hair.

"Where?" I asked, suspicious of the people who looked like they would rather be anywhere but here when previously they were

211

persistent on. What were they so persistent on? My eyes narrowed at them, scanning their black clothing.

"Uh . . ."

"Well . . ."

"You see . . ."

"The thing is . . ."

They all spoke simultaneously.

I had a sneaky suspicion that there was something weird going on here; not just now, but this whole week. I took a step towards them, feeling like they held answers. *Where had I met them?*

"What were you doing just now? Who are you? Guards? Patrol? Who were you calling that was just here?"

They all looked away from me. The tall woman with a scar over her eyebrow spoke with caution as if her words were carefully picked.

"We are guards, but we're specific guardians. We can't tell you what we're guarding, and please don't ask why. As to who we were calling . . . we weren't calling anyone." She looked at me firmly in the eyes, seeming sure of her own words.

Why do I feel like I'm being lied to?

"So, you didn't call a 'her' and that it was just a mistake?" I asked, crossing my hands over my chest. They shook their heads in denial.

"So, I'm hearing things now?" They said nothing.

There was something bothering me here, and I knew just how to fix it. I had a hunch on one thing, and I wanted to know if I was right.

I was still confused as to what was going on around me; even the ground I was walking on didn't seem right. Could it be that my gut was telling me something was wrong and these four were part of it?

I reached into my pocket and pulled out my phone. Their eyes widened, and they all took a step forward.

"What are you doing?" the red-headed guy said. His green eyes panicked and flickered from my phone to my face.

"I'm just going to return the call I missed," I said nonchalantly, shrugging and swiping the screen. The missed call number on my screen was in bold red, indicating that my phone didn't have the caller ID.

"I'm sure it's nothing important," the girl without a scar said with her face chaining to a panicked reassuring smile as if she was sure.

"Yes, nothing important at all," the woman with the scar said, hands outstretched in front of her, ready to snatch the phone from me at any chance.

"Yeah, besides, didn't your parents ever tell you that it's bad manners to make a call mid conversation?" The blond scolded me.

I narrowed my eyes at them all, noticing how fast their hearts were all beating. The slow shuffling of their feet discreetly made their way closer to me.

"You're right. It maybe nothing important, and my parents do talk to me about manners," I said slowly to them. They all let out a relieved sigh and dropped their stances.

Beep.

"But I really should return this; could be important." I smiled at their surprise and horrified expressions.

My sensitive ears picked up a sound—the vibration of a phone. My eyes scanned them, realizing it was coming from the red headed guy.

I lifted a brow at him.

"Aren't you going to get that? Might be *important.*"

Shaking his head, he reached into his pocket and took the phone out with a grimace. Pressing the *answer* button, he brought the phone up to his pale face, which just seemed to lose more and more color over time.

The other line answered.

"Hello?" he mumbled, looking straight at me.

The line on the other side followed his exact same words.

"*Mmhh,*" I mumbled, ending the call and pocketing my phone.

"Okay, spill. Who are you and why do you have my number, which then leads me to asking why are you following me?" I ask them seriously. I wanted to know what these familiar people were up to and where we met, not to mention why they appeared to be following me.

"Look," the tall blond spoke. His voice sounded very serious. "If you want answers, we will give them to you tomorrow. Meet us up here. We have to go." The others around him looked at him with surprise and immediately began to protest, but he gave them a look I couldn't decipher. It made me realize they might have been using their pack link.

After a while, they all nodded at each other and turned to look at me with the same odd looks on their faces. The other man spoke this time.

"Yes, meet us here same time tomorrow for answers."

I was getting a sneaky suspicion that if I agreed to this, I would be stood up and ditched.

"No, wait—" I tried.

They all began running off in separate directions before I could open my mouth. Even with the new speed I seemed to have, their movements were still too confusing, and I didn't want to run after them.

213

With a huff and a look in all directions, they went off. I decided to go back home to go over this puzzle. Maybe they wouldn't ditch me. It was a long shot.

By the time I made it back home, the house was empty, making me realize how much time that whole little fiasco took up of my morning. Going straight to my room, I sat on my bed only to stand back up, not being able to sit still with what just happened.

Who the hell where those four? What were they doing? And why did I know them? Where they really talking about me? Trying to wake me up to go home for what? Why were they even worried? The question on where I had met them bothered me the most because I felt like it would unlock something within my mind.

I undid my ponytail and shook out my hair, letting it lay in a mess around me. I had been getting a lot of déjà vu lately, and they were only triggered by small things that felt like reminders . . . but why? And why did I feel like I was now partly complete as soon as I saw them as if blank spots in my head had been filled once more? Something in my head shifted around.

I frowned as my wolf began pacing back and forth in my mind and then stopping as if confused before shaking her wolf head vigorously. For some reason, I mirrored her actions slowly. I moved my head back and forth slowly as if denying something before I shook harder, trying to shake something out of my mind. I stopped as soon as I felt pounding in my head. Ugh, why did I do that? I stilled.

Even though my head was pounding, I felt as if something in my mind was . . . off. I was faintly reminded of the Avengers movie when Loki overpowered everyone's will with the staff and the Black Widow broke Hawk Eye out of it by banging his head. I wonder why that came to mind? I could feel things pushing to the front of my thoughts, hoping that whatever had gotten free in my weird mind scramble would help me make sense of why I was feeling so off.

I let out a scream, bringing my hands to my head to stop the pained memory. Countless memories forced themselves in front of my eyes, not letting me rest to think or breath. I heard so many voices in my memory and my wolf's that I did know what to listen to. My head spun faster and faster and felt as if it was heating up on overload. My body began to shake and quiver, making me drop to the ground and move around as if I was having uncontrollable muscle spasms. It was like a restrained power that began growing in me and pushing forward like a bullet to surge through my body like hot molten lava.

My eyes began to roll in the back of my head as I gasped for a breath, wanting to feel cool air in my overworked body and mind. As I remembered blue eyes and dark hair, I felt a trickle of something thick

214

that felt like liquid slowly beginning to make its way down my face from my nose. Blue eyes were the last thing I saw before I passed out.

"Zaliver," I whispered in a breath as darkness claimed me.

~•~

I didn't know what time I woke up but when I did, I was on the ground—sore, tired, hungry, and mad as hell.

I remembered. I remembered everything. *Everything.*

Picking myself off the floor, I, for the first time since waking up in my old house, didn't feel like I was missing something important. No, everything was clear. I knew what I was missing or, better yet, who I was missing. I didn't need a mirror to know that my face was serious or of someone not to be messed with.

Moving to the bathroom, I pushed open the door, and without flicking the lights, I stood in front of the mirror. My eyesight was slowly making everything clear.

Not taking my eyes off the mirror, I reached up to my hood and pulled it down roughly to bare my mark that was slowly appearing under my eyes.

I snarled as an anger I had never felt in my entire life build up in me. Boiling lava was nothing compared to it. Even Satan couldn't overpass the dark emotions swirling in me and the rage flowing in my veins. I was so angry that I was shaking, feeling hot and cold.

Looking back at myself in the mirror, I didn't bother wiping the dried blood that trailed down my face. I shook my head as emotions and thoughts swarmed in me. I took a breath to control myself, making sure not to use the bond like he had been doing, so as not to alarm him. Even though he could possibly get a feeling of what I was feeling if he wasn't distracted.

I let out a humorless laugh that had it not come from me, it would have chilled me to the bones. I kept my mind, my body, and my emotions cold. I would have time to explode later and on the right person too. Underneath, I could feel anger, betrayal, and a dark twisted need to take those feelings out on the ones who brought them on.

"I'm so going to kill you for this," I murmured under my breath with a bitter and horrid taste on the tip of my tongue.

I didn't clean my face, knowing it would help with my first step.

Storming out of my room, I stopped in the kitchen to grab something and then exited the house, making a quick plan. Knowing the guards I had, they'd be watching me from a far. Since they were now cautious of being sensed by me since this morning, I had no doubt they were too far for me to tail now.

They were far, but they were watching.

Making my way back to the park, I made my way quickly and made sure I looked like I was in a hurry, keeping my head down to avoid having the blood on my face seen by others and get stopped before I'd even make it. The sun was low in the sky, giving off a dramatic and beautiful flare of different shades in the sky. It was perfect.

Once I made it a few steps, I began probably one of the best performances in my life.

I began pacing back and forth, looking down and shaking my head. I stopped and sat down, bringing my knees to my chest and rocking back and forth very quickly. I then let out sounds of distress. My ears caught the sound of mumbles and slow approaching steps of four hearts. Without having to smell the air, I knew it would be them.

They weren't nearing me fast enough as if not sure what was going on.

"Ohhh! I'm so confused! So lonely!" I cried out pathetically. I was feeling so emotionally cold that I was finding it hard not to snort at how flat it sounded.

The moment I stood up, they halted. Continuing, I began pacing back and forth again, running my hands through my already crazy hair. I lifted up my head, pushed my hair out of my face, and made sure the side with the dried blood faced them.

"Oh, the pain!" I yelled out.

It worked. Their horrified gasps made them quicken their pace towards me.

Hmmm, let's see if they can move faster.

"I can no longer go on with this hollow emptiness that lives on in me! Life no longer holds value to me! I'm done! Finished! Oh!" I cried out. I pulled out the large knife I grabbed from the kitchen and held it up, letting it gleam.

I almost rolled my eyes as they began to run faster to me; they shot out of the trees and shadows, not stopping. Luke was in the lead. His face was pale but fierce as he ran as fast as he could. I didn't think he even cared how to get the knife out of my hand as long as I was out of danger from . . . well, myself.

I tensed my body as he neared, knowing that at the speed he was moving, he wouldn't be able to stop and that he planned on tackling me to the floor. His hand was already out to take the knife from me.

Nope, not how this was gonna work.

As soon as he grabbed onto the knife, my eyes flashed. I grabbed his arm and flipped his body on the ground and then loomed over him with knife still in hand.

As time continued, Luke let out a breath as he caught up with the impact of his body on the ground. He blinked before looking confused and dazed up at me. I heard the heavy breathing of the others around me.

I smiled down at him.

"Hello, Luke," I said too sweetly, coldly gazing at him. His eyes widened.

I turned to the others and opened both arms to them as if ready for embrace.

"Hello, Johnson, Mila, and Courtney. Long time no see, huh. I wouldn't count this morning as a meeting. I wasn't myself. You see, I seemed to have forgotten some things like meeting you. My memories had just seemed to go . . . *poof.* Odd, right?" I said, looking them straight in the eyes while I spoke sardonically but managed to add the right amount of sticky sweetness to my tone to make them flinch.

I looked at the knife in my hand, ignoring their intake of breath. I began to toss the knife in the air like a ball, catching it by its tip. Luke scrambled to his feet and slowly backed away from me as if he could feel the quiet anger in me under the façade of calmness I was portraying, which they all probably could. The others said nothing, which just fueled my anger more.

I caught the knife by the handle and pointed it in their direction.

"Oh no, don't stay quiet now! You've done it all week. Speak. I'm sure you're dying to say something," I bantered at them.

Stone-faced, they said nothing but stood tall like soldiers, not looking directly into my eyes. My jaw clenched and the darkening emotions in me tried to burst out. I clenched the knife tighter, feeling the handle under my strength.

"It's not our place to say anything, Luna," Johnson said blankly, looking forward. My eyes flickered to his face. I knew he saw me because he looked tensed.

"Not your place, huh?" I murmured, running my fingers softly over the edge of the knife.

I knew exactly whose place it was. Fine then. I looked at the knife in fascination as if it meant something dearly to me.

"Fine. I know you've been in contact with him. Tell him you're taking me back. I don't care what you say to him, but make sure he knows I'm coming back," I said coolly, making sure not to say his name because I knew I'd combust.

There was a moment of silence before Luke spoke hesitantly.

"Luna, we can't."

Moving faster than he could blink, I turned and threw the knife in his direction. I made sure it didn't actually hit him, but he felt it whizzed by his head and landed its tip into a tree a few feet away from

217

him. The sound of the knife wiggling due to the force of impact rang out like shots fired from a gun through the forest.

He froze, eyes wide like the others. Their hearts pounded fast.

"This is not a request. It's an *order*," I snarled out through my teeth, my hands clenching by my sides.

Luke tried to compose himself and nodded at me. His face and voice were blank like the others beside him.

"We understand." They all nodded and waited for further instructions from me.

I began walking past them and back home after telling them to come find me at my house.

As I made my way home, I began to make a plan, letting my emotions lead my actions. He was going to pay. He was going to pay for playing me the way he did.
I was going to make him learn that he couldn't just step all over people and think he'd get away with it. Oh no, he was going to learn, and he wasn't going to like my methods.

He was about to learn why messing with Vivian Grey was the biggest mistake he had ever made in his life. Mate or not, Zaliver was going to pay.

~•~

ZALIVER AZRALA

I stood in front of the metal bolted black door, hearing Jack Ruston struggle against the chains that held him to his chair. If I focused enough, I would see his immense body heat moving through the door, but I didn't.

I heard footsteps approaching me from my right.

"Is this what I asked for you to set?" I asked without turning to look at Albericus who grunted out a *yes*. I nodded at him, making him walk away.

My beast grew more and more excited at the prospect of having fun now, finally having someone he was going to sink his claws into for this whole mess. I couldn't agree more. He paced back and forth within me, lifting its head up and then looking at the black door in front of me. He lunged at it as if he was really doing it. He tried to force me to do so, but I held him back.

"Patience . . . You will get your turn," I murmured to him.

When Albericus informed me of the quick and efficient capture and imprisonment of Jack, I was glad. The little rat sat with panic and fear filtering through his body as if he could feel his death standing on the other side of the door.

218

That made very much sense because that's what I was going to deliver to the guy.

Relinquishing half of my control to my beast, I took a deep breath, focusing on letting half of my control go and giving him what he wanted.

Immediately, my body and mind went through the change. My build grew a bit. I could feel my facial features sharpen, my eyes go black, and the veins under my eyes raise. My claws grew frighteningly sharp and long while the teeth in my mouth shifted and lengthened. My fangs poked out of my mouth. My eyes opened. I could feel the change. I could see my beasts' eyes in me.

This half transformation was very unique. No one but Albericus knew of me doing this. Well, there were a few, but they only saw this form before they died.

The beast reached out and opened the door. We stepped into the dimly lit room with concrete walls and floors. In the center of the room sat Jack Ruston with his back to me. Breathing deeply, he was frozen in his seat as I closed the door loudly behind me. I knew he could feel my presence through his shaking body. From the back, all I could see was his buzz cut head.

Coward.

I purposely let my boots make noise as I made my way slowly to him, stopping behind his chair. The cold room grew even colder as my beast released some of the darkness swallowing him. Jack began to cough as the darkness swarmed around him, cutting off his oxygen and making him gasp and breathe in the negativity that choked my beast for so long. My beast had grown comforted by violence. I chuckled as I heard his desperate panting for air as if his lungs refused to take in all the air in the room.

"It's all in your head, Jack. Breathe," I said loudly. My voice sounded rougher and harsher with a sort of wild animal snarl to it.

After a few seconds, he took my advice and realized that it was—as I said—all in his head. He could breathe; he just thought he couldn't. That's what the darkness in me could do to anyone around me; it would mess with their minds, play around, and manipulate them as if it had a mind of its own. After years of living with it, I figured how to control the little curse and then learned how to turn it into a gift of sort. The beast wasn't going to use the direct command. Oh no, he was going to drag this out.

Jack sat in his chair, gulping in air as if it was water. I let out a chuckle, which must have made him remember I was behind him. The beast smirked at his prey even though he knew he couldn't see our face; at least, not yet.

219

Poor Jack tried to turn his head to look at me over his shoulder but couldn't, not only was it too dark in here with no windows but I also wore black. Darkness was also swimming through the air like clouds, fogging his eyes.

"So, Jack Ruston, let's get down to business. I'm going to give you two choices. What I want is simple: the names of the people you gave the information to and how you got it in the first place.

First, give me what I want, then I'll snap your neck like how I snapped your mate's or I can torture it out of you. Either which you die. So really, the *how* is what you would want to worry about. Which will it be?" I put my hand on his shoulder, letting him feel my claws on top of his shirt. His heart that had calmed a bit took off again.

"F-fuck you," he managed to say out of fear.

I let out a small snarl at his disrespect but let it go since I was going to kill him anyway.

I walked in front of Jack, taking a sick joy at how his eyes widened and face paled at the sight of me. I gave him a wide smile, flashing my fangs. My eyes took in the sweat trickling down the side of the brown-eyed snitch in front of me. I brought my hand in front of me and pointed a long claw at him.

"Last chance, Jack. Tell me what I want to know and make this a lot less painful than it has to be."

He shook his head at me, eyes looking at the ground as if it would swallow him whole. He'd be a lucky son of a bitch if it did. I could feel the wolf within him trying to submit to me out of fear but also trying to hold on to his decision to avenge his mate.

"Alright then." I smiled down at him.

Walking around him to other corner of the room, I pulled the small cart over to him. He tensed as he heard the wheels near him. Once in front, he looked at what was on the tray and froze. His breathing stopped, and for a moment, so did his heart before he tried getting out of his chains.

I felt an emotion from the bond begin to make its way to me, but I closed it off, not wanting Vivian to distract me. I'd check on her later.

"Don't worry. That's for later. Right now, I'm just going to rip all the flesh off of you and then break some bones. I'd punch you, but I'm afraid I'd kill you instantly," I said cheerfully at him. My beast was growling in anticipation for the fun to really begin. The darkness was coming for Jack again.

×

I swiped my hand across his chest, leaving four deep claw marks over his chest to which he immediately let out a cry. His wounds began to bleed out and then slowly, so slowly, it began to heal.

I made eye contact with him. Pale and sweaty, he glared at me with as much hatred as he could. We hadn't even begun but he was already throwing glares at me.

Swiping at the remaining part of his shirt, I tore it away from his top body, not wanting anything to stand in the way of the next process. He'd be lucky if I didn't get to his back; that is if he died in this process, of course.

"You can't heal flesh if you don't have any," I said darkly, humor thick in my wild-like voice.

The beast enjoyed it.

He reached out and dug his claws in the top part of Jack's left shoulder, ignoring the boy's cry and cutting out the shape of a square on both of his sides. Looking at Jack deeply in the eyes, the beast put his claws under Jack's skin before it could begin to heal, and pulled downward, yanking the skin all the way down to his elbow.

Jack howled in pain. He thrashed in his chair as the flesh was ripped off of his arm. Taking a chunk of bloody meat with me, I pulled it completely. His head snapped down to look at his arm and when he saw it, his eyes widened in horror. I backed away as I heard his stomach reacting to the not so pretty picture painted in red. He turned his head and began vomiting on the other side of his chair. I scrunched up my nose in disgust at the smell.

Vomit was the one thing I hated out of this process.

"Alright whimp, ready for the other arm?" I asked coldly, already doing the same to his other arm and yanking the meat down before he could process what I had said. His pained scream was music to my ears.

With blood seeping out, I neared his arm and looked down at it, watching as his body tried to heal what wasn't there anymore. His muscles clenched on their own. Red, pink, and little chunks of remaining meat were all over my sight.

Holding both chunks of stripped meat from his arms, I looked down at him, which made him seem like he was about to faint.

"Wake up, bitch! This is only going to get worse if you don't tell me what I want to know. Think about it, Jack. The quicker I kill you, the faster you can be with her—Martha." Saying her name had him snap his eyes wide open and try to lunge at me with bared teeth.

"Shut up! You don't deserve to say her name! The only pleasure I'm getting through all of this is knowing how he'll kill her like you killed my mate! You'll have to suffer the way I do but worse. He promised a painfully slow death for your bitch—"

I had my hand around his throat in a flash. I pulled him up along the chair he was chained to. I brought him close to my furious face.

"So, it's a *he* then?" I asked calmly even though my face said anything.

Jack's eyes began to roll in the back of his head, so I drop him back down.

"You'll talk. They always do. And don't think I'll forget the *bitch* comment."

Reaching down, I forcefully lifted up his right leg high into the air in an uncomfortable position. With one hand, I grabbed his foot and pulled hard to the side, snapping it clean off his leg with the bone sticking out.

He let out a bellow so loud I had to drop his leg and foot on the ground where his ripped flesh laid.

Once his yelling went down to grunts and moans, I reached for his other leg. In an attempt to avoid me, he tried to kick me away from his last foot. I smiled at him when I grasped onto it tightly and repeated the same process. He screamed once more, but I was ready this time. Using my unnatural speed, I dropped his foot in the pile and reached down for one of the strips of flesh I had torn from him. Standing back up, I shoved it in his mouth.

This would most definitely be mental torture—a bloody and torn piece of his own flesh in his mouth? Most definitely. This was for calling Vivian a *bitch*.

He stopped screaming and looked down, then began trying to spit out his flesh. When he did, he began coughing and spitting on the ground with saliva trailing down his face. Tears began to stream down his eyes as he held his legs straight so as not to touch the ground, but that also meant he could see that he no longer had both feet. His legs began shaking with effort and weakness, and his blood was pooling around the chair.

"Now for the part I'm sure you've been waiting for," I murmured. His hate-filled crying brown eyes flickered from me to what was on the tray. I nodded.

I reached for the little hot box that had been giving off steam this whole time and opened the lid. I dipped the tip of my claw inside, doing the same thing with the other claws. Turning back to Jack, I smiled viciously.

"As you've probably suspected, I'm no wolf. I can't help but wonder, how do wolves react to silver?" I said, nearing him. His skin was ashen and almost transparent. The veins in his body were popping up because of a massive blood loss. Of course, I knew how they would react. This wasn't my first rodeo but still, every time was a first time.

"Come now, Jack. Give me a name," I snarled at him and put one finger in the middle of his chest, letting the tip of my finger hover over his skin. He tried to push himself back further into the chair.

"N-no," he stuttered out with his eyes screwed shut.

I sighed but then pushed my finger forcefully into his chest.

I watched in amazement as his skin began to sizzle and bubble around my clawed fingertip, sinking the rest of my fingers into his chest and spreading his skin out. He screamed an agonizing scream, worse than the others. With my other hand, I swiped at his stomach, making sure to remove the skin with me. I removed my claws from his chest and watched as he withered in agony while his body could no longer heal itself from the wound. He shook his head side to side with tears streaming down his face at what I imagined was a horrific pain.

Whistling, I walked around him and whipped my fingers on my shirt.

I wrapped my hand around his neck and lifted him out of the chair, making him thrash once more.

"Ready to talk? No? Okay. This ought to change your mind," I said after he spat on the ground as an answer.

With one hand around his neck, I thrust my other hand into his lower mid back, going through the skin and pushing my hand into his flesh. I wrapped my hand around his spinal cord and pulled.

Snap!

His lower half slumped. I pulled my hand out and left half of his spine hanging out of his back. Walking to the front again, I whipped my bloodied hand on his face and smiled as he gave little twitches. His eyes were wide with horror and pain. He seemed to be frozen in shock.

"Y-you're a monster. You'll go to h-hell," he managed to say.

"Of course I will. *Someone* needs to take the throne."

I laughed and walked back around him.

~•~

I clasped the back of Jack's shoulder and shook him roughly, leaning forward in a serious and slightly mocking voice.

"What did I say Jack? Breathe. It's all in your head," I said.

Jack's head slowly lifted to look up at me. He took deep shaky breath multiple times. As the darkness pulled away from him, he realized everything he just went through happened only in his head. He looked down and lifted both feet. He looked down and saw he still had the flesh on both arms. Looking around, his eyes scanned for blood but saw none.

He began to cry.

I rolled my eyes and walked in front of him.

223

"B-but it was real! I f-felt the p-pain! My body still hurts!" he yelled out in disbelief and confusion. His eyes were getting a crazed glint as things drove him insane. The mind could only withstand so much.

Jack was mentally weak the moment he let the darkness enter him. I, having the power over him and the darkness, morphed what he saw and felt. This all happened within three minutes but for Jack, it felt like hours of slowly bleeding out, making his body and mind exhausted and weak.

I stood in front of him and grabbed his face roughly to look at him coldly.

"I should make you go through that again and make it real. I don't have to though because looking at you now, I can tell you've already lost your mind. No mate, no sense of reality, and you still feel the pain of something that never happened. Now, for that information," I said, ridiculing.

Placing both hands on his head, I forced my mind into his, searching it. He screamed as I forcefully and painfully pulled his mind apart from the inside. His weak mind was not able to do anything because of the exhaustion and mental torture. This was more than his shaken and grieving mind and spirit could handle.

In his mind, I pushed past the moments he cherished most and went into the deeper and deepest section of his mind where he felt his mate's death. The bind that had barely begun to form was breaking and leaving him cold and alone for the first time in his life. His world darkened as he realized what happened. I sorted through until I found the part I was looking for.

"Hmmm," I hummed under my breath, focusing more. This was strange, very strange.

Looking through his mind carefully and making sure to get everything I needed, I pulled back and watched the man slump in his chair. Passed out or dead, I didn't really care.

"Kill me." Jack whimpered in his chair, lifting his head slowly.

I lowered myself to his eye level, making sure he was looking at me in the eyes.

"I should keep you locked up in a concrete room like this, feeling this same physical pain you feel now and making you think you'll never heal. All the while having your mate's things in the same room to let you ponder on what your life could have been like if I hadn't killed her." I stood and walked around him while he began to weep again.

I took hold of his head.

"But I'm on a busy schedule." I snapped his neck.

Walking out of there, I called for two of the men in the building to clean up.

224

Once back in my office, I began walking back and forth, going over what I saw at Albericus when I felt a strong wave of fear from the four wolves I was very in tuned with to check on Vivian.

Seeing my expression halted Albericus mid sentence.

"What is it?" he asked, frowning at me. I lifted a hand at him for a moment.

I remembered I had tuned out on the bond and brought it back to focus, but when I felt nothing from Vivian's side, I began to worry. I could feel her, but I couldn't feel her emotions. She was cold, but I knew she wasn't asleep.

A few seconds later, Luke, one of the guards positioned to guard Vivian, contacted me. His voice was business-like even if I could detect the strain he was trying to hide.

"Alpha."

"Speak. What just happened? Is Vivian alright?"

There was a pause from him that made me freeze and go cold. My beast growled in anxiety.

"She remembers and demanded I let you know that she is to come back, sir."

His voice shook a little at the next part.

"And it's not a request."

My mind was in shock that she knows. Fuck!

"How?" I growled out at him loudly, making Albericus jump.

"She . . . saw us."

"You fucking let her see you?!" I roared at him.

"Well . . ."

He began explaining everything that happened and as he did, I walked over to my chair and slumped down.

"All right. I'll send the plane tomorrow. Take her whenever she wants. Keep me informed."

"Alright sir."

I sighed and ran my hands down my face. She remembered . . .

She. Fucking. Remembered.

"What is it, man? What's the problem now?" Albericus said, turning to look at me while setting his documents down. I looked at him with a tired look on my face.

"She remembers," I said, making him look at me with surprise.

"But . . . how? I mean, what?" he sputtered out, not seeming to believe she outdid a direct command. I felt pride swell at me at her ignoring my command.

225

"She saw the guards and remembered. She's closed her side of the bond off," I mumbled the last part unhappily. He shook his head at me and whistled.

"Don't worry. I'm sure you'll work out your problems," he said with an edge to his voice. We were on the same boat—he and I.

I shook my head at him, making him tilt his head at me in question.

"What? What am I missing?" he asked.

"She threw a knife at Luke, and that was after appearing with blood on her face and pretending to stab herself to get them to come out," he said with his eyes widening on each word.

"Yeaaa, no! You're fucked," he said in a matter-of-fact tone and amused green eyes.

Fucker. I nodded at him.

"Very."

CHAPTER 21

You would think being an eighteen-year-old werewolf would lessen your parents' control over you. Not really.

After storming back home, I began planning what was going to happen step by step, trying to make sure nothing was left out, including my parents. In the end, I decided I didn't want them to be involved just yet. For all I knew, I'd go and beat Zaliver's ass and come back without them getting involved, seeing how well it worked out last time.

During lunch, I couldn't eat just thinking about that conniving, lying blue-eyed little shit. My stomach twisted. Instead, I went up to my room to pack a small bag of clothes and necessities, not knowing if I would even manage to be around Zaliver for long. I wasn't sure how he'd react. A few minutes after packing, Courtney knocked on my door, pale-faced but serious, to let me know that a plane would be on standby for me when I wanted to leave. Eyeing her, I decided tomorrow would be a better day to leave to give me more time to plan.

When my parents came home, I told them in probably the most evasive way possible that I was going on a trip and didn't know when I'd be back. I probably shouldn't have put it like that, but I was being very blunt today with my mood. Of course, they weren't very happy and tried to ask me where I was going and if I was going with anyone. But after pulling the I-am-eighteen-and-more-of-a-supernatural-being-than-you-think rebuttal, they didn't have much to argue with. It was not like I wasn't going to grow up and go one day.

I also pointed out that, at least, I informed them that I was leaving and not just (cough) disappearing randomly. They realized how true that little statement was and left me alone, very much unhappy and worried. Perhaps they did it because of the I-am-not-changing-my-mind look on my face.

Sleeping that night wasn't much of an option for me. A large, if not, a small part of a me believed Zaliver would take advantage of me while sleeping and mess with my head once more. Pacing back and forth that night, I decided that tomorrow—glancing at the clock and knowing it was two in the morning—or actually today I would dress according to my feelings.

Black, it is.

Thanks to the calm storm running in my veins, I didn't feel tired but eager and ready for action.

I went into my closet and decided on an ass-kicking black jeans and a long-sleeved gray shirt, top with a flowy black open vest made of lace. Looking down, I smiled at the only good pair of shoes that matched my outfit—black combat boots. The irony wasn't lost in me. Once dressed, I went into the bathroom and applied black eyeliner. I had used it a few times, but I was feeling dramatic lately, so I sat down on my bed with my fingers drumming an impatient beat.

What the hell was he thinking? Why? Why did he send me home after basically giving me a big speech on how I was his? Bipolar bastard.

Questions and more questions made their way to my head, but I tried to push them out. I needed a strong plan, a back up, and a sideways one. Better safe than sorry.

Zaliver was physically stronger than me; no questions asked. But if some of the things he had told me were even true, especially about how he felt, then I had to use them to my advantage. I smiled as a plan began forming in my head. I recalled everything Zaliver had done to me and came up with an equal payback. I know some people say revenge is unhealthy, but fuck that, he did me dirty and was not about to get away with it.

Morning couldn't have come slower. All night I had walked back and forth, planning and adding on to my diabolical plans. When my parents came, they were both surprised and unhappy to see me awake and ready for my sudden trip. After a lot of hugs, kisses, and are-you-sure questions, I walked out of the house with a promise to call sometime later. I had told Courtney when she came yesterday evening that I would meet them at the park. I didn't want them coming to the house and giving my parents the opportunity to get information out of them.

I tightened the straps of my carrier bag and quickly made my way, knowing there was at least one guard on watch even though it was barely 6:24 in the morning. I was proven correct when from behind me, Mila walked out of the trees and walked up to me with a wary expression on her face a few minutes later. I raised a brow at her and looked away.

"Shall I tell the others to come, Luna?" she asked me. I nodded in her direction and then went to go lean on a tree, not in a talking mood. At least, not with her. I had questions, but I would only get them from one person.

The others got to us twenty minutes later, not bringing anything with them, which made me suspect they had already loaded their things onto the plane. As soon as they were in my line of sight, I stood from the tree and walked in their direction.

"Is the plane ready?" I asked Luke. He nodded briskly with his eyes casted away from me.

"Then let's go." Without another word, he turned and began walking into a different direction. The others followed behind much slower. It wasn't until I looked back that I noticed I had the girls on either side of me and the men behind us. I rolled my eyes.

If anyone should be protected from my wrath, it would be Zaliver.

And even that wouldn't be enough.

I looked down and let out a dark chuckle, my dark locks covering the large smirk on my face. I felt the wariness and hesitation in the others as if they were my own emotions, but they said nothing.

I was surprised when we walked back into plain sight, there were a few wolves out even if it was still early—something they hadn't said anything about. Last night, I guessed they snuck into the pack but now, I was beginning to realize that it might not be that. The thought just seemed to darken my already black mood.

"We're going to take a car out of pack grounds and go to the closest airport," Luke murmured, stopping to look at me as if asking if it was alright.

"Fine," I responded, faking the boredom. He nodded and jogged in front of me, stopping at a black BMW. He pulled out some keys and unlocked the door. I was ready to walk around to hit up front, but when Johnson opened the back door, I looked up at him with narrowed eyes. He just gave me a polite smile in return. Courtney went to sit up front.

"Whatever," I mumbled. I almost felt like they thought I would jump out the passenger seat or something. With Mila and Johnson on each side and Luke and Courtney up front, the car ride was tense and awkward. It didn't help that I was probably emitting hostility and resentment at them too.

I looked out of the window as we drove out of my old pack home, watching the trees as we passed them by. The whole week that I had been inside left me confused. I felt strange and lonely, and I couldn't put my finger on what but I knew now. The moment Zaliver sank his teeth into my neck, I became a part of his pack—his personal pack. Of course, I still felt attached to my old pack but not the same way when I was surrounded by the wolves of the island. I was a little unsure how my life got so complicated.

229

We got to the borders, but instead of pack guards stopping us like they should, a group of wolves opened the gates and let us drive out like nothing and then closed the gates without a glance. As soon as we were out, four large black SUVs surrounded the car, driving in front and behind us. I sat up and looked around, but no one else in the car even blinked at the cars.

"What is this? Who are in those cars?" I asked. Luke looked at me through the mirror.

"More security," he said.

"How many people are in the cars?" I asked with narrowed eyes.

He looked back in front of him and then glanced at me before his green eyes flickered back to the road. I was about to ask him again when he answered.

"Counting all four cars together, twenty guards." Even in my state of mind, I was shocked into silence for a few moments. *Twenty?*

"Why so many?" I choked out after the shock had let me think again.

Who the hell kicks someone to the curve and then give them twenty guards plus four?

"Protection," Johnson said next to me, eyeing on the window with his face tensing.

I opened my mouth to ask something but then shut it. I wanted my answers from Zaliver. I could wait for him to explain this whole mess. I sat back into my seat, crossing my arms over my chest.

When we began driving out of the forest trail and onto the road, I suddenly got very . . . uncomfortable. It wasn't me though; I knew that. But my skin began to itch on the inside, so maybe it was me. I tried not to fidget though I wanted to. All I ended up doing was tensed up. The closer we got to civilization, the stranger I felt. It was almost like a growing irritation and fidgety annoyance.

What is going on with me? Are these some sort of side effects for being away from Zaliver for so long?

It sounded more reasonable. Last time, I ended up throwing up blood. You know what, I would prefer fidgety annoyance over the blood one. I tsked and shook my head, another thing to add to Zaliver's list of fuck ups.

The cars finally stopped at an airport. We went straight to where they kept the planes without being checked up and down. I noted with interest that all the escorts and security we passed were werewolves. They nodded at us and dropped their heads when I passed, which got a few odd stares from humans. It did seem strange though. Imagine a large group of people all dressed in black moving together without even trying to blend in at the airport. Not suspicious at all. No not at all.

230

Something was telling me discretion wasn't on these wolves' priorities.

I was surrounded from all sides by men and women of various figures who stood as equally frightening. I felt oddly at ease even though I knew some of them had their eyes on me. I just lifted my head, pushing back the uncomfortable, irritating, and bad attitude that was becoming very unstable within me. I could feel it bubbling and ready to pop. When we got down to where they kept the planes, Luke stopped in front of a large one that was already open with stairs out and began talking rapidly to a man at the top of the stairs. I checked out the wicked-looking plane. Of course, Zaliver had a plane that matched him.

The whole plane was painted in glossy black with silver outlines. Hell, the plane door was silver in color, and in neat large cursive writing, it read:

Z.A. Line Black Beauty 2

Black beauty 2? I had an incline of hearing that before from somewhere.

"Luna, all seat." Mila nudged me gently, snapping me out of my thoughts.

Everyone was looking at me as if asking for permission to enter. I nodded at her and began ascending the stairs after Luke and Courtney, who seemed to be making sure the coast was clear before relaxing a bit. Everyone else got into the huge plane after me. Entering it, I was surprised to see that unlike the outside, the inside was decorated with white and silver with spacious room, puff chairs, and sturdy white tables. The bastard traveled with taste. I would give him that.

Moving with confidence and a bit of my attitude from earlier, I walked over to the left side of the plane and sat by the window, looking out and letting the others leave me be. There was a brief pause in the plane, so I looked over with a serious face and raised a brow at everyone. They looked away and began to get comfortable. I ignored the plane safety talk, buckled in, and waited for take off.

I wasn't usually this rude to people I had never met, but I really just didn't give a damn at the moment. I had plans and I was ready to get started. As I looked out of the window, I smiled viciously at the reflection of myself. My usual awkward flushed skin was surrounded with my dark strands of hair. My dark brown almost black eyes stared back at me with purpose. I wasn't blind to the almost dark halo surrounding me, but I didn't mind it. I felt like it understood my pain and anger.

I didn't move when the plane took off, holding my breath and releasing it once the turbulence was over. Thankfully, whatever had bothered me calmed down a lot, even my wolf who usually complained about planes was quiet, sulking in the back of my mind. I would think

231

she was completely sad if it weren't for the way her claws came out every five minutes and the feeling of resentment.

"The plane ride is going to be about six hours, Luna," someone standing from behind my seat said. I didn't look and just nodded.

Six hours, huh? Well that would give me enough time to revise my next steps. Whenever one of the guards offered me something, I just shook my head at them or wouldn't even respond, which made them take the hint. I took out my iPod and put my headphones in. If I wouldn't able to block out the feeling from the curious eyes on me, at least I could try to block out noise. It was almost as if God knew my mood because Heavy in Your Arms by Florence + The Machine came on. I sat back and closed my eyes, letting the melody and the lyrics float into me and become one until my body became the words and the melody. I felt the music both in my soul and body.

I couldn't help but hum it softly as the plane flew, knowing the others could both hear my humming and the lyrics. Annoyingly, something I couldn't turn off or control was sensing the emotions of the wolves near me, so I just turned up the music and focused on the next few hours.

Honey, here I come.

Five hours and thirty minutes later, I was ready to face Zaliver.

Anticipation, curiosity, longing, rage, hurt, betrayal, anger, and a lot more emotions overwhelmed my system that I had to continuously take a deep breath to calm down. Sitting in one seat for hours and now realizing how close I was made me antsy. I tapped my nails on the armrest impatiently as I looked out the window to gaze at the now familiar deep blue sea, but this wasn't the kind of blue I wanted to see. I wanted to see the electric blue eyes that pushed me away and left anger lingering in my body.

That man's actions confused me to no end.

Does he or does he not want me? Why? Why send me to my home only to take me back? Why give me guards? Why?

The questions were just building up heavily on my head and in my heart.

How dare he? How dare he confuse me like this?

I shook my head and looked back out the window. This time, I was focusing on my reflection rather than the sea below. An angry woman with narrowed eyes stared back at me, but something was off. I didn't know if it was the way the corner of her lips lifted at one side that left a wicked smirk in place or the melted silver eyes that seemed to glint with malicious promise, but I liked what I saw.

Something was raising in me at the thought of revenge, being played, and disrespected.

Am I just a chewing toy for him? A toy he can toss around and call back?

I felt used once more. It repulsed me to even consider that I was a sweetening chip from the gods to calm Zaliver. It completely shattered and disarmed me to even think that he exactly saw me as a bargaining chip. Not an equal.

My claws had come out and were impaled into the armrest, digging into the fluff. I didn't care as my rage and hurt grew. I wanted to scream. I wanted to shout so loud that my throat burned and hurt. I wanted to laugh until my energy would leave me and tears would take place. I wanted to get rid of the darkness that seemed to be gluing itself to me, calling *pain* home.

But I didn't because I was strong. I wouldn't let these emotions take over me. I took a deep breath, letting the air rush to my head.

Mates. I chuckled at the one word that had so much meaning and so much power.

I was aware of the fact that I was scaring the guards with my random burst of little chuckles and smiles, but who were they to judge?

As the minutes ticked by and the tension in the plane grew, my devious smile did as well, including my grin that was now as large as the cat's from Alice in Wonderland. When the plane finally landed and we all unbuckled, the tension in the room grew even more as a presence I had never felt before became known to me.

I could feel it. I could feel his power, his radiance, his will over others, his presence, and his warmth

His side of the bond. I could feel him.

I closed my eyes and for a brief moment in time, I savored those feelings before closing myself completely and putting on my mask.

The grin fell from my face as a cold and indifferent look replaced it.

Let's see how he would like this.

When the door opened, I didn't come out first. Instead, I let the others go before me. They gave me wry glances, but with a careless gesture, I pushed them forward until I was the last one left. With one last breath, I walked out and onto the stairs. I didn't look at him. No. That would be too easy. I went down with my eyes on my feet, making sure I didn't fall and then looked up.

I almost gasped at the sight of him. Memory did no justice compared to the real man—no, god in front of me. Jet black hair that I knew was as soft as silk. Mysterious electric blue eyes that held so many secrets and silent words gazed at me with breathless intensity. Plump lips that kissed with passion and fever were parted. A face with angled beauty and yet masculine, strong, and fierce feature.

233

What a god he was. My mate as well. Who was in big trouble.

I wouldn't be dazzled by his beauty, not with the way he made me feel. I knew what I had to do, and I knew that I had to do it, not only for me but to show him the error of his ways. My mask didn't break in the outside, but it did crack on the inside.

We glanced at each other for less than what could be a second and then began walking towards each other. Everyone around us were statues and had they been anything else, I doubt I would notice. When we were mere inches apart, we stopped.

He looked down at me with an incomprehensible expression. His lips parted to breath out one word.

"Vivian."

My name. How pretty it sounded coming out of his mouth. My eyes gazed at him blankly as images of the last time I saw him flashed, his words and the previous week shaking the control I had over my anger.

"Why?" I asked him with my voice ringing out clearly for once, loud and cold. His brows came together.

"I had to," he said softly. His hand was coming up to stroke my face, but with one hand, I blocked it from actually touching me, the contact sending a shock through my system. He looked hurt but he understood, dropping his arm and standing stiffly with his eyes looking longingly at me.

You have no right, I said to myself.

"You're the Lupus Deus. You don't have to do anything," I pointed out harshly. My tone came out as animalistic as the raging emotions in me.

"You were in danger. I had to act fast and protect you and your family. I couldn't have you here until it was safe," he explained with his voice hardening along with his face. His words almost distracted me.

No, I needed him calm.

Taking more self-control than I knew I had, I reached up and put my hand on his chest right on his heart. He tensed and then began relaxing again. I softened my facial features, so his guard backed down. I let him reach out to touch my face, allowing him and myself to enjoy this small heaven.

"I've missed you, my little cloud," he whispered softly only for me to hear. He leaned down closer to me, his scent filling my senses.

I trailed my hand up to cup his face, doing the same with the other. I pulled his face down closer to mine until our lips were a breath apart, getting up on the tips of my toes. I gazed into his eyes and replied in the same low murmur.

"And I've missed you as well." I brought our lips together and let him lead us into a soft kiss, which quickly began to turn into much

234

more. I kissed him back with equal energy. I pulled back before we ran out of air and caressed his face with my thumbs. He closed his eyes and leaned into my touch as my mask came back on.

"But I'm sick of your shit." Before he could open his eyes, I snapped his head to the side, breaking his neck.

Zaliver dropped to my feet like a boulder, hitting his head harshly to the ground. I flinched and sighed. Oh well, the damage was already done. Nowhere to go but forward now. Questions would wait a few moments longer.

Gasps and shock range around me. I looked up with a bit of a smirk.

"Oh shit!" Algebra gasped a few feet from me. His eyes widened on the slumped man at my feet. I narrowed my eyes at him.

I then looked to the black dodge challenger behind him, turning to look at the pale-faced and bugged-eyed Luke and Johnson.

"You two, put him in the car," I told them. They came forward slowly and sluggishly.

"B-but you killed him!" Johnson exclaimed with horror. I rolled my eyes.

"He's not dead. Immortal, remember? Besides, had I really killed him, don't you think your mind link would have broke and your wolf would have probably even gone a bit wild?" With the tip of my foot, I nudged Zaliver's shoulder and pushed him to roll over, face up. A bit of his shirt lifted over his abdomen, causing a sudden hunger to come over me. I forced it back before it could become more.

The others could also see the steady rise and fall of his chest. It was like he was sleeping—just a bit unwillingly—and dead, but still sleeping.

Man, will he be pissed when he wakes up? I had to work fast because I wasn't exactly sure how fast he could heal from a broken neck.

They hesitantly walked over to him. At first, I thought they would be enough to pick him up, but when it became evident that they couldn't, two other buff men came over to help. Even then seemed like a struggle. I wasn't very comfortable with them touching him, but I couldn't help.

I decided after knocking out Zaliver, it would be best that I didn't touch him, just in case my touch might bring him back. Something told me it would, besides, better safe than sorry. I turned back to Algebra who seemed to be trying to sneak away by backing up.

"Come here," I said to him. Just by looking at the expression on his face, I could tell he was going to run for it. He would not ruin my plans.

"Algebra, come here. Now!" I demanded, filling my words with power.

235

He scowled at me, his green cat-like eyes narrowing in slits. He made his way robotically with displeasure but with a bit of respect in his face.

"Albericus. Say it with me. Al-be-ri-cus. Albericus," he said slowly, stopping in front of me.

"Yeah, yeah. Albert-help-us and whatever. Listen. I have something to ask you," I said. He looked at me skeptically before his eyes went over my shoulder. He shook his head and sighed.

"Oh for the love of everything holy, give him to me." He walked over to the struggling guys and took Zaliver's side, wrapping a hand under his waist and throwing Zaliver's arm over his own shoulder to keep him upright.

The two other strange guards backed up as Johnson and Luke took up the other side. *Damn. How heavy is Zaliver?* I followed them as they made their way to the car. Johnson opened the car door before they laid my brute out well. They stuffed him in the back seat awkwardly, but he still looked semi relaxed. He looked calm. They closed the door and with an odd look, my way went back to the gaping and whispering guards who were now looking at me with a new expression.

I told Algebra to get into the car and drive me back to the house Zaliver and I had stayed, but first . . .

"As his beta, I'm sure you know how much of a . . . beast Zaliver is, right?" I asked, turning to look at him. He glanced at me and then nodded. I smiled.

"So I'm guessing, at some point, you two figured out a way to keep him down if he ever goes on a rampage, right?" I said sweetly. He nodded after a pause.

"And what do you use?" I asked innocently.

He pursed his lips and shook his head.

"Tell me," I demanded harshly, my face an annoyed scowl.

"Shots."

"Oh," I said, disappointed. I didn't want him drugged. That's the last thing I would want. Then, an idea came to mind.

"Stop by the pack house for a sec." He frowned at me but did so.

Stopping at the pack house, I got out and left a bewildered beta and the car door opened as I ran up. When I got back in the car, Algebra eyed me.

"What's that?" he asked.

"Improvisation," I said blankly.

"I knew he was fucked," he muttered under his breath, and I gave him an evil look.

Algebra drove to the beautiful house that was surprisingly open, muttering to himself the whole time on how I should be helping him. I just rolled my eyes at him and pushed the doors open.

"Lay him on the bed, face up," I stated.

"Oh sure, no problem. Do you want me to undress the god whose neck you snapped as well?" he said sarcastically. I made a face at him.

"I don't know. Do you want to?" He gave me the finger.

"Okay. You can leave. Thanks," I said, standing at the end of the bed and looking down at my very much unconscious mate. Algebra surprised me when he hesitated.

"Are you sure? He's gonna be pissed beyond fuck when he wakes up. I should stay—"

"No, it is fine. Thanks though." With one disapproving, worried yet amused look, he went out the door.

I carefully undid Zaliver's boots, making sure not to touch him too much. When that was done, I moved on to the trickier part of my plan. My heart beat loudly as I carefully moved around him. When I was done, I let out a relieved breath. Now all I had to do was wait . . . or I could have fun with this. I smiled.

Removing my shoes and carry on bag, I gently climbed onto the bed. When he didn't stir, I smiled to myself and carefully threw a leg over him until I was straddling him. Then, I carefully lowered my top half onto him.

Bingo.

He began to lift his head slowly and move it side to side until a pop could be heard. He groaned immediately afterwards, making me tighten my legs together. This must have made him realize I was on top of him because with a few flutters, his eyes snapped open. Furious black eyes met mine.

Boy, is he angry? I smiled down sweetly at him.

"Doesn't this just bring back memories?" I asked him, trailing down the side of his face with my nose. He hissed at me and I giggled.

Rolling off of him as soon as I felt movement, I stood back up and walked to the edge of the bed to look at him with dark glee. He slowly sat up and brought his hands to cup the back of his neck but stopped very quickly. His face grew angrier.

"What the fuck is this? What is this shit?" he growled out at me, grabbing hold of the chains that hung from his wrists.

"Props," I answered.

"What the hell is that suppose to mean?" he snapped, throwing his legs over the bed and standing stiffly on his legs. He stayed still by the bed, glaring down at me. I lifted my head at him.

237

"Never mind that. Now, do you want to explain to me why the fuck you almost killed my dad and then shipped us off? Or why you made me forget? What the hell is going on?" I asked with a demanding tone in my voice.

"First of all, I wasn't going to really kill him. I would never hurt you like that." I snorted at his answer.

"But you would ship me off without telling me why or anything right then and there, right?" He glared at me but continued. I bared my teeth at him in annoyance.

"It was never my intention to hurt you, but if I had to choose between that or your safety, without a doubt—"

"There you go again! Always making decisions without consulting me. We're supposed to be in this together, not one but two people for good and bad moments. It wasn't your call to make on whether I stayed or not. It was mine." I threw my hands up in exasperation, taking steps to him and poking his chest with my finger to emphasize my last words.

He stared down at me with pitch black eyes. His nose flared as he breathed heavily. I realized how close we were and before anything would happen, I quickly backed up, a serious expression took place. No contact.

"There was a leak of information about you. When I was dressing that day to meet your parents, Albericus informed me that a pack member did it for revenge against us," he spoke softly. His eyes moved away from me to look over my shoulder.

I tensed at the news. *So, that's what this was about? Someone shared information about me, but what type? Medical records? Who?*

"What type of information? Who? And to whom?" I asked, my brows coming together.

"The girl that tripped you in the field, whose neck I snapped, apparently met her mate earlier that day. He wasn't too happy about me killing her. He didn't get much information on you, but just with him telling anyone that you were my mate put you in danger. We just learned of that. We weren't sure who and where the person was, so I had to get you away from me incase the first place they would look was here. The island had been attacked before. If you went back to your pack, then no one would question someone they've known their whole lives. I knew you wouldn't go without a fight, so I thought that if I erased your memories, you'd stay away. Although, it would make you hate me and stay away from me once you recalled everything."

His confession left me speechless for a moment as it was a lot to take in. I dropped my head, letting my hair cover my face from him. I could feel his gaze on me.

The girl he killed in the clearing? Her mate wanted revenge and had told someone I was the great Lupus Deus' mate? So . . . Zaliver hadn't been playing with me after all. He just wanted to keep me safe. The insecure part of me exhaled in relief after hearing what he said, but that still didn't excuse the way he did things. The fact that if I let this slide like everything else, he will just do it all over again.

I lifted my head and pursed my lips at him. His eyes widened a bit as if surprised I didn't say, "Oh my hero!" Nope, not here.

"That still isn't an excuse for your previous actions."

He glared at me and opened his mouth to probably start yelling, but I stopped him.

"Shut up." I didn't stop to dwell on my surprise at the fact that his mouth began shutting, eyes still furious.

"Now, I'm going to teach your old ass"—he growled but I ignored him—"something all your years apparently haven't seem to grasp yet. The definition of relationship is equal to partners. As you can tell, I'm also going to get even with you for all the shit you pulled on me. Starting with the forced unconsciousness, then with the waking up with someone over you, and as you can tell, being chained." Slowly, the bastard began to grin at me.

"You do realize I can break out of these anytime, right?" he said, cocky like he defeated some great plan, which he did. I grinned back at him.

"Oh, I know that, but do you want to know something else?" He stayed silent, eyeing me now with caution. His guard wouldn't be dropping around me anytime soon, so he sat back down on the bed. Exhaustion was clear on his face. I felt a pinch of worry bubbled through his façade.

"You won't break out of these chains. You won't break out of them because I'm asking you not to and because you owe it to me. If you truly meant all that mate crap you told me, then by doing all of this, you might just get a chance at getting back on my good side. I don't know about you, but I've been single my whole life and right now, it's not looking so bad." His eyes lightened to his familiar blue as shock and comprehension made way to his face. He sat still and thought for a long time. After a few moments, he spoke with a rough voice.

"Is that what you want?" he asked. His expression was that of someone thinking very hard about something that was yet to come. I crossed my arms over my chest and looked down at him, not saying anything.

"Fine. I'll play along," he gritted out, leaning back against the bed to glare at me.

"Welcome to my version of couple therapy."

239

"So this is it, huh? You know I expected you to be angry and everything, but I never in a million years thought you'd kill me."

"You're talking and breathing, aren't you? So, I never really killed you. I just put you in an unwilling, unconscious form of sleep or at least, that's how I like to think about it."

"So, you're just going to leave me here chained up until you feel better?" he asked with his eyes steady at me, calculating and alert. I shook my head and laughed sarcastically.

"Oh no, that wouldn't do us very well if I just left you here. Nope. What this is going to do is teach you how to communicate with me and make you learn some self-control over your actions. As you put it, you can break out of those chains anytime, but you have two choices. First, break out and continue your road to loneliness because I just refuse to be with someone who keeps things from me, commands, and constantly steps over to control me. That's not how a relationship works. The second is that you can stay here and show me I can actually trust you and learn something out of this. I know it's a bit ironic how I'm going about it, but I'm sure you get the point. Unlike you, I give choices, so the choice is up to you," I said, challenging him with my eyes.

He lifted his chin high and looked me straight in the eyes. As he responded, his face became intense and determined.

"You know I'll stay here if that's what you wish." His answer made me chuckle.

"Why don't I believe you?" His jaw visibly clenched.

"You can," he said roughly but earnestly.

"I guess you'll just have to prove it to me then, won't you?" He nodded briskly at me.

"I guess I will. And when I win you back, I'll—"

"Let's not get ahead of ourselves," I said, holding my hands up. He smirked devilishly at me and stayed quiet, something about the glint in his eyes throwing me off. What was he going to say? Oh well, too late to know now.

I nodded at him, studying him in silence and him, me. I noted how tired he looked, exhausted even, but the aura he gave off didn't change a bit. Power and an animalistic feeling were still coming off of him.

After deciding to give him time to rest, I grabbed my bag and shoes and began walking to the door. Immediately, I heard him stand from the bed.

"Where are you going? Come back," Zaliver said behind me. I turned around and smirked wickedly at him.

"Careful there. Sounds like it might just . . . break." He froze with his hands outstretched and looked down at his chains with clear distaste and annoyance but didn't go any further.

"Where are you going? You just got here." He demanded. Anger was making his skin flush.

"Out," I said casually, riling him up. I was going to be doing that a lot.

"Where is out? With who? Where?" he gritted out, hands clenching into tight fists.

"Where is out? Out is outside. With who? People. Where? Somewhere," I answered coyly. He growled at me and took a step forward but stopped and cursed when a creaking sound was heard from where I attached the chains.

"Vivian."

"Zaliver," I responded with the same tone, mirroring his expression playfully and mockingly.

"You can't leave me here alone," he said as if it would stop me.

"Oh really? Because what I could recall, you had no problem leaving me chained up and alone in your room," I snapped at him. He began running his hands through his hair, the look on his face becoming a bit desperate.

"What about when I'm bored?"

"You have a mind link to every werewolf in the world. Be creative. But here." I walked around him and then back, handing him the laptop he gave me when he left me in his room.

He took hold of it stiffly.

"Entertain yourself." I smiled victoriously and walked out of the room.

"Vivian!" he roared out. With a large smile, I walked downstairs and out the front door, ignoring his infuriated growls.

Now for step three.

"Oh, this is going to be fun," I muttered under my breath, whistling to myself in malicious happiness.

CHAPTER 22

"You're killing me! I can't breathe! Oh my god, my baby!" Hannah wheezed out, breathless.

I rolled my eyes at her over dramatic laughter, but let a few chuckles escape while popping another grape into my mouth as I watched my friend gasp for breath.

"Oh god, I can't believe you left him chained," she said in between laughters, "in the room all alone at home with a computer for company! Oh my god! Beyoncé may be Queen B, Zaliver may be a god, but you're my role model. All hail Queen V!" She began making small bowing motions by raising and dropping her hand.

"Queen V?" I questioned her with a raised brow. I shifted a bit, crossing my legs on the foot stool with her.

"Queen Vengeance." She smirked at me.

I threw my head back and laughed.

"Nice." I clapped with glee.

"Thanks. Man, I missed you while you were gone, and since you took my brother with you, I had no one else but Mark to bother and made him decorate the baby's room like five times," she confessed softly. My smile dropped a bit. I didn't want to damper my mood that had finally lightened with Hannah. She was probably the only person I wasn't angry at.

"So, how is Mark?" I asked. She averted her eyes and plucked a grape, chewing slowly. I narrowed my eyes at her innocent look.

"Hannah, where's Mark?" I asked, amused. *What had she done to the poor guy?*

"Buying a new can of paint, so he can remodel the room again," she said sheepishly before she laughed while I threw a grape at her.

"You are horrible. Poor Mark." I threw another grape at her to which she caught with her mouth.

"Hey, I torture my mate. You torture yours." Her laughter flowed through the house, and I shook my head at her.

The TV suddenly got a bit louder when a certain commercial about medicines came on, making us look at it. I laughed, causing Hannah to eye me.

"What?"

"These make me laugh," I confessed.

"Why?" she asked, surprised.

I cleared my throat and sat up straighter, faking a serious and pleased look on my face.

"Helps you control your problem. Side effects include loss of feeling, depression, weight loss, numbing of the limbs, active allergies, dizziness, fatigue, muscle spasms, and headaches. If you are pregnant or planning to be, ask your doctor before taking the said medicine. If you are middle-aged or elderly, do not take; under or over eighteen, ask your doctor. Possible mood swings, heat strokes, strokes, and even death may occur. If any do happen, please do tell your doctor."

I ended up laughing at the end with Hannah joining me.

"A-as if you can tell your doctor after you die!" Hannah wheezed out.

"They really should just call it what it is! Death in a bottle!" I laughed out, bending over. After a long period of laughter, we sighed and talked a bit more.

"So, what are you gonna do next?" she asked, leaning her head on her hand and turned to look at me.

I put the plate of grapes back on her table and stood in front of her with my hands on my hips and a smile on my face. Hannah sat up and eyed me.

"What?"

"Well, I didn't just come here to say hi. I actually need a hand in the nearby future," I asked a bit slowly.

She became excited, dancing mischievously in her baby blue eyes. She clapped her hands and began bounding on the couch.

"Okay! Okay! I'm in. What do you need?" she asked.

I smiled.

~•~

It was around three in the afternoon when I walked into the house. I closed the door and listened for a moment. When I heard nothing, I made my way upstairs and stood at the doorway to our room.

Zaliver was bundled under the bed with his large frame huddled together; his breathing was deep and even. I stared at him for a moment and went down the hall to a room two doors down. I most definitely would not be staying with him, and I could almost hear him arguing when he found out. I would still need to get my things from the

243

room though. I really didn't want to go in while he's sleeping because knowing him, he'd just end up scaring me with his super senses and caging me in his arms. I dropped the bags in the guest closet; I could handle them later. Going back, I decided to cook something to eat. Luckily, all the food in this house was good. For some reason, I thought that with me being gone, Zaliver would somehow mess the beautiful house up.

I decided on something easy and fast as it was probably the only thing I knew because other than that, I was useless in the kitchen. I knew Zaliver cooked and since I couldn't, I wasn't too happy about living off. I was considering giving him free rein in the kitchen and only the kitchen. I'd have to think it through though. How long could I survive with cereal?

I began cooking spaghetti with garlic bread. Gotta love it. While I was cooking, I gazed out of the kitchen window, not really seeing but thinking. I sighed and continued to cook. Minutes later, I heard Zaliver stirring and then grumbling.

"Vivian!" he shouted out. There was no use in ignoring him since he could probably both hear and smell me and the food.

"What?" I shouted back with a smile on my face as I heard him stand and go as far as his chains allowed him, then curse.

How does it feel to be limited and caged?

Somehow, knowing I had Zaliver right where I wanted him took a lot of my resentment and anger away. By no means was I even thinking of forgiving him, but it did mean that I felt amused knowing he'd be going through what I went through . . . and a bit more.

"Vivian!" he yelled again, and I rolled my eyes.

"What!" I repeated.

"Come up here!"

"Nah!" he responded with a growl and I laughed.

After finishing in the kitchen, I made two plates and put them on trays. Why there were trays here? I didn't know. I put two cups of water on them and carried them skillfully upstairs to an unhappy and very much awake Zaliver. Pushing the rest of the door open with my hip, I walked in. His eyes flickered between me and the food suspiciously. I rolled my eyes at him as I set the plate down next to the bed. I took my plate before sitting on the small couch.

He picked up the plate and fork and poked the food.

"You know, to the person who cooked it, that's pretty damn offensive. And no, I didn't poison it. Where the hell am I supposed to buy poison anyway? I'm sure they don't just sell that shit at the dollar store," I said before I began eating, watching him.

After watching me for a few seconds, he sighed and began eating the food down. It made me stop to look at him, cocking my head

244

to the side. He was eating like a mad man or a really hungry one. Looking at him devour his food, I knew he'd want more, so I sat my plate down next to me and stood. His head snapped up to look at me with alert and worried eyes. I said nothing as I went down to fetch him a another plate and fill it just in case.

Ugh, this will be a pain to wash.

As I entered, I knew I was right to get more when I saw he had cleaned the plate and was currently looking at mine. I handed him the other plate and set the extra on the nightstand with his water.

"Thanks," he managed to say between mouthfuls. I nodded. He was being oddly quiet and non-Zaliver-y.

When we both finished, he drank his glass and set it down on the floor. He sat crisscross on the bed, looking at me with a fixed look on his face. Onto business, I crossed my legs.

"So . . . how was your day?" I asked politely, blinking innocently at him.

"It's been fine. Thanks for asking," he responded dryly. I nodded at him.

"I see you took a nap. That's good," I said while he stared at me. I could guess what was going through his head.

"What's with the small talk?" he asked with suspicion in his tone, shrugging. I leaned back against the couch.

"Did you use the computer?" He nodded slowly.

"What for?"

"Work."

"Your mind link?" I asked again.

"Yes, work related as well."

"What's that supposed to mean? Work related, I mean," I specified when he looked momentarily confused.

"That I used both for my work," he said slowly as if stating the obvious. I controlled the urge to roll my eyes.

"Yes, but I mean like, what do you do? You're a god, so what type of work does that enlist?" I asked, shaking my crossed foot a bit.

He studied my face and skimmed his eyes down my body. I resisted the shiver that wanted to take place.

"What is this? An interrogation?" he asked, amused.

I shook my head with a small smile on my face.

"Nope. I'm calling this official day one of couples therapy, which is focused on you. Welcome to Zaliver 101." I smirked at the end.

He smirked back at me with his hand coming to rub at his jaw. I noted that he was slowly beginning to grow a bit of hair, barely noticeable.

"Oh baby, if you want to know me, I have an idea of where we can start," he said huskily. His eyes were going darker into midnight blue.

"Oh, I'm sure you do. Too bad. I'm not too impressed with what I do know. So just answer the question, will you?" I said, pointing a finger at him.

His expression dropped and became a disturbing dark expression. He looked down, causing his hair to fall over his forehead and cover his eyes. His dark locks were partly hiding his expression. When he looked back up, he had a . . . bothersome grin on his face with his pearly whites showing. Unease grew in me, but I shouldn't be intimidated. I couldn't.

His head was slightly lifted up but also turned to an angle. He looked a bit unstable to be honest.

"So you . . . don't like me then?" he said calmly, but I detected the edge within it. The question actually took me by surprise. I didn't expect that to come out of his mouth.

"That's not what I said or meant," I said quickly, wanting to clear up the misunderstanding. He immediately lifted his head with his grin dropping and blue eyes looking a bit lost and relieved.

"Oh."

Holy shit, why is my heart pounding? It took me a second. After a few blinks and a clearing of my throat, I spoke again, "It just means that you've shown me both positive and negative sides of you, more so the latter. I just want to get to know you better. Since you went through my head without my permission, I'm sort of left with the good old-fashioned way of asking a person—the straight forward route," I explained, trying to lighten the mood.

He looked back down and began to softly run his fingers on top of the unmade bed cover. I watched him closely. When he said nothing, I spoke again, needing to push this further for this steep to work in the future.

"Of course. Unlike you, I won't be able to tell if you're honest or not," I said coolly.

He looked up with a hurt yet fierce expression, his eyes narrowing at me.

"I will always be honest with you," he spoke seriously.

"Will you?" I raised a brow.

"I am."

"Starting now?" I asked, uncrossing my legs and leaning in.

He seemed to grasp what I said and stayed silent, struggling in a mental battle. His brows were furrowed and gaze were calculating. After a moment, he dropped his head, hiding whatever expression he had.

"Even if it hurts me? Even if I don't like it and probably don't want to hear it?" I pushed on. I stood up and then walked up to him on the bed, making sure not to get too close.

He didn't lift his head for a moment, and just when I thought he wouldn't answer, he lifted his head and said, "Yes. I give you my word that I will be honest with you from this point forward even when you don't want me to be," he said with his blue eyes glowing with something I had never seen him with before.

Respect.

I looked down into his unblinking eyes for a moment, seeing the way he gazed back up—worried, vulnerable, and most of all, open. I gave him a small smile. It seemed Zaliver was a fast learner.

"Okay," I said, walking around him to collect the plate and cup.

"Okay?" he repeated, confused.

I went into the closet and grabbed my pj's as fast as possible to change my clothes and threw them over my shoulder. Walking back out, I saw him sat on the bed.

When I walked out, he stood up from the bed.

"Okay? That's it? No questions? I didn't even answer the one you gave me on my work," he said, sounding confused and annoyed.

"Yup," I said, walking in front of him and picking up his glass and then going for my plates. When I turned back around, he was as far as the chains would allow him, making sure it wouldn't snap. His eyes were on the clothes over my shoulders. That's my cue to go.

"What's with the clothes? You're going to come back and change anyway. Just leave them here," he said with a hint of a soft but slightly panicked order from him.

I backed up to the door, and when I stood in the hallway, I turned to smirk.

"Enjoy the bed, babe. I'll be enjoying two doors down. Good night." I shut the door with my hip and saw his eyes went black.

"Vivian, come back here. We're not done talking!" he yelled out.

"Yes we are," I muttered, knowing he could hear me very well. He was just being dramatic by shouting.

"Come back up here! I-I'll answer anything you want!" I smirked and placed the plates and glasses in the sink. I rolled up my sleeves, placing both hands on either side of the sink. I looked up.

"No thanks. I'm no longer interested." With a flick of my wrist, I turned the water on, letting the sound of rushing water out. I heard a crunch upstairs.

Welcome to Vivian 101.

After washing and drying, I quickly ran upstairs, turning off the lights I passed. I ignored the booming Zaliver and went into the guest bedroom. I left the door wide open and made sure to check for any squeaky floorboards. None. Good.

I whipped out my phone and set the alarm for a few hours. Changing into my pj's, I sat on my bed and tried not to sleep, knowing that if I did, I would end up hitting snooze and not get up. I need to do this to complete the last part of this steep as much as I hate waking up in the middle of the night.

It took Zaliver about twenty-eight minutes and forty-three seconds to realize that no amount of shouting would get me to respond to him, so he began to make whining noises. At first, I couldn't tell what they were because I honestly never thought he'd make them. It took me off guard completely. I even got to the door before I stopped myself, reigning in my wolf who was pushing to comfort my mate. After seven minutes and ten seconds of this whining and groaning, he began to growl. I rolled my eyes at this and resisted the urge to laugh at his mood swings. I could most definitely tell who was in the lead of what he must have labeled "Operation Get Vivian Into Bed With Me." I was impressed.

If his wolf—uh, beast—was mostly in control and he hadn't ripped the chains off, then that meant he was respecting my wishes, which was not something I had taken into consideration but should have. When twelve o'clock hit, Zaliver went around and finally laid down. He made his distaste on sleeping alone very clear to me before his breaths evened out, but I knew he'd be a light sleeper tonight, knowing I wouldn't be with him in the same room. It was Basic Mating 101. Gosh, I'm using 101 as an excuse to label stuff . . . eh.

I laid still while counting down the minutes. When I felt my alarm was close, I reached for it and checked the time, 2:08 AM. Good. Before it went off at 2:10 AM, I turned it off quietly as possible and rolled out of bed near the window. It was completely dark and lonely outside. The house was surrounded by what I was guessing was its own gate warding off snooping wolves, but other than that, I didn't know if Zaliver had any guards on duty. Time to see.

Tiptoeing out of my room and past Zaliver's was easier said than done. For one, I knew he was in the room. That alone made my heart race. Sneaking out of the house just made it all the more exciting as adrenaline rushed through my system, making every little sound my enemy and every little movement a barrier. I somehow made it downstairs before Zaliver's heartbeat suddenly took off. I heard him spring silently to his feet before standing still and then seemingly relaxing.

"Vivian."

For the first time since—well, the first time—Zaliver was using the mind link.

"*Yes?*" I answered.

"*What are you doing?*"

He spoke quickly as his emotions strongly shone through the bond, almost knocking me over. Hysterical panic and alarm rang through to me.

"*Nothing. Go to sleep.*"

"*Like hell I will. When my mate is leaving in the middle of the night!*"

He roared mentally and I grimaced.

"*I'm not leaving. I'm just going out for a moment.*"

I began making my way to the door. His heart rate picked up to the point of worrying me a bit. Calm down, Vivian. Knowing Zaliver couldn't die really took a lot of stress off of me.

"*Vivian, wait. Let me go with you!*"

He spoke hurriedly. I heard the faint sound of metal bending and narrowed my eyes upstairs as if actually glaring at him.

"*Not needed. I'll be back soon.*"

I waited with a bit of anticipation for his response.

"*But—*"

"*Trust me that I will be able to take care of myself, especially in our backyard,*"

I said, softening my tone down to persuade him a little. Taking silence as his answer, I walked over to the door and walked out, shutting it quietly.

When I stood on the front yard, I sighed and looked up at the glowing moon that seemed to be considerably brighter tonight. I took a few steps away from the house and walked around to the back, passing by the large pool.

When I was a safe distance away, I focused on bringing my wolf forward. I blinked a bit as it became hard to focus on finding her in me, but I could still see her. She was waiting for me to reach for her. Weird. I took in a deep breath. A moment later, I began to shift after giving control over to her. The back of my head suddenly exploded in a brief moment of pain and then it was gone. I thought my eyesight went red for a moment.

I shook my wolf's head out to shake out the odd feeling my body was having. How long has it been since I shifted? Too long, I guess. I began a steady pace into the trees and around, exploring how far the yard was. It was pretty damn far. We would give an amusement park a run for their money. Why did Zaliver need so much running room? Never mind.

I knew getting up in the middle of the night to go for a run was shady even under the best circumstances, but I had to do it for two reasons. First, because I had to let my wolf out for a run. Second, Zaliver was protective, and I understood that to a certain extent. He had enemies as a god, but his overprotectiveness sometimes made me feel as if he thought he had to protect me from *me*. I had no doubt that if I were ever in any serious danger, I'd let him take charge, but it would be easier if he could see that I had a mind of my own. Perhaps running at night wasn't the best way to go about it, but if I could go for a late night jog, then maybe he'd relax a bit.

I felt like I had been running for a long time. Zaliver's worry was beginning to drive me crazy, so I decided to go back. Stopping in front of the porch, I began to change back, but something was wrong.

Usually when I changed back, it was a painless and quick process where if you blinked, you would miss it. But as the process finished, I suddenly became very much aware of the glow around my body only because it was dimming as if clouds above were passing. A hot and pounding pain exploded in the back of my head. I snapped my eyes open as a tint of fury red and oranges covered everything in my sight, making me gasp.

As the transformation finished, my left wrist suddenly snapped at an unfamiliar angle. I let out a choked scream but clamped my lips shut. I held my breath, letting both the burning need in my lungs and the need to scream to try and overcome the pain from my wrist, which I cradled to my chest. I faintly made out the sound of something snapping as I dropped to the ground from shock at the sudden pain. I took in a shaky breath as my hand and forearm began to throb and yet go numb at the same time. I couldn't tell which it was.

The front door suddenly slammed open, but I didn't look up. I was too busy grunting from shock and pain. I had never broke a bone before the first shift and certainly not after shifting back years later.

A shadow loomed over me and then lowered down to my level. A large pale hand reached out towards my injured hand, making me bare and snap my teeth at it.

"Shh, shh, it's alright. Let me take a look, Vivian," Zaliver's soothing voice called out to me. I looked up at him slowly.

His blue eyes glowed and contrasted against his softly colored skin. His lips were parted and turned down at the corners. Under the moonlight, his jet black locks that were tossed all over his head seemed to have silvery outlines. His hand reached out to me with caution and care. Looking at his hand, I noticed the shackles were still there along with their chains, hanging long and uneven from his wrists. I glared at him. It was dumb, but it took my mind off of the pain even just for a moment.

"You broke out," I accused through clenched teeth. His worried features grew annoyed.

"Give me your hand, Vivian," he said harshly.

Hesitantly giving him my injured wrist, he took hold of it gently. His face may have been hard and harsh, but his touch was comforting. His fingers began to glow a startling white that slowly began to make my hand glow. From our bond, I felt an odd pulling sensation like something within me was being called out. The feeling alone made me take in a breath.

Slowly, a warm sensation came over me, not just in my wrist but the lower half of my body. My lower muscles tightened, making me clench my legs together. My face flushed at the intense feeling. Zaliver was looking completely focused on the task he was on. My wrist began hurting lesser and lesser but suddenly snapped back. I flinched, expecting pain but when none came, I looked at it curiously. As soon as he pulled his hand away from me, the glow ceased and so did the feeling that his hand brought. We were both breathing heavily.

"What was that?" I asked him, looking at my wrist and moving it. It didn't hurt that much now. It was like I just spent two hours straight writing an English essay.

He pulled away a bit and sighed, closing his eyes and rolling his neck from side to side. When he opened them, his bright blue eyes were back. He took hold of my hand and seemed to be pleased with his examination. Worrying it would somehow magically snap again, I brought it protectively to my chest.

"You have around three to four days before your new form is completely ready to come out for a shift. I'm guessing your hand breaking had to do with that. Your body is going through a change to make more room for your other form, so to speak, that can sometimes trigger a false change." As he spoke, I felt the blood drain from my face.

"Three to four? You guess? What do you mean you guess it had to do with my shifting? *You're* the one who god damn bit me. You can't go telling me you're guessing all of a sudden!" I snapped at him.

"Yes, three to four. I said I guess because unlike you, I don't have a wolf, so your transformation will probably end up a tad bit different from mine," he explained, pursing his lips.

I glared at him. I didn't feel entirely sure I wanted to even think about this. The fact that something odd happened in the middle of the night made it safe to say we should put pause on things and head back inside. Speaking of inside . . .

"You broke out," I said, repeating my sentence from earlier.

"Are you fucking kidding me? Are you serious right now? You break a bloody bone and all you care about is me breaking out of these shits to see if you're alright?!" he scowled down at me.

251

"Yes, I'm serious as well as stubborn. You broke out of your chains and left the house." He rolled his eyes and spoke with a weary tone, looking at me.

"Technically, I'm still chained . . . and since I am standing on the last step of the porch . . . I'm still home. See?" He lifted a chained hand and then pointed to the steep he was on. True to his word, he was on the last step and chained. The smug bastard was grinning a bit.

"Fine. Get inside and don't leave then." His eyes narrowed on me and to my cradled hand and then back to my face.

"Hey! Hey, put me down! I broke my wrist, not my legs!" I yelled when he suddenly picked me up and began carrying me bridal style into the house. At first, I began thrashing but it was taking too much energy, and I didn't necessarily feel like being dropped.

"Don't care," he mumbled out, carrying me upstairs.

When he made a turn to go into our bedroom, I straightened my legs and braced my feet on either side so he couldn't enter. I shook my head at him to which he frowned and set me down.

"I'm sleeping down there." I pointed two doors down and began backing up to my room slowly. He took a step but stopped when I narrowed my eyes at him. He looked down at me astutely.

"Thank you for the wrist thing . . . and for not coming out to stop me before that. Good night," I said slowly, and before he could say anything other than good night, I made my way into the room and shut the door.

I threw myself on the bed and exhaled, letting today's stress and tiredness wash over me. Zaliver stood in the hall for a good minute before going into the room.

I rolled under the bed cover and began to get comfortable when I heard bare feet walking in my direction and then some shuffling outside of my door. My eyes snapped open. He is not . . .

I threw my covers off of me and walked quietly over to the door and slowly opened it. I looked down and just like I suspected, Zaliver was on the floor next to my door with a large blanket wrapped around him and two pillows under his head. He looked up at me cheekily. I dropped down next to him.

"What are you doing? Go back to bed," I told him. Sleeping on the floor would probably hurt his back.

"Nope," he said, popping the "p." I shook my head at him disapprovingly.

"Why not?"

"Because that bed isn't comfortable without you. No bed is," he said seriously. I opened my mouth but nothing came back.

"Idiot." He opened his mouth to say something, but I leaned in and kissed his cheek and stood up all in one.

252

"Fuck your back then, but don't come crying to me when you need a hip replacement," I said sarcastically, not wanting him to get away with that.

He growled at me.

"I'm still angry at you," I said, closing the door and climbing into bed.

"I know," he said softly, "and you have the right to be. I can see now that I'm a bit of a jackass when it comes to doing things with you," he whispered the last part, almost like he was speaking to himself. I listened, holding my breath from surprise.

"So . . . I'm sorry," he said in a breath.

"Apology not accepted, especially when it comes from a talking door at like three in the morning," I said playfully, not knowing what to say. He chuckled.

"I'm beginning to sense that sarcasm is a defense of yours when you don't know what to say."

"Good night, Zaliver."

"Good night, my little cloud." I rolled my eyes at him.

It was my only defense.

CHAPTER 23

Waking up wasn't so hard to do, knowing Zaliver was outside of my door. Sleeping did not come easy even though I was beyond exhausted. Being a mastermind was a bit tiring. Didn't know how he could do it for so long.

When I rolled out of bed, I walked over to the bathroom and looked at my reflection. My hair was all over the place, the faint mark of the pillow was on my face, and my eyes looked tired. All in all, I looked like crap. Turning on the sink, I splashed some cold water to wake myself up and rubbed my eyes.

I felt a bit foggy inside, unclear and disoriented. I felt sick for having chills but felt like I wasn't at the same time. Damn. I think it was my wolf who was feeling sick. I gave her a mental nudge, and she gave one back. Okay then. Oh, the miracles of water. I looked into the mirror and was glad to see myself look decent. Looking for a hairbrush and toothbrush was easy. I combed my hair into place and held it down with a spare hair band before brushing my teeth. After using the bathroom and having a quick stretch, I was ready to face Zaliver.

Opening the door, I saw he wasn't there, not even the blankets and pillows. I heard rummaging in the kitchen, so I went downstairs. I didn't really care if he walked around the house, especially if it was to make food. When I walked into the kitchen, I sort of froze at the sight in front of me.

Zaliver was cooking shirtless.

Holy mother of everything tight, tan, and perfectly sculpted. I had to agree with my wolf here; there was definitely a god of all of the above. There had to be, and I was staring at their work.

He turned his head in my direction and smiled at me. His eyes were staring at my gaped mouth. The only thing he had on was a pair of light blue cotton pj pants that were already hanging pretty damn loose on his hips and the swaying chains from his wrist. I'm wide awake now. I shuffled slowly into the kitchen, standing on the other side of the countertop to leave room between us. I licked my bottom lip and then cleared my throat.

"Morning. Where's your shirt?" I asked casually, looking at his muscles as he moved around. Whatever he was cooking smelled wonderful. He kept his back to me as he cooked, but I could hear the smile in his voice.

"Took it off. Didn't really match my chains, so I think I'll just go shirtless for now," he stated.

I hummed in response. Those muscles . . . damn. His back looked so soft and smooth that I just wanted to run my fingers to it and over his shoulders. I didn't know what it was about a guy's back and shoulders that I found hot but man, did I want to feel on Zaliver at the moment.

I guess I must have been too distracted with my daydreaming because I wasn't looking at his firm well-built back but his front. He began to walk towards me with a plate of food and a smirk on his face. I blushed and smiled down at the table.

"Breakfast today will be french toast with cinnamon sticks, fruit salad, orange juice, and a very much willing mate on the side." My eyes snapped up to him with an embarrassed and mortified expression covering my face.

"I'll take all but the last one. Thanks," I said, taking the plate from his hands. He leaned onto the counter and smiled flirtatiously at me with eyes twinkling.

"Are you sure?" he asked, leaning in closer to me while his large frame was towering over mine.

"Yeah," I said a bit too quickly, nerves rattling in me.

"Okay. Later than," he said, pulling away from me and walking back to the stove. I know I probably shouldn't have, but I couldn't help it.

"Definitely later," I said softly. Zaliver's head whipped back around to look at me with a mixture of surprise and excitement that made my heart race in my chest. He actually looked really cute right now.

Right when he was about to say something, a knock was heard on the door. Taking the chance, I hopped out of my seat and ran to open it only to find an annoyed looking Algebra looking down at me. I beamed up at him.

"Hello, Algebra," I said happily and side-stepped to let him in. He pointed a finger at me with narrowed green eyes.

"You have made my job twenty times harder. Stop it." He stepped inside and closed the door. I rolled my eyes at him and then lifted a brow, crossing my hands over my chest.

"It's a pleasure to see you too, Algebra," I said sarcastically. At the at same moment, Zaliver walked out of the kitchen with his eyes going back and forth between Algebra and me unhappily.

255

Algebra walked up to him and took a black messenger bag I just noticed hanging on his shoulders and handed it to Zaliver.

"Thanks. How's everything else?" he asked, opening the bag and pulling out a small stack of folders and what I was guessing was his personal laptop. He pulled out a thick black folder labeled "Private" in red before pushing it back inside. *Hmmm . . .*

"Everything is running good, man. Vivian," he turned to look at me, "let the man work! Now, I'm stuck doing his job. I have a life too you know." He whined at me.

"Shut up," Zaliver snapped at him.

"I thought betas were supposed to be good at handling alpha jobs when it came to it?" I asked jokingly. He shook his head at me.

"Yeah, when it comes to normal alphas not the alpha of all alphas. I'm Beta, one of many," he explained dryly. This was news to me. I looked over him to Zaliver who was skimming his eyes over some papers.

"You have more betas out here?" I asked. He shook his head.

"Out in every pack. You didn't really think alphas chose their betas, did you?" he asked, looking up. I nodded. "Well, they don't. I give each pack a beta that the pack will be comfortable with. He does more work than the alpha themselves—handles paperwork and physical work other alphas won't do and knows more, if not all, of the alphas tricks and decisions. They report back to me, and I decide if an alpha needs to be removed or not," he explained seriously.

"Oh," I said stupidly. My head throbbed a bit but not enough to make me comment on it. I felt like something was . . . tapping. It reminded me when people tap on glass to get someone's attention or out of curiosity. My wolf was huffing. Algebra brought me out of my thoughts.

"See! Everyone is always forgetting and underestimating the beta. We're hard workers too, you know. Now, I have more work to do with his royal highness gone. Come on, Luna. Cut the guy a break."

Zaliver smacked the back of Algebra's head with a little too much force, then I thought he should have given.

"Ow! Shit, man! That hurt! All I'm trying to do is help a buddy out and what happens? I get hit. This is abuse of power, Zaliver! If I didn't know you enough, I'd protest but I'm sure you'd kill me!" Algebra shouted while rubbing the back of his head repeatedly. Muttering under his breath, he began walking back to the front door.

"Later losers," he said and then he was gone.

I looked after him and then turned to Zaliver. He was shaking his head with displeasure and annoyance.

"Your beta is weird."

256

"I know but he's good at his job and loyal, so I like to keep him around," he responded dryly. I looked at him and his paper stack.

"Are you gonna work?" I asked him. Those were a lot of papers, like enough to have me wanting to procrastinate on finishing them and they weren't even for me.

"Yeah, unless you—"

I shook my head. There was no way I was about to pull him away from all the work he had to do. I'm sure even Algebra would strangle me if he got less back than what he brought. He'd find a way.

"Go ahead. I'm gonna go do stuff around the house."

Before he could say more, I went into the kitchen to finish eating and then went upstairs when I was done.

Back in our room, I couldn't help but change with a small frown on my face, not completely sure why I was displeased at the moment. I decided I wanted to go for a swim in the pool. Why not? It was a part of the house that needed to be enjoyed and so far, I hadn't paid it much mind. I picked out probably the only bikini I could pull off. It was a deep midnight blue top tied around my neck and back while the bottom was black from the back and blue from the front. On top of it, I threw on a long somewhat see-through loose dress. I found some flip-flops and a towel and went downstairs. Zaliver wasn't in the living room or anywhere I passed, so I assumed he had a home office here.

When I made it to the pool, I threw my towel and took my sandals off along with the dress. Removing the hair band, I ran my fingers into my hair and soothed my scalp. Sometimes ponytails did more damage than help. I was a bit self-conscious about Zaliver seeing me, but I had always done things that made me feel uncomfortable to get out from my comfort zone. Him being my mate somewhat made it worse, but I just kept chanting, "He's my mate. He's attracted to me. If he complains, fuck him. I'm beautiful." That seemed to work even though I was sure that if he did say something, I would end up feelings a little hurt.

Jumping into the pool was a bad idea since I came back up sputtering and laughing at how cold the water was. Soon enough, my body became used to the temperature. For the most part, it was always sunny and warm on the island, but today was the perfect weather for swimming. I took in a breath, went under water, and began to swim. Playing in the water, I couldn't help but think about Algebra's complaining.

In a sense, he was right. Telling Zaliver not to leave the house was causing a bit of a problem for him. I was guessing Zaliver could leave at any given time he wanted, but he couldn't because I had asked him not to. I went over to a wall of the pool and stood, staring into the

257

clear blue water. I put the tips of my fingers into the pool and moved them around, feeling the lightness of my hand.

This led me to think that maybe trying to teach Zaliver a lesson made me seem childish. Was this childish? Getting back at him? Hmm . . .

I was breaking down part of his walls but in doing so, I might not be doing it correctly. Maybe I should allow him to leave the house when he pleases? I mean he did keep me chained to the bed for like a full day but spent the rest of his time with me. Besides, it's not like he won't be around me when he wanted to, which used to be all the time. Let's be honest here, Zaliver didn't seem like he liked me hanging out with people without him. He would check in either to see if everything was alright or to remind me of him as if he was easily forgettable. I snorted. Not even mind control got me to forget about the bastard.

I'd just have to get back at him from a different angle that would have the same effect as the one I was doing now. Or should I drop it?

I don't think so . . . but . . .

We could just sit down and talk. Those would all just be words and promises that might get broken. I thought we were more of a hands-on couple.

Couple. Did we even behave like a couple? But if I did let him be, I could use it to an advantage. Him being not around the house I mean. That made it sound better I guess.

I groaned. I was overthinking and overanalyzing everything, messing with my head. I was beginning to doubt myself. I felt a little bit of annoyance grow in me, but it wasn't mine or my wolf's since it wasn't coming from the bond. I took a guess. It was coming from what was probably my new growing beast's consciousness. This was the source of my extra feelings lately. My new beast.

Ugh, something else to think about.

I looked up into the sky and closed my eyes, feeling the relaxing breeze drift by. I loved the tropical smell and the richness of the scents the island gave off; the sea wasn't even a problem once my wolf got used to it.

Was I ready to take on a new form? I didn't know much about it; how it worked and the difference between a werewolf and a lycan. I'd have to ask Zaliver and he'd have to answer. I thought I had avoided even thinking about taking on a new form. All my life, I had only known my wolf. Just thinking about changing into something other than a wolf was frightening. It didn't help that the new form I was taking on was one that you'd only hear in horror stories. How would my parents react? Shit! I forgot to call them. I hit the water with a groan. I would have to call them later.

I went underwater and began swimming, letting my thoughts just float away. It wasn't until an hour later when I finally got out of the water and dried myself. I steamed into the house wrapped in a towel. I saw Zaliver pacing back and forth in the hallway with an open door in front of him. I stopped to watch, leaning on a wall. I knew that he knew I was there because of the brief pause, but he didn't stop, so I assumed he didn't care if I overheard.

"Find the damn entrance. That door doesn't just disappear and you know it. I expect you to be able to do this while I'm out but if you can't, do that . . ." his voice trailed off.

"I will find the door, sir. I apologize for my call. I will be done before you return," the man on the phone spoke. Zaliver scowled at the ground.

"You better and fast," Zaliver snarled into the phone. He ended the call without another word. Closing his eyes, he took in a deep breath and cracked his neck side to side. When he opened his eyes, he turned to face me slowly, but his face lost some of its harshness as seconds passed.

"Work problems?" I murmured. He nodded but roamed his eyes. I clutched the towel closer to me. I was suddenly much aware of his masculinity and my lack of cover.

His hair was in the same messy style that worked for him with a few long strands over his face. His stance was strong and alert. He tucked his phone into the pocket of his pj bottoms and tilted his head to the side with a particular look sparking in his eyes. It was as if I hadn't just been sore from swimming and was suddenly energized.

"You went for a swim," he stated simply, walking over with long strides.

"Yeah, the pool is awesome—" I began to talk, but he interrupted me.

"You, love, are very beautiful and certainly ravishing," he said huskily. I froze mid sentence and saw the look on his face halting me. My wolf raised her head, interested and flattered.

"*Take me now then,*" my wolf said.

"*Shut it,*" I snapped at her.

"*Look at that body. Mmhh, I'd like to run my tongue down those abs.*"

"*What part of "shut it down" do you not understand? Not helping.*"

"*Girl, I don't want to shut. I want to hump, thump, and fuck—*"

I tuned her out even if she did have a point.

I eyed him as he leaned over me. His hand outreached to cup my face with gentleness. His thumb moved back and forth on my skin. He leaned down closer. His face above mine studied me with twinkling eyes that reminded me of gems; there was lightness in them. My lower muscles tightened. Was he always this hot? I was getting a strong urge to

259

do something with him that would get me a first class ticket to hell. It didn't help that my wolf was adding little comments on how it would feel to have his arms around us and something else in us. She'd get a separate ticket too.

He leaned his head in closer, skimming his nose down the side of my neck and inhaling.

"You smell wonderful," he whispered. I let out a high-pitched laugh out of both nerves and confusion. It was one of those cringe-worthy laughs that you wish you could take back as soon as you heard it.

"I smell like chemicals . . . like a pool, you know?" He pulled back and shook his head, looking at me as if seeing me not for the first time but with new eyes. It made me feel raw and on display.

"No. You smell . . . different. Sweeter. Mouth-watering. Makes me want to taste . . ." he trailed off. The corner of his mouth pulled up to smirk devilishly at me. I took a step back for the sake of my heart and because I shouldn't be seduced.

"Okay weirdo," I joked. He rolled his eyes and dropped his hands, making the chains shake. I looked at them for a moment and sighed.

"You can take them off," I said warily at him.

"Are you aware of what you're saying?" he asked, raising his hand. He put his right hand around his left wrist and paused.

"Yeah."

"I'm free?" he asked.

"From the house, yes. From me? Not so much." He grinned down at me.

"And I wouldn't want to be," he said. A second later, he clamped down on the chain before his hand fully got to my face. The chains crumpled under his strength like styrofoam, breaking into little pieces around his fingers. I watched in surprise.

"Damn." When I looked up at Zaliver, he had a proud look on his face.

I'm gonna go shower, are you?

"Yes," he replied fast. I frowned at him in confusion.

"What?" How did he know what I was going to ask?

"Yes, I will join you." He took hold of my towel and began tugging gently. I smacked his hand away and backed up.

"I wasn't going to ask that, dummy. I was gonna ask if you were going to leave," I said over my shoulder, moving away from him but his footsteps followed.

"I'll stay here for the rest of the day." I went up the stairs and into the bedroom to grab some of my clothing. When I walked out of the room, Zaliver followed me into the room I was staying at with an annoyed look on his face but didn't say anything. When I tried to close the door on his face, he put out his hands and stopped me.

"What?" I asked, pursing my lips at him. My suspicion was obvious. I bet he was going to say something stupid.

"We really should shower together, save water, and all that shit," he said earnestly.

See. I shook my head at him and looked up at the ceiling as if asking for divine guidance.

"Wanna really save water?" I asked slowly, smiling up at him as if I would actually consider his idea. His face lit up with excitement.

"Go shower in the ocean then." I pushed him away from my door, knowing he let me with a scowl. I laughed though the door.

I was washing the conditioner out of hair when the faint tapping began again; this time with a pounding force. I started rubbing at my head not to wash out but to sort of massage my head. When it went away, I began washing my body. The water seemed really warm.

I didn't realize it, but I was breathing a bit harshly. I turned up the cold water and turned down the hot water. I put my head on the wall tile and let the water rain down on me. It wasn't as if I couldn't catch air but rather as if I wasn't getting enough. My limbs left me feeling weak, almost heavy at the same time. My head had a dull throbbing, which was stronger this time.

My body felt warm inside out. I could actually feel myself sweat a bit, which was as alarming as the pounding returned into my skull. It felt like I was coming from one part of my brain and echoing throughout the rest of it. I raised my head and decided I should get out with the way I was feeling. The water was not helping at all.

I turned the water off and immediately felt like I had just been hit in the back with a metal bat as the surprise of the sudden pain made me stumble back and almost fall. My body was suddenly super sensitive and yet fully aware of new incoming pains as well as my back, my chest, and my mouth. My eyes seemed to be having a hard time focusing.

I clutched onto the side railing quickly as the pain progressed. Wrapping a towel over me and grabbing onto the sink, I looked into the foggy mirror. I raised a shaky hand and wiped the mirror. My claws were back out, lengthening and shortening without my control. It hurt. My fingertips hurt. My wolf was letting out distressed whimpers.

My wet hair clung to my skin, making the dark locks show just how pale I looked. My eyes were wide with pain and panic while my pupil was growing larger than the iris. The iris, on the other hand, was outlining it in a constant chaining brown. From what I could see, my dark brown was lightening and then darkening back and forth. I opened my mouth to see how red my gums were. They hurt like mad. I instinctively raised my hand to feel on them but stopped at the sight of my claws. I'd cut myself if I put them near me.

Where the hell did this suddenly come from? My back began to throb. A single spot felt as if someone was pinching me from the inside or better yet digging claws into me; the sharpness was making me gasp. My eyes began to water as I slid down the floor. My energy was leaving me as my body was suddenly taking so many different attacks from itself. What's happening to me? I began crawling out of the bathroom. Zaliver. I need Zaliver.

I managed to get out of the bathroom and towards the edge of the bed before I gave up. I was half wishing to pass out and half wanting to call out to Zaliver, but I couldn't think straight. I couldn't find my voice. I didn't recognize my own mind.

My heart was pounding in my chest. My lungs were begging for air as all I could only manage to do was gasp as my mind tried to focus on one singular pain out of all. My hands began to fist, my claws cut into my palm, and the scent of blood filled my nose.

Not even a second had passed when the bedroom door burst open. Zaliver ran into the room with a crazed look on his face as he saw me half crawling and half lying on the floor. He dropped down onto his knees and leaned over me with hands outstretched to touch me while I looked up at him with watery eyes.

"It hurts," I moaned out to him. Pain was laced in my words.

Zaliver looked down at me with anguish and despair on his face. His eyes flickered all over my crumpled body. After a painful minute, he cursed and scooped me into his arms. I let out a bellow as my body protested at the sudden movement.

"I'm so sorry. It's okay. It's alright. You're going to be fine. You're okay. I've got you. It's okay," he repeated over and over. He spoke in a way I had never heard him speak before. He almost sounded sacred, which in turn frightened me.

I could feel him moving with me in his arms, but I closed my eyes and placed my face where his neck met his shoulder, letting his scent soothe me as much as it could. As he moved, he kissed my forehead and nuzzled me, mumbling in between kisses and touches. It was a small but welcoming distraction.

His woodsy scent calmed me down. I felt the cool air rush past my face. When he stopped, I opened my eyes, looking forward and not daring to move my head. Knowing a new pain would start, I could almost feel a soft throb behind my ears as if my muscles were tight and unused. My heart beated so fast that it was beginning to hurt me. Was I going to have a heart attack? I wondered through my pain and infused thoughts.

We were in the forest with many trees and vines. It couldn't possibly be used to go on runs. The large amount of clumped-up trees and dangling wild vines blocked out some of the sun in the sky, providing shade, but the sun shone out through some places, creating spots on the small patch of grass Zaliver must have walked on. I heard a sound of rushing water and wanted to turn and look but a sharp pain in my chest made me cry out. He began to walk faster. When the sound neared and my feet felt icy cold, the towel around me was becoming heavy. I realized Zaliver had carried me into the water. Over his shoulder, I made out the shape of a waterfall a few feet away.

The cold water made my body go numb and the green scenery and air made my senses calm, but the pain were still there. Zaliver walked deeper into the water until a part of my face felt the splashing of the small waves all the way to his mid chest. I still clutched to his shirtless chest.

"Vivian, I need you to shift for me into your wolf form," he pleaded frantically.

I made a sound in the back of my throat, not having enough energy to even think about his words. I just wanted to sleep and let darkness claim me. I felt so heavy. So tired.

"Hey! Hey! Baby stay with me. Come on. I know you can do it. Please Vivian, I need you . . . Shift for me," he implored. His voice took on a new tone. I shifted my head to look up at him. His expression was unreadable.

"Okay," I whispered.

I closed my eyes and called out to my wolf, but she wouldn't listen to me. She couldn't hear me. She was whimpering in a corner. Her paws were over her ears as if blocking something out. I tried to call out to her again to no success as I was losing energy.

"I can't," I said hopelessly. Zaliver's arms tightened around me. He shook me when I closed my eyes. My eyes fluttered.

"No, no, baby. Try again. Come on, my little cloud. I know you're tired, but you have to shift. You'll feel better, I promise. Come on. Yes, that's it." I closed my eyes tightly and instead of calling out to her, I focused on the feel of Zaliver's skin against mine and how his warmth emanated from him even in the cold waters.

I focused on the sound of his voice as he begged softly. I could hear the sound of his heart. Oh, his heart called out to me. Strong and loud. My wolf raised her head at the familiar and welcoming thumping.

"Home. Safe," she whispered.

I called out to her and she listened.

"Oh thank god," Zaliver said once I began shifting in his arms, slowly but surely.

Once I was done, my wolf wasn't comfortable. Feeling she would drown, she tried to paddle. Zaliver shook his head.

"It's alright. I've got you," he said. His face looked relieved. He soothed me.

He supported my wolf's head on his shoulder and kept one hand under my body for me to lay in the water and float. The cool water soothed whatever remaining pain I had. I let out a relieved breath.

"Better?" he asked, cupping some water and wetting my fur.

"*Yes.*" I responded through the link.

"I'm glad," he said. After a moment of silence, he leaned down and nuzzled me.

"*What's happening?*" I asked, looking out into the quiet forest. The animals hid at the presence of larger predators. He sighed.

"We've been away from each other for so long—"

"*And who's fault is that?*" I couldn't stop the comment from slipping out even if my life depended on it.

"And it seems like every time we're apart, our bodies or in this case, your body can't take it. I'm a lycan and you're born a werewolf. Werewolf bonds can last up to months without the need of pushing for a marking or mating, but a lycan's mark is different. Our bond isn't like any other, Vivian. We might not die, but being apart from each other might be the closest thing we'll get to it. We're pushing a bond that I'm not even sure how it works. We're one of a kind. Now that your body is getting closer to the shifting day, it's panicking. Like I said, you're a born shifter and now a new form is trying to adjust. I was just created with one form. I'm sorry you have to go through so much for me.

"You're right. I am a jerk. I forced a mark on you without your consent and altered your life in more than I had the right to do. I can't tell you how sorry I am that you're stuck with a pathetic excuse of a man who's only a shell of what he used to be. I'm sorry I'm a complete domineering monster who craves you to be at my side at all times and that I'm never going to let you leave me because I'm selfish enough to put my happiness over yours. I'm sorry that out of all the men in the world you could have been mated to, you got the broken one with baggage. I'm so—"

"*Stop,*" I pleaded. My heart broke into little fragments at his tormented blue eyes.

"But—" He frowned at me. His brows pulled together as if he didn't understand that his apology hurt me.

"*Don't talk about yourself like that,*" I said.

If it weren't for the fact that I was tired both emotionally and physically, I would have shifted back to both kiss and yell at him.

He looked at me intensely for a long time. His eyes searched mine as mine were to his. I felt him search through the bond, so I opened and dropped my walls. I was not entirely comfortable with dropping my walls and being so vulnerable, but I needed him to see that it truly upset me on the way he talked about himself. It seemed like more than just self hatred; it was as if he had no idea what to do with himself anymore and was just living to do so.

"*You're not a monster. You're Zaliver. My Zaliver,*" I spoke softly, letting him both hear and see that I meant every word I said.

"Okay," he said but I could hear the uncertainty in his voice. I wanted to distract both him and myself from those dark thoughts.

"*Can you talk about something else? I don't really care. I just want to hear your voice.*"

He nodded at me and did the most surprising thing; he began to sing. He looked away from me and just focused on wetting my fur, running his hands soothingly though my body. I looked at him as he sang softly. His voice had a deep melody of its own. I had once asked Zaliver what his favorite song was but he responded negatively. I realized he didn't tell me because the words to the song would give his vulnerable heart away. I recognized this song. It was Underneath by Adam Lambert. It was beautiful. It was heartbreaking. It was somehow Zaliver.

I think this was it. He sang to a beat only he memorized. My eyes closed as his voice made its way to me. His own deep voice added depth to his words without cracking or breaking. He was steady. Somehow his voice complemented the song, giving it what I was sure was a new form of itself. He was beautiful. Listening to him sing made me fall into a peaceful zone. And so there we were, two people with totally different backgrounds and upbringings trying to understand and give each other what we needed. At the end of the day, something finally stood out. Love. I fell asleep in my mate's arms, listening to him singing a sad melody.

CHAPTER 24

Waking up in Zaliver's arms and feeling the cool water around me was comforting. I felt much more energized and rested. Zaliver still stood with me in his arms, but he was quiet as he ran his fingers through my fur. He must have been doing this for a while. His body tensed and his breathing harsh. There was still light in the sky. I didn't know how long I slept.

Without saying anything, I shifted back into my human form in his arms. My body no longer hurt. If anything, I felt like I just woke up after a long and hard work out. Zaliver looked down at me blankly, not sure what to say. I just looked at him while his arms were wrapped around my waist. Bringing myself close, I put my hands on his shoulders and looked into his piercing blue eyes.

"How long have I been asleep?" I asked. My voice had a slight rasp to it from crying. He didn't respond and just looked down at me, not saying anything. He lifted a hand and cupped the side of my face and pulled me in closer.

"What?" I asked. Why was he so quiet?

He answered me by quickly leaning down and capturing my lips with his. Taken off guard, I didn't respond immediately, but I did when he snarled between tugging on my bottom and top lip. I responded eagerly even if his sudden action left me surprised. His kissing was not sweet and gentle like other kisses. This one was rough, fast, and passionate. His lips moved all over me, making me respond just as he was.

I wrapped my arms around his neck and took his hair roughly in my hand, pushing him closer to me. He made a sound that flared me up even more. The cold water didn't help in stopping my temperature from rising. Zaliver grabbed my hair and pulled with the same force I used on him, making me gasp out not in pain but at the strange sensation that it gave. He took the opportunity and slid his tongue into my mouth without hesitation, claiming my mouth. His taste invaded my mouth out of instinct I guess. I began sort of massaging his tongue with my mouth.

We made out for a very long time, and when I felt his hand slither down my leg and under my butt, my eyes snapped open. I realized I was just in a soaking towel that felt pretty damn loose, like really damn loose.

Snatching my hands away from him quickly, I tugged the towel back up my chest and tried to backup only to realize that he was supporting my body in the water. It felt like I wasn't even standing on anything. He pulled me back to him with hooded black eyes, gripping my waist. With the hand that was still under my butt, he pulled me to him, hoisting my leg around him. I blushed when I felt the towel rise.

Where the hell is this coming from? Oh, who cares!

He leaned down and began trailing wet kisses down my neck, not trying to be quiet about it either.

"What are you doing?" I asked him, my voice a breath away from a whisper and yet wanton at the same time.

"Mine," he growled out. His voice was rough and disoriented.

"What—" I interrupted myself by letting out the loudest moan I had probably ever released in my life. I couldn't even feel embarrassed because he had began kissing and nipping at his mark.

I had forgotten how it felt to have him touch me there, even more feeling him kiss me where his mark was. He pulled at the bond. My skin felt like it was on fire every time his skin touched mine. I forgot about my towel and let go to wrap my arms back around him. My lower half pushed itself closer to him. I felt him do the same.

The blood in my veins rushed through my body faster. My heart was beating out of control as my body begged only for his touch. His hand slowly slid down from my back to the bottom of the towel. He halted and pulled back his face to look at me. I was stuck in a hazy fog of lust for him that I didn't care if he was about to ask me if he could. I just pulled his hair and his head to the side and brought my lips to his neck at the same time that he slid his hand under the towel to cup my butt. Skin on skin.

I wrapped my other leg around him, making his other hand released my hair and cupped my other cheek under the towel. I took the opportunity and leveled myself a bit higher than him. I kissed down from his jaw to his neck, going back and forth like he did. When his neck met my shoulder where my mark was, I nipped at him, wanting to see if he would feel anything.

His hands that had been slowly mending my flesh suddenly squeezed hard, causing me to let out a squeak. His hips bucked forward and grounded me onto him. He let out a long moan that caused a pleased and mischievous smile on my face, making me want to hear it again. I bit at the same spot and then blew gently on his skin, making him grind onto me again. The cold water had caused his pj pants to stick

267

to him that I could feel everything. Everything. His erection pushed into me as much as I pushed into him.

I ran the hand that wasn't holding onto his hair down his back, scraping my nails as I did so. He pulled his head from me and brought his lips back to mine. I wanted to feel him closer. I wanted him, needed him. Zaliver's emotions and himself seemed to be all I could think about, to feel him both emotionally and physically. It felt like if I didn't have him now, I would die.

I had red lights flashing in the back of my mind. I should know what was happening, but I couldn't quite grasp it.

He pushed my bottom half onto him with a grunt as I let out a shaky breath. Something in me was pushing for more, needing for more. My wolf was on the same boat. Zaliver suddenly pulled back with a groan. I did as well. Both of our breathing were fast and loud.

"Fuck," he muttered. I laughed.

"You can say that again," I said, looking at how red and swollen his lips were, which made me want to kiss them some more. I hadn't noticed I was leaning forward until Zaliver pushed me back. I pouted at him, not liking how far he was from my lips. The nagging feeling came back . . . but why?

"Oh man, never thought I'd be the one pulling away," he muttered under his breath, slowly releasing me until his hands were placed firmly on my waist. My arms that were still wrapped around him tried to pull him down to no avail.

"So don't," I stated. He raised a brow.

"As much as I'd like to take you, I'd rather do it when we both have a clear head and you're not beginning your heat," he said.

His words made the nagging in my head come forward with a big ass sighed that read, "Told Yah!" My eyes widened up and my body was freezing.

I was beginning my heat?

Seeing my expression, Zaliver sighed and hugged me, taking my head and placing it on his chest where his heart was.

"When a female werewolf goes into heat as you probably know, she's the one to feel all the side effects unless taken cared of by a male or her mate. Her scent changes, pulling in other males who aren't mated. However, it seems like in our case, your scent riles me up into a lust craze that makes me attack you, pushing your heat forefront. You changing into your new form might add to your heat. How interesting," he mused the last part to himself.

Of course, it's interesting to him. In the end, he would get to mate with me and complete the bond. I was frozen in his arms.

I was going into heat? Damn.

True to his word, when a female werewolf was in heat, her body would go into different heating stages that could only be eased with sexual contact with a male or her mate. If not, the female could suffer alone with medical aid. Males going through a similar stage had never been heard of. The males would usually just become much more aware of the females' stage and would be eager to mate and produce pups. But if what Zaliver said was true, then what? Every time I had a brief moment of heat and he caught my scent, he would get turned on, turn me on and then fully activate the whole lust cloud? Damn.

Was I ready to mate? That question brought a whole lot of mixed feelings and thoughts. I was not sure what I felt to be honest. I had been through the heat cycle before when I hit sixteen. That shit hurts worse than cramps. It was like getting punched from inside out or getting your insides set on fire, then hosed down with a fire hose at full pressure. It felt like you got millions of tiny little crystals stabbed into you and then separately at the same time.

Could I take that pain again? Nope. But, could I do *it* with Zaliver?

I pulled back a little to look at him. At the moment, he looked peaceful and calm. He looked down with his blue eyes gleaming in the natural lighting with his arms tightened around me. It seemed as if mother nature herself rooted for him, making him look irresistible to me or maybe it was my heat beginning to start.

Pulling me out of the water, Zaliver scooped me up again the way we got here and made his way out. I secured my towel to myself, now realizing he actually got to feel my butt and I let him. I began to turn scarlet. He lifted a brow at me that just made me shake my head and put it on his chest.

Ahh! Oh my god, he felt my butt! I didn't know why I suddenly felt all strange with him. Midway to the house, I finally figured out why.

It was real.

This whole situation was real. I was really changing. I indeed had a mate and we were going to mate together, binding each other forever. My fingers began to twitch a bit.

Remember when I said I could usually take a sudden event without fully freaking out because I usually had late reactions? Yeah, I thought this was it.

I guess knowing you have a mate whom your supposed to be with and live happily ever after was way different from actually living day by day with them. I somehow felt like through all of the ups and downs with Zaliver, I had held back on him. Knowing Zaliver was there for me was nice and comforting, but was I holding back on him because I

269

wasn't ready? Because I didn't trust him? I was such a hypocrite. Here I was trying to get the man to trust me when I didn't know if I did myself.

Being in a relationship and giving yourself fully to your partner were leaps of faith and trust that were easier said than done. These thoughts began clouding my mind, making me review some things. Why was I doubting myself all of a sudden? Or had these thoughts always been there and were now resurfacing when things were about to get real and serious between us? I didn't have commitment issues, so was I just scared of getting hurt?

When we got to the house, Zaliver put me down and stood there looking at me. I looked back at him with a frown on my face. His expression dropped to one of concern for me. I turned and began making my way up the stairs with my wet towel, not really knowing what to say. And this all started with a butt grab from him.

I stopped mid stairway and turned back around to look at Zaliver. His forehead creased as he looked at me silently with his hands crossed over his chest. I began going down the stairs again, keeping my eyes on his. When I stepped off the last one and passed him, he began to turn around as well to face me but jumped in the air when he felt both of my hands on his ass.

"Whoa! Not what I was expecting!" he said loudly.

Maybe if I felt on his butt, my doubt would clear?

I looked down at my hands that were on him. His bottoms were wet just like my towel. It clung to his form. He had a really nice and firm butt. To prove my point, I pinched a cheek.

"Okay!" he said, jumping out of reach from me. I looked up with a serious expression, ready to tell him to come back, but my expression morphed to that of surprise at his red face. His blue eyes kept flickering over me and then away, repeatedly blinking and clearing his throat. The tips of his ears and face became red and flustered. His expression made me laugh out loudly.

It wasn't exactly how I thought this would go, but I liked this flustered, embarrassed looking Zaliver. I gasped as I continued to laugh, needing air as I bent slightly. I made sure my towel was securely under both of my arms as I laughed. The water weighed heavy to go against. His face became a mixture of grim happiness. He crossed his arms over his chest again and shook his head at me. His face was cooling down, but the tips of his ears were still red.

"Well, I'm glad to see you enjoying yourself at my expense. Even got a feel, huh?" he muttered in a sulky, teasing voice. I walked up to him in a better mood and in the moment, reached up and pinched his cheeks.

"Aww, you look so cute all—" I forgot that my towel was held up by the pressure from my arms, so when it dropped to the floor with a loud swish, we both froze.

Hahaha, yesss! The moment I've been waiting for, my wolf hissed.

Why did I somehow always manage to get myself in situations out of my league?

Before I could blink, I was slammed up against a wall and had Zaliver's lips on mine. His body loomed over me. His hand pinned me up and the other had my leg wrapped around him. In the back of my head, I wondered if he saw anything. Of course he did, didn't he?

My body temperature began to rise while a little vaguely familiar heat slowly began to form in my stomach, slowly traveling all over until I was hot and bothered and back to fogged up with lust.

Fudge.

This was nowhere near the pain from my other heat cycles. Was it because Zaliver was with me? Probably.

Bringing my hand up, I scratched until I cupped his neck and brought his lips roughly onto mine. I kissed him with a new fevered goal. My other hand squeezed at his hand, liking how he squeezed back. It somehow seemed more of a comforting touch than . . . well, everything else.

He began to kiss down my neck and I tilted my head, giving him more room. I closed my eyes, letting the sensation of him overwhelm me completely. His erection was once again placed against me in the most pleasurable way.

I could hear my wolf's voice sounding differently into my ears. Maybe it was the clouding fog, but it sounded older, wiser, and a hell lot seductive. Actually, it sounded like someone else's.

I moaned when Zaliver grinded himself against me. The friction made me push myself against him. He began nipping at my mark, causing tingles to spark up all over my body, especially·where his flesh met mine. Since that was everywhere, I felt pretty damn high. I pushed my chest against his and began rubbing myself against him wantingly. He growled deep in his chest, causing me to purr back.

Red lights. Why did it seem like we only moved make out places? Like from outside to inside?

His hand left my leg, but I kept it wrapped around him as it traveled up my waist and skimmed lightly over my ribs. His hand began shaking and slowing down under my breast. I tensed in anticipation.

"Mmm . . . ahhh," he moaned with a sound changing towards the end as if he were struggling with something.

He came back up and kissed my lips roughly before his hand under my breast moved away. He began making struggling sounds and

271

suddenly punched a hole in the wall next to me, startling me awake from my fogged state. Then suddenly he was off of me and gone.

I stood wide-eyed, shaking and nude. I dropped to my knees and put my face in my hands.

I had no idea what would have happened if Zaliver didn't pull away. This was twice now. I knew I was going to do it. My mind was too clouded. I had to give the guy credit. Other males probably had taken advantage of the chance to mate their other half without hesitation. What stopped him? I knew he wasn't in the house because I couldn't feel him anywhere near. He probably ran for the hills.

"Oh god, what's happening to me?" I spoke out loud. My emotions and body were suddenly at war with each other. While my body wanted him to take me here and now, my mind brought up everything he did and his crazed reactions to the most bizarre situation.

"*You're changing, silly. Of course, your mind is trying to recall everything so I can build a new perspective.*"

That was not my voice. I aint say squat. It was a new voice. I lifted my face out of my hands.

"You were in my head when . . ." I said out loud, looking forward blankly.

"*When you were grinding on our mate? Yes. It's a pity he stopped. We must find out why.*"

I swallowed and began shaking for a new reason. She said mate which means . . .

"Are you the—"

"*The newer, better beast in you? Yes. Yes I am.*"

I felt like I just got slapped in the face with reality. She was the ultimate piece that's finally showing me that nothing would ever be the same. I really was changing. I can no longer ignore it. It was much easier to do when the other side didn't talk.

"*Oh yes, about that. You seemed to subconsciously block me from you.*"

"What?" I asked in a daze, my chest feeling heavy.

"*You blocked out my voice from forming thus the headaches, the tapping, and the pain. Your wolf went along, which wasn't nice by the way. So here's some advice, do it again and I will painfully force my way to the front.*" The voice grew malicious and angry with a clear warning.

"You are the one doing all that?" I asked.

"*No, it was you. By trying to deny me, you left me no other choice but to force myself into your head and out of the little glass box you placed me in. Embrace me, Vivian. I've been the one lending you strength, will, and courage to do all the things you've done. Who did you think blocked out the hysterical thoughts when you snapped our mate's neck? You did it after all.*"

I looked down at my hands in horror. I did plan that, but I had no intention on hurting him no matter how angry I was.

272

"That was you," I stated.

Unlike my wolf who was as far away from the voice, this new voice wasn't a solid shape in my mind. I could see my wolf clear as day. I could see her fur, snout, and body as if she were in front of me, but this voice? She was an unidentifiable form of black and dark red smoke moving around. If I focused hard enough, I could make out a blurry outline of a large figure.

A figure that stood on two. A figure of a beast that had once chased me in the forest.

I brought both hands to my head and squeezed my eyes, not wanting to see or hear anything.

"No, no, no," I chanted over and over.

"Wishing me away won't do anything, but I'll leave you for now," she said. Just like that, she was gone and out of sight from my mind, but I could still feel her in the back of my mind. My wolf moved forward. I felt like I was all over the place.

I needed to go do something to distract me. First things first, getting off the ground and putting some clothes on. I stood up shakily on my feet, picked up the towel, and went up to the room for some clothes, noting the giant hole in the wall. While I dressed, I couldn't decide if I should stay in the room tonight. Did it even matter? But then again, I probably shouldn't just to be safe.

I sat in the guest room for about three seconds before deciding that I wouldn't just sit around and think about anything. Thinking might just give me a headache, besides, I really needed to call my parents before they decide I died on my "road trip."

I pulled out my phone before remembering that it probably wouldn't work without being pinned by Zaliver. Great. I guess I'd have to wait for him to come home . . . if he did. I wondered why he pulled away. Nope. Don't think about it, not now.

I needed a distraction that wouldn't involve anyone incase I flipped a switch and ended up either humping the shit out of them or trying to claw their eyes out. That's how I found myself in the library of our house. It was ginormous and styled to look classic and homey with cool-looking chairs and comforters everywhere. There were couches and bean bags. It even had a table in the middle. I loved it.

When lunch time came, I was calmer, reading a book while eating some things from the fridge. After a while, I got bored and went upstairs into our room. I was looking for the laptop around the bed—since that was where most people leave them—when I found something else instead.

Lifting Zaliver's pillow, I found two things: First was a folded peach dress that looked familiar. I lifted it up and saw a small white square. I picked both up and flipped the white square.

273

"Of all the damn photos he could have of me, he had my driver's license." I shook my head. It's not that it was a bad photo, but it most definitely not the best. I put it in my pants pocket. I'd keep this one.

I frowned at the dress and unfolded it. When it dropped, the scent hit my nose.

My scent, which made this dress mine. Why would Zaliver have my dress under his pillow? Wasn't this the dress I wore when my parents came here? I sat on his side of the bed, looking at the floor with it in my hands.

I brought it up to my face and inhaled. His scent was all over it, masking mine that still lingered. Why? Wait, had he been sleeping with it and the picture since I had been gone? I closed my eyes and sighed. There was no point in trying to ignore my problems with a good book. It seemed like they follow me everywhere.

I didn't think I could even look at him. I mean, the man saw me naked for God's sake! I was sure he took a peek before I basically moaned out for him like a hoe. God, I was so embarrassed! I laid down in the bed face down and muttered to myself into the comforter. We already had Zaliver's obvious revenge plans, which I was sure wouldn't end pretty for anyone. With the heat, the change, and my new-found personal conflict issues, I didn't know how many more problems I could take.

Mating was a big step, especially when one partner was inexperienced and the other . . . well, I doubt Zaliver was a virgin.

The thought of him with anyone else brought a bitter and nasty taste to the tip of my tongue. I bit back a growl. And then, there was his apology earlier today. Huh. The man got a way with words and had the voice of an angel when it came to singing. He most definitely would sing our kids to sle—

Wait. Oh man, did he even want kids? What if he didn't? What if he did and wanted them now? I was not ready!

These were startling new questions that really needed to be asked. Most mates didn't wait long to have kids, which was fine by me, but that's probably because they're not my kids. It was not that I disliked having kids. I just didn't know how to handle them. I loved them really. They're all cute, cuddly, and adorable, as well as funny, but I never had spent every waking moment with one or had sat down and scolded them. I was sure as soon as I would hold my first child, all my doubts would probably melt away, but when?

Before any kids, there had to be mating though, which mother nature seemed to be pushing for way earlier than necessary and with extreme actions. I had never heard of the male igniting the spark to begin the female's heat. Must be a lycan thing.

Uhh, and then there was the lycan problem. I felt her stir, so I shut that train of thoughts down.

See all of these problems? Why couldn't I have one easy problem to solve like running out of toilet paper? I would just run to the store and—

Wait. I didn't have a job nor money, and living off of Zaliver still felt wrong. Great. I couldn't even solve a toilet paper problem. I screamed into the bed.

"Well, doesn't that look like fun," an amused voice spoke from the doorway. Right away, I knew who it was. I turned a bit to his direction. My hair curtained my face and then turned back.

He saw me *naked*.

The thought popped up into my head, and mortification rushed into my body. Oh bed, close up on me now like in those movies! He moved closer to me and stood by the bed.

"Vivian?" His voice was soft and cautious. "What's wrong?"

I wanted to say everything but just grunted in response. I felt the bed dip and tensed when his large hand laid flat on my back.

"Talk to me," he said. After a moment, I turned my face to the side. Having your face flat on the bed didn't really feel comfortable at all.

"You saw me naked, and I'm not sure how I feel about the mating yet or if I want to mate at all. Plus, I'm not sure if you want kids, or what will happen if we do mate because I'm pretty sure you didn't keep your dick in your pants," I muttered lowly and fast that it almost sounded inaudible.

"I'm sorry. What was that?" Zaliver asked politely. I took a breath and began again.

"I said you saw me naked, and I'm not sure how I feel about the mating yet, or if I want to mate at all. Plus, I'm not sure if you want kids, or what will happen if we do mate because I'm pretty sure you didn't keep your dick in your pants?" I said all in one breath with the last part coming out more like a question.

"Hmm," he said. I frowned and turned my head more to face him, but he wasn't looking at me. His eyes were elsewhere, his face blank.

"What?" I asked him, curious to know what he was thinking. Zaliver always reacted differently than I expected him to sometimes, most times actually. He then took in a deep breath.

"I can't say I didn't look when the towel drop because that would be a lie. I can't change what happened today and I sure as hell wouldn't want to. I love your body the way it is and that's all I'm going to say on the matter. As for the mating thing, I'm actually not surprised."

"Why the hell not?" I snapped, happy about his words but peeved after. *What's that supposed to mean?*

"Well, it's no secret that I haven't been the best mate. I'd actually be surprised if you didn't have doubts about mating with a monster." The bitterness in his tone made me feel bad, but when I opened my mouth to explain, he shook his head.

"Dont. I don't want to know. I'm not going to try to persuade you to choose me. That's why I stopped us at times from doing anything . . . damaging in the morning. If there's something that you've taught me, it's that I haven't given you choices in matters that I should have and so, this one's yours. If you choose to not mate with me, I will respect that begrudgingly. But don't be mistaken, you are mine," he said with his voice lowering as he spoke. His last words made me laugh.

The words "a thousand-year-old virgin" came to mind. That's actually really . . . different from Zaliver's part. Hmm, change.

"And as for the kids. I've gone most of my existence surrounded by people, watching them form their families and memories. I've not had much interaction with kids, but I have a feeling that if it's ours, I'll be honored. So really, again, the choice is yours. If you want kids, you have a willing contestant—the only contestant matter-of-fact. The choice is yours, baby," he said, staring down softly at me. He moved the hand from my back to move strands of hair away from my face. I smiled shyly at him.

I was somehow feeling more like myself. I still held a bit of resentment against him, but people made mistakes, right? Yeah, no one fucked up more than Zaliver, but he was improving, even changing.

"And yes, I fucked a lot of women in my life," I snarled at him to which he frowned at.

Way to fuck up the mood. I turned my head away from him and gave him my back.

"I don't see why you're angry. It's not like you didn't know—"

"No female would ever like to know that the dick that's meant for her had fucked others."

Did . . . did I really just say that out loud?

"*You go girl!*" my wolf praised.

"*Oh, shut it.*"

As soon as the words left my mouth, I regretted them. Well, not the words but by saying them out loud. Oh Jesus take me outta here! Zaliver was quiet for a long time, like uncomfortably long.

"Are . . . Are you jealous of women who knew they meant nothing to me and were just meaningless fucks to relieve myself with?" he asked, sounding angry. My eyes widened at his words.

Well, when he puts it like that . . .

276

I didn't turn around. Now, I really didn't want to see him. Well, what was I supposed to say to that?

"Vivian!" he snapped. I jumped and slowly turned to look at him, my lips parted at his infuriated expression.

"Why are you mad?" I whispered at him. He stood up quickly and threw his hands in the air.

"Because you're putting yourself into a category of women who don't matter to me, not them, and most importantly, not now or ever. You're jealous of something of the past, which I would have changed had I known you would come along. Vivian, when you live thinking you're meant to be alone and unloved, physical pleasure is high on the list of musts. I don't want you poisoning your mind with this, so please just forget about them," he said, calming down towards the end of his rant.

"But I bet if I told you that I had slept with guys before—" I began.

"But you haven't." He frowned.

"But if I did—"

"But you didn't," he pressed.

"Well if I do—"

"You won't," he snarled.

"I dunno. Dylan O' Brien and Jensen Ackles call to me." I had to send a quick prayer to the god of reflex when I rolled over and off of the bed as soon as Zaliver lunged for me.

He was quick to bounce up, narrowing his eyes on me with his blue eyes in slits. He parted his lips to bare his teeth at me. He didn't look very happy.

I turned to crawl away and in that split second, he had me pinned to the floor. One hand held both of mine while his legs parted mine. His body weight was shifted partly on my back, stopping all movements and struggles without hurting me. He leaned over me. His breath was hot and heavy. See what I meant by putting myself in difficult situation? Why didn't I just nod my head and move along?

"Why do you make things so hard for me. Here I am, fighting every instinct to claim you, and you go on about not one but two males," he said calmly. I tried wiggling my hands out of his.

For some reason, instead of being bothered or anything, I found myself feeling amused. I let out a chuckle that turned into a giggle and escalated into a full-blown laughter. Zaliver huffed and got off of me, picking my shaking body and dumping me on the bed not so gracefully.

"H-hey!" I shouted between laughs. He rolled his eyes at me. When I was calm enough, he raised a brow at me to which I just shrugged. I ran my hands next to me and felt my dress.

277

"Oh yeah, this reminds me. Why do you have this and a very not-so-good picture of me under your pillow?" I asked. His lips thinned before answering me unhappily.

"What else was I supposed to hug and cuddle while you were gone? And that's a lovely photo of you."

I sat up and looked at him, eyeing him from bottom to top.

"Who are you, and what have you done to Zaliver?" I asked. He shook his head and reached for my hand that was holding the dress. He took the cloth out of my hand and folded the dress with delicate care before setting it down. He then kissed my knuckles while looking me in the eye.

"I believe the question, my beautiful little mate, is what have *you* done to Zaliver?" he said seriously.

"I don't know. Why don't tell me?" He smiled.

"Nope. Now, hurry and change," he said quickly, letting go of my hand and walking into the closet.

"What? Why? What's wrong with what I'm wearing?" I asked.

"It's not appropriate for where and what we'll be doing," he said, stopping at the door.

"And what will that be?" I asked curiously. He turned and looked at me over his shoulder with a smirk in place.

"Well, our first date, of course."

CHAPTER 25

"You know, it's not that I'm complaining or anything, but when you said date, I thought dinner and maybe a nice drive while we played twenty questions not god damn walking," I complained.

We were currently walking down a neighborhood in a steady pace. It almost looked like a movie with all the little stores and kids playing in the park with their friends and family. The sun was low in the sky, but we still had a couple of hours before it set. Some of the trees were covered in fairy lights, stretching as far as the eye could see.

Zaliver rolled his eyes and threw his arm around me, kissing the top of my head as I scowled at the ground and laughed.

"Patience. The place we're going to is a neighborhood I thought you'd like to see up close and personal," he said, looking down, amused at me.

"And you could have parked the car closer. Besides, I can see this place up close and personal through the window as you drive the car," I muttered the last parts to myself. I hated walking or anything that could be avoided.

His whole body shook as he let out a loud laugh, causing others to look at us with smiles. As he laughed, his weight shifted a bit on me.

"God damn, giant," I whispered under my breath, which just caused him to laugh some more.

When we finally stopped walking, Zaliver pulled open the door to a bakery shop. I frowned in confusion as we entered the place. There were around ten couples, including us, in the building. The walls were painted with soft pink and purple outlines; there were tables spread all over the place with cooking utensils on them.

When we walked in, all the couples quieted down and stared at us or me in wonder. I fidgeted a bit. I felt Zaliver place a hand on my shoulder and spoke behind me.

"Don't mind us," he said pleasantly with clear order.

A few of them were still staring at us, but no one said anything, so I didn't mind. Zaliver walked me over to a table and handed me an apron.

There was a sign on the wall that read, "Couples Night. Bake when you're ready. Eat when you're ready. We do not take responsibility for bad cooking and food poisoning. Enjoy."

Well then.

"So we're going to bake?" I asked, amused as he put the apron on without a pause. He looked really cute with the baby blue apron on. It brought out his eyes.

"Yes, now put yours on." I did as told and looked up at him, giggling a bit.

"What?" he asked with his face becoming slightly wry.

"Do you come here often? To take baking classes I mean?" Please say yes! That would be so funny to imagine. Zaliver taking classes and trying to learn how to bake while the teacher trying to scold him but saying it nicely. He shook his head with a small smile and poked my cheek.

"Wouldn't you wish? I'm letting you know I'm a natural chef and baker," he said with pride.

"Oh really?" I questioned. I didn't doubt it, but he'd have to take one class at least once right? It would make me feel better since I can't cook at all to save my life.

"Yes really. Shall we test this?" he said, leaning in to me with a smirk. A strand of his combed-back hair fell forward, making him look very tempting.

"Yes. I bet my cake will look better than your cake," I taunted. I said look not taste.

"Then let's see."

~•~

"Oh god, why did you let me taste my cake?" I cried out, trying not to gag at the horrid taste in my mouth. It was like charcoal and rotten egg mixed with sour milk and chunks of I don't know what.

Zaliver watched me with worried and amused eyes. He stood beside his pretty-looking cake that probably tasted as good as it looked, not like my piece of shit of a cake. I wiped my mouth with a napkin and lowered myself, glaring at my cake.

"You have disappointed me. After all my hard work, you went and sucked? You have dishonored me, you disgraceful cake," I said, looking at the lumpy, burnt, and ugly cake.

"Dishonored the *chef*. Don't forget that one," Zaliver added. My head snapped over and bared my teeth at him.

He lifted his hands in mock surrender and then grinned at me. I stood up and crossed my hands over my chest, looking at his cake in perfect form. The lavender icing was smooth. White designs decorated the sides and it had a large Z+V on top.

I couldn't even be fully mad at him. I pouted at the cake.

"At least, we can assume that I will be cooking from now on and forever," he said, stepping to my side and wrapping his arms over me. He looked down at me with a happy smile and blue eyes sparkling. It was hard to hate the cake, especially when the baker was hot.

"Yeah. Well . . . whatever. Let's see if your cake tastes better than mine." I huffed. I attempted to get out of his arms, but he just spun me around.

"Let's be honest. Anything tastes better than your cake—"

"Hey!" I exclaimed.

"It's true!" he said jokingly. I rolled my eyes and slumped in his arms.

"Yeah," I agreed solemnly.

"But it was pretty," he said softly as my BS detector went off. I gave out a loud laugh along with a few quiet giggles from around us. I was sure we entertained the couples of tonight.

"Nah, that shit was ugly. I'll agree to that," I confessed, looking at the cake on the table.

"All right. I'm not saying anything else about your cake. Now come on, we're still not done," he said, making way for me.

"What about tasting your cake?" I asked, removing my apron. He motioned for someone to come over, and a red-haired woman brought over a blue box that would fit the cake. She smiled at us and walked away.

"Later," he said, placing the cake in the box and closing it. He picked it up and held up his other hand for me to take. He eyed my cake on the table. The corner of his lip twitching as he fought off a smile.

"Do you want to take—" he began.

"Oh, shut up!" I took hold of the ugly, nasty, and disgrace of a cake and threw it away in the trash at the end of the table.

I marched back over to Zaliver and took hold of his hand. He stared down at me with an odd look on his face but didn't say anything, leading me back to the car.

Once in the car, Zaliver asked me to put the cake in the back, but I looked at him like he was crazy.

"What?" he asked, holding the back door open.

"Hell no. The cake will just slide around and possibly fall. I'll just place it on my lap."

He shrugged, closed the front door, and opened the passenger door for me. I thanked him and went to sit. The sun was slowly setting. The sky was in a mixture of orange, yellow, pink, and purple.

"So, where to next?" I asked excitedly since baking with him was so much fun. He concentrated on his cake as we talked, but he was still somehow aware enough to prevent me from both burning myself multiple times and almost slipping on the floor because of the flour.

"You'll see soon," he said.

I looked out the car as he drove. It wasn't an awkward ride. We weren't waiting for the other to begin a conversation but just sat and looked. When the car finally stopped, we got out and faced a forest that seemed to have mini mountains in it. I turned to look at Zaliver.

"Please tell me we're not walking in there," I said.

"We're not," he assured me. I nodded happily.

"We're hiking." He took the cake from my hand and marched straight forward.

"Yipeee," I said dryly, lifting my hand and twirling an imagery twirly thing at parties.

"Oh wait, before we go—" he stopped and turned to look at me with expectation. "Can I call my parents? It only works with a pin from you so . . ." I trailed off.

He nodded and reached into his back pocket, tossing his phone to me which I caught gracefully. I dialed my house phone and waited for it to ring.

"Hello?"

"Hey, Dad. It's me," I said with a smile while Zaliver studied my face.

"'It's me' can be any of my children," he joked. A second later, I heard a smack and yelling from my mom.

"Hey, Vivian," he said a moment later, sounding much more sheepish.

"Yes, Dad. It is me. The only child you have," I said into the phone, smiling stupidly.

"It's good to hear from you, young lady. You said you'll call as soon as possible. It's been—"

"Yeah, sorry about that, but I have to make this quick since I'm about to go on a hike like right now and—"

"Are you on some sort of drugs?" I blinked.

"What?" I asked.

"Are you on drugs? Because I know for a fact that my daughter doesn't walk around for fun. She sure as hell doesn't to hike. Are you sure you're my child?" he asked, lowering his voice. I pursed my lips. Zaliver nodded as if agreeing with something.

"Har har. I can hike, but yeah, I just called to let you know I'm good," I stated.

"Well, that's good to know. I'll let you go 'hike' now. Your mother sends hugs and kisses, as well as glares my way," he said. I heard a scoff come from the other end.

"Love you, two. Bye," I said before hanging up and making out a few words.

"Any of my children, huh?"

"It was a joke—" The line ended.

I handed Zaliver the phone back. He put it in his back pocket. Once again, the same odd look came back on his face. It looked like he was contemplating on something and, at the same time, discovering something that both surprised and pleased him.

"Ready?" he asked. I nodded, and we began to walk into the forest. I sighed and stomped on after him.

"So, is there a reason why you decided to take me on a date?" I asked him. I stepped over a fallen tree trunk while he gave me his hand.

"I just figured you needed something to take your mind off of things. What type of mate would I be if I didn't take my mate out?" he questioned.

"Eh, I wouldn't know," I said truthfully.

"So besides walking and hiking, should there be anything else I should add to the list of physical activities you don't like to do?" he asked me, turning half around to wiggle his brows at me. My eyes widened at the way he asked it.

"I don't like rollerblading or anything to do with heights," I answered, trying not to let his question get to me. His eyes widened a bit but quickly went back to normal.

"Oh," he said slowly. I narrowed my eyes on his back, about to question him.

"Well, I'm just glad sex isn't on that list," he said quickly.

"Not yet," I said snippy.

"Or ever. I'll make sure of that," he stated haughtily. He ducked under a large branch and lifted it up for me to duck under.

What the hell am I supposed to say? Oh, I'm glad you'll make sure I'll love you screwing my brains out?

Oh! Oh! Try this one: Prove it, my wolf chimed in, but I ignored her.

"Hmmm," I hummed in response.

"So, am I correct to guess that you still harbor ill feeling at my previous actions and will figure out a new way to get back at me?" he said out of the blue. His question caused me to stop and look at his back for a moment. He turned around and looked at me with a curious look on his face.

283

Where did that come from? And did I? I knew I still felt some anger to a degree on what he had done, but honestly, I was more worried about my transformation and the upcoming heat that I didn't even feel like pondering over it.

"I do feel ill about your past actions but not as much as I did before. I don't know if it's because I'm more worried about the transformation or the heat, but I . . . I don't know," I confessed, looking down and staring blankly at the dirt on the ground.

I heard Zaliver stepped closer to me and felt his hand softly grab my chin to tilt my head. In the dark shading and earthly colors of the forest, Zaliver's eyes seemed brighter and bluer than ever as he looked down at me. Instead of piercing into me, they seemed tender and softer.

"I'm sorry that all I seem to be giving you are headaches and heartaches. I'm not a very good mate, am I?" His voice was low and tremulous. My lips parted and my forehead creased as he gave me one expression but said something else.

"Headaches? Yes. Heartache? Not so much," I said softly. His head tilted to the side.

"But still aches?"

"Only the good kind," I said.

"Oh really?" he asked, his thumb moving back and forth on my skin, which was a bit distracting.

"I think no matter how angry I was or how many problems arose between us didn't matter anymore. At the end of the day, we overcame them and got to know each others' needs and wants a bit better. So, I think the road so far has been a bumpy but an informative one. You're not a bad mate. You're just figuring out things you didn't have to think much about before just like I'm figuring out the new sides to myself," I said, just saying what was on my mind and hoping it helped him. I felt like my words were true though. We could have been in worse situations.

"I really don't deserve you, but you're mine now," he said. I was about to say something when I found my back pressed against a tree and his lips against my own.

As we kissed, his lips were soft and tender on me, but as I felt a stirring heat pool in my lower half, he began to quicken the kiss. I wrapped my hands around his back and one in his hair. Still having more sense than the other times, I began to move away, trying to slide out from him and step to the side but he followed me.

I must have ran into a tree because I was suddenly falling back with Zaliver on top of me.

"Save the cake!" I managed to yell out as I braced for the ground.

284

I jolted. I was suddenly on top of a bewildered looking Zaliver, one hand on my lower waist and the other held the blue box in the air, waiter style.

"Save the cake?" he choked out, repeating after me.

"Yes, is it okay?" I asked, pushing myself up by putting my hands on his chest and straddling him. I went to grab the box, but he moved his hand away.

"You didn't even make it, and you're worried about the cake? And yes, I'm fine. Thank you for asking," he said sarcastically. I put my hands on my hips and narrowed my eyes at him. He looked quite nice under me—messy black hair, relaxed muscles . . . Wait, what? Oh yeah.

"Yes, I'm worried about the cake. You'll heal. The cake won't. Mine didn't work, so I'm adopting yours," I stated.

"You adopted my cake?" he said with satire.

"No, *my* cake. It's mine," I corrected.

His smile dropped and he looked at me seriously for a moment, unnerving me a bit. What was with his mood swings and odd looks?

"I'm yours," he said unwaveringly.

I felt like my breath was stolen for me as his words met my ears. He looked at me head on, clearly and honestly. What was this feeling in my chest? Zaliver always pulled the you-are-mine card, so to hear him say that he was mine was like a slap to the face. I gulped and gave a small smile.

"I guess you are, aren't you?" He nodded at me. We stared into each others eyes, savoring the moment.

"You know, I like this position. I say we forget about the rest of the date and just stay like this," he said. I chuckled and shook my head while I moved off of him and stood up. He did so as well.

"I did not just hike all the way up here to straddle you," I said, putting a hand on my hip as if to prove something.

"But you kinda did," he pressed. My cheeks warmed as I realized he was slightly right. I pushed my hair behind my ear and turned away from him, walking forward in the direction he was headed before.

"Don't get smart with me."

"How about I get sexy with you instead?" I turned around to start yelling things at him when I realized his eyes weren't even on my face. They were on my ass. When I turned fully around, his eyes snapped up quickly. He blinked innocently at me, but the corner of his lips were pulled up.

"Thirsty?" I muttered.

He frowned at me in confusion.

"What?" he asked. I chuckled and shook my head.

285

"Never mind. Come on." I went back down and got behind him, pushing him in front of me.

"Oh, I see how it is. You wanna check my ass out," he spoke mockingly.

"No I don't! Just bloody walk will you!" I yelled at him.

He muttered under his breath and began walking again. When we finally stopped and walked out from the trees, I gasped.

Zaliver brought us to a clearing to the side of the island, high enough to get a perfect angle of the beach, rivers, trees, cliffs, the sea, and the sky. Illuminated by the glow of the night, I could hear and see the ocean waves pull towards the beach. I could see how the last bit of sun went down and gave the sky a captivating and beautiful look. The air up here was colder but not enough to denture the sight in front of me.

"Wow," I said, trying to take all the beauty before my eyes.

"Was it worth the hike?" he asked. I nodded, wide-eyed at him.

"One more surprise," he said, taking hold of my hand and leading me towards the middle of the clearing. I wasn't usually good with heights, but with his hand, my nerves were put to rest.

Among the lively green grass mixed in with various flowers, I seemed to notice a large thick-looking blanket. It had a picnic basket in the middle, pillows, a folded blanket, two bottles of wine in a bucket of ice, and a mini speaker. It was . . .

Zaliver set the cake down next to the basket and pulled me into the blanket. We sat facing the beautiful view.

"Wait," he said, pulling out his phone and tapping something on the screen. I recognized Fire In The Water by Feist playing through the speaker. He then turned off his phone and a few seconds later, fairy lights of different colors turned on one by one, going around us in a huge circle once, twice and then a third time. They twinkled and changed colors around us slowly, bringing a magical feeling to the atmosphere. I felt my heart swell with how much there was to take in. I looked back at him to see he was already looking at me, giving me a shy smile.

"Do you like it?" he asked.

How could he just ask that with everything around us?

"Zaliver," I whispered in awe.

How could he be so brutish and make me want to pull my hair out in one minute but melt my heart and be a kind as a gentle guy the next? All of this was just so . . . I didn't have words.

His eyes flickered over my face, reading my expressions as my face softened while I just stared at him.

"So yes?" he said, unsure. He began bunching up the bottom blanket as if he was nervous.

286

I sat on my knees and in the sweet and gentle moment, I leaned into him and planted a peck on his lips. He brought me closer with one hand on the back of my head, not letting me move back while the other gripped my waist. The kiss was unlike the others we shared; there was no insanely unfightable lust from both sides, and it wasn't rough and fast. It was slow and sweet with every inch of passion.

When we pulled back, we breathed hard and had goofy grins on our faces. I rested my forehead on his and looked into his eyes.

"It's a yes," I whispered to him.

"I'm glad," he replied.

We separated and took out the plates and glasses, putting the still hot pasta and vegetables on the plate. I learned Zaliver had some members watch and bring the food, but he cooked and set them up himself. He made sure I knew of it too. I just smiled and nodded at him, still taken aback by how much detail and thought he put into this. When we fished the food, he served me some wine. We drank while we talked to each other.

I learned so many new things about him: interests, likes, dislikes, and how he struggled with understanding why I got angry at him sometimes. I learned he missed his brother when he brought him up. We laid back, looking at the stars side by side.

"I miss my brother terribly," he muttered after a moment of silence.

"Joshula?" I asked softly, not completely sure on how to approach such a delicate topic. We never really brought up the brother he was forced to kill.

"Yeah, I don't have many memories of my human days or of any family besides him, but I do remember how much fun it was to have him around. I wish he was here. You would have liked him. He always scolded me. Being the oldest, I should have been the one who took care of him," he said, sounding distant and distracted. He spoke calmly and with fondness until his voice lowered. I turned my head to look at him.

"I think I would have liked him too, especially that he always scolded you," I added.

He laughed and changed the topic as A Drop In The Ocean by Ron Pope & The District played in the back. We moved on to talk about what I liked and didn't like. He was very persistent on knowing the names of kids who bothered me during my school years from kindergarten to my senior years, but I didn't tell him. I was not trying to be responsible for a hit list.

When dessert time came, he grabbed the box and a fork, pulled me on his lap, and took a pice of the cake. I gave him a look, which he ignored. I didn't try to move away because truth be told, I was feeling very comfortable in his lap.

287

"So what? You gonna feed me?" I asked when he lifted the fork up to my mouth.

"Yes, so open," he demanded, his blue eyes looking at my eyes with something dark.

I rolled my eyes at him but did so. When the cake's flavor and rich goodness met my mouth, I moaned out and jumped up and down with excitement and glee. I thought that the cake would taste weird since it wasn't warm anymore, but it was one of those rare cakes that tasted better when cold. I felt Zaliver freeze under me.

"Are you trying to give me blue balls? Because if you are, it's working," he said through clenched teeth. I stopped bouncing and reached for the fork and cake, but he moved them away and just continued to give me some.

"This is awesome. I think I'm in love with this cake," I said after another spoonful.

I closed my eyes and smiled. When I opened them, Zaliver was looking at me with a look on his face. He leaned in close to me and surprised me by kissing the corner of my mouth to the other and lastly pecking my lips.

"Only the cake?"

CHAPTER 26

"And what did you say?" Hannah asked, leaning in eagerly.

Courtney and Mila did so as well while Mark rolled his eyes. Luke and Johnson stopped playing their game of cards, glancing over as well with curious gazes. It wasn't every day you got to hear a god's love life. I took in a breath and pushed a fallen strand of hair behind my ear. I brought my knees up to my chest and hugged them, hiding my face.

"I didn't say anything."

"What do you mean you didn't say anything?" Hannah shrieked. I heard Mark shuffle in his seat next to her.

"His question caught me off guard . . . I choked . . . on the cake in my mouth," I mumbled.

I had to jump off of Zaliver's lap to stand up and move my arms around like an idiot as if that would help. He immediately raced to my side and began patting my back, out of panic. He must have forgotten that he was about a million times stronger because it felt like my backbone seemed to break. I thought it was safe to say I would forever be embarrassed to even eat cake with him. Thankfully, he forgot about his question and gave me a small lecture on the importance of chewing and swallowing.

Or he decided not bring it up, my wolf whispered.

Or that.

I looked up to see all the half amused, half pitying looks on their faces, except for Johnson who looked honestly disappointed.

You and me, honey, my wolf muttered.

"Awww, you left the guy hanging," Johnson said, shaking his head. Luke kicked him under the table with a cautious look.

I wonder if I did.

But how did I feel about Zaliver? I knew I liked him, a lot, but to what point? Better yet, what was love? After spending an hour with Hannah and the others, I asked them to take me to the nearest drug store. I think it was safe to say that something was going to happen next time. Best be prepared.

If I was comfortable thinking like this, did it mean I trusted Zaliver like this? With myself? With my heart? I felt like my time was ticking.

~•~

"You know, you never really told me what to expect in my transformation," I brought up after lunch with Zaliver.

He had begun some paperwork, and out of boredom and a curiosity to see his home office, I followed him. He didn't seem to mind, so I just sat near the window on his large and fluffy black couch. I threw his small cotton blanket over my head and made sure that only my face was visible.

Zaliver dropped whatever he was working on, placing his fancy looking pen back to where it was. He shifted in his chair to look at me. His face was blank yet polite. I couldn't tell what he was thinking.

"Ask what you want." He waved a hand at me. I pondered for a second before organizing my questions.

"Will it hurt?" I asked that first, feeling it was the most important.

"I'm not going to lie to you. Yes it will. Unlike the first werewolf shift where you only remember the pain of your bones breaking and rearranging, in this transformation, you will feel everything."

"Everything?" I asked, my voice sounding distant

"The bone breaking, the rough texture, and the feeling of whatever you're wearing or laying on. Each and every cell in your body hardens to create rougher skin and at the same time, each and every hair grows out off the skin that felt like little needles growing out of your skin. The way your ribs break and then grow larger, how your organs tighten up, the expanding of your face to make the snout, and the most painful part has to be your spine breaking in order for all of this to happen. You'd think that would mean everything goes numb . . . but it's the opposite actually," he said.

I listened attentively. A vivid picture was painting itself in my mind. His words made me want to run for the hills and hide, but what would that do?

"And after. Will every shift hurt?"

"No. It will be quicker. The more times you shift, the more the pain turns into nothing." That wasn't an actual no. Well, at least, it wasn't going to be like the first time. Maybe if I thought positively, then it wouldn't seem so bad.

"What about after the shift?" I asked.

"Well, I've never seen anyone else after the shift. Being the only one, I suppose we'll see that after," he said, cracking a small smile with his eyes softening.

"Well, that's true. What about the voice in my head, will her . . . personality grow onto mine?" I asked, a bit hesitant. Zaliver sat up in his chair, brows furrowed as he looked at me in confusion and intrigue.

"Voice?"

"Yeah," I answered, suddenly unsure. He looked surprised and bothered by what I just told him.

"Vivian, beasts don't come with voices. They communicate with strong emotions. Every once in a while, they take over to use our voice to speak, but they don't have one of their own."

"W-what?" I asked. Now this one was surprising. If beasts didn't have voices, then why did mine have one? Great. I'm a freak among freaks.

"How many times have you heard the voice?" he asked, clamping his hands together.

"Uh, once, but I could always feel her around my head trying to get through. She said I had been blocking her voice out thus my headaches."

"You've been getting headaches?"

"Yeah," I said shortly, feeling his annoyance that slipped through the bond.

"Why haven't you told me!" he snapped, slamming a hand on the table.

"I didn't think it was all that serious," I said and pursed my lips.

"Vivian, be it big or small, I want to know what's happening to you. I don't care if it is even a paper cut. Inform me next time," he said through clenched teeth, leaning back in his chair to look at me as if trying to catch something else I could have possibly kept to myself.

"Okay."

"As for the voice, the only plausible explanation is that your beast has mingled with your wolf and figured out how to speak on her own. Hmmm, interesting."

"So, you don't get a voice?"

He shook his head, and I slumped a bit. Out of all voices, I seemed to have gotten the mean one. I felt a sliver of annoyance from the beast.

"So if a werewolf shift is three to five hours, how long will this one be?" I asked him. He tilted his head to the side as if recalling a memory.

"Back then, time wasn't really cared for, but recalling my shift"—his expression and voice darkened—"I have to say eight hours."

291

"What?" I gasped.

He said nothing as I looked at him in shocked horror. Eight hours. Eight horrific hours in pain sounded like labor. Oh god, no. I could only handle three to five. Shit, I did, but eight was something I believe I never wanted to go through. What would happen during that time? Did this mean everything he just said during the shift would happen slowly and painfully as if it was dragging me out? Perhaps I would be knocked out that I couldn't even run in my new form at the first time. Then, a startling thought came to mind.

What about my heat? If my guess was right, then wouldn't my heat become full blown as soon as I transformed? The thought of actually having to go through the mating soon made my eyes widen. How much time did I have left?

"Something else you want to ask me?" Zaliver asked, snapping me out of my thoughts. His eyes skimmed over me, and his body turned more in my direction. I looked at him and opened my mouth only to gulp and give a false smile.

"Nope." His eyes narrowed down on me with a frown on his lips.

"Are you sure?" he asked.

"Yup."

Nope.

~•~

I stared at Zaliver as he walked around the room with his back at me. It was around five in the morning. This had to be the first time he had ever gotten up so early since we had met. None of the lights were turned on; the only light was from the little light from the rising sun through the curtain.

Something about his behavior made me feel . . . I don't know, cautious, odd, and worried. The thing was he wasn't doing anything to make me feel that way. Besides, maybe he was just being more quiet and serious than usual. Maybe it was my imagination at work.

"I'll be back later. I've got things I have to take care of." He walked over to my side of the bed and leaned over, kissing my forehead. I stared at him silently for a moment. When he began walking to the door I spoke.

"Zaliver? Is everything okay?" I asked softly. I could feel the hair on my forearms rising.

He opened the door and stopped. Without fully turning his head to look at me, he spoke calmly

My wolf shifted uneasily; she could feel it too.

"Everything's . . . going to be fine. Don't go outside. Looks like it's going to rain." Without another word, he left and closed the door behind him.

I looked out from the side window. Even through the curtains, I could see that today would not be a pretty day. I suddenly felt something strange. I grabbed Zaliver's pillow and hugged it to my chest, trying to get rid of the feeling.

What was he up to that seemed to make his blue eyes glint in that dangerous light? And why did I not like the way he responded.

Zaliver, what are you up to?

I felt like the answer was on the tip of my tongue, but I couldn't quite grasp it. A hazy fog surrounded my mind, leaving only so much room for clear thoughts. My body was heavy and sore, but I hadn't done much yesterday. At the same time, I was feeling antsy and alert.

Maybe I should stay in. It felt as if nothing from the outside could get me, but I forgot about the inside.

People said to expect the unexpected, but what if you had been waiting for it? I think the only real shock was when it finally happened.

~•~

ZALIVER AZRALA

Walking out of the room, I knew I probably should have at least tried to act casual in front of her, but I couldn't. Not now because I was so close to my revenge. I traveled in the last cover of darkness in the forest surrounding the house. The clouds in the sky was darkening and as the minutes passed, the air smelled like it was about to rain.

As I entered the premises of the farthest corner of the island, I nodded at the two men in front. Entering the cave, I went down further and further until I reached the war room.

Hogan, Albericus, Lexero, Venom, and Fern were already in deep discussion, leaning over the large table with countless maps and papers. The men all quieted down as I entered, their faces concealing whatever emotions they were feeling.

"Report," I ordered. They were quick to respond, knowing my patience had gone far on this mission.

"We've discovered where the door was hidden, and I've managed to lock it down in place. We now await for your command, my lord," Venom spoke in his gloomy tone with a hiss, making it somehow difficult to understand. He couldn't help it.

Venom, as named, was a snake shifter of a different sense. He got hell of a lot of loyalty than most gave him credit for. At a whopping seven feet, slicked back white hair, golden eyes with black vertical narrowed pupils, and a very lean yet muscular build, he was someone who had a dark story that rivaled even my own. In the beginning, it was difficult talking to the venomous snake, but once we became friends, he somehow saw me more as a master or a lord than a friend, no matter how many times I tried to explain to him that I ruled werewolves and not snakes.

"The men are ready and have been preparing themselves with the dosages you've ordered. Four hundred in front line, forty thousand in second line, and another four hundred for backup," Lexero said informatively. He was in charge of the men in the mission, training and preparing them.

Lexero was actually a half human half lion shifter. He wasn't able to fully shift into his animal form, which he had already accepted but not before making his way to the top to dominate his race after years of taunts and mockery for being a halfbreed. His long dark locks were messily pulled up onto his head. He had chocolate skin. His chest and arms were covered with scars of the many battles he had gone through—something he displayed proudly. One of his eyes was black and outlined in gold while the other was golden, outlined in black. He carried himself with just as much pride as the rest of us. Being the shortest in the group at five foot eleven, he was no different in our eyes.

"There have been reports of gods and goddesses' presence in the last three weeks, more so the last few days worldwide. Important artifacts have been reported stolen from supernatural temples—things with origin no one knew about or what the objects represented. Werewolves in the East Coast mentioned about the tension in the air. Although it appeared that no actual crimes and murders have been committed, leading me to suspect that their hideout may be in that direction and that they aren't trying to hide or bothered to hide their uneasiness. The bad weather and negativity has shown on the population of werewolves living there," Hogan said quickly yet professionally. His eyes flickered from mine to elsewhere.

I said nothing to him, but he knew I caught everything. I knew Hogan was uneasy with the others in the room, but I never cared why. He was pushed in a corner of the room, clutching a heavy clipboard and notebook in his hand, staying far from the others in the room.

"As for the information about the rat, Jack Ruston has been released. I managed to pin down four small people he had spoken to, but it seemed everyone was so sure you have no soul, thus no soul mate. They just waved him off. I've spread some rumors in their location just in case. The only two things bothering me are how he managed to get that information and who was the first person he told that matches the description you gave," Albericus spoke seriously. His brows lowered as he frowned. I saw his eye twitched as if he was going to look somewhere but then he held himself blankly again.

He was onto something. He'd tell me when he had a solid trail.

I ignored how the others eyed me curiously over the confirmation that I indeed had a mate. They could wonder all they want.

The last to report was Fern. He was a werewolf with an odd sense, but he was great when it came to getting information even if it was questionable and suspicious sometimes. He was of Filipino descendant. His skin was darker and unlike most werewolves, his canines were always out. His dark hair was cut clean, his stark light eyes contrasted him, and his iris was as white as sclera. He was quite the sight but just like Venom, he was loyal to the end.

"My sources tell me that something odd is happening up in the sky; that the gods do have an army of their own that have begun to prepare, but something else seems to be hanging over their heads. It seems like they have a secret weapon or something they've secluded themselves in their golden castle in the clouds," Fern said with contemplative eyes. This made me stare at him for a moment longer, waiting for more, but he shook his head, which made me give him a brisk nod. I walked around them to the map in the center of the table.

I hadn't introduced Vivian to Venom, Lexero, and Fern because I didn't want to involve her more in this than she already was. There was also the fact that I didn't introduce her to many people. I saw that it truly bothered her to know that she was just a peace offering to me and that she was created to tame the beast. I guessed that was what made her push herself out a bit of whatever she used to be, which made me happy and wry. She seemed to have a way with getting me where she wanted.

"Well, if they do have a secret weapon, then they better hope I don't have one of my own," I said darkly.

I had spent at least three hundred years away from them, perfecting my kills, skills, and gaining more power than they had ever wanted to give me. If I used to be their secret weapon, then I would have no doubt that they would try to outdo themselves again. Idiots could try, but my power and rage during a kill had no match. None.

"So what's the plan, Zaliver?" Lexero asked, crossing his arms over his chest.

"How long do you think you can hold the door in place, Venom?" I asked without glancing at him. I was focusing on where they said the door was located in. The Amazon jungle. It is located in its deepest part too.

"Up to a month if it's not summoned or if they try to relocate it again. If they do, then it will be a limit of fourteen days," he answered immediately. I got used to the way his voice chilled me long ago, so I wasn't bothered by it anymore; but others still tensed when he spoke even after a few years. This was another reason why Venom tried to speak very little.

The door we were talking about was a door suspected as a portal. As soon as you stepped through it, you would be instantly transported to the other opening of the door's original makings. This door was the only door the gods and goddesses could use to come down and interact with others. Unfortunately for them, we could also use the same door to get to them. Not many knew that however, almost like the doors in Monsters Inc.

Yes, I had seen the movie. Vivian was obsessed with showing it to me after making a reference about some purple lizard thing and after mistakenly telling her I had no idea of what it was. I hadn't really paid attention. I was secretly watching her reaction to the movie and mind linking other betas for check ins.

Multitasking was one of many talents of mine.

"Alright. I'm going to count those fourteen days as our maximum. At this point, they're not taking any chances and will probably be moving the door in the next ten days. Be prepared for anything. I won't put it behind Alstha to try and send attacks to drop our numbers. She always does like a little blood before battle," I warned the men, and they nodded back at me.

"Your packs, tribes, and family are welcome to stay on the island if you want. There is sufficient room for all and more. The island's magic protection will be cranked up in the next three days, so if you are to move in, I suggest you do so now."

Venom stayed quiet for obvious reasons. He had no one—no family, and not so many friends. At least, that's what he said.

Fren shook his head. He had very few family from what I had known over the years. I knew they were both strong enough to protect themselves and odd enough to somehow manage the impossible, especially if it was necessary to survive.

"My pride will stay as they are. My second-in-command handles them now, but I would like to move my wife and kids here until it is over," Lexero spoke.

"That is fine with me. I will have you set up near my own place if you'd like," I said and he agreed.

"All I ask is to keep Aurora where she is now. This will both keep her and others out of danger," Albericus said seriously. The room temperature dropped to a few degrees, but I didn't stop to look at Fern who probably had a nasty look on his face at the name of the witch.

Those two were like water and oil ever since they first met. It got a bit worse after she and Albericus . . . split, for a better word. Aurora had caused a large mess in trying to flee from her first trackers.

"That's fine with me. Just make sure she doesn't even try to tamper the island's magic. I'm telling you this because anyone who does try to enter or escape dies a very painful death." He stared at me for a moment before speaking.

"We both know she's not just going to stay here for another week without leverage."

"So give her a reason to stay. She's your mate," Fern muttered. Albericus tensed but kept his eyes on me. I could see his fisted hands and hear the growls his wolf was giving off mentally.

"I can't help you there, Albericus, but if you need the witches' cooperation, you know where to find me."

I long ago realized that no matter how many or how long people knew me, no one could really stand the sight of my beast. It wasn't until Vivian ran from me that it actually hurt, but I knew her actions were justified.

It seemed that even in moments when I wasn't supposed to show my thoughts, it strayed her. I gave myself a mental shake.

Focus.

"No, that's fine. I'll find a way," Albericus quickly denied my help. In human form, Aurora was as sarcastic and sassy to me as she was with anyone else. She thought I annoyed her. During my first transformation, she fainted in front of me, making that the last transformation she ever saw. It was safe to say she pushed me but made sure that it was enough not to push me over the edge, which would transform me into my beast. Not that anything she could ever say or do would get me to do so.

"If any of you change your minds, just inform Hogan, and he will take care of it. Now, let's talk about strategy, statistics, and what else are needed for next week."

After three hours of entirely talking about strategies in the war room, I ended the meeting. Something was bothering me, and it wasn't the war talk. My beast seemed to be on edge as we felt the atmosphere change. Was it the weather? Even from the inside of the deep cave, I could hear the sounds of rain hitting the walls and the smell of wet earth.

It was only these three men who could enter and leave the island as they pleased. They would do it so rarely, so when they would, it must be important, except for Venom. For some reason, he felt the need to check in every once in a while. I didn't know if it was to check in on me or to let me know he still existed. I always told him it wasn't needed, but he ignored that.

"I'll call you in the next twelve hours to confirm. The men are getting antsy. They want to fight already," Lexero said, twisting the golden band wrapped around his left bicep.

"I can imagine. Two years of training can make a man mad," I said dryly.

Those pups should try twenty-four human years of training and then add forty non-human years. That could drive a man mad.

"I'm going to take care of some things, Alpha," Hogan said loudly.

"Alright. Make sure to rewrite the notes we had today," I said, looking over at him. He nodded briskly and steadily walked off.

"I've got several things to do as well. It was nice seeing you all today," Albericus said seriously and left without letting the others speak.

"What's up with his ass?" Fren asked, pulling out a bag of chips from nowhere and began to eat them.

I stayed quiet as I silently tracked Albericus state of mind. He was calm but also seemed to be in deep thought, but I left him to it.

"So how about you, Venom? Met any pretty girls?" Lexero asked, amused to hear his answer.

Venom's gloomy golden eyes snapped over to Lexero and stared unblinkingly at him with what appeared to be sharp and alert eye. I was sure he was actually just annoyed that even the prideful lion looked away awkwardly.

"Okay then. How about you Fren—"

"No," he answered flatly. Lexero sulked a bit but then a look crossed his face.

"Well, I am mated, married, and have kids. So Zaliver, what about your mate?" he said smugly as if he confronted me about some deep dark secret I had been trying to hide that had just been revealed, which in a way had.

I rolled my eyes. Now that we were out of the seriousness of the war room, everyone seemed to be acting like their normal selves, except for me. I had an odd feeling in the lower pit of my stomach. It wasn't painful, but it wasn't pleasant. Somehow, I felt it was more of a mental feeling than anything.

Why do I feel like something was wrong?

"Zaliver? You there?" Fern asked me, waving a chip in front of me.

"Yes," I answered. They were all looking at me as if I were some foreign object.

"So . . . mate?" Lexero asked again.

"Yes. Mate." I walked in front of him and hoped he got the idea to either return back home to his own mate or leave mine alone.

Unfortunately, he didn't seem to grasp the clue and just followed close behind with the other two trailing me as well.

"So, what's her name?" he asked.

"None of your business," I said lowly, speeding up to get out of the cave.

"Damn, just trying to know the lady's name. You know with that attitude, I bet she has to put up with a lot of your shit," he said. I felt my eye twitch.

"Hmmm, if you won't even give out her name but confirmed to having one, I assume you've marked but haven't mated, yes?" Fern asked. Another twitch and smoother foot steps. Thankfully, Venom stayed quiet, not that he talked much.

"Oh come on, Zaliver. It's not like we're going to try anything on her man—" I snarled and turned around to face them.

"You would be dead before you even tried."

"Must really like her," Lexero mumbled under his breath.

"And you must really want to die," Fren whispered to Lexero as if I weren't glaring at the two.

"I swear I don't understand how I have managed not to kill you when all you two do is annoy—" I stopped talking and froze.

The mating bond opened up itself. Through it, I felt Vivian's end flaring with emotions like crazy. I froze as I tried to make sense of them all. The golden wire that seemed to connect us was glowing and throwing out sparks like mad.

"Hey man, you don't look too good." I could barely even hear Fern speak as I was so attuned to what was going on.

"Zaliver!"

I took off running in her direction and moved faster than I had ever gone, only getting damp in the pouring rain. Her voice sounded pained and scared. The image of the last time I saw her in pain flashed in my mind. Usually, it took me five minutes to reach the cave from the house but surprisingly, it was less than one when I arrived.

I crashed through the door and stopped to listen for her heartbeat. It was pounding like mad as if it was a drum getting hit repeatedly over and over. The loud and fast thumping was hitting my ears and not letting me focus on her exact location. I whipped my head over and climbed up the stairs when I heard a whimper.

I was in our room in a flash and had Vivian in my arms on the floor. She appeared two shades paler than normal, and her skin was boiling hot, enough to leave sweat where her skin touched mine. Her hair strands stuck to her damp forehead, and her eyes rolled in the back of her head, showing me only the white part. She thrashed in my arms and clung to whatever she could. Her pale lips parted as she gasped for air.

"Vivian!" I shouted at her when she began to shake like crazy in my arms. I brought her closer to me and inhaled her scent only to pull back wide-eyed.

The smell of sweet lavender, fruits, and earth assaulted my senses, but her innocent scent grew more and more intoxicating, rousing the beast within as a new smell emerged from her.

I looked at my trembling mate in my arms. Vivian was transforming. She was transforming now.

Her hands pulled away from me as her teeth began to chatter. She tried pushing me away from her, and when I wouldn't let her, she began scratching at her skin, digging her nails in and drawing blood.

"No! Get off! You hurt! You all hurt!" she yelled out, lifting her legs and kicking wildly.

I knew my next move would cause her great pain, but I had no other choice. I carefully and securely wrapped my arms around her, ignoring her whimpers and snarls, and ran as fast as I could into the pouring rain and forest.

~•~

VIVIAN GREY

It started with me throwing up.

I didn't even eat much that morning, but it didn't matter because it came right back up. I hated throwing up mostly because I was the type of person that once I started, I couldn't seem to stop. This was no exception. My stomach was empty when lunch time came around. I could feel my organs clench tighter, pushing whatever food was left out even the water I had tried to drink.

When I finally calmed down, I was shaking with cold sweat. Lying in bed made it worse since the usually soft texture of the silk and cotton seemed like sandpaper to my skin, so I sat down on the cold floor. I put my head in between my knees, hoping to feel better. If I had sex with Zaliver, I would have said I was pregnant with the way I was throwing up.

At least, my humor was still intact but then the voice came. She was back and she seemed so loud. Her voice rang too loud and clear in my head.

"*Missed me?*" she purred.

I squeezed my eyes shut tightly, not wanting to hear her, but I had no energy to try and block her out. Her presence was visibly noticeable in my mind while my wolf was pushed back to a distant corner. Her figure was still clouded by the fog in my mind, but her

300

outline was noticeable. She was crouched down with her head tilted to the side as if watching me back.

I brought my hands up to my head, holding it as if to block out her voice, but it was useless. My fingers shook as I pulled my hair.

"You know, it's really not fair how mean you are to me. Just think about everything I've done for you."

"You've done nothing," I said through clenched teeth, feeling as if her words echoed in my head.

"Oh really? Then who gave you the strength and speed when you needed it? Who gave you the courage to plan out your revenge without hesitation and skill? I gave that to you. I am you!" she hissed mockingly.

"You are not me!" I screamed. Oh god, the voice was trying to drive me crazy.

"No, but you fear the beast so you fear me. I am—"

"SHUT UP!" I growled out.

"I will not be silenced now that I have a voice. You will learn to accept me over time. You'll see," she said coldly.

I think I spent five minutes straight trying hard to ignore her, but she didn't leave my mind. Oh no, she stayed forward in my mind.

I couldn't even think about my wolf as the beast took over the majority of my thoughts. My body shook with aftershocks. I felt cold; oh, so cold. I tried to stand slowly, but it seemed as if I had pins and needles under my feet. I could see my legs, but I couldn't remember how to move them. My stomach twisted and tightened with every movement. My lips and throat felt dry. I put my forehead on the ground to try and balance out my body. I needed to feel sturdy, but I was all over the place. And then my heart took off faster than I could handle.

I began thrashing on the ground. My eyes rolled to the back of my head as darkness took my sight away. I felt my fingers try to grab onto something, but I couldn't. There was nothing near me and yet I kept trying to hold onto the ground.

Panic, fear, dread, shock, and an overwhelming sense of loneliness hit me all at once. Was I dying? It felt like it. I didn't want to die alone. My mind was a mess and was not thinking straight. Every fast beat my heart gave was like an electric shock to my system.

"Zaliver!"

I screamed in my mind. Only thinking of his name. My skin felt as if it were on fire, but I was so cold on the inside. My body felt as if it was engulfed in flames while every uncontrollable movement was like rolling around in a pile of needles and knives. I was jolted and then pushed up by something touching me; a familiar but painful touch. No! I couldn't bare it!

It was like each nerve in my body, every cell, and every fast thump of my heart were working through fire and ice, pushing my body

301

to an end. I could feel the touch, but it hurt like everything around me—on me. I tried to force my eyes to stop flickering, but my body wouldn't stop as if something was controlling me. I was powerless. Weak.

No, don't touch me. Please. I am suffocating. Don't touch me! Zaliver! Where are you?!

"No! Get off! You hurt! You all hurt!" I heard a pained shrill of a voice scream.

I was moving and the air around me was changing—confining and cold but liberating and open.

The air was colder and so was the ground. I was laying flat on my back. I could sense earth and an overpowering sense of freedom, then the familiar touch moved away. My eyes closed shut. My fingers dug into the ground. Something made way for my fingers, and I clenched my hand around it.

I opened my mouth for air, then I realized I could feel multiple hits on my body. They hit my bare flesh and cooled the fire surrounding me, but I didn't care. I'd rather die frozen than burned.

My body tingled through the multiple attacks on me, but the strongest was in my lower back. I forced my eyes to open and then had to squint up as dark gray angry colors looked down at me. I turned my head to avoid the attacks on my face. A blurry dark outline was next to me with a pale face and darkness surrounding him, but he had beautiful blue electric eyes.

A dark beautiful angel with a sad face.

I blinked slowly. My vision was blurring in and out on details. I felt my arm slowly move on the cold ground and reach for the sad angel. My fingers felt something rough as he moved. Something wrapped around my hand, flesh to flesh. His hand. I blinked up at him with a frown on my face. How could I focus on him when my body was under a heavy attack? My ears were assaulted with the sound of heavy pattering when something was sliding followed by a splash that sounded as if a bomb went off next to my ear.

My head throbbed. I whimpered as more bombs went off, making me flinch. My breathing was heavy. I felt as if something was leaving me and clouding around my face. Something squeezed my hand, making me look back at the sad angel.

He looked so familiar; his touch, his eyes. His name was on the tip of my tongue, but the understanding was so far from my mind. My back tingled stronger.

"Why," I tried to croak out but I couldn't finish.

Not when the tingling turned into a fierce stabbing.

Not when the bottom of my spine suddenly broke, making my back lift off the ground. I gave out a painful scream that didn't seem to end until my lungs burned. I screamed to the top of my lungs as the tingling that had turned into stabbing made its way up my skin slowly and painfully. Something made a sound next to me, but I drowned them out with my wails.

The more my spine broke, the harder my back lifted itself off the ground only to drop back down. My legs lifted and hit the ground with the ball of my feet repeatedly. I shouldn't have been able to move my legs, I knew that, but I could feel them. I could thrash and kick.

When the breaking seemed to finally stop, it seemed as if my back was still intact, but I wouldn't know because my insides felt as if they were being torn out and ripped apart inside of me. I gave out a breathless scream, a stinging sensation in my eyes. The dark and gray clouds started to surround me.

The clouds looked so angry at the unbearable pain I was having.

Something leaned in closer, blocking the clouds as more ripping and tightening began on the inside. I wanted to shout, but it would tighten my muscles, so I just shook my head back and forth.

Pain. Pain. Pain.

So much pain filled me all over and for so long. I couldn't tell how long I withered there on the ground. Minutes, hours, days possibly. My skin was torn; it bled and pulled until it broke. I broke. Nothing was safe. Nothing filled me with comfort. There was no ending or beginning. No lesser pain or worse. There was just pain.

"Please. Kill me," I pleaded to the angels.

He could put me out of my misery. He had to.

My senses snapped to something that grabbed my face and forced me to look up. The angel leaned over me with a new look on his face. Was he in pain too?

Something about him was taking a layer of the coldness that I had. I felt like drowning in cold waters. We were drowning.

His lips moved but no words came out. I tried to turn my head away, but he didn't let me. The pain was so strong it made me bare my teeth and bang my head on the ground. My fingers tingle and something seemed to be pushing itself out as well as my toes while another odd sensation formed from the tip of my toes to my knees. His lips moved faster. This time, I managed to catch his words.

"Vivian, listen to me! Do you understand me?" he shouted with neither too little nor too much sound. It was too much of everything.

Vivian . . . Was that me? Was that my name?

My blurry eyes squinted on him, ignoring what he was trying to communicate with me. I forced my breaths to slow, pushed through the pain, and focused on his face. His lips were looking even more alluring. His black hair was wet. Some strands were sticking to his forehead as he leaned over me. Those big blue eyes that seemed so scared, worried and yet so determined stared down at me.

"Zaliver," I cried out, recognizing him.

"Shh baby. It's all going to be alright," he said. His voice sounded relieved.

A sharp and very loud crack met our ears. I groaned and choked back a scream as one of my ribs broke. Zaliver called my name, but I didn't answer, my body curling up and wanting to die. It hurt with so much hurt.

"No! No! Vivian, look at me! Look at me!" he demanded. I looked at him through painful eyes while feeling that same rib closing in.

"P-please," I cried out, not sure of what I was even asking him.

"Do you trust me?" I heard him ask me.

I frowned at his question. Why would he ask that in a time like this?! I moaned as a tingling began on another rib.

No. No. No. Please don't break.

My body felt bruised, beaten, burned, and sensitive to everything around me. I felt like burning and freezing in hell. My lungs felt like being burned.

Trust? He asked me about trust when I wanted to die? I opened my mouth to give him a piece of my mind but ended up sucking in a breath when the same horrible cracking sound met our ears.

"Vivian, do you trust me?" he asked again. Without thinking, I responded.

"Yes!"

Zaliver moved fast over me and with tears in his eyes, I watched his hands lift in the air and grow out his claws. A moment later, I felt cool air and something that was clinging to my skin left me. My eyes widened as I felt Zaliver remove my pj's, leaving me in my black and polka-dotted garments. I didn't have the will or strength to fight him off if he decided to mate then and there, but if I trusted him . . .

I saw him remove his shirt and waited to hear him remove his pants, which he didn't. I felt an annoying feeling grow in the back of my throat and suddenly began coughing. That had to be the worse for me. An uncontrollable cough forced me to double over and tightened my organs. My broken ribs were stabbing my organs from the inside. It wasn't long before I felt a thick substance make its way up and out of my mouth. Zaliver cursed and suddenly took hold of one of my hands.

At first, nothing happened but then I felt a large amount of pain left my body. I could still feel the tingles, but I couldn't feel anything else. I was going numb.

My head cleared. I could think without the pain. I gave out a hesitant breath, waiting to feel pain but nothing came. It was a small victory in a battle. I was laying in a field of vibrant green grass that stood out in the dark and gloomy weather. I didn't look down at my body. All I did was carefully turn on my front and sat on my knees just as Zaliver was, but his head was down.

His hand was still wrapped tightly around mine. His hand was gripping my wrist. I didn't even feel it. I was numb to almost everything. I'd get a sharp pain every once in a while, but I could take that than the full blast pain.

"Zaliver, it doesn't hurt," I said softly, wiping at what must have been the blood I had coughed up.

I felt another rib tingle, but it was soft. When a snap came, I heard it but I didn't feel it.

But then I heard something else.

A low pained grunt.

My head snapped down to Zaliver, his head down and hand clutched. His muscles were taunt and tensed, then his shoulder shook.

"Zaliver?" I whispered, a knowing thought crossing my mind.

His breathing was loud and harsh . . . like mine had been a while ago. I reached down with a shaky hand and took hold of his chin and brought his face up. His face was that of a man in agony. His eyes were shut, his jaw was clenched, and his lips were parted, baring his teeth.

My eyes flickered at Zaliver and watched in horror as his leg began to kick out as if trying to shake off pain. He suddenly gave out a loud low moan with my rib and leg snapping.

He was taking the pain for me.

I tried to pull my hand out from him to get him to lay down, but he wouldn't let my hand go.

I tried to get him to take my other hand, so I could maneuver him down, but he refused. *Did he need to hold my hand?*

I tried even harder to pull away from him, realizing that each whimper and grunt was being taken away. It lightened my chest to know he would take the pain for me, but he didn't have to.

"No!" he spit out through gritted teeth.

"Why?" I choked out with tears streaming down my face under the never-ending rain that was drowning us. *Was he drowning as I was?*

He lifted his head slowly. His wet black hair was dripping all over his face. His agonized, fierce, watery blue eyes looked straight at me while the corner of his lip turned up to a soft smile. That expression broke my heart.

"Because if going through this torture again means taking the pain away from you, then I'll do it a million times over," he said, strangled. I let out a small sob and shook my head at him.

305

"No. Give it back, Zaliver. You shouldn't have—"

"No," he said and then scrunched his face up in pain.

I reached for his other hand with my free one and put my head on his shoulder.

"No. Together," I said with my voice stronger than I felt.

Slowly, I felt my own pain go back into me, but it wasn't as sharp and impacting at the full force because Zaliver was taking half of it.

And that's how we went through my shift. We whimpered and groaned together, holding each other's hands. My body was breaking and rearranging itself while my skin was hardening and my blood was boiling under my skin.

As time passed, I felt like I was breaking the freezing coldness inside me; as if I could almost feel the deliverance on the other side. I just had to break the surface. I was still drowning . . . but I was no longer alone. I squeezed Zaliver's hand and without a beat, he squeezed mine back. The simple gesture was lending me strength.

Furs began to show on my body. My hands and feet began to fully shift. I could tell I was almost there.

"I can't help you in these last few stages, baby, but I'm right here," Zaliver said. I felt him lift his head, but I didn't move from my position.

"Okay." He squeezed my hand before letting go.

I was hit with a wall of pain but instead of crumpling down to it, I gritted my teeth and sucked it up. I could do this. I had to do this. The icy sensation in me was melting. I could feel my body elongating. My claws were forming. I could feel the painful after-sensation as my organs fit back into place and how my teeth grew out of my gums, leaving a metalic taste into my mouth.

My senses were sharpening and shifting which others didn't experience. My sense of smell was helping me inhale Zaliver's scent; now that I couldn't touch him. My heartbeat slowed down, but it sounded stronger to my ears somehow. I didn't think about how different my limbs felt and how odd it was to feel smooth fur when I could still think as if I were in my human form. The rain had stopped a few moments ago, but the ground was still cold and wet yet I wasn't.

When the pain in my body seemed to retract and make its way to my chest, I let out a strange gasp and my mouth opened with my large teeth. This was it; my pain was ending.

With one last painful twist in my chest, it all suddenly stopped—the pain, the sore muscles, and my tiredness. My eyes were still shut, but when I heard Zaliver shifting and his bones breaking, I knew he was in his beast form.

306

I now realized that the beast in my mind was no longer crouching and had her head tilted to the side.

Because now I was the couched beast.

I felt as if I was reborn.

Without opening my eyes, I slowly straightened myself up. I had expected myself to fumble and fall like a newly-shifted wolf, but I stood with grace and ease, my muscles feeling strong and agile. With a deep breath, my eyes snapped open.

My eyesight was sharper than ever. I could see every detail on trees and rocks from a distance just as I could see Zaliver in front of me clearly even without the moon light. I was so afraid and terrified the first time I saw him that I hadn't truly looked at him. His fur was the same color of his pitch black hair; it seemed to give a silvery bounce every once in a while. Judging with how high off the ground I felt, I could tell that even in this new form, Zaliver's physical traits would remain the dominant one. His build was larger than me with packed on muscles. He still towered over me but not as much as if we were in human form. He looked down at me with intelligent black eyes that seemed to be looking at me over as well.

"*Vivian?*" His voice rang clear in my head.

Something stirred in me at the sound of his voice in my new form.

"*Yes?*" I responded to him. My mind was clear and unexpectedly organized.

"*Come, run with me,*" he said. His build was crouched down, looking at me expectantly.

Hmmm. Running must feel like running as a human, but the choice of four legs seemed to be an option because I could feel how my new form would work with me.

"*Alright.*" I felt excitement and adrenaline fill me. Running had always been something that called to me no matter the form. Most of the time, anyway.

I took off first. I felt the atmosphere change with the thrill of a chase in this place. I was faster than I had ever thought I could move. My speed was able to make everything I passed both splendidly clear and blurry at the same time for me. I was aware of everything too. My reflexes were making me jump, duck, and avoid hitting anything in my path before I fully acknowledged them. My senses were high and strong. I could see the trees miles away. I could smell the scent of both old and new animals that had been in the area as well as the wolves that were miles away. I could hear the pounding heartbeat of every little critter hiding as two deadly new beasts prowled through their territory at night.

Because that's what we were.

Deadly. Strong. Powerful. Together.

We ran for the longest of times. I didn't tire fast but I was still new, so I stopped near a large pond, drinking its water. Zaliver stopped a few feet away from me. His beauty was deadly and attractive to me as he stood at the top of the small cliff in front the pond. He gazed down at me.

I looked down at the pond, startled a little at the animal before me. It had large black eyes that watched every move stared back at me and had dark chocolate fur covering a lean and fit build. My beast's body was larger than I thought. I looked down at my clawed hands and raised one, watching as the reflection did the same. When I dipped a claw into the pond, I watched the ripples work on my reflection.

I looked back up into Zaliver's gazing beast.

He looked at me for a minute more and then up at the moon. His snout opened, showing the razor-sharp teeth that I both feared and felt at first. He let out a loud howl.

A few seconds later, I heard hundreds of howls fill the air. I kept looking around as if trying to see the wolves that were howling, but there were so many from different directions. I just looked back at the beast before me. Through the bond, I felt his side filled with pride, possessiveness, protection, care, and an emotion that had me stopping for a moment.

He lifted his head back up and howled but this time, I joined in with him.

When we ran back to the clearing, Zaliver showed me how to shift back after doing so himself. He stood naked before me with no shame at all, which I found very . . . arousing. A voice in the back of my head said *heat* repeatedly. When I finally did shift back to my human form, Zaliver was ready, catching me as I finally felt the energy drain from my body. I felt him place his black shirt over me before taking me into his arms gently and sitting down for a moment.

I began dozing off quickly in his arms after realizing something important through all of this chaos.

I not only trusted Zaliver but . . . I might just love him as well. I had a lot to do.

CHAPTER 27

When I woke up the next day, I felt different from other mornings—refreshed and energized—but there was something else. I could feel the beast in my mind. My wolf seemed unafraid and contented, so I let her be.

I could hear things both inside and outside. I could see the dust partials in the air and smell different scents. The heaviest and most intoxicating part was hearing very, very faint conversations though I couldn't understand them as they seemed to be so far away.

How good was my hearing?

I was surrounded by soft and smooth material, but warm arms wrapped my body, pushing me against a solid chest that was breathing up and down slowly. I could tell the sun was high and bright in the sky because the room was illuminated with a soft glow, lighting up the room. The sunlight covered the end of the bed as if reaching for us. If I stared for too long, I felt as if my eyes would burn for some reason. I wasn't thinking much; it was a rare moment where my mind was blank and went on instinct.

I inhaled slowly and closed my eyes as the scent of pure male and unique woody scent filled my mind. As soon as I thought about turning, I realized I was already facing Zaliver's direction, not disturbing his sleep. He laid with one hand under his head and the other under me; his hold was loose. His face looked so relaxed and peaceful. His long dark lashes made his face structure stand out somehow. My eyes trailed down to his slightly parted lips and stared.

I raised a hand and touched a strand of his black hair. His dark locks fanned around the pillow. His hair was silky between my fingers and was long enough to wrap around my finger. I felt as if I was looking at him for the first time.

His eyes opened and without trouble, he focused on me as if he wasn't just sleeping a minute ago. His expression was still relaxed but with anxiousness. He pulled me closer, and I felt his thumb make soothing motions on my back.

I tilted my head to the side, feeling my hair move. It shouldn't have felt this heavy. Zaliver removed the hand behind his head and reached for my hair. I wasn't surprised to see a long chocolate strand. It seemed as if my hair had grown longer during the change. I wonder what else changed.

As he gazed and studied my hair, I studied his eyes.

His eyes were the color of the clear ocean and a thunderstorm. I began to lean in closer to him while an electric spark got stronger as I got closer. His eyes flickered up to look into my eyes and let got of the strand, then cupped my face. I leaned into his touch. His hands were smooth yet rough. Hmmm, his warm touch was comforting.

He studied my face and whatever expression I had must have pleased him because he smiled at me. The corners of his lips were lifting slowly, but even then, I could still see some tightness around his eyes.

I smiled back, mimicking his action. Everything felt new somehow and yet not. And those voices still didn't seem to be clearing up, almost like a buzz in my head, but I tried to ignore them.

I felt new, but I also felt the same somehow like it was my birthday and didn't feel older.

When we got out of bed, showered, and changed, Zaliver told me not to rush because I wouldn't be going anywhere for a while. When I looked into the mirror, I was relieved to see that not much had changed in me. If anything, my hair was longer and healthier. My skin seemed smoother; old scars and blemishes were almost non-existent. Zaliver's words made a small amount of defiance grow in me for no reason.

"Oh yeah? And why is that?" I asked, leaning on one leg and popping the other with hands on hips.

If I wanted to go outside, I could.

"For one, your eyes are more sensitive than ever to light," he said softly.

He walked over to the window and with one glance at me, he opened the curtain.

I didn't expect the burning sensation my eyes went through, and I did not realize I jumped back until I hit something. The light filling the room was blinding me. Zaliver closed the curtains. It took a few seconds before I got my sight back by blinking.

"So, are your ears." I watched him with weary eyes now, knowing I wouldn't like what he was going to do next.

He grabbed a remote from the nightstand. I covered my ears when a horrible static sound filled the air, including voices that seemed to be screaming in my ears. Zaliver turned it off. I uncovered my ears and shook my head to get rid of the ringing.

"Then, there's your lack of understanding in your new strength, speed, and so on," he said, walking up to me. He took hold of my hand and pulled me closely to him and then turned me around.

My brows furrowed at the cracked and damaged drawer with a shape that could be identified as my back hitting it. Talk about back bone.

"Then, there's your touch," he whispered next to my ear.

I felt the tips of his index finger skim down my bare right arm. My lips parted at the positive tingles he left in the process. His nose skimmed the side of my face softly. My breath hitched when I felt the same index finger jumped over to my hip and then slipped under my night shirt and onto my bare skin.

His other fingers moved with his index finger softly over my stomach. My eyes widened in surprise at the heat that began churning in the pit of my belly. He laid his hand flat on my skin and pushed me back onto him. I felt something dig into my back. I let my head fall back and took a step back, almost to get closer while my breathing was getting heavy. I felt myself overwhelmed in all of my emotions and senses.

"Your emotions are heightened as well," he said, trailing hot kisses from the side of my neck to my face. His husky voice made me snap out of my trance. If I didn't get a hold of myself, I had a one hundred and fifty percent idea that something would be going down.

"*And hopefully in as well*," my wolf muttered while my beast hummed in agreement.

Ahhh, this is going to take a while to get used to. Why do I feel like I just gained a pervert with the beast? My wolf and her together . . . great. I could feel the headaches and arguments coming already.

"O-okay, so what now?" I asked, jumping away from him. His arms dropped as a knowing look made its way to his smug face.

On a second thought, staying inside looked just as comfortable.

"Now, let me show you how to control your new self," he said, a hint of amusement and excitement in his voice. I narrowed my eyes at him. A happy Zaliver was good, but it was also suspicious and dangerous.

"Why do you look so happy? What are you planning, Zaliver?" He crossed his arms over his broad chest and looked down at me with playful sternness while the corners of his lips pulling up.

"You will refer to me as Mr. Azrala from now on because I am your teacher. I must warn you though," he said and walked around me slowly, "rewards will only be given when you succeed. And when you don't . . ." He trailed off.

I bit my bottom lips to hold back a smile but didn't stop my head from shaking at his joke. Him? A teacher? Please. I felt goosebumps rise on my body and heard the shift in the air. I tried to move but even with my heightened senses and speed, I couldn't dodge

311

him because he was better experienced than me and I couldn't quite comprehend what was going on until it happened.

I squeaked as a hard smack hit my behind. I covered my butt and turned around to glare at Zaliver who had a smirk on his face.

"You—"

"Now, get downstairs so we can start, or you get detention in five, four—"

"You can't be—"

"I think I have a ruler good enough for spanking somewhere, or would you prefer just my hand?" I ran past him and down the stairs faster than I had ever moved in my life. His laughter was booming through the house as he made his way down. I rubbed my butt and muttered under my breath. I could feel both shifters in my mind stirring with amusement. A need to play along with him grew but mostly, all I felt was the sting on my butt.

"Jackass . . . I'll give you a good old-fashioned Vivian detention. There will be tears," I muttered under my breath, knowing he could hear me but not caring.

"Oh really?" he said, coming into sight. I stayed silent and just stuck my tongue out at him. He raised a brow with his eyes sparkling in amusement.

I looked away from him and then moved my attention around the living room. Every little thing distracted me and had me snapping my head to look at something else. A clearing throat had me remembering   Zaliver.

"Ready?" he asked, leaning on the stairway bars.

"What? No food first?" I whined unthinkingly. Just the thought of food alone made me feel as if I hadn't eaten for days, and my stomach itself seemed like a black hole in need of consuming sustenance.

He rolled his eyes and shook his head. My eyes flickered to the smooth skin on his neck, then back to his face.

"If you want to eat, you'll have to learn how to control your senses first. I can cook for you, but your sense of smell has gotten so much stronger that you will be able to smell all of the individual ingredients. It will probably make you nauseated, and that's the last thing I want. So, this first and then food. Okay?" he explained. My lips made a little opened "o" shape in understanding and a bit of displeasure.

I'd let him lead on my training. Besides, the faster I became a master at controlling myself, then the faster I could get food.

"*Food*," the beast said with hunger.

"*Foood.*" My wolf followed along, a bit more childish.

"*Focus*," I said, sighing in my head at the two.

312

"Okay. Let's get started then," I said, cracking my fingers only to regret when I broke one. There was no real pain, just a stinging sensation.

Before I could let out a surprised yell, it snapped itself back into place. By that point, Zaliver had leaned up and was shaking his head at me, reaching for my hand.

"What part of you not understanding how much more strength you have, do you not get?" he muttered, both annoyed and concerned while looking over my finger.

"Well, excuse me for purposely breaking my finger, teacher. Won't do it again," I said, both distracted and amazed at how fast it healed. I bent my pointer finger to see how it was. It was instant. How cool! Imagine if a broken finger healed that fast, then I would be invincible when it came to paper cuts. I felt strong but it somehow felt just the same as my other strength, so it seemed natural to ignore it. I usually had to call upon my strength; I guess lycan strength just stays with us at all time. It was a bubbling energy in my body, waiting to be used.

"*Yup*," the beast said.

"*Well, thanks for the info.*"

"*No problem*," she said mockingly.

Zaliver let go of my hand, a serious look crossed his face.

"All right. Let's get started. I can already see the side effects of starving," he joked.

"Hey!" I exclaimed.

~•~

For three hours, Zaliver had spent teaching me various things. From controlling how much focus I should put in my sense of smell, how to hold back on my strength if I thought everything around me was an egg-shell (Harder than you think), and to focus my eyes on what I wanted and tune things out.

I also learned three important things about Zaliver: First, he was insanely good at motivating me. Second, he was good at telling when I pretended to understand his lecture. Third, he was one of *those* teachers.

"Zaliver, I swear to—" I said through clenched teeth.

"It's Mr. Azrala!" he interrupted by being playfully harsh. I didn't even know there could be such a tone until now. Man, it would have been a turn on if we weren't in the situation we were now.

"It's Mr. Asshaha," I mimicked him, ignoring his loud and not so playful snarl.

313

I struggled not to let go of the bar inside the gym; maybe not to drop to my death but certainly to a painful fall. I had no idea how high up I was, and I really didn't want to think about it.

"Get me down from here! I don't see how having me hang from here is anything helpful!" I yelled at him. My clammy hands were making it hard to grip the bar.

"That's because you're not suppose to hang. You're supposed to pull yourself up to the top," he said tautly.

The top of mother fucking what? The rainbow?

I don't think he noticed because I sure as hell couldn't even imagine pulling myself up. What made him think I wanna even try?

I looked down around my arms and threw him the meanest glare I could give. He was looking up at me with an expectant look on his face. His eyes narrowed.

"*Studying this ass,*" my wolf said.

My legs swung in all directions under me as I tried to move myself down onto something but couldn't because I myself didn't know how I even ended up here. Maybe if I had paid more attention to him, I wouldn't be in this position.

I gave up and let out a breath, adjusting my grip on the bar as my hands began slipping. My beast and my wolf were just onlookers, and I could feel it. Neither of them was helping me at all. Traitors.

"Powerful and improved my ass," I muttered.

What good was strength if I couldn't even pull myself up? I would either not use enough of it or too much of it and break something. I still wasn't exactly sure how strong or fast I was since we had mostly been doing breathing and listening exercises and focusing stuff.

"*You'll thank us later,*" they both said.

I growled, annoyed at them and Zaliver. It seemed like the bars were giving up. It wasn't that I was that heavy, but I had began to grip them harder than I should and was beginning to bend them. Shit.

"Zaliver, get me down from here! I'm hungry and I want food!" I shouted at him. I didn't want to give my all in this because I counted this as unnecessary when I could be eating. I kept that last thought to myself. Maybe that's why I was fat?

Nah.

It was silent for a few seconds before he sighed and then I felt the small shift of air that was letting me know he was moving. I learned that Zaliver was by far faster than me even now, but I was at least fast enough to know when he was moving. I wonder who would win in a race? A second later, I felt my feet land on the ground softly. I dropped to the ground and threw my arms over my face. My body felt off and yet pumped and alert, which was weird. It was like a rush and need to do something unbelievable.

"Hmmm," I heard from him. I moved an arm to glare at him. He stood above me with his legs parted and his hands on his hips.

"Hmmm, what?" I asked. He shook his head, but the decisive and suspicious look didn't leave his face. I wonder if he knew I wasn't giving it my all? Probably.

"I'll tell you after breakfast." I perked up at that and ran quickly to the kitchen, waiting on the counter with an eager smile. Well, I certainly couldn't cook, and I don't think becoming a lycan changed that.

As Zaliver cooked, I focused my eyes on him, ignoring the distraction my body and senses from everything else going on—the sound and smell of what he was cooking. As I watched his body move swiftly in the kitchen, the way he gracefully moved and tossed the pancakes in the air only to swiftly catch them, how concentrated he looked, and most definitely, how good his ass looked in those pants, I felt a low-key hum begin in me.

I felt the same sensation from this morning arise as I studied my mate work in front of me. He was a mighty fine man too with a body that made me want to explore everything hidden from sight. When he turned around with the sky-high pile of pancakes and a plate of fruit salad and bread spread with jam, I forced my eyes to look away from him. The voices in my head were not helping with their own wanton thoughts, pushing onto mine.

As a werewolf, I had always eaten a lot, but after five huge pancakes, four slices of bread, three pieces of bacon and two cups of coffee, I think I could beat a record. I eyed the empty plate in front of me with a bit of disbelief and then eyed Zaliver who was eating twice as much as I was as if nothing out of the ordinary.

"Was that all right?" he asked, pausing.

"Oh yeah. It tasted good," I said stupidly.

"I mean, were you able to see why I had you practice your sense of smell first before you ate?" he clarified, reaching over for his coffee. My eyes flickered to how his hand wrapped securely around the coffee mug and how he brought it up to his mouth. Since when was drinking coffee so attractive?

"Oh, it was okay. I found a good method for distracting myself from everything," I said coyly at him. He lifted a brow at me but didn't ask.

"*That ass,*" my wolf howled. I almost choked on my air, but let out a small cough.

His amusement and pleasure rang through me. He was happy that I checked him out. Of course, he was. He knew he was fine-looking,

315

and he was all mine. After he finished, we cleaned everything. I was surprised to see him growl agitatedly before he pulled out his phone and began walking away from me. *Were we done for the day?* I thought excitedly.

"So, does this mean I can go out without you?" I asked, already eager to see the outside.

He turned half to me with a scolding yet sorry look on his face.

"Not even close. Can you give me a moment? I have a call to make," he asked. I nodded and he began to walk away.

"You know, I'll probably be able to hear you no matter how far you go now." I taunted out to him, sitting crisscross on the couch.

"Yes, but I doubt you'll be able to focus on this conversation out of everything that makes a sound or moves. Besides, the farther I get from you, the lesser the phone static will bother your ears," he said, already far away. He was fast even when he was slow. Dang.

"Hmmm." I pouted as he disappeared, but I wasn't planning on listening to that painful sound that the tv made this morning. My ears hurt just from thinking about it.

Instead, what I did was get up and head to the living room curtain. Zaliver had all of them closed, saying that direct sunlight would hurt and that it would be easier to ease my eyes to bright things.

The bright light poked out from the curtain. I lifted my hand and put it in the sunlight, basking in on the natural warmth. I closed my eyes and just felt it. I felt a strong pull and longing to go outside from both animals. I wanted to feel the wind move my hair all over the place as well as the sounds of the island and waves. Being in the house after a shift wasn't good. I really, really wanted to go outside.

There was a tug somewhere in me; a familiar yet odd feeling. The buzzing of conversations continued stronger. I still couldn't tell what everyone was saying since they were overlapping, but there was a conversation or two voices that rang stronger than the two. Even then, I couldn't hear them. I wanted to say it was like when we used the pack link, but this felt different.

I must have spaced out because my ears caught the sound of Zaliver's boots making their way back to me. He must have finished talking to whoever he was talking to. I turned to face him.

"Who'd you call?" I asked. He put his hands in his pants' back pocket. My eyes flickered to his muscles as they flexed. The humming vibrated through me a bit louder. My fingers twitched.

"A friend and Dr. Leonard is coming over," he said slowly with a contemplative look. His blue eyes were at me for a reaction. The name rang a bell, but I paid it no mind.

"Why?" I asked after a brief pause.

"I want to see if everything is alright with you. That's all."

Does anyone else smell B.S.?

"And why wouldn't you be able to tell if I was alright? Why the doctor?" I asked suspiciously for his reasons not that I didn't trust Zaliver but after going to the doctor with him, I learned that things always took uncomfortable turns.

"Because besides your lack of control on the basic senses, speed, and strength, you're oddly . . . calm. When I changed, I was very unstable for the lack of a better word. You shouldn't be this calm. You just went through a huge transformation last night, Vivian. You do realize that right?" he said, walking up to me and putting one hand on my shoulder.

"Yeah," I stopped talking. As soon as his hand made contact with my shoulder, the humming vibrated through me again as if someone had pulled the string of a guitar and the cord's vibration were in me. This was different though. At the end of the hum, something seemed to start—a candle's heat, small and warm but growing with each second his hand stayed on me. I was about to lift my hand and place it on his chest when I heard tires pull up closer to the house. A guest.

Doc?

Zaliver must have heard too because he gave me a comforting smile and removed his hand.

As soon as he did so, the candle flickered out. I then felt cold; a coldness I didn't realize I had been living with my whole life until now. The startling feeling made me stand still and furrow my brows.

Why did I now just realize how absolutely hollow and boring my life was before meeting Zaliver? Even if he was a jackass who was a pain sometimes, he still seemed to bring life and joy to my world. He was my . . . warmth. The front door opened. A strong wind must have blown from outside because a scent that I must have smelt at some point but couldn't register at that moment hit me. It was as if nothing else in this world that I could relate to.

It was like I was shoved back into my head and forced to watch my body react as the beast took over.

As soon as the scent hit me, my immediate thought was danger and to protect Zaliver from it. My head snapped in the direction of the smell. Two hearts: one was welcoming and the other, a threat. My eyes flashed silver, and as soon as the threat came into sight, I lunged with a snarl at the right body, ignoring the other.

I landed on top of a bewildered male.

"Threat. Must eliminate the threat. Protect, Mate," the beast snarled viciously in my mind.

I could feel her anger at his presence. She craved the need to see him cry out in pain and for a mercy that wouldn't be given to him. Her thoughts both frightened and pulled me in. We lifted our clawed

317

hand to swipe at him, moving faster than he could understand. I could see in his face that in his mind, he was still falling.

I was suddenly lifted from him and being pulled back. I roared in anger and tried to remove the strong arms and hands from me, but they moved faster than me. My hands were restrained by one hand while the other solidly pushed me close to their body. I thrashed and shrieked, snarled and snapped at nothing. My eyes were seeing red, but my vision was a perfect silver. I was, no, she was angry; thoughts clouded with need to get rid of the unknown male wolf in our home who was too close to our mate. We didn't know him. The blond-haired man with golden hazel eyes backed away, frightened. My restrained arms outreached for him, but the hand around me gripped tighter.

"Now, this makes more sense to me," a throaty voice said behind me. My anger and thrashing lessened a bit but not by much. My body was recognizing the body wrapped around mine.

"A-alpha, m-maybe I should g-g-go?" the male asked. His voice was shaking as he spoke. I pushed my body forward and tried reaching for him again. Zaliver grunted behind me.

"Shut up. I so knew you weren't trying earlier. Come on, Vivian. Snap out of it," he cooed to me, picking me up and bringing me up his body. I felt his hand push firmly on my stomach. My feet kicked out now that I wasn't on the ground. The beast didn't like this.

Her eyes were still on the quivering male in front of her. My eyes narrowed at him as I pulled my lips back and barred my elongated canines at him.

"Vivian," he whispered lowly in my ear, his breath tickling my ear. A humming began again.

"Vivian," he said again, nuzzling my neck with the side of his face.

My beast seemed to like this because slowly the anger and distrust seemed to melt away. The humming took its place, and when Zaliver's lips skimmed the mark on the side of my neck, my whole body seemed to have slumped in relaxation.

"Gotcha," Zaliver murmured to me. I was pushed forward again and in control.

"C-can I g-go now—"

"Shut. Up." Zaliver snapped.

I shook my head to clear my thoughts. I felt like I just walked out of a dark movie theater. I pulled my hands back while Zaliver was slowly letting them go. I looked at the poor man I had tried to kill apologetically.

"I'm sorry. My um . . . well, I didn't recognize you at first. I'm really sorry about that just now. Do you think you could forgive me for that and maybe start all over again?" I asked sheepishly and sort of mortified.

"*Nice, you crazy animal. Now, the doctor thinks we are a violent luna with the Lupus Deus as her mate, who was known to be pretty violent himself.*"

"*We're the perfect violent couple then, aren't we?*" she scoffed.

I muttered things under my breath and then gave the doctor a small smile. He stared back at me as if I was crazy and then without missing a beat, he gave me a big smile.

"Of course, Luna. I wouldn't even hesitate to forgive you. Attacking me and almost ripping my god damn . . . I mean attacking me was totally understandable. There's nothing to forgive . . . not at all . . . "
He trailed off oddly. His body shook as his eyes flickered from behind me to my eyes.

"Are you glaring at him, Zaliver?" I asked dryly.

"No," he said calmly behind me.

"You sure?" I asked again.

"Yes, right Dr. Leonard?" he asked or more like ordered. I rolled my eyes.

"Oh yes," Dr. Leonard answered quickly.

"*I don't think his answer counts anymore. Our mate made the doctor his bitch,*" my wolf whispered. I and the beast agreed.

It was silent for a minute before I looked down and swung my dangling legs.

"Sooo, you gonna put me down or . . . " I trailed off. Zaliver slowly slid me down his body but didn't remove his hand from in front of me.

"Alright, Dr. Leonard. Besides that little test, I need you to check Vivian and then get the heck out," Zaliver said briskly. The doc nodded and walked out quickly from the house. His car door opened and I heard him rummage around.

"So, what was that?" I asked, lifting and then turning my head to look up around him.

"That, was what I had thought was happening. When I turned, I attacked anyone near me. It didn't matter that I already knew them. I was wondering why you didn't attack me in the morning, and now I can see it was the bond preventing that. Everyone else however is not included," he explained to me. I frowned as he talked, focusing on what he was saying and not on the humming.

"Are you telling me you knew there was a chance I would attack you, and your stupid ass still slept with me even though I woke up first and I could have clawed your eyes out?" I asked angrily at him. What type of first degree idiot—

"First of all, I'm not stupid at all. Second, I was awake the whole night, making sure you were alright while your body calmed down and adjusted. Just because I let you stare at me this morning didn't mean I wasn't awake. Third, even if you did attack me, as you saw earlier, you are no threat to me," he growled out.

"No threat, huh."

"Yes."

"Really?"

"Yes, really."

"Says the one who got his neck snapped by this not-so-threatening chick," I mocked. His body tensed.

"Gotcha," I said.

I was surprised when he gave me a wicked smirk in return, the humming became the candle again and my breathing became harder. His eyes narrowed down on me—bright, blue, and burning.

"Oh, did you, now?" he said huskily. I was suddenly flipped around and my front was pushed against his. Now, his hand was on my lower back, pushing me against his body while his other hand gripped the back of my head softly yet firmly.

"*Wow. What the fuck just happened now?*"

"*I don't know, but don't fuck it up,*" my wolf muttered.

Both of us had began to lean into each other, eyes focused on one another. The air around us charged and became intense. Why did it feel as if once our lips touched, we'd start something that needed to be finished. The candle-like fire burned through my body. I could hear Zaliver's heart speeding up just as mine was. Our lips were mere seconds away from touching—

"I've got everything ready for ohh . . . " Dr. Leonard spoke behind us.

Damn doc, I thought with a bit of anger.

Zaliver looked at me with clear wanting and a burning passion that I felt as equally for a moment before his jaw clenched as he took a deep breath and then looked over at the doctor.

"Just hurry," he snapped, releasing me.

After a brief pause, Dr. Leonard hurried in and set everything up. He checked my eyes, ears, and all the rest. Luckily, he didn't even ask about my weight. I didn't say much on the topic, but I didn't doubt we would have a repeat of earlier. Zaliver stood nearby with watchful eyes. I noted and quite frankly found a sort of pleasure of watching how his body tensed every time the doc had to touch my face or skin in general; the scowl on his face amused me though. By the time Dr. Leonard finished, he had written plenty on his clipboard.

"So, what's the verdict doc?" I asked jokingly.

Zaliver came closer to me and the doc discreetly backed away. His heart had been pounding since the moment he got here. Sweat trickled down the side of his face.

Was he like this the last time I saw him? No, I don't think so.

Hmmm, it was obvious he was frightened of Zaliver but now, was he also afraid of me?

"*You did try to kill him,*" my beast reminded me.

"*No, you tried to kill him for which I apologized for.*"

"*Me, you, us, we, same thing.*"

"*Whatever.*"

"Well, everything seems to be fine and going smoothly. Umm, just like any other . . . transformation. You have muscles and unused strength that needs to be exercised," the doctor said. I made a horrified expression at where he was going with this.

"So, I recommend training for the luna until she gets a good grasp on her new abilities and physical level," he said, looking up from his clipboard.

"No thanks."

"Alright. How much time should she be spending physical activities? Recommendations?"

My head snapped back to look at Zaliver who had his arms crossed over his chest. He looked at the doctor seriously, ignoring my daggered eyes.

"At least one or two hours a day until she gets the hang of her physical limitations and abilities. It will also help her reach full capacity but besides that, everything seems fine," he answered.

"Hey, I don't want—"

"For how long will this have to go on?" Zaliver asked, completely ignoring me. I knew that he knew I didn't want to work out because through the bond, he was sending comforting emotions. He placed his hand on my shoulder and gave me a soft squeeze.

"Maybe a week or more. It really just depends on how much effort Luna will put in," Dr. Leonard said, glancing at me. I huffed at them and turned my head away from them. I wasn't going to do shit, and they could say what they wanted. I ran as a wolf and now, I could do it as a lycan. Surely that equaled to a physical work out.

"Oh, I'm sure she'll give her one hundred percent," Zaliver said confidently. His other hand landing beside my mark. I tensed as he began rubbing the mark slowly and softly with his thumb. My body damn near turned to mush, enjoying the tingles his contact brought. The humming didn't start, but a direct call to my heat did.

They talked for a second and then the doctor was out. All the while, my body was still unavailable to move as Zaliver's thumb played my body like a puppet with just one touch. Zaliver removed his hands and walked the doctor out, giving me a moment to breathe and collect myself. There was someone else with him but only Zaliver entered. The second new person stayed outside. When he came back in, I managed a good expression. Not to this, not to that.

"More like 'Fuck me now. Did you just volunteer me for exercise?'" my wolf joked.

"What was that?" I asked with a leveled tone. He ran a hand through his hair. I wanted to do that for a moment.

"I knew you would reject the idea if we even asked you, so I made the decision for you. It's for your well-being and you know it too," he said, walking up to me. I put my hands on my hips and looked or scowled up at him.

"True or not, it's unnecessary physical movement that Vivian does not approve of," I said with a bit of attitude. Me and workouts were a no; me and food however . . .

His eyes became amused as his lips parted and then closed before he spoke, clearly enjoying himself.

"Vivian, doesn't approve? Are you speaking in third person?" he asked, chuckling.

"And if she is?" I asked. I could be weird if I wanted to. Besides, it would hopefully distract him from the real topic and of exercise in general.

"Well then, Zaliver wants to join of course," he answered mockingly serious, playing along.

"Can I be the narrator then?" a male's voice said from behind the door. I frowned at Zaliver and looked behind him.

Who the heck is that and why do they sound so familiarly annoying?

Zaliver rolled his eyes and shook his head and then looked down at me seriously.

Albericus is at the door. Don't attack him, was all he said before walking over to open the door.

"Why would I attack Algeb—" As soon as his foot landed in the house, I saw red again and lunged.

"Jez-us woman!" he exclaimed as he bounced back, narrowly escaping my grasp as arms wrapped around me again in a tight grip.

"It was worth a try," Zaliver said, picking me up and turning me around. I tried to get out to get rid of the male in the house.

"You knew she was gonna attack me and you still told me to come?! What type of alpha has his luna kill his good-looking main beta that has done nothing but be loyal and hard working! Are you mad—"

"SHUT UP!" Zaliver growled. He pushed me against the wall and had both of my hands pinned above me. I bared my teeth to the green-eyed male who bared his teeth back at me. I snarled at him, but Zaliver forced my focus back on him.

"Come on, Vivian. It's Alber—Algebra as you call him—" he said into my ear but was cut off by a wail from the male at the door.

"No! Not you too man," the male whined, putting his hands on his head and shaking back and forth. I knew it was Algebra, but why the heck did I try to claw his eyes out? Actually, I didn't. The beast did.

I took a deep breath, forcefully, then closed my eyes. It took me a moment. After focusing on pushing the beast back and keeping her there, I opened my eyes. Zaliver loosened his hold on me but didn't remove his body from mine. My wolf and my beast quite liked this position.

"Why do I keep attacking people who walk into the house?" I asked no one in particular. I tried to ignore how Zaliver's chest rubbed on me with every breath he took, mmmhhh . . . so warm and sturdy . . . focus. . . on his chest . . . no, no.

"Because you're crazy to want to get rid of all of this fine piece of ass . . . " Algebra muttered, throwing me a dirty look with eyes narrowing on me.

"Because your beast knows these people by your memory, but she hasn't actually interacted with them. It doesn't help that it's in our house, which she sees as her territory. Are you in control?" Zaliver asked me. I nodded and after a moment, he took a step back.

"Nah man. Don't let her go. She tried to kill me!" Algebra exclaimed, pointing a finger at me. I smiled at him with his narrowed eyes again.

"So, am I going to be attacking everyone?" I said, worried. If that was the case, then I didn't eat to hurt any of my friends, especially Hannah and the baby.

"No . . . but there's also something else," Zaliver said mysteriously, looking down at me with an odd expectant look.

"What?" I asked, really wanting to know.

"I'll tell you later." I sighed at his answer, still as cryptic as ever.

"*Nah, tell me now,*" my wolf said, shaking her wolf head. I looked over at the annoyed looking beta in our house.

"Sorry about that, Algebra," I ignored his groan, "but as you've heard, I'm not the one responsible for my violent outburst or not completely," I said, moving away from the wall. The guys watched my every movement with caution.

"Right. Right. What did you call me for anyway, Zaliver?" He asked, deciding to ignore me. I snorted at the look on his face. He looked like one of those little kids who were just told they couldn't go out to recess, aggrieved.

"I need you to look after Vivian for an hour or less. I've got to do something." My head snapped over at him in surprise.

"You're leaving?" I couldn't hide the disappointment in my voice. I couldn't help but want him near even though at least seventy percent of it came from within.

Why the heck didn't he tell me?

My beast and wolf growled in my head, not liking that he was going to leave us. I suddenly felt a hundred times more possessive of him than before. Scary.

"Just for a moment. I'll be back soon though. Don't worry," he said, walking up to me and kissing my forehead. He pulled away before the humming could begin again.

"Albericus—"

"Yeah, yeah. I know the whole protect-her-with-your-life thing even though now she'd be the one protecting me . . . " he grumbled, displeased, looking off to the side. Zaliver stared blankly at him for a moment. Albericus tensed and his body posture changed as his face went grim. My head buzzed again with voices and the same thing happened from before; two voices stood out. I squinted at both of the guys as a thought crossed my mind at what was going on.

Were they mind linking?

And if they were, was I somewhat listening to them. I could hear them but for some reason , I couldn't understand them like they were talking underwater in my mind. Algebra's lips parted to a small "o" in understanding of something I wasn't aware of.

"Oh," he said and then nodded. I narrowed my eyes at Zaliver.

What was he keeping from me? I'd get it out of him one way or another even if it kill—

Nope, can't die. Damn. What was I supposed to say then? I guess I couldn't use any dead puns now.

"So, would you like to tell me what's the reason for leaving?" I asked, crossing my arms over my chest to look at Zaliver who glanced at me with an unidentifiable look.

"I will. I promise. For now, I have to go have a talk with an over curious snake," he muttered, both annoyed and thoughtful at the same time.

Curious snake? Is that code for something? Before I could say more, I felt the air shift and gave up because the next second, he was gone and it was now just me and a butt hurt beta.

"So, are you going to tell me what that meant?" I asked him. He pursed his lips and shook his head at me.

My beast and my wolf were muttering to themselves, wanting to know where and what he was doing.

Does curious little snake mean slippery little bitch as in a woman? I felt anger and annoyance at a possible chick my mate was meeting. My gums

324

began to ache in my mouth, but my canines didn't come out. I felt the need to bite something hard.

I looked at Algebra seriously. He was the only one who really knew. He saw the look on my face and began shaking his head at me, already saying no.

I am Luna. His Luna. He had to tell me.

"Oh no. Sorry, Vivian, but I'm under sworn oath not to tell," he began saying.

"Tell me," I said softly, but my tone was strong, menacing, and fierce. A command he couldn't deny. His eyes widened and his hands went up to his throat to grasp it as he looked at me in shock. As his face pained and reddened, I began to worry that he was choking himself when strained. He began to speak.

"No! Ahhh! Alpha, no, no . . . went to go talk to Venom about still being here. Shit. He's not—ahh, damn—supposed to be here this long and Alpha wants to know why he still is. I'm dead." He coughed out, rubbing at his temples and throat.

As he slowly recovered, I looked down at him, surprised and confused for many reasons. At least, I now knew it was a guy Zaliver was going to meet. Who was this Venom guy then? Who would name their kid Venom, and why did it seem odd for him to still be around Zaliver? Did he not live in the pack? And what the heck did I do to Algebra? I walked up to him and patted him on the back, concerned.

"I'm sorry. Are you alright? Do you want some water?" I asked him.

That's odd. Usually, the luna command wouldn't hurt the ordered person then again, this wasn't a normal mated couple. Most lunas only got their official command power when they were are fully mated. I hadn't mated and yet . . . I still commanded him. It just seemed to hurt him though. I frowned as he stood and patted his chest.

"Nah, I'm good. You know, I just had my luna almost attack me and then had her force information literally out of my throat. You'll probably have to look for a new beta, but no one will ever be as good-looking and hardworking as me. Let's not even forget the fact that my own bloody mate won't let me go near her—" He cut himself off mid rant and his face paled.

My head snapped back in shock as I blinked at his ashen face.

"Mate? You have a mate?" I asked. Why hadn't I heard? Matter-of-fact, why hadn't Zaliver told me? I groaned inwardly. I was going to have serious talk with Zaliver about communication. Algebra's little confession distracted me.

Algebra nodded slowly without looking at me. He walked over to the couch and sat down on it, putting his head in his hands and pulling on his brown curls. Did he get a haircut? Man, I'm out of it. I

325

hesitated over to the couch, feeling both guilt for hurting him and curiosity over who his mate was. Who is she? Do I know her? The oddest sensation came over me as I looked at him sitting on the couch. It was as if all my emotions suddenly . . . stopped and disappeared. Emotions made their way to my chest—sadness, ache, anger, and despair.

These weren't my emotions. They were his.

I blinked as the emotions swarmed my chest, making my eyes sting at the sharp and raw emotions. Algebra was hurting about something.

"Want to talk about it?" I asked him softly, sitting beside him. He sighed and looked up at me. His expression was guarded and serious. For the first time, he looked like the beta who kidnapped me when we first met. If it weren't for the sorrow I knew he was feeling, I might have backed off.

"It's fine. I'm alright, Luna," he lied, trying to brush off his pain.

"What's her name?" I asked. I didn't feel comfortable knowing he was hurting and not doing anything about it. His pain felt like my pain. I almost felt protective and in need to help him feel better. After a brief pause, he slumped and lost his façade and threw his head back onto the couch, looking at the ceiling. I copied his position.

"Aurora," he said softly. The pain was clear in that one breath of a name. I said nothing, giving him a moment. I didn't have anything else to ask or at least nothing that wasn't too personal. I wanted him to tell me just what he wanted if anything at all.

"We met about seventy years ago when I was running some errands for Zaliver since he never left the island back then. It was purely out of chance that we even bumped into each other. If she had decided not to cross the street the same time I did, then we would never have seen each other since the street was so busy. She caught my eyes immediately," he spoke. His voice that of someone far away in their own thoughts.

"What does she look like?" I asked curiously.

"Long black hair, black eyes, pale white skin, slim, and around my height," he said. There was something about his description that seemed off. Maybe it was the way he explained it or maybe it was the way his body tensed besides mine.

"Or at least that's how she looks like now," he muttered. He was neither disappointed nor very happy. My brows came together.

"Now? Did she have a makeover?" I asked out loud and he shook his head.

"When I first met her, she could have been the modern-looking Snow White, but now . . . . she turned into a dark, heartless, and

326

cruel woman who's not the same. We fell in love at first sight, courted, and then mated. It was hard with me being a werewolf and her family not liking our kind—"

"Wait. She's not a werewolf?" I asked, shocked. A werewolf and different type of species mating was very rare.

"*Look who's talking,*" my wolf piped in.

"*True.*"

"No."

"Then, what is she?" He turned his head to look at me seriously.

"A witch."

"Oh," I said.

Witches were very unique and secretive creatures that even wolves tried to stay away from them, so hearing on how they were mates came as a huge shock, more so than me and Zaliver.

"You said that she was . . . cold now?" I asked him.

Why would she be cold towards her mate after they mated? It was impossible for couples to turn on each other, cheat, or even purposely hurt one another. It would be like wanting to hurt yourself.

"Yes she is," he answered flatly. His green eyes hardened, but a flicker of pain reflected sorrow back at me.

"Why is that? If you don't mind me asking," I said. He didn't have to tell me, but I didn't want him to sit here and beat himself up. Maybe I should tell Zaliver to speak with him?

Algebra slapped both hands on his thighs and then rubbed them up and down; an expression I had never seen on the playful beta just showed up. He stood and began pacing the room back and forth. His hand came up to cup the back of his head as he walked but then he stopped in front of the living room window and gave his back to me.

My beast and my wolf looked to him curiously, feeling the tension in him grow. I was about to open my mouth to tell him he didn't have to say anything when he spoke to me. His hands fisted and his structure tensed. I had a feeling that whatever he was going to say was not what I would expect.

"Because she tried to cheat death."

"What?" I asked, surprised by his answer.

"I am much older than I look, Luna. Even in all my years, I've always known that nothing good comes from playing with black magic, especially when death is involved," he spoke, still facing the window. His hands clenched even harder. I could hear his teeth working against each other. His heart pounded in his chest as emotions stirred a storm in him.

Black magic was not something I knew much of, but from what I did know, it was bad. Very bad. The usage of it was bad, but the actual price for using it was even worse. I heard of all types of side effects of witches, but to cheat death with it? Why?

"Who did she save?"

"Our son," he responded with a choked whisper.

Oh my god.

Algebra and Aurora had a . . . child? Cheated death? Did that mean . . . it was just horrible thinking about it. My heart clenched in pain and sorrow for the beta that was alway laughing and joking whenever I saw him. Under all his laughters and smiles, he was in serious pain.

Those who made us laugh with joy really were the saddest of us all.

To lose a child . . . I tried picturing me and Zaliver in that situation. I, myself, almost wanted to cry from the painful thought. My beast and my wolf howled and growled at the mere thought of our child hurt, not something they liked to think and the loss of a mate.

"Did it work?" I asked with a hopeful spark making its way in my heart. I held my breath, waiting for his answer. The longer he stayed silent, the clearer his answer became. An iciness crept through my body at the reality of this situation.

He was quiet. His heart slowed and after a few heartbeats, I smelled it. He slowly turned to me with a single tear streaming down his pained face, his eyes clenched. He was pale and tensed. I was sure that if he actually had his eyes open, I would see a pained and tortured soul.

My heart broke for Albericus at this moment.

"No," he cried out, agonized. He dropped to his knees and wept.

CHAPTER 28

People said comforting someone was a hard job but personally, I think being able to let out heart-wrenching sobs in front of someone would be the hardest part.

My instinct kicked in as soon as he dropped to the ground. I wrapped my arms around the much bigger but shaken beta as he cried over the loss of his child. He shook and sobbed. All I could do was rocked back and forth, whispered comforting words, pushed his hair back, and let him cry out some of his pain. My wolf's sadness mirrored mine, and the beast felt compassion as well as a new bond to the beta. She didn't know what to expect from him and now, she regretted attacking him and felt guilty. I think we must have sat there for at least twenty minutes. He slowly recovered and just stopped at some point, but he didn't move. I could feel his stormy emotions calm a bit and then as if they were bottled, they slowly became distant. He was pushing them back.

"Sorry about that, Luna," he croaked out. He gave a shaky laugh and with one hand, wiped at the tears on his face. His red eyes rimmed his slightly reddened face.

Who said guys don't cry? I thought sadly.

"Don't worry about that. I'm just glad you at least got it out of your system. How do you feel?" I asked softly. I could already guess but it was best not tell him that.

"I'm fine, really," he said gruffly. Pulling away and standing, I looked up at him with a raised brow but said nothing. If he didn't want to talk, that would be all right. The death of a child was probably not something that rolled off one's tongue.

"Well, what can you do now that you are all mighty and powerful?" he asked, chaining the question. I could see the changes as they happen in his behavior. Algebra was pushing everything back and bringing only positivity forward. I was a bit surprised but impressed. I stood up and stretched. The smell of salty tears was still in my senses, but I ignored them.

"How about attack anyone entering my house," I joked, feeling his need to lighten and forget the mood.

"I've noticed," he said with dry humor. I could already see his eyes lightening, its color returning to his face. He healed fast; we all did. I scratched the back of my head sheepishly and looked around the room, mentally scolding my beast again.

"I really am sorry about that, Albericus. I didn't know." His eyes widened in surprise and shock as his head snapped over to look at me with both hands raised to point in me.

"D-did you just say my name?" he whispered, clear bewilderment in his voice before a dramatic pause. I rolled my eyes and dropped my hand, crossing my arms over my chest.

"Yes, yes. I did say your name," I confirmed, amused and relieved that he was joking now. He clapped his hands and bounced on his feet, pointing at me with excitement on his face and his green eyes glowing. He reached his phone in his back pocket and tapped on something, then pointed it at me.

"Okay, okay, go. I've got to get this on tape," he said, leaning in while looking all expectant.

"This just makes me not want to say it even more."

"Awww, come on. I just cried in front of you!" I huffed and smiled at him before shaking my head.

"Fine."

"Annnd go," he cued.

"Albericus," I said into the phone.

His expression went blank for a minute before he dropped the phone. He began laughing uncontrollably until he dropped to the floor and began to roll. I frowned, worried that this was a side effect from all the crying. Maybe he wasn't alright after all . . . until I heard what he said.

"*Dayyuummmm.* That shit was dry." He laughed again, hitting the ground with his palms.

He was fine. I scowled at him and unthinkingly nudged him really hard with my foot.

Me being me, forgot how strong I was and sent him flying into the wall. He crashed into the TV and dropped. My eyes widened as the flat screen TV cracked and pieces fell to the floor. Algebra moaned on the ground.

I raised my hands as if to catch the TV mid-air, but the damage was already done. I let it land on Algebra, my mouth hung open and my beast whistled.

"*Run, bitch, run,*" my wolf whispered to me.

"No, no, no, no, no, no, shit. This can't be happening to me. Oh my god, he's going to kill—" I stopped my panic mumbling and walked over to a moaning Algebra. He squinted up at me with a grimace. I didn't even nudge him that hard.

330

"*You.* He's going to kill *you* because this is *your* fault," I stated, pointing a finger at him with a glare on my face.

His face looked outraged. He lifted the top part of his body off the ground and pushed the TV off of him and back in its place, but what was the point now?

"Me? Da Fuck did I miss? Because I know for a fact I didn't 'superman' my ass over to the TV on purpose. Nah, this is on you," he said sarcastically.

I growled at him and stomped my foot, then regretted it when I felt the floorboard crunch under it. I lifted my foot to see a dent on the ground. I groaned. Algebra cursed and stood up to go over the damage. His eyes went back and forth from the missing cracks on the screen to the dent on the ground.

"Do you think he'll notice?" I asked with a nervous voice.

I knew Zaliver wouldn't be mad over the fact that I broke the TV or dented the floor, but he would be disappointed that I hadn't been more careful. Somehow, that made it all seem worse than it really was.

"No, not if you keep him away from the living room for like . . . ever," he said, dusting himself off.

"This is your fault," I turned to Algebra. "If you hadn't made fun of me for saying your name, I wouldn't have nudged you."

"Well, I'm sorry if I now understand why you made a nickname for me. It just sounds wrong when you say it, and you did not 'nudge' me. You Bruce Lee, Hulk fan girl kicked me. Those three combinations are deadly. Vivian, I think my ribs are bruised," he muttered, lifting his shirt to reveal a firm tan and an eight pack with a large already forming purple bruise.

Gasping, I felt a bit guilty and then unthinkingly poked it. He let out a shocked yelp and put his shirt back down.

"What the hell!" he exclaimed.

"Sorry." I shrugged, looking back at the damage before me.

Zaliver hadn't even been gone for thirty minutes, and I already made his beta cry , broke the TV, and made a dent on the floor, not to mention I bruised his beta.

"Yeah, yeah. Now, I might have a plan on how to fix this," Algebra stated. My head snapped over to him with a hopeful look.

"Are you going to call a clean up crew and tell them to keep their mouths shut?" I asked excitedly. I had always seen it in the movies. He snorted before asking me and shook his head.

"No, I have a better plan."

~•~

331

"My plan was better. You have to be the stupidest beta I have ever met," I muttered.

"This is perfect," he argued.

Turned out Algebra's plan was to go outside, which was something I couldn't do. As soon as he opened the door, my eyes were blinded and my senses went crazy. I came back in after four minutes of looking and placed a huge rock on the dent on the floor. Then, he went to Zaliver's study, grabbed a blank piece of paper, and taped it over the cracks. See what I mean by stupid?

I sank down to the couch and covered my face. I was surrounded by idiots, and their idiocy was rubbing off on me because I was acting stupid.

"Oh, come on. Just tell him that you are decorating, then stand in front of the TV while you tell him," he explained his plan, looking pretty damn proud.

Note to self: Betas should stick to their level of expertise.

I rubbed at my temples as a pounding began; the same thing that happened where I kept hearing "underwater" conversations. Algebra's expression changed from playful to serious in a beat, dropping down in front of me to get a better look at my face.

"I was just playing. I can call an actual clean up crew, Luna," he said, sounding apologetic. Sometimes, I forget that when a luna showed clear distress and not just playful panic, the wolves around would feel compelled to fix the situation.

I shook my head at him, not even caring about the mess anymore. Heck, I would just try and make out with Zaliver as soon as he walked in, in hopes of distracting him and finishing what we couldn't start earlier.

"No, it's not that. I'm just having a little headache," I said, rubbing a bit harder as if to rub the pain away.

"I'll call—" Worry was evident in his voice.

"No, it's fine. He'll be here soon anyway," I interrupted him.

"I don't think it'll matter to him. I'd rather let him know now than later when anything could happen to you, Luna. I know this might be odd for me to say, but thank you, Vivian," he said with sincerity, looking into my eyes.

"Why?" I asked him. The distraction made the pain begin to fade.

"Because you make Zaliver happy. In all the time I have been with that guy, I've never seen him so happy without hating himself or his existence. So, thank you for making Alpha happy," he answered honestly, smiling a bit.

Tears stung my eyes a bit at what he said. I smiled at him, not knowing what else to say.

"Well, I'm not going to stand here and look at his mess. Wanna play a game?"

"What game?" I asked, both excited and weary of the usual beta.

"Well . . ." he started.

~•~

Why the hell did Algebra carry around four Nerf guns with him in the car? I thought as I peaked around the corner of the hallway.

Turned out, Algebra's idea of fun was the game of Nerf war. He said it might help with getting attuned with my new self, which was surprisingly true as I could focus a lot better when playing.

My competitive nature wouldn't let me lose, and my wolf kept whispering at me not to fuck up. That helped too. The beast just watched in curiosity at the way the game worked. Now that I was a lycan, she seemed more like a curious creature than a scary, angry voice in my head.

I could hear Algebra's heart beating at the end of the hall. It was almost like my mind was on some "super aware" mode because I swear, I could even make out his body by the heat of it. I just sort of knew that he had both guns raised and was crouched down.

"I can hear your heart, Luna. You should give up now," he taunted.

"And I can actually see you. If anyone should give up, it should be you." I smiled to myself. I peaked around the corner and saw his body tensed, his head moving a little hesitant.

"Damn. You and him shouldn't be allowed to play with others unless it's against one another," he said, walking around the corner. I did the same with narrowed eyes. My guns raised at him when he tried something.

He raised his weapons in defeat.

"Hey, I give up. You keep ending up in the hiding spot I chose. You two are no fun," he confessed.

"And how do I know I can trust you?" I questioned.

Until he died or called defeat, I would keep an eye on him. I was so not into losing.

"I don't know what you—" He started rolling his eyes at me.

I did the only thing I could think of. I shot him in the forehead. I think he wasn't expecting it because it shot him dead straight. I blinked at him innocently while his green eyes slowly darkened.

"Did you just—"

I shot him again and then I ran.

333

As I ducked, dived, and sped all over the house, I could hear his slow heavy steps behind me. I could also hear every click of the Nerf gun as he shot at me, making me laugh like crazy when I moved at the last second and made him miss.

"Stop moving and let me shoot you!" he yelled, frustrated.

"Never!" I yelled, spinning around and firing at him. He tried dodging them with his heightened reflexes, but I had calculated his movements. My advanced senses made him move sluggishly to me.

"Stop shooting me!" he yelled, ducking behind the kitchen counter.

"Suck it up!"

He mumbled under his breath. My ears caught the sound of tires from outside. I looked up at the kitchen clock.

Zaliver is back!

I felt happiness at the thought of seeing him again. I suddenly felt an urgent need to have physical contact with him and smell his scent. Something began humming again within me.

"Zaliver is back," I whispered, knowing Algebra would be able to hear me. He suddenly hopped up off the ground with a devious expression and mischievous green eyes.

I tilted my head at him in question. He pointed his gun to the door and made a shooting motion. Ohh. I nodded with a grin of my own. I totally wanted to see how this turned out. Algebra tiptoed to the door and got behind the couch where he had access to Zaliver first. I looked around. I had to think fast.

I couldn't hide behind the stairs because the door would block me and the fake bullets would be too slow for him. Algebra already had the couch and was already in position one. I was running out of time.

Algebra was making frantic motions as I stood there, so I just stood a bit more in front of the door as if greeting him home. I hid my guns behind my back. I knew I looked suspicious, but oh well.

Algebra nodded at me and gave me a thumbs up. At the sound of footsteps, I tensed in anticipation and excitement. I wasn't sure if I wanted to shoot him first or jump on him. I was just so overfilled with emotions of knowing he was back. My wolf was howling and my beast was crouching as if she were the one about to pounce on him.

When I saw the doorknob begin to turn, I looked at Algebra for a moment as he too prepared himself with a wide grin on his face. It was as if the whole thing went in slow motion as soon as the door fully opened because what happened then was not what I was expecting to happen.

Zaliver pushed the door open. When his piercing blue eyes met mine, electricity pulsed through my body for a second before I remembered the guns behind me. I pulled them out and began firing at him.

As each round flew out of my guns, I could see them slowly spin in the air towards him. Algebra gave out a warrior's cry as he shot out his own. It wasn't until Zaliver's blue eyes flashed black and began running at a blinding speed.

As Zaliver ran towards me, I managed to catch an unbelievably tall white-haired man with golden snake-like eyes run in after him. I wasn't even sure how. Let's just say Algebra was in the air before I even comprehended it.

My eyes moved back to Zaliver who had a smirk on his face as he neared me. My lips parted to let out a shriek. I flew back and Zaliver surrounded me before we landed on the ground. He somehow landed underneath me but then switched positions. He had my arms pinned above me with the guns laying down far away. I let out a gasp as time seemed to catch up.

"Well, hello, Vivian. You weren't actually planning on shooting me, were you?" Zaliver purred above me. His face was extremely close to mine, and the tips of his black hair tickled my forehead.

Feeling him this close made me forget about Algebra and the strangely tall white-haired man in our house. All I cared about was that my mate was home and very much on top of me.

"Zaliver!" I exclaimed happily, grinning at him. I moved my legs and wrapped them around him. I could tell I had caught him off guard because his eyes widened and then began darkening oh so slowly.

"Vivian?" he murmured huskily. His voice was strained as his hands tightened on my own.

"Hmm?" I asked, lifting my head and rubbing the tip of my nose on his affectionately. He closed his eyes and did the same. My wolf and beast were purring.

He opened his stormy blue eyes that expressed his desire as much my very own. His eyes flickered down to my lips, and I parted them a little. He seemed to like my reaction because his waist pushed down and began to lean down when—

"Awww, hell no. No grinding while I'm here!" I heard Algebra yell out.

I snarled at him as Zaliver moved his head and dropped it on my shoulder, breathing in deeply. I heard a similar snarl build up in his chest.

"*Cockblockers! Cockblockers everywhere!*" my wolf growled, unamused.

Zaliver got off of me and offered me a hand, which I gladly took. Algebra was laying on the ground by the TV again. The tall white-

335

haired man stood in front of him with his head down and arms behind his back in a sort of . . . submissive stance.

Weird. He didn't smell like a wolf.

I heard my beast begin to growl and felt her try to push to the front to try and attack again, but I fought her off this time. I turned to Zaliver and wrapped my arms around his waist, burying my face into his chest and inhaling his familiar and calming scent. He wrapped his arms around me without hesitation and rubbed circles on my back, seeming to understand what I was doing.

Turning back to the two, I walked up cautiously to the guy. His aura was . . . odd. I really did not know how to explain it, but he looked dangerous. He acted docile yet I had the feeling that behind that bad boy angel's face was a striking predator with the grace to kill.

It was odd . . . very odd. But he was really tall, so it was cool.

"Hi, I'm Vivian. How tall are you?" I asked right away. He was taller than Zaliver, who stood very close behind me with an arm wrapped around my waist.

The man looked at Zaliver and then those striking and alert golden eyes were on me. The fact that his pupil was vertical made looking into his eyes very hypnotizing. He looked down and I frowned.

He was wearing white pants with a long-sleeved black shirt on top of a white vest and white shoe that didn't seem to have a speck of dirt on them. He had a muscular build, but he was lean as well. I could tell he was athletic. What interested me besides his eyes was his hair that caught light, making the tips seemed almost see through.

"I apologize, Luna Vivian, for my previous actions. I am not worthy of your recognition. I am Venom, a snake . . . shifter, and I am seven feet tall." The man's voice was cold but appealing to the ears that it sent an automatic shiver through my spine.

I knew that he didn't mean for it to come out the way it did, but his words were a hiss. It was threatening, but I think he couldn't help it. I just knew right there, that if this guy wanted, he could be the scariest mofo I had ever met. Maybe even Zaliver.

My wolf and my beast didn't know what to think, but I found myself interested in the snake shifter and forced myself to relax.

"Oh, don't be so down, Venom. I think we're going to get along just great. Nice meeting you," I said truthfully. He peered at me. His golden eyes was seemingly endless, but I think I caught curiosity swirling through them.

"Oh yeah. I'm fine. Thanks," Algebra said sarcastically, dusting himself off. I rolled my eyes at him but then stopped when I thought of a plan.

I walked over to Algebra who eyed me suspiciously even though he was already up. I walked over to him and made sure to softly

336

pat him on the back while ripping the paper off the TV and kicking the rock away. It hit the wall with a loud noise to which I just ignored with a fake concerned look.

"I'm sure you'll be fine but oh, would you look at that? The TV is cracked and what's this? A dent on the floor? What a shame really. . . oh well." I tsked, pretending to be saddened at the destruction.

I looked over at Zaliver who was more busy eyeing my hand on Algebra's back than the actual mess while Venom actually looked sorry.

"Yes. What a pity," Zaliver said darkly for some reason. His expression was blank. His eyes flickered from me to his beta in suspicion.

"I'm so sorry about—"

I felt guilty that Venom thought he had done this.

"Oh, don't worry, really. Don't worry. At all. Like no. Like stooop," I said, stretching out my words to make it clear.

"Yup, accident happens," Algebra said. We both made eye contact and a look of understanding passed. No one ever had to know what really happened.

Zaliver cleared his throat, and I walked over to him. Something was telling me that we needed a close contact.

"*Not close enough*," my wolf pushed.

"*You are a horny wolf. You know that?*" I said to her.

"*Bitch, please. I need the d—*"

"*Shut the hell up.*"

I blocked her out after that, not ready to hear her perverted mind at the moment.

"Vivian, since the doctor said that you need to train to get use to your new muscles, and since you agreed—" I interrupted him. His lips pursed but he didn't say anything.

"Hold up, hold up, *hold up*. Ain't nobody agree to anything. Because see, from what I remembered, he said some words, you said some words but I didn't say anything. So, I don't know what you're talking about," I cleared. Zaliver must have really thought I would go down without a fight.

He must have forgotten who he was talking to. He sighed and looked at the ceiling as if reconsidering his choice for his sake. I hope he was.

"It's really not that bad. You'll be working out at max three weeks—"

"Nah."

"You haven't even—"

"Nope."

"Let me tell you—"

337

"Mhhh ummm . . . "

"Viv—"

"Nah Man."

"Viv—" He was beginning to get angry and I could tell, but I hadn't been paying attention.

"Que no."

"Vivian!" He boomed.

The room went completely silent. My wolf lowered herself, even my beast seemed a bit quiet. The atmosphere changed to a cold and dark one. I took a peek at Zaliver and realized something.

Maybe pushing your god or alpha mate who witnessed and went through a big change that involved a hell lot of pain was not a good idea.

Zaliver's stance was dominating and intense. His head was held high and his blue eyes glowed with a brewing storm inside. He looked down at me with a truly blank and yet controlled expression. I had never wanted to both shrink and say sorry so fast in my life. I may have . . . pushed it.

"Vivian," he said calmly.

"Yes?" My voice was no less than a whisper. I wasn't scared of Zaliver. I knew he would never hurt me, but my god, he did look ready to rule the world. Like, I think even Beyoncé would do a double take and then leave, like real fast.

"I know you don't want to do this, but you heard Dr. Leonard. This is for your health and well-being. It's just for a little while. I will never ever take risks with your health. Do you understand that?" he asked me, staring unblinkingly into my eyes.

I felt as if my soul was exposed to him. It both felt good and nerve-wracking. I nodded. His face softened a bit, and his hand came up to cup my face. Instinctively, I leaned into his touch.

"I rather choose you be mad at me than you being unhealthy when I could have done something," he confessed.

I felt like a bitch—a small one, but still. Here, my mate was trying to look out for me and all I was doing was making it hard on the poor guy.

"I'm sorry," I said, looking up at him.

He leaned down and put his forehead on mine, looking into my eyes.

"Never apologize for being you. Just don't fight with me when I'm trying to help. How about that?" he asked, smiling at me. The atmosphere went back to normal, and he was my Zaliver again.

"Okay," I said, grinning up at him. He pulled away but not before quickly kissing my forehead.

"That's my girl."

338

That's when I remembered we weren't alone.

Something that I just realized is that Zaliver wouldn't hide how affectionate he was towards me and I liked it . . . a lot actually.

I turned around with a sheepish look on my face, not surprised seeing Venom looking at the ground the whole time it seemed while Algebra . . . Algebra had his back towards us and his arms wrapped around him as if he were passionately kissing someone. In short, he was mocking us.

"Oh, shut it," I said, feeling my face heat up.

"So, you're blushing because you're having a conversation with your mate but not because you had your legs wrapped around his waist earlier? my wolf asked mockingly.

"I thought I blocked you out."

"We all fail at things."

"I gave a mental groan."

"Oh yes, Venom will be training you," Zaliver stated a bit displeased.

"Really?" I asked, surprised.

"Yes, he is the man for the job and the only one I trust with training you," he stated, leaning in and nuzzling my neck. I pulled back a little to look at him with a confused look on my face.

"Why not you?" I turned to Venom. "No offense."

"None taken, Luna."

"Well shit, I'm offended." We ignored Algebra.

Zaliver hesitated before answering me.

"We'll talk later." I rolled my eyes at him and shook my head to which he looked at me apologetically.

Yes, I realize we have a lot to talk about "later". I turned back to Venom.

"So, when and where do we start?" I asked.

I figure since it's Monday, he'll probably want to start next week to clear off his schedule since this must have been sudden. Giving me a few rest days—

"Tomorrow at 7:50 AM in the training field."

"Fuck."

~•~

Later that night in bed, sitting crisscrossed, I was just watching Zaliver walk around and get his things ready for tomorrow, which I had begrudgingly done so as well. I decided it was time for "later."

"So, it's later now. I want my explanations." I caught Zaliver off guard. He stopped mid step and then sighed, putting down his things and running his hands through his hair.

339

"Yes you do," he said, turning to face me.

"Yes I do, so are you going to start or . . . " I trailed off while he stayed quiet. Rolling his eyes, he stood at the end of the bed. I tried to keep my eyes on his eyes and not check out his chest in his white pajama shirt.

"Remembered how earlier I had told you there was a reason you kept attacking everyone?" he asked seriously and I nodded. Was there more to it than just my beast being territorial and not trusting everyone?

"Well, beside it being a natural instinct to attack the unknown to an animal and then release some steam, your beast was also trying to eliminate any possible . . . competitors," he said. I frowned, not understanding what he was trying to tell me.

"Let off steam? Get rid of the competition? How were those guys competition? To what?" I asked, more confused than ever.

"Ask your beast," he said. I frowned but did as he asked and closed my eyes. She had already been listening to the conversation and was ready for me.

"*What's up with the letting off the steam with violence?*" I asked. She snorted.

"*We have a mate who hasn't mated us yet. Excuse me if I become a little violent.*"

Oh. I felt my face heat up, but I didn't open my eyes just yet.

"*Why did you attack the guys?*" I asked her.

"*Because they could have stolen Zaliver away from us and took him for themselves. He's ours.*"

My eyes snapped open as the pieces finally fit together. Zaliver was looking at me with amusement in his eyes. My face just seemed to get redder by the second, so I grabbed a pillow and covered my face. I was so mortified. My beast thought the guys were *that* kind of competition. Oh man.

I heard Zaliver let out a chuckle. I pulled the pillow low enough to glare at him, showing him how unamused I was.

"This is so not funny, Zaliver," I stated, annoyed at him.

"It kinda is," he said, chuckling again at me.

"No it's not. My beast tried to maul the guys because . . . Well, you know." I couldn't even say it. I pulled the pillow back up.

"It's completely normal. It's fine," he said. After my face calmed down, I felt like I could look him in the eyes before we spoke again.

"Algebra told me about Aurora and . . . " I trailed off sadly. He didn't look surprise, which surprised me.

"And Andrew," he said.

340

I didn't actually know the child's name but somehow, that just made it sadder—the three As. I nodded.

"I thought he did. I always check up on your emotional levels and since his was depressingly low, I figured there was only one thing to get him that low," he said with a mournful tone.

Zaliver seemed to know the kid too as his eyes got a far away look. We were quiet for a mournful second. I didn't know anything about the child, but I won't ask Zaliver anything because it was not really his story to tell.

"So, why exactly is Venom the man for the job?" I asked Zaliver. His eyes moved away from me, and he scratched the back of his head before sighing.

"For many reasons."

"Like?" I pushed, raising my brow at his secrecy.

"I only have two instincts when training: to kill or seriously injure my opponent until they learn from their mistakes. I'm with full force, and I'd rather not risk you when Venom can do it. He's aware of everything because of his senses. He's always in control of himself and most importantly, he knows where the boundaries lie when it comes to you, so he'll know how far to push you," he explained.

I bit my lip, thinking it over. It made sense. I knew by this point that Zaliver was usually correct when it came to things like this, but that didn't mean I didn't want him to train me.

"So, you're not going to train me at all?" I pouted, saddened by the thought of not putting him on his ass at least once.

"Oh, don't worry. I'll be around. In fact, I'll probably be attending more than not. You are going to be in the warriors' train field after all," he pointed out.

"What? With the professionals? Are you out of your mind? I'll look like a kid in the adult section of a sports section," I said.

"Don't worry about them. If anything, everyone will be happy to have their luna improving beside them. It'll probably make them feel better knowing that while they are training, you are watching them. It will let them prove their abilities to you," he spoke, trying to comfort me as well as sound quite proud of his warriors. I smiled at him and nodded.

"Fine, but if it all goes downhill, then I will tell Venom to train me in the front yard," I stated.

"No," he said with finality in his voice, his eyes darkening.

"Why not?"

"You will not be alone with him at any point," he said. I was about to retort when I remembered something he said before we went off topic.

"And?" I asked. His expression became confused.

341

"And what was the other reason for not being able to train me yourself?" I clarified.

His expression morphed to one clear and utter seduction in the blink of an eye.

He put a hand on the bed, then another and then he was over me, laying me down. Both of his arms were on either side of me as he loomed over me.

The look in his eyes were hypnotizing me, and everything but him blurred to the background. I just knew that I was his and he was mine. We belonged together. I could feel his every muscle and movement as if it were one of my own. My arms wrapped themselves over his strong build, feeling each muscle flex and tense as my fingers skimmed over his skin lightly.

His lips neared my ear as he whispered slowly.

"I can't train you because I know that seeing you all hot and sweaty under me will make me want to fuck you then and there," he said huskily.

My back pushed off the bed and touched his chest as emotions stirred up a storm in me at his words. I closed my eyes for a moment and let him nuzzle his face into my neck before planting soft kisses on my skin and trail up and reach my lips. Electric. Pulsing. Hot. Heavy. Totally consuming.

I was beginning to understand that kissing Zaliver was just something that would never stop being shocking and exciting to me. It was as if Zaliver and I were two clashing fires trying to destroy everything in our path. Together, we were an invincible force of destruction. A dangerous one that not only destroyed everything around us but consumed us from the inside out until we were so intertwined that we weren't two fires but one. He must have felt the pulsing electricity that I felt.

My everything was focused on him. The way his woodsy and clean scent surrounded me had infiltrated my mind and recorded itself. His lips were so soft yet aggressively playful were making me moan wantingly. It was so much more than a kiss of two lovers reuniting. That's for sure. When we pulled back, we were both breathing hard and had goofy grins on our faces. Zaliver was still on top of me and kept dipping his head to steal another peck.

"Wow."

"Indeed, wow."

I think my wolf passed out again somewhere in the back of my mind while my beast tried to wake it up.

I wanted to kiss him again.

So I did.

342

~•~

"This is an unholy hour. I don't care what you say," I complained as I drank my orange juice in the car. I would never admit it to Zaliver, but getting up in the morning was actually helping my eyes adjust to the natural lighting. My eyes didn't burn at all. He'd see it as a win and be smug about it all day.

"Vivian, I'm pretty sure any hour before 11 PM to you is unholy," Zaliver joked as he pulled into the training field that seemed to be already filled with sweaty warriors. How long have they been here?

"That just maybe true," I said, before stepping out of the car.

It was as if we were waiting neon suits to an all black party because everyone stopped their training to look at us. Jeez, they acted like they had never seen an alpha pair in matching workout outfits. Yes, yes. I said matching.

I told Zaliver that if he wanted me to feel good, then he had to match with me. That, and I really wanted to see him in some skin-tight clothing—all hot and sweaty. So, I picked out black basketball shorts for him with a skin-tight shirt vest, which was unsurprisingly black. Instead of the shorts for me, I had on some Nike leggings. The really cool part about our outfits was that I made Zaliver wear my other pink sweatband. Yup, pink. Let's just say that he was rocking it better than I do.

Zaliver nodded at everyone while I just gave a smile. Most responded back with a smile while others bowed. Still odd. When they continued, I found Venom set up in a space no one seemed to be using. There was a large green mat and all types of equipment. He wore black shorts like Zaliver, except he had on a white track jacket. I noticed how some wolves kept eyeing him with untrusting eyes.

The training field had obstacle courses that honestly made me want to cry just by looking at them. They had a grand track and everything you'd see in a military outdoor gym and possibly every torture device someone like me hated, unless it was walking to the fridge.

"Hello, Luna Vivian, Alpha Zaliver. It's a pleasure to see you both this early morning," Venom said lowly, but I still unconsciously shivered. Damn.

"Good morning, Venom," I said while Zaliver nodded at him. "So what are we doing today, coach?" I asked him, just wanting to get this over with.

Subconsciously biting at the top of my water bottle with the last of my orange juice, Zaliver found it weird that I liked the taste of orange after brushing my teeth, but I just ignored him. The corner of Venom's lips lifted only for a moment before he explained.

343

"We aren't going to do anything to heavy today, Luna. Just stretching, warming up, jogging, and a few exercises to let me know where you're at and that's pretty much it. Just an hour and thirty today," he said. I glanced at Zaliver who seemed to be going over my schedule before nodding.

"See, that doesn't sound too bad now, does it?" he asked, turning to face me with a smile on his face.

"Yeah, yeah. Now go, run along, or whatever it is with people who can't fight because they might actually kill the test dummy," I said, pushing him away.

"Oh yeah. Now, you want me to go? Fine, fine, but first . . . " He turned around and stole a kiss from me.

"I'll be around if you need me. Venom, I don't have to say anything, do I?" Zaliver asked, confusing me. What did that mean?

"No sir. Don't worry. She will be absolutely safe in my care," Venom said, completely serious. His eyes looking straight into Zaliver's. Usually that would piss off a dominant alpha, but with Venom, it almost seemed like he was proving something to Zaliver by doing that.

"Well okay. Good luck," Zaliver said before jogging over to a group of young wolves.

As the time passed, I realize working with Venom wasn't bad at all. He even made the workout fun by joining in, and even though he tried not to talk to me for what seemed to be respect, I got him too. Zaliver passed by every once in a while to give me words of encouragement and a kiss, no matter how many times I told him not to touch me while he or I was sweaty. He'd just laugh it off, making me realize many things.

First, I never imagined playing out the way I did in my whole life. Out of all of the problems I had gotten in since I met Zaliver, all I kept thinking was that it somehow was just not going to work because well . . . they seemed impossible, but look at us now—together and happy.

Second, seeing Zaliver so interactive and supportive yet still a bit strict to his warriors made me realize what a big heart he had even if he didn't see it. Heck, even if they didn't feel it.

Third, I realized I was undoubtedly in love with my mate, Zaliver. Through our ups and downs, I realized that together we made each other better. Yeah, we fought like crazy and got back at each other in the oddest of ways, but we weren't a normal couple. I didn't think we were meant to be. Sure, there were still some things I didn't know about him and things he didn't know about me, but we had all the time in the world to learn about each other and then more. I knew that we'd be put in interesting situations that would drive us both insane, but as long as we were together, I knew nothing would ever break our bond.

344

As Zaliver's electric blue eyes found mine and a smile graced his face, I knew right then and there what I had to do. I was going to seduce my mate into mating with me. I was ready.

CHAPTER 29

"Bye, Venom. Thanks for today. See ya tomorrow." I waved to the calm looking snake man who didn't seem to care at all that he was surrounded by wolves. His golden eyes were seemingly happy, but it was hard to tell. He bowed his head at me as if saying goodbye.

"I'll talk to you later, man," Zaliver called out and then took my hand, pulling me to the car. I had to resist both pulling my hand back from the emotions it brought and jumping on him then and there because we were in a crowded area.

As we got into the car, I tried not to fidget all the way, aware that he was looking me over to make sure I wasn't hurt or pulled something from today's workout. I was avoiding eye contact.

"You must be really tired. You haven't said a word since we got in the car," Zaliver said, sounding concerned. I felt his eyes on the side of my face, but I didn't turn to him. I gave him a hum as a response and looked out of the car window, watching as the sensory passed by quickly. I could feel Zaliver's eyes on me as we made our way home. It made me even more self-aware and tensed than I was, and being all sweaty didn't help too.

But how the hell was one suppose to act when they realized they were in love with someone? Because I'm pretty sure, most couldn't even act normal around their crush. Through the bond, I could begin to feel Zaliver's frustration and anxiousness grow. I knew that I would have to do something about that before he took this to a whole new and unnecessary level. But first, I had to organize my thoughts. When he pulled up to the driveway, he hadn't even fully parked the car before I was out. Running towards the front door in a mad dash, I heard his outraged yell but paid it no attention.

I was in our room and had all my stuff ready for the shower when I felt the air shift. Before curses left my mouth, Zaliver loomed over me with an unamused look on his face. His arms crossed over his broad, firm . . . sexy looking chest . . .

Fuck, focus!

His piercing blue eyes froze me at where I was. I felt as if my legs were cemented onto the ground. His long black locks sort of clung to his head with dampened sweat. His skin had a faint flush from his workout, and the tight clothes seemed impossibly tighter on his form. He was mad, but boy he was sexy as hell.

"All right, what is it? What made you upset?" he demanded with an edge to his voice as he looked down at me. My brows came together, and I gave him a dramatic surprised expression.

"Me? Upset? What?" My voice came out more high-pitched than I had expected it. I gave a nervous laugh as his eyes narrowed in slits. He took a step towards me, and I took one too around him.

"You've been acting odd ever since the work out. Are you still upset about that because if you are—"

"Oh no, really Zaliver, I'm fine. I just don't like being sweaty that all."

"*Well, it isn't a complete* lie," my wolf snorted at me.

"*So you don't like sweat, but you plan on getting down and dirty with him?*" She probed.

My eyes widened and I looked away from Zaliver's eyes as my face suddenly flushed. I felt like slapping my palm on my forehead at the both of us. It was one thing to have your wolf be perverted. It was another when your perverted wolf was irrevocably correct. I glanced at the bathroom door and then glared at Zaliver. His face looked as if he knew that I was trying to avoid this conversation. I took a step towards the bathroom to get ready to dash for it, but a heated large hand wrapped around my upper arm, stopping me. I looked up.

"Wait, why are you—" he began. His expression showing just how confused and worried he was about my weird behavior.

It made my heart swell and pound at the same time. I wanted to say it, but it wasn't the right time. When would be the right time to tell someone that you loved them?

I opened my mouth.

"Nope," I said, yanking my arm out harshly and ignoring some of the things that fell out of my hands.

I dashed to the bathroom and shut the door behind me, locking it. Leaning against the door for a moment of breath, I shook myself off and put my things on the sink, then stripped down and got into the shower to think. It wasn't until thirty minutes was over when I realized that some of the things I dropped and left hastily were much-needed.

Like my bra or my underwear.

I facepalmed and shook my head, ignoring the barking laughter of the two in my head as if I needed more on my plate. I wrapped the towel around me securely and took a breath.

What was the possibility of Zaliver storming off after I ran in here and completely not looking down? I got very close to the door,

347

turned the door handle quietly, poked my head out, then looked around the room and died.

There on the bed was the freshly showered Zaliver, sitting with only a white towel around his waist and with legs slightly parted. He had both my bra and underwear in both hands. He then twirled my bra with one finger.

I made a choking sound and stepped out, not knowing what to do. I wanted to storm over, snatch my undergarments, and curse his name while stomping back to the bathroom and slamming my head on the sink. I also wanted to snatch his towel, and well, see if he too had dropped and had misplaced his belongings. He looked up slowly. His wet black hair somehow looked darker and hung over his eyes, hiding them from me. All I could see was how the corner of his lips were turned up in a wicked smile towards me. Even my wolf and beast froze at this image. All three of us were not sure what to make of it.

"Why don't you come over here and get these from me?" he prompted, saying the words slowly and making sure to pronounce them each.

I gulped, and with brave slow steps, I inched closer to him. When I was a foot away from him, he stopped twirling my dark purple wine-colored bra and set it down on his lap. My teeth clicked. I hesitantly put my hand out for him to give them to me. I was not reaching down there to get it.

"*You should*," my beast encouraged, whispering.

I knew he could hear how fast my heart was pounding in my chest because his smirk widened a bit, showing me his white teeth.

"You know," my eyes widened when he took hold of my underwear with both hands and held it up in front of him, "I'd really like to see you in this."

I was completely speechless. None of my sarcastic remarks could come to mind. Not with him and me in towels. I was already planning to jump at his bones.

I take back what I said earlier. I was not ready at all for Zaliver.

The man was sex on legs. Hell, the man was sex itself. Someone help me!

"Umm . . ." I replied smartly.

He chuckled and shook his head, water dripping over the bed. I noted how relaxed his body seemed but then I caught sight of one of his fingers tapping on the bed slowly.

He took both my undergarments in one hand. Without looking at me, he held them out for me to grab. My outreached hand grabbed onto the two, but before I could pull them out of his grasp, he yanked me down on top of him and flipped us with me underneath him.

348

He ripped the undergarments from my hand and threw them across the room.

My breaths were coming harsh and fast. My heart was pumping in my chest like never before. His body pushed and pinned me down to the bed, and his hands held mine above my head. He dropped his head to the crook of my neck and took in a deep breath only to let out a small moan that shook my to the core. When he lifted his head back up, I was surprised to see pitch black eyes staring back at me.

"You, my dear, smell mouth-watering. Now, why don't you tell me what's on your mind?" he stated calmly.

I should have realized the moment the tingling sensation began in my stomach; the moment I unconsciously curled my toes and pushed myself closer, ignoring how the towel loosened up around my chest; and the moment my beast let out a pleasure growl and then whispered in the most seductive voice that she was back.

I should have realized that it was my heat talking, but I didn't.

So, when I grinned up at Zaliver and flipped us over, reversing our positions faster than he could even think, his black eyes snapped back to blue, looking surprised.

"Now, why does there has to be something wrong with me? Can't a girl just say nothing?" I purred at him, liking how he felt underneath me.

"Vivian—" He took a deep breath. His nose flared as if he smelled something he liked very much. I leaned down and planted my lips on his shoulder.

"Hmmm?" I asked him, flipping my hair onto the other side of my neck, looking at him through hooded eyes.

He moved his hands out of my hold. I let his one hand go around my waist and the other went under my hair to grip it. I wrapped one arm around his neck to bring him closer to me and placed one on his chest.

I watched as his blue eyes darkened to a stormy blue. His arm kept tightening and loosening around me. His hand was bunching up the back of my towel as his jaw clenched and unclenched. By the way he was holding me, I could tell he was having a battle within himself, and I was not going to make it easy for him.

"I see your heat is back," he said through clenched teeth. I hummed as a response and kissed up from his shoulder to his ear.

"And what are you going to do about that?" I whispered before softly biting his ear.

He pushed me down with his hand at the same time that his hips lifted off the bed. His hand pulled my hair back, forcing my lips away from his skin. He looked at me, and I smiled at him wantingly.

"I really should leave. I should let you calm down and leave to avoid taking advantage on you," he said, trailing off as he looked down from my lips to my neck and then lingered on my chest.

"Oh really?" I asked mockingly, tightening my legs around his waist.

"Yeah, I really should," he said, bringing my face down to capture my lips.

I smirked as he kissed me roughly. I bit his bottom lip playfully and then squeaked when he returned it. As we kissed, I trailed my hand down from his chest to his abs, feeling the muscle flex as he breathed. When my hand inched lower towards the knot where the towel held itself together loosely, he froze. With my index finger, I skimmed his lower abdomen, feeling a light trail of hair, and then went to slip my hand under—

Then he was gone.

I bounced on the bed a bit and then sat up, looking around the room for him, but I already knew he was across the house. I sighed and closed my eyes.

When I opened them, I was much calmer . . . and much more aware of what I had been doing.

"Great," I muttered to myself, standing up and readjusting the towel on me. I walked over to the far wall to pick up my undergarments. He didn't need to throw them away.

I felt slightly mortified and very . . . pleased in a sense that . . . I don't know, happy and excited. I quickly dressed, seeing how flush my face was. I combed my hair, seeing how long it was above my breasts. I sighed and bit my lip as I figured what I would do now because I doubt Zaliver would stick around after that. I loved Zaliver. I was in love with my mate.

I think it was safe to say that he loved me to a certain degree. I wasn't worried if he was at the same level as how I felt as long as he got there one day. I think it was stupid to say, but the only real thing I was intimidated was that he wouldn't . . . want me. I didn't know how to explain it, but in a way, I felt insecure that maybe he'd reject me right before anything serious would happen. I knew it wasn't going to happen because of everything he had said and done.

Sometimes, being a girl sucked.

I went down to the kitchen to get something to eat after the morning work out. I think I ended up making like seven sandwiches before I was full. I grabbed a water bottle and then listened in for where Zaliver was. I heard a low hum and focused on that. I closed my eyes and strained my hearing. As if I were standing on the other side of a door, I heard the words clearly.

"What do you fucking mean the door is gone?" Zaliver yelled out. I flinched back from the anger and menacing tone.

"Yes sir. The door destroyed everything holding it down and disappeared two hours ago. I already have the men move location," a male's voice said. I frowned. Zaliver's breathing was coming out harshly.

"Find that fucking door," he said.

Door? I walked in the direction of his office, wanting to check up on him. Through the bond, his end of the line was covered in darkness. Dark emotions were coming from his end. I didn't like it. I felt the need to comfort him rising. He rarely had the chance to be happy and calm.

"Will do." The line clicked before something shattered in his office. I knocked on his door before opening it. He stood with his back towards me as he looked out the window. His hands were balled up at his sides. I walked up behind him and carefully wrapped my arms around his waist. It took a long moment before his form relaxed. He sighed and turned around in my arms. I peered up at him curiously, and he gave me a forced smile that didn't meet his eyes.

"Now, it seems it is my turn to ask you what's wrong?" I asked him, reaching up with one hand to stroke his cheek. He leaned down into my hand and closed his eyes briefly.

"Just having some problems with the gods up there," he answered. I tensed and he opened his eyes.

"I didn't want to tell you until after it was taken care of, but I have a feeling you would have castrated me if I did," he confessed. I blinked up at him, feeling both perplexed and curious.

"What kind of trouble?" I asked.

"To get to where they are, I have to find the door that lets them come down to earth because it also works the other way."

"Why do you need to find the door?" His face went cold. He took a step back and turned from me.

He answered me with silence, and my mind processed his information. Me as a peace offering. Dead brother. Trouble with the gods. Finding a door that would lead him to them.

The word rang in my head. Revenge.

"Oh," I said.

I walked back to him and wrapped him in my arms again, putting my face in his chest. I felt him move and wrap his arms around me.

"Don't you have anything else to say?" he asked, not saying it rudely but as a true question. I shook my head.

"Not now. One thing at a time," I regretted my words as soon as they slipped my mouth, so I shut the hell up, but he had already caught onto my little pause.

351

"Vivian? I believe we have a talk due, don't you?" he asked. I cursed and looked at him, innocently blinking my lashes at him. I was relieved to see him looking down at me more amused than worried now.

"Nope."

"You know you can tell me anything, right? That I'll always be here if you need me right?" he asked.

I beamed up at him and grabbed the back of his head, pulling him down to peck him on the lips.

"Yup." He pursed his lips at me, his expression softer than before.

"So, you're not going to tell me?" he asked. I thought about it for a moment before answering.

"Not yet.'

He sighed and looked down at me with amusement and happiness shining in his eyes.

"I'll take that for now," he stated.

"*Take this for now so that you can take us* later," my wolf yelled in my head. I think my eye twitched.

"So . . . what are you going to do for the rest of the day?" I asked. He pulled out his phone, stared at it for a moment, and sighed.

"I have four online meetings, check over some paper requests, check in with betas." He stopped at my dry expression.

"You lost me at the word *meetings*. So, you'll be holed up in here all day?" I asked casually.

"Yes, so if you want to go out, just tell me so that I can—"

"No, no. It's fine. I wasn't really planning on doing much today," I said.

Since my hand was still in his head, I tugged at a black lock and twirled it in my hand. He looked down at me with an peculiar look.

"Your hair's getting longer," I pointed out, tugging again. He smiled and pulled back until I released the lock.

"Do you want me to cut it?" he asked. His question caught me off guard.

"Why does it matter what I think of your hair?" I asked, confused, subconsciously reaching up to tug on it as if it would disappear. He smiled softly and took a hold of my hand, bringing it to his lips to kiss my hand and looking at me with grand admiration and care.

"Is it a crime to please my beautiful mate?" he asked. I rolled my eyes, but he knew his words had gotten to me. He could hear my heart flutter.

"No, I don't think you should cut it, not yet at least," I said. I backed up and went to head out to let him work, but I stopped at the open door.

352

"So, are we ever gonna talk about what happened up there?" I asked him, forcing myself not to grip the door tightly. I didn't need to go breaking more things. He put his hands behind his back and cocked a brow at me. I huffed at him.

"Fine."

"Why do you keep pulling away?" I asked him seriously. His eyes skimmed my face. I wanted to know.

"Because when we do mate, I don't want it to be out of the heat. I most definitely don't want you to wake up and regret it later and hate me for not being strong enough to resist you. I want you to be completely sure," he answered, staring at me through his fierce blue eyes. My heart skipped a beat, or two.

We looked at each other for a moment as if remembering the moment upstairs.

"Well, it seems we agree on something," I said coyly. He tilted his head to the side, trying to understand what it was.

"And what would that be?" he asked.

"I'm completely sure of what I want now." I closed the door and walked down the hall.

"*Like a* boss," my wolf said, wagging her tail.

While Zaliver worked in the office, I went upstairs and paused at the beginning of the hall. After a second, I went into the guest room I had stayed in when I returned and went to the closet. Opening, I was relieved to see that the bag I had bought with Hannah was still there. I picked it up and went into the room, locking the door just in case.

I took a breath before dumping everything on the bed. I bit my lip as I looked at everything. Hannah had good taste, but the longer I looked at the lingerie on the bed, the more I got displeased. It was beautiful. All the pieces were, but they didn't . . . I don't know, seem important. Besides that they would eventually come off. I wanted to do this in a way that showed me but also showed us.

When Zaliver and I met—even in the oddest of situations—there was no pretense. It was all raw and bold. I wasn't expecting to meet my mate, and he didn't believe he had one. I closed my eyes and smiled. I knew what I would do. Picking up all the lingerie, I put it back in the bag and put it up in the closet. Maybe not now but definitely someday.

I went into the bathroom and grabbed my brush, combing my hair always calmed me down or gave me time to think. I combed my hair by the bedroom window. After this morning's workout, the clouds seemed to be turning gray but not the type that made one believe it would rain.

I liked this type of gray. It was the type that made you want to stay inside and read a book by the window or listen to music. So that's what I did, but instead of going to the library for a book, I got my computer and regrettably opened Zaliver's office door.

I gave him a *sorry* smile as I entered. His face went from cold and business-like to confusion and curiosity. He was on his computer. I could hear people speaking, but I was too busy looking for some goddamn blank paper. He watched me basically dig through his office with amused eyes, not even paying attention to the computer anymore.

When I couldn't find it, I looked at his desk with my hands on my hips. There had to be a paper drawer there somewhere. He cocked a brow at me, but I shook my head at him and motioned for him to pay attention to the sacred-sounding guy. I dropped to my knees and crawled around to his side of the desk. His eyes widened. I stopped at a drawer and pulled the bottom one. Nope. I closed it. I pulled open the second one and found stacks of paper, blank colorful sticky notes. You name it, he had it all. I pulled out a small stack and closed the drawer softly. With my paper, I crawled from around the desk and stood up. I plucked two pencils from his desk and mouthed a *thanks* and went out. I heard him give out a strained chuckle.

Back in our room, I plugged my headphones into the computer and downloaded music. I turned to the window and began to draw what I saw. It must have been lunch time because my stomach growled or maybe my wolf did; I couldn't tell the difference. When I went down to the kitchen to make another sandwich, I rubbed my eyes when I saw what was on the counter. Grilled cheese with tomato soup. How did he even have the time? Next to the plate was a note in Zaliver's handwriting.

My beloved mate,
Eat it all and tell me if you want more.
P.s. You're mine.
- Zaliver

I laughed out loud at his signature. The first time he wrote me a letter was when we were in the pack house, telling me to lock both doors. I quickly ate the warm food, wondering when he would come down. Had he already eaten as well? When I went up stairs, I continued where I left off, letting Wait by M83 decide my mood for me. Every once in a while, I'd hear the "underwater" conversations, but it was brief enough that it didn't give me a headache like last time. I should really mention this to Zaliver.

The more I drew, the calmer my body felt. My mind was focused on how lightly I held the pencil. I always loved drawing when I was a child and now, it was just a hobby. When the sun began to set, I realized that even though I could still see everything perfectly well, it still wasn't the same— beautiful, but not the same. I collected the scattered drawings and took out my headphones, closing the computer and placing it on the couch. I stretched and was glad that my fast healing didn't make me feel sore from today's workout. I was pretty sure that would have sucked but with that, working out didn't seem so bad now.

Venom was odd, polite, and scary, but there was something about him that if you looked past the murderous aura he gave off, you'd see something very interesting. I just still hadn't figured out what that was. I heard Zaliver's boots coming upstairs and stilled for a moment before reminding myself to relax. He opened the door and looked at me with a smile.

"Did you like lunch?" he said, walking up to the bed couch and sitting next to me. He crossed one leg over the other and turned to face me.

"Yup, loved it. My favorite actually," I stated, leaning into him and placing my hands a few inches from making contact to his thigh.

"Good. Do you want dinner now or later?" he murmured, reaching out and combing his fingers through my hair before taking his hand back.

"Now please. I'll even help!" I said happily. He made a face between a grimace and dramatic horror, his blue eyes widening. A small laugh escaped me at his expression even if it was at my own expense. I probably would get in the way more then I would help.

"Fine. I'll watch," I said, pouting.

"That's both better and safer." He grabbed my hand and pulled me off the couch, leading us to the kitchen.

"Safer for who?" I asked, narrowing my eyes on his back.

"Both of us. We'll get food poisoning if you cook," he answered without hesitation.

I gasped and slapped his shoulder. I was glad and annoyed that he was so good in the kitchen. I mean it's not like it would kill him to eat something I made. I pushed the memory of my cake to the back of my mind. No one was good when it came to doing things first time around.

"Immortal, remember?" I snapped. He turned to look at me over his shoulder.

"Good cook," he pointed to himself, grinning largely. "Bad cook, remember?" he pointed to me. I stuck my tongue out at him and went to go sit on the chair at the kitchen table.

"What does the lady desire tonight?" he asked, bowing down playfully. I blinked at him for a moment, my mind going blank.

"You," my wolf howled.

"Oh, um, anything is fine."

"Anything it is then."

~•~

355

"You go up. I have one last thing to do before I finish. I'll be there in five," Zaliver said, heading to his office. I went upstairs feeling as if each step echoed through my head, but I knew that wasn't the case. It was all of my imaginations and nerves. I hurried up and went into the closet, looking through Zaliver's shirts. Aside from the black ones, he always wore a dark midnight blue with white button down shirt.

I took off my pants and shirt. I wore it on top of my bra and underwear. I rolled up the sleeves to my elbow and looked in the mirror. The shirt was large on me. I only buttoned up three of the buttons in the middle of the shirt that ended mid-thigh. I quickly went into the bathroom and brushed whatever knots were in my hair, hoping it would perhaps brush away the knots forming in my stomach. I ran my fingers through it, making it a bit messy. It wasn't until I placed my hand down that I realized they were shaking. I clenched my hand and took a deep breath. I love him. Everything would be fine.

My body was going on overdrive. I gritted my teeth and shook myself out. Opening my eyes and looking at my reflection for a moment, I could see my big brown eyes that were bright and nervous but still happy. My skin had a pink hue, and my dark locks for once looked good—all messy and out. Over all, I looked happier than I could ever remembered. Nervous? Yes, but still happy. I was happy with Zaliver, and I wanted to stay that way with him, forever.

I smiled at myself before turning off the bathroom lights and walking out. I walked to where the nightstand lights were and dimmed them both, giving the room a soft glow. I walked back to the front of the bed and sat in the middle of it, sitting crisscross on the bed. Now, all I needed was Zaliver.

Two minutes later, when I heard him make his way up the stairs, I closed my eyes tightly. My heart was pounding in my chest wildly. I was shaking a bit, but I didn't dare move from my position. With each step that he took, I felt like my air was leaving me.

"*Every step you take, every move I make—*" my wolf sang.

"*Shut the hell up.*" I took a shaky breath, focusing on that only.

When the doorknob began to turn, I could feel my nerves spike. When the door began to open a bit, it stopped and then slowly opened to reveal him. He stared at me with glowing blue eyes. In this type of light, he really stood out.

"Vivian?" he asked. He stepped into the room slowly and closed the door behind him, not moving from his spot. His gaze was intense and focused solely on me. His hands fisted at his sides close to his body. I let out a small breath and looked down momentarily at his boots.

"Well, it's definitely later . . ." I trailed off, knowing he would get me. I glanced up from under my lashes, wanting to know what he was thinking. His bright eyes were electrifying and piercing right through me as if he was looking straight into my soul, which maybe he was. I didn't really care. He could stare all he wanted. He took slow steps to the front of the bed until he stood at the end. Once there, he didn't move. Up close, I could barely hear him breathing, but the sound of his heart was louder than usual.

"You don't have to—"

"I know I don't." I gave him a nervous smile. "I want to though, if possible." His gaze intensified on me. It was slightly unnerving having his full attention on me like that, but it was somehow empowering.

"And what is it that you want exactly, Vivian?" he murmured softly. I looked at him in the eyes for a moment before answering.

"You," I whispered.

His breath hitched in his throat. He closed his eyes and a barely audible growl began from his chest, not a threatening one however. It was a new growl that I hadn't heard him make before. It was a mixture of a purr and something else. Whatever it was, it made me want to give one in return. When he opened his eyes again, they were a stormy midnight blue, almost matching the dark shade. I knew there was a reason why I liked this shirt.

"You don't know what—"

"I do. I'm sure, Zaliver," I said. My fingers gripped the covers as each word came out of me.

"But how do you know? How can you be sure that this is what you want? How do I know that if you wake up tomorrow morning, you won't regret it?" he said, almost pleading me to give him an answer. His words were showing me just as much as his eyes. He would be beyond hurt if that were to happen, but it wouldn't.

"Because I love you, Zaliver."

It was like a moment suspended in time. I could both see and hear that he had stopped breathing. Now it was out. I felt liberated. It was almost too easy to say and felt *right* to say. But what did he feel? Zaliver took a shaky breath. It surprised me when his hands went to his heart with a surprised look on his face mixed with awe and disbelief.

"You . . . love . . . me?" he choked out.

I nodded at him, noting how his breaths were speeding up. I clenched my hands, almost making them go numb. I released my hold and forced my hands to hold still. To wait.

"Are you sure?" he asked, still not comprehending.

"Yes, Zaliver. I am completely sure that I am in love with you, and I want you to make me yours completely," I said with a hint of sass

357

in my voice. I couldn't help it. Of course, I had to have the one mate that had "superman" self-control now of all times.

He ran a hand through his hair and pushed it back, showing me his smoldering blue eyes that reflected the strong emotions within him like ocean waves colliding.

"Are you—"

"Yes. I'm bloody sure that I love you, and yes, I'm bloody sure that I want you to take me here and now. But if you're having trouble with that, I'm sure there are others out there—" He cut me off with a growl so loud and quite frankly, it was rough that it shook the frame of the house. I feared for the man's throat sometimes, with all the force he used. My eyes widened at him as he looked down at me with pitch black eyes.

"This is for all eternity, Vivian. Once you become mine, there will be no going back. No teasing, no flirting, no touching. Just you and me. No one else," he stated seriously.

"Right back at yah," I murmured.

He gripped the bottom of his black shirt and pulled it over his head, throwing the shirt somewhere. My eyes moved all over his strong build, and my fingers gripped tighter if possible at the covers. Just seeing his physique made me want to do things.

"Once we start, I don't think I'll be able to stop. You've tempted the beast one to too many times, Vivian. Back out now while you still can," he said; kicking off his boots, taking off his socks, and unbuckling his belt.

My eyes went back up to meet his eyes. My body hummed in anticipation.

"No," I challenged. He smirked at me and began pulling his pants off of his body. I gulped.

As he pulled off his pants, he kept his eyes firmly on mine, trying to see any sign of regret or a change of mind, but he wouldn't. All he could see would be nervousness and excitement.

He stood in front of me with only his black briefs on, unashamed or shy. A bulge was outlined in the front. My insides tightened.

He put both knees onto the bed slowly. With one hand, he slowly pushed me back onto the bed to lay on my back, making the shirt rise up considerably. I looked at him as he looked down at me hungrily. My breaths were coming out rapidly, and the man hadn't even really touched me.

He tapped my knees with his fingers twice, making me believe he wanted me to uncross my legs, which I did slowly. I kept my knees together, feeling both intensely frightened of the situation and intrigued by the new meaning of exposure.

358

He climbed up higher to the bed, pressing up against my legs. He looked down at me, checking one last time. The look on his face warned me to back out, but I shook my head. I felt his fingers skim up from my calf ever so slowly and then he gripped both of my knees in each hand firmly. He smirked at me and then spread my legs open in front of him. I gasped at his boldness. He didn't even bother hiding where his eyes were when he looked down. Wherever his skin touched me left a tingle like a strong current, adding to the passion I felt for him.

He rubbed one of my legs up and down sensuously with his hand while he trailed it up softly with the other hand from my knee to my inner thigh. My body shook in anticipation while he continued up until he undid the tree buttons holding the shirt open.

I bit my lip harshly, watching his mesmerized expression as his eyes took in their fill. I liked the expression on his face. He first flipped open one side of the shirt and then the other. Both of my arms that were on either side of me gripped the covers. Zaliver's eyes looked all over my body from top to bottom. His eyes then met mine again with a dark passionate blue burning right through me.

"You're everything I imagined you'd look like under this shirt. Beautiful. Perfect. Curvy. Unbelievably sexy, and all mine," he said huskily. He leaned down and kissed me with scorching fever.

Our kiss wasn't soft and sweet but passionate and animalistic. He wasn't holding back, and I wasn't going to either. I sure as hell wasn't going to be shy either. His lips played with mine without any hesitation. He plunged his tongue into my mouth, which I did the same. I explored his mouth while he staked claim of mine. My arms came up around him with one hand tangled itself in his hair while the other gripped at his back, enjoying the feeling of his broad shoulders. He trailed off of my lips to let me breath. I gasped as he made his way down to his mark.

My hips bucked forward in response to his hard bite, which he soothed a second later with his slick, wet tongue. His hand moved over to my chest and firmly cupped my breast with his hand while my eyes closed shut. I felt his lips make their way down to the top of my other breast as he began to softly suck at the flesh on top of my bra. His other hand fondled my breast, palming it. His pressure was neither soft nor harsh. I pushed my chest forward. My nipples hardened under my bra, feeling sensitive against the rough-feeling material.

"Zaliver," I whispered in a breath. His lips trailed back up to my neck as his other hand slid down slowly from my breast and then lower.

"Shh, I know," he whispered into my ear. I moaned loudly when he began to suck on my mark, creating a fiery sensation to spread all over. The hand that had slowly been trailing down my stomach

359

slipped into my underwear. My eyes opened in surprise and then shut in pleasure. My hips bucked up because of the unexpected yet welcomed new touch.

Zaliver's fingers played and teased me until I was tensed with want and need of a release. I gripped onto his bicep tightly. I opened my eyes to find him already looking down at me. My lips parted to let out a moan when he stroked harder. My ears heard only my gasps and moans and the frantic beating of my heart. Oh, how I pleaded for him to give me the final stroke, but he just shook his head and captured my lips in a sort of torture kisses. My stomach muscles tightened.

"Please," I moaned with my back lifting off the bed. He nuzzled my neck, planted small kisses and then pulled back.

"Not yet, baby. You'll get what you want only when I'm fully and completely buried in you," he said huskily. He leaned down to peck me on the lips. "I want to feel your hot little body tighten around me," he said, grinning at me.

With a sudden burst of confidence, I grabbed his hand and pulled it out, flipping him and making me on top of him. My chest lifted up and down quickly as I tried to control myself. Zaliver's wicked eyes looked at me as he lifted his fingers to his mouth. My eyes widened.

"I always wondered what you tasted like. Now, I get to know . . . and you're going to remind me everyday," he stated. My insides throbbed and clenched at his words.

"You are very wicked, mate of mine." I narrowed my eyes at him and then grinned when I felt his hard member underneath me. Being just as bold as he was, I first kissed his lips and then down to his chest, making sure to look up at him. He let out a hiss as a breath. "My turn," I said, kissing his toned chest and playfully biting his left nipple. He let out a small growl.

The more I kissed his body, the more my hands explored, feeling his chest, biceps, abs, and slowly dragging my fingers down to where my mind really wanted to explore. My eyes snapped back to his eyes, smiling smugly at me.

"Unbelievable? Aren't I?" he joked.

I squeezed him and was rewarded with a buck of his hips while his lips parted. Let's see how he likes to be played with I thought wickedly. I felt a strong sense of possessiveness that I had never felt before. I made my way back to kiss his lips while keeping my hand firmly on his manhood, feeling him though the thin fabric of his briefs. Even with the cloth, I could still feel how hard and hot his length was; it both frightened and excite the crap out of me.

I kissed him and he kissed me back. Our lips were meeting one another with fiery passion and desire for one another. His arms wrapped around me to pull me closer. I pulled on his bottom lip with

360

my teeth with my hand rubbing at him, earning a groan out of him that pleased me to the core. I did it for a little longer before he took hold of my hand in his and put one of my fingers in his mouth, sucking softly. The warmth of his mouth made it feel like it was the only thing I knew. I pulled my finger from his mouth and with my thumb, I skimmed his swollen lips.

He caught me off guard when I was suddenly back under him with both of his arms on either side of me, hovering above me. I felt his hips pushing and aligning perfectly well with the junction between my thighs, making me let out a groan. I put both of my hands around his neck and pulled his down to me, wrapping my legs around his waist and causing more friction between the two. With one hand supporting his upper half, he reached for my underwear with the other and looked me in the eyes before ripping it off and tossing it elsewhere. I squirmed at the sensation of having something rub up against my naked flesh. With that same hand, I felt him do the same to himself. My heart began beating faster at the sound of his last remaining scraps of clothes being torn off.

I shuddered a bit when I felt the hot and pulsing manhood push up against me, tensing a bit. Zaliver loomed over me. He closed his eyes and took a deep breath. I felt his firm abdomen flex against me, and because I couldn't hold still, I ended up rubbing against him. His eyes snapped open; vibrant and glowing blue eyes clashed with my light brown ones. His expression was hungry and just as lustful as mine but with softness to it. His body pushed down on me, making me feel all of him just as he could feel all of mine.

I gave him a shy smile. He looked at me for a second before bowing down to kiss my forehead for a long moment.

"You are my life, my reason for breathing and fighting. Never forget that," he murmured against my skin. I felt tears sting my eyes. If that wasn't an "I love you" in Zaliver's way, then I didn't know what is.

"I love you too," I whispered to him. I felt his form shake. I could feel his emotions coursing through me like they were my own. It was an opening of his will. The shielded wall protecting or hiding his doubts and worries and vulnerabilities were replaced with disbelief, awe, uncertainty, fear, unbelievable happiness, and an ever-growing love. I felt the moisture spill over my eye in a single tear drop of happiness. He pulled back. With the pad of his thumb, he removed it and kissed me where the tear had been.

"I'll try to make it quick," he whispered lowly as he pulled back. I nodded and took in a breath. He reached over to his nightstand and pulled out a pack of condoms. I gave him a questioning look, and he gave me half sheepish half I-have-been-waiting-for-this look. I just laughed. When people thought of sex, they thought of painting and the world rocking bliss; most people craved for that. But what I realized that moment was that what I craved and what Zaliver craved was the trust and intimacy of two people who loved each other very much. What we craved, needed, and wanted was each other.

He reached down, aligning himself to me. I tensed at the feel of his head at my entrance but told myself to relax. I distracted myself by looking at his concentrated look, how his brows furrowed, and how his lips parted as he took in a shaky breath. I smiled as he glanced up at me with his blue eyes momentarily surprising me. That was all he needed to push in with one big thrust. I cried out as a sharp pain hit my lower muscles. He leaned down and captured my cry with his mouth. He didn't stop until he was fully buried in me. I was breathing and shuddering heavily as pain and the new sensation became one with me. Thankfully, I was a fast healer. He held very still above me while his tongue plunged into my mouth, making me focus on him.

I focused on the kiss and the way his hand reached up to cup the side of my face as he poured all of his emotions and senses in the kiss. Our lips met to a private dance only we knew—a dance that connected us as whole as we both gave it our all. When we both pulled back, we were panting and gazing into each other's eyes with unspoken words and promises. The pain was long forgotten as he caressed my face with love in his eyes. He began to plant gentle kisses all over my face, my cheeks, my nose, my forehead, the corner of my lips and then he pulled his hips back.

I gasped and unthinkingly drove my hips forward to get the sensation back. He must have realized that whatever pain he thought I felt was gone because he grinned down at me and with brutal force plunged back into me.

"Ahh!" I exclaimed, feeling full and enjoying the feeling that his actions gave me.

He did it again and again and again without holding back; we both didn't. I gave into the sensation and let the animalistic side of me take over, giving in to my desires. I let myself get tangled and lost in the man I loved, in the way he responded to my kisses and touch, and to the sound of his groans and moans of pleasure. The way he touched my face with gentle care, joy, and pleasured look on his face. How he wrapped his body around my own as if shielding me from the world and wrapping me up in his own.

His hands removed my bra. He drove his face into my breasts, kissing and nipping, making me pant. He took his time with my chest, sucking on my nipples only to blow softly on them. Everything he did drove me crazy to the point of no return.

The closer we got to the edge, the more I drew closer to him. I lifted my back off the bed and straddled him, not breaking the sensual

362

rhythm we had. His head was thrown back and his mouth was open in an unheard moan. I began shaking as a new sensation started from the tip of my toes to my heart. The more I looked at him, the stronger it got. It wasn't just my body but my soul.

I began planting kisses on his shoulder and went up and down his neck, feeling my gums ace. Without warning, he plunged deeply into me, causing my canines to come out. I let out a gasp as his thrusts became harder, faster, and more intoxicating. Just when I thought life couldn't get any better, it did as stars exploded behind my eyes. My body shook and tightened around Zaliver as he called out my name in a strained voice.

Without knowing why, I threw my head back in the middle of the new earth-shattering sensation and sunk my teeth into Zaliver's neck. It had caught us both off guard. Instead of his angered growls of pain, he let out a sound of absolute pleasure—one I hadn't heard before. His hips "jackhammered" into me, making me squeak at the sensation.

At the same time, my mind seemed to explode with voices, but instead of being murky and not being able to understand them, I could hear the thousands of voice clearly. I could feel them all. It felt like I knew all of them. It all happened in less than a second but in that one second when I heard the voices and felt the people, power coursed through me. It was pushed to the back of my head as Zaliver moved his head away from me and sunk his teeth into me this time, remarking me.

We laid there for a long moment. I was wrapped in his arms as he pulled the covers over us. He had his head on top of my head while my head was on his chest, listening to his heart and returning back to normal. His beats sounded very much like my own. His hand rubbed up and down my back while I did the same on his thigh. What? He had a hot, firm ass. the heck was I supposed to do? Ignore it? After a long time had passed, he spoke into the darkness.

"You marked me," he stated. His tone was not indicating how he felt.

"I guess I did. Are you angry?" I asked him, shuffling around to see his expression.

I realized the answer right away when his soft blue eyes looked down at me with mirth and love. He smiled down at me softly.

"No. Never. Now everyone knows I'm yours just as much as you are mine," he stated proudly, leaning down to peck my lips. I smiled up at him.

"Damn right. You're mine," I growled out playfully.

"So . . . we still have some cond—" I stated but before I could finish. He threw himself on top of me with a wicked smile.

As I fell asleep in my mate's warm embrace with low-toned voice in the back of my mind and a new-found power that made me feel

363

complete and unwaveringly attached to Zaliver like nothing before, I felt his arms squeezed me as he planted a long kiss to the side of my face.

"I love you too, my little cloud. I love you too," he whispered into the darkness of the night.

CHAPTER 30

I woke up to the feeling of a feather-light touch on my face. Something was trailing from the corner of my eye down to the side of my face, then to the corner of my lips before going over my bottom lip. Recognizing the familiar pattern, I parted my lips and softly bit his finger. I heard him inhale sharply before opening my eyes. Laying half on top of me and his face hovering above mine, Zaliver's blue eyes were bright and full of adoration.

"Good morning," he murmured softly.

With the tip of my tongue, I swiped over his finger. He narrowed his eyes on me playfully. I let go and gave him a wide smile, wrapping my arms back around him and pushing myself against him.

Wait—

"You're naked. Stupid." My wolf reminded me in a happily dazed voice. She was laying down with one of her back legs twitching repeatedly. The beast was in the same position. My eyes widened as the memory of last night resurfaced. My lips parted. Seeing my expression, Zaliver swept down and captured my lips in a wakening kiss. When he pulled back, I was breathless and very much wake. All of my senses were focused solely on him, not even noting the thin wall holding off a large power source in the back of my mind.

"Well, I'm awake now," I muttered. I snuggled into him and kissed his smooth chest. His arms tightened around me as he rolled me on top of him.

"I'm glad to see that."

I shifted a bit.

"I can feel that." And boy was he glad.

He let out a laugh before kissing my forehead tenderly. I looked up at him with a smile, and he grinned. It was gonna be a good day.

~•~

"Fuck today, matter-of-fact, fuck everyone, especially you," I muttered under my breath, annoyed. Zaliver smirked proudly as we

365

made our way to the car that early morning or at least, as I tried to make my way to the car. He got to the car before me and stood with my door open, waiting for me to reach the car. I glared at him as I took tentative steps, making sure not to move too fast.

"Oh, of course you're happy. You're not the one walking like an unbalanced drunk and feeling like I've just been pounded by a jackhammer." His grin widened when I got to him.

"Not a jackhammer, just me," he stated, closing my door. When he got into the car and began driving, he spoke again, taking hold of my hand and bringing it up to his mouth. It seemed like he couldn't stop touching me ever since last night. In the kitchen, he would find little ways to touch me—be it my hand, face, or hips. It was really distracting in a good way.

"I'm sorry about the unbalanced drunk part, but I can't help but feel proud to have been given the utmost honor of bringing you pleasure repeatedly last night," he said, turning to look at me when we got to a red light. His blue eyes still left me breathless.

"You smooth-talk your way out on this one, huh," I stated, playfully glaring at him. His eyes lit up in the early morning sunlight, looking lighter than I've ever seen them, almost crystal-like. "I did, didn't I?"

I laughed at him. Today, Zaliver was just going to drop me off at the training field but would come pick me up in two hours. I was mostly going for the stretches today. Lord knew I needed them. It was odd though as we drove not because we had mated last night but because I could feel something was going on in my head; I just didn't know what. It was the same feeling of frustration and confusion someone gets when they realize they had forgotten something but couldn't remember what. I knew I hadn't forgotten anything.

There was a wall blocking the very active and moving section of the back of my mind as it gave off a strong sense. There was something nagging at me. When we pulled into the training field and got out, everyone stopped and dropped to one knee instead of bowing.

I looked at Zaliver in question, but he looked forward with a blank look on his face. The only assurance I got from him was the squeeze of his hand. I looked back and saw that all of their heads had lifted to show me silver eyes. I gasped, almost as if practiced, they raised their right hand and crossed it over their chest.

"We bind our lives and loyalty to Luna Vivian. We fight, breathe, and shall bleed for the luna of all wolves," they said in unison.

I felt every single one of their emotions as if they were my own. My mind was processing it like crazy. Zaliver didn't have to say anything for me to know that this was a situation I had to handle. It was instinctive, like breathing, to respond, my voice sounding strong and sure of my words.

"And I, in return, promise to you that I shall protect and cherish our pack, our family." They all lifted their heads up and gave out wolf howls. When they stopped, their eyes were back to normal. The power that soured though me didn't disappear but went to the back of my mind where that mystery wall was.

It was hard to ignore the proud and heated look from Zaliver, who was next to me. He leaned down closer to my face, hovering just inches from my lips.

"That was perfect." He quickly pecked me and reluctantly pulled back. He was filled with buzzing energy that was overwhelming him with irresistible happiness.

"What was that exactly?" I asked him.

"That," he nodded in their direction, "is something that will be happening a lot today. Wolves will be pledging themselves to you. Your response depending on their rank will be different. These are warrior wolves you swore to protect.

"But . . . why now?" I asked, still not getting it. Zaliver smiled.

"Because they know you're completely mine. You've just become the Luna of all packs. They want to be the first to let you know they're loyal." My mouth hung open at his words.

"B-but . . . you said 'all packs'. I thought . . . Just this—" He cut me off with a smirk on his handsome face.

"Baby. You were not just mated to the god of all wolves to get handed with one section. You get the full deal. Remember what you said to me when I first marked you?" he asked. I gave him a look.

"I remembered a lot of 'please no' and a lot of 'oh my gods.' " He grimaced but shook his head.

"You said and I quote, 'No man should have all this power.' And I answered with—"

"'I get to share all this power with you'," I answered with a whisper. He nodded.

"I know you have questions. We'll talk later. don't worry for now. There's Venom," he said. I turned to see the quiet snake standing under a tree far away with his hands at his back.

"Okay, I've gotta run, but you can contact me anytime."

"Okay," I said, still a little dazed.

He leaned down and took my lips into a leg-weakening kiss. He tried to pull away but memories of what we did last night still held me and made me nip at his bottom lip. He growled into the kiss, and I felt his hand grip the back of my head and pull me closer. This time, he kissed me with the same passion, making me want to gasp and do something inappropriate for the crowd watching, but he still held on for a bit. When he let go, I took in a deep breath. My lungs was feeling the cool air, and my heart was pounding like a hummingbird's wings while my body ached for the man standing in front of me with dark-hooded eyes.

"Later," he said before leaving. I stood there watching him drive away. Did he mean "see you later" or "later as in later? I wondered.

"I don't care. As long as one of those "laters" means he'll be screwing our brains out," my beast mumbled.

"Preach it sista'" My wolf sighed.

"True." I added.

I turned around to walk to Venom but let out a startled yell when I saw him standing a few feet behind me.

"Mother of—" I cut myself off and slapped my hand on my chest. My eyes were wide at the golden-eyed giant while he bowed his head in guilt.

"I'm sorry, Luna. I didn't mean to frighten you. I should have warned you that I'm much quieter than a wolf," he muttered lowly.

"Damn. I didn't even hear your heart," I muttered the last part mostly to myself. It must have been a part of my imagination, but I couldn't tell if his eyes tightened a bit.

"Well, let's start," I muttered, taking a few awkward steps towards where we were yesterday but he stopped me.

"Actually," he hissed, not meaning to sound menacing and cleared his throat, "I have something else in mind. Now that you are completely in sense with yourself, your balance in power must be crazed and in need of workout." I tilted my head to the side, curious as to what was in his mind.

"Like what?" I asked. He opened his mouth but then closed it and then opened it again.

"I'll tell you, but uhh . . . I'll do it while we stretch. I believe you are in need of one, yes?" he asked. His words coming out with an odd sense since I could see that he felt mortified in saying them but meaning well. I blushed.

"Yup."

After stretching for about twenty minutes, turned out Venom wanted me to go through an obstacle course. I thought that I would complain at first, but I was oddly excited at the thought of jumping over things, climbing, and all that stuff. When I was done, I wasn't even winded a bit. I skipped over to Venom whose eyes hadn't left me since I began.

His arms were crossed over his chest. His face was blank along with his golden eyes. They really were very pretty and chilling to look into. Something about his eyes made it feel as if he saw more than he should have. As if he knew more than he should have. He had old eyes, I thought.

"Well?" I asked him, wanting to know the verdict of my work out.

He tilted his head to the side slowly and without realizing, I did the same subconsciously, not wanting to look away from his odd eyes. He blinked and shook his head. His white strands were falling out from his pulled-back hair. I blinked. Wow, what was that?

"Sorry," he hissed. "I've got a theory I like to try out tomorrow if you don't mind?" he asked.

"Sure. What theory? Is it that I'm not meant to be working out? Because if it is, I'm all for it," I joked. The corners of his lips lifted up the smallest bits. When he opened his mouth to speak, I caught the sight of his sharp teeth and something else that looked like fangs. I held back a shiver.

"Wow. Why is it now that I'm noticing this?" I gasped to myself.

"You're mind has expanded. That's why," my beast muttered.

"I'm sorry, but no, that isn't the case. You are, however, probably going to finish sooner than you planned," he muttered lowly.

"Really? Why's that?" I asked, rocking forward and back on my feet. He uncrossed his arms and pulled them behind his back.

"If you don't mind me asking, do you have medical training?" he asked randomly.

"Uhh, no," I stated, bewildered by his odd comment. I knew how to wrap a bandage in a pretty comfortable grip, but that's about as far as my knowledge goes.

"Alright. Thank you for returning today, Luna Vivian. See you tomorrow," he said quickly and walked off gracefully into the shadows before I could ask anything more.

"What was that about?" my wolf asked.

"I have no idea."

"Weird snake," my beast muttered, narrowing her eyes in the direction Venom went to.

"Maybe just a little."

~•~

"We bind our lives and loyalty to the luna of all wolves. We give our lives and support to all of your choices," Mark, Hannah, and all the guards stated.

"And I, to you, will support and help you within my care," I stated.

369

After a release of breath, Hannah came squealing into my arms, waddling over with open arms with a large grin on her face. Her round belly was covered by a large flower printed shirt, but I most definitely felt it in the hug.

"Wow! You're mated! Oh my gosh, this is great!" she yelled out in glee. I laughed with her and tried to calm my flaming face. No point in denying it. It so weird though. I mean, who would go around congratulating someone for having sex?

"Yup. And look at you, I swear it feels like I haven't seen you in months. Your baby's gotten so big!" I pointed to her stomach. Mark came up behind her and placed his hand on her stomach with love in his eyes.

"Hey, Mark. Have you guys finally picked a style for the baby's room, or has she still got you remodeling?" I asked jokingly.

"We've finally decided on the last one," he confessed with a relieved smile and green eyes lighting up at the fact. I heard Johnson snort beside me. I turned to him with a raised brow.

"Only because I refused to keep returning their things every time she wanted a change. I swear, my sister makes me feel like a donkey running errands," Johnson stated, wagging his finger at Hannah who stuck her tongue out at him.

"Maybe because you look like a donkey," Mila muttered not so discreetly under her breath. He turned to glare at her.

"Damn," Courtney said. Luke shook his head with a small smile.

Hannah slipped from under Mark's arms and speedwalked as much as she could into the kitchen and came back with something in her hands. She handed it to Johnson and moved back with a smirk on her face. Johnson looked at the object with confusion with his blond curls falling forward.

"Why did you bring me ice?"

"To apply to that burn." We all burst out laughing while Johnson's confusion morphed into annoyance, but the corners of his lips twitched once or twice.

"Man, I missed you guys," I stated between chuckles.

"I'm glad to hear that because we have too. It's been so boring without you here, and I'm sure Luke misses Alpha taking his body. Isn't that right, Luke?" Johnson asked with all sickeningly sweet voice, blinking innocently at a glaring Luke

"I oughta hit you for that, but since we're in the presence of the luna, I will not," Luke stated. Johnson raised his arms and shook them.

"Ohhh no, look at me shake," he said sarcastically.

I laughed harder, feeling my eyes water a bit at both of the guys, acting younger than their actual age. Yes, I did miss them.

"Do you want to stay for lunch?" Mark asked me.

"If you don't mind."

"I'll start cooking then. Hey, Johnson. Where did you leave the stake?" he asked, beginning to make his way to the kitchen.

"Why the hell should I know?" Johnson asked, following behind with the pack of ice.

"Maybe because you were the last one seen with it?" Luke pointed out, trailing behind the guys. I was guessing they were going to give us some girl time.

"You've got no proof," I heard Johnson state smugly. All the girls rolled eyes at the bickering guys.

"These are your teeth marks, you ass. It's not even cooked yet!" Mark exclaimed. The sound of someone's hand moving in the air let me know Johnson was about to get smacked.

"I swear living with Johnson in the house is like living with another pregnant lady. I feel bad for Mark sometimes. He already has me to deal with," Hannah stated.

"I thought Johnson lives in the pack house?" I asked, confused. Hannah nodded but it was Mila who answered, moving closer to sit with us.

"He does, but since Hannah's five months pregnant, he wants to help around. He said he's not leaving until after the second month to the baby's birth," she stated with hidden fondness. Eyeing her, I saw a hint of pink on her face. Hmm . . . It was like she actually glowed in pink.

"Awww, that's so cute," I said. He really cared for his sister.

"Yeah, when he's not fighting me for the last slice of pizza, or who should get a foot message from Mark. I swear . . . " She shook her head.

"As long as he's here and not knocking at my door every five minutes at the pack house," Mila said. Courtney nudged her with a secret small smile.

"Oh, don't act like you don't like his knocking on your door every five minutes." She snickered. Why am I getting the sense of a little romance coming from Mila and Johnson here?

"Because they're mates," my beast stated. My eyes widened at Mila who was too busy denying Courtney to notice me.

"What? How do you know?"

"Look at them. Notice how they seemed to be giving off a pink hazy glow when they're together. You can tell who are mates," my beast stated.

"Cool." It slipped out before I could stop it.

371

"What's cool?" Courtney asked curiously.

"Don't say anything yet," my beast warned.

"Why not?"

"Just don't."

I hesitated but agreed.

"Nothing. Hey, Hannah. Do you know what you're having? I just realized all this time I've never actually asked you." It was a good change of topic because she jumped up and down in her seat.

"We're having a little girl! Oh my gosh. I'm so happy! More shopping and then telling her the do and don't of high school," she said, tearing up a bit.

"Congrats! Do you guys have a name yet?" I asked, curious for the baby.

"A developing mind link," my beast said.

We all went into a deep conversation about names, nicknames, and ideas for the baby.

"So . . . " Hannah asked after a brief pause in the group. She looked at me with innocent eyes, but the way she was leaning forward threw me off. The gleam in her eyes and the almost rabidly hungry look should have warned me.

"What?" I asked. The other girls looked at Hannah as well, wondering what was going on.

"Oh you know . . . " She snickered and I frowned.

"No, what?" She sighed and rolled her eyes.

"How was the sex?" she blurted out.

"Umm . . . you know . . . private," I said sarcastically. I hoped she wasn't expecting any details from me because she wasn't going to get any.

Mila and Courtney laughed and then smothered it with an all too obvious fake cough. Hannah made a whiny sound and ran her fingers through her light locks of hair.

"Oh, don't be like that. I know that you know that everyone wants to know what Alpha is like in bed. Don't be like that. Feed the hungry!" Hannah yelled out, begging. At the exact same moment when my face flushed, Mark's head poked out from around the kitchen.

"You hungry? Foods almost—" He ducked as Hannah's shoe flew through the air.

"Nevermind!" he yelled out. Hannah turned back to me.

"We're all hungry for some info. Come on, spill the beans. Was he good? I mean he had to be good, right? Right?" She turned to ask the girls who had blank expressions but amused eyes.

"This is all that I'm saying because I can tell that you're not dropping this and because I'm sure some of the people noticed as well." I sighed, half mortified and embarrassed. Hannah squeaked and nodded

372

with her bright eyes and eagerness for information. If I didn't know any better, I would have presumed she was a reporter.

"Well, don't hold back!" she said. Even Mila and Courtney who had tried not to look too interested were looking at me now.

"Fine. All I'm going to say on the matter is that even my super fast healing ability did not get me out of the soreness this morning. And that's it!" I stated, pointing a finger at a giggling and bouncy Hannah.

"Ahhh! I don't know how to process this! My inner fangirl is going nuts!" She clapped in glee. I raised a brow at her odd statement.

"Your inner . . . fangirl?" I asked.

"Yeah, so ever since you came to the island, Alpha's been seen doing his work much faster than before. We don't see him as much because as soon as he's done, he goes straight home. And guess who's home? You! So, of course, I couldn't help but be a fangirl over it. You guys are so cute!" Hannah gushed.

"It's true, Luna. Alpha used to be seen doing his work every once in a while on the island but then he would spend the majority of his time sparring and training with the wolves," Courtney imputed.

"It is quite adorable." Mila nodded.

"Yes. . . I guess it is," I muttered, distracted. I didn't know Zaliver rushed home, but I guessed I should have with all the time we spent together these last few days. When Mark was done with the cooking, we all had lunch together. I left soon after with a promise to come back to a teary-eyed Hannah.

"You have to or else I'll come break you out. I don't care how good the sex is," she promised with a wave. Mark apologized with an amused face.

It was hard but not impossible to get the guards off of me. At first, they were pretty persistent but with a firm voice, I told them that I could take care of myself. It wasn't that I didn't want them with me, but I just felt like having a bit of me time to wrap my mind around everything.

Luna of this pack—that I could wrap my mind around. But Luna of all packs? No. No way. What would happen to the other lunas? What would be my job? Did I have to do what Zaliver did? What did he do? I sighed and ran my fingers through my hair, pulling a bit as it got tangled towards the end. I was walking down a busy street with cafes, parks, and random little shops. I caught the sight of an elementary school nearby with lots of little kids playing on the playground.

School. I hadn't thought about it in a while, well college, that is. Did I still want to go? Probably, but would I have the time? I had so much free time and had no idea what I was supposed to do with it.

"*Well, you're immortal for one. It's not like the colleges are going anywhere,*" my wolf pointed out.

373

I decided it was best to go home. I began walking home when I decided to try something. Zaliver was always flashing all over the place, so wouldn't that mean that I could do the same? I closed my eyes and took a breath. I felt my body begin to heat up a bit. It could have been excitement or adrenaline that was beginning to pump through me. I began taking some steps and then jogging lightly. I could see people looking at me, but I didn't stop. I took three more steps before breaking out in an eye-missing speed.

I could see everything around me moving slowly, but unlike the other times, I moved quickly. I knew that I was moving beyond normal speed. When the house came into sight, I stopped a few feet in front of the house. My body still felt a bit heated, ready for more action but I was done for the moment.

I went into the kitchen and grabbed a glass of water. Looking out the window, my mind traveled to my visit to Hannah. I was glad to finally be able to see her with the others. I wished I could see my parents as well. I began to wonder what they were doing and was surprised when a spark went off in my mind. As if by choice, I took hold of the spark mentally and was almost pulled into my mind as the spark took off and suddenly stopped. In a blink of an eye, I was suddenly in both of my parents' mind.

It was like mind linking them by looking into their eyes through my mind. I could see my dad sitting next to my mom with his hand over her shoulder as they watched a late night movie while my mom was thinking about me.

"What do you think Vivian is doing now?" my mom whispered sadly. It broke my heart to hear her like that.

"I don't know, but I hope she's safe," my dad muttered, kissing the top of her head and thinking about me. I mentally let go of their spark and had the full sight of the outside window. What the heck was that? I just thought about them and then suddenly it was like I was in their minds.

This time, I closed my eyes and thought of an old friend of mine from high school before a spark went off in my mind, but instead of thinking about it, I followed and was plunged into a mall. I spent I don't know how long jumping from people to people and entranced on what they were doing. Distance was not important as I did so. It seemed something like what Zaliver could do, but instead of taking over, I sort of just . . . spied. It was wrong but fascinating. This was how Zaliver found me in the kitchen with my eyes closed, seeing through the eyes of someone I knew.

I jumped when I felt arms wrap themselves around me. I let go of the spark and opened my eyes. Outside was dark, and I could see my reflection. My face flushed and my brown eyes went wide with both

374

excitement and interest. Zaliver's chin rested on my head as his blue eyes stared at me through our reflection as well with a soft smile on his face. Unlike our other hugs, this front to back hug was different. He didn't have to be careful of not being too close, instead, he both pulled me closer and pushed the hard planes of his body onto mine, not leaving anything untouched. He moved down to whisper in my ear.

"Honey, I'm home," he whispered softly and then playfully nipped at my ear. I grinned and turned in his arms to face him, wrapping my arms around his waist and locking my fingers.

"How was work, dear?" I played along, looking up at him with a smile. My wolf's ears perked up and her tail began to wag like a happy dog. He sighed and shook his head with mock disappointment.

"More boring than usual. I wonder why?" he asked me, looking down.

"I don't know. Why do you think?" I asked, kissing right above his mark softly. I felt him tense and then shudder. I felt a joy run through me at his reaction. He pulled back and looked down at me with heated eyes. He pushed me back further into the sink and let me felt the bulge in the front of his pants.

"You little tease. I think you know exactly why working was more boring than usual, but how about I tell you why?" he murmured. I nodded with my breath coming out slower and my body feeling hot all over. He leaned down and began trailing kisses from my jaw across my chin and then back down, nipping and sucking on my skin softly. I slipped my fingers under his shirt and gripped his firm waist.

"Well, for one, I was at work when I could have been with you," he stated with his mouth touching my skin, "on you . . . in you." I shivered at his statements and at the feel of one of his hands lifting the bottom of my shirt and placing his hand on my waist. His thumb made a circling motion that drove me crazy like it did.

"Really . . ." I muttered in a shaky breath.

"Mhh, hmm." His teeth slightly felt like hot electricity running through me and was collected in the pit of my stomach that my hips squirmed against his.

I was not used to this at all, but I wanted him. Now.

"Zaliver—"

"So, how was your day?" He pulled back completely and walked around the counter to look at me with his blinking innocent blue eyes and a taunting smile.

He left me hot and bothered on the sink. I narrowed my eyes at him. My wolf growled.

"*Boiii, bring that dick here!*" she snapped, unamused.

Zaliver closed his eyes and chuckled, shaking his head a bit. I froze. He opened his eyes with much amusement.

375

"Your wolf greatly amuses me. She makes it quite hard to talk to you with a straight face sometimes, if I'm honest."

I made a horrified, embarrassed choking sound.

"Nooo! Please nooo! Tell me you haven't been able to hear her the whole time!" I slapped my hands over my face and shook my head. My wolf was deadly silent. I couldn't tell if she was embarrassed or holding her breath to pass out.

Zaliver walked over to me and held me in his arms again. I still didn't move. He leaned down to speak next to my ear.

"I must not tell lies. My mate has forbidden me from doing so," he whispered mockingly. I made another sound in between a laugh and a murder-me-now sound.

"It's really not that bad," he tried saying but I shook my head.

"It is when I now know you've heard some pretty damn perverted things." I shrieked.

"Most of which I've agreed with," he confessed. I shook my head and removed my hands.

"*See? Now, he knows how perverted your mutt ass is,*" I said to my wolf.

"*Hey, technically, I'm a manifestation of you . . . so. . . . I'm your inner pervert. Hey, baby!*" she yelled out towards Zaliver who shook with laughter.

"Hello," he answered. I smacked his chest.

"Don't encourage her! She'll just be more perverted now," I grumbled. A heated look grew in his eyes.

"I'm all up for that baby." I rolled my eyes with a smile.

"I'm sure you are now." I stepped out of his arms and this time, I walked around the counter. "It's 'later' and I want my morning answers." A somber and annoyed look grew on his face, but I knew it wasn't directed at me. He turned and began rummaging through the fridge.

"Yes, but first, what do you want to eat?"

"I'm not hungry." I was much too nervous and full of questions to think about food, not to mention the fine view of his behind I was awarded with. He stopped and pulled out to look at me with narrowed eyes.

"Have you eaten?"

"Lunch with Hannah." He was nodding before I was done.

"Yes I know, but have you eaten here?" he pushed. I shook my head.

"I'm not hungry though." He pursed his lips at me.

"What?" I asked, exasperated. Was he avoiding the subject?

"Do you want a fruit smoothie?" he asked, already pulling out materials and fruit.

376

"Sure," I said.

"Good," he said, pleased.

"When you marked me last night, did you notice anything?" he asked. His voice was casual while cutting a fruit.

He couldn't see it, but I was giving him a "really?" look.

"You're going to have to be a bit more specific when you talk about last night and me noticing certain things," I said dryly. I felt his pleasure at my admission though the bond. If anything, I noticed a little too much . . . not that it was bad.

"What I'm asking is that while you were marking me, did you feel a rush of power? A sense of not only everything but everyone? It was brief but still present." I thought about it for a second and then went over my thoughts.

"Yeah, actually. Why's that?"

"That my dear was you calming not only me but your luna right to all pack links and wolves. I'm also guessing you've noticed some changes today besides from this morning?" he asked. He turned to look at me so I nodded.

"You're now connected to every wolf pack to ever live. I'm not sure how far or what new advanced powers you might get. It's sort of new for me as well because I've only got my experience to rely on." He tossed all of the cut-up fruit into the blender and put the lid on.

"So, what does that mean now? I mean I probably have to do things, right? Like I don't know, work? I've never really been trained for this," I muttered, feeling a bit anxious. I didn't know what lunas do.

"Well, for starters, you don't ever have to work, but leave that to me. There is something else . . . " He trailed off hesitantly with a hint of annoyance.

This made me worry.

Oh no! Do I have to take some sort of luna assessment test? I can't do that! I fail at ever very test I take, no matter how much I study.

"What?"

"The thing is that when you marked me and claimed your position, you also made all wolves alert to the new hierarchy change. Wolves and alphas everywhere have been banging on my mental shields all day," he growled the last part with distaste.

Oh shit. They know I mated Zaliver. Well, I mean, they knew the top boss was mated. It must have been a huge ass shock since before I met him he was considered a monster. They didn't necessarily know it was me—yet.

"So what's next?" I whispered, knowing I wasn't going to like his answer by the grimace on his face.

377

"They aren't going to leave us alone until they know why the power structure has been changed, so that means we're going to have to follow through with a meeting."

"Are you saying that the great Lupus Deus is going to leave his cave and go talk to the alphas?" I asked, surprised. This wasn't so bad. He cocked his brow at me for a long moment, then I got it.

"Wait . . . I have to go too?" I asked, horrified. He smirked at me, blended the fruit and then poured it in two cups. He walked over and placed one in front of me. Leaning down, he took the opportunity of me being surprised to steal a kiss. He answered my question.

"Seems like we're throwing a ball."

What the fuck!

While getting ready for bed, I sat on the bed, looking at Zaliver while he was tapping away on his computer.

"You can't just leave me in charge of throwing a ball I don't even want to go to. It's ridiculous," I exclaimed.

"I've already told you. Just write down what you want—colors, tables, theme, all that stuff. I'll have someone make sure it happens before we arrive," he stated firmly, glancing at me for a moment and then going back onto the computer. Something he said caught my attention.

"Well, if I get to do that, then why can't I make sure it's all put together?" I asked. He snorted and turned in his chair to look at me.

"Like hell am I going to allow a whole bunch of alphas and their own people to our island. Knowing some of them, they'll try to find a way to fuck shit up or take over. We're going to have to leave the island for a few days," he said, walking over to me and placing his hands on the bed, slowly crawling over to me. I wrapped my arms around him and looked up into his smoldering blue eyes that were hinting at something very promising.

"So, all I have to do is . . . "

"Tell me what you want. Your wish is your command," he said huskily.

I thought for a moment and then beamed up at him with excitement. Without thinking, I wrapped my legs around his hips and squeezed out of excitement, ignoring how his eyes turned black. His hands bunched up the pillows under me, too busy thinking about how to turn everything into an awesome ball.

"Ahhh, can we have a masquerade ball where you and me wear unique masks!" I asked.

He leaned down and began kissing my throat.

"Mhh hmm," he answered immediately.

"Should we wear the same color, like I wear—"

378

"Whatever you want baby," he answered quickly, trailing over to the other side of my neck where my mark was.

That made me snap out of my planning and realized he was totally not paying any attention to what I had said. I think I could ask him to punch someone and he would agree.

Well then.

I lifted head closer to his ear and with a wicked smile, asked him for something I knew he'd pay attention to. He pulled back with a challenging look.

"Naughty cloud," he said before giving me what I asked for.

~•~

I looked over to where Venom and Zaliver were talking or more like, where Zaliver was talking rapidly with an unamused look on his face while Venom looked on with a blank look. I saw Zaliver point a finger at Venom and then shake his head. Venom whispered something. Zaliver paused and then looked over at me with a blank look that made me worry. What was going on? Zaliver turned back at Venom and without another word, he nodded. I looked up at him with a questioning look on my face. He crossed his hands over his chest and stood next to me with a tensed stance.

"What?" I asked him, but he shook his head and nodded in Venom's direction who seemed to be rearranging mats on the floor. When he was done, he walked over to the weapons section and picked up something I couldn't see. I looked from the mat to Zaliver and then to Venom.

"Are you fighting, Venom?" Is that why he wanted Zaliver to come today? I didn't know how to feel about that since both looked like they could take on an army. Zaliver looked down at me with blank blue eyes and shook his head. My beast raised her head in malicious interested.

"Not me. You." My eyes widened at him with fear and panic.

"What? Nuh, uh. I've never been in a fight in my life. He'll pulverize me. He'll turn me into wolf-shabab, wolf nip. Hell, I bet you five buck one punch and I'll die or get paralyzed from waist down. Hope you like being on top for the rest of your life," I stated, dramatically watching as Venom neared.

"He will not hurt you. He's got better self-control than everyone I know—"

"Not hurt me?! What the fuck is in his hand? Is that a knife? Ah hell nah, fuck this. I'm out." I narrowed my eyes at the long dagger-looking knives. I turned to Zaliver with an incredulous look on my face.

379

"What the hell, man?!" I turned back to Venom who now stood near us.

Venom stuck out his hand and held the daggers out of me to take, which I did without hesitation. It would be better in my hands than him holding it. There were two of them with the same plain design and shape.

"I have a theory I like to test out, Luna Vivian. I don't know if you remembered yesterday I had—" Venom began, but I cut him off.

"If your theory involves proving how you can knock me on my ass in less than a nano second, then it's not needed."

I wasn't trying to keep my voice down and the warriors weren't even trying to pretend they weren't listening. A crowd had formed around us. Venom shook his head at me.

"Not at all, Luna. I will not even strike you—"

"And how do you fight without hitting?" I asked sarcastically, putting my hands on my hips.

"Control," he said.

Control my ass. I'd go down swinging. Maybe this wasn't such—

No. I'd get my ass handed to me and then everyone around would watch what a bad luna I was. I shook my head.

"Alpha has already consented to this," Venom mumbled.

I turned to glare at "Alpha."

"Oh really. Well, Alpha is sleeping on the couch tonight." His eyes narrowed the tiniest of bit at me.

"Please just trust us, Luna Vivian. There's a reason—" Venom was cut off as the crowd around us began growling with angered faces.

"This is unbelievable!"

"Not the luna!"

"It'll take her place, you slippery snake!"

"Can't believe he'd try to fight her—" The crowd was silenced with a loud snarl from Zaliver. They quieted down and bowed their heads in a submissive position, but some still had displeased and uncomfortable looks on their faces. That was really heart warming. They didn't know me and yet felt protective already.

"Vivian . . . " Zaliver's said in a strangled voice.

I turned to face him with a frown and was about to ask what the hell was his problem when I took a better look at his eyes. They were worried and wild-looking. He didn't want me to fight with Venom but . . . then why?

"Just trust us on this, please?" he asked softly. I looked into his eyes for a long moment before hesitantly nodding.

Venom and I walked over to the mats and took positions. I stood while his knees bent and spread. His upper torso turned towards

380

me with his hands raised with fists and then there was me with my awkward ass position. Legs were spread, knees were bent, hands were raised, and my daggers were held down because I felt that would be better.

I was sort of a mess, and I was gonna have my ass handed to me.

I glanced over to the crowd who all had different expressions ranging from worry to curiosity to excitement, then I looked at Zaliver. He looked grim and worried more than anything, but I didn't miss the look of encouragement in his eyes. That look made me want to make him proud and show that I wasn't going to go down without a fight.

"*Y'all ready?*" I asked my wolf and my beast who were alert and serious the minute my foot set on the mat.

"*Ready. We've got your back,*" they both said.

At that exact moment, I felt their combined strengths, agility, and senses go through me along with something stronger than anything I had ever felt before. Something without a name or word.

In an instant, my eyes flashed as a sense of power and dominance coursed through me. My legs shifted position, and my feet on the tips were giving me a better chance to move. My arms moved from in front of me, slightly lowered and spread. My back straightened and my head cocked to the side. The corner of my lips lifted.

Venom took notice of the change with his alert and watchful golden eyes. If possible the small black vertical line in his eyes narrowed. He nodded at me forward.

"Yeah, no thanks," I said sarcastically. My voice came out strong and sickeningly sweet. He nodded and in a flash our little dance began.

The air tensed for a split second that Venom's foot lifted off the ground. Everyone's breath stopped and in that moment, I felt truly and unwaveringly powerful. I entered a sort of calm mood that I put my mind in a sharp one goal set with my emotions cut off.

Venom was fast. I knew he wasn't trying to avoid real damage. Had I not been alert, he could have seriously hurt me.

He flashed over to me and instead of fearing the looming snake, I didn't move, waiting for him to arrive. The moment his hand shot out, my eyes travel over his physique in a way I had never heard of. He was taller than me by all standards. His knees were bent a lot. He had to reach down to push me, leaving his right side momentarily thrown off-balance but because of high differentiation, I knew I wouldn't get to him in time.

The instance I felt the air shift around my chest, I knew his hand was getting dangerously close. Using my speed, I twisted my top half to lean away from his outreached hand, knowing I had less than a

381

second to move myself from the position. I shifted my weight onto my back leg and wrapped my other one around his knee.

It threw us momentarily off-balance, but that wasn't what we cared for. Most of my weight was pushed onto the leg locked around Venom's knee, not allowing him to fully move. With both hands, he tried to grab onto my shoulders to hold me in place while his other knee aimed for my ribs. I pushed at his chest, making us both fall back.

While falling, his knee still raised itself to hit me, so I quickly loosened my hold on his leg, and as soon as I felt the jolts of his shoulder hitting the mat, I threw all of my weight sideways in a quick roll and looked back at Venom who was doing the same. We both stood up slowly. It was much harder for me to grab hold of him with both daggers, so my goals subconsciously changed much to mine and everyone's surprise. Venom was fast and quick in bouncing. If he managed to wrap his arms around me, I'd be done. I calculated my choices.

My smaller size would work to my advantage but not so much speed because we'd end up dodging each other like a cat and a mouse. That would be a bore. It was all about size and strength. I just had to get him good. Just once.

I looked over his frame, ignoring how his eyes stayed focus on my face. He was well-built and muscular. He didn't limp or stand unevenly. His weight was distributed equally. That meant I'd have to make him weak.

He lunged at me and without thinking, I waited until the last second to cart-wheel next to his lunging body. The exact moment he realized that, he began turning his head to look for me. I was on one hand upside down, one dagger lodging itself behind his knee.

I pulled it out and stood upright in a ready position. He bucked and started to go down, fighting his body's natural reaction to curl in on itself.

"Didn't know I could cartwheel. Nice," I said, genuinely surprised. Venom summer salted himself upright, looking down briefly at his knee and then back up at me.

The next time he came for me, I did it as well. I caught him off guard and punched him in the throat, cutting off his oxygen. I would give him credit though because he acted as if it didn't bother him. He was on defense. While I punched and jabbed, he blocked and tried to grab hold of me, which I quickly slipped out of. In one moment, he had taken hold of my ankle when I tried to kick him away. I didn't think he was expecting me to grin at him and spin kicked his ass with my other foot, making him release it. He flew back but quickly recovered and brought his hand up to his jaw. A click went through the field. I felt a brief moment of regret and worry, but as quickly as it came, a calming sense pushed it down. Venom was resistant as hell because he didn't back down or slow down after that, which was very much annoying for me.

Stay down. Releasing an annoyed growl, I sped towards Venom. When I had the chance, I kicked his hip, thinking this would make him stumble, but he let himself pushed instead so that he could quickly turn around to face me once more. But that was his mistake.

Never give your opponent your back. I had a clear shot and I took it.

I raised my hand and plunged the dagger into his back directly where his heart would be if he were facing forward.

He froze.

Without thinking, I plunge the other one in his lower back where the bottom of his spine was located.

He began to shake, standing up.

My calm and alert senses faded.

My eyes widened in horror at the two very large daggers that stuck from out of a shaking Venom's back. I began to panic.

"Oh my god! Oh my god. What did I do? What do I—"

I felt Zaliver's presence next to me and looked over at him with teary eyes. He put both hands on my face and cupped my cheeks, forcing me to look at him.

"It's all right, baby. Breath—" He tried to sooth me.

"No, it's not! Venom, are you okay? Of course not. Oh my god. We need a doctor! Zaliver call a doc—"

"It's really quite alright, Luna Vivian," Venom said, turning his shaking body around to face me with a small smile. No pain was reflected in his golden eyes but of course, I didn't see that in my state of panic and dread.

Please don't die!

"Shh, it's alright. You're in shock. I'm so sorry. I don't know what came over me—" Venom reached around his back, and while looking at me in the eyes, he pulled out both daggers out of his front and back and immediately stopped shaking.

"See, no blood. I don't bleed," Venom spoke quietly. He showed me the daggers that, true to his word, were clean.

"But I-I stabbed you . . . three times!" I shrieked. Zaliver's made soothing patterns on my back.

"I am not easy to harm which is why I am honored to have been the one to spar and prove my theory correct," Venom said, pulling his arms behind his back and standing up straight as if nothing. I was breathing rapidly. My mind had a whirl of thoughts, and my emotions were even worse.

383

"And what theory exactly was that?" I asked shakily. I stabbed him. I actually stabbed someone.

"That you, Luna, have killer instincts. Literally," Venom mumbled.

"I'm so proud of you, Vivian. You held your own against Venom," Zaliver said.

"Ha ha ha ha ha! Ahh . . . shit," I said. At that moment, I didn't know how his statement made me feel. Apparently, it made everyone else happy because they cheered and clapped. They were all screaming, but it was like my ears couldn't make out the sound. All of it were sounding like babble. I couldn't link them to their definitions.

I gave Venom a weak smile to which his brows furrowed in a look of worry. He was starting to blur around the edges. I blinked slowly.

"Hey Zaliver?" I asked.

"Yeah, baby?"

"Catch me."

Then, I fainted.

CHAPTER 31

I stared at the strong metal door before me in hesitation. I wasn't sure how this was going to go, but it was not like I could just give up.

I clenched my hands and took a breath before opening the heavily bolted door. Once I was immediately casted into darkness, the only light was coming from behind me. Even that was about to disappear. The sound of the door shutting echoed in the dark room and then my sensitive ears caught the sound of a shuffling.

Her scent lingered through the air. I breathed it in and felt the long but not forgotten feeling of our bond coursing through me. My head knew as well as my body who was near me, but unlike my head, my heart refused to believe the truth.

"Look who's back. My persistent annoyance of a mate," a female's bitter voice called out in the dark. With my eyes, I could see her outline. I could hear her steady heartbeat unlike my wild one. My fists clenched at her tone.

The room she was in was made out of cold cement walls. It had a bed, a chair, and a bathroom that was added for her benefit. Other than that, she had nothing else. Whatever she needed was brought in and then taken out to avoid giving her a chance to escape. The only light peeked from under the door crack. That was all I needed to see her but for her, even that wasn't enough. Her face showed boredom, which wasn't used to be. I didn't move or respond. I didn't how to. I just looked on to the face of someone I knew who had changed. What was I supposed to say?

"So, are you going to stand there like a muscle mute, or are you going to release me?" she asked. Again, I stayed silent, making her release a sigh.

"Muscle mute it is. You know, there's really no point in holding me here anymore. I already gave Zaliver his reading. The world doesn't revolve around him you know. Just let me go—"

"Do you need anything?" I asked, walking a few inches closer to her and feeling as if my body's molecules were trying to drag me even closer. My wolf whined at being close to his mate.

"Besides my freedom?" she snapped at me, shuffling around in her chair. She was good at hiding her uneasiness at being left in the dark and at having me nearby, but you could never fool a wolf's nose. She smelled restless.

Her long black hair was pulled back up. She wore a long gray dress with a thick black jacket thrown over. At least, she accepted some of the things I had sent over to her. The only thing she seemed to refuse was the food. Witches were picky eaters. At least, that hadn't changed. I used to find it adorable when she would complain about dinner and then the next day, she would comment on how well it was but would then mention how she would never eat it again. Now, it just worried me. She was becoming skin and bones before my eyes.

In the dark, she wouldn't be able to use her magic to try to escape. It wasn't that she couldn't do it, but more of the fact that she too would be afraid to try. Even now as a dark witch, her nature was light. Without it, she was in a state of mind and power dysfunction. She could perform magic. She just wouldn't know which one she would be tapping into. For a witch, that was a purgatory. Nothing was worse than not knowing what you did and what it would cost you.

"Aurora . . . " I sighed. I took a hesitant step in her direction, watching how she crossed her ankles. Her bindings were fairly loose, but it was the blindfold that I could tell she wanted off. It looked ragged and pulled on but still in place. I sent a thanks to Zaliver's weaponry of magic—the only place where they hold an enemy. She wasn't my enemy, but she wasn't mine either. Not in this state.

"Albericus . . . stop being a sentimental fool and release me. I no longer want you. Truth be told, I don't know why I ever did. We didn't work." She shook her head as if truly bewildered. My heart clenched at her words, but I knew I couldn't take it personally. It wasn't just because after everything that had happened that those were her true feelings. This wasn't her speaking. Not fully.

I lowered myself to my knees in front of her and firmly placed my hand on one of her knees, savoring the warm and electric current that sparked as our skin touched. It had been a long time since we had contact. She even froze before trying to shake it off. In the darkness of the room, I watched her closer as the internal struggle began.

"Aurora . . . I know you're still in there. I won't give up now or ever. I know you're still hurting over Andrew. So am I. But you and I know he wouldn't want you to let your magic take over. You have to let go and restore the balance in you. Come back and let the magic be," I whispered, looking up at her.

386

She pursed her lips and clenched her jaw before a dark smile graced her face. She leaned in close and tilted her head in the direction of where she thought I was.

"And what makes you so sure that I didn't already do that, and that the Aurora you fell in love with simply just died . . . Personally, I love this version of me way better." She snickered to herself on the last part while leaning back. I could only stare at her.

It was possible that she did that a long time ago, but the Aurora I knew and loved would never act this way, even at the loss of Andrew.

When I met Aurora, she was what people called a light witch. She barely practiced any magic and when she did, it was all herbs, plants, and small good spells. She rarely used her own gifts; something even she herself had admitted were not something to be taken lightly. When Andrew died, she lost it and turned to the only source so she could bring our son back—dark magic.

It was too late when I realized what she had begun, but once it was obvious that the black magic wouldn't bring him back, it all went to hell. I did not only lose my son, but my mate as well all in one instant. Instead of beginning a grief process for my son, I had to watch as black magic drain her life and consume her to the point of pushing her true self and coming out into someone she was not.

As soon as her eyes opened, I knew I lost her. She fled with a cruel smile. I looked for her for years and years without end, but I quickly realized that she didn't want to be found.

Dark magic took my mate hostage; black magic stared me right back in the face.

"That maybe true . . . but I don't believe it," I confessed, looking down at where my hand laid on her leg. She snorted at me and slouched in her chair. My thumb creased her skin for a moment. I looked back up to focused on her expression to watch any changes. She rolled her neck but didn't look down. She directed herself to where she thought I was. She wanted me to go away and never come back. Neither my wolf nor I had ever thought that we would finally find her after more than twenty years of searching.

She had to come out of this state even if I had to force her out of it. I took hold of the blindfold and pulled on it, being the only one granted with the right of removing it. Her dark eyes blinked for a moment and then narrowed in the dark. With my other hand, I reached up and took hold of her chin in a soft yet unbreakable hold, turning her head back to me. Her suspicious black eyes were on mine. My own eyes narrowed on her.

"Enough. I want my woman back, and I want her back now," I stated firmly, no longer having the patience of walking on eggshells and trying to coat my mate out of this situation. Now, I would take matters into my own hands. She smirked at me with malicious intent and lifted a brow as if mocking me.

"Give me my mate back," I demanded, watching her dark black eyes swirl with dangerous power. The air thickened and heated. I wasn't sure if it was her doing, or if it was just because of how close our bodies were. She leaned in once more and whispered hauntingly.

"I can't bring the dead back to life. You should know that by now," she said and I snapped.

Before she could pull back, I brought her face down to mine, taking her lips with my own which she resisted. I felt her hands push against my chest. Everywhere we touched felt heated. Tingles erupted on my body, wanting me to get closer to her. The long unused bond was igniting and rekindling, wanting something to bring it to life and pull it together. I stood up and took her with me. Her body tried to pull away, but that just made me kiss her rougher, forcing her lips to part with my own.

She was alive. She had to be. She was alive. My mate was alive. She had to be. I couldn't be alone. She was alive. She had to be.

My hands fisted behind her waist when I realized that the warm sparks of heat we shared when we kissed before weren't present in this kiss. I felt my body begin to shake as dread and fear entered my soul. My body felt like it was going numb with the realization that I might truly be alone and that the woman in my arms was like a lifeless, empty shell.

My eyes opened up to find angered black eyes glaring at me with hatred. I slowly pulled my lips off of her and looked back at her. She pulled her head back from me since my hold on her body was iron tight. I couldn't seem to remember how to move a numb body.

I was. . . alone.

"Get off of me, you dirty mutt," she snapped with anger.

Her words actually forced me to snap back. I took a step and my arms began unwinding themselves slowly. I looked into her eyes as I pulled away. I didn't bother trying to a hide my hurt expression.

And then there was hope. It was fast, but I noticed it.

Her black eyes stared at me with anger, but for a brief moment, her eyes flashed to a light hazel brown that was barely a shade lighter like a flicker of a candle. A familiar, heartwarming brown set of eyes. I realized I wasn't alone.

Before my arm dropped completely from her waist, her hand reached out and gripped my forearm with force. Her nails digged into my skin. Her expression became that of a woman in pain; a woman fighting something off.

For a moment, I was looking back into warm hazel eyes instead of a pool of darkness.

Her lips parted. My heart began pounding in my chest as I waited for what could be said. Those words could rebuild me or finish me off.

"B-berry, mark m . . . " she whispered in pain.

And suddenly she was gone. She snatched her hand back and stumbled away from me. She turned her back to a me as I listened to her heart pounding in her chest.

She wasn't gone. She wasn't gone. I wasn't alone and now, I knew it.

I watched as she turned around with black eyes.

"She's still in there," I stated.

She gave out a cold laugh and shrugged at me.

"So what? That doesn't change anything." She snickered at me. I took fast strides in her direction. At first, she did nothing, but as soon as my canines came out her face, she became horrified and panicked. She began backing up, trying to get away from me.

But I wouldn't let her. Not this time.

I held her shoulders and pushed her back against the wall roughly. I pinned her body with my own, limiting her movement as I took hold of her hair and pushed it to the side.

"No! Get off of me, you piece of shit! I'll burn you! I'll—" She let out a shriek of agony as my teeth sank into her skin, remarking her as mine.

The bond that had been dying and weakening over the years was suddenly back at full force, making me sink my teeth deeper into her flesh as if it was my way of making sure she knew she was mine.

When I pulled back, I watched with a pounding heart as her hand went up to her neck. Horrified, she looked at me before she slid down the wall. I took shaky steps back until I got to the door to make sure I had her attention.

"You're wrong." She looked up with dazed eyes. Her black eyes were fading and darkening back and forth. "This changes everything."

I opened the door and quickly stepped out, closing it behind me.

"Fuck," she muttered under her breath.

I walked out of the cell with a lighter heart and settled for a chance of bringing my mate back.

~•~

You are invited to the celebration in honor of my newly found mate.

You and the top class of your pack are expected to appear in the directions listed below in the next two days.

This is not a request: Be punctual. Those who do not show will suffer dire consequences if one of the reasons listed below is not the reason for the absence.

Only exceptions: Your death.

Consequences of not showing for the reason above: Your death.

Your pack's safety and security will be taken cared of. You are to pack for a two-day stay and no more than that. The alpha, luna, beta, and related children must come. The choice of who comes as well is yours. The mates of the fated pairs must attend as well.

The event's theme is a black and white masquerade ball; no other colors will be allowed in or out.

Sincerely, the one you wolves call,

Lupus Deus

"The amount of sass you put in this invitation has surpassed me. I'm impressed," I said to Zaliver, flipping over the black and golden card to put it back with the others. I looked up to catch him grinning. He crossed his arms over his broad chest and tilted his head up, still managing to look down at me.

"I'm glad I've impressed you. So, what was it about the clothing that—" I jumped up and down and ran across the room and took hold of his shoulders.

"I found the dress! It's so pretty. I'm not showing you though, so don't peek through the luggage!" I eyed him with seriousness as he gazed down at me with his blue eyes filled with amusement.

"Deal?" I asked. He uncrossed his hands and wrapped them around my waist, pulling me closer.

"Oh, I don't know. What will I get out of it if I do?" he asked mischievously. I narrowed my eyes on him and then gave my own mischievous smile.

"If you don't peek, I'll let you take it off of me when the night's done." His eyes widened and then darkened to a delicious blue.

"Deal," he answered quickly. No hesitation whatsoever. I smirked and then moved over to his laptop and opened a tab, leaning over his desk a bit. Zaliver stepped behind me to see what I was doing.

"Okay, you have two choices since you've already stated that you're wearing all black . . . again. I swear one day I'm going to get you in some color other than black . . . maybe midnight blue. That's pretty, right? Anyway, your handkerchief can be either one of these two colors. My dress color is between any of these," I explained, looking at the two

390

colors with glee. Just thinking about the ball excited me, but it was mainly the dressing up concept, not the talking to people who wanted to growl, snarl, snap, command, demand, and probably a whole lot of other stuff to Zaliver and I. When he didn't answer, I looked up at him in confusion.

"What?" I asked, thinking that maybe he didn't like the color. Tough nuts if he didn't. He was gonna wear one of the two even if I had to superglue it to his suit.

"I don't really mind. You chose," he said. He held my hips and pushed my back side against his front. I rolled my eyes. Nope. Mother nature was not feeling Zaliver's mood and neither was I.

I moved out of his arms after closing the tab and went around his desk, amused when he slouched in his chair with an expectant and desperate look on his face.

"One more day, just one more day," he muttered under his breath as if reminding himself of when my period was to leave. I chuckled, making him look up at me innocently. I shook my head at him.

"So, I already packed our things, sent the list of decorations and supplies for Jesse to set up, left the food for the turtles to eat—" Zaliver interrupted me with a raised brow.

"We don't have turtles," he stated, giving me a suspicious look.

I placed my hands on my hips.

"Not yet." He lifted his hands in surrender and opened a file, signing something. I sat down in front of him, crossing my feet. "So, what's with Algebra staying here while we're gone? Are you sure that's a good idea? Don't you need him if something goes wrong?" I asked, worried.

I wasn't sure how I felt with Zaliver leaving Algebra behind while we went to party with curious group of badass, bossy, and temperamental alphas, lunas, and betas. That just seemed to be asking for problems. I could already picture everything that could go wrong. Someone could try to hurt Zaliver. There could be an angry mob that even he couldn't control. There, the list was endless, and I didn't exactly like that.

Feeling my distress, Zaliver looked up, surprised and worried. He reached out for my hand, which I gave him. The contact immediately calmed me down. I gave him a small smile, but he didn't return it.

"Don't worry, baby. He has to stay to take care of things and make sure his mate doesn't try to escape. Even if I will need him, which I won't, someone is coming with us," he said, looking me in the eyes. I tilted my head.

"Who?" I asked, Zaliver gave a peculiar smile.

391

"Your personal bodyguard for moments like this," he said. I frowned at his words. Personal bodyguard, not guards.

"My normal guards aren't coming?"

He shook his head with his long black hair falling over his eyes.

"While they are the best for you here outside and in the presence of important figures, I will feel more comfortable with this guard with you for now," he explained, rubbing his thumb against my knuckles.

"I can take care of myself you know." I huffed. He smiled at me and kissed my palm. I felt tingles erupted on my skin like sunshine traveling up my arm.

"I'm very much aware of that. Do you want to know who your personal guard is?" he questioned me knowing I did.

"Venom," he said.

"Venom?" I asked actually taken by surprise.

"Yup."

"But I kicked his ass." I pointed out to him with confusion in my tone. Zaliver chuckled and shook his head.

"You're very good, my dear, but even you must have noticed that Venom was holding back. Yes?" He cocked his brow at me in question. I begrudgingly nodded at him.

"Venom, besides myself, is the only person I really trust with your safety outside of this island," he stated seriously. I stayed silent for a moment before asking.

"What about you?" I asked him with suspicion. "What about me?" he asked with furrowed brows, not comprehending what I meant.

"I know you can kick ass, but who's going to protect you from angry crowd. The rock-looking alphas?" I asked, slightly joking. Zaliver seemed to get a bit offended. His jaw ticked because he pulled me out of the office at that same moment. I trailed after him, bewildered and curious.

"Where are we going?" I asked as he took the car keys and marched out the front door with me behind him. The man was actually stomping around, and it was cute.

"To show you just how well your mate can kick ass," he declared, glaring at everything in front of him but still opening the door for me to get in. I smiled and kissed his cheek, making his glare lessen just a bit. Talk about wounding a man's ego.

"Well, let's see," I joked.

~•~

Zaliver drove all the way to the training field, grumbling and giving me the eye, but he'd reach over every once in a while to touch me in a way. Be it moving my hair, placing his hand on my leg, or taking hold of my hand.

It had been two days since I no longer had to come to the training field. After the whole Venom thing, I was released from all work out activities. It was odd because I hadn't shifted since the night I gained my beast, but Zaliver said that I now had a better tolerance for shifting. It hadn't bothered my wolf, so I didn't think much of it. Just to be sure, I knew I had to shift in the next few days.

Pulling into the field, Zaliver jumped out and opened my door, taking my hand. He walked up to the sparing warriors who glistened in the sun as if they had planned for this very moment and wanted to be caught as their very best.

Don't they ever take a break? I swear, they're here like every day.

"Everyone," Zaliver called out. His voice boomed through the field immediately, making everyone stop. "It seems our luna here is worried over our departure. I want to show her that everything will be alright. I need a group of volunteers. Anyone willing?" Zaliver asked, taking a step forward and meeting everyone's gaze.

Many hands went up; some were from the largest of the groups of both male and female. Zaliver nodded at all of them and beckoned them forward with a nod. The crowd parted and made a circle around us. Zaliver turned to face me. I narrowed my eyes at him. He wasn't really considering . . .

He reached back with one hand and removed his shirt from the back of his collar, pulling it over his head. Immediately, I felt possessiveness and anger towards him. The first emotion was obvious.

Zaliver handed me his shirt with a devious smile, feeling my emotions through the bond.

"Hold that for me, will you?" I took the shirt from his and held it tightly in my hands. He walked off, stretching his arms and back. I enjoyed watching his muscular back flex. I was sure others did too.

I watched him plant himself in the middle of the volunteers. In total, there could have been around fifteen wolves. I felt worried for Zaliver as well as the wolves. I mind linked Zaliver as they all got into position.

"You aren't seriously going to fight all of those wolves, right? You'll get tired before you even get through the ninth one. You could get hurt."

He looked over at me, his blue eyes piercing through mine. I think everyone knew we were mind linking, so they stayed very quiet.

393

"Calm down, Vivian. Before you get worked up over nothing, I can take care of you and myself. Trust me."

I stared into his eyes and didn't hesitate in answering.

"I do. I know I do. I just can't help it. Move your hair back so that you can see better."

Zaliver smiled and ran his fingers through his hair, pushing it back and out of the way.

"Yes dear."

"Don't sass me when I'm worried about you! Who are you going to fight first?"

I clenched his shirt tightly in my hands as it brought me a small amount of comfort. I scanned the crowd of volunteers. All of them were of different shapes and sizes. I eyed the big ones a little longer.

Zaliver bent his knees and brought his hands up in a ready position. Everyone else around him did the same. My eyes widened at the sight of him surrounded at all angles. He looked over at me before winking and then nodding his head.

The crowd went wild as they all lunged at my mate.

CHAPTER 32

I think there's always a moment in someone's life when they finally realized something had always been there, something painfully obvious like the fact that my mate was a god and a badass one.

They came at him from all angles—back, front, and sides. Three of the biggest guys lunged at Zaliver as if to tackle him to the ground. I watched my mate with attentive and worry-filled eyes. I was able to keep up with him after they all lunged, and it might have been because a part of me was a lycan.

Zaliver struck his palm out and hit the guy in front of him in the chest that sent him flying back. His bottom half didn't move at all. He moved that same hand to the side, took hold of the nearest arm to him, and pulled the body over his figure, crashing it with the attacking body beside his.

Zaliver was not on the defense.

"*Body slam, bitch! You can't see me!*" my wolf yelled out, jumping around in excitement.

"*Mhhh,*" my beast hummed, leaning forward, impressed already.

My eyes took in the show.

He spun around and blocked three punches thrown at him from three different people with his forearm, throwing his own fast and efficient power-filled punches. He dropped four fighters by striking three spots quickly for all. They dropped like dead weights and didn't get back up. The crowd gasped at the sight of four very large fighters dropping to the ground. The atmosphere was filled with excitement and anticipation as Zaliver looked at his next opponents. I gripped his black shirt not from fear anymore but from something completely different. Something was stirring in me while watching him in action.

Zaliver wasn't even winded or sweaty. He was surrounded by dressed guards, and being the only shirtless one, his muscular build stood out. It wasn't just that his black jeans were that perfect loose yet tight combination, showing off his long toned legs or the fact that his very build projected that dark and dangerous power. His blue eyes were alert and serious, not cocky or uncaring like other professional fighters would be. He was a serious fighter who didn't underestimate his opponent.

There were two female fighters to his left, seeming to plan a simultaneous attack. This intrigued me because Zaliver seemed to realize this as well. A man from behind went to kick Zaliver in the back to push him forward, but Zaliver surprised us all when he jumped up and flipped his body in the air, landing in a handstand.

I noticed his muscles tensed as they supported his weight and yet he looked unbothered. The leg that the man had been kicking out retreated. But by then, Zaliver spun on one hand and kicked his leg, sweeping the man's leg from under him and knocking him on his ass. Still spinning from his handstand position, Zaliver's other leg kicked out once more, getting the man in the face and knocking him out. Zaliver's other hand went down. He braced and then pushed, folding his body for a moment before kicking out and standing back on his feet.

He ducked a punch a millisecond right after both his feet touched the ground, then spiked on his heels. He confused us by putting himself between the two females. Without thinking, my eyes narrowed at the sight. Okay.

Besides the two females, there were still a good handful of fighters left for him to take, but it seemed like they were watching and taking in his moves, looking for weaknesses. Hell. Even I was looking for a weakness.

The short female in front of him must have been hesitating to strike. I couldn't really blame her because from where I was standing, I could really notice the height difference. The one behind Zaliver wasn't though. She went for a good old kick in the balls, but Zaliver wasn't having that.

At the same time, she kicked out behind him. The one in front sent a quick kick that would have gotten him directly in the stomach if he hadn't taken a step to the side.

A step to the side and pushed from behind.

Zaliver flashed out from between the two females and appeared behind the second one, pushing her forward a bit. They didn't notice. No one noticed, but I did.

So, I understood why they both kicked each other and stumbled back bewildered.

Everyone else looked at each other, confused. They then looked at Zaliver with admired suspicion. I let out a small laugh. The only way I knew he heard me above everyone else was the slight shift of his head and the quirk at the corner of his lips, holding back a smile. The two females moved back. This time, the remaining males followed. The pack members buzzed, wanting to know how this would end.

With newly determination, the remaining fighters slowly circled Zaliver, who slowly spun in a circle to keep his eyes on them all. I knew that if he wanted to, he could end it before they all knew what hit them, but he was giving them a chance.

Was. Apparently, not anymore.

I don't know exactly how Zaliver did it but in the next moment, he moved like a ninja fighting snails. The moment one of the warriors stepped forward as if to force him to take one back, Zaliver jumped up in a twist over the man, taking him by the neck and throwing him down backwards. As soon as he dropped to the ground beside the now unconscious man, he spun on his knees, and in a move that I could only relate to a tornado, he used his unbelievable speed to dashed through the wolves who couldn't keep up with his movement. I watched as he struck some on the knees, dropping them and knocking them out. Like rag dolls, he crashed others with the others hard enough to make them stay down and then finally just end it.

Because he moved so fast, all the crowd saw was their alpha disappear as the rest of the fighters dropped, flew, and stayed down. They saw him in the middle of all the guards in the same position that he began in.

It was completely silent for a moment before everyone began clapping and whistling. Without hesitation, he turned to me with an attentive look on his face after straightening up. While my face . . . Well, my face showed how impressed and very much proud I was.

He walked past everyone and stopped in front of me. He placed his hands on my waist. With hair all over his face, he looked down at me. I could still see a glimpse of his bright blue eyes.

"Well?" he asked huskily. I smiled up at him while strong emotions coursed through me. Some were mine and some were from the crowd and others from him.

"One more day," I reminded him.

"*You don't need to wait a day to get down and freaky with it. That's why God gave you hands and a mou*—" I tried shutting my wolf in my head as my face flushed.

His hands tightened on my waist. He leaned down closer to me and bit my bottom lip for a second before pulling away.

"Mmhmm, she's got a point you know," he said. I handed him his shirt and watched him put it on.

"Shut the hell up." I took in a breath to calm my heated face and then realized something.

"You're not even sweaty! What the heck?" I looked at him, astonished.

He shook his head with a secretive smile and turned the still pumped-up crowd. He held up his hand, which immediately silenced them.

"Thank you for your support. Now, get back to practice and attend to your unconscious partners. The next time we spar, I do expect at least one hit," he said with full authority. The wolves all nodded and seemingly went back to work with more energy than before.

Zaliver turned to face me. It took me a moment to recall why we were even there in the first place, my mind still filled with him fighting.

"I retract my earlier statement of you needing guards," I said. He smirked and took hold of my hand, leading me back to the car.

"Good. Now, I've got to get the preparations for tonight's flight and check up on things for the ball. Do you want to tag along, or do you want me to drop you off?" he asked, opening the car door for me.

"Can I tag along with you? You still haven't exactly told me what my job is. I'm pretty sure it doesn't consist of me doing nothing. Besides that, I'm not exactly sure how the ball is going to go down. This is the one thing I'm so not winging," I confessed, strapping in. He rolled his eyes but nodded.

Tagging along with Zaliver was both fun and boring. Fun because I got to tag along and put my thoughts on important things for the pack. Boring because he began talking about pack calculations, number of members, and put a side pack documents. It was already afternoon and we were on our way home when he brought my attention back to the car with an important question.

"Do you want to invite your parents to the ball?" he asked.

My head snapped over to look at him wide-eyed, surprise and horror coursed through me. Surprise because I had completely forgotten about them with everything that had been going on, and horror at the thought of them going.

"By the look on your face, I'll take that as a no," he muttered.

"Well, I mean yeah, no. Thanks for reminding me. I rather prefer them not to be in the presence of a room full of possessive, territorial, easily offended, and aggressive wolves." I shuddered at the thought of them. They would totally cower and flinch. They'd be uncomfortable all night with downcast eyes. They wouldn't exactly know why they were invited to such a party because they wouldn't know who my mate was . . . and who I was now.

"If you want them to go, I'll make sure everyone knows not to bother them. They will be fine." He started sending me a comforting look.

"Thanks, but I rather not chance it. Can we have them come on the next day after the ball. Everything should be calm enough by then."

"All right. What I meant to say was if you want, I can return their memory—"

"No. I know it's wrong, but I seriously do not want them to hate you because of that. I mean, we moved on. There's no need to start something again," I objected.

Although my parents probably deserved to know that they had once met Zaliver, it really just wasn't worth the drama and having to sit through awkward family dinners. What they didn't know wouldn't hurt them.

Zaliver's disapproving stare caught me off guard.

"What? You disagree? And here I thought you'll be the happiest out of the two of us," I said. He sighed and took hold of my hand, bringing it up to his lips. He kissed my knuckles and squeezed my hand.

"It doesn't matter if I disagree or agree with it. I just don't want you to regret this later and hope that by not returning their memory of how our first meeting went, the next one will be better. Let's not fool ourselves, love. My reputation isn't something any parent will welcome with open arms," he said as if trying to make a stubborn child understand something. I narrowed my eyes at him.

"I know. I heard. But I'm sure that if my parents get to meet you and you don't freak out at something they say and you don't do your whole Zaliver's-A-to-Z-plans-on-keeping-Vivian-to-himself, we should all be good.

"Zaliver's A to Z plans on keeping Vivian to himself," he repeated, amused. He looked at me with twinkling eyes. I rolled my own.

"Yes, your plans that usually end up with you not telling me what's going on or what makes you hysterical that usually ends with us fighting. So as long as you don't panic, we should all be fine." He huffed and shook his head.

"So as long as I don't panic, huh. Well, that should be easy," he answered.

"It should."

"Well then, I guess we have nothing to worry about."

"Yup."

"*Why you lyin'? Why you always lyin', stop f—*"

I interrupted my wolf. Zaliver pretended not to hear us argue in my head.

"*Stop. Just stop.*"

"Then stop lying. We all know something is going to go down. You don't just put alphas, lunas, betas, and their hormonal ass kids in a room with you and Zaliver. You just don't."

How I hated when she was right.

~•~

"Dude, don't worry. I got this bro." Algebra patted Zaliver on his back while my mate made a sour face at his beta. I laughed.

"I can never trust an island to someone who uses the words *dude* and *bro* in the same sentence. I can almost picture fire when we return," I joked. Zaliver cracked a smile that made Algebra scowl at me playfully.

"I hope you step on your dress and trip in front of everyone," he muttered under his breath. My breath hitched at that, my mouth falling open.

"Not cool! That's actually a girl's worst fear when wearing a long dress to a party. You better have not jinxed me!" I pointed a finger at him, and he gave me a mocking smile.

"Fine. Do you rather I say I hope you sit on something that stains your dress an ugly color and no one tells you?" My eyes narrowed on him.

"I hope you fall off a mountain and don't get found until we get back." He shook his head at me.

"I'm too irresistible to go unnoticed." His brow raised as if it had a mind of its own.

"I hope that one of the newly shifted wolves bites out of your groin." He flinched.

"Mean, but I'm not in charge of them."

"Then, I hope you forget to do something important that will make Zaliver kick your ass when we get back." I held in a giggle at his truly horrified expression.

"Damn. You're scary. You think that's a joke? He actually did that once." He subconsciously glanced at Zaliver who lifted a brow tauntingly at him, and took a step back. I made a face at him to which he just shrugged.

"Well, good luck on your trip. I don't hope any of that stuff to happen to you. That will be really messed up if they do," Algebra said. He gave me a quick hug and then moved away from me before Zaliver's hand made contact with his head.

"And don't worry Alpha, I shall run everything smoothly," he said to Zaliver. Zaliver nodded at him before they did the whole handshake back patting things guys do.

"I know you will, man." Zaliver's face went serious for the next part, which was a bit scary. "But if you fuck up, I will kick your ass again like I did last time." Zaliver took my hand and pulled me up the plane's stairs. I looked back at a slightly amused and yet frightened Algebra.

"I'll miss you too, buddy. No pressure or anything . . . no not at all," he muttered that last part under his breath, waved at me, and stalked off. We got onto the plane and waited while everything was checked and loaded.

"I can't believe you said that to him," I said, shaking my head at Zaliver while strapping myself to my seat. He shrugged and crossed his arms over his chest.

"I like to keep him on his toes every once in a while," he said.

"Well, I'm sure his feet aren't even touching the ground now. So, how long is the flight?" I asked, taking out my carry on bag and putting it on my lap.

"Five hours and then we're going to check in in one of the hotels that I own. It's an all-werewolves hotel so that should take the strain off of the guest. We'll be checking onto the top floor so that we aren't disturbed," he said nonchalantly as if he hadn't just told me we were checking into one of his hotels. This man.

"Is Jesse going to be there when we arrive?" I asked him.

Jesse was the person in charge of arranging the ball, following my instructions. Zaliver had introduced us over phone the day after telling me about the ball. At first, it was awkward but then as minutes turned to hours, we clicked.

"Yes, but she won't be able to stay for the actual ball. She's been working nonstop and from what I've heard and glimpsed in her mind, it's going great," he answered.

"Do you plan on sleeping on the plane or at the hotel?" Zaliver asked.

"Hotel. I've never been able to sleep on planes." He nodded. I began rummaging through my bag for something to distract me.

"So, about the dress—" My head snapped up and my eyes narrowed at him with warning.

"Stay away from my dress," I snarled out while he lifted his hands up in defense.

"I know. I've got no plans on messing up our deal. I just wanted to ask something."

I pursed my lips at him but nodded. Staring at me seriously and with a hard tone, he asked.

"So, just how much skin will you be showing?"

"Probably not as much as you're imagining," I stated. I could basically feel his possessiveness bringing up different dress styles to his mind.

"Good."

When the plane finally landed, I was ready to shower and go to bed. Before we got out of the plane, Zaliver had taken out a large sweater out of his travel back and put it over my head while I gave him a look. I was already wearing a sweater and this one was three sizes bigger.

"It's much colder than you think. Don't argue." He pulled up the hood over my head, tucking my hair in. It smelled like him. I liked it.

"Fine, but you might not get it back," I said, wrapping my arms around his waist. He smiled down at me and kissed my forehead.

"That's alright as long as I get to keep you forever," he murmured, nuzzling the side of his face against my own.

"Deal," I whispered.

Making our way out of the plane, Zaliver said our bags would be in the room by the time we got to the hotel, then I realized something.

"Where's Venom?" I asked.

Zaliver fished out car keys from his front pocket and unlocked the car. He had a longing and happy look on his face as he gazed at the car.

"Oh, he's here already. Don't worry. You'll see him before the ball."

"Oh, okay." I got into the car without another word, tiredness begging me to fall asleep but I really needed a shower and a bed.

After a long drive, Zaliver pulled up to this grand looking hotel that seemed more like a palace than anything. It was gothic but modern-looking. Zaliver went right past the front and went around the hotel and into a sort of underground parking. Getting out, he held my hand while I just followed, drowsy. I had all day tomorrow to explore before the ball the next day.

The inside was beautiful as the outside with luxurious decorations, making the rooms and halls stand out. I was not sure if it was completely coincidental or if Zaliver had made it so, but the halls were empty on our way in. We didn't enter through the front, but wherever we did was completely abandoned of all staff members. Maybe it was also because it was so late. We stepped into an elevator, and he punched in a complicated ass code.

"I'll give you the code in the morning," he promised softly. He was very much aware that I probably wouldn't have liked it if he spoke loudly at this late hour. With my hearing, he still sounded loud.

When the doors finally opened, they showed a grand and spacious room that screamed out royalty and riches. The rooms' theme showed just who owned this hotel with its black and silver walls and bed covering. I saw my bag and rushed over to it.

"Yay," I said. Grabbing my things and without another word, I went into what must have been god's personal bathroom and came out thirty minutes later, still sleepy but refreshed. Zaliver was seated on the bed with a lot of different papers in his hands. He looked up when I came out, smiling at me.

"Better?" he asked . I nodded and stretched. I climbed into the bed and hugged a pillow, blinking sleepily at him.

He stood up and went into the bathroom. I heard the water get turned back on. I must have dozed off for a moment because I felt him climb into the bed later on. His bare chest touched my face. I felt his arms wrapped around me to pull me closer to him. I let go of the pillow and wrapped my arms around him instead.

"Night." I whispered.

"Good night, my little cloud. Rest." He kissed my forehead and sighed content.

~•~

"No, no, no. If you think I'll let you put their table in the center or the front of the room, then you must be looking for a new job. Who the hell told you to place their table right there? Do you want them to be surrounded and then attacked? Do you not like my face the way it is? Because I know I do. Put their table up there." Jesse's voice could be heard loud and totally angry from where I was standing.

I had never met her in person, so I didn't know what she'd look like, but I could take a wild guess that she was the short black woman with the dark red mohawk. She stood in the center of the room, ordering staff members to rearrange the tables and chairs with a scowl on her face and glaring at somebody who was doing her orders.

I was standing by the door. I was actually just passing by the room when I heard her voice. I smiled and went to step into the room. I ignored the stares and worried glances from the staff, understanding yet not completely believing I had an aura similar to Zaliver's.

I wondered how I came across to people?

Sassy. Sarcastic. Rude. Nice. Indecisive. Anti-social. Hungry. Moody.

I thought we were listing me, not you.

Honey, I'm doing both.

"Oh my, could it be? Is it she? Well, I'll be damned. Hello, Luna," Jesse said playfully, turning around with a large smile on her face.

"Hey, Jesse. It's nice to finally meet you in person. This is looking," I looked around at the unfinished walls, plastic-covered
403

furniture, and opened cans of paint as well as the sticking out wire cables, "uhh . . ."

"Unfinished?" She suggested, amused, picking up a clipboard and pen.

"Yeah, pretty much," I said sheepishly.

She nodded at me. With an exasperated voice, she said, "I know. I was hoping to have it all done by tonight, but it seems like it won't be finished until early morning tomorrow and that's not counting the food and lighting. But don't worry. It will be finished by the time the ball starts. Now that you're here what do you think about . . . "

~•~

I spent the whole morning going over decorations, lighting, music, and food before I had to leave Jesse. To say it was a busy but fun morning would be putting it lightly. I made my way back up to the room where Zaliver said lunch would be waiting for us. Unsurprisingly, I found him there with the untouched food. He was slumping over a large pile of papers with an unpleasant and angry look on his face.

"You okay?" I asked, concerned, as I entered the room. I took a seat at the table and took a garlic stick from the table. He sighed and ran a hand down his face.

"No. It seems like tomorrow night, I will have to be doing a lot of firing and promotions. Some people are bloody fools. Do you know of Alpha Stone? From the Leanzar pack?" he grumbled. He moved to sit across from me and picked up his own bread stick, taking a bite out of it.

"I've heard of him, but I've never directly seen him. Why?" I asked.

Man, this garlic bread is good.

The Leanzar pack was known for its strict rules and procedures. Getting in and out of that pack was like going to school the whole day only to get picked up ten minutes before school was out, and getting told that if you left, you'd be marked absent all day. It fucked you over. Badly.

"It seems as if he's been overlooking forced mating in his pack. Instead of mating with their true other half, they decided to do it in the old fashion business trade. Males and females alike," he said, disgusted. I stopped chewing and blinked at him. My beast and my wolf growled in my head.

"They're mating for business?" I asked, feeling sick for a moment. He nodded at me.

"It seems like you do have a lot of firing to do. What about the mated wolves? What will happen to them?" I asked, feeling sad

404

about the people who had the chances of mating with their other half taken from them. It also made me feel hatred towards Alpha Stone. How dare he choose who belonged with who? Did he not care for his own mate?

"I'm not sure. I usually just take care of the root of the problem. I don't really know how to deal with the emotional aftermath if you haven't been able to tell," Zaliver said.

I looked down at the table for a moment. Something deep within me couldn't just let the pieces fall where they may. I wanted to do something about it. I knew I needed to do something about it.

"Since the mated pairs aren't true mates, won't the marks just fade after a while if a separating process begins? I mean, if their mates are still out there, then don't they deserve to find them and be with them? I think that all wolves that want to find their true mates should be able to separate from the ones forced upon them. Hopefully, no procreating happened while mating but if so, then I guess it depends on their own choices whether or not to stay together or raise the child in turn," I muttered mostly to myself. My voice grew more as I thought about it. Looking up, I found Zaliver looking at me with an impressed look on his face.

"You never fail to astonish me. You don't need me to tell you what your job as luna is, Vivian. You fill it just perfectly when you need to," he said with pride and joy in his voice.

I smiled at his compliment. It filled me with happiness to hear that coming from him, especially when I felt like this whole luna of all left me walking in unstable ground.

"If that is your wish, then I shall make it happen," he stated.

"Good."

While Zaliver was going over different pack reports and documents, I took the chance of going into the walk-in closet with our luggage and took out the dress. I wasn't worried about it getting wrinkled. It didn't matter to me if it did. It's not like it would show. A black bag covered the dress, so unless Zaliver unzipped it, he wouldn't be able to see it. I put the matching shoes above and the masks on top.

Zaliver's suit was hanging across from mine in his own black bag. It was still a little early, but I figured I might as well take out my straightener and hair curler even though I wasn't exactly sure how I'd do my hair yet. It had grown since I met Zaliver. It was now at mid chest length. Speaking of hair, I walked out and unceremoniously threw myself on top of Zaliver's back, making him the bed and the papers bounce for a moment. He didn't say anything, so I decided to poke him repetitively.

Poke cheek.

Poke cheek.

Poke forehead

Poke stomach.

Poke thigh.

Poke cheek.

Poke butt cheek.

"Okay!" he muttered lowly. He rolled over and placed himself on top of me with a blank look on his face but acceptance in his eyes. I laughed at him. He knew I wouldn't leave him alone.

"Yes, Ms. Pokey?" Reaching up, I took a long black strand of hair and twirled it in my fingers.

"You need a haircut." I started, remembering that time he told me he'd cut it if I asked him to.

"Really?"

"Yes. I want my man looking on point for tomorrow's ball," I said earnestly to him.

He leaned down and nuzzled his face in my neck, kissing the skin above his mark. I shivered.

"I like how you said that," he whispered into my ear.

"Me too." I wrapped my arms around his neck and brought his lips to my own.

"As long as he wouldn't shave it all off, a haircut would make a huge difference you know," my wolf grumbled.

Zaliver broke from the kiss with a loud laugh, rolling off of me. I narrowed my eyes at the ceiling as if to glare at her.

"What? It's true."

"And you couldn't have waited to input your thoughts later?" I asked her, crossing my arms over my chest.

"No, I had to do it while his attention was elsewhere. If you know what I—"

"I get it."

"Damn. Someone's moody. PMSing ass bitch."

"You—"

"You know, as amusing as hearing you two bicker back and forth is, I don't exactly like ignoring that fine piece of man looking at us like we are the light of his life."

At that moment, I looked over at Zaliver who had been looking at us just as she had said. His head was being supported by his other arm. His blue eyes were sparkling with warmth and tenderness.

"Yes?" I asked. He said nothing, but a secretive smile hinting at the edges of his lips.

"So just to go over tomorrow night event, correct me if I'm wrong," I started and he nodded at me. "We go state ourselves, greet, and meet everyone. Then later on at night, eat and mingle to which at some point, you'll sort out the alphas and I'll greet the lunas. Then, we dance the night away while trying to prevent fights, murders, and scandals from out breaking. Correct?" I asked.

He reached over and took a strand of my hair. Now, he was the one twirling at it. Shifting so that he was closer to me, he laid his head on my shoulder, which was funny since he had to shift his lower body for being so much taller and bigger than me. He shook his head in response to what I has said.

"And pray tell what I missed."

"You forgot the part where we show them just how truly badass and beautiful their Alpha and Luna are. Or how about if any of those dumb decision-making alpha kids look at you in any inappropriate way, I'll—" I cut him off, making a small growl leave his chest.

"Then, the same goes for you. If I see any female touch you, I'm stating it now that I won't be held responsible for my actions," I said jokingly.

I wouldn't be held responsible for my actions.

They would.

He smirked at me.

"Noted."

~•~

The next day was hectic from the moment I opened my eyes to the moment my feet touched the ground to get up. Zaliver and I parted in the morning. He went to check his arrangements, so he could get ready later while I spent the whole day getting ready. In the end, I decided to go to a spa and get my legs waxed, just my legs. I would have shaved like usual, but I swear it seemed it decided to grow overnight. It was annoying as hell.

I got my hair trimmed a bit to get rid of split ends, had my nails and toe nails painted, spent the majority of the time in the steam room to open my pores, and make my skin glow a bit before a cool shower.

Zaliver would check in every once in a while through our mate link. The poor guy sounded excited to see how I would look like.

I went into the bathroom and grabbed my lotion bottle and made sure to cover myself in a good amount. While the lotion dried a bit on my skin, I went over to the dress, shoes, and masks and set them all on the bed. I went back into the bathroom and blow dried my hair and then straightened it.

When I felt it was time, I slipped into the dress with a smile on my face at the fabulous design and then into the kick ass shoes. I went to the mirror and did my makeup. I did a bold and cat-like eyeliner with mascara, then grabbed the lipstick. It made an intense contrast against my skin, but I liked it.

I grabbed my brush and pulled back my hair in a low but tight ponytail using a bit of hairspray to hold the stubborn hairs down. I dug through my small bag.

"Where are you? Where . . . oh, gotcha." I pulled out what I was looking for and began reading the directions. After feeling like I had a good enough idea on how it worked, I began to work.

Fifteen minutes later, I was completely done and ready for the night. Excitement, worry, delight, and happiness ran through me for different reasons. I looked at my reflection and knew for once, I didn't have one bad thing to point out.

I stood in front of the mirror with a red laced long-sleeved dress that fitted me tightly from my bust down to mid waist. It slowly began gaining volume from under the silver ribbon that separated my waist from my hips in the dress. It wasn't just the red-flowered lace pattern that I liked on my sleeves or the equally impressive black stiletto heels or even the silkiness of the dress from the sweetheart neckline but the temporary mask tattooed on my bare face.

It evened out all the red in the dress. Around my eyes was a black temporary face tattoo with classy patterns coming together to make a mask. It made my brown eyes pop out and made my eyelashes seemed longer than they really were. Once I'd put on my other mask, it wouldn't be seen until I took it off, which I thought would be really cool. I decided to go with simple pearl earrings and three rings that I had thought would match along with a long gladiator sort of bracelet. I had a hollow flower patterned black choker necklace around my neck. My nails were painted the same cool silver shade as my ribbon made them look super pretty.

Instead of doing the normal red lipstick like it was sure most of the women were going to do, I decided to turn it around and instead of red, I painted my lips black. Instead of looking as odd as I thought I would, the mask made me look dramatic.

Over all, I looked like a kick ass luna and damn well felt like one too.

I walked over to the bed with steady feet and took hold of the two masks. Right in time, my hunk of a sexy mate walked in looking as fine as I felt.

He strolled in in confident strides with full power and dominance. His newly cut black hair was shorter from the sides and was neatly slicked back just a few inches from the front. His dark blue eyes darkened even more as he took me in my attire and I took him in.

His toned and muscular body was covered in a black custom-made Armani black suit. The first two buttons of his black shirt were closed. For some reason, it drove me mad, wanting them to be open as the shirts material stretched over his broad chest. In his suit pocket, his handkerchief had the same shade of my red dress, letting all know he was mine. Unlike the normal dress pants, Zaliver wore the ones that were tight around the ankles, which he pulled off wonderfully. A pair of black dress shoes rested at his feet.

Over all, if I looked badass, Zaliver looked sexy and ready for action.

He briefly stopped at the sight of me before rushing over and stopping in front of me with a heated look in his eyes. His lips parted as his tongue stroked out to lick his bottom lip. My heart pounded in my chest at the familiar feeling stirring in my core. And he didn't even know what I had on under the dress yet. He finally spoke, "Can I take the dress off now?" he asked huskily. His eyes trailing down and lingering at my chest.

I laughed a breathless laugh and shook my head at him.

"No, I just put it on. Later though," I promised. He looked up, dazed. His eyes trailed back down but to my lips this time. He lifted his index finger and very lightly traced my bottom lip.

He swallowed loudly.

"Yes. Later."

Something dropped in my stomach at the dark and promising tone in his voice that I wished for the night to end sooner.

"I'm a bit worried on meeting the alphas and lunas," I blurted out.

The heated look didn't leave his eyes, but he did frown a bit.

"Why is that?" he asked. I looked away to the side for a moment.

"Well, besides you and Algebra, I never had much contact with other alphas. Not even from my old pack. I grew up being told to look down and away from them, to not challenge them, but since I never had the chance, I never had to do that. With you, it was different because you're my mate but . . . they . . . "

"Are under your command, Vivian. Whether they like it or not, you are their luna. You do not look down or away. You do not have to hold your tongue or thoughts around them, they do. You will not have to excuse or pardon yourself for anything, you do not have to explain or justify yourself, they do. They do not have any power whatsoever over you nor I my love. Only one person does and she's standing in this room. Now tell me who that is," Zaliver said softly.

I looked into the vast blue of his eyes and answered.

"Me," I said firmly. He smiled sensually at me and held my chin softly, tipping my head back so that I'd look up at him more.

409

"That's right. You hold the power Vivian, and I want you to show them that tonight. Be the sarcastic, witty, beautiful, bold girl who I've fallen madly in love with. Can you do that for me, baby?" he asked, leaning in closer to whisper the words into my ear.

I nodded, feeling my legs shake but refusing to fall. His words gave me strength and belief in where I stood by his side. His equal. His luna.

Remembering the masks in my hand, I handed him his. He took it, and after reluctantly removing his eyes off of me, he looked at it and smirked at the masks.

"This is both ironic and amusing from your part, Vivian. I like them," he said, putting his mask on and wrapping one arm around my waist, which I did too.

We turned simultaneously at the same time to look into the mirror, together wearing silver lycan masks. Walking out of the room and closing it, Zaliver leaned down to my ear.

"The next time we walk back to that room, I plan on removing that dress and showing you just how sexy you look." He pulled back, showing his expressive wild expressive blue eyes.

"Looking forward to that," I said.

"Wait. Where's Venom?" I asked. I felt Zaliver tense for a moment before he relaxed and turned to face me, stopping completely.

"Can you keep an open mind?" he asked. I lifted a brow and then remembered he couldn't see so I spoke.

"It depends on how open you're talking about." He sighed and took my hand once more, pulling me down the hall and into a different direction—a balcony.

A tall familiar figure in all white with white hair stood still at the balcony. Hearing us coming, Venom turned to us. Venom will forever be the only seven-foot male with golden snake eyes and white slicked back hair that I know who could pull off wearing all white with a cute little golden bow.

"Luna, Alpha, you both look exceptionally good," he greeted.

"Thank you."

"As do you. Nice bow," I complimented and he bowed his head.

Zaliver turned to me with his back to Venom and put both hands on my shoulders, then looked at me in the eyes. Through our bond, I could feel a small amount of weariness coming off of him.

"All right, spit it out already," I demanded.

"How comfortable are you with snakes?" I gaped at him. That wasn't exactly what I thought would come out.

"What do you mean?" I asked, suspiciously eyeing the calm snake man behind him.

410

"When I said Venom would be your personal bodyguard, I wasn't just giving him a title. I actually meant it. Venom has particular . . . gifts," Zaliver said.

I looked over his shoulder and at Venom.

"You're not going to turn into a snake, are you? Because I cannot talk to anyone if there's a seven-foot snake following me throughout the whole night," I said, already picturing the screaming people running away from me every time I went to get food.

Yeah. Snakes were bad at conversations.

Venom smiled slightly and shook his head.

"That would truly be impertinent, if I may show you? Perhaps that would be better?" he asked. I nodded and Zaliver stepped to the side to let Venom closer.

I was surprised when Venom reached out his hand as if asking me to shake his. Hesitantly, I reached for it. I was confused when he disappeared as soon as our hands touched.

"What in the . . . ?" I said out loud, looking for Venom. Zaliver stood silently next to me, looking down in amusement.

"Where's Venom? Oh my god. It cannot be this hard to lose a seven foot white snake . . . What the heck is that?" I stopped mid rant and noticed the shiny white snake looking arm band around my upper arm.

"Is . . . is that—"

"Venom? Yes," Zaliver responded. I lifted up my arm, astonished. I just looked at the snake band.

"He . . . looks like jewelry. He's . . . wrapped around my arm . . . how?" I asked, bewildered by the odd phenomenon.

He was neither light nor heavy. Venom's tall figure was now a small white arm jewelry bracelet. He was cold and made up of some hard material. Out of curiousity, I poked him, expecting to hear an outraged cry but silence met my ears.

"Venom has many gifts, my dear. Too many to talk about right now. Maybe you can ask him yourself after tonight. I under—"

"It's actually kind cool," I said, distracted.

And it was better than having a real snake over me. Zaliver looked surprised but shrugged and took my arms again.

When we walked into the hall, I could hear and smell various scents around us. Zaliver opened the door and grinned at me. His eyes were mischievous.

"Want to have a little fun?" he asked. I nodded.

The whole room was large and open. There were also stairs leading to an indoor theater room. He quickly pulled me to our table at the balcony of the ballroom using our super speed. We were so fast that

411

we were unnoticed by the wolves who were mingling with each other. We looked down at the sight around us.

We were unseen and unnoticed but not unsensed.

Not only was Zaliver's presence felt but so was mine. I could tell by how some wolves began looking around nervously. Zaliver and I glanced at each other, having the same thought in our minds.

Let the party begins.

CHAPTER 33

I looked around the room, taking the opportunity now that I was yet to be seen to scan the room and people.

Jesse did wonders to the room. She had it painted with different mixture of black, white, silver, gold, and a little bit of blood-red. The outreached half wall was decorated with circular small mirrors. The see-through net curtains that hung from different parts of the room were colored in deep red, touching the ground and bunching up at the floor to show its long length.

The tables were all positioned half across the room with the dancefloor in between. Once you entered, you could see the table for desserts positioned towards the back of the room, sort of where Zaliver and I stood now. The dj was on the right side of the room in a small podium of his own, playing background music. I had actually given Jesse my playlist for a certain time for the night. I figured since it was a party dedicated in my greeting, I shouldn't have to suffer and listen to old classical music that needed to be remixed quickly.

The tables had black cloths on top that matched the chairs with golden and silver legs. In the middle of every table was a small decorative piece. I hated that in the other parties. They would always look awkward when talking to people, so I told Jesse to make it small. She was a genius because instead of a huge bouquet of extravagant yet odd-looking pieces, she went for a medium-sized wolf with every packs logo hanging over it on the moon, letting the alphas know their designated tables.

Hanging in the middle of the dance floor was a large crystal chandelier that looked medieval and of gothic architecture. There were small lights on the walls that were all turned down low, including the chandelier. The room was casted in a soft glow, giving the room a serious yet mysterious mood. While I loved it, I could see it made everyone else nervous. The mysterious and dark mood of the room gave them no hints as to how the night would go.

Zaliver and I were on the second floor of the ballroom where our table was set up. We were positioned in the outward part of the inward balcony, so we could see everyone even when we were seated.

I needed to remember to praise Jesse after this.

A squeeze to my hand brought my mind back to Zaliver, who had a crooked smile on his face. With his eyes, he motioned down below. Through the whispering crowd, black and white dresses, and mask covered faces. I noticed what had caught his attention.

Barely entering the door and deciding to be rebellious as hell, a young alpha pair walked in. The pair must have been around my age. Although they followed wearing black and white, they did not wear their masks but their scowls and snooty looks. The guy with wavy blond locks wore his suit unbuttoned and his shirt half-open as if to flash skin purposely.

The red-haired girl beside him must have had as much confidence as a Victoria's Secret model because although she wasn't tall and skinny, her body was curvy and she wasn't hiding that. Her black dress, if that's what she thought she had brought, covered only the essentials. Instead of her boobs almost sticking out, it was as if she wanted the world to see the bottom of her boobs by the design of it. There was a strip covering her nipples, and there was nothing more than that for her chest. Strings crossed over her stomach until they got to her waist where the bottom material just seemed to get more and more to see, not even ending close to her thighs. It was obvious what choice of undergarments she chose to wear.

I could see mates watched them with shock. The males turned their heads away quickly, looking at their mates who had annoyed looks. I myself just felt amused.

She looked like she was wearing a belt and her version of a scarf for a skirt. I mind linked Zaliver who just shook his head. I could see the amusement and annoyance in him.

"*I didn't think I'd have to state how much skin was too much. I honestly doubted that's his mate*," he responded.

His eyes left the young couple and scanned the room once more. I looked away as well, already sensing the trouble they would be giving tonight.

Some families huddled up together, whispering among themselves. From what I could tell through their displeased facial expressions, some alphas were speaking aggressively with other alphas and betas. The tension between certain alphas and lunas made an interesting night.

Not caring for their drama, I looked over to my right in the middle of the tables but slightly closer to the wall.

I felt my heart warm a bit at the sight of a certain pair of mates who huddled. While the guy was certainly older than the female with bronze brown hair who looked uncomfortable, he still heartened his skittish caramel-skinned looking mate who continued to look around the room. She had on a small cream and green colored mask that reminded me of leaves from different seasons. He turned slightly, giving me enough time to catch sight of his mask that was made up of various types of twigs and branches.

They were a good match. She was the leaves to his branches. Cute. They both had a sort of orange-green aura around them, matching each other.

I must have stared at them for a very long time because I felt Zaliver look over as well.

Slowly the guests began catching on and looking up. They had now realized who had been standing here the whole time.

Zaliver shook out his other hand from his pocket and checked the time on his wrist watch. At the same time that the dj cut the music and the last of the guest had entered, two large wolves with the same copper-colored masks closed the doors and stood in front of them. Their eyes flashed silver, making those near step back. They were Zaliver's wolves.

He turned towards me and unlocked our arms, skimming his hand down my arm until he took hold of my hand and kissed my knuckles. His blue eyes stood out with a devilish hint in them. Zaliver was about to be on his alpha of all alpha approach, and I was about to learn just what that meant.

He stepped forward, closer to the edge of the balcony. With each step that he took, I could feel darkness in him growing. His power surged, including mine, as he activated something animalistic and primal in him.

He placed both hands firmly on the railing, leaned on it for a moment and looked down at the crowd, scanning and making sure he held everyone's attention.

The alphas tensed and blinked at the direct eye contact.

The lunas shifted around and stared at their mates in surprise.

The betas and their mates looked away quickly.

A dark smile curled up at the corners of his lips before speaking through his dark, sensual, and dominant voice.

"Welcome to tonight's ball. My name is Zaliver Azrala, and I am your Alpha. Bow down."

Surprised and scared gasps left the crowd as their bodies bent to Zaliver's will. The alphas tried to fight it but were no match for his command. Angry growls and snarls came from everyone who tried to fight off his will. He lifted his hand and flicked his wrist as if to shoo something. They immediately stood back up with different mixtures of emotions. I could feel fear, anger, shock, curiosity, disdain, and hatred in the air.

415

I was surprised that not one alpha spoke out at his declaration. Perhaps, they held their tongue out of fear or they, themselves, knew that it was not a declaration but a solid fact. Some of the wolves near the doors tried to leave immediately. An alpha stood in front of them, holding his mate tightly.

"Move!" He boomed across the room. I could even feel his power from where I stood, but it was like walking on a windy day. You could feel it, but it would not stop you from walking..

The wolves bared their teeth at him and held still.

The surprised look on everyone around them made Zaliver chuckle, bringing the attention back to us. The alpha stepped away from the copper masked wolves with confusion.

"As I was saying, I am your alpha. But most of you have heard only stories of me under the nickname Lupus Deus. Does that ring any bells?" he asked sarcastically.

Whispers grew in the crowd. Through the masks, I could see eyes widening and hear hearts beat quicker as recognition flashed through them. Had they truly come here thinking the invitation was some sort of a joke? Even so, this joke must have had enough punch to it that they followed the rules. Zaliver carried on.

"Tonight's ball is in honor of my mate who I've been looking for quite a while." Zaliver glanced back at me. His eyes were softening as he held out his hand for me to take, which I did. "Your luna, Vivian. Clap."

Hands went into the air as people began to clap. Women and men looked down at their hands and then to us. I didn't cower away from the eyes of everyone. I looked over at Zaliver.

He was in full swing, enjoying showing them who was in charge.

He flicked his wrist again and looked at me with twinkling eyes. He wanted me to talk.

Taking some of the power he had and mustering up as much confidence, I joined him in his show. I felt my beast pull forward slightly. Her dominance was mixing in with my attitude. I turned my face back to the audience and spoke.

"It'll be a pleasure to speak to each and every one of you. I do hope you enjoy the night," I purred out softly but loud enough to hold everyone's attention.

"So do I. It seems there are some changes to be done in the werewolf community. Enjoy," he said hauntingly.

He pulled me back. We watched as their eyes tried to follow us but being able to see only so far because of the railing. The dj began playing music again though it did nothing to calm the tense atmosphere.

I turned to him and laughed.

"I knew you were secretly dramatic under all the hard expressions. I told him in my mind."

He clasped both hands on my waist and pulled me abruptly close to him. I gasped.

"Those aren't the only hard things," he said.

I shook my head at him but didn't pull back.

"So, shall we mingle?" I asked him, turning around in his arms to look down at the tensed guest. He placed his chin on top of my head and shook his head. I reached behind and swatted his butt. No. I don't trust them not to try and pull something. I smell at least three guns in the room, and I tensed.

"Don't worry. I'll keep you safe," he said, tightening his arms around me. We wouldn't die, and we're probably faster than a bullet.

"It's not me I'm worried about."

For some reason, my eyes went over to the skittish girl and her mate. There was just something about the pair that seemed to get my attention. I wanted to go talk to them later.

"Let everyone calm down first. Dinner will be served in a few minutes anyway."

I nodded and then just let him rock me back and forth. True to his word, a few minutes later everyone was forced to sit down at their tables as waiters in uniform and fully face covering theater masks came out to place plates on tables. Wow.

I thought as I watched them move as one. They were graceful and quick. Two waiters came up the stairs and placed two plates on our table along with a champagne bottle. While some families dug in without thought, others held back and looked up at us with distrust. I rolled my eyes and walked up to the edge.

You do not waste a meal in my presence. It just isn't about to happen.

"We aren't going to poison any of you if that's what you're thinking. There are much faster ways to kill someone you know. Besides, we're eating from the same meal. It will just be rude to murder a guest," I said, ending it with an exasperated sigh.

I saw a few bold females gave a reluctant smile and after shushing their mates, they started to dig in. I went back to the table but not before hearing a whiny voice say.

"I can't eat this. What are the carbs on this? Is that real pasta? Gross."

I rolled my eyes. I think I could take a wild guess and still be right about who said that.

Zaliver pulled out my chair and pushed it back in with a smile and then sat across from me. Tonight's dinner was some fancy ass pasta that tasted really good, but what I enjoyed the most was watching

417

Zaliver try to eat without hitting the mask. He glared at the fork for a second. I chuckled, which made his eyes snap over to me.

"You find your mate's struggle funny?" he asked darkly.

"Frankly, yes. Here." I held up my fork and fed him, watching his lips close around the fork. I pulled back and swallowed when he licked his bottom lip.

"My turn." He then did the same to me.

I chewed and took a sip of the cool champagne, his eyes not leaving mine as he did the same.

After eating, the waiters came back out and took our plates. Since dessert was served on the lower floor from us, I found that as the perfect excuse to go and mingle. So did Zaliver.

He held my arm and wrapped it around his own. Before we reached the stairs, he stopped and tapped Venom twice.

"Be on guard," he said.

I was surprised when Venom responded by sticking his tongue out like a real snake hissing. It was both frightening and cool. After that, he did nothing more.

When we got to the stairs, some of the wolves began to quiet down and stare. With one hand Zaliver supported me, I grabbed my dress to make sure I didn't fall with the other. I'd kick Algebra's ass if he jinxed me and I ended up falling.

Luckily for me, when we reached the bottom of the stairs, no accidents happened. Zaliver squeezed my hand and then walked off in the direction of the alpha males who were huddled up. He walked with confidence and power, and I did the same.

Approaching the snack table, I wanted to try the cute fruit and yogurt salad.

I tried not to let it bother me that some of the people slowly walked away from me until they were gone. I didn't need Zaliver to know that it had actually been my presence that scared them.

Since his alpha was present full front, my luna was as well.

I turned around and scanned the room for the skittish couple. When I found them towards the back of the room, I made eye contact with the girl and smiled as nice as possible. Even though she paled, I still began making my way to their table, knowing all eyes were watching and judging me. With a high head, I made my way to the back. I recognized my music playing now, Shades of Golden by Sea Oleana. The wolves parted and made way for me as I walked by, ignoring the looks they threw me. Some were nice, others were not. Some were a little too nice, others were beyond unfriendly. My heels made a loud clicking sound as I moved as the end of my dress floated around my feet.

When I reached the table, I noticed how tensed the male was. He was slowly shifting himself in case of an attack. His partner clung

418

onto him by the arm. Her large brown eyes were wide with fear with a hint of curiosity.

I stopped in front of the table. It was only the two of them there, and judging from the male's basic form and radiance, he was a beta. Where was the alpha?

"May I join you?" I asked softly. I made sure to look at them both while I spoke, letting them know the choice was theirs to take.

The male looked set on wanting to say no but held his answer. The girl glanced at him, to me, and around the room hesitantly. She even paled at the realization that people were looking and turning back, but she nodded slowly.

Making my movements slow and deliberate for them both to see, I took the chair in front of them and sat down, placing my cup in front of me.

"Hello, I'm Vivian. Who are you two?" I started.

I stretched my hand for the male to shake first. He looked at me with distrust, but to not shake my hand would be insulting to a pack structure. I opened my senses up and focused on him.

He was guarded up mentally and physically, but most of his concern and worry was for his mate besides him. I could sense his wolf could sense that my intentions were pure. Ahh, it was an internal struggle against his instincts.

He reluctantly shook my hand. I actually laughed when his eyes widened at my grip.

"I'm sorry. I've yet to get a grasp on how much I should use," I confessed. He pulled back, shocked and then quickly on guard.

"I am Beta Theo from the Crawn Pack. This is my mate, Melly." His voice was gruff but soft when he spoke of his mate.

I looked over to her and held out my hand. She took it faster than he did, but I was careful with my grip this time.

"It's a pleasure to meet the two of you. I'm sorry for the suddenness, but where is your alpha?" I asked. His eyes, although looking at me, did not show hatred.

"He is over there." He nodded in the direction of a very much overweight alpha who seemed to be on the better section of the room, where all the snobby-looking alphas were. I turned around.

"Ahh," I said.

It was Melly who then spoke with her soft, reluctant voice.

"Are you not to go speak with him? He is of importance, yes?" She looked regretful as soon as she spoke. I smiled at her, noticing her Spanish accent.

"Yes. He is of importance, but it's you two who I want to talk to. Would you mind if I keep you company?" I asked, taking my spoon and eat my snack.

419

They looked genuinely surprised, something about their reaction didn't sit well with me.

"No not at all, Luna," Theo said. His voice sounded at ease.

"You two are very adorable, you know that? You actually caught my attention. How long have you two been together?" I asked. Melly blushed under her mask while Theo looked at her and smiled fondly.

"Three years next month," he said. I awed and then chuckled at the next shade of red she turned.

"I'm sorry. I can be a bit blunt. What do you like to do?" I asked Melly. She coughed softly and turned her head back to look at me with an excited look in her eyes. She looked at her mate who gave her an encouraging look.

"I like creating arts and crafts. I actually . . . made the masks we're wearing," she answered humbly.

"I know. I thought they actually smelled like true leaves and sticks. That's amazing. You're very talented."

"Thank you." She sort of shuffled in embarrassment in her seat, trying to hide herself from my eyes. I just wanted to pinch her cheeks! She was so adorable.

I turned to look at Theo who now seemed to be totally relaxed with a hint of thankfulness in his eyes. By now, the music had slowly shifted to a more upbeat one. I could see some people nodding their heads to the beat.

"How about you, Theo? What do you like to do?" I asked, taking the chance to eat.

"I am not a man of many activities, Luna. I just like to keep Melly happy," he said. I could sense it was his wolf who was uncomfortable around me.

"So tell me, what is your pack like? I've never heard of the Crawn Pack before," I said. Not all packs kept contact with one another so when a new pack is created, it depends on how long it would last and the number of its members. If it became official, then a pack had been decided. They looked at each other before looking back at me. I felt unease and tension now roll off of them.

"Actually—" Theo began but was interrupted as a group of multiple people began to walk to the table.

It seemed as if people nearby had listened and wanted to talk to me personally.

"Hello I'm . . ."

I was slowly crowded, and seeing their uncomfortable faces, I turned to them with an apologetic smile.

"I'll talk to you guys later. Yes?" Theo gave me a brisk nod, but I felt as if he didn't believe I would come back.

420

I talked for a while with a good chunk of wolves from all ranks. Some were genuinely curious while others were snooping for information, which I quickly swerved. It seemed that after watching and listening to me, people were beginning to understand that I was like any other luna.

But not all thought that.

As I walked to the bathroom, I passed by the snooty table of older women with masks that didn't hide their displeasure and criticism. They were talking smack about me as I walked past them, not knowing that my senses were more sensitive than theirs. They seemed to forget that werewolves could hear from far away, especially if I was as close as I was now.

"Look at her wearing such a bright shade of red that reminds me of the color that whores wear."

"She looks no older than the age of twelve. What could she possibly know about being a luna?"

"She's just a little girl playing dress up."

I didn't even fully stop to respond to them. Those who heard them looked at me intensely, waiting to see how I would respond.

"Grandma number one, you must be color blind because this is crimson not whore red. Grandma number two, I'm eighteen about to be nineteen. I'm learning, and I've just realized that old age doesn't always mature people. It just makes them wrinkly and bitter. And grandma number three, I'm not a little girl playing dress up. I'm a grown woman enjoying a party. Now, sit your flat old asses down before yall break a hip."

I didn't even look back to see the horrified, humiliated, and angry looks on their faces as I passed by them carelessly. I did, however, hear the hooting laughter of those around them.

Man, I'm glad I'm not going to age. I walked around the red mirror wall and made my way down the hall.

Sensing that no one was in the bathroom, I entered and grabbed a paper towel to wipe the yogurt on my hands gone sticky. I washed my hands and looked up in the mirror.

Still on point.

I dried my hands and was walking out of the bathroom when I caught sight of the belt-scarf-dressed girl walk around the red wall and stop. Jeez, it was worse up close.

Since she didn't have a mask on—what a rebel—I could see her brown eyes outlined in black and the annoyed look on her face, ready for trouble to anyone she encountered.

Yay me.

She saw me and a devious expression crossed her face. I didn't like it. She suddenly began walking towards me as if to talk with her head held high. Can't see what she must have been proud of but okay.

This ought to get interesting. I met her halfway. She stopped in front of me, and because of her stripper heels, she leaned over me with a smirk.

Looks good on her, I thought sarcastically.

I could hear my wolf growling softly at her.

"Hello," I said politely.

"Yes, hello. Vivian, is it?" she asked mockingly as if finding something funny.

"This bitch must not want to live long," my wolf snapped. I shushed her.

"Yes, and you are?" I asked, clasping my hands behind my back.

She looked at her nails and took her sweet time answering me. When she finally answered, she turned her back to me with a smirk on her face.

"I am the real luna of all wolves. I know your secret," she said.

She couldn't see it, but my brow lifted at her. I smiled with amusement.

"Really? And what would that be?" I asked.

She leaned down towards me, close enough that the smell of her cheap perfume and way too much cosmetics made its way to my nose. I wrinkled my face.

"I know that you got my mate believing that you were his true mate. I knew I was made for Oliver as soon as I walked in. I could sense our power connecting," she said snarkily.

I felt a mixture of emotions at her exclamation but amusement won.

"You mean, Zaliver?" I asked, holding in a long and unladylike snort.

Heat flushed to her face as she realized her mistake, so she changed tactics to remove the attention.

"Do not laugh at me. You will respect me," she snarled out harshly.

My eyes narrowed at her tone while I could hear her heart speed up in her chest. She stood her ground.

"I'm not laughing at you *yet*. And if anyone's disrespecting you, it's yourself. Did you even realize what you grabbed when you put it on?" I pointed out.

She looked down at her dress and then at mine with clear envy showing in her eyes, but she beat it down.

422

"At least, I know what to wear to grab by mate's attention. Zaliver's eyes haven't left my body since I walked in." She smirked.

I felt fury enter my body at her accusation, and even though I knew she was lying, it still pissed me off to no end and to what she was implying.

"Probably because he's been deciding whether to kick you out for dressing like a skank, but since *my mate* is a gentleman, he's probably just decided to ignore you like the lying, attention seeking, little girl you're acting out to be. Now, walk away. Your attitude, attire, disrespect to me and to yourself are not wanted," I said calmly.

Her eyes grew larger and larger with every word I said. Her face turned redder than a tomato in seconds. I pursed my lips and took a step sideways to leave when she did the same. Her anger was not letting her say anything.

I narrowed my eyes once more at her. My patience for her was becoming thinner than ice.

I could feel Zaliver checking up on my emotional mood, but I blocked him out for a moment.

"Move. I do not wish to speak to you until you've changed your attitude and clothing," I warned. I knew I could have commanded her to move, but something in me wanted her to do it on her own will and realized how she looked and sounded.

The luna in me wanted to push her to the right direction even though she didn't seem to deserve it.

"No one talks to me like that—" she growled out.

"And gets away with it, right? Is that what you were going to say?" I said, annoyed. People seriously needed new phrases.

She got a new look in her eyes.

"I'm going to get my man. I'm going to kiss him, and he'll realize that I'm the one he wants—"

I didn't mean to bitch-slap her that hard, I didn't. Okay, *maybe* I did. But the bitch had it coming.

As soon as my mind made an image for her words, my hand flew up and I smacked her hard across the face not only did her head turn to the other direction forcefully but so did her body.

She flew up in a spectacular twirl and crashed through the glass wall, shattering the glass in the middle. All the guests stopped to look at her as she landed with a pleasingly painful thud. Everyone's eyes snapped over to look at me in shock while I just picked up my dress and walked through the gap her body made through the glass wall with a scowl on my face. Zaliver was at my side in a flash, earning another round of gasps. I ignored him and walked over to the girl's direction, the sound of my heels on the breaking glass rang loud and clear.

423

She was coughing and moaning as she tried to get up. When she heard me nearing her, she turned her head in my direction. Her hair fell away from her face, showing what my hand had done—a large and deep black imprint of the back of my hand like a tattoo. It looked beyond painful with her eye on that same side twitched and looked swollen. I wouldn't be surprised if she had internal bleeding.

"*Oh well. Tough luck for* her," my wolf said darkly

"*I doubt she'll be the same after she heals. If she heals,*" my beast added with dark malicious intent.

"I'm s-sorry! I'm . . . " she stuttered. She was half standing half crouching, cupping herself mid section. I smelled blood and noted gashes from the glass. It had cut her and her landing probably got her a few broken ribs.

The guy she came with showed up through the front of the crowd and took a step in her direction. I snarled at him. His head snapped over at me and his eyes widened. He didn't even look back a step towards her before raising his hands and disappearing in the crowd.

"You want to be a little bitch? Fine," I stated darkly, feeling the thickening air around me and getting electrified with power. My eyes had flashed silver a long time ago.

"N-no! I'm s-sor—" she tried again, looking fearful. I walked up to her face and interrupted her.

"Sit." She dropped to the ground and let out a cry of pain. Her legs came up to her body as her arms went to her sides. Looking down, I ordered again.

"Stay." Her eyes widened in fear as her back and head straightened up and then froze like that. Only her eyes moved frantically like an obedient little bitch.

I felt Zaliver walk up beside me and put his arm on my shoulder. My eyes flashed back, then I relaxed my shoulders.

"Clean this up," Zaliver barked at someone. There were scuttling noises behind us and the sound of fast sweeping of glass. Zaliver pulled me a few inches to the side to get the glass cleaned.

He looked towards the dj who continued to play the music from where it had left off. People looked and whispered while the girl whose name I never did get was frozen on the ground, unmoving and would remain that way until I said so. Zaliver turned me around to face him. I expected to see anger or disbelief at what I had just done, but all I saw in his eyes was concern for me.

He grabbed me and in an instant, we were back up in the second floor, away from curious ears and eyes.

"You alright?" he asked, running his hands up and down my back as he pulled me closer to him.

424

"I just bitch-slapped a girl, threw her through a glass, and made her sit like a dog, and you're asking me if I'm okay?" I pulled back to ask.

"Yes. Are you?" he repeated.

I rolled my eyes but nodded and then looked at him.

"Why aren't you . . . I don't know, asking why I did that," I spoke. His lips parted to speak but then he closed them and instead reached up with his hand and tugged on my ear softly.

"You heard?" He nodded.

"You were polite when she wasn't. You gave her warnings when she didn't deserve any and then she crossed the line. She's lucky you're the one who punished her and not me," he grumbled out.

I sighed and then decided to take off my mask. Zaliver watched with intrigued eyes as I removed it. I sighed and wrapped my arms around his waist again, liking how firm he felt. He reached, touched my lips, and traced it with the tip of his finger.

"Pretty," he said and I smiled.

When the commotion had died down, couples were dancing to some of the slower songs, looking like they were having fun. I did feel a bit bad when I saw some of them dance around the belt-scarf-dressed girl who looked utterly humiliated, but even now, I could still sense her holding into some deeply rooted anger, so I just let her be for now.

"How did talking to some of the alphas go?" I asked.

He sighed and shook his head.

"I didn't realize how corrupt and truly bothersome those old traditional alphas were. In the span of two hours, I had to remind them that not all alphas die of old age," he said darkly.

"Have you talked to Alpha Stone yet?" He shook his head.

"I sense him here and I assume he knows I've got to talk to him because he's been avoiding me. I've seen him though. I plan to talk to a whole bunch of fools tonight," he answered with his eyes getting a far away look. He walked me to the table, and we began talking for a while.

At some point, Zaliver removed his own mask. I took the chance to peck at his cheek while he was talking. When a new song began, I was surprised when Zaliver suddenly stood up. Since I was sitting on his lap, I was jolted up as well.

"I just realized we've never danced together. How silly of me not to ask you earlier. Will you dance with me?" he asked, already pulling me along with him. I giggled at his panicked tone.

"I would be honored," I said, holding the hand he offered me.

Zaliver flashed us to the middle of the dance floor. Some couples jumped and danced into each other as we appeared. I ignored the gawking and surprised gasps from females as they took in Zaliver's

425

face without the mask. Salvatore by Lana Del Rey began to play in the background. Zaliver gripped my waist and brought me closer to his front. I wrapped my arms around his neck and let him take the lead as he moved us gracefully around the room.

I looked at him and just let myself get lost in his deep blue eyes, his electric blue eyes. He looked down at me with tenderness and love, making my insides tightened. Not only did it say love but it promised darker, pleasurable things. He leaned down and whispered into my ear huskily.

"I love you." I shivered from the declaration of affection.

"I love you too," I whispered breathlessly.

He smirked at the knowledge of the effect that he had on me and suddenly in one smooth move, he twirled me in his arms. He stopped me with my back to his front and pushed himself against me. I could feel his hardened manhood against the back of my dress. I gasped.

His arms came over me. He held me to him by putting his full palm on the lower part of my stomach, which was a little too close to where I really wanted it. He swayed us to the sound of the music, somehow making the music his own seductive piece. He didn't hold back either, instead, he dipped his head and planted a kiss right on his mark, making me push back against him and close my eyes.

I had to repeatedly tell myself that there were people in the room who I could feel staring at us.

"Behave," I whispered, knowing he'd hear me perfectly clear.

I felt his chest shake with laughter as he twirled me back around in his arms. His eyes reflected his inner thought as we continued to dance.

"But why? Being naughty is much more fun. Don't you think?" He dipped his head and took hold of my bottom lip between his own and softly bit it before releasing it. I looked up at him with heated eyes. The man was torturing me and he knew it.

"I do, but we've got ears on us," I reminded.

He shook his head.

"One of my talents is the ability to control what senses they can and cannot use in my presence, and I've chosen hearing," he explained, looking around his shoulder. I noted the confused looks on some wolves faces. He leaned down.

"Which is why I can say that I can't wait to get you back into our room and fuck you nice and hard without them hearing. Isn't that great?" he whispered.

I gulped. My legs shook. My insides quivered.

"Very," I choked out.

"I thought so too." He kissed my forehead.

426

"Then, I guess you can say that I am not wearing a bra under this dress and that I'm wearing stockings," I purred at him.

He suddenly twirled me, catching me by surprise and loomed over me with wild animalistic eyes.

"Did I say nice and hard? I meant to say long, hot, and hard. I'm going to have fun watching you scream for me, my love," he purred back.

He captured my mouth in a hot punishing kiss that expressed his longing and desire. He forced his tongue into mine that my legs almost gave out as he began thrusting it into my mouth. He pulled away far too quickly. He pulled me back up and twirled me all at the same time. We continued to dance. I was struggling the whole time not to let my legs give up. Zaliver refused to let me go, so we just continued to dance to What Kind of Man by Florence and The Machine.

We were all calm when an alpha came onto the dance floor with confidence. His were eyes on me. All ready, I felt Zaliver tensed around me. The rock built alpha came up to us and nodded at Zaliver quickly with dismissal.

"*Oh shit,*" my wolf said.

I glanced at Zaliver who stood as still as ice. I calculated how I could hold my mate back if a fight broke out. I couldn't.

"Dance with me, will you?" the alpha asked or more so demanded.

"No, thank you." I turned him down. His face went red under the purple mask with fury.

His hand reached out as if to grab me. I blinked, and when I opened my eyes again, there was a wall of white in front of me.

Venom.

I glanced at my arm and saw that the snake band was gone. Zaliver stood beside me with a cool look over his face.

"Who the hell are you?" the alpha yelled out. I looked around Venom to see the alpha about to take a step back and then seemed to remember he was the alpha.

The whole room froze as they took in the sight of the seven-foot, golden eyed and white-haired male in front of me.

"She said no. Now, hand over your weapon." If Venom's voice made me shiver before and that was just his whispers, then I must have died now.

His voice was still soft but loud enough to be heard over the music. The hiss mixed with the coldness that seemed to seep from his voice was like listening to your killer explain how he was going to burn your flesh off of you alive. Scary.

The alpha, regardless, took a step back and turned white but managed to keep the fury in his voice. I noted how it seemed hard for

427

him to even glance at Venom's face. I wondered what expression he had.

"How dare you speak to an alpha like that you"—he paused for a second as a question rang in his mind—"What the hell are you?" The alpha tried to appear dominant over Venom.

"I guess no one told him you can't intimidate people ten inches taller than you," My wolf tsked.

"I will not repeat myself after this. Hand over your weapon or I will be forced to remove it myself," Venom hissed out, threatening. With each word he spoke, he took a step forward, forcing the alpha to stumble back.

"Fine! You want it, here it is. That's right I've got a gun. Now, what are you going to do about that? Nothing! Now step aside. I want a piece of that ass on the dance floor." My mouth fell open at his crude words while Zaliver let out a low growl but did not move.

The alpha looked around Venom and winked at me with a pistol in his hand. I was surprised when two other large men stood up and neared the alpha, pulling out guns.

Something tells me they're from the same pack.

"I think it's the masks." My wolf butted in.

I wasn't exactly scared. I mean I and Zaliver couldn't die. I'm pretty sure if we if we did get shot, we'd heal quickly but not with the people around us.

"Hand them over," Venom said, unaffected.

I heard a clicking noise and saw the alpha point a gun at Venom's direction.

"Shut up, you little freak. You're all freaks, and when I'm done with you, everyone will be thankful. Alpha of the alphas, my ass." He snorted and a second later, pulled the trigger.

I had thought Venom would dodge, move, or at least stop the bullet. He didn't.

He took it like a man—in the chest.

I gasped along with everyone in the room who screamed and was getting ready to catch him when I realized he was standing perfectly upright. Zaliver held my arm to stop me from moving anywhere.

The alpha looked at Venom, to his chest, and paled. The men at his side glanced at each other nervously. They were no longer confident like their alpha. Venom moved, and with one of his hands, he dug the bullet out of his chest without blinking at the alpha. He held up the bullet between his middle and pointer finger.

"Shall I give the bullet back, Alpha Zaliver?" Venom asked without turning around.

428

"Yes, it would be quite rude not to return to him his belonging," Zaliver said coldly. His hand was tightening briefly on my arm.

"And the other two, sir?" Venom asked.

"I need just one," Zaliver's answered.

"Understood."

The alpha dropped the gun and began backing up. He panicked while sweat trickled down his face.

"If there are children in the room, I recommend you cover their eyes," Venom hissed out to no one in particular.

Before he could take another step back, Venom's wrist flickered at the direction of the alpha who later dropped to the ground with a bullet between his panicked eyes.

"*And that's when they knew, they fucked up,*" my wolf whispered.

My stomach churned at the sight, so I looked away.

All I saw was a white blur as Venom disappeared in front of me and two other bodies joined the floor and then gone. Venom stood back in front of me with his head bowed.

"Good job, Venom." Zaliver said.

"Alpha," he responded.

Venom turned to me and held out his hand.

I hesitated for a second but gave him my hand, then the familiar pressure was felt on my arm.

I took a shaky breath and looked around the room. To say I wasn't the only wondering what the hell just happened was belittling it.

"Resume as if nothing happened," Zaliver's voice boomed through the room.

Like that could happen.

Zaliver pulled me by the arm up the stairs since I was lost in my thoughts when a familiar scent hit me. Familiar because I had grown up wearing that same scent to recognize where I was from. It was my old alpha from the Delfuo pack.

I stopped and pulled my hand out of Zaliver's and walked over to them. At first, Alpha Daniel shifted nervously as I neared, and when he could no longer look away, he blinked and shock covered his face.

"Vivian? Vivian Grey?" he asked, shocked. His mate, Luna Holly gasped. I was honestly surprised he even knew my name since I had never spoken or actually even seen the guy face to face until now.

"Yes, Hello Alpha Daniel, Luna Holly. How are you?" I asked casually while they gaped.

Awkward. I had thought that meeting my old alphas would be . . . odd. I mean it was, but I thought I would still feel under them. Now, I don't really feel anything.

"B-but how? When? You were . . . wha . . . " Alpha Daniel said. I shrugged in response.

"It's a long story. How are my parents?" I asked.

"I can sense that they are all right, but then again, I'm guessing you can as well." Luna Holly answered softly and I smiled back.

"Do they know—" I cut off Alpha Daniels sentence, paying no mind to the tightness around his eyes.

"No, and I will appreciate it tremendously if you won't say anything to them yet." I hinted and he nodded.

After a few minutes of talking with them, I wandered off, sensing Zaliver's eyes on me every once in a while until he seemed to think I was okay on my own.

I ended up chatting with some really funny lunas who explained what they did around the pack and how they helped out, which helped me in the end. Every once in a while, I would talk with an alpha or beta and their kids since I was closer to their kids' age and conversations went by a lot faster.

I even got their phone numbers. I don't think Zaliver would understand when I tell him they were just for friendship.

I was near the snack table when I caught sight of Melly with Theo beside her. He was filling her plate.

"The fruit yogurt salad is good, but I haven't tried those yet. Are they any good?" I asked, standing next to Melly who gripped her plate tightly and began to shake.

She was easily scared, huh. Theo looked up and swallowed harshly. He pulled her a bit closer to him while I lifted a brow at him.

One step forward, thirty-six steps back. I could guess why.

"*You don't say?*" my wolf said sarcastically.

I opened my mouth to say something when my eyes caught the sight of four very large purple marks on Melly's side, almost by her shoulder. They were finger marks. She shifted enough for me to catch them as the dress opened a bit. She was so thin.

It couldn't possibly be Theo. I knew that from instinct. I looked at Theo with fury but realized he had the same mark too.

Peeking out from his throat, I saw his shirt collar was not long enough to hide the changing of his skin tone that seemed to be in the state of healing.

My mouth opened up in horror at the sight of them. Theo's eyes became confused at the expression on my face.

The bruises were on both of the beta couple. A beta couple. Melly was skittish and easily scared. Theo was more protective than any other mate I'd seen here. I could say that his hobby was making her happy. He only relaxed around me when I had shown kindness to her. I noticed their uneasiness at the mention of their pack, and they weren't seated with their alpha—the only one in the pack who could land a blow on his beta.

My expression became livid, and my anger was like nothing I had been before. My blood began to boil in my veins as I looked at the couple before me. Theo stood in front of Melly who had dropped her plate.

Not wanting to scare them, I turned around and looked for Zaliver. I found him talking with a group of people. Everyone else paled when they saw me. I wouldn't judge if I would be known as the Lupus Deus' short-tempered mate.

Zaliver turned around to face me, and before he could ask anything, I spoke.

"You said you can promote or take ranks. How do you do it without killing anyone?" I asked. I'd appreciate him later for not hesitating to answer.

"Put your hand on their heart, and you'll know what to do. Then, place your hand on the heart you want to promote and let go," he answered.

I nodded and began to walk away, ignoring him calling my name. I thought he would try to stop me and ask what was going on, but he just looked at me for a moment and said, "Be careful."

He trusted me. The thought calmed me a little; it was not much but was enough.

I walked over to the table where the worthless beating alpha was seated, chatting with an older woman. When he saw me and tried giving me a charming smile, I didn't respond and kept my face blank.

"Are you the alpha of the Crawn pack?" I asked.

"Why, yes I am. What can I help you with, sugar?"

The old perverted wolf must have actually thought that I was going to sit on his lap when I walked around the table, but to his surprise, I did just as Zaliver said and placed my hand on his heart.

Immediately, I felt his heart pound in his chest as if trying to leave him and get into my hand. His eyes widened while power surged through me as if I was pulling something out of him. His body shook and his face began to change to purple as I collected the power from his bloodline. When I felt like he would get a heart attack, I removed my hand to which he sank down in his chair and began weeping, realizing what I just did.

I walked back to Theo and Melly who were cleaning up the food they had dropped.

When Theo saw me, he stood in front of Melly but was surprised when instead of going for her, I went for him instead.

Placing my hand on his chest, I relaxed the hot energy that my hand was holding. He began to shake and groan and fell from my grasp. Melly was horrified and crouched over him, calling his name.

His body suddenly stopped shaking and I felt drained. His eyes opened and he grinned up at Melly who looked at him, surprised. He stood up slowly with her help, looked down at his hands and then up at me.

"Congrats, Alpha Theo, Luna Melly," I said, smiling.

I walked away from the shell-shocked couple and made my way up to our table, needing to sit down for a bit. Before I reached the stairs, I remembered the girl on the floor and went over to her. She had particularly healed everywhere but where I hit her. I tapped her on the shoulder twice and watched her groan and stretch. I leaned down to her level.

"Now listen, loud and clear. If you don't change your attitude and way of living, you're going to bump into people who aren't going be as nice as I am. You can stay bitchy forever and end up alone, or you can find a way to deal with all that resentment and loneliness you've got in there and get true friends. Your choice, but I'll go for the second one." I didn't give her a chance to respond as I made my way upstairs. I found Zaliver already there with a proud look on his eyes.

"What do you say we end the party?" he asked.

He stepped up to the edge and grasped the bars. He waited to have everyone's attention.

"The party is over. Go home. I expect all alphas to be present in tomorrow's meeting. I will find you if you do not show up, and you will not like my reaction when I get my hands on you. Good night," Zaliver said. As soon as he said that, the wolves who stood at the entrance stepped aside and unlocked the doors.

He held my hand and pulled me along with him. Once out in the hallway, he stopped and tapped on the snake band twice, and when I blinked, Venom stood next to me.

"Thank you for your help, Venom. I'll speak to you tomorrow. Good night," Zaliver said hurriedly.

"Night, Venom," I said, waving to him. He waved back.

I was surprised and curious as to why Zaliver was in such a rush until he opened the room and shoved me in, slamming the door loudly.

I turned around to yell at him when I made eye contact with two black eyes.

"Now, what shall I do with you first?" he purred.

432

CHAPTER 34

He gazed at me with hunger and dark carnal promises while his black eyes seemed to glow with raw and bold statements. In the silent and dark room, his question made my body burn with eager anticipation. My tongue stuck out to lick my bottom lip. His eyes didn't miss that as his head tilted to the side. Slowly, I watched as the corners of his lips curled up to give me a wicked smirk.

He chuckled and took slow, deliberate steps in my direction. My eyes followed his every movement as he took of his blazer and threw it on the floor. I watched as his fingers slowly unbuttoned the first three on his suit.

Zaliver stopped in front of me for a brief moment. He loomed over me, and instead of looking up to meet his gaze, I looked at the fourth button and the smooth skin that he revealed to me. I could feel his presence in the room more than I could feel my own; it was consuming. He took slow steps around me and placed the lightest of touches on my bare forearm with his index finger. He trailed up slowly from my arm to my shoulder while his finger was leaving a path that was the only thing my body knew how to follow and yet made me shiver from the want for more.

He stood behind me, very close behind me. I could feel him purposely pressed up against my back side. His finger moved from my shoulder to my back and then to my other shoulder. I could tell it was his other finger because after trailing down my arm, he wrapped his arm around my waist and brought me closer to him. My mouth parted as my body came forward. He spoke close to my ear, and the hand that wasn't holding me reached back and slowly pulled on the ribbon.

"I'm so lucky to have you. You've made me very, very happy tonight. I think it's time to return the favor and claim my mate. Don't you think?" he purred into my ear, placing a kiss on my neck.

My sensitive ears caught the sound of the silky fabric of the ribbon being undone. Somehow, that just turned me on even more. Dropping our masks, my hands reached behind me to grab hold of him not only did I feel the way my body was reacting to my own desire but

433

to his as well. I felt like even breathing became a struggle. My body felt sensitive around him.

"So, which will you do first?" I asked with my voice coming out breathless.

He gave out a low and dark chuckle while his hand suddenly pushed firmly against the lower part of my stomach. He began sliding it down to the bottom half of my body and cupped me through the dress.

"Both. Always both with you," he murmured.

My body didn't know whether to push against his hand or back against his body. He began trailing kisses around my neck and shoulders, but I spun around. Taking hold of his face in between both of my hands, his black eyes blinked down at me and reopened into a midnight blue. I loved that color.

I smiled up at him and loved how his breath hitched for a moment. Not waiting any longer, he leaned down and brought our lips together in a passionate kiss, and I returned the feeling. He reached down and hooked both of his hands under my thighs, picking me up effortlessly. Taking advantage of this, I wrapped my legs around his hips and my arms around him. I broke the kiss with a gasp as my back felt the coldness of a wall all of a sudden. Zaliver didn't break off from kissing me. He just trailed down to my jaw and neck, taking special care to scrape his teeth on his mark.

With his bottom half, he pushed and maintained my body against the wall. He let go for a moment and reached under me for his pants. I heard the sound of his belt and zipper being undone.

Zaliver went to find the zipper of the dress in my back, but I guess his mind must have been clouded because he gave a growl before reaching for the front of the dress, and with brutal strength, he tore the front into two. I gave out a surprised yell that halted him. He pulled away from kissing my neck to look at me with worry.

"Are you—"

"I like this dress!" I exclaimed, a bit annoyed but mostly amused.

He was not thinking with his head. Understanding grew in his eyes before he rolled them.

"I'll buy you fifty more," he said before completely separating it. I rolled my eyes and looked at his face as he gazed at my bare chest.

Because he had torn the bust in two all the way, which was the heaviest part, it fell to the sides, taking the dress with it and showing the stockings.

Zaliver was quiet for a long time until he looked back up slowly. His expression momentarily frightened me with the intensity of it. It was like he'd been drowning and was taking in his first breath in a long time as if he were looking into my soul and taking a part for himself. That look made me squirm against him.

"Mine," he murmured quietly.

I smiled softly at him and nuzzled my nose with his, feeling like it was the correct thing to do. "So you like it?" I asked.

"Yes, you should go like this more often," he cut himself off with a quick snarl, "only around me though. No one else can see. No one," he said more to himself. I had a feeling he was more of an animal than a man now.

I kissed his cheek and then trailed down to where his mark was. When my teeth softly bit at my mark, he threw his head back and gave a groan. He leaned back down and took my lips in an almost punishing kiss with rough and frantic movement. He brought a hand around the back of my neck to keep me there as if I were trying to get away. Realizing my hair was in a ponytail, he pulled at the hair band until it came off and tangled his hand in my hair with a firm grip. One of his hands reached down and just ripped the undergarment off of me and was about to push in when I remembered something, barely managing to get my lips off of his on time.

"Condom," I whispered breathlessly. I felt his entire body freeze momentarily before he shifted a bit and must have rummaged through his pocket.

"Right," he said. If I had not been thinking straight, I would have caught the tiny flare of ambivalence coming from his part. Once he had it on, there was nothing stopping him. I gasped at the size of him, still not used to it. He paused for a moment to let me adjust.

My arms tightened around his neck as he began to move while the heat of both of our bodies, making the mirror next to us fog up immediately. His hips grounded onto my own, causing pleasure and making my eyes shut. I threw my head back with a silent moan. I clung to him and him to me. I felt one of his hands cup my breast and enjoyed the sensations his body was giving me. Using the position I was in, I brought my hips down to his every time his came up. I didn't know how long that went on but at some point, his shirt had annoyed me, so I ripped it off of him like he did to my dress.

My fingers clung to his back and probably left marks. I trailed one hand up and took hold of his hair roughly, capturing one of his silent moans with my lips. When my body began to tremor and tighten, he responded with harder strokes and nonstop friction until my body could no longer hold it and shattered. He pulled out and surprised me by placing me on my shaky legs. I looked up half-dazed and half confused. I hadn't felt him—

"I'm not even close to being done with you. I don't think I ever will," he said huskily with eyes filled with fire.

435

He grinned down at me with twinkling eyes. I opened my mouth to ask when he suddenly took hold of me and I was bent over the couch across the room with him fully buried in me once more.

"Ahhh!"

I took hold of the back of the couch with a solid grip, not caring for the cracking sound the wood made. My body was not completely over from the aftershocks of my first orgasm, and Zaliver knew that as he moved relentlessly behind me. He held my hips and moved even faster. I bit my lip at the strong sensation, and seeing this, he reached around with one hand and without pausing, his movement played my body like an instrument with his fingers. He spoke with a deep voice.

"Don't hold it in, baby. I want to hear you scream. I want to hear your moans I want to hear it all," he said so I did.

Not missing a beat, Zaliver reached for one of my legs and held it up. This caused him to go deeper and much further than I could believe. I dropped my head and let out a loud scream.

"Oh god. Oh my god. Oh god. Oh my god" I repeated over and over again incoherently in a muddled state of mind.

Zaliver wrapped his arm around my chest and brought me up against his firm chest, bringing about more pleasurable sounds from me.

"That's right. I'm your god," he whispered into my ear, nibbling at it softly with his teeth.

"Mine," I responded, feeling my body begin to tighten around him again.

"Forever and always," he said. Releasing my leg, he moved his hips back, but before he could push forward, I moved. Taking his moment of surprise, I flashed us over to the bed. This time, I was the one on top of him.

He clasped his hands behind his head. His lustful eyes and a smirk encouraged me to continue. I placed both hands on his chest firmly and leaned down until our faces were inches apart and spoke in a hoarse voice said.

"My turn."

I rotated my hips against his, letting my instincts take me along. I liked the way Zaliver's abdomen tightened and flexed under me. He removed his hands from under his head and wrapped them around me, bringing me down for his mouth to take my breasts. I put one arm on the bed next to his head and wasn't surprised when it folded, bringing me closer to him. Our bodies were slick with sweat and the scent of sex hung in the air. I opened my eyes to see Zaliver already gazing at me.

"I love you. I love you. I love you," he repeated over and over intensely. He reached up with one hand to cup the back of my neck and

436

brought me down to his lips with so much intensity, emotion, sensation, and so much love for another being that I didn't know if my body could handle the extreme sensations at the same time.

I don't think he could either. Our bodies were connected along with our souls, bringing the ultimate soul and body shaking connection between us two. I collapsed on top of Zaliver, breathing heavily with my forehead rested on his chest that was rising with his own harsh breathing.

"Oh no. I'm still not done with you," he said with a laugh that shook me with him. My eyes widened in surprise, and I moved to look at him.

"What?" I exclaimed, shock. Oh god, I don't know if my body could handle this man.

He rolled us over so that he was on top now and grinned down at me.

"Not even close."

~•~

"Geez, if we keep this up, I'll need a wheelchair," I muttered under my breath, twisting my back to see if I could stretch out some of my sore muscles. Zaliver leaned down and kissed my forehead with a smile.

"If you want, I can just carry you?" he said, already reaching for me. I swatted him away, knowing damn well that he was secretly pleased by my soreness.

"I'm good, no thanks." He pouted at my answer and just took hold of my hand as we walked down the hall.

We were heading down for Zaliver's meeting with the other alphas. He said I could come if I wanted to so I just tagged along. I wanted to see how the meeting would go.

I could also smell the dominance and tension in the air from all of the alphas being put together in a small space.

"Do you think a fight will break out?" I asked Zaliver randomly. I turned to look up at him.

"Do you?" he responded with a question. I shrugged.

"Your parents will arrive sometime during lunch. Alpha Daniel said that they are confused as to why they were called," he said. My mouth parted when I remembered that we were supposed to meet them today. I stopped us before we got to the door and narrowed my eyes at Zaliver who lifted a brow at me in question.

"You're not going to pull anything last-minute like last time, right? Because technically to them this is the first time meeting you." He

437

shook his head and pulled me in for a hug. I buried my nose in his chest and inhaled his comforting scent.

"Not this time. I'll have you know that if I want to, I can charm people," he said with pride. I pulled away and looked at him.

"Oh, I have no doubt of that." I stepped away from him. "But I'll be impressed when you go an hour without threats, growls, or even a glare. Good luck, buddy." I patted his back, ignored his growl and opened the door for the meeting room.

All of the alphas were standing as far as they possibly could from one another. I wasn't surprised to see some of their mates in the same room with them. The ladies were much more civil. At least, they didn't glare at one another but smiled.

I walked in front of Zaliver—who, to me, seemed grumpy—but by the look on some of the others' faces, he looked ready to kill. I smiled brightly at everyone.

"Hello, everyone. I hope you all had a wonderful night's rest." Lord knows I didn't.

Some alphas nodded briskly at me while some started with curious yet polite looks on their faces. Some of the lunas returned my smile. I even recognized a few from last night's conversations. I also noted some of the unpleasant ones.

Cough, cough. "*Grandma squad*," my wolf coughed out.

I couldn't help but chuckle when my eyes skimmed over them. They averted their gazes. Zaliver stepped in and stood beside me, making sure to look at every single person in the room until they looked away, much to the alphas' displeasure.

"Good morning, everyone. Take a seat in the next room. Our meeting will begin," he said without any further instructions or greeting.

Some alphas walked in with their mates and took seats, but there were a few alphas who stopped their mate from entering; those who looked over at Zaliver and then at me in question.

"Are you seriously considering letting the females join in on the meeting?" one alpha questioned.

Other alphas glared and gave low growls at the alphas while some gave annoyed looks. Zaliver looked at them coldly. His expression was not giving anything away. I was not. My beast sent a wave of annoyance my way.

"Dude, this is the 21st century. Does the phrase same-sex equality or the word equality in general mean anything to you?" I asked. Zaliver pulled out my seat and pushed me in.

The alpha not only ignored me but just looked at Zaliver, waiting for a response.

"Your luna spoke to you. If you feel that she is below that of the power you believe you have, then perhaps I shall hand the pack over to your mate to see who truly runs it better, Alpha Stone. But then again, she isn't your mate now, is she?" Zaliver stated coldly.

When he said that, everyone looked over to his supposed mate, taking a closer look at Alpha Stone. I realized he was totally . . . ugly, and I wasn't just talking about appearance. He appeared to have more stress lines and greying hair than anyone in this room. His body was not as tone as the others because he slouched a bit as if he were getting ready to bolt. I had a mouth brain malfunction and spoke without thinking.

"Damnnn, Alpha Stone . . . You look more like Alpha Pebble . . ." I whispered. The giggles and chuckles from the lunas and alphas made me realize I said that out loud.

Alpha Stone's face flushed red with anger. He made it seem as if he were going to take a threatening step in my direction, but before he could, he was suddenly surrounded by a wall of snarling alphas.

He blanched and took a step back with disbelief on his face. Even the ones that hesitated on letting their mates in stepped away from him. Zaliver spoke as he walked to the seat next to me, which was the head of the table.

"Now, now gentlemen, don't fret. We have a lot to discuss, and I'd rather not meet the in-laws with blood all over me. Sit," he stated. He took out a bunch of folders from the bag he carried.

Everyone took a step back and sat down. It was an awkward adjustment because the alphas didn't know where to place their mates so that they would be both safe and away from the other male alphas. I rolled my eyes.

Three hours, two arguments, three almost fights, one shift, a begging alpha, and a pissed off Zaliver later, I was done. I knew that me being there reduced Zaliver's anger, but I was done. Some of the people in the room honestly deserved some of his wrath, and I was tired of hearing wacky explanations on stupidly obvious things.

"Does any of you ladies want to go for a lunch break with me?" I asked and stood up from the meeting, interrupting another begging alpha.

Immediately, three stood up. Their mates didn't even try to hold them back and just pecked their cheeks. Two other females nudged their mates until they begrudgingly agreed.

"Shit, can I go?" a young guy asked with his eyes begging. I raised a brow at him.

"Aren't you an alpha?" I asked. He shook his head and nodded to the girl sitting next to him. I caught on immediately.

"Nah, my mate is. So can I?" he asked, begging. I shrugged, amused at how he asked me. He hopped up immediately and patted his stomach.

"Thank god. I thought I was going to starve in here." He kissed his mate on the cheek who rolled her eyes at him.

"I'll bring you back a sandwich . . . half a sandwich . . . if I don't get hungry on the way back," he promised and walked out to seemingly wait for us outside.

Even the granny squad stood up and went to the door. I caught sight of Melly and Theo and smiled.

I walked over to her and smiled at Theo. He surprisingly returned it and squeezed her arm affectionately.

"Go on. I'm sure you're hungry," he said soothingly. *So cute*!

I could feel Zaliver's eyes on me, so I turned around to catch his unhappy eyes looking back at me. I could tell he wanted me to stay. We gazed at each other.

"*Stay. Don't leave me here with these people.*"

"*Too bad, suck it up,*" I said.

"*You calm me down,*" he said with longing clear in his voice.

"*And sometimes being angry gets things done faster. Just don't murder anyone and we should be good.*"

"*I won't if you give me something in return.*"

Just by how his voice deepened in my mind, I could tell where his mind was going to. I was too sure for this!

"*Never mind. Bye, Zaliver. Be good.*"

I walked out without another glance, not trying to end up in that wheelchair sooner than later.

All of us went down the hall and into the hotel's cafeteria, which could become my new favorite place to eat. The walls were bright and colorful, reminding me of the forest, which was odd.

Since we're here on meeting, the food was free for alphas and lunas. I figured that out when some went to pay after getting what they wanted, but we're told that the food was on the hotel.

What took me by surprise, however, was when I went to eat.

Since they had said it was on the hotel, I hadn't bothered to even get in line to pay and went to sit down, but as soon as I opened my Naked to drink from it, all of the wolves from the cashiers jumped up and ran after me.

It startled me enough that I placed it down and waited for them to reach me. Werewolves always this slow? Huh. When they reached me, they had fear on their faces and checked my tray with frantic movement.

"Is everything okay?" I asked them.

A brown-eyed blond closest one to me answered.

"Did you eat or drink anything from this tray, Luna?" she asked, looking at me. I shook my head, which seemed to calm her down immediately. She brought her hand up to her mouth, showing one of those little wrist devices you could speak into.

"Snow has not taken a bite out of the apple. I repeat, Snow has not taken a bite out of the apple. Bring down the food," she said.

My table was cleared away along with my opened Naked. Some of the lunas looked on in confusion and then looked down at their food with distrust.

"I wanted that," I murmured sadly, watching it get carried off.

The blond-haired girl smiled at me apologetically.

"I'm sorry, Luna. Alpha Azrala gave clear instructions to follow protocol. All of your food is to be tested and served from a specific and guarded fridge while you are here. That also applies to anything you grab," she explained. A few minutes later, the same people came back, carrying what looked like the same things, but this time, my Naked was closed. They placed it down in front of me with smiles and went back to their earlier positions.

"Oh," I said.

"It's to prevent poisoning or something related to dangers of your health or well-being. Did Alpha not tell you?" she asked.

Poison. I just gave her a tensed smile and sat down.

"Thank you anyway," I said. She nodded and walked back to her previous position. By now, the other lunas had gone back to eating but had thoughtful looks on their faces. The guy from the meeting didn't even bother to stop eating. He was half done from eating two full sandwiches from what I could tell.

"*You have my food tested?*" I asked Zaliver through our bond link. It took him no time to answer even though he was in a meeting.

"*Always. Why?*" he responded, confused. I frowned as I picked at my chips.

"*We can't die, so even if I am poisoned, I don't see why you should get someone to taste the food. What if they die?*" I asked, worried. It took him a moment to respond, thinking out his answer carefully.

"*That's true, but it . . . hurts me to even think of you in pain. I don't make anyone taste your food by force. Wolves volunteer, Vivian. They would give up their lives for yours as I would. Don't think too much about it.*"

"*Hmmm,*" I responded before pulling out of our bond and ate.

Melly, who sat next to me, was gazing at me nervously.

"You okay?" I asked after taking a bite out of my pizza. She gave me a comforting smile.

"I want to thank you for what you did last night. Our previous alpha has been abusive for years after his mate left him. Theo had to step into the beta position by bloodline and was horrified after seeing the violent changes that came with the work," Melly said. Her voice was barely a whisper.

441

"He never told anyone how abusive the previous alpha was to him or anyone in the pack house because he wasn't allowed to. No one was. When we found out we were mates, I was hurt because he tried to keep me away from him at first. I thought he rejected me, but it wasn't until I went into the pack house to speak to him that I realized what was happening. When the alpha realized I was Theo's mate, he punished him by beating me. Theo tried to stop him but sometimes . . ." she trailed off.

I felt my stomach churn at what she was telling me. Her resentment and hatred for her previous alpha welled up in me. I wanted to find him and beat him, but I knew that taking his alpha position had and would probably the only thing to hurt him.

"But after last night, you gave us both the power to fix things in the pack and to change the rules he made and help the ones that have been hurting for so long. Thank you, Luna Vivian. I promise we will make you proud," she said, hesitating only a little to reach out for my hands and giving me a squeeze. I held onto her hands and looked into her eyes seriously. Her eyes widened.

"You already have." For the first time since meeting Melly, she gave me a smile so warm. I knew she'd be okay. They would all be okay.

~•~

"I'm going to really miss some of those girls. They're so nice and funny," I said to Zaliver after saying goodbye to them.

The meeting finished soon after lunch, and they were quick to leave back to their packs. I was really going to miss some of them. Zaliver shook his head and placed his head in his hands. I laughed.

When we returned from lunch and walked into the meeting room, it was a mess, and by mess, I mean alphas cowered away from a very, very pissed off Zaliver, who was barking orders and new regulations left and right. He gave up on trying to listen to them all and decided to just rummage through their head—Zaliver style that, of course, freaked them out. He had to order them to stand still that caused them to freak out even more and scream and shout.

When we walked in, they all stood up straight like statues with fearful eyes while Zaliver sat at the table, going over some documents calmly in a silent room if you ignored the pounding hearts.

"You're so mean to them. You'll never make friends if you keep ordering them to stand still and shut up," I exclaimed mockingly. I walked up behind him and placed my hands on his shoulders. He groaned.

"I don't want friends," he said. I held in a laugh. My big giant mate who could control the werewolf population was sullen.

442

"Sure you do. Who else are you going to complain about me too?" I asked, playing with his hair. He turned around and made me stand between his legs, so he could pay his head on my chest.

"You, all I need is you," he said. I smiled at him and bent down to peck him, but he took hold of my face between both of his hands. I got lost in the kiss and was about to straddle him when a knock came on the door.

I jumped back from him as far as his arms would allow me to. I knew what that knock meant. My parents were here.

"Come on. Time to meet the in-laws . . . again." I added after a quick thought.

He stood up and stretched his arms over his head. Unthinkingly, my eyes went to the exposed skin that appeared. When I looked back up shyly, his eyes were closed as he took in a deep breath.

"I'm trying really hard to remind myself that your parents are waiting for us. Don't make it harder by looking at me like that, love," he said.

From the look of his crotch, it wasn't the only hard thing. I took his hand and led him to the door.

"Sorry. Ready?" I asked him before we walked out.

He squeezed my hand as an answer. The garden where my parents were waiting for us was three floors down. The funny thing of this whole situation was the fact that my parents had absolutely no idea as to why they were here and who they were going to meet.

This was just one big balloon waiting to pop. Can't wait.

As we neared the garden, I could see my parents standing by the small pond. My mom pointed eagerly at the little fishes while my dad looked at her in amusement with love in his eyes. I always liked that about my parents. No matter where or what they were doing, they always showed their affection in what they did.

As we neared, I was guessing they could feel our presence because my mom frowned in confusion. She then stood up straight along with my dad who brought her closer to his side protectively. When they caught sight of us, their eyes first fixed themselves on me with shock and then excitement, which then morphed into disbelief and curiosity when they finally looked at Zaliver's way. They really didn't remember him. I knew that they wouldn't, but it didn't make it any less weird for me.

My mom was the first to speak. Her eyes were shining with unshed tears of joy. She took a step away from my dad to come and hug me. I let go of Zaliver's hand and went to hug her.

"Vivian?"

443

"Hi, Mom. Hi, Dad." I hugged her tightly and then went to my dad who stood gape-mouthed. He hugged me back. I could feel his hesitation on letting me go to step beside Zaliver again.

"Honey, what are you doing here? I thought you were traveling?" my dad asked me. His eyes flicked momentarily to Zaliver who had a calm and polite smile on his face. There really was no way of introducing your mate to your parents, so I might as well wing it.

"I was and then I found my mate. Mom, Dad, this is Zaliver Azrala," I introduced him proudly. He took a step forward and gave my dad his hand who took it.

"Hello, sir. It's a pleasure to meet you," he said politely. My dad who was still shocked over my revelation blinked up at Zaliver.

Zaliver took my mother's wonderstruck hand and kissed her knuckles.

"Ma'am, such an honor." He stepped back and placed his hand on my back.

My parents looked at him, to me, then back to him. Since they were all ready surprised, I prefered for them to know now.

"Before you guys say anything, I love him and he loves me. You guys told me not to judge a book by its cover. Zaliver is known as Lupus Deus to werewolves . . . so have you guys had lunch or . . ." I said all in one breath. My mother's eyes became impossibly big while my father's mind immediately clicked and went into overdrive.

"Wait, you mean—" my mother began.

"Vivian, get aw—" my dad said, panicked.

"Is that a mark—" My mom noticed.

"Oh my god—" My dad did too.

"Am I gonna be a grandma?" That question cleared any other. All three of us snapped to look at my mom.

My dad stared at her like he was trying to figure out how they were still married after all of this time. I stared at my mother with disbelief, and when I turned to look at Zaliver expression, he had already composed it to a calm expression.

"Really Alison? Grandkids? That's the first thing that comes to mind after our only daughter says she's mated to a guy known for destruction. Grandkids?" my dad asked. My mom turned to face him with happy eyes.

"Oh, calm down, Chace. She's obviously happy, and he obviously loves her. We did tell her not to judge, so let's not be hypocrites. So . . . about my grandbabies?" My mom turned back to face me with suggestive eyebrows. My dad shook his head and looked at Zaliver far longer than any other alpha had. He nodded after a few minutes.

"Just keep her safe and happy. That's all I'm asking for," he said.

"That's all I want," Zaliver responded.

"Well, I want grandkids," my mom added in after. I rolled my eyes.

"Well, this went better than last time," I muttered.

"What?" my dad asked. My eyes widened and I coughed.

"Oh nothing. So, have you guys eaten? They have wonderful . . . " I began blabbing about random things. Knowing what I meant, Zaliver began talking to my dad. They ended up wandering away from me and my mom. Every once in a while, I'd see them both look in our direction.

"I can see that you love him, and that he loves you." My mother's voice broke me out of my thoughts. I smiled at her happily.

"I'm so happy with him. I never knew finding your mate would feel so fulfilling." I sighed in content.

She smiled and brushed some of my hair away from my face in a way that only a mother would do.

"It is once you get past all the fighting and arguing and getting to know one another," she said wisely. I snorted.

"Tell me about it," I muttered.

"You to seem to be in sync. It's interesting for a newly mated couple. How long have you two been together?" she asked with searching eyes. I squirmed a bit.

"Oh not long . . . " If we ignored the days I was knocked out, had my memory taken from me, and arguments with him, not long at all.

"Hmmm, so what is he like? For being the Lupus Deus, he isn't as wild or savage like I pictured him to be," my mother asked, not meaning any offense.

"It's a long story, but he truly is one of a kind. He's intelligent, brave, stubborn, caring, thick-headed, loveable, adorable, and just has a way with getting his way. At first, he can be intense, but once you get to you him, you just . . . Mom?" I asked once I saw the way her eyes were tearing up. She smiled and swatted my hands away.

"Oh, my baby's in love. I'm gonna get my grandkids sooner than later," she said, sniffling.

"Really, Mom?" I said dryly.

She gave a small laugh.

"Hey, Mom. How you and Dad feel about moving to where me and Zaliver are staying? I mean it's better protected than anywhere else, and it's beautiful place to retire," I said excitedly.

My mom's sad smile answered me.

"That sounds lovely, but it's just too late in our lives to get up and move. Don't worry. We'll always visit wherever you're staying." She hugged me. I sagged a bit in disappointment but I understood.

"I guess, but if you ever change your mind—"

"You'll be the first to know." We smiled at each other.

After having a long and overdue conversation with my parents, Zaliver and I had to go back to the island. He told my parents they were welcomed to stay at the hotel for how long they pleased and that all expenses were paid. If they wished to go back home, all they had to do was tell the staff and the plane would be ready for them. My mom really liked that. She convinced my dad to stay for a little vacation. This time, when I said goodbye to them, I felt a lot better knowing they knew I was fine and with Zaliver. On the plane, I sat on his lap and played with his hair while he cuddled me.

"That went great. My parents love you," I said sleepily and he agreed silently.

"What were you and my dad talking about? You guys kept looking at us," I asked him.

"Just guy stuff," he answered.

"Oh," I said, drifting off.

When the plane landed, I was feeling a bit sluggish even after the nap. I thought it was because I hadn't shifted in a long time. When we got off of the plane, it was raining really hard. The skies were a stormy gray. One great thing about having advanced capabilities was that you could flash to the car without getting wet.

"I won't be able to go home right away. I've got to check on everything I left for Albericus and make sure he didn't mess anything up," Zaliver said, running his hand through his hair.

I did the same with mine and looked up at him. I pulled him down to kiss his cheek. He gave me a soft smile.

"What was that for?" he asked, holding my hand.

"Just felt like doing it." I shrugged.

"Well, don't hold back."

"Are you going to be fine by yourself, or do you want me to send the guards over?" he asked. I shook my head. The car stopped at his destination.

"No, it's fine. I think I'll go for a run first and then just rest. I feel like I need a run," I said. He looked down at me anxiously.

"Don't worry. I'm fine. Say hi to Algebra for me. I love you," I said, shoving him out. He chuckled and kissed me quickly. I waved at him.

"I love you too. Be careful!" he yelled out.

"Always am!" I replied. The driver pulled up in front of the house and helped me unload the bags. Once inside, I changed my clothing and went out through the back door that lead to our humongous backyard. It technically was a forest.

The rain was really coming down heavily but sometimes, it was good to just enjoy nature and its gifts. I paused and lifted my face and hands to the rain, letting my hair and body get soaked; it felt great. I continued to walk and breathed in the scent of rain and earth.

I felt at home. I felt happy.

I stood under a large tree with large branches and patted the bark, letting my body relax I closed my eyes.

I could smell everything. Hear everything. Sense everything.

I opened my mind to prepare to shift when it felt like my body was suddenly on fire from the inside out.

"I wanted to go. I wanted to go."

I frowned at the sound of them both arguing. Suddenly, both of them shoved me to the back of my mind while I was still in human form. My body began to shake.

"I wanted to shift," my beast growled out.

I felt my mind begin to split in half as she pushed her will over mine and began to command my body to follow her will.

My human body didn't know what was going on and began shaking even harder. I couldn't control my body. I couldn't open my eyes. I couldn't move. My body shook as both sides fought for control of the other half. It felt like pins, needles, and fire. My body was in such agony. It prepared for a shift, but unsure of which one, and suspended in some half state.

"Stop fighting!" I yelled.

They didn't seem to hear me as they growled and snarled at each other.

It rained harder and something crackled nearby.

"Stop!" I yelled out again.

No, not a crackle, but more like a deep, maniacal laughter.

Harder.

I felt as if my body was being torn from the inside out, and there was nothing I could do to stop it. The rain hitting my skin was feeling like cold metal hitting me repeatedly.

BOOM!

As my body burned and fought itself on the inside, something loud was heard overhead.

Tearing. Breaking. Falling.

As if fate had this planned, the rain hit its ultimate peak. Through the sound of my blood rushing, something that sounded like whistle, but I couldn't be sure.

Falling.

447

I stood frozen and shaking as both animalistic sides of me fought for dominance.

Falling.

"Stop!"

"*Me?*"

"*No, me!*"

"Please stop this!"

Something was falling.

Pain.

And then silence.

CHAPTER 35

Awaken, my child. I shall see you soon enough.

My body felt cold, yet warm at the same time. It wasn't unpleasant at all. I moved my fingers and felt something soft under my fingertips. I lifted my tongue a little and then pushed it out, forcing my lips to open. It took a little more effort than it should have.

I was parched.

My head felt foggy. Everything was quiet without the constant beating of a loud ping, and it had been annoying my ears. I wiggled my toes and sighed. Where was I? I tried to recall how I got where I was for a moment.

Rain. It was raining. Something was arguing before a loud sound happened, then pain. I frowned and felt as if the muscles in my face were tensed.

My body felt fine, but I was mentally exhausted. I opened my eyes and immediately shut them when bright lights appeared. I blinked repeatedly, raised my back a bit, and looked around the room the large light brown-painted room filled with lots of colorful flowers.

I stretched my arms around my head for a moment and stared at my fingers. I felt so tired though I was pretty sure I had rested well. Next to my bed was an equipment with wires connected to me.

I threw the top covering off my body and got up slowly, and put my feet on the floor. I wiggled my toes again and sighed.

Standing up was hard as my balance was a bit off that I had to grab the bars on the bed. I looked at the window and saw a pinkish orange tint peeking through the white curtains—must be the sunrise. With a harsh tug, I ripped them out from me which just made the sound became loud and prolonged that seemed to never end.

"Noo!!" My head snapped over to the door.

A frightening, animalistic, and painful sound came from somewhere, coming closer to the room. I held my breath as it neared like my heart took off from my chest. I flinched when the door was thrown open violently. There at the door stood a giant man who looked ruggedly handsome and tired with wild blue eyes and a muscular-shaking figure. His chest lifted up and down with his harsh breaths while his nose was flaring, and his eyes were all over the room.

His eyes looked at the bed and then looked up to me. A flicked of different emotions crossed over his face. He didn't stop shaking but he began taking slow steps towards me. I tilted my head to the side and looked at him. He looked so familiar.

I could feel the gears in my head turning. Things were clicking into place as those deep and pained blue eyes were gazing at me.

He stood before me and looked at me with wide fearful eyes. Lifting his shaking hand, he reached out for my cheek. I felt as if my whole body was jolted by the mere contact of our skin.

Zaliver—a name of emotions and memories.

"Zaliver," I croaked.

His arms were around me before I could blink. He repeatedly nuzzled my neck, face, and anywhere he could reach. I could hear the pounding of his heart. I caught the sight of pale-faced people standing by the door who wore scrubs.

Zaliver must have sensed the people in the room. He didn't move from his spot near me but made a small space and turned to face them.

"Check her," he ordered.

They immediately came to me and while they were fussing, I looked at Zaliver who watched them with hawk-like eyes, making sure not to miss anything. A blond-haired man with a long white coat waved them away. I looked at him with curious eyes. He smiled at me sympathetically.

"Hello, Luna. My name is Dr. Leonard, remember? Can you tell me your name, please?" he asked, blinking his pretty hazel eyes at me. He brought out a clipboard and wrote something on it. Of course, I knew my name.

"Uh . . . Uh . . ." I closed my mouth and looked at the floor with confusion. Zaliver rubbed his hands on my arms comfortingly.

"It's alright—"

"V-Vivian . . . Grey?" I said.

I didn't like this feeling at all. My chest lifted up with shudders. Dr. Leonard smiled at me and nodded while Zaliver kissed the side of my head. I repeated my name a multiple times in my head. I didn't want to forget my name. Ever.

"How old are you?" My answer came a bit faster than last time thankfully.

"Eighteen," I responded.

"Birthday?"

"In a few weeks. December 8th." He nodded, but his eyes flicked back to Zaliver who hadn't said anything.

450

"Do you know why you're here? What's the last thing you remember?" he asked, putting his clipboard down by his lap and keeping his hands in front of him calmly.

"I remembered coming back from the party. It was dark, and it was raining. There was a loud sound, then something fell . . ." My voice trailed off as I recalled.

I reached for my head and felt it to see if I had anything weird back there but nothing. Was I hit with something? I think I was . . . was I?

"You went to the forest when it was raining . . ." Dr. Leonard said, confirming what I was saying.

"I found you under a branch," a dark voice spoke behind me. I looked at Zaliver who came up to me hugging me closer to his chest.

"A branch . . ." I whispered.

"When I removed it from you . . ." I touched my face and was glad that my skin felt fine and was not disfigured.

"Your healing process had already kicked in by the time Alpha found you so don't worry about any facial damage. Your entire body is fine." Dr. Leandro explained quickly. My eyes narrowed on him.

"But . . ." I asked.

"When Alpha Zaliver shifts, he does it swiftly. You, on the other hand, are a different case. You have a wolf and beast in you. When you shift, your body releases a chemical that pushes it to shift. That's what made your werewolf transformation so quick.

Gaining your beast caused both animal sides to become more aggressive, thus the disagreement as to who would shift. After doing some scanning on your body and brain, I realized that during your preparation for a shift, your mind enters a vulnerable state where all parts of you come forward in your mind.

You, your beast, and your wolf are pulled to the front and in that moment of vulnerability, you can not control your body or senses, making you extremely easy to be taken advantage of, or in this case harmed. When lightning hit a tree, its branch broke off and landed on your head."

My memory started to clear as he spoke, and I couldn't believe what I was hearing.

"I can't hear my beast or wolf. Why is that?" I asked him anxiously.

I didn't want to lose them. It wasn't their fault I was here; not exactly. He pursed his lips but answered me hesitantly.

"You were hit on the head with at least a twenty-pound tree branch—" My eyes widened. "And you've been unconscious for a week and seventy-three hours. For safety precautions—" Zaliver cut him off.

"I had them knock your beast and wolf out," he stated.

451

"What?! Why—" I asked, looking at Zaliver.

His eyes weren't the same. There was something dark and frightening about those eyes.

I turned back around stiffly without another word and faced the doctor. Zaliver nuzzled the side of my neck, and I swallowed.

"When will they return?" I asked Dr. Leandro.

"Since you're finally up, your body should be burning the drug as we speak; roughly two or three hours if we don't inject you again," he stated.

"When can I go home?" I asked softly.

My mind had a lot of catching up to do for a full week, and I missed it. Wow!

I felt uneasy and scared to be honest, as if there was something in the air . . . something dark. Dr. Leonard looked at his clipboard for a few moments and then looked back up.

"Well, your pulse and body seem to be functioning just fine, and your memory should be returning slowly. I'd usually ask the patient to stay for an overnight evaluation, but your rapid healing process has left that precaution needless. I do however . . . have a warning." His face turned grave as he spoke, and his face paled as he's looked behind me.

Zaliver's arms tightened around me. Something was off about him.

"What warning?" I asked.

The doctor moved around uncomfortably before sighing and looking at me seriously.

"The state of vulnerability that you are put in every time you shift will never stop. In every shift you take, it controls and decides who would take over . . . and may be the most dangerous point in your life."

I blinked up at the doctor, not sure of how to feel about his words.

"So what you're saying is . . ." My voice came out weaker than I wanted it to, and my throat felt as dry as it truly was.

"Luna . . . you may not be able to die, but if you are attacked while in mid shift process, then your mind will protect itself and you will enter a sleep-like coma state. Even I, can not tell you if you will ever wake up from it," he said. Without another word, he looked behind me and became deathly pale before turning to leave the room. I looked after him in mind numbing shock.

~•~

I watched Zaliver for the last two days with worried eyes. He was silent most of the time and was being patient with me. While he attended to me and gave me whatever I asked, he seemed to be . . . I

452

didn't know what to say. It was like he was afraid that I would fall and hit my head.

Every time I tried to speak to him, he would do or say something to distract me.

To say I was mad about missing thanksgiving was a bust, then having to call my parents and make up some excuses as to why we didn't call or text was even harder. Ugh, food, I missed food.

Zaliver softly whispered a promise on making a big dinner one of these days, but the way he said it distracted me from fantasizing about food.

We were together but seemed like we weren't. I felt him with me but he was also distant. His eyes would look at me and become dazed as if he was remembering something and then he would refocus on me, more intense than before. He was starting to scare me.

His cold and silent eyes would follow me. He had even closed his side of the bond from me that I couldn't even catch an inkling of his emotions. If it weren't for the gentle touches every time he thought I was asleep, or the way he nuzzled his face on my neck in the middle of the night and whimper, I'd be more worried about us.

In a sense, I understood he was scared on what had happened, and I felt the same too.

I felt like I was better both physically and mentally on what the doctor said. I'd be better prepared and guarded when I went to shift—if he would let me out.

Both my beast and wolf apologized dramatically when I got them back. Even they didn't understand where all the aggression had come from. All three of us watched Zaliver with concern. While my body was rested, Zaliver looked . . . tired.

He had dark circles under his eyes. His hair was a mess. He had a dark stubble on his face from not shaving. I'd love the look on him if he didn't look weary. I didn't even think he slept. Sometimes I'd get the same feeling that he was watching me even as we slept. He'd walk around the house in a black t-shirt and black sweats, and even in his pjs.

I felt like I was the one needed to take care of him. Sometimes, I'd hear him yelling down stairs at someone, he'd tell them to take care of something without him that he didn't have the time for it. He'd come back up with a calm expression as if he hadn't just threatened anyone. He would break things when I wasn't around. I would always hear something tearing or shattering and his soft growls.

I think it was time we talked. At the moment, he was downstairs cooking breakfast. He would push me down gently when I tried to get up, but I would always try to get up by myself. The room was casted in dark light. The curtains were closed tightly but even then, I could see that it was a bit stormy outside. Dark clouds covered the sun. I shook my thoughts away. It was a new day, and I had to start living in it.

As soon as my bare feet landed softly on the floor, he was in front of me, looking crazy with his hands outstretched towards me.

"What are you doing? You need to rest." He was already going to grab me but I took hold of his hands and stood up.

"Zaliver, I'm fine. I've laid down for two days straight, I'm okay." I tried to move around him but he just kept taking steps in front of me to block any movement. I sighed.

He shook his head quickly.

"No, no, no, no! You have to sit and rest. Do you want something? I can get it for you. Just tell me," he said.

His voice rose towards the end while stepped on his side. I shook my head at him, and I raised one of my hands and placed it on his face. My thumb was feeling his stubble.

"You're the one who needs rest and a long hot shower. When was the last time you shaved or ate for the matter?" I asked. He had always bought me my meals but never ate with me; he was just watching saying he had already eaten, or was waiting for something—some type of an excuse.

"I am not important. You—"

"Of course, you're important Zaliver! I know you want to take care of me, but let me take care of you now. I'm okay. See?" I exclaimed angrily. I turned around, trying to calm him down. He was not amused.

"Go lay down, Vivian," he ordered softly.

I frowned up at him, brows coming together.

"Zali—"

"Go."

"No."

His eyes hardened. He took a step towards me as if he was about to pick me up to lay me down himself. I took a couple of steps backward and raised my arms.

"Zaliver I'm okay, it's okay—"

"Stop saying that," he said. I glanced down to see his hands fisting. For the first time, I caught something from his side of the bond—a flare of emotion like a scorching flame. It was scary.

"What's going on, Zaliver? You're different and not exactly in a good way. Let me in," I whispered to him, and he began shaking again.

His eyes closed. He took in a deep breath and shook his head as he grimaced.

"It's alright, Vivian. Everything's fine, just go to bed sweetheart—"

"Bullshit!"

454

"ENOUGH!"

"NO! Let me in. What's bothering you?! Just tell me and we can work on it together—"

He cracked and took a step towards me and then a step back. He began pacing, growling, and snarling as he lets his canines out.

"Work on it? Work on it?! We can't. There is nothing to fix. You don't know. You don't know . . . don't know. She doesn't know," he shouted, turning to me, and began muttering to himself.

I reached out to grab him but he flinched away from me, leaving me frozen. He had never done that before. I felt cold, colder than I had ever felt in my life. His emotions were hitting me like crazy, and I could feel it through our bond. There all felt like a heavy chain around my neck

"Z-Zaliv—"

"I couldn't save you. I DIDN'T SAVE YOU! I failed. I'm a failure as a mate," he yelled. He stopped a few inches from me and looked down at his hands in horror.

"All these tests and precautions I made for you were useless. It's my fault. It's me."

My chest suddenly felt heavy with a forced breath of air parting my lips in a silent cry. My eyes welled up with tears. My mind couldn't bear the burden as I looked at my mate in so much pain.

Guilt. He was drowning himself in guilt.

"No," I whispered, horrified for blaming himself.

"Zaliver, it wasn't your fault—"

His head snapped up to look at me with his dark eyes becoming darker.

"Yes it was."

"I was standing under a tree, it was raining," I tried to explain.

"I let you go. I should have gone with you," his voice cracked, his breaths coming out harsher.

"It's was just a coincidence, a bad one but—" I stepped closer towards him, and he took another one back.

"I saw what the weather was like, but I didn't go with you. I didn't."

"You're not expected to be with me at all times."

I slowly got down on my knees in front of him and put my hands firmly on his shoulders.

"You're wrong. You did save me. I'm right here." He raised his head slowly. His expression was heart-wrenching, and broken as tears fell from his eyes.

"You died."

His words caught me off guard.

"W-What?" I choked, surprised.

455

As he cried silently, he removed his hands from his hair and with a shaky movement, he took my hands from his shoulders. He held them together and brought them to his lips, closing his eyes and kissed them. He took a sharp, broken breath before exhaling heavily through his mouth.

I just looked down at him not sure what . . . to think or what to say. He opened his eyes and smiled softly at me.

"I felt you die."

"But—" I couldn't breath. It felt as if I couldn't find it in me.

"You died, Vivian. I felt it. "He pulled my hands away from his face and placed them on his beating heart. "In here."

"I felt the exact moment your heart stopped beating," he whispered. He looked up and blinked quickly as he shook his head.

"Oh god, it hurt . . . so fucking much." He whimpered while his hands tightened around mine.

Me? dead?

His behavior was that of someone who had blamed themselves for the fall of a loved one.

I closed my eyes with my hands on his chest and listened to his heartbeat. Though my eyes were closed, I could see myself through our mating bond.

Darkness drowned him, covered him, and pulled him in deeper, and he had it for a long time. He was so used to the darkness that it had become his home—the only thing he knew would never abandon him.

He couldn't tell if light meant good, or if light was really just emptiness or pure nothing.

He didn't even know if darkness was bad, or if it would make him blind, but he didn't care.

A sob escaped my body as I shook from the strong emotions that overcame me. He was hurting and punishing himself.

Fear. Anger. Regret. Hurt. Pain. Horror. Disgust. Shock. All of these negative emotions beat against him, and he let them, believing he deserved it.

I opened my eyes. My vision was blurry for a moment because of my tears. He looked at me with a haunted look.

"Oh Zaliver," I said. My chest felt hollow when he didn't even look up.

I didn't like seeing him so . . . broken. It wasn't him. He was supposed to be my big, strong, confident brute who always knew what to do even if it was completely wrong in the eyes of others. I had to bring him out of this.

Determination fired up through my veins.

I pulled my hands out from his hold and wiped my tears with the back of my hands.

"What good am I if I can't even keep the love of my life safe?" he whispered to himself.

I took a breath and shook my head. I reached for him and grabbed his face in between my hands, forcing him to look at me. His haunted blue eyes blinked at me without seeing me.

"Hey! Stop thinking like that, Zaliver. Nothing that happened was your fault, do you hear me? Absolutely nothing. You and I couldn't have known this was going to happen, and there's no doubt that there's nothing you wouldn't do to prevent me from dying because that's who you are. You have a heart to help and protect."

He blinked at me slowly. His eyes were still looking dead, but he was beginning to hear me.

"I'm so sorry you had to go through that. I'm so sorry that I didn't pay enough attention to where or what I was doing that you had to go through that alone. But you're not alone anymore, don't you see? I'm right here and I'm with you because you did save me, Zaliver. Yes I died, but I'm immortal remember? I'm not going anywhere you won't be."

He blinked, and I could see him agree with me.

"Don't blame yourself for this. It's not your fault, Zaliver. Bad luck. It happens to the best of us, and you are the best mate anyone could ever have. You're always telling me how lucky you are to have me, but I don't think I've ever told you how happy and lucky I am to have you."

His eyes began to lighten up slowly as he focused on me. His hands came up shakily to my waist where he held me softly.

"Yes, I whine and complain about some of the things that you do, but I would never trade a single moment that we've had; everything good and bad. I'm the lucky one. You're generous, protective, caring, smart, charming, romantic, thoughtful, supportive, loveable and the list is endless. I'm the lucky one, and I will forever be thankful that we're together.

So please. . . please, don't blame yourself for something that isn't true. Let me in, Zaliver. Let me love you the way I do because I do love you. I love you, Zaliver."

I leaned my forehead against his and closed my eyes that took a few moments. When his nose nuzzled mine and his hands on my waist pulled me closer and then tightened, I knew he'd fought the darkness inside of him and won.

I opened my eyes to see his baby blue eyes gazing into mine with strong emotions that meant just one word—love.

457

I smiled softly at him. My lips trembled along with my whole body. He raised one of his hands from my waist and wiped a tear from my eye.

"Shhh, baby. It's okay. It all okay now," he whispered.

I gulped and nodded. I was about to pull away when he held my head firmly in place. He planted his lips down softly onto mine.

The kiss shook me to my core—soft yet unbreakable; firm yet gentle; dark yet light; full of fear and love. My hands that were still holding onto his face pulled him closer. I needed him and wanted to be closer to him.

He must have felt the same because our lips moved quicker, harder against each other, hungrily searching and funding our other half. One of my hands went to his shoulder and down, pushing his chest against mine. I felt as if I couldn't get enough of him; as if I hadn't in a long while and as if we were still distant.

We both pulled away when we needed air. Our loud breaths and pounding hearts could be heard loud and clear. I placed my head on his chest as I caught my breath.

"I want you," I whispered breathlessly.

He didn't say anything. He didn't have to. In one motion, we stood together, and he had me in his arms bridal style. In a few seconds, he was laying me down on the bed. He laid himself on top of me carefully.

One arm was positioned beside me while tracing my temple to my lips using his finger. He gazed into my eyes with tender love.

I raised my arms and wrapped them around him. He lowered his face to kiss me. No words had to be spoken and no apologies or explanations.

We weren't fucking, having sex, or even making love.

What we were doing was so much more than words or emotions could convey. We were confiding in the most intimate way. Our souls were intertwining and reconnecting between each other in every touch, skim, kiss, crease or look.

We were more than one. We were whole.

I laid my check on Zaliver's chest. His arms wrapped around me tightly as his kissed the top of my head and sighed.

"You do realize that I'll be annoyingly overprotective now right?" he said gruffly.

"Yup," I answered.

"And that I'll bring you with me almost everywhere I go?" he asked skeptical of my answer. I smiled and kissed his chest.

"Figured." He huffed at my response, still not believing that I was so calm and collected at his statements.

458

"Your oddly calm about it," he pointed out. I could hear the question in his voice.

I rolled my eyes and looked up at him. He was already gazing down at me with half playful, narrowed eyes.

"Because at some point you'll lay off yourself. Maybe not in days but in weeks or months definitely." His eyes tightened a little. He rubbed his thumb in a circular motion on my waist.

"I don't think I ever will," he whispered softly.

"What . . . What did it feel like?" I asked softly, unsure if he was going to answer.

I didn't have to explain my question, but he answered without looking my way.

"It felt as if my heart had been set on fire as if half of my beating heart had been ripped out of my chest. I felt as if the whole world had suddenly grew forty times its size, and here I was standing in one spot. This meaningless shell of a man with no direction, no meaning, no purpose, and with no one," he said with his voice sounding strained as if just thinking about it brought the pain back.

I rubbed my hand against his abdomen to remind him that I was still here. He looked down and smiled gratefully.

"You did begin to heal as soon as it landed on you, but not properly until I reached you and removed the tree branch. You were . . . bleeding." I flinched at that and I could just imagine. If I was under a tree branch as big and as heavy as the doctor said, then it must have completely crushed my skull. I shivered at the thought that Zaliver had to see that. No wonder his eyes looked haunted, lost, and pained.

"When I got you to the hospital, you were all ready healing from the outside, but I didn't know what kind of damage could have happened on the inside. Then the doctor began explaining. I lost control when he said that you could never wake up again. Here you were, alive but not living." He shook his head and looked up.

That almost seemed ironic.

"Alive but not living," I repeated the words softly, and it honestly frightened me to the core. Spending the rest of eternity in a coma was like sleeping in darkness without a hint of what the word outside was going though; what Zaliver would go through—alone by himself.

"And then seconds turned into minutes and hours, next thing I know, it became days. I-I didn't know what to do without you. I was so lost. I was so scared. I was tired, oh so tired. I began wondering how an immortal man could release himself from a pointless word. I felt like I was living without being alive," Zaliver confessed.

His words alarmed me, making me jolt up and look at him with uneasy eyes. I made sure he was focused on me before speaking.

459

"You must never, ever think like that. I don't care how bad the situation is. It always gets better if you want it." I straddled him and took his face in between my hands again. "Even in the darkest of times when everything seems hopeless, where no one is there to help or care, where it seems pointless and impossible, and you feel tired, just remember that even a blind man knows what light means.

You can only drown for so long before your lungs get used to it and crave for change, crave for oxygen. The surface will always wait for you. You just have to be strong enough to want it. If you can have hope for me than I can have hope for you. I've always believed in you, why don't we believe together? Yeah?" I asked him seriously.

He smiled at me with awed eyes. He reached up and tucked a strand of hair behind my ear.

"I will forever love you Vivian Grey, and I will forever spend my life proving to you that I am the lucky one to have been granted the opportunity to love you as I do," he said with an enchanting voice.

I leaned down and nuzzled his nose with mine.

"And I love you Zaliver Azrala. I'll try my best not to take over your space because I find it adorable," I joked. He laughed and pulled me to him, rolling me while he landed on top and making me laugh with him.

"Your facial hair tickles, shave the damn thing off," I said.

He pulled back with amused eyes, gazing down at me.

"Really?" he asked offended.

"Duh, did my laughter not give me away. I am not going to apologize if I wake you up in the middle of the night laughing. Go shave it off," I commanded. His eyes narrowed down on me before he got that familiar and welcoming wicked hint in his eyes.

"Maybe later, but right now . . ." he trailed off huskily.

~•~

"Oh my god Hannah, for the ninety-what?" I turned to ask Zaliver. He answered without looking up from the stack of papers.

"Sixth."

"For the ninety-sixth time, I'm fine today. Just like I was fine yesterday and the day before that, and the day before that, and the day before that until today. Girl, I love you but if I get another question, I'll be dropping hints to Mark on what you really think about his favorite TV show obsession," I threatened.

I heard her huff and then tsked me. I walked over to the couch in Zaliver's office and crossed one leg under my butt, knowing damn well it was going to fall asleep in like three minutes, and I'd regret sitting like this later.

460

"Fine, fine. But if you faint, don't wait up for a concerned Hannah at your doorstep. I'm just saying. Johnson says hi, get the hell away from me with that! MARK, JOHNNY'S GOT THE BACK SCRATCHER AGAIN. Dammit, I'm not itchy anymore! Vivian, I'll call you back in a few." I heard some shuffling and the sound of running feet on the other line.

"It's fine, tell him I said hi." I laughed as I heard Johnson let out a very girly scream on the other line.

"They are family is quite interesting," Zaliver said, pushing his papers all together and stacking them neatly, finishing up apparently.

"Yup, Hannah's someone special, Mark is adorably patient with her and Johnson . . . well." I laughed.

"And then there's his mate who refuses to acknowledge his existence until he returns the teddy bear he stole from her in high school. Quite the pair," he added absentmindedly.

I sat up quickly, surprised by what he said.

"Mila? That's why they aren't together? Over a stolen teddy bear?" I asked.

He nodded, stacking up some papers. "They have a long history of stealing each other's things before they knew they were mates. It sort of just happened that they decided that until everything was returned that they would actually acknowledge it."

My eyes narrowed on him.

"How do you know?" I asked suspicious and bewildered. He looked up with a raised brow.

"What don't I know?" he asked sarcastically and I rolled my eyes.

True to his words, Zaliver kept me by his side everywhere. It was rare for him to leave me alone. He would freak out for a minute and make me promise to call him whenever needed. He would always remind me not to shift at all, and he'd call the guards to hang with me to be sure.

He'd been able to calm down. A week passed since we spoke about it, so I'd call that progress. We chatted for a few minutes before someone knocked on the door. It was one of those days where he got to stay home and work. He stood it and grabbed my hand pulling me along with his.

It was Algebra.

I'd finally gotten to talk to him after I woke up three days later, and I was touched when he brought flowers and a little algebraic stuffed shape with him. He hugged me and told me how relieved he was to see that the only one with humor was still alive.

461

Zaliver kept quiet; quiet but not kind. When Zaliver opened the door, Algebra's expression made us both sober up from the happy mood.

"What is it?" Zaliver asked immediately.

"We found the door. It's now or later man. The men are ready. Your call Alpha," he said.

With the first sentence, I knew what he was talking about. The door which would allow them entrance up into the heavens where the gods who forced him to kill his brother and turned him into the powerful yet dangerously exotic beast that he is. Zaliver's hand tightened in mine, and his body tensed.

I wasn't going to lie. I was deathly afraid of what he was doing but this was beyond me. I knew that this was something that he needed to do. Even if I wanted to, I couldn't stop him from going, and I feared for the outcome but I trusted Zaliver.

He knew his limits. He wouldn't have gone through with this if there was a chance that he'd leave me alone. I squeezed his hand, snapping him back. He turned to look down at me with wild emotions. I could already see what he was thinking.

I shook my head.

"I'll be fine. Go. This is what you've been waiting for Zaliver. Go end this," I whispered urgently.

He looked down at me, searching for something in my expression. After a long pause, he turned to look at Algebra.

He nodded, without another word Algebra took off, to get ready I assume. Zaliver wrapped his arms around me and I did the same. We held onto each other tightly, breathing in one another. Both of our hearts pounded quickly, sensing what was about to happen.

He pulled away and brought my lips to his. I poured all of my love and fear into the kiss. We kissed with fiery passion and pulled back reluctantly.

"I'll be back soon," he promised.

"You better or I'll come up there looking for you myself," I said.

He smiled and kissed my forehead before pulling away, and as he walked out, I held onto his hand until I had to let go. I gripped the door hard as I watched him go. He turned back to look at me one last time.

"I love you," he yelled.

"I love you too, come back in one piece," I yelled back. He sped off without another glance.

I went back into the house and did something I haven't done in a really long time.

462

I prayed for hours, days, weeks. I didn't know how long had passed that I had lost count. I was hopeful and fearful. I cried, yelled, and believed. You would never know how truly desperately you love a person until you realize you could no longer function without them.

I couldn't help but think of everything that could go wrong and of everything that could fail, but I fought those thoughts for Zaliver.

It must have been early into the next morning when I heard the door open, and without even thinking, I flee off of the couch and ran to the door. There he stood covered with blood, beaten, and healing; all in one piece. I ran into his arms not caring that I was getting blood on me. I knew I probably looked as bad as he did but I didn't care. I wrapped my arms tightly around his as he did to me.

I let out a breath of sweet relief. I felt as if my soul and being could finally breathe.

"You're back," I said shakily and was about to cry.

"I am. I promised," he said happily.

I pulled away and was about to say something when I noticed a figure standing by the open door. I frowned and studied the person at the door.

This figure was unknown to me, and their slightly muscular figure that stood straight with their hands behind there back was a stranger to me. This figure stood with odd-looking clothing, something that seemed to come out of a movie where time was yet unknown and not comprehended yet.

However, the soft curl of their lips to show a polite smile, the strong jaw and sharp cheeks, the pitch black hair seemed familiar. The only thing that did not was this person's eyes, the lightest shade of green that was mesmerizing to look into with a mixture of the softest of the blue and green together.

The facial features were new yet familiar to me, and my eyes widened as something clicked. The facial features were familiar because . . . I looked towards Zaliver who had a grin on his face.

"Vivian, meet my brother—" he said. I looked back to the door and noticed him identical to my mate's facial features.

"Joshula."

CHAPTER 36

ZALIVER AZRALA

Death.

It lingers in the air, infiltrates our lungs and cuts off our oxygen. In some cases it even keeps the heart or mind alive just to carry out the pain through the body

From what I could remember, I've never truly feared death, at least not my own. I never thought that the mere thought of someone I love dying could cripple me that their death alone would cause me to want to follow, but that's what death does to people. It changes and morphs them, bringing out their true personality to the light of day.

I had died a thousand deaths and I knew there would be more to come, but death is never expected or welcomed most of the time. It's a constant reminder that what began can be put to an end at any given moment. That a loved one could be ripped from your caring arms and thrown into the embrace of cold and lost ones. Their whole essence were being tainted, taken and stripped. What is on the other side is something only those who have stayed can answer. Death is something that should not be trifled with, and yet here I stand today after a thousand deaths of my own.

I guess I should be thankful for the loopholes death had given me in my life, but sometimes . . . What gets down should stay down.

~•~

"I'll be back," I promised Vivian, looking down at her deep brown eyes filled with so much warmth—warmth and love for me. Just looking at her made me feel like a better person in general. She narrowed her adorable eyes on me.

"You better or I'll come up there looking for you," she responded. From the way her eyes held mine, I knew she wasn't playing. It caused mixed feelings to grow in me—amusement, worry, exasperation, and fear, but the first one won over.

464

She had no self-preservation sometimes, but I love her. That would be quite the sight, I had no doubt that Vivian would cause quite a scene if she somehow managed a way up there. That just made me want to finish things faster. I'd be home soon enough back in her arms spoiling her to her heart's desires. With her by my side alone pleases me; the rest was just a bonus.

I leaned down and kissed her forehead. I closed my eyes tightly and forcefully pulled away knowing fully well that if I dared to even look at her lips, I might never leave. I pulled away with weakening will power. My beast and I were both going haywire on leaving her so soon after just getting her back. But I had to do this, not only for me and my brother, but for her as well now.

I wouldn't have this hanging over her head like this . . . too soon.

I began walking away but I knew that I needed just one last glance at her. She wasn't wearing designer jeans or a red ball gown. Her hair sat on her shoulders a bit tangled while she unknowingly clutched onto the bottom of her sweater that was bigger than her size. Her big brown eyes looked my way with worry, fear, love, pride and belief. Because she believed her mate could do this.

She believed in me and in that moment I knew that whatever lingering doubts or worries I had were none existent because if she knew and believed that I would succeed, then I was beyond ready.

"I love you!" I yelled out knowing fully well that I could have whispered it and she would have heard just fine, but I wanted to yell it out. I wanted the world—or island in this case, to hear. Her face lit up as well as my unsteady heart.

"I love you too, come back in one piece!" She yelled back with just as much force as I did.

I stored the image of her standing there yelling her heartwarming words at me, and ran off without another glance for I knew I would be back. I would not leave her alone. Ever.

I made sure to close our link tightly, I didn't want her seeing or feeling anything from my end of the bond. I made it to the others in a matter of minutes. Lexero, Albericus, and Fern were all there in their battle wear. Venom stood off to the side. Each uniquely representing their brotherhood to their past.

Lexero had his long locks pulled up as usual. Two golden lines were painted under his black and gold outlined eyes. He wore golden arm bands around his biceps. From his neck to the top of his shoulders, he wore something that looked like a golden collar (both decorative and protective), bare footed and baggy jeans. The brutal lion gave me an excited nod as greeting and walked off to a group of waiting soldiers.

465

Albericus had changed from his casual wear to a more appropriate attire. His usual curly hair was pulled back. He wore armored vest and pants that would stay on him during and after his shift—a reluctant present from Aurora.

Fern lounged away from the others. His eyes closed as he meditated for battle, calling in his calm zone. Fern was one of the few werewolves who prefered to channel all the perks of being a wolf in human form. His favorite blade sat in front of him polished. I had no doubt that he had weapons under his black cloak. I looked over to Venom who was already nodding at me.

Venom was . . . a special case. He wore a white T-shirt with white dress pants and white converse on his feet. I nodded back at him; he knew what his role was and I had no doubt in his skill. He walked off and disappeared. He knew when I would need him. I went to the back of the cave, passing and preparing soldiers and went to change myself.

I stopped in front of the large glass case and took a moment to take it in again. What was in front of me had come from the darkest times of my life, had been with me in each, and every moment blood had been spilled by my hands.

Blood. Death. Fear. Hatred. Beauty and Evil. It all clung to it before it had all clung to me.

The beast inside traced all the familiar patterns with recognition, but instead of longing it looked at it with neutral acceptance. This would be the last time I wore this because as soon as I was done. I would enjoy my new life with my mate beside me. I opened the case and prepared standing in front of the mirror. I couldn't help but look on at the sight before me.

A dark-haired man with blue eyes looked back at me. His features were attractive and alluring to the viewer, but he was surrounded by darkness. Black intricate armor covered my body, clinging to my muscular form with perfection. The armor was both a form of art and something that would make any stay away from me.

My legs and the front of my thighs were covered in a thin layer of black material that moved easily with my form but would not tear at the attack of just any material. I had black protective armor over me covering my groin and the front of my thighs. The material stretched all over my body to stop at the beginning of my neck. My chest was covered with the same black armor from the top to the bottom of my abdomen, strapped together in the back with two silver chains. The top of my feet were covered with the same armor and leather soils for my feet and nothing else.

The reason for fearing the armor was because of its artistic detail carved to perfection. A story of brutality, violence, blood, fear, and power. But that was the thing; it wasn't just a story. Long ago, I had

466

discovered two things about my armor in battle. Firstly, with each and every kill, an image would carve itself upon my armor. Secondly, if those before me were to stand too close . . . the images would move to show not only all of my kills but their death as well. An enchanted armor with a brutal tale.

On both of my wrists were two thick silver bands with enchanting patterns on it. I looked down at my hands and sighed. I strapped both of the old customer silver swords onto my side, for gods to be fighting over it was never done with the modern-day technology because it would never be seen as a battle where blows and force were interchanged between a man and his opponent. I looked back at the glass case which had the last piece of my suit.

Every hero and every villain had a piece that they were recognized with. Batman by the bat sign, the Flash by the lightning bolt, the Joker by his maniacal smile, and the devil with his horns. I was no different.

I reached in and took the piece off, holding it in my hands. I could feel power surge through me. My memory was trying to surface at the sight of it, but I pushed them down. I put it on, strapping it on tightly to the back of my head and turned to look at the mirror once more.

On my face was a type of mask for the lower half though. In the shape of a protruding lycan snout and jaw, a set of an outlined sharp teeth attached. It was made to accommodate my real snout when I shifted the lower half of my face, half man, half lycan on the battlefield.

In the mask I could open my mouth and take a bite out of anything or mainly, anyone. It was both protective gear and a sign of who I was. It was like the crown of a king. I half shifted my face and felt as the lower half of my face filled out the familiar piece. When I bared my teeth, my canines would pass the masks showing an even more frightening effect.

A silver crown for a silver king.

My eyes completed the process. In an instant, the blue was tainted by the black, taking over completely. Gone was Zaliver Azrala and in his place was the all feared and brutal Lupus Deus.

Power, dominance, and darkness radiated from every pore in my body. I let go of a portion of my control over the darkness within. The nails on my fingers grew out to claws while a thin layer of smooth, shiny black fur sprouted, seemingly blending in with the material I wore underneath. My muscles tensed and relaxed as they thickened and my build grew twice in size. The beast smiled back at me in my reflection.

Leaving the room and exiting, I wasn't surprised to see the soldiers here all lined up outside in rows. At the sight of me, recognition, fear, and respect were shown on their faces as I walked past them with radiating power. One by one they dropped to their knees as a show of respect and submission. There was a time when wolves would scream at the mere sight of me walking by, the body armor and mask giving my intentions away.

Death.

I found the others in the front of the lines with respect and grim-faced. They too had interaction with the silver crowned king at his worst. Lexero whistled and shook his head at me.

"You're pretty freaking scary when you want to be, you know that?" he said gravely, the lion was not one for lying so I just nodded at him.

Fern, although a friend, was still a werewolf so he too dropped to his knees and then stood. Albericus too made his way to my right side after. He gave me a brisk shake of his head and the air-filled with excitement, tension and seriousness in an instant.

I looked at the soldiers in front of me, but I opened my mid link to all of the soldiers already in place elsewhere so they too would hear the words I spoke.

"Today you will either die a hero or live to become a legacy, but you will not have both. You will all help me accomplish something that has been panning out for more than the years you have all lived. By doing this you are proving to your Alpha what true loyalty is, what true family is, and for that I am grateful.

You have been training, sparring, and preparing for this day half of your lives. I know that each and every one of you has something to lose and I promise you here and now as each other's witnesses that for those of you that do not return home, your loved one will be taken cared of. Today will be a day to never forget.

You will fight beside me, you will die beside me and you will be remembered by me. You will go into this battle not as tools or pawns but as my soldiers, my warriors and I'll be damned, my killing machines!" I smirked at the last part with a dark twisted humor growing in me.

The air thickened at my emotions while the other wolves were feeding off of it and began buzzing with anticipation; blood lust was stirring in their veins.

"You have all prepared for this battle with bravery and in return, I will give you the power of a hundred men, the brutality of a scorned women, the blood lust of Satan himself and the taste of true darkness," I said invigorating.

Without a second to spare I found each and every one of their silver linings, their individual strings in my mind and let the darkness within me touch them. Every soldier in the crowd grew twice their size, their claws coming out, snarls and howls filled the air. All at the same

468

time their eyes flashed silver and stayed silver. This is what I like to call the Lupus Deus effect.

Addicting. Strong. Powerful. Deadly.

I had once almost told Vivian what it meant for a wolf to have silver eyes. Luckily, she never asked again how I stayed strong with so many wolves using my strength. Easy. With each death of a wolf, I got stronger.

It was unfortunate for them but great for me. I let out a little chuckle at the sight of the overly excited wolves. There was only one way for a man like me to get so powerful so quickly and that was by the death of others. Simple. Twisted.

My beast hummed with dark intent and impatience. He had been far away from a true battle in years and if this was to be his last he sure as hell was going to make it a bloody one.

Albericus let out a small cough, bringing my attention back. His eyes held weariness and a hint of pity for the wolves but he concealed the rest. The others eyed me, reminding me that we weren't out on the battlefield and that I had to calm down a little.

"Venom said that as soon as you're ready, we'll have thirty-six seconds to teleport to their location and then an eight minute window to get through the door with all of the soldiers," Fern informed me calmly.

"Is he ready?" I asked.

Teleportation was a very unique and dangerous thing to do in this world, not only because it was something only the teleporter should do, but because we were teleporting so many people.

"Venom has some shady contacts. The snake holds his tongue on how he met him though," Lexero murmured, looking at the means of our transportation. A shady looking guy indeed.

"You are faster than you will ever be in your life again. Move as soon as he opened the portal and do not stop to wonder about where your are, just go. Run and do not stop until you reach Venom," I ordered the men.

They all nodded at the same time in understanding, momentarily calming down and returning to their still state.

A blue haired man with a twitching eye and arm who appeared to be sick and insomniac walked up nervously but with an alertness to him, obviously wanting to bolt but we all caught the words he mumbled under his breath.

"Damn snake. Out of all the ways I could start paying him off, this is how he wants me to do it. Fucking Vipers fault . . . Gonna kill her if I get the chance for getting me in this mess with her brother. . ." He quieted down once he got to us. I wasn't the only one who lifted a brow at his ramblings.

Shuffling unsteadily on his feet his jaw clenched when he neared us, we easily towered over the lanky guy.

"I'll try to hold it open for as long as possible but thirty-six seconds is as much as I can promise with the amount of people here . . ." he trailed off. His mouth was thinning.

"Just give us a warning," I ordered. My voice waas thick with animalistic intent.

"Fine. At the count of three have your men run over there," he pointed a few feet away. "And don't stop," he stated. I ignored the way he leaned away from me.

I didn't have to give the order out again as all the men were prepared, although I knew I would be in before any of them could. After all, out of everyone I was the one who had the vendetta here.

"Ready?" he asked loudly, rolling his sleeves up to his bony elbows and showing off two tattoos that looked identical on each arm.

Two clocks. Looking closely I noticed that they weren't identical. On one hand, it looked to be going clockwise while on the other it was counter-clockwise. Past and future. Here and there. I assumed.

"Just count," I said gruffly, my knees bending slightly.

"One, two, three!"

I took off as soon as I caught sight of a purple electric spark in the direction, the blue haired guy pointed in. Passing everyone who were barely lifting their feet up to spring, I was the first one through as I thought, for a moment my body felt weightless and uneven.

It made me uncomfortable, but I pushed past the feeling that was telling me that I was not in control due to me not standing firmly on the ground with both feet. I was blind for a moment but I told myself not to stop running even if I couldn't tell up from down.

Altogether it ended as soon as it began. When I had my eyesight and gravitational balance back, my feet silently dashed over dirt and moved me past large trees. I caught both sight and sound of a large group a few feet ahead and halted all movement.

All forty thousand and eight hundred men now present. My beast paced in my mind back and forth, snarling and snapping his teeth at any outer movement. His mouth was salivating at the thought of what was going to go down in a few minutes.

I didn't have to turn around and check for all of my companions. I could sense them all moving as one, running without stopping until they got to their destination. Albericus, Lexero, and Fern appeared beside me.

"Never realized how many we recruited . . ." Fern whispered a bit beguiled. I caught a faint sense of where his thoughts where amount of chaos and fighting were going on at the same time. Battlefield tactics and possible attack ideas—an ultimate game of Call of Duty.

"From Venom's directions, the door is just past those trees over there," Albericus informed me. "All we're waiting on is your say Alpha and this begins. What's your call?" he asked me seriously. His eyes were looking for something. Hesitation or a change of heart maybe?

I looked in the direction of which he had pointed to, past all the eager soldiers, through the trees until my eyes caught sight of the door.

"Gather your group of men and prepare yourselves for the bloodiest battle you'll ever get the pleasure of getting to fight in. We're going into the war zone," I declared. I turned back to look at my beta who acted on my command.

"Well I guess this is it. Gather around you over excited pups, you're about to become real wolves!" Fern yelled out, collecting his section of skilled wolves.

"Damn, we'll I guess we're doing this," Lexero muttered with his usual mediocre humor dimmed. The lion was lazy until provoked. Someone would have to stab him before he'd become a real beast on the battlefield.

Albericus didn't have to say anything. He already had the attention of his men which left the rest to me. I walked over to them and made sure to project my voice both physically and mentally for those in the back.

"We will be going in first so it is likely we will be attacked first and some of you will instantly die. There's also a chance that that won't happen and that they have something else up their sleeves. As soon as we enter move to the right side no matter what you see, hear or smell, a majority of the time whatever is haunting you is really just in you head.

We will be the group guiding the others through, they will follow our lead. If you find something alarming, do not hold it in. You will get yourself and those around you killed. Your strength will allow you to take on a large group but remember your training. Don't try to show off how many kills you can do. Take on only the amount you know will not end up with you dead. Good luck to you all."

With that, I turned around and marched through the dense trees, noting how foggy and moist everything was. The side of me that was still active and not focused completely on what was to come could sense a small pack close by. I could sense their alphas need to check on the reason for so many wolves uniting near his pack, thinking it could be attack he wasn't sure on what steps to take so I sent a calming message only his wolf would comprehend to calm him down. The last thing I needed was an alpha getting in my way and delaying us.

Past the trees and hidden for the sight of certain creatures, I saw the familiar door. Although the appearance of the "door" was ever changing,. If anything it resembled a ruined and old doorway of what could have been an impressive medieval structure now. In the middle of a forest however, medieval old ruined structures did not omit their own force field for protection and have an aurora that kept not only any being from getting closely but animals as well.

As I made my way to the door Lexero, Albericus, Fern, and Venom appeared one by one behind me or to my side with their own group of soldiers trailing behind them. Their own energy and anticipation mixed in with the beasts blood lust which they feed off of created for a tense and thick air.

As a god who's used this door many times in the past to come down to do the others bidding, I could enter the force field without trouble, but the others would fare differently. I was proven correct when I set a foot into the force field with no trouble and an overeager soldier behind me followed too closely. He immediately caught fire and turned to ash. I turned to look over my shoulder at the pile of ash while the others immediately halted and froze unsure. My teeth flashed at them in what must have been a threatening way when it really was an amusement.

"Ah, fuck man. I got kids. I have to go home after this. Don't tell me I'm gonna die before I even get to the actual battle field," Lexero cursed. I could tell from his fidgeting that he wanted to try to step into the force field. Curiosity would kill the cat.

"Give me a moment and you'll all be able to enter. Unless you decide that sticking your toe is worth never seeing your kids again Lexero, but go ahead, be my guest," I muttered.

I would be the one to both open the door for the others to pass through the and grant them all permission to enter. The other gods might have banned me from coming back up there by their own rule, but once a god always a god. I had as much right as they did to use the door. Walking closer to the ruins of the door, I stood before it and knew that once. I activated it there would be no going back. Each God had their own unique way of activating the door. Even after all of these years I still remembered mine.

With one clawed hand, I raised it to the air and swiped as if I were clawing at something, four long, animalistic glowing marks appeared mid-air within seconds. As they grew and expanded until reaching the edges of the door, white fog and glowing light see need to make its way from out of the door. I wasn't done though. One last thing needed to be done to remove the outer force field that would allowed the others to enter with me.

Throwing my head back I released a ground shaking howl that warned my enemies that I was coming for them.

I ended it is with a snarl as soon as I saw the barriers coming down. My group wasted no time and marched in with me. Unstrapping both of my swords, I held them in both hands.

I heard it before I even saw it, swishing and maneuvering my sword in a swinging motion over my face. I cut an arrow as it neared my face and let out an annoyed snarl. This did not detain me or my men as we marched in through the thick fog nearly blinding us. I knew that it would not hold out for long. Fog was most definitely not Alstha's strength. I couldn't wait to stab that bitch in the gut for years of brutal punishments.

My ears caught the sound of more arrows flying through the air, hitting their targets and angered growls from hit soldiers, but those that wanted to shift couldn't because it would leave them uncovered. I was the first to make it out of the cover of the fog and was prepared for the wave of arrows sent my ways.

"There he is. Aim to kill!" A strong female voice yelled over the sound of pained cries. Before all arrows were sent my way, I caught sight of a tall woman with a sword in her crossed hands as she stood beside a row of thousands of archers in red. The blond-haired, glowing green-eyed bitch smirked at me.

"Fire!!" As soon as the first arrow was released into the air in my direction, the others followed suit.

I gripped my swords tightly and at a blinding speed began cutting arrows in half as I moved forward, I crossed my arms and moved my wrists in repetitive short movements like a fan would do but in all half directions. For a long moment, I was buried in a sea of brown, and the only thing I concentrated on was slicing down every single thing.

Even through all of the chaos, I could not ignore each silver lining that dimmed and transferred its strength to me adding to my speed and focus. When the last arrow was cut, I stood straight knowing that if I were to look down I would no doubt see the fallen bodies of those who did not service the assault.

My black eyes met with grim green ones. Alstha uncrossed her arms and stood up straighter, taking step forward her armor gleamed in the suddenly gloomy and deserted field. She had the power to manipulate the setting outside of the entrance of the temple they loved so much.

"Zalvius, there really is no need for all of this, honestly, we should be able to talk about this, get both sides of the story and then," she said in her critiquing tone, the one that irked me to no end. The usage of that name caused my eyes to narrow on her threateningly that I pointed a sword at her. All I heard was bullshit coming from her mouth.

"It's Zaliver and you're right, there isn't. So why don't you stay right there and call off your new play toys so that I can enjoy watching you suffer by my sword?" I taunted her, watching as the black rims that outlined her green eyes turn red. "Guess not. Either way I'll still enjoy your pain before anyone else's." Her eyes went large before she finally composed herself, but it was too late.

In the battle field, you are not to show your enemy your fear. In the vast distance between us with all the beating and silent hearts, I caught scent of something that excited both the beast and me something more exciting than a predator's kill or hunt—the scent of the prey's fear.

"I am trying to tell you something but if you want to do this the hard why, then I am fine by it. You have been on this earth for far too long, doing as you pleased and taking the lives of others. You are under the impression that I fear you. The great Lupus Deus. You are mistaken, boy. I taught you everything you know. I will cut you down like the useless waste of space you always were." She spat out, trying to cover her slip up with anger.

"Turns out you were a lousy teacher." I began walking in her direction, prepared for any movement that would come from their side. I was on a schedule and had no time from this wrench unless it was to make her suffer.

She too began taking steps towards me, slower more deliberate steps. It wasn't until I was but a few feet from her that the six foot three woman notice that in the build I was in that I towered over her by many inches. In most of the fights that she had with me she had never fought me at this size and I hadn't even fully shifted.

Oh, this was going to be quick.

Taking our proximity, I flashed over to her and swiped my sword above her head which she ducked in time and turned. With that movement, the fighting began from both sides as they ran towards each other. No one from her side or mine tried to interfere with our own fight. Snarling, clashing, and growls filled the air.

I held both swords up on either side of me, blocking, and cutting off any advance moves, she threw my way. I couldn't help but open my mouth and let my tongue go over my sharp teeth. My gums were suggesting I take a bite out of her at that very moment. Her own eyes caught sight of my canines and clenched her jaw tight.

The tip of her sword poked at the side of my rib in a sudden movement of hers that would have been painful if I hadn't blocked the rest just in time. She pulled back and dropped to the ground, and brought her swords up. I jumped into the air and curled up in a ball and then sparing back down in front of her, spinning around her and giving her playful nudge that could have been a deadly blow if I wished for it to be. She stumbled before twisting to face me with a pale face.

"You've slowed. Old age maybe?" I jumped backwards when she made a jab move at me at the last moment.

She managed a scratch to the left side of my face when I went for her side. She quickly backed up when I let out a hiss. I quickly healed just as fast,but it still pissed me off. Triumph flashed in her eyes until I returned the action. Unlike me, she didn't possess the quick healing gene.

From the corner of my eye, I caught Albericus unarm one of the soldiers and duck under him. He spun back around and decapitated the soldier. Without wasting another moment, he threw the sword in the air, shifted and threw himself on top of the enemy and took a chunk out of him before shifting back to catch the sword and plunge it into the man's heart. I looked back to my fight.

Alstha had began to bore me.

I swung a sword down to try to amputate one of her legs but she jumped upped into the air. Anticipating this movement, I stuck out my other which she blocked and then tried to swing her other sword for my head. I truly did love how gravity worked sometimes.

As she came down from her high jump, she was so focused on trying to stab me with one of her swords that she didn't notice the sword that went to amputate one of her legs swung back in a second attempt.

The sound of my sword slicing through her flesh and then cutting the bone in clean half met my ears out of everything going on in the field.

Her pain filled shout beat all of the others coming from the field. Immediately the cloudy and deserted field began to faulted as her concentration wavered. She fell over and much to my surprise instead of cradling her bloodied leg held up a sword and pointed it to me with gritted teeth. I could see her sweating. Those around us seemed to stop what they were doing which just so happened to get them killed since I did tell my men that distractions would get them killed. I guess Alstha didn't believe in the same thing because only her warriors stopped to gap at her in disbelief and horror.

I picked up her leg with my claws and walked over to her. In all of her years, I'm guessing the great and mighty Alstha was ever defeated. I don't know what was bothering her more. The fact that she lost or the fact that I had her leg in my hand.

"As a god, we can not die. Of course, you knew that but did you know that even if one of our limbs is to be removed that we can still reattach it?" I asked her calmly. Her paling green eyes narrowed as much as they could on me and then flickered to her leg.

"I was bored one day. But that's not the best part." I waved her bloodied leg in front of her. "No, the best part is that even when unattached to the body, you can still feel whatever is happening to your leg." To prove myself I dug my claws into her leg, blood began trickling down my hand.

She dropped her swords and clung to her half leg that was bleeding heavily on the dead grass. Screams and pleads left her lips as she kicked out with her only good leg as a reaction to the pain.

Years of having others do her dirty work have made her slow and pitiful. She wasn't even half of the warrior that I remembered. It was embarrassing really.

"Music to my ears. What's that?" I barked out a humorless laugh that sounded disturbing even to my ears.

"I am sorry, I did you horribly wrong many time. I was wrong to have done what I did. Just stop, I beg of you!!" she screamed. This time when the sky flickered again, it became clear as she lost full concentration. Now I could enter the grounds without having to go through all of that mental bullshit she loved to play with.

I stepped up to her crouched body with her hateful and fearful eyes looking up at me. Leaning down, I made sure her leg was out of her reach as I dug my claws in deeper. She opened her mouth in that silent scream type of way. My gums once more made me want to take a chunk out of her face with my teeth but I held back. That was for later.

"If I accepted every 'Sorry' that came my way, I wouldn't be where I am today now, would I? And besides, I doubt you mean it." I pulled away with another laugh, she glared at me with livid pain filled green eyes, the rims of her eyes turning a nasty shade of yellow.

"Venom!" I called out, not removing my eyes from her until caught I caught the sight of something white making its way in my direction.

Only Venom would manage to remain blood free on a battlefield, not a white hair out-of-place. As he made his way past the fighting warriors with his hands in his pockets completely relaxed, a group of Alstha's soldiers caught sight of the seven-foot, completely blood free snake and decided to attack him in a group.

There was a reason as to why Venom needed absolutely no body armor on the battlefield.

As he caught sight of the four armed warriors making their way to him, he rolled his golden eyes and sighed as if in annoyance. I noted how I wasn't the only one watching anymore. Alstha had followed my eyes and stared weakly at Venom in confusion and worry.

Venom's skin suddenly seemed to be covered with faint outlines of scales. His facial features becoming more defined and sharper if possible. His vertical pupil expanding for a second before quickly coming back thinner than before. When the men neared Venom, he stopped and waited for them to get closer. His jaw opened for a moment allowing me to catch a glimpse of his snake-like tongue darting out.

When the men surrounded him he didn't move which surprised them but they all went to lunge at him with their weapons. Did no one teach them to fear anything that was fearless when faced with death?

Venom opened his mouth and blew out a large breath, something that resembled white smoke in the shape of a long snake left his mouth. The white smoke began slithering around the four men quickly until it had them all in its hold. Venom stood in the middle and watched as the men swiped their swords at the smoke to try to get it away but nothing they did stopped it from tightening its grasp on their necks.

Their swords dropped as they clawed at their throats with their eyes growing large. Their faces were turning red until I caught the distinctive sound of four necks snapping at the same time. The snake released its hold on the slumping bodies and slithered its way around Venom's neck and suddenly disappeared.

Venoms face returned back to normal as he stepped over the bodies and made his way to me. I looked down with half amused eyes to the supposed war-goddess who had turned paler than was probably good. Her eyes showed horror and disbelief. As Venom stepped next to me, she began crawling away slowly so I put the end of my foot on her leg with force. At the sound of a snap I realized I had applied too much force and broke her ankle.

My beast and I found the sound of her whimpers amusing.

"This is my good friend, Venom, who specializes in many things, but I asked him for one of his special abilities just for you." I handed Venom the leg which he took without even blinking and opened his mouth showing two long fangs. Biting into it, I turned to look at the moaning Alstha on the ground, bloodied, broken and clueless as to how much I had waited for this day.

Alstha who had already began moaning in pain suddenly stopped and looked up at me or more specifically to her leg which Venom had finished biting into. Her eyes were focusing in and out, and her pupils growing and shrinking.

"W-What have you d-done—" She didn't even get to finish her sentence because in the next moment, her body began thrashing, shaking, and spasming all over the place as she lost all control over her movement. A revolting green foam began coughing out of her mouth uncontrollably, the stench of it possibly even more so.

"See Venom? If you didn't take it by his name is venomous, but luckily for you, I only asked for one of his specific gifts. Right now, your nerves must be on fire as the venom enters your system and heads towards your heart. Instead of stopping it because you're immortal, all it is going to do is help keep it in your system as you pump it even more into your own body as your body continues to come back after every death. I've been told that it's worse than being burned alive because you're still conscious enough to feel the venom turn into acid. Bet that hurts, huh?" I mused knowing fully well that my words probably meant nothing to her at the moment.

I began to turn away when I looked over my shoulder once more.

"One more thing. In order to get this to stop, you must remove the poison from the origin of bite. Why don't you go hide that leg somewhere in this large planet of ours we live in Venom?" I said as he nodded and took a step back into the chaos, disappearing from my sight. I turned away from the fallen warrior god.

Now that the sky and the path ahead of me was clear of Alstha's mind games, I could now get through without wasting time. As I walked through the fighting, I felt the edge of a sword point against my side. No doubt, one of her soldiers was being brave. Without turning, I reached behind me and grabbed onto a scrawny neck with my bare claws.

Pulling the brown-haired kid in front of me, I brought him up to my face with his feet dangling as he gasped for air.

"Now, why don't you give me a good reason not to snap your neck?" I snarled out quietly, making sure to bare my canines at him. His eyes went down to my teeth as his body began thrashing violently. He couldn't breath.

I relaxed my hold on his neck for a moment, enough to let him gasp for air.

"That's what I thought," I muttered, all ready getting ready to take a bite out of his face.

"W-Wait! I can be o-of val-value," he rasped out, tapping his hand on my own. I narrowed my eyes and then thought about something.

I dropped him and then grabbed the back of his head, dragging him along by the hair as I pushed past everyone. I had to snap some necks along the way but after a while they soon stopped approaching me. The cowards.

"What do you need the kid for?" Fern yelled a few feet away, pulling out a gun from his back pocket and shooting an upcoming enemy. He jogged over to me and pointed to the kid. I shouldn't have been surprised to see the gun, but it still seemed wrong to have it during battle. To easy.

Without looking at him, I answered squinting my eyes before me. I could see the temples ahead, but the trouble would be getting there without trouble, Alstha was down but that didn't mean they didn't plan back up. Fate would have made sure they were ready for anything, but so was I.

"He's going to be my pebble," I said with a malicious grin.

"What?" Fern asked confused, but that didn't matter.

"Where's Lexero?" I asked him, turning back to look into the vast space filled with fighting, falling and dying men. Both sides. Each death strengthening me as my power returned in double fold.

"Look for the cat playing with his food," Fern muttered uninterested as he pointed across from me with end of his gun.

"Dammit Lexero! Finish him and get your ass over here!" I snapped out to him.

Without turning to look at me Lexero held up his hand with a thumbs up before lunging at the much large soldier and from the sight of it, ripping his throat out with his bare teeth. He stood up and walked over to us with blood all over his face. He wiped at it messily with the side of his arm. His black and golden eyes were bright with excitement.

"Kill joys!" he sang. I looked at him, he lifted up his hands. "Okay, I'm good. I'm good," he added.

Without saying anything else I turned and went in the direction of the temple. They followed behind, I mind linked Albericus.

Take care of this field, keep me informed if you see anything suspicious.

Okay. He answered quickly.

Unlike below, here the sky was a mixture of different colors blended all together or just near each other, the stars were always out at every point of the day as well as the moon and the sun. On my right was the sun with all of the lighter colors while on the left the moon glowed in a side of darker shades,the temple looked large, modern and yet very ancient all at the same time. The pasty to the temple was a clear one, however we were surrounded by forests, rivers, clouds, and magic. Anything could be manipulated by anyone.

After walking for a moment, I paused at the stoned river. All I had to do was walk across the stones and that would be it.

Easy.

"Stop," I commanded the two who seemed not to mind the calmness of the river, their instincts telling them there was no danger in the calming waters. I knew better though. I knew who this river was made to represent.

Fern and Lexero looked at me confused and they looked around before shaking their heads at each other and looking back at me.

"What—"

"There's nothing—"

"Shh," I hushed them quickly.

479

I had almost forgotten about the kid in my grasp, but his struggling made me look back down at him. He looked up at me. I grinned down at him which caused him to begin to thrash around.

"Hello, Pebble," I said sardonically.

Without another world, I rung the kid with all of my strength in front of me in front of the river. He let out a terrified scream. His body was mid way of making it across the river when from the very calming waters something that would only appear out of your nightmares, set itself free out of the water.

A humongous slimy, purple monster jumped out, clumps and gut jutting out from the almost transparent thin skin. Two deformed fins at its sides opened up to show multiple eyes in different colors and sizes blinking at us. The front where it's face was supposed to be had two empty sockets, but as it opened its mouth, its tongue which was made out of what appeared to be multiple rotten and decaying human hands stuck together stuck out and reached for the boy's body.

It made a sound of an innocent little girl laughing and swallowed the boy whole and dived back into the calming waters without a splash.

"Good bye, Pebble."

Next to me, Fern turned and began throwing up while Lexero scrunched up his face with disgust.

"This is why I tell my kids to stick to meat you can hunt on land," Lexero muttered.

"I'm gonna be sick . . . shit, I am sick. What in hell's name was that?" Fern coughed out horrified.

"You really don't want to know," I muttered, looking around for the owner and sole creator.

"Yeah, you might be right," he mumbled, wiping at his mouth, both men now stood more alert of their surroundings.

I narrowed my eyes ahead of me at the sight of a hunched figure appeared behind of a tree far away from us. The figure neared us calmly, at its own pace. I felt the hairs on my arm stand on end. Fern and Lexero crouched down as they caught sight of the figure approaching, they looked up at me in explanation, but I didn't have to give one.

"I told them you wouldn't fall for old Berna's trick. You're much too aware of your instincts and you never did like animals, didn't you Zalvius? It's been awhile, boy," the long-haired man with olive skin spoke grimly, his orange eyes scanning over me and my companions. Before me was the god of intelligence and instinct.

"Eccasto, it's Zaliver like I told Alstha; and no I did not. How could I when you had Berna swallow me too once?" His face tighten at the mention of Alstha, but other than that he did not show much more.

"Zalvius . . . you must stop now, we have wronged you, yes. But I'm here to tell you on behalf of everyone that—" he began in a calming voice, instead of coining that exactly it just pissed me off even more.

"What? You're sorry? Yeah thanks, that's all I've wanted to hear all along. Now I can happily go on my way. Even you can't be as stupid as to believe that an apology is what I will accept from you all." I snarled at him, anger pulsing through me at the mere thought of a stupid and worthless apology. Years. I spent years of torture and humiliations for their entertainment before I had any power.

He was god of instinct and if his instincts were not telling him to run, then something was seriously wrong because he was about to pay. He grounded his teeth before speaking once more.

"No, I understand that after everything we put you and your brother through that you'd have motive to want our lives, but we were young and foolish. Times have aged and matured us,we even tried to do you good by—"

By the direction his words were going, I knew what he was going to say and I did not like it at all. Abhor twisted in the pit of my stomach at the thought of his lips uttering her very name. My body began to tremble a bit, I took a calming breath and then whispered lowly.

"If you even mention her name, I will make sure that pain is worse than what Alstha is going through becomes your companion," I said slowly and calmly. This was not a threat, it was a promise.

He halted and blinked at me an expression that conveyed both dread and showed just how truly bothered, he was by fighting his own instincts that must have warned him that I was something he would not be able to handle.

Perhaps in the past he might have been able to take me on, but he himself made sure that long ago I would be invincible.

He nodded in understanding, his eyes looked over at Fern and Lexero, who had stood in listening to the conversation. I had once briefed them over who each of the gods where and what they represented.

"Where is Fate, Eccasto?" I asked knowing fully well that he would not give up his friend's position for nothing in the world. Couldn't hurt to try.

"You and I both know that I will not say and nothing you do to me will make me. Zalvius, years have passed, you were human when it happened, the human memory is a poor thing to depend on." I bared my teeth at him in agitation.

"You speak of things I do not wish, nor care to hear about Eccasto, if you will not tell me where the old coward is than perhaps your time has come. I will ask you only once more, where is the old fool who likes to play with the lives of others as he pleases?" I demanded from him. Eccasto shook his head in silence, orange eyes showing his refusal. I tsked at him.

"All right then." I turned to look at Lexero. He understood what I meant without having to say anything.

"How do I get across the river without getting eaten by the ugly version of Finding Nemo here?" he asked, looking into the river with concern.

"You can cross without a problem. Eccasto here can only summon Berna once and that already takes most of his strength, you really shouldn't have done that. For the god of intelligence and instinct you sure do make stupid mistakes," I said, walking over the stones, crossing over the river. "You did then and you continue to do so now. You truly do not learn from your mistakes," I pointed out.

Eccasto took some steps back and believing I was going to pounce on him crouched himself in preparation for a fight. Lexero crossed over, followed by a weary Fern who kept looking into the water with uneasiness.

"I will take you down Zalivus, I am weakened, not weak," he spoke with calculation as if he already had a plan on taking me down, which no doubt would not have worked.

"Not much of a difference, but it is not me you will be fighting. Revenge does not necessarily have to be by my hand," I said with a smirk.

His face showed confusion so I looked over to Lexero who waved at Eccasto with a large grin. Eccasto let out a laugh and stood up straight, putting his hands on his stomach. Lexero's eyes narrowed on Eccasto. He just offended a prideful lion.

"Him? You're having me fight a weakling like him, a half-breed cat? With you I'll admit that I would have not had a very good chance but I'm beginning to think you've lost your touch by having me fight this," He pointed at Lexero without looking at him. "disappointment of a thing. He can't even fully shift." Eccasto snorted in disbelief.

I shook my head and took a step back.

Lexero's shoulders lifted up and down with his heavy breaths. His claws were coming out from his fingertips. His teeth were sharpening as he bared his teeth at the distracted god of instinct while his face was half transforming into that of a lion.

"Actually, quite the opposite. See, I knew that you being the cocky son of a bitch that you are wouldn't take anyone else but me serious, so what I did was place my very prideful lion friend in front of you.You did the insulting yourself, but I think now would be a good time to warn you that he doesn't like being told what he can and can't do. As long as you don't bring up the half-breed thing you should be slightly okay . . . oh wait."

Eccasto frowned, his face morphed into one of realization, but of course it was too late to realize his mistake. He had underestimated, insulted, and seriously pissed off his opponent. He turned to look at Lexero with his eyes widening on the sight of his match he turned back to look at me with anger in his eyes.

"You—" Before he had the chance to finish what would have probably been insult for me, Lexero lunged at him, knocking him straight down with the force of the impact.

They immediately began fighting but it was clear that even though Eccasto was the god in the fight, Lexero's anger and brutal strength overpowered him, not to mention the anger that fueled him to show that he was better than the god. Better than a full shifter. It was a sore subject.

I nodded at Fern to stay here with the two of them if something was to go wrong, but I doubted that. Lexero's fresh anger and wounded pride would do Eccasto untreatable damage; much more than any anger I had towards him. As I said, revenge does not always have to be done by your own hands.

I made my way to the temple, alert for anyone who would try to stop my entrance. Both doors were ajar, showing the open space and cream marble walls with many passages and hallways. I looked around trying to sense anyone when I caught the familiar scent of a frolicsome she-wolf.

I followed the scent down a long hallway passage, kicking down a large dark brown wooden door I palled in without a care.

There on the couch with popcorn in her lap sat the silver-haired, black-eyed, graceful Mother Luna. Her dainty little features making her extremely feminine, and I'm sure that had she stood up her curves would have pointed it out as well, but I did not care much for her.

I had nothing against the her. She did not interact with me at all when I was here for all of those years. If she hid Fate, however, I will hurt her even if in some way she is like some long distance relative of mine.

"Where is he Luna?" I asked, straight to the point.

She blinked her big dark eyes at me and then reached down into the bowl for popcorn, putting it in her mouth and chewing slowly. Something about the action reminded me of someone.

When she was done, she spoke. "Well, hello Zaliver. Long time no see. How are you?" Her eyes scanned me. "Never mind, you do not have to answer that, you look busy," she muttered while standing up.

Instead of feeling annoyed, I just sighed and shook my head. Even my beast was not angered by her unimportant rambling.

"Luna, where?" I asked again. She sighed and stood up. I watched her carefully as she walked past me.

"Come on, I'm not picking sides. Just so you know, next time people try to tell you something you should stop and listen, even if they are people who you despise," she said. My eyes narrowed on her back.

"What do you—" I tried asking but she interrupted me.

"Now he wants to listen," she muttered under her breath, eating some popcorn.

She led me deep into the temple. If my memory serves me right, we were on Fate's private wing. He'd never let anyone go near his wing, and there would always be guards making sure of that and to see not here made me suspicious of his true where abouts.

Luna stopped at two large doors and without stopping opened them up. Looking in, I felt my energize begin to tense up at the sight before me.

"I should have known that you would have brought him to me Luna," a wistful voice said. At the end of the room and covered in fine silk and sitting on his throne of his own mighty power, sat the all mighty Fate. To any person, be they human or not, the calm, brown-haired man with the charming smile would have seem like the nicest person on the face of the earth but I knew better. I knew that under that mask of calm and knowledge the man was worse than anyone could ever imagine.

"I'm a sucker for a live fight. Sue me." She walked away from me and stood far away from both of us.

"Fate," I said with disdain.

He gave me a forced smile. Her amber eyes were not being able to hide how uneasy he was with me in the same room.

"Zalvius, I see you made it past everyone. As I knew you would," he said, not bothering to hide his disappointment at that.

"Your attempts on stopping this from happening have honestly been pitiful, Fate. I'm surprised you even thought they would work."

"Not all of my attempts have failed," he said smugly. I didn't understand what he meant which made me feel uneasy. Luna snarled at him and glared but said nothing on the matter.

" You killed my brother Fate." He rolled his eyes and waved his hand as if the accusation was preposterous.

"No I didn't, you did," he pointed out.

"On your order and under your control, you bastard! At least have the balls to accept what you did!" I yelled out in anger.

484

"Fine I had you kill your brother. And I'll have you do it again if you want to get to me," he stated firmly. Something about the gleam in his eyes, the seriousness. These weren't just words to him. He meant them.

I froze.

"What are you talking about?" I asked, strained. The large grin on his face had me feeling sick to my stomach, a bad feeling growing and spreading through my body.

"What have you done Fate?" I snarled.

"Why don't you see for yourself." He snapped his fingers and the sound of footsteps from afar neared us. From behind Fate a door was opened and in he walked.

I felt as if I could not breathe, as if my lungs refused to use the air that they were given. I was washed over by so many emotions. Guilt, happiness, confusion, recollection, guilt, an overwhelming need to hug my brother.

My brother who was alive. My younger brother

"Joshula." I breathed out, blinking in disbelief at the sight before me. I felt as if my gravitational pull had changed.

Joshula and I had always been mistaken for twins back then but on closer inspection, you could clearly see that I was the oldest and then there was the fact that while my eyes were blue. His were a mixture of green and blue. We shared the same dark hair and strong facial features but due to me being both older and aging more than him I had a rougher look, but there was no mistaken us for being related to one another. He was a bit slimmer and shorter than me but not but much.

"Incredible what I can do, isn't it? You really tore him to shreds." I looked away from Joshula to look at Fate with a flinch. "So it took me a few years to piece him back together and then another few for him to heal enough to stay intact but he came out pretty good. Now, as I was saying, if you want to get to me, you're going to have to get through your brother again. Can you do that, Zalvius? Can you rip your brother apart again?" Fate asked with sick glee in his voice, clapping his hands.

I couldn't say anything, but look at my brother who had just stood beside Fate with a blank expression on his face. As if he weren't actually there . . . was he? Was this merely a puppet?

"I've even improved him, I bet he can last in a fight with you now. Maybe even win." Fate smirked, Luna who had stood quiet this whole time gasped in outrage.

"This is why you needed all of those wolves for? Your experiments? No, I will not have this." She growled out, her face morphing from a delicate female to a brutal wolf. Fate narrowed his eyes on her and shook his head.

485

"If you are not with me you stand against me. Joshua, dispose of theses two," he ordered.

Joshua reacted immediately at the order and began advancing to us. I did not move. For once, I did not know how to react or what to do. Luna however, did. She barked out a laugh and then raised her hand in front of her and moved it around in an interesting way.

Joshula stopped mid step and stared at her. Fate looked at her in angered shock.

"What are you doing to him. Stop it immediately."

"You seem to be under the impression that I am below you, I am a goddess. You have somehow manipulated this boy but you forget that he is here because of the power that I lent you under a false impression. I am in control of him not you. He is a wolf. Not your puppet. I'm over-riding your power. You've been so obsessed on trying to stop Zaliver that you have crossed a line that should not be messed with."

Luna snapped her fingers and Joshula walked over to her calmly. She placed her hands on his temples and began whispering something in an odd language. He closed his eyes and slowly sank to the floor.

She looked at me.

"When he wakes up, you will have your brother back, but I do not know of what the side effects of him returning will be. So beware," she warned and then she looked at a pale Fate.

"I can not believe you would do such a thing Fate," she said in honest disappointment and almost betrayal. He looked around in panic and gripped the edge of his chair, looking for an exit no doubt.

"Oh come on Luna, it's not that big of a deal. You can't leave me defenseless against him like this. I thought you understood. I've done no wrong. The World goes as I please, because it must," he said quickly.

"You hurt one of my innocent children when I told you not to. I warned you," Luna's tone grew sharper than I had ever hear the laid back woman speak in, she turned to look at me.

I did not remove my eye from Fate's. He would pay for trying to get me to kill my brother, again, the sick bastard.

"Fate is the reason your mate was hurt the other day, and his attempt on keeping your attention elsewhere." She turned back around to speak to Fate before walking out. " That's right, I snitched. You deserve whatever he does to you."

It took me a second to process her words and that's when it hit me. All of it.

Anger would not be a strong enough word. Hate would not express what I felt. Disgust could not be hidden.

486

What I felt towards Fate before was nothing compared to what I felt for him now. Now, in this exact moment what I felt was raw, unbelievable, and ever-growing abomination for the man in front of me. The monster that would try to harm the only person on the entire planet that had done nothing wrong in her entire life, and had somehow ended up with me. He had reached into the field of flowers and tried to pluck the only flower that I had laid my eyes on with his tainted hands.

My body trembled with the boiling fury in my body, I could feel the shift completing from half beast and human to fully beast. I relinquished my absolute control to the darkness swirling in me.

Without removing my eyes from Fate, I walked over to the side of room where he had a wall made of different textures like metal, marble, and other impenetrable material. With my claws on the wall, I swiped down and then back up. It made a loud screeching sound that might have bothered me if my fury didn't make me so focused.

I was sharpening my claws.

Fate flinched at the sound of my claws but he did not move from his spot. Lifting his arms as if in defense he began speaking.

"I will admit to doing that. I apologize for the damage I caused but don't you see Zalvius? It was I who thought of giving you a mate, without me you would still be roaming the world on your own, you would have never had a taste of true happiness. You should be thanking me, you would have none of this, power or control if it wasn't for me. I gave you a future and I returned your past," he declared. His eyes were narrowing down at me towards the day end of his idiotic speech.

I walked away from the wall and slowly walked to him, closer and closer until I loomed over him in his stupid throne. His face paled. He pushed himself into the back of his chair as I neared my snout next to his face. The stench of fear rolled off of him, but the faint scent of hope made me let out a small growl.

What did he hoped for? For someone to save him from his unstoppable demise? For me to reconsider my actions after what's just learned? Because whatever he hoped for what not come soon.

"You will pay for your actions against my family Fate. You will suffer by my hand," I whispered cruelly. My voice was half more animalistic than human. Fate had the audacity to give out a weak laugh.

"What can you do to me that I will not recover from. I am a god, I can not die," he boasted.

I gave out my own humorless laugh and pulled back. I grabbed him with both hands, digging my claws into his shoulders, tainting his white silk clothing in crimson red.

"I was counting on that," I informed him.

487

His eyes widened in absolute fear as I opened my mouth to reveal my sharp teeth, my tongue went over my teeth, making them glisten. There was a reason for my gums aching so much on the battlefield, why I had the insatiable urge to bite into my enemy.

Just like Venom, I had a venomous bite but mine was just a different type of poison.

I looked Fate in the eyes as I spoke, making sure he understood each and every word that left my mouth because those would be the only words he would hear for the next few millennium.

"Every life, every death, every tortured soul you have played with and destroyed out of careless fun will show you their pain. You have sat on your throne and turned a blind eye on those in need of you, your choices have led you to today. I will bring hell to you." With that I threw my head back and then bit into his shoulder without holding back, sinking my teeth firmly into his flesh as he screamed and withered before me.

I opened my eyes and with one hand, I dug my claws into his chest until I held his heart in my hand. I closed my eyes and collected all of the darkness that had grown and drowned me for so long, with one final breath I transferred it from me into him.

Immediately I could feel as if I was being sucked dry of all negativity. All evil and hatred in my body were leaving me. When I felt as if I were going to fall with the amount of drawing done from me, I knew that it was time to pull away. I removed my teeth and claws from his chest.

Fate fell to the floor like dead weight. His eyes were wide opened, and his facial expression forever stuck on that of one in unimaginable, everlasting torture.

I shifted back into my normal human form, feeling as if a weight had been removed from my shoulders. I kneaded next to his paralyzed body.

"I had saved that bite for you, and I can finally say that revenge has never felt sweeter. Enjoy your nap, Fate and remember that once you're done with your nightmares, I will still be on this earth when you awaken. As I always will be." I patted his cheek and stood up.

I turned and with a shaky breath walked over to my brother who was lumped on the floor. What would he say? Would he forgive me? Did I deserve it? What do I do? I've never felt this way before, my heart pounded in my chest, my body trembled, but not from anger but from fear.

I nearly down to shake his shoulder softly. Warm, he was warm. I could hear his heart. He was here.

As his eyes fluttered opened he blinked repeatedly for a long moment. When it seemed as if he was finally stable enough, he pulled himself up and groaned. He looked tame and narrowed his eyes before an odd tint covered his eyes and then he smiled largely.

"Hello, brother," he said happily.

I felt my heart clutch at the sound of his voice and those words leaving him, I suddenly could speak.

"I-I'm S—"

"It's okay, you don't have to say anything. I already know," he said patting me on the back. He was strong, perhaps even as strong as me.

"What do you say on leaving this place?" I asked, helping him stand up.

"And go where?" he asked me.

"Home."

"Home?" he repeated. I nodded and helped him to the door when he stumbled.

"Yeah, I have some one I want you to meet," I said, excited at the realization that my brother was alive and that I had my mate. I had a family of my own.

"Who?" he asked frowning in confusion. I grinned largely at him.

"My mate, Vivian," I said happily, turning away for a moment to open the door.

"Oh . . . Vivian . . ." he said slowly, trying out her name. I turned back to look at him to catch the corners of his lips curled up.

"Yeah, Vivian."

He looked at me with an unreadable expression on his face for a moment, I'm guessing trying to take it all in, I know I was. It was a second before he spoke.

"Well, I can't wait to meet your Vivian then," he said. His voice and avid his eyes were intense.

CHAPTER 37

I looked at the guy at the door, to Zaliver and then back and forth.

"B-Brother?" I stuttered out.

Zaliver nodded happily at me and then looked back at the doorway where his brother stood.

"Come in, Joshula. This is where we live," he said to his brother, who walked in slowly.

He approached me with a small smile on his face up close. I could see just how similar he looked to Zaliver, but in his own way he was different. His eyes weren't Zaliver's deep blue; they had more green to them and was slimmer but still muscular in his own way.

"Hello, you must be Vivian. It's nice to meet the woman who has captured my brother's heart. I'm Joshula," he said. His voice was smooth and controlled.

"Uh, H-Hi, yeah um. . .ha, uh, wow. Yeah," I said.

I couldn't help it. It's not every day your mate brings home his brother whom he said he killed. I was bewildered and honestly caught off guard. My emotions were still all over the place with all of my worrying that I had done about Zaliver's safety. Joshula's smile widened at my response and looked up at Zaliver with amusement.

"She is quite adorable," he said honestly.

Zaliver nodded and looked down at me with a smile before kissing my forehead.

"Yes she is," he agreed wholeheartedly. That made me snap out of my moment of shock, slightly, if anything.

"She's right here you know," I said with narrowed eyes at both of them. Zaliver just chuckled while Joshula raised a brow.

"So . . . you're alive . . . how?" I asked after a brief pause.

Joshula's eyes darkened momentarily as he looked down at me and then in the blink of his eyes they were back to their normal green. His eyes flickered up to look at Zaliver that happened very quickly.

490

"Why don't we discuss that later? For now I'm sure that everyone is hungry, and I'm in need of a shower. Joshula, do you want me to show you to your room or . . ." Zaliver asked looking at Joshula in question who looked down at me before nodding.

I followed behind the two as the went up the stairs, still going over everything. I had a lot of questions, some more pressing than others.

"Here, this can be your room if you want. There are other rooms to choose from if you wish to do so," Zaliver said, stopping at a room two doors down from where our room was.

Joshula stopped in front of the open door and looked into it. He stepped in cautiously and examined the room. I stood at the doorway of the room Zaliver and I stayed at, and looked from afar at the expression on my mate's expression.

Even covered in dirt and dried blood, he was still the most precious thing I have ever seen in the world. He didn't seem tired or grim from coming back from a war zone where I'm sure many died, even with the knowledge that his brother was alive and in front of him. I couldn't fathom why the air around Zaliver felt so much lighter.

He still had his side of the bond closed off but I couldn't just sense it. I could see and hear it as he spoke calmly.

"No, this room is fine," Joshula replied stepping out a bit. Zaliver grinned and clasped his brother by the shoulder and gave him a squeeze.

"It's good to have you back little brother," Zaliver said, his voice with thick emotion.

Joshula looked at him and smiled. His light green eyes looked my way for a brief moment before looking back at Zaliver once more.

"It's good to be back," he whispered.

They looked at each other for a moment; a moment of reconnection after so much time lost before they both turned from each other.

Zaliver stepped back and then went into our bedroom and headed straight for the bathroom. I lingered at the doorway of our room when I saw that Joshula did as well. I gave him a smile that I hoped resembled both comfort and support, rather than conveying the small amount of awkwardness I felt about being around him.

I was never one to adjust well with meeting new people and knowing that it was Zaliver's brother just made it more nerve wrecking for me. I needed one of those "How to get on the good side of the brother of your mate who he killed-but came back somehow" guides.

He turned his head to the side in a form of curiosity before slowly smiling at me. Both my beat and wolf were quiet, not knowing how to feel about the sudden guest, but knowing that it was someone

491

important to Zaliver made then both more willing to try to form a bond to the new family member. I gave a short of nod before retreating into the room and closing the door, I could hear Zaliver shuffling around in the bathroom.

I walked in without knocking, Zaliver didn't even look up from what he was doing. I closed the door and pulled myself up on the sink counter. Now having more of a chance to study him I frowned at what I saw.

He was wearing some odd black material that clung to his body form, by no means did I find the look bad, but how could ge have gone in just that? He was peeling the material off of his body, off of his top half and followed by his lower half, he stood naked before me.

"You didn't go in just that, right?" I asked worried

Although most of the blood had been on the outer suit, some must have soaked through because there were a few spots on his upper and lower chest. Half of his face was covered in small blood splatter patterns. I knew that it should have bothered me, but just seeing no open wounds coming from him made everything else seem bleak. He looked at me with a small secretive smile.

"No, I had body armor on top that I took off as soon as I got back. Why? Afraid I might have gotten this torn and then had gone off fighting nude?" he joked with a raised brow, and I rolled my eyes at him.

"No, but it's good to know your not an idiot who enters the battlefield without armour on," I stated. He looked at me for a moment and then hummed in response. Before he turned around my eyes, I caught something that had me pause briefly.

He entered the shower and the hot water was turned on a moment later. I didn't have to shower but I just wanted to get in after him to get close. I got to remove my own large sweater when my ears caught the sound of something odd outside of the room. Curiosity got the best of me and with one look at the shower, I left the bathroom and went out of the room.

I listened for the sound again and when my ears twitched, I followed the sound. It was coming from Joshula's room. It sounded like an odd pulling of metal or something.

"Hey, are you alright?" I asked him through the door. When no one answere,d I knocked on the door.

"Umm . . . Vivian? Can you possibly help me with something?"

I gave a weary smile at the awkward and panicked voice. Did he break something?

Well at least it wasn't us this time. My wolf piped in.

Pushing the door open, I looked around the large room for a body and found none, I stepped into the room just as a towel clad

492

Joshula walked out of the bathroom. I kept my eyes firmly on his green eyes and nowhere near what I thought could be a six-pack.

No comment. No comment for the love of god. My wolf muttered.

None from me either, keep those eyes up. My beast said firmly.

"You need help with something?" I began quickly. I wasn't very comfortable with a half-naked male who wasn't my mate but looked like the younger version of him.

"I can not work that thing. I've heard and read of them but I do not know how to use one," he said with annoyance and a bit of shame.

My mouth opened in confusion, not sure what he was asking about. Looking at my expression, he pointed behind him into the bathroom. "Where is the water suppose to come out of exactly?" he asked.

It immediately clicked as to what he was talking about and I couldn't help but let out a small laugh, I walked past him and into the bathroom and over to the shower. I made sure that he was watching when I turned on the water, he looked on with a fascinated and intrigued look.

"See this? It's the hot water handle. You just turn it this way and hot water pours out from up there. This is the cold water handle. You balance the hot water with the cold to get the right temperature. To get it to turn off, you just turn them back the opposite way. When you're ready for it to come from the top, you push this button here. Got it?" I asked him, I put my finger under the water to make sure it was okay.

Turning around, I caught his eyes flickering to mine quickly, paying it no mind I asked again to which he nodded.

"Glad to help," I said truthfully.

"I'm not sure what I would have done if not for you, I had tried pulling the this from the wall but they seem firmly in place," he confessed sheepishly. I looked to the handles and did in fact see cracked tile around the handles.

It's a good thing Zaliver proofed the house. That must have been what my ears had caught.

"Don't worry, we all get confused when it come to showering in strange bathrooms, not just you, buddy. Let me know if you need help with anything else that I can help with," I said, walking out of his room.

"I will, thank you," he said courteously with his green eyes following me out of the room until I closed the door.

I shook my head as I walked back into the room and head back into the bathroom. Poor kid . . . wait, technically he was older than me but . . . huh. Wonder how this age thing works?

I stripped once in the bathroom and opened the glass door and then closed it behind me. Zaliver had most of the hot water on and

493

had caused fog to form everywhere. He turned around once he heard me open the door, pushing a button on the side of the handles the back side of the shower where I had just entered related more water to spray me as well.

"Where'd you go?" he asked.

"Your brother didn't know how to turn the water on so I showed him how," I said distracted by what I was seeing.

Zaliver seemed to be simply enthralled me under the sprays of the water as drops travels down his skin quickly and followed every trace of his body. His black hair seemingly darker as they became silky strands and stuck to his face.

"Oh . . ." he said and then paused and narrowed his eyes. "Was he decent?" he asked skeptically.

"Oh shut up," I said, playfully staring at his forearm.

"Wait, does that mean he wasn't—" his voice rose a level.

"Shh!" I said, reaching up to cup his face in my hands.

I looked at what had caught my attention earlier and stared deeply. Zaliver's arms wrapped around me and pulled me closer. His body made me instantly feel warmer even under the scorching water.

"What?" he asked with a soft smile, subconsciously I had begun creasing his face with one hand and moving strands of his hair away from his face.

"Your eyes, they're so much lighter than they were when you left," I murmured mesmerized. He let out a soft chuckle raised his brow.

"Oh really?" he asked with no true care. It didn't seem to get his attention but it did mine.

It was true. Before his eyes had been a the color of the sky before a storm and now they were more like the lightest blue in the sky or even of what a frozen lake might look like. There were different shades of blue mixed in which made them even harder to look away from.

I traced under his eyes with my fingertips which he quickly took hold of and brought to his lips. Keeping his eyes on me he kissed all of my fingers before kissing my palm and placing it on his face. The simple romantic action made my heart stutter and made all of the emotions of before come rushing back.

I couldn't help the happy sob that left my mouth as his expression changed quickly to that of heartache and sorrow. He pushed my body against the wall, and I gasped at the feel of the cold tiles against my bare side.

"Don't be sad. Please don't be sad. Everything is fine, I'm okay. Everything is okay Vivian," he whispered softly, kissing the side of my face and bringing me to his chest and inhaled deeply.

494

I wrapped my arms around his body and pulled his as close as I could. I needed this—the feel of his body against mine knowing that he was here, and the steady thumping of his heart against my ear. The way his arms wrapped around my body as his covered me.

"I was scared," I whispered breathlessly. My eyes were stinging as I felt tears well up. "I didn't know if you were going to come back in one piece or if you weren't going to come back at all," I said, still tormented by the thought alone.

My life was tied to his, no matter what happened I knew that if he wasn't in my life I wasn't living. Just the thought of not being with him pained me physically.

"Hey, hey, look at me," he said, pulling away. I looked up as his eyes gazed down at me with intensity that hadn't been there before.

One of his hands went to the back of head and cupped my neck with a firm grip making sure I couldn't turn away. He leaned down and kissed me with a soul-shaking passion, his lips against mine brought on a frantically, I clutched onto him tightly.

His lips parted as he traced my bottom lip with the tip of his tongue and then began a hypnotic rhythm with his lips. He started off slow and tenderly which then grew into fervent and all soul consuming. I was long past gasping, and the burning in my lungs was nothing compared to the amount of open emotion Zaliver was transmitting through his lips. He pulled away shakily, but he didn't seem to be able to keep himself from kissing me again and again in small pecks. Repeatedly, he did so until he just pressed his lips to mine roughly before pulling back once more to plant a soft one on me. He opened his tightly clenched eyes and looked down at me.

"I will always find my way back to you Vivian, no matter where I am in this world. No matter how many people or who I have to go through, you are the one who my heart will fight for to be with at the end because I love you.

So do not worry, my little cloud. I will not be far from you. It is impossible to keep me from where and who I want to be, who is you. Keep calm my love, we are together as we should be. As we always will be," he said. I sniffed as I looked up at him with amazement.

"I love you too," I said, laughing softly for no reason. I suddenly felt calmer and just happy. He smiled down at me and pulled me to his chest.

"Good." He said putting his head on top of my head.

This was more than something sex could give us, this was a physical connect without lust. An emotional and spiritual connecting back together after too long apart by worry some circumstances. This was us. We stood there for a few second before I felt his side of the bond opening up.

I jerked back in his arms from the surprise of what his side of the bond felt like. Usually even when he left it opened I'd never really ventured past my line because there was something eerie about his side, something dark and dangerous.

But now as he opened his side of the bond I felt none of that, all I felt was peace and absolute happiness coming from his side. It reminded me of what laying down under a willow tree on a hot sunny day would feel like. Tranquil. Peaceful. Calm. Absolute.

I looked up into his eyes and realized that something huge had shifted in him.

"What happened out there?" I asked him. He kissed the top of my head before pulling away.

"I did what I had planned all this time and in return came back with a surprise." He evaded the question, my eyes narrowed on him, it wasn't the brutal details that I wanted.

"A very good surprise." I said, emphasizing on the surprise.

I took hold of a bath sponge behind him and put soap on it. I began rubbing small circles on his bicep and then went over his shoulder. His eyes lightened up with tremendous joy and excitement.

"My brothers back, I almost can't believe it. Oh god, there's so many things I have to tell him, show him . . ." His eyes saddened for a moment before he spoke in a sad tone.

"If he will allow me to, I killed him Vivian. I took his life from him in cold blood. How could he even forgive me. I myself don't," he whispered. His hands squeezed my waist and pulled me closer for comfort.

"He's your brother and even though you did that, it wasn't by choice, he'll know that. Once he sees the person you've become he'll remember why his big brother is so awesome and totally forgivable or I'll kick his ass. Politely of course," I added when he gave me a light disapproving look.

Shaking his head softly at me he leaned down to kiss me. When he pulled back I surprised him by scrubbing the side of his face harshly. He pulled back and glared at me.

"What? You had blood on your cheek, that stuff is hard to get rid off!" I defended myself, he scoffed and rubbed at his red cheek.

"Your lucky I love you because that hurt like hell." He pouted, faking hurt.

"Oh you big baby! You just got out of a fight, don't tell me a little scrubbing—" He cut me off with a breath stealing kiss.

~•~

My stomach grumbled loudly as I pulled Zaliver's hoodie over my head. He looked over from towel drying his hair and gave me an apologetic smile. His black hair was shiny and sticking up in all directions as he walked over.

"Have you eaten anything since I left?" he asked, standing behind me and began towel drying my damp hair.

"I don't remember, I was sort of busy worrying about you to, for once, care about food," I confessed. I turned around to face him. He had a frown on his face so I poked him repeatedly to which he gave a mock growl to.

"Don't do that—"

"Poke you?" I asked confused. Tough luck, I liked poking people especially him.

"No, I mean don't worry to the point of not eating Vivian," he cleared. I wrapped my arms around his waist and leaned back. I felt him bend his knees a bit and plant his feet firmly on the ground to keep us steady.

"I promise to never, ever, ever forget to eat if you promise to never, ever, ever get into a fight with other gods again. Deal?" I asked. His lips thinned as he grimaced. He groaned and looked up before looking back down at me.

"How about I promise to try to not get into fights with other gods and you promise to at least order take out if I'm gone?" he suggested.

I let out a laugh, I knew he wouldn't be able to resist starting a fight with someone just like I knew that as long as he did I would worry myself to exhaustion.

"Fine," I answered after calming down.

"Fine," he copied.

Fine, now that we've all agreed to these terms, can you please feed this body before I contemplate eating myself from inside out? My wolf added too friendly.

This time it was Zaliver's turn to laugh and laugh he did. You just had to add something didn't you? I asked her.

Well duh, since you're not taking the responsibility of feeding the body we share, I figure I took matters into my own hands. She responded smartly.

Claws, your own claws. We don't have hands. My beast corrected with a mocking tone.

My wolf growled.

Ha. I snickered.

Who's side are you on?

The side that feeds us, being neither of you two. Aka, him over there. She said.

Zaliver took hold of my hand as he listened on. He dragged me down the stairs with him. I wasn't surprised to see a freshly showered Joshula in a pair of what must have been Zaliver pjs because they looked slightly large on him.

"Now that we're all showered, I think it's time for dinner. You hungry Joshula or . . ." Zaliver asked walking to the fridge and began pulling things out only to stop and turn to face his brother in question. Joshula face twisted in confusion as he looked from Zaliver to me as I made my way onto a stool across from him.

"What?" I asked as he stared at me.

"You do not cook?" he asked. I narrowed my eyes at him. Behind him Zaliver made a face before closing the fridge. He walked over and stood next to his very confused and possibly endangered brother.

"Uh Joshula, times have changed and women are no longer expected to do the work of home," He explained awkwardly, bringing his hand up to scratch the back of his head. Joshula nodded in understanding but still seemed unsure of something.

"I'm very much aware that times and customs have changed, Fate kept me vaguely informed as the world progressed but it's different hearing and experiencing," he explained slowly, choosing his words. My glare lessened in understanding.

"For a second, I thought you were implying that I should be doing all of the kitchen work because I'm a female." I tsked and shook my head at him. "I could cook, if you want food poisoning that is."

His soft green eyes widened before he turned to look at Zaliver who confirmed my statement. Zaliver went back to being masterchef.

"So my brother does all the cooking?" he asked bewildered. I nodded eagerly, knowing exactly why it would seem so odd. His reason was probably different from mine, but I think we were on the same ground. He half turned to look at Zaliver who had his back to him.

"When did this happen? Last time I recall, you couldn't even catch a fish with a spear even when it was in a small puddle in front of you?" He asked amused. Something in Zaliver's hands dropped in the sink before he quickly picked it up.

"Really now?" I asked, a large grin on my face as I watched Zaliver's back stiffen.

Joshula turned around with the same grin I was giving him, green eyes sparkling with purpose. He leaned forward, placing both arms on the table.

"He might have been older, but I was most definitely the guardian. He was far too heedless and young spirited," He whispered the last part to himself.

498

"But so were you," I pointed out. His head turned to the side as his eyes narrowed slightly.

"What do you mean?" he asked after a moment of pause.

"Young, you were young too. So what did you do?" I clarified quickly, hopping I hadn't offended him. Without turning around Zaliver answered just as Joshula opened his mouth.

"He trained for fun with the others who liked the adrenaline fighting brought. That or keeping me on a leash whenever he thought I was going to do something idiotic. Am I right brother?" Zaliver asked, my nose caught the smell of meat.

Joshula looked down and shook his head, letting out a deep chuckle before lifting his head back up.

"Oh yes. Right you are. Like always," he said flatly.

"Not always and for your information the only reason I didn't catch the fish was because it looked like a pile of shit. I was not going to eat shit," Zaliver defended himself. Walking over to the stove and moving some stuff around before coming to sit next to me.

"Oh yes, that is why," Joshula muttered, rolling his eyes.

Although I think we all knew that we were delaying the real conversation for later, the air was still a bit tense as if they waited for either one two bring up the big question. Or questions and accusations in this case. Not this is for sure though, I was so not asking it.

Not only was it not my place, but I'd honestly rather not be the one to bring it up. I liked seeing Zaliver have a normal conversation, especially with his brother, even if they were both a bit tense.

"What you are you making?" I asked Zaliver.

"Ribs, mac and cheese with mashed potatoes and gravy, a small serving of vegetable soup and ice cream for dessert if you still have room," he said.

My mouth dropped as I looked over Joshula to see the kitchen counter.

"I didn't even see you pull that many things out . . ." I mumbled under my breath, looking around him to see that he had pulled various sized containers and ingredients that seemed to have been already finished. Had be planned the meal yesterday?

"You certainly do know your way around the kitchen," Joshula said, looking at Zaliver with a hint of surprise."

You kind of have to learn if you want to eat. I didn't trust people feeding me after you—" Zaliver suddenly cut himself off.

My eyes widened as I understood what he was going to say. Joshula's smile didn't leave his face but you'd have to be an idiot not to notice the way his smile became a bit strained.

"So what exactly is the age difference between you two?" I asked quickly.

499

"He is . . . was." I flinched, maybe not the best question to ask. "four years older than I," Joshula answered, slowly turning his head in my direction.

A "What to bring up to your revived brother-in-law who was killed by his brother-your mate" guide is needed very much now. My wolf muttered.

I didn't need to tune into Zaliver to sense the disapproval he felt towards that comment. I gave a mental growl to my wolf.

Sorry, sorry. It's just so damn awkward and tense in here, I just can't. She sighed.

I hated to agree with her but she was right.

Thankfully whatever Zaliver was finishing cooking was done so he stood up and went to get the food so I stood up as well to get the plates and silverware.

"Do you need assistance?" Joshula asked, reaching out to grab plate out of my hand.

"Sure," I said, handing him the plates. When one of his fingers made contact with mine, I felt something odd course through me. The feeling passed through me leaving a subtle and mute sort of sense. It left my wolf and beast alarmed and uneasy. I passed it off as it just being from his cold temperature. He had a pondering expression on his face as he tried to figure out where to put the plates.

It made me freeze for a moment while him and Zaliver setup and prepared everything. I recuperated quickly and grabbed the cups. When everything was step I sat down back at my spot.

We had a dinner table, but we didn't really use it as there were too many empty seats. I guess we still weren't using it and that was okay since this would be much better placement than sitting far away from each other in awkward silence.

Once we were all sat down and eating, I decided to be that one person to ask a question while we ate. Admittedly, I disliked those people but I figured it couldn't help since Joshula looked honestly confused by what he was eating while I felt uncomfortable eating in front of him. It took me a while to feel comfortable eating in front of anyone new. Zaliver seemed alright, confident, and uncaring as always.

"So Joshula, I can't help but bring up the fact that your eyes have green in them. Which parent did you get that from?" I asked, hitting two birds with one stone since Zaliver never mentioned his parents.

Joshula put down his fork and leaned back into his chair, I reached for my juice as he answered.

"I have very little memory of our parents but I do believe I inherited mother's eyes while Zalvius inherited—" Zaliver's head whipped over to look at me with wide anxious eyes. Guilt filled eyes.

500

I sputtered a bit of juice and began to pat my chest as I coughed. Still coughing I turned to glare at Zaliver whose eyes had widened comically, ribs sauce all over his lips as he smiled sheepishly.

"Are you alright?" Joshula asked concerned as he had his hand half outstretched towards me. I nodded at him as I calmed down.

"Just fine," I rasped out. He frowned as he leaned back into his chair. "What did you just call him?" I asked.

"Zalivus?" he asked, looking over to my lying ass mate with momentary confusion before a large grin made way to his face, understanding making its way to his eyes.

"You renamed yourself didn't you?" Joshula asked crossing his arms over his chest.

"Apparently he did," I muttered. Zaliver wiped his mouth with a napkin before speaking quickly, a nervous hint in his voice as he looked at me.

"It's not that big of a deal. I never liked the name so I figured it wouldn't hurt anyone to change my name after a good hundred and five years with it. Zaliver seemed more appropriate," he said, placing his arm behind my chair.

I felt more annoyed at finding out late out of everything but he didn't know that. I could see the worry in his blue eyes at the thought of hurting my feelings by not telling me.

"Oh yeah, right. Anything else you might want to share with me that you've been holding out on? Long lost wife with six kids? Another secret island? A pet goldfish you've been keeping in the basement maybe?" I asked sarcastically. His face went serious as he answered me next.

"Two," he said.

I frowned at him in confusion, he sighed regretfully.

"Two kids and the goldfish died last week," he answered.

My mouth dropped in shock before I caught onto the amusement flaring in his eyes. He threw his head back and laughed. I began smacking him with my hand to which he laughed even harder

I gave up after realizing that he really just didn't give a damn about my smacks, so I took my smacks back. I sat petulant in my chair with crossed arms, ignoring the engrossed look on Joshula's face,I looked off to the side and began muttering to myself.

"Two kids my ass . . ."

We should make him sleep on the couch just for that last one. My wolf muttered herself.

". . . get my name changed . . . gonna be the last one I tell, let see how he likes that." Zaliver's laughter died down as I felt his arms pull me closer.

"Oh come on, I'm sorry, don't change your name," he said, putting his chin on top of my head.

I love it very much like I do you. He said softly through the mind link.

I softened at that and relaxed in his hands. I chuckled to myself as I turned to look at his brother.

"See what I have to deal with?" I complained. He nodded, playing along.

"Oh yes, it amuses me that you both have no concern over the pet fish he named Gold and let die last week," he said, shaking his head at Zaliver in mock disgust.

We both looked at each other with confusion before it dawned on us what Joshula was trying to say.

"No,no, the fish it's not named Gold—Well, I mean it technically is a golden fish, but it's the type of fish and it was a joke. The fish it's not really really . . . I'll explain later," I said, realizing that I was probably just confusing him even more.

"Ice cream?" I asked instead.

"No, thank you. The food was very well prepared but I just do not have much of an appetite," Joshula apologized.

I looked down at his plate to see that he had barely even eaten a third of his food. Momentarily I wondered if his lack of food was a side effect of some sort. Was I hungry when I came back from the dead? Huh.

Zaliver also seemed bothered by the lack of Joshula's appetite, but he did not bring it up and instead finished what he had eaten. I, on the other hand, completely cleared my plate deciding that they really should have a talk alone, and made sure to get them out of the kitchen while I cleaned. That's a first.

Zaliver's eyes panicked and shook his head as he realized what I was doing. I shook my head back. He'd thank me for this eventually. Some conversations were just not meant to be evaded or prolonged.

I heard them make their way to the living room slowly and then sit. I would have at least thought Zaliver would be the first to say something, apparently not. I didn't even strain my ears, they weren't making any sounds that hinted towards any conversation of sorts. Not even a small talk. I shook my head when they did just that for a good five minutes, all through my washing and drying.

Shit, they might as well come in and helped instead of sitting there like two rocks. My wolf muttered annoyed. They can't be serious, I thought turning off the water and drying my hands.

I fished and walked into the living room to see Zaliver on the couch while Joshula sat on the lone chair in front of him. What good that did them, both had their heads turned away from each other as if whatever they were looking at was much more interesting than one another.

I stomped my foot and groaned as I looked up, marching over to them I placed my hand on my hips. They would actually rather sit in silence then talk to one another. I could not believe these two.

I can. My wolf coughed.

I so do not feel like being Dr.Phil right now.

We'll if not you then who? My beast asked.

"I know you guys don't really want to talk about this and if you're both really bad at expressing yourselves, then suck it up because I'm not living in a house with awkward ass tension every time I say something totally inappropriate about this situation. I know I will at some point.

You're brothers, not enemies. Sure it's going to take some time to get over your issues but you can't get over them if you refuse to acknowledge and sort them out first. Now come on boys, speak up," I said firmly, making sure to look at both of them.

Zaliver blinked at me before looking away, his posture becoming stronger, his eyes fiercer, but underneath I could feel his hesitation and fear for what the outcome was going to be.

Joshula's eyes looked at me with appreciativeness, he nodded at me and then turned back to look at Zaliver with carefully calculated eyes.

I was about to take a step to give them privacy but Joshula lifted a hand and shook his head.

"No, stay. You are a part of this just as much as him now," he said, giving me an attentive look. I didn't move from my spot.

"I'm sorry for killing you," Zaliver stated, looking straight at his brother.

Joshula didn't hesitate to nod, he placed both hands in front of him and clasped his hands together.

"I know you are," he said.

Zaliver took in a breath and ran a hand through his hair pushing it back before continuing.

"I would have never done that, ever, had I had the choice. My human memory if very vague of how we ended up the way we did, but I can clearly remember during and after. I'm truly sorry for doing that to you when all you did was take care of me, when it should have been the other way around," Zaliver said thickly.

Joshula looked at Zaliver with a bleak expression, green eyes not showing what was going through his mind as he listened to Zaliver.

"I hated myself more than you could ever imagine after realizing what I had done, I had broken out from the compulsion to late. I can't what you hist have felt, what you are feeling and I understand if

503

you do not forgive me but I wish for you to know that I had planned revenge on you and I have done so. Had I known what Fate had been doing to you . . ." Zaliver broke off and just looked at Joshula in question.

I too waited for his reaction, we both looked on at the pensive Joshula. The amount of tension, fear, worry, and hope coming from Zaliver had not only my heart reacting out for him but me physically as well. I walked behind him and placed my hand on his shoulde. He reached up and gave me a soft squeeze of his own.

His thanks I guess, towards the gesture. I honestly wish that they both get past this because it would break my heart if Zaliver has to live know that now that his brother is alive, he wants nothing to do with him.

It seemed like it was forever that Joshula sat there quietly, his eyes focused on Zaliver. He tilted his head to the side slowly and then his eyes meet mine. For shorter than a second his empty green eyes gazed at me and then we got a reaction.

Zaliver stood as well and waited for Joshula to say something with his back strained and flexed in reaction to the moment. A large grin slowly spread in his face as he hopped off of his chair and walked over to us.

"Of course, I forgive you brother. You are not to blame here. I can not hold you responsible for something that happened so many years ago, under special circumstances. Your mate," His eyes looked at me with a twinkle in his eyes. "is correct. We are brothers not enemies. Having any ill feelings or ill plans towards you would be no good. I do indeed forgive you Zaliver."

I smiled at the amount of happiness and disbelief coming from Zaliver, even though I couldn't see the expression his face I could almost sense his large grin. They embraced. I smiled at Joshula, happy that the two brothers would be getting along. Joshula responded by giving me a smile of his own.

When they pulled back, they sat back down in their original spots and I decided to sit next to Zaliver.

"So, if you don't mind me asking . . . how are you . . . you know . . . here?" I asked, tucking my feet under me.

Joshula lifted a brow at the way I framed my question, but all I did in return was shrug. Beside me, Zaliver pulled me closer to him but turned to look at his brother.

"It's true, Fate wasn't very specific about how . . ." He trailed off, his happy dying down at the name of Fate, voice turning serious.

"It's an odd thing, really. I don't remember much myself. I can only recall to the point of my body being filled with more power than I understood. Healing began soon after, but I was under while my body

504

pulled itself back together. Apparently that was a very long process. It was always dark where I was, but I could recall Fate coming in every once in a while and speaking to me, telling me things."

"What things?" Zaliver asked leaning in.

Joshula shifted a bit in his chair, looking down for a moment before looking up again, his expression clear.

"Just odd thing, informing me of the advances of the world. His own thoughts and ramblings, nothing of true importance. I could not respond of course, so I just had to listen. There were moment when I was able to move but only brief. In those moments he showered clear joy and delight in my progress," Joshula explained looking off to the side, something in the way he spoke of Fate made my brows furrow.

"Why did Fate keep you to himself all this time?" I asked him.

"I am not sure," he said uninterested, as if the question was not of importance.

"I do." Zaliver said beside me, I looked at him in question.

"When I got to Fate he had planned on using you to fight me, defeat me. The shock of you being alive would have been all he needed. He knew I would not purposely harm you again." Zaliver explained grimly, looking at his brother. My eyes widened at the news.

"He was going to make you fight your brother? Again?" I asked no one in particular. My face scrunched up in disgust. " That's so messed up in so many ways," Zaliver voiced out his agreement.

"Well I guess he was," Joshula said shortly before clearing his throat. " When I was fully wakened he told me of all of these amazing things could do and then proved to me just how strong I was," he said.

The tone he was using once more made me look at him in question. He almost sounded . . . fond. That can't be right, my ears might be deceiving me.

"Luna said something—" Zaliver began but I interrupted him. I turned to look at him and began smacking him without thought.

"Oh my gosh, Luna? As in mother Luna!? You saw her? What is she like? What does she look like? Tell me!" I whisper-shouted with excitement. I couldn't help it, every wolf would want to know about their creator.

His blue eyes widened from the surprise attack, but he quickly took hold of my flailing as in his hands but that didn't stop my excited bouncing on the couch. An eager and excited expression made its way to my face.

"She's . . . uh . . . actually," Zaliver began narrowing his eyes suspiciously on me. "She reminded me of you in a way," he said, more to himself than to me.

"Really?" I whispered, searching his face for any hint of a joke.

"Yeah," he responded, looking down at me with affectionate eyes but I didn't really pay attention I was too busy.

She reminded him of me . . . cool.

"Any way," Zaliver said glancing at the large dazed grin on my expression with amusement, " she said. He had asked a favor from her, from what I got he must have asked her to give him the power of multiple wolves to make you heal quickly, stronger, faster and who knows what more," Zaliver stated, Joshula nodded in agreement.

"Perhaps we should test just why it is Fate believed you could take me down." Zaliver said out loud in thought.

"You do not believe that I could defeat you?" Joshula asked with an edge to his voice. This made me snap out of my thoughts.

"I'm not a werewolf, Joshula. I assume that it what power courses through you as we speak," Zaliver mentioned, leaning back.

"Hmmm," Joshula said.

"You mentioned that Fate spoke to you of the advancements of the world. Does that mean that he never showered you the outside world?" I asked.

"You are correct. He brought pictures, books, those things called movies and documentaries, but I was forbidden to leave," he said looking towards the window which showed the rising sun outside. Seeing that reminded me that I actually hadn't sleep all night yesterday and neither had Zaliver. Perhaps Joshula as well.

Just realizing this made my exhaustion suddenly pulled full front. I looked at the clock on the wall that read six fifty-five in the morning.

Dear god, why? It was so early. Huh, I guess what we actually had was breakfast Instead of dinner. Odd.

"I know you guys probably have a lot of catching up to do, but I haven't slept since lord knows when so I'm going to take a nap. Peace," I said standing up. I wasn't surprised when Zaliver did so as well. He must also be tired.

"I think we can finish this conversation later Joshula. What do you think?" Zaliver said holding me to him as he waited for his brothers response. Joshula stood up as well and walked from his spot to be in front of us.

"I agree, I do believe we all need the rest," he said. Zaliver patted his brother on the back with an easy-going smile and nodded. We all walked up stairs and went into our rooms to sleep.

"Good morning slash night Joshula. See you in a few," I yelled out. His laughter was my response.

I jumped onto the bed and bounced, then just laid there in a star position. Zaliver chuckled as he climbed in after me, he got under the covers and pulled me to him, somehow getting the covers from under me to cover me. He turned me on my side as he did the same. He let out a happy sigh as we laid there.

"I can't believe everything that's happening, Vivian. I have my brother, I got my revenge, and I have you. I truly believe I'm dreaming," he whispered into my ear. I wrapped my arms around him and snuggled into his chest. Then I thought of something and giggled.

"Ouch!" he exclaimed, pulling back to look at me in question. I didn't move from my spot. "What was that for?" he asked, clearly taken by surprise.

"I pinched you to show you that you weren't dreaming," I said in a "duh" type of tone. He let out a small growl.

"Why'd you pinch my ass?" he asked grumbled.

"That was purely for my benefit," I confessed. I felt him shake his head at me.

"Of course it was." He said, adoration clear in his voice.

It was silent and I was close to falling completely asleep, but I had to get this out before I forgot later.

"You were right," I mumbled into his chest.

"Hmmm?" he asked, clearly almost falling asleep himself.

"Zaliver suits you much better. You were right." I explained in one breath.

His arms tightened around me before he pulled back and shifted down a bit to firmly kiss my lips. This unintentionally or perhaps intentionally woke me up a bit. My eyes fluttered open as I blinked. Darkening clear blue eyes gazed at me.

My breath hitched.

"What was that for?" I asked in a whisper.

"Being you," he said softly.

"Oh." I said, suddenly feeling shy under his darkening gaze.

He leaned down slowly and then gave me a back arching kiss that made me do exactly that. I gasped for breath as he pulled back only an inch.

"And that one?" I asked.

A grin covered his handsome face before he answered in a husky voice.

"Being mine."

CHAPTER 38

VIVIAN GREY

Screaming. Someone was screaming.

I shot up off the bed with a pounding and startled heart the same time Zaliver did, in a brief pause we looked at each other, making sure the other wasn't hurt. And then another scream came, but not from us.

Zaliver ran out of the room in a blur. I followed behind with wild, panicked eyes. The sound was coming from Joshula's room. It was the sound of a dying man, of a man experiencing unbelievable pain.

When we entered his room Zaliver stood frozen at the door. His expression that of despair and fear. It was like his whole body was glue to the floor as he looked at his withering brother who screamed on the bed, his eyes shut tightly as he clenched his fists.

It was obvious Joshula was having a nightmare and Zaliver himself seemed lost on what to do so I pushed past him and got as close as I dared to the bed.

You don't ever physically try to wake someone up who's come back from the dead when they're having nightmares. That shit should be common sense.

I picked up one of the many pillows on the ground he must have knocked over and held it tightly between my hands as his sweaty face scrunched up in pain, another scream left his pale lips.

"Joshula!" I yelled, throwing the pillow with all of my strength at his head.

I was right on my theory.

As soon as the pillow hit Joshula's forehead with what was probably too much strength, he grabbed onto it quickly with clawed hands and tore into it with sharp canines. His eyes flew opened, instead of dark green eyes, a dark mustard yellow glowed in the dark with hatred.

I gasped at the sight of him and his eyes flew to mine. Zaliver, who had been at the door moments ago, flashed in front of me and half crouched as if preparing to defend if Joshula pounced.

Joshula stopped ripping into the pillow and released it, spitting it out he closed his eyes and took a deep breath. When he opened his eyes again they were his normal green, a tired green, but still. He brought his hand up, the movement making Zaliver twitch slightly, and ran it through his damp hair.

"I apologize for the disturbance," he said, shaking his head. "But I seemed to have had a . . . nightmare," he said, chuckling without humor as he looked up at Zaliver.

It might have been because I was startled out of sleep but my instincts were telling me that maybe it should have been me in front of Zaliver, crouching.

"Are you okay?" Zaliver asked after a beat, straightening up and taking a hesitant step forward. Uncertainty in his voice

"Yes," he responded too quickly, and his form was still shaking though. His eyes were too wide, his smile too calm.

"What happened? What were you dreaming about that had you sound like you were dying?" I asked, stepping behind Zaliver and to his left.

"I do not remember. It has left my conscious state of mind," he answered and too quickly to be believable. His eyes tightened as he looked around the room, not looking at us. I think he wanted us to go. Zaliver must have caught on.

"Is there anything we can do?"

"Not at the moment," Joshula said through thin pursed lips.

"Alright, we'll leave you to rest then." Zaliver sighed, worry clear in his tone.

"Thank you."

As I followed behind Zaliver, a sudden grasp at my wrist had me stopping. A familiar cold and mute-like feeling passed through me, it made goose bumps appear on my arms. I looked down to Joshula in question.

Zaliver stopped at the door once he no longer heard my footsteps, his hand all ready on the door handle, he turned with a questioning look on his face and looked at Joshula.

"I'd like a moment with her if you don't mind," Joshula said. My brows furrowed as I looked at Joshula. What would he have to tell me that he could say in front of Zaliver?

Zaliver looked at us for an awfully long pause before nodding his head stiffly, his jaw clenched as he closed the door softly.

Joshula waited until he heard the sound of Zaliver walking away before turning to look at me. The feeling of Joshula's hand around my wrist was unintentionally causing my wolf to slowly curl her lip up to bare her teeth in a low crouch. My beast as well felt unreasonable annoyance and some sense of alarment towards his grasp.

509

I pulled my hand out of his, he looked down at his still outstretched grasping hand where my wrist was a moment ago. Flexing and then clenching his fingers he looked at me.

"You wanted to say something to me?" I asked slowly, still pondering over my now quit wolf and beast. Their behavior was sudden and very odd.

"Yes," he whispered.

"Why are you whispering?" I asked him.

"If don't want him to hear," he whispered again, and I laughed.

"All of the rooms are sound proof, he didn't want to hear anything going on in the rooms because of his hearing so he sound proofed them," I explained.

I had laughed back then when he told me that, but after changing myself I realized that it was actually necessary. I got headaches just from being in Hannah's house sometimes because I could hear everything inside and outside. If Zaliver wanted to he could probably hear us, but he'd have to focus his hearing and that was easier said than done.

"Really?" Joshula asked taken off guard, interest in his voice.

"Yeah, So what did you want to talk to me about?" I asked, wondering what was so important the Zaliver had to be asked out. It's not like I wasn't going to tell him if he asked me later.

"My dream," he said seriously.

"The one you had right now?" I frowned.

"Yes. It wasn't a dream. It was memory."

I felt my stomach sink at the tone of his voice, my mind already knowing what he was hinting at, but I asked anyway.

"Of what?"

"The day Zaliver killed me," he whispered.

I took in a sharp breath. I closed my eyes briefly and let out a sigh. This, this would surely bring up tension, and I could feel it. Even though Joshula had forgiven Zaliver, just by seeing how Zaliver stood at the door unsure, I'm sure just knowing that he was behind the reason for those screams would make him feel even more than he was letting on. I opened my eyes and sat at the end of the bed with my hands on my lap. Well this ought to get deep.

"You said you didn't remember what your nightmare was about to spare Zaliver's feelings," I stated more than asked.

Joshula's nodded and sat up straighter. He brought both of his hands together in front of him.

"Thank you for that," I said sincerely. Zaliver would have been totally saddened by that and just seeing him as happy as he was this morning had me happy. He smiled at me for a second before his expression turned grim.

"I would not harm him purposely, but you on the other hand, must understand that I have nightmares on that horrible event and I'm afraid that if this were to happen continuously he will begin to suspect," he spoke, looking at me seriously. I looked away and thought about it.

It was true, one forgotten nightmare, Zaliver could let pass, but two, three . . . He'd get worried and would begin doing what he does best. Trying to find the root of the problem to try to eliminate it.

Only in this case he was the root.

"That is a problem. But what can I do to help? I don't exactly have a Bachelors in the art of making people forget," I said crossing my arms over my chest. His face morphed to confusion before he shook his head and continued.

"I just need help in distracting myself, perhaps if someone were to tell me and show me the Zaliver of today then my subconscious mind would come to the realization that what happened long ago was just misfortune. Who better than my brothers mate?" he explained, lifting a brow at me with his tired green eyes suddenly seemed large and innocent looking.

The way he spoke was careful and planned and yet his eyes were large and innocent looking, but the twist of his lips said something else. Over all something about him seemed off. It left me staring at him, feeling as if for once my eyes were actually taking him in. I couldn't tell what exactly he made me feel but I must have looked long enough because he frowned and ran a hand down his face and sighed.

"I apologize. I'll understand if you do not want to, you must be extremely—"

"No . . . it's fine," I said after a hesitant moment. I couldn't put my finger on it exactly but if I spent more time with him than I could see what exactly was what was bothering me.

It was odd. Usually I knew exactly what I thought about a person but since Joshula was so polite and seemed oddly preserved I shrugged it off, Zaliver hadn't mentioned anything on his brothers behavior so I just assumed it was normal.

"Really?" he asked cheerfully.

"Yeah, I mean, whatever I can help in is good with me," I said, standing up.

"You're a dear Vivian. Thank you," he said.

I gave him a little nod before walking to the door and opening it, walking out. As I closed the door, I noted how odd the door handle felt, quickly looking down I saw that the material of the door had sunken in the forms of long fingers. As if someone had been squeezing the door handle with incredible strength.

511

Closing the door, I made my way to the room, and noticed that I felt very sad and sort of . . . grieving. But it wasn't really coming from me so that left me a bit under the weather.

I found Zaliver slipping on a pair of black pants on when I walked into our room. He gave me a brief glance before walking into the closet. I walked over to the bed and sat on it, looking over at the clock on his side of the bed I noted that it said 10:57 AM.

I groaned, we only slept for four hours but I guess it would be a shame to waste the day inside. I guess since Zaliver was up and changing that he also agreed. Standing up and making my into the closet I paused briefly at the sight of Zaliver's muscular back flexing as he rummaged for a shirt.

Mmmmh, that is a mighty fine back. My wolf sighed dreamy, setting her head on her paws.

Mmmhmmm. I agreed taking my clothes off.

All it's missing are some scratch marks. She added.

"I agree," Zaliver said without turning around.

I threw my hoodie at him, and it landed on his head, covering his face.

"Of course you and the perverted wolf would agree," I muttered.

I took a pair of leggings out of one of the draws where I put my bottoms which weren't pants and put them on. I personally thought leggings were a girl's best friend. I put on a long sleeve white shirt and went to turn around to look for a sweater when I froze.

"Is . . . is that a white shirt?" I asked hoarsely, completely blown away.

Zaliver rolled his eyes, but nodded as he pulled it down his abdomen. I felt my throat tighten at the sight of my mate in a tight white T-shirt instead of his regular black ones. I knew Zaliver would look hot in anything that he put on but oh god.

Unlike the black shirt, you could practically see through this shirt. It clung to his muscular build, expanded over his broad chest as he flexed, you could see his abdomen tense. I felt my mouth water.

Mate . . . touch . . . shirt . . . oh . . . god . . . mine. My wolf and I thought in uncontrolled and jumbled thoughts.

Zaliver watched in amusement as I neared him with outreached hands. He stood perfectly still as my hands felt over the white material over his chest with shaky hands and loud breath. My heart pounded in my chest as my eyes took in the sight before me, a rush coursing through my body.

"Vivian?" he said with a husky voice. I looked up slowly and batted my lashes at him.

512

I don't think either of us was totally ready for my reaction to him wearing something other than a black shirt.

In less than a second, I jumped on him, wrapping my legs around his waist tightly and forcefully pulled on his hair, bringing his lips to mine.

He responded a second behind and placed both of his hands on my ass, pulling me closer to the bulge in his pants. Spinning us around my back was roughly pushed against one of the closet walls as he kissed me back.

My body sort of shook against him as I kissed him roughly, not knowing where this was coming from exactly but not caring either way. I pulled at his hair making him give out a deep groan as I pulled his head back. My lips didn't leave his skin as they trailed down to the mark I gave him and began to nibble at the skin.

The reaction was immediate as his lower half began to grind against my front, giving me as much pleasure as he must have been feeling. Skimming my teeth over the mark he let out a small non threatening growl.

"Vivian," he said thickly, pushing his front onto me harder when I sucked on the mark softly. "Stop, before I have to change my pants." He breathed out.

Smiling against his neck, I trailed kisses up to his ear; he let out a partially relieved breath.

"No," I whispered, nibbling on the bottom of his ear.

His hands pushed my ass closer to him at this, he let out a hiss of air. I trailed down back to his mark, tightening my legs around him.

"Vivian . . . seriously . . . I don't want to change—— He tried to say through clenched teeth. Even though he could have pulled away from me himself, all he seemed to be doing was pulling me closer.

I let out a small moan as the pressure of his front left a pleasurable sensation. All this made him squeeze my ass in his hands. I ran one hand down his back as my tongue pushed past my lips and barely skimmed over his mark.

But that did it.

"Fuck!" he cursed, tensing all around me as he pulled me impossibly close to him.

I planted a kiss on his mark and smiled deviously to myself. His breathing was heavy and loud as he pulled back to look at me with dark and intense narrowed eyes as he caught the smile on my face.

"I like the shirt. A lot," I said as some sort of defense which was quickly ruined by the giggle that came out from my lips.

His eyes narrowed down even further but there was playfulness to them this time as he leaned down and whispered into my ear.

"I'm going to get you back for this," he promised, pressing a kiss below my ear. I shivered.

"Oh I hope you do," I whispered back.

He pulled back slowly and sat me down on shaky legs. He looked down and groaned and then threw me a look.

"Now I have to change," he said, wagging his finger in me in a sort of scolding way. I blinked back innocently.

I laughed my way out of the closet, taking what I needed I walked over to the bed and sat down. Zaliver walked out of the closet with what I assume was a new pair of pants and underwear.

I put a pair of black converse and a black cardigan on and then went to brush my hair. I put on a pair of small diamond earrings with a matching necklace and mascara on with a soft pink lipstick. Putting my hair in a ponytail I decided I looked pretty decent this morning.

Define decent? My wolf asked jokingly.

My expression became dry in the mirror as I flipped her and myself off.

When I heard the bathroom door open slowly, I turned around. Zaliver had his upper half out as he looked at me with suspicious eyes. My lips twitched as I fought off a smile.

"If I tell you I'm wearing blue jeans will you jump me again?" he asked. I bit my bottom lip and thought about it before answering.

"I don't know. Now let me see," I demanded eagerly.

He rolled his eyes before opening the door fully and walking out and walking over to me. I restrained myself from jumping him as I caught sight of the dark blue jeans that clung onto him perfectly.

"Good girl," he said once in front of me, I chuckled. Taking hold of his hands I pulled back a little to look him over, he still had his combat boots so I guess not everything was gone. I sort of liked that.

"Where the hell have you been keeping this from me? Are you hiding Narnia on your side of the closet? Because I sure as hell missed it," I accused, not ever seeing any other colors stick out from his black wardrobe.

"Oh yeah, it's right behind the Where's Waldo sweater. Can't believe you missed that!" he exclaimed sarcastically.

I stuck my tongue out at him to which he opened his mouth and made a biting motion.

"Well from now on I'm making a new rule, you're to wear different colored outfits from now on," I stated. He lifted a dark brow at me.

"And if I don't?" he asked.

"Then you won't ever find out which outfits make me want to jump you. Who knows I might even jump some other hot guy wearing

514

an outfit I thought you would have worn," I continued to talk over Zaliver furious growl. "Hell, they might even wear it better than you."

"The only person you'll be jumping like that will be me, do you understand?" he said darkly, taking my chin in his hands.

"Do I take this as a yes?" I asked coyly. He nodded once.

"Okay." He pressed his lips onto mine in a dominating kiss, sealing the deal and reminding me that he was the only one I'd ever be able to jump.

As we walked down the stairs, I couldn't help but check his ass out in those jeans.

That ass, those jeans, why are we not back in that room people? My wolf asked peeved.

"Because I have grieving wolves to talk to. Today's going to be a busy day," Zaliver responded absentmindedly, reading something on his phone that made his frown.

"Oh." I guess that explained the sad feeling I was getting, they were coming from the grieving wolves.

Of course, lives were taken in the battle. It was just sad to think that it was from our side but I guess every success must have its own losses. That sort of lowered the mood but it also gave me an idea, I felt like helping today.

"I'm going to go out and socialize with the pack today, see what I can do to help," I told Zaliver who looked up from his phone and gave me an approving smile.

"Do you mind if I come with?" a voice said behind us. Standing at the top of the stairs Joshula stood in his pjs.

"You should, you need clothes to go out anyway," I said. He walked down the stairs and stood next to me. I looked up to Zaliver who looked from me to his brother before nodding.

"Joshula, when things calm down I'll have you announced to the pack as my brother and they'll—" Joshula interrupted Zaliver quickly.

"If it's alright with you I'd rather you didn't." Both Zaliver and I looked at Joshula with surprised and confused expressions.

"Why?" I asked perplexed.

"I'd just rather not," he said. Zaliver stood silent for a moment before clearing his throat and straightening up.

"All right, if that is what you want," he said monotonously.

"It is, thank you," Joshula responded, looking at Zaliver seriously. Well, that was a weird request. Why wouldn't Joshula want to be recognized as Zaliver only living family relative? His own brother? He was an odd cookie, a very odd cookie indeed.

Zaliver's phone beeped making him look down at it, another frown made its way to his face, Alpha business. He looked back up and sighed.

"I have to go, you two, be careful. Wait for your guards. Bye," he said, giving us each a look before walking out of the front door. I turned to Joshula and clapped.

"Are you hungry or do you just want to go now?" I asked.

"Why? Are you offering to cook breakfast?" he asked me. I rolled my eyes and waved a hand at him.

"Oh please, I was just asking to let you know that there is some delicious cereal in the cabinet if you were." I pointed in the direction of the kitchen.

"Oh."

Oh is right buddy, if I don't cook for myself or my mate, what made him think I was going to suddenly try cooking for you?

"I am ready to go—"

"Right after you change that is." I piped up. He opened his mouth and then closed it, turning around he made his way up the stairs.

"All right then. I shall be down shortly." As he made his way up I went into the kitchen.

We might have eaten a few hours ago but that didn't mean I wasn't hungry.

"Let's see what is in cabinet number one. . ." I muttered under my breath. Opening the door I pumped my fist at the sight of my pop tarts and fruit snacks behind all of the healthy snacks. A.k.a Zaliver's snacks.

I took out one of each and leaned against the counter as I ate them. This was the life.

As my ears caught the sight of Joshula making his way down the stairs, I looked down at my half-finished open bag of fruit snacks and thought fast. I couldn't eat them all because then, I wouldn't truly enjoy them and if he'd seen them there was a fifty-fifty chance he would say yes if I offered him some out of courtesy. That was a chance I wasn't willing to take.

Stuffing them in the pocket of my cardigan, I smiled at Joshula innocently as he caught sight of me in the kitchen.

Sorry, Joshula. I thought to myself.

No you're not. My wolf laughed.

Ignoring her, I grabbed my purse and keys and made my way out of the kitchen. Joshula was wearing black pants and a button down dark green shirt, which must have been Zaliver's since they were kind of lose on his form. Just seeing the shirt had me narrowing my eyes in suspicion.

516

"Remind me to raid his side of the closet later because seriously, where is he hiding all of the colored cloths?" I said to no one in particular.

Done. My beast said, eyeing the shirt as well. I could tell that in her mind she to was wondering where he hid them.

"Ready to go Joshula?" I asked him. He put his hands behind his back and looked at me.

"Where to?" he asked.

I thought about it, he needed clothes badly so that had to be the first of many stops, then after that I'd see where to go, but I had a vague idea of how things were going to happen.

"First, the mall to get you your own clothes and personal things, after that I guess I ask one of my guards to give you a tour since I still don't know the island as well and after that we'll see." I said to him looking in the direction of the door, I could hear tires making their way closer to the house.

"Guards?" he asked. His tone making me turn to look at him.

"Yeah, Zaliver had guards on me whenever I leave the house even though I can take care of myself just fine. Don't worry though, they're pretty cool," I said with a fond smile.

"Mhhh." He lifted his head a bit, looking down at me. "I'm sure they are."

As soon as the honk came outside and then a slap to the head I figured that my guards were indeed outside.

"Come on, they're here." I moved my head in the direction of the door.

"How do you know?" he asked confused.

I tapped my ears, and his eyes narrowed slightly.

"You are as strong and have the same heightened senses as Zaliver?" he asked me.

There it was again, that tone. It almost reminded me of someone fishing for information, but there was something else in there.

"Yup, so beware," I warned slightly joking.

"I will, it's good to know," he responded

I opened the door and motioned for him to step out, locking the door behind him. I turned and saw four confused and alert faces looking at Joshula with suspicion. I smiled inwardly at their protective behavior.

Perhaps today, all this time with Joshula will give me a hint of what type of person he really is.

~•~

ALBERICUS WILT

517

She was not in a good mood. Well, I mean, she never was when I came to see her but still, from what I heard she was extremely cranky today which was both a good and bad thing for me.

Good, because that meant that the mark was working its mojo, bringing my Aurora closer to reclaiming full control of herself.

Bad, because cranky Aurora was just plain mean.

A few days after marking her, I gave the order to have her moved somewhere else. Seeing as how now marked, I couldn't just keep my mate all in the dark and locked up. She was still locked up . . . she just wasn't in the dark. That had to count for something . . . right?

Today was a busy day, but I couldn't think straight if I didn't see her even if she didn't give me a smile just knowing she was closer than before was a huge relief.

Now marked, Aurora had slim chances of escaping or even hurting someone else and not because it was something I or anyone else was doing. She had slimmer chances because now marked she would feel the need to be around me, need me and any attempt to leave would emotionally and spirituality hurt her.

She couldn't leave her other half, especially if the true her didn't want to go. The dark magic in her had taken hold of her pure momental desperation, but it wouldn't be able to fight both her and the bond no matter how long of a hold it had on Aurora.

I knocked on the wooden door before opening it. As expected, the room was a mess with things thrown all over the place and like last time I began cleaning.

"Why can't you just pick one section to destroy? Why does it have to be the whole room?" I muttered, not looking up from what I was picking up. I could sense her crouching on the far wall to my right.

"What fun would that be? Especially if I don't have to be the one to clean it up," she responded, boredom clear in her voice. I looked over at her with a raised brow.

Whatever snippy remark she was about to spit out seemed to have stopped at her throat when her dark brown eyes met me. For a moment, I got to enjoy watching my mate gape at me with a fluttering heart. I got to watch her mouth open and then close in a breathless and confused second. I couldn't help myself but winked at her.

"Hmp." She turned her face away from me, hiding behind herself behind her long hair, but I still saw the flush of her cheeks.

I, myself, felt my chest warm up at the sight of her lost but not unfamiliar emotions rising up. Longing to hold her in my arms and help her to the way she was before everything went down; when she was happy, when she walked around with flowers in her hair and good luck charms for the pack.

My wolf whimpered, feeling the emptiness of our arms.

Soon. I promised.

"You can look all you want baby, I'm all yours," I said coyly. Her hands fisted up but she still didn't turn to look at me.

I chuckled at her silence and picked up the flipped chair, setting it up correctly. I found her empty plate on the ground. At least she was eating now, when she first got here she seemed an unhealthy thin, I'm guessing dark magic doesn't need food sustenance.

"Look Albericus—" she said in an exasperated tone.

"Ah, ah, ah. You can only negotiate with Berry, none of this formality." I tsked at her standing up and crossing my arms over my chest.

"Well then." Her tongue went over her bottom lip, distracting me. "Berry, how about you remove these chains and take me out for a stroll like a gentleman who do. Or are you really a little mutt, like I suspect?" She taunted, tilting her head to the side, brown eyes gleaming wickedly.

I narrowed my eyes at her. The way her pupils expanded and shrunk made me instantly aware of the fact that a part of her didn't really mean all of the insults she threw my way. But that didn't mean that the beta in me didn't like it.

"And why would I do that?" I lifted a brow at her, leaning in the wall and pretending to be disinterested.

She shuffled up and slowly dragged herself to me as if her body was unbalanced and heavy. I knew it was more of an inner process at war, but that didn't stop me from reaching out to make sure she stayed up right.

She tensed at my grasp but surprisingly didn't pull away, instead she supported most of her weight on me and lifted her head back, fluttering her long lashes at me. I could taste blood in my mouth as I bit the inside of my mouth, fighting the urge to pull her closer, fighting the urge to replace the blood in mouth for a taste of her lips, ignoring the sudden tightness of my pants at her close contact.

She placed her hands on my chest and stroked softly, as if with care. I felt my knees weakening at her gentle touch, her closeness. It's been so long.

"How about." She leaned in closely, her sweet breath fanning my face. "I let you feel up this body you seem to adore so much. Maybe after you get what you want you'll leave me alone," she murmured seductively. Her words were bitter.

I pulled back without thought. Aurora was still under the dark influence. This was not my Aurora.

" That's not what I want," I said shaking my head sadly as I watched her eyes flash with annoyance. " Perhaps if you gave up and just released." She pulled back with a sudden jerked and shuffled away.

"Oh poor Berry, can't wait until his mate is full one hundred percent huh? Well guess what you moron? The day she does will be the day I die and since I'm inside of her so does she. Boo hoo." She hissed.

I couldn't control the growl that felt my mouth, or the force in which I gripped her arm, turning her back around to face me.

Looking directly into those dark, bitter eyes I made sure to make myself clear.

"I will get my mate, my woman, and my wife back. Even if I have to reach into her body and pull you out myself because at the end of the day, I know that she'd prefer the pain of me doing that then the thought of lasting more than she possibly has to with you." I snarled out.

It might have been the adrenaline, the anger or even the rage in my body that caused me to see this, but I could have sworn I saw a spark of life in those dark eyes staring back at me. She once more pulled back, this time with slower, almost hesitant movement.

Damn right. I thought, taking in breaths to calm myself.

"Whatever. You gonna let me out or what?" She grumbled, sliding down the wall to sit down on the ground. Why wouldn't she sit in a chair?

"So that you can play peek a boo with me again? No thanks." I scoffed.

Now that my mark was in place she could try to escape the island, but seeing how no one left the island without Zaliver's permission, no matter the species, all she was now was a bitter witch with bad mojo jojo.

"I'll let you count to ten this time, fair warning, I swear," she promised sarcastically.

I rolled my eyes at her attitude, what was with the sudden need to go outside anyway? She hadn't asked for anything before. So why now?

"Look . . ." She seemed really uncomfortable as she spoke, eyes looking everywhere but me. " As much as she completely annoys me, your little witch is that of light, meaning she needs natural surroundings and if you haven't notice, I ain't feeling the breeze in this bitch."

I thought about it for a moment before sighing. This was either an escape attempt which would result in pain for me or she was telling the truth but would somehow end up giving me pain.

"Fine," I started, noticing how the corners of her lips twisted up in the slightest.

"But don't think for a moment you're going out alone, we're going outside together," I said firmly. She let out a deep groan and stood up.

520

"Why must you come with me? Your need to be around this body is very inconvenient for me." She frowned. I rolled my eyes.

"We're mates. We're she goes, I go. If you don't like it, you can leave. The bond only needs us two," I pointed out, waving a hand between me and well . . . her.

"There's no 'we' in 'mates,'" she said.

"But there sure as hell is a 'team' if you rearrange the words and that's good enough for me," I said with a smirk at her glare. Grabbing on to her hands I made sure to look her in the eyes wearily.

"Don't try anything, because if you do I promise that there will be a spanking," Her eyes widened in surprise. "I'm joking . . . maybe . . . possibly . . . not at all," I whispered the last part under my breath, her glare becoming frosty.

Well someone's a grouch.

"You lying sack of crap. I dare you to try, I'll roast you alive before you touch me." She hissed out, yanking her hands out of mine and storming over to the door, waiting for me to open it.

Damn. This woman.

I felt two emotions come from her through the incomplete bond. One was amusement which I could bet came from Aurora and the other was uneasiness which I could also bet came from the darkness. It wasn't sure if I was playing or not, my advances and promises towards her meant that the bond would always throw her off-balance. It's a hard life when you're controlling someone who doesn't want to be controlled anymore, especially when they have a mate who mentions spanking.

"I was only jokin g. . . sorta," I said, walking over to the door and unlocking it. She eyed me and then the door. I eyed her back.

"Go ahead, try something funny. Just remember it when you're over my lap." She stormed out and I followed right behind her.

She might have been in one of her long dark and oddly made yet weirdly attractive dresses, but it did nothing to hide her curves from me. I wept mentally, making my wolf roll his eyes at me. It's been so long. . .

I didn't need to guide her for her to find the exist, once outside she paused before taking a deep breath. I crossed my arms over my chest as I watched her.

The sun made her long hair gleam, usually her hair was pin strength but I could see a hit of curls beginning to form. She used to have curls.

She walked over to the trees, I followed and watched her lowered herself to the ground and dig her hands into the dirt, wiggling her fingers into the dirt.

I couldn't help myself.

"That's right, enjoy the breeze, wiggle those fingers, play with that dirt," I teased. Her head snapped up to look at me, boy was she not amused.

"You're the mutt, not me," she said before the rocks, leaves and dirt began flying in my direction.

I ducked the rocks, but had to cover my face for the dirt. I could feel cuts form and heal just as fast as they came. I caught sight of her standing, both hands extended on her sides as her hair moved all over the place.

"Okay!Okay! I'm sorry!" I yelled out, dodging a large rock that seemed suspiciously aimed at my crotch.

"I'm so sick of you! If it weren't for you stupid werewolves and your mating bonds I'd be halfway around the world right now!" she yelled out. I ran for cover behind a tree, my breath quick

This was nothing like war and I couldn't just tackle her to the ground.

Well . . . I could . . My wolf snarled at the idea of harming our mate even if she was trying to harm us.

"I know, I know." I muttered. All around me dirt, rocks and earth flew at me and around the tree.

"Come on babe, don't you think your being a little—" A sudden force wrapped itself around my ankles, knocking me over and dragging me from the tree.

I looked over at her, both hands lifted into the air and I suddenly went with them. My feet were pulled up forcing me to hang in the air upside down. I snarled out at her.

I was a wolf, a beta at that.

I was not meant to be upside down.

"Put me down now! Or I wear to—" A sudden hit to my abdomen had me releasing a hiss of breath.

"Shut it."

"Oh I'm going to get you for this!" I snapped out, point a finger at her.

She smirked at me and took a step forward. On the bright side she no longer made things fly in my direction.

"And how are you going to do that while mid-air? See, it's easy really, I'm going to go and your just going to. . .hang." she mocked.

"You think this is funny don't you?"

"Yes, yes I do."

She began walking away when her step faulted and she brought her hands to her head. Just in that moment whatever hold her magic had on me faltered enough for me to get out of it.

Dropping to the ground I twisted my upper torso mid-air, changing the way my body dropped and manage a somersault. I didn't waste any time and rushed over to her.

"What's wrong?" I asked taking her face in my hands. She had her eyes shut tightly, hands fisted into her hair.

"Ughh."

"Hey, hey, look at me." I whispered softly, concern filling every pour in my body.

Her eyes opened slowly, to reveal darkening and lightening brown eyes. It seemed as if she was. . .fighting something.

Or someone.

"Aurora?" I asked hopeful.

She gave me a pained grimace.

"Hey Berry," she responded.

I let out a shaky breath and pulled her closer to me. Her hands wrapped around my waist, just the feel of her pulling me closer was enough to make my whole being weaken.

"I don't know how long I have but I'm guessing that by using dark magic now will loosen the hold on me." She said, breathing harshly, she closed her eyes.

"So basically, piss you off when it's in control, enough to get it to use magic and weaken its hold?" I asked, brining one hand through her hair.

"Mmhmm."

"I missed you. I still do." Her eyes fluttered open, sadness swimming in her eyes

"I'm so sorry Berry—" She choked out. "I left you all alone, I'm so sorry." Tears began streaming down her face, seeing her like this was slowly breaking my heart.

"No, no. I know why you did it. All that matters is getting you back,after that we can talk. Just focus on getting better okay?" I kissed her forehead and held her to me.

"I'm sorry."

"Shhhh, it's okay, it's okay." I closed my eyes and cherished this moment because I wasn't sure how long this was going to last.

"I'm so sorry."

~•~

After getting Aurora back into her room and letting her rest, I went to work. Today was going to be both busy and depressing.

A day after battle always is, especially when as beta you were in change of getting head count of all of the wolves lost in battle and their family.

523

Walking into Zaliver's office, I wasn't surprised to see him there leaning over stacks of papers, Hogan on his lap top, he looked up and then back down quickly.

I stared at him with narrowed eyes for a moment before walking past him.

Zaliver didn't even look up as he handed me a stack of papers. Sitting in front of him I began working. It was two hours in when he finally spoke.

"Why do you smell of dirt and dark magic?"

"Long story."

"Hmm."

"How's the brother?" I asked looking up curiously, it was odd to think of Zaliver with a brother. Just knowing was still odd.

"Good. He's shopping with Vivian," he said slowly.

I lifted a brow at him.

"I'm sorry can you repeat that? I don't think I heard correctly the first time." I leaned back and shook my head.

"What?"

"Well I mean, I just find it odd that your letting your brother, whom you killed, roam around with your mate. I just figured you'd be more . . . I don't know, cautious," I said carefully, aware that my words might cause my unpredictable alpha to act.

Zaliver stared at me for a moment and for a moment I thought about jumping out of my chair and running the fuck out of here but then he shook his head.

"We already talked about it, we're alright," he said gruffly.

"Y-Your alright?" I asked bewildered. "Shit, if it was me I'd hold a grudge." His eyes turned a fierce blue, unflinching and unnerving.

"Do you want me to kill you? Because I can do that." He snapped, I shook my head and lifted my hands as surrender.

I collected all of the files we looked over and handed then to Hogan. He looked up with a half-smile, this time he was wearing a red shirt and black tie.

"Get all the addresses and names printed on the same paper, we're going to need it for family visits. Contract the pack funeral services and have them make all of the coffins needed along with any other personal decisions family members might make for their loved ones," I ordered.

"Yes Beta, right away," I watched him stand and leave in a hurry. I turned around and sat back down, picking up more work.

Jesus, I hate paperwork.

"I need you to sign—" I was cut off by a beeping from Zaliver's phone when he received a message.

524

He looked down for a second before picking it up and reading, he clicked something on the screen before shutting his phone off and looking at it. He took in a breath and then closed his laptop, pushed back the files and stood up.

I looked up confused.

"Are you leaving? Dude you can't leave me with all of this paper work!" I hated paperwork, I felt the panic begin to set in.

He rolled his eyes and walked around his desk, making his way to the door.

"I've got to pick something up, then I'll be right back."

"What do you have to pick up that's so important?" I asked him. I'll be damned if I get stuck on paperwork while he goes pick up some lunch.

He stopped at the door, half facing me and half facing away so I couldn't see his expression clearly.

"A ring."

My mind stopped working for a moment.

And then my mind caught up and I shot up from my chair. Zaliver turned around with a grin.

"Dude!" I yelled surprised, excited and totally happy for him.

I walked up to him and gave him a half hug, patting him on the back. Oh man! oh man! this was huge!

"I can't believe it! I can't!" I exclaimed again, shaking my head in surprise. Zaliver had the biggest grin I've ever seen on his face.

"I'm gonna do it. I'm going to ask Vivian to marry me."

CHAPTER 39

VIVIAN GREY

Joshula was officially testing my nerves.

"How about these?"

"Lovely."

"And these?"

"Very colorful—"

"I swear to god I will beat you with these socks if you don't tell me what you really think about them." I snapped.He blinked in caught off guard.

"I-I'm sorry?" he asked.

Damn right, you should be.

I set the socks back in the pile and turned to look at him with a serious expression. Two hours. Two hours in and I was officially ready to explain to Zaliver why his brother had been strangled in a horrible sock accident.

"Joshula it's okay to say no to things you don't like, especially when you're going to be wearing them. No one will judge you if you say no to muffin patterned socks. I swear."

Behind me, Johnson snickered. I'd strangle him too if I had to.

Joshula looked at me with suspicion before giving a hesitant nod. He reached in and began taking out all of the things I'm guessing he didn't really like from the cart.

"Thank you for helping me by the way, I'm sure you don't have this much trouble when with Zaliver," he said, looking over a dark orange shirt before taking it out. It wasn't his color anyway.

"We've never gone shopping together so I wouldn't know," I said, realizing how true that was. Huh, never even thought about going shopping with Zaliver.

Sort of made me wonder what type of shopper he was. Maybe I should buy him something, since I'd brought almost everyone something while in the mall.

What should I get the guy that has everything and commands everything? I pondered.

How about . . . Some socks? My wolf said.

You're so funny . . . not.

Oh come on, how about some shorts?

An odd sound came out of my throat, I shook my head in muted horror, a grimace making its way onto my face.

I can't give the love of my life some shorts, hell, I can't even picture him in shorts. The heck is wrong with you!

Okay, okay, I see your point. So what, oh wise one should we give our mate?

How about—

"Vivian?"

"Huh?" I snapped out of my mind to find Joshula staring at me with a lifted brow. Zaliver did that to, was it a family trait or something?

"I was just asking what was next." He gestured down to the cart that had a whole less than what we began with but what must have been what he wanted.

What was next . . . oh . . . OH.

"Um, let me just go pay for this. Luke!" I called, waving him over from his post by the shop door. I think he'd do a much better job than Johnson on this next one. He walked over quickly, eyes alarmed.

"Yes Luna?" he asked, eyeing Joshula worriedly with new scepticism.

I think it's safe to say my guards were a bit cautious around Joshula. A fifteen minute car ride didn't seem to do any help. To say the car ride was awkward was an understatement. Apparently car games were not cool if you were above eight.

"I'm going to go pay for this, can you uh, help him buy . . . you know. The underpants for his under pants." I awkwardly gestured from my waist and down.

Luke and Joshula tilted their heads to the side, both looked at me with open gazes.

"What?"

"You know, the shorts that aren't shorts but go inside his pants?"

They blinked.

"That thing that holds your junk in the trunk?"

Luke frowned.

"Oh for-boxers, briefs. I don't give a damn, can you just help him buy it! I am not going to stand there and ask him what fabric makes him feel liberated or flexible!" I whisper-shouted, my face turning red.

I stalked off with the cart, almost breaking the bar when I jerked it to the right sharply. "Why can't guys ever get hints. What? They

527

want me to spell it out for them?" I muttered to myself while I got in line.

A few wolves around me smiled or just plainly avoided my eyes, but the amusement coming off of them was too much to hide. Three minutes huffing in line was all it took for me to calm down. By the time it was my turn to pay I was able to muster up a reluctant smile to the bubbly cashier.

"Hello Luna, I hope you've had a good shop?" she said, doing that thing cashiers do and began scanning. Beside me Johnson appeared and silently helped bag.

"Yup, great," I muttered, taking out the black card Zaliver gave to me for when I wanted to go shopping. I noted how much slower she was moving now. She began eyeing Johnson with appreciation. Great, my checkout girl was checking out my bodyguard.

Hey, better him than you. I don't think Zaliver would be happy if we let our sexiness distract her. And at least he's free of charge! My wolf added with a snicker.

"Your good with packing. Any experience?" The girl suddenly asked, batting her eyelashes at Johnson who couldn't look more serious while on the job.

"Nope," he responded without looking up.

"Oh . . . well—" she tried again.

"Can you hand me that?" Johnson asked without looking up. The checkout girl flushed but did as he asked. I rolled my eyes and paid for the things.

"Come back soon!" she called out, probably directed towards Johnson more than me.

"Johnson you're a heartbreaker," I teased him.

"Eh?" He turned to look at me with confusion, that made it all the more amusing.

We left the bags in the car and then I had to go back in, searching for a present for Zaliver. A little while later, I think I had found the perfect present. I went back in look for Joshula and Luke, turns out they were all ready waiting for me at the car. I secretly think Mila and Cort just like watching me yell out their names and turn around in circles like an idiot. When you think you've lost your mates brother, you tend to panic.

While driving, my happy mood dropped as I was hit with strong negative emotions. I blinked back tears as I was assaulted by the sudden waves. It took me a full second before I comprehended what was going on.

"Luke, can you drive to the nearest hospital?" I asked, my voice coming sadder than I was aware of. I don't know if it was my voice or the words that came from my mouth that made his step on it, lurching the car forward while everyone began fretting over me as if I had been shot and they had just noticed.

"Luna are you hurt? Where's the pain?" Luke asked frantic looking back every few seconds through the mirror, his expression both panicked and pained.

"No, I'm fine—" I swatted Milla's hands away from my sides. "I just have to go do something." I explained.

"In the hospital?" Johnson asked, voice an octave higher than usual.

I turned around to look at Joshula, I had Johnson sit behind so that he wouldn't feel excluded by the seat arrangement. I had tried to sit in the back but Luke began rambling about protocol and my protection.

"Do you want to head back home? Luke can drop you off." I asked softly, taking a deep breath so as not to drown in the overwhelming grief that grew the closer we got to the hospital. Have you ever noticed how sad hospitals were, even with bright colors?

Joshula was looking at me with worry, I felt cold so I was sure I looked paler than my normal.

"Are you alright Vivian?" he asked, not answering the question.

"I'm fine, so do you want to be dropped off—"

"If it's alright with you I'd rather keep an eye on you," he answered with a frown. I nodded and turned back around.

I knew I was supposed to be giving him a better welcome back to "life" tour but compared to everything going on now, it just didn't seem that important. Besides, that's what Google maps is for.

Luke pulled into the parking lot of the hospital, not even bothering to turn the car off before he was turned around in his seat looking me over.

"I'm fine, seriously," I said, motioning for Mila to open the door so that I could get out. When everyone was out they were looking as if they we're ready to catch me in case I fainted.

I rolled my eyes at them but understood that it was just their way of showing they cared about why we were all here in the first place. I couldn't tell them it was because I was sad but it wasn't exactly my grief. I couldn't explain to them the overwhelming and crushing sensation of total loss I was feeling. The only thing I could do was show them what I was feeling.

Making my way into the front entrance of the hospital, they all trailed behind me, looking around with me as if searching for whatever had pulled me here. Even I myself wasn't aware of what force was pulling me into the hospital but in a sense I knew what it was, it was the Luna in me wanting to comfort those in pain. I'm assuming that after the battle even we had casualties, even we have wolves we had lost and

529

even we had wolves that were hurt. The emotional pain I was feeling was coming from them and their loved ones, as Luna it was my job to comfort and tell them everything would be better, and I was going to do my job.

I wasn't looking for anyone in particular but closed my eyes and let the strongest sense of emotions lead the way. It was as if I was following, a silver string down the hall to the left and into a room, patients, and staff saw me and just stared with curiosity, some of them moved out-of-the-way while others stared. Before I entered I turned to Luke, Johnson, Milla, Cort, and Joshula, telling them not to follow me in. I could see their hesitation on letting me enter alone but they did as asked.

There on the hospital bed laid a large battered man covered in scratches and thick bandages, but the faint scent of blood was still in the air. Beside him sat a woman asleep on a chair her dark brown hair covered her face but still her small frame showed a sense of tension and fatigue.

I stepped into the room and stood beside her chair. I placed my hand on her shoulder, startling her awake. She looked momentarily confused as anyone who had just woken up would. She was frightened when she looked at the man but felt relief when she saw him still breathing. She was so focused on him she had yet to feel my hand on her shoulder so I removed it, then she turned to look at me.

Her eyes were dark brown, but they looked to large for her as if she had cried which I believe she had. Exhaustion rolled off of her in waves and for a brief second, I could tell that she wasn't completely focused on me even if she was looking at me. Her mind was still on the man on the bed. Focusing my eyes, I could see that she was outlined in a faint orange colors that mimic the exact same color of the man on the bed. They were mates and she was watching over him. She didn't stand.

"Who are you?" she asked softly. Her voice was hoarse. I smiled softly, feeling an odd tenderness and calm come over me and into the room, relaxing everyone present. She looked older than me by many years and yet I felt almost a motherly instinct to comfort her and anyone else in this building.

It felt . . . right.

I wasn't all that surprised. She didn't sense I was her luna. If Zaliver were hurt, I wouldn't give a damn if the president, Pope or Miley Cyrus stood next to me with their name on their foreheads. I would only focus on him.

"I'm Vivian. That's your mate isn't it? How is he?" I asked, lowering myself into a squat and taking her hands into mine. She didn't seem to mind, in fact, she looked a bit more relaxed and tranquil.

She nodded and looked over to the bed with sad yet full of love eyes.

"Yeah, that's Jans. His real name is Junior but I don't think it fits him. He doesn't like me calling him that but he still let me. He-he was in that war that just went on, he's a good fighter. I've seen him practice. He's the best!" she said with conviction.

"He saved one of his friends, and he's always doing stuff like that." She smiled but her eyes began to water so I knew that his brave actions had cost a great pain. "But whatever weapons he was hurt with slowed his healing, he began to be bleed out without healing but he still fought," she explained.

"He's not healing now?" I asked with a frown. She shook her head. I turned to look at Jans.

He was a large muscular man with a neatly trimmed beard,with honey colored blonde hair. His skin was a bit yellow. Dark purple circles were under his eyes as greenish blue veins came forward. The smell of faint blood had grown a little in the time I was here. He wasn't healing.

The need to take hold of his hand and talk to him surged in me so I did so. Letting one of her hands go I took one of his so that we were all connected.

"Hello, Jans, do you mind if I call you Jans? Your mate says it suits you much better than Junior. I hear you're a brave warrior, so thank you for your part, but I think it's time you began to heal. Your mate seems very worried about you, I doubt you're planning on leaving her, right?" I spoke as if he were awake, because that was what I wished to believe.

My beast and wolf were both quiet but very much aware of what was going on, I could feel all three of us connect full front. We were all Lunas and together we were stronger, to comfort our own.

"I just want him to heal so he can get better. We don't even have kids yet, he's too young to . . ." She couldn't finish the sentence and I didn't want to hear the rest.

"And he shall. Just you wait and see," I said with more force and sureness than I was feeling.

I squeezed both of their hands to comfort them both even if it wouldn't better the situation. To my surprise, some sort of electric spark zapped all three of us, both I and the woman pulled our hands apart in shock. And Jans? Jans began to heal.

I wasn't the one to notice, his mate did, with a surprised shriek she pointed to a large cut on his forearm that began to heal, slowly. A presence I hadn't noticed was needed appeared. Jans wolf must have been knocked out cold because it was faint, but I could feel it now.

The woman began to cry happy tears as she leaned over her mate and hugged him, whispering soothing words. Feeling as if it was

531

time to go I stepped out of the room, not noticed but with a relieved breath. One down, Lord knows how many to go.

The guards and Joshula were where I had left them with worried yet understanding looks on their faces. It seemed that they had heard the woman's cries of happiness and immediately understood that I wasn't not here because I was hurt but because I was comforting those who were hurt.

"I have to admit that I believe you were hurt at first, we've never actually seen you do. . .Luna things like this before," Cort said with a hint of embarrassment.

I shook my head in understanding, it was true. I had never really done anything to prove I was luna, I was younger than most thought me to be and Zaliver had never really pushed me into my position, not that it was his fault. This was something that I was supposed to do and I wasn't surprised it would seem as a shock to them. Being a Luna was going to take getting used to, for them and me.

I went into the next room, next person, and next silver string. I wiped away a stray tear and went to go sit down at the bench in the empty hall. I had told the guards to go on break, ordered was more like it, they needed it.

Ever since I got to the hospital I had gone up and down, room to room, patient to family member to try to comfort people. Sometimes it was quick and light other times it was dark and heavy. Some people were getting better while others were getting use to the idea of their loved ones being gone. The last one was the hardest.

The last family I had just gone to see had lost a brother and father in the fight, the mother was devastated. A mate and a son. I was still connected to her, her grief was mine. As was her anger. Not all of the victims reacted the same. And yet all I could do was try my hardest to help lessen the pain, the anger and the fear.

I saw him from the corner of my eyes but said nothing, reining my emotions in, breathing in deeply and letting out a breath. I closed my eyes. Thanks to me going around some of the emotion destroys had lessened greatly but it had left me exhausted mentally and physically.

"You're a very compassionate person, I hadn't realized," he said next to me. I kept my eyes closed. Sometimes hospitals were too bright.

Wanna be heaven. My wolf mumbled without lifting her head off her paws, resting.

"I get that a lot, most people just remember me by my sarcasm. You know," I opened my eyes and turned to look at him. "Your brother is compassionate too."

Emphasis on "passionate" honey. My wolf muttered again.

532

"He must be if you say so, I'm just having trouble believing it. He's always been full front and careless when it comes to the being of others," he said.

"Oh, he was in the beginning. Trust me, I should know. He was all 'act first, questions later.' " I shook my head at the memory. Who knew I'd be able to look back and not feel like kicking his ass?

"Pardon my curiosity, but just how did you and my brother meet?"he asked. I couldn't help that bubbling laughter that came out of me.When I was calm enough I spoke.

"His beta kidnapped me and I woke up with Zaliver on top of me," I said bluntly. It must have not been the answer he was expecting because he looked dumbfounded.

"So yeah, believe me when I tell you I know a little about how Zaliver was, but you can also believe me when I say that he's changed." I was happy to say that, it showed change had happened and not just to Zaliver but to me as well.

Joshula leaned back against the wall, arms crossed over his chest. His eyes were closed as well and for a moment he truly did look like a younger version of Zaliver. I felt both pity and guilt at once.

"I'm sorry for today. I'm sure you were expecting a much better outcome of how things were going to go," I said, his eyes opened to show me not blue, but green eyes.

"It's alright. War caused casualties and pain, this is something I'm very much aware of. Besides, this day hasn't been a complete waste. I've learned a lot today," he said leaning towards me.

I lifted a surprised brow. What could he have learned today in the hospital? How to sanitize his hands? Because I'm sure we passed at least fifty of those little boxes by now.

"Like what?" I asked intrigued.

"Well what I've learned is more about what type of person you are. You're funny, short-tempered, your stance is relaxed which leads me to believe that you're not a fighter or have ever fought, you care deeply for others but don't show the full extent and as I said before you're compassionate," he said casually but his eyes were focused on my reaction.

I smiled, while some of those things I knew just from being me, were completely wrong I didn't bother correcting him. What would be the point?

"Really?"

"Yes."

"Interesting how you view me," I said with amusement.

"What do you mean?" he asked.

"Well, do you want to know what I've learned from you?" I asked closing my eyes and leaning forward, putting my elbows on my knees, hunched forward.

It was horrible posture and probably made me look like I was Egor, but I was half ready to kick it and let the doctor's wheel me away. I was so exhausted. I didn't wait for his reply.

"You're distant from everyone, you keep to yourself, you like to watch and observe people and learn their habits. You're polite and yet I get the sense that you know exactly what people like to hear, you hold back. You're smart and have most definitely trained. I'm going to also take a wild guess and say that you have a hole in you somewhere and you just can't figure out what that's about." I opened my eyes and turned to look at him after a long moment of silence.

Joshula looked at me with genuine shock. He slowly composed his face but his eyes were expressive. He seemed disturbed, as if I had seen him naked or something. So what, he can study me but I can't study him?

"How—"

"And after years in school, not only do you get good at seeing under people's armor but you get real good at seeing past what people want you to see. People do some pretty odd things to get cheat sheets and notes," I said with a small smile but he didn't return it.

Later on, when the guards left Joshula and me in the house, I was surprised when Joshula muttered something about resting in his room and then vanished, leaving only the sound of his bedroom door slamming. Weirdo.

I didn't really care to pay any attention to that even if my mind stored it somewhere for whatever reason. Instead, I went into the room and prepared for a shower. My mother had always talked about how even if hospitals were all 'kill germs, keep clean' most of the time, that they probably had the most germs because of all the viruses, sick and hurt people.

Because we left in the afternoon, it was pretty late when we got back. I was honestly surprised not to see Zaliver home, but I knew that it was a matter of time before he contacted me or showed up.

I quickly showered, messily towel dried my hair and did something I hadn't done in a long time, but should most definitely do so in the future. I took a nap.

I climbed into bed and pulled the covers over me, grabbing hold of Zaliver's pillow and went to sleep faster than I thought possible. I dreamt of night sky with blazing stars, fallen flower petals, warm kisses and blue eyes. Actually, that last part might have been a lie.

Opening my eyes, I realized blue eyes were in fact looking back at me, Zaliver gazed at me, his arms wrapped around me. A loving smile made its way to his face, making me respond with the same back.

"Hi," I whispered. I brought my hands up to rubbed away the sleep.

He brought up his hand and cupped my face tenderly. I unwrapped my arms from his pillow and instead wrapped them around him.

"Hello to you too sleepyhead," he said huskily, as if he had been the one asleep. I ran my fingers through his thick hair, tugging on the strands. "I hear you've been busy today."

I nodded and threw my leg over him, snuggling closer. He growled softly and ran the tip of his nose along the side of my face.

"You—are—my—world," he said between kisses.

He ran his hand up my leg and took a firm of my thigh. I let out a gasp as I was suddenly pinned under him. I was surprised when Zaliver pulled away from my neck, his usually blue eyes were black, his canines were out.

"Zaliver?" I asked, he usually had to be at an extreme emotional state for this to happen.

"Mine."

"Yeah, I think we already established that," I joked, still trying to guess what had him riled up.

"Ma—" He cut himself off with a growl and ripped himself away from me. I blinked in bewilderment.

I pushed myself up onto my elbows to see him pacing back and forth, pulling at the roots of his hair roughly, snarling under his breath.

"Okay, what's up with you?" I asked him, beginning to actually worry. He turned to face me, his face back to normal, this time a large grin on his face.

"Nothing, sorry, long day. Not that you haven't had a long day but yeah. Let's go down to eat. I'm guessing you haven't eaten right? Well let's go, can't have you starving, can we?" He leaned down and took hold of my hand, yanking me up with so much power that I flew onto him.

Is he rambling? My wolf asked.

"What the fu—"

He didn't even bother letting me finish my sentence and raced down the stairs. When we got to the kitchen he sat me down and began taking things out of the fridge. I watched him with suspicious eyes.

Now, I was worried. He suddenly froze, chuckled and took a breath. Umm, I was usually prepared for most things, but a hectic and bizarre Zaliver was not one of them.

535

"Okay, I'm sorry about that. I'm usually not this . . .unorganized," he said, looking at me with an apologetic grin on his face.

"Really? Never noticed," I said slowly. He shrugged and began moving much slower than before.

"I just have a lot on my mind, a lot to plan and prepare that's all," he said seriously.

"Like?" I asked going around the counter to stand next to him while he made what I believe was a sandwich.

"Well for one, the next three days are going to be full with funeral services, families to console,which you did today." He didn't bother hiding his pride. "After that we have two days of silence for the fallen, those days might be worse than the actual funerals." He grimaced.

I nodded in agreement, silence days for wolves were not days of prayer, not days of silence and not days for remembrance. They were two days. One day to remember the human and one day to remember the wolf.

And they were the worst because it was then and only then when people realized that we had lost two souls that would never be seen again. After that the true healing could begin.

"And then of course there's your birthday . . ." he said.

My mouth opened in surprise, I had forgotten my birthday was coming up soon.

"You forgot didn't you?" Zaliver said, wagging a finger at me. Amusement lighting up his eyes.

"Yeah," I admitted.

He walked over to me, putting both arms on either side on me and pushing my hips back with his own, my lips parted. He leaned over me with smoldering electric blue eye, a smirk made its way across his face as he leaned down even more, strands of black hair fell forward framing his face.

Was it possible to fall in love even more with the man you were in love with? Because I felt like that was what was happening.

"Well I'm going to promise you something. Do you want to know what that is?" he asked. His voice suddenly low and very much alluring.

I hadn't noticed but I had begun to tremble a bit, Zaliver was emitting his presence more than I've ever felt him do when he was with me.

Strength. Desire. Lust. Raw and utter dominance. Power. Control. Love.

"Yeah," I said in one breath.

He reached up with a hand and look a lock of my hair, twirling it and then putting it behind my ear. Dropping his hand back down I felt him wrap it around my waist.

536

"I'll make sure it's unforgettable. You can count on that my love."

CHAPTER 40

VIVIAN GREY

Those next few days were full of gloom, black clothing and tears of mourning from grieving family members. Both Zaliver and I being Alpha and Luna meant that we had to attend every funeral, making sure everything ran smoothly. Depression was friends with funerals.

During all of those days and events Zaliver made wonderful speeches, rendering even myself surprised by how well and detailed he would speak of a fallen warrior. He spoke of each individual with so much knowledge that some of the family members came over afterwards to thank him for getting to know their fallen member. I never had to go to a funeral before, not much happened in my life before I met Zaliver. I wasn't sure on how to go about but after bumping into some kids it seemed like I had some sort of magnet turned on after that. And believe me when I say I tried to turn it off.

Kids of all ages would seem to at first just drift near by me and then suddenly follow me around. I didn't notice but they were like ants, or a pack of wolves in this case. I wasn't sure what to do and I didn't want to ask Zaliver about it since he was busy, he looked hot as usual in dressed cloths but he also seemed tired. I decided to take charge of the situation. Literally.

I turned around and asked all of the kids their names and ages, it was sort of adorable. It seemed I had a talent for attracting toddlers who could barely walk and five-year old with large quiet eyes. Asking them why they were following me was easy but their response threw me off guard. They all seemed to be thinking along the lines of 'Follow the leader,' and when I asked them why they didn't follow Zaliver, they just shrugged. Kids.

Not wanting them to get lost and have to deal with an over emotional parent I told them to take a buddy and grab each other's hands, in each of my own, I held the hand of the youngest, afraid they would fall with all of their stumbling. And thus I spent not one but three days with kids trailing behind me while holding hands.

My wolf had called it 'The cute squad', I had to refrain from telling her to shut it, in the temple, not wanting to get struck by a bolt. I wasn't really religious but you could believe that if I could avoid getting struck for insolence, I would.

With all of this going on, Joshula had stayed away and out of sight and yet I could see him every once in a while. He had made a friend, a tall muscular man who was alway well dressed with ties and seemed to always have a clipboard and papers in his hand. Out of distraction, I forgot to ask him who his new friend was, he was always in his room so that didn't help. So much for family bonding, I felt sort of bad, I'm sure this was not the welcome party he had envisioned.

It was around these days that I first saw Zaliver whip out the hard liquor. I found him in his home office after returning from a meeting, I had found it odd that he hadn't come up to tell me he was home like usual, he just went straight to his office. Upon open the door, I had found him slumped down in his chair, turned to the window which showed the gloomy sky. All of the lights were off casting him in shadows. His hair looked especially black in the room. Walking closer to him, I realized his black tie was on the table desk and the first three buttons on his black shirt were undone.

When the scent of alcohol met my nose, I hesitated but quickly made my way to stand beside him. He didn't even look up, his side of the bond was blocked. I felt worry build up in me, but for once I wasn't sure how to comfort him so I began patting his hair, playing with it.

"Is there anything I can do?" I asked softly.

He brought the ice filled drink to his lips and took a long gulp. Setting it down, he reached up with one hand to grab my hands on his hair and began pulling me from behind him until I was on his lap. He tucked my head under his and sighed.

"No. Just stay like this with me for a while," he said roughly.

It was moments like this when I came to the realization of everything that had happened, when my life caught up to my brain. I was mated to an alpha, and we had just lost wolves and yet the world moved on. It was scary and left me with unreasonable panic. I wanted to get up and do something but Zaliver needed me,so I snuggled deeper into his chest, feeling his arms tighten around me as if he knew what I had just been feeling.

I'm not sure how long we stayed there in silence, but it was a sad yet peaceful time until I opened my mouth.

"Zaliver . . ." I said slowly, trailing off. His hand which had drawn small patterns on my back stilled and then continued as I broke silence.

"Yes?" he asked, sounding more relaxed and tranquil.

I paused and took a breath knowing this wasn't what he needed now, but it was what I needed.

"I need to go for a run." His reaction was instantaneous.

His whole body tensed under mine, the arms around me suddenly restraining as if to keep me from getting away from him, a rumbling began from his chest and I didn't need to look up to know his teeth were bared.

"Absolutely not." He snarled.

I sighed and tried pulling away but his arms wouldn't allow it. I rolled my eyes but stopped trying and instead put a hand on his fast beating heart.

"I need to shift and you know it. Last time didn't go so well, but this is why I'm telling you now. So that you can come with me," I explained. I gave him a few minutes to think about it, when his arms began to slowly relax around me I pulled back slowly as to not startle him into changing his mind.

His reaction to my request was aggressive and yet when I pulled back to look at him I realized that his eyes were filled with fear and pain. My heart broke a little.

"Oh Zaliver," I said sadly. He cupped my face in his hands and shook his head.

"I can't lose you too, not again. Not you. I-I can't." He choked out, his frame shaking, I blinked away the upcoming tears forcing in my eyes.

"And you won't." He opened his mouth to say something but I placed a finger over his mouth. ", Will you protect me?" I asked removing my finger from over his mouth.

Blue eyes flashed fiercely at me, almost offended at the question.

"Always," he said seriously.

"Do you believe you can keep me safe?" I continued, intertwining my fingers in his hair.

"Yes," he answered without a doubt. I smiled at him, tilting my head to the side a little.

"Then I don't see what the problem is. I mean, my big bad alpha mate will be there, watching over me. My hero," I said, half jokingly. After a brief pause Zaliver relaxed and gave me a reluctant smile.

"I can not find any holes in your logic," he said. My chin lifted up with mock pride.

"Of course not. I'm right, I'm always right." At this, his brow lifted, my eyes narrowed warningly.

"Do you have something to say?" I questioned leaning in, there was a certain edge to my voice.

540

"I love you." I laughed and kissed both of his cheeks.

"Good answer."

Jumping off of his lap I spun around quickly, the cloth of my dress twisting around with me, I took hold of both of Zaliver hands and began the process of trying to pull up my heavy mate. He watched with amused eyes.

"Cooperate with me!" I whined, yanking at him with all my straight, all of it, if anything I saw him plant himself firmer into his chair. A crooked grin made its way onto his face, my heart skipped a beat.

"And why should I do so, what will I get?" he asked, eyeing me from head to toe with wanting eyes. This man goes from depressed to horny unbelievably fast.

I let go of his hands and placed them on my hip, I couldn't look down at him because even sitting down he still made it seem as if he had the upper hand. That didn't mean I wouldn't try.

"Why is it always negotiations with you? Why can't your heavy ass just stand the hell up?"

"I prefer the term 'fit'."

"And I'm getting ready to prefer the term 'hit' if you don't stand up. Do you want me to go alone?" I asked annoyed.

This cleaned off any amusement from his face, with a groan he stood up and placed his hands on my shoulders, turning me around.

"No," he muttered.

"So let's go." I began walking to the doorway.

"Fine. At least I'll get to watch you strip," he said more to himself.

"I don't know, I might make you turn the other way," I said, a bit peeved. My emotions had been growing and turning into relentless energy that I hadn't been able to burn off in my natural form or forms.

Zaliver chuckled behind me, his breath fanning over his mark on my shoulder making me shiver.

"Do you really think I'd turn away from the chance of watching you strip? My little cloud, so naïve. " He leaned down and skimmed his lips down my neck, I tilted my head to give him better access, until he planted a firm kiss on his mark.

I couldn't help the soft groan that came from my mouth but I knew better than to let Zaliver seduce me, he was trying to distract me from going outside and shifting. He was doing it because he cared but I couldn't go on forever without shifting, I'd need to do it eventually and better now than later.

Taking a step away from him and looking over my shoulder I stuck my tongue out at him and walked out of his office, knowing he'd follow behind me. I was correct when I hear soft footsteps behind me.

When we made our way to the front of the house we were surprised to see Joshula walking in, returning. Everyone paused, surprise and confusion as well as a bit of guilt flooded my system, once more remembering how easy it was to push Joshula to the back of our heads when everything was going on. Zaliver came up to greet Joshula and then stood back and next to me.

"Hey, are you just getting home?" Zaliver asked, surprise thick in his voice. Joshula looked momentarily uncertain before he took composure.

"Yes, I was with a friend," he said cooly, showing nothing in both his tone or expression.

Zaliver tilted his head to the side but didn't further question his brother as if getting some unsaid hint that Joshula wouldn't like it if he were nosy. I didn't get that hint.

"A girl-friend?" I asked, feeling a sort of mocking amusement, like when you want to tease someone who's just gotten caught returning from a naughty night out.

Joshula looked appalled, a frown making its way to his face, his eyes flashed momentarily to that startling and bizarre murky yellow. I wasn't sure if it was intentional or not from his part, but Zaliver took a sudden step in front of me.

"Joshula . . ."

"No, I was not out with a female. A friend, that is all," he answered me, ignoring Zaliver who stood partly in front of me.

I didn't say anything but just nodded. There was a pull in my gut, some feeling of. . .what exactly?

"Joshula," Zaliver said again. "We're going for a run, would you like to come with? Perhaps you-"

"No."

I held my breath.

Even I was taken back by how quick and harsh it came from him, as was Zaliver as his side of the bond opened up with flared emotions. While as a brother he was momentarily bothered and hurt by his brothers reply, the alpha in him was furious at the interruption and was not in the mood but thankfully had enough self-control to not deck his brother then and there.

"Well then," Zaliver said. His voice just as cold as Joshula's had been. With everything going on Zaliver was running on high emotions, low energy and a lot of will.

"Vivian," Zaliver said as he took my hand and walked us around Joshula who gave me a skeeving look.

We were out of the door and into the forest faster than I could fish my sentence. When he turned around to face me I opened my mouth to say something about what happened back there but something

542

about his expression to told me to leave it, that he didn't want to talk about it, not at the moment. So I did.

"Are you going to shift with me?" I asked him.

"And give your wolf a heart attack at the realization of how much bigger I am beside her?" He asked putting his hands in his pants pocket. He looked really hot doing that—snap out of it!

"True, true, maybe next time," I said.

" Maybe, wait here, don't move," he said before I felt the air shift around me in warning of his departure.

Zaliver made me wait before I shifted, checked the area, made me stand in the least crowded spot and then gave me the go. While he watched. Like a hawk. Okay maybe not like a hawk but he was pretty damn intense.

I shook my head and closed my eyes, taking a deep breath.

Who wants to go? I asked my beast and wolf who were suddenly full of energy.

To avoid last time I say we got at this slowly and cautiously. I'll let the wolf go first since I can last the longest without a run, she has not gone into long. My beast said calmly.

Yeah, what she said. My wolf barked.

Okay than, wolf first. Are you two going to be okay or are you going to clash when I try to change? I asked seriously.

Just focus on bringing the wolf forward instead of all three of us connecting together. It should work. My beast though, logically it made sense but that still didn't stop me from worried it wouldn't. Last time all three of us were full front in my mind it did not end well.

Focusing on just my wolf was easy, pulling only her forward was harder than I thought. Both of them were equal in my mind and to leave one behind felt as if I were almost rejecting a part of myself but my beast assured me that she did not feel it and that it was the moral side of my human side effecting the process. After sometime I felt the shift come over me and when I opened my eyes I was on all fours.

Oh god baby yesssssss. This is the body. My wolf hissed out, for a wolf she was very. . .non wolf like sometimes.

Strains, exhaustion, aches and emotional baggage I didn't know I was carrying suddenly left me, filling me with positive things. My wolf made her way to Zaliver with a wolfish grin and barked at him. He looked down with adoring amusement in his sparkling blue eyes.

"Well hello little wolf," he said, petting my head with his hand. Jeezus he's gonna pull the ear—He pulled the ear.

My wolf let out a loud purr as Zaliver pulled on my left ear making her rub her fur onto his leg as if marking him with our scent.

Zaliver smirked a very proud, very pleased smirk. My wolf pulled back a bit and looked over our mate and said.

I'll be back for your fine ass in a few, don't go anywhere suga', I'll be right back.

And ran off without another glance. I buried myself further in my mind with mortification as Zaliver laugh boomed through the air.

Why do you always do this to me!? I screamed at my wolf.

She hopped over a log and gave a very human like snort. She caught sight of a sleeping bunny and decided to scare the crap out of it by growling, waking it up and then giving chase to it.

Because if I don't then who else will? Besides, you think it, I just, you know. . .say it. In a completely different way. That mortifies you. Because it's fun.

If I could hit you.

You'd hit yourself. My beast said.

My wolf caught the bunny but didn't eat it, instead she let it go and ran back to Zaliver whose eyes were focused on us even before we left the cover of the forest. I briefly wondered if his eyesight was good enough to see me from all the way to where I had run.

Running back to Zaliver my wolf eyes caught sight of a figure standing behind a window of our house. Joshula.

Was he watching? The thought made my fur stand up, a disturbing chill made me slow my running. When I got to Zaliver my eyes had not moved from the house so he turned to look at what had caused my distraction.

Oh no officer I wasn't stalking, no, just observing from afar without the other person knowing they were being observed. My wolf mumbled. Starts with windows, ends with trees and then a restraining order and we all know how well waving around a piece of paper goes. . .

It was hard but I shut her up.

With both of us now looking Joshula stood at the window for a few more seconds, his expression unclear with my wolf eyes because of far he was and through the window, but he suddenly turned and disappeared.

Zaliver turned with a frown but said nothing on his brothers odd behavior. I'd never had a brother but was that normal? I didn't think so. If he wanted to come with us he should have just said so, maybe he was having second thoughts now?

I shifted mid step and now stood before Zaliver in human form. I stretched my arms above my head and across my chest. Giving out a relieved sigh I draped myself over Zaliver, automatically his arms opened around me to hold me steady. I felt like I was on cloud nine, the high after a long time without shifting.

"Better?" he murmured.

544

"Almost? You sure you don't want to shift with me? I'll feel weird going around like bigfoot," I said with a pout. Huffing Zaliver agreed and began pulling me deeper into the forest until we got to a large tree where he began stripping down.

Doing so eagerly I took my dress and undergarments. Since my beast was ready for her turn, pulling her forward was a bit easier now that I knew what to expect. Opening my eyes I saw that Zaliver was already a beast with shiny black fur who stood proudly, black predator eyes took me in.

In this form we stayed longer, ran further and eventually I was exhausted. Going back to our cloths I dressed quickly, but Zaliver? He decided to tease his poor little mate by putting on every layer slowly, sensually and with his eyes on me.

I swear, by the time the buttoning of his shirt began I was going crazy and the man wasn't even undressing himself! If anything, he was putting it back on!

"See something you like?" he asked me, knowing damn well I did.

Grumbling I gave him the finger and stalked off to the house, planning on getting a nice shower before bed, I wasn't all that hungry. Not for food at least.

As the days and nights passed the atmosphere on the island slowly began to lighten thankfully. It was odd, in between cheerful because of the holidays and bittersweet. Zaliver had been going around doing lots of things and when I tried to ask him about his day he'd just look at me oddly so I let him be.

Joshula had kept mostly to himself when in the house, which was less and less as the days passed. When he was around though the room seemed tense to me, Zaliver had tried to catch Joshula whenever he could but it was almost as if the younger brother was avoiding him. I'd have to talk to him next time I saw him.

It was a day before my birthday when I woke up in the middle of the night groggy, not completely sure what had woken me up. It had almost felt as if someone was playing with my fingers. Beside me Zaliver shifted a bit, it almost felt as if he was looming over me, blaming my sleepy state I reached out and wrapped an arm around his waist. He tensed.

He shifted a bit and grabbed hold of that same arm, it almost felt as if he had removed something from my fingers but I knew that was impossible because I hadn't gone to sleep with anything on.

"What are you doing?" I mumbled, barely understandable.

"Nothing," he whispered in the dark, wrapping how own arm around me and pulling me on top of his chest, I relaxed, believing him and went back to sleep.

He let out a shaky breath.

~•~

On the morning of my birthday I was awakened by screaming people. Beautiful right?

"Happy Birthday!"

If it weren't for Zaliver's arms which he had wrapped around me, ready for my reaction, I would have sprung at everyone in the room since they startled my beast. They froze for a moment at the bared teeth and silver eyes and then when Hannah began laughing they joined.

"Happy birthday," Zaliver whispered in my ear.

Now that I was more aware as to what was going on and not on defense mode a large grin made its way across my face.

Hannah, Mark, Luke, Mila, Johnson and Cort stood in front of me with party hats. Even the two twins Drake and Blake and the other three girls Amber, Leslie and Angela. I hadn't seen them in the longest of times, Leslie was a redhead who was Luke's younger sister while Amber was a tall dark girl with light hazel eyes, Angela was a caramel colored girl with brown eyes. They stood behind everyone with sheepish yet excited expressions. Behind them a calm and sort of separated Joshula stood.

"Umm . . ." I said in a bubbling grin.

Hannah rubbed her very pregnant belly and rolled her eyes sky blue eyes, her hair was much shorter than I remember it being. She was wearing a light summer dress with what looked like splatter painted flowers. I noted that for once the guards were out of their normal black gear and actually in normal clothing.

Of course I would be caught while still in bed. . . A part of me cringed on the inside.

"Either she's speechless or can't think of anything to say. It's 'Oh my god you guys!' by the way." Hannah said humorously. That snapped me out of my half dumb mental state.

"Well I was just sleeping like a few seconds ago," I pointed out, raising a brow as if to further my point. She pointed at me.

"And now you're awake so . . ." she trailed off. I laughed and then shook my head at her, she rolled her hands as if saying 'continue'.

"Oh my god you guys!" I gushed with a much false as real pretense as I could. I felt Zaliver's chest shake with his silent chuckles.

"We wanted to say it as soon as possible so we asked Alpha," Johnson said happily.

"Well thank you for startling me awake. I really appreciate it," I said, and he nodded.

"I know we haven't really talked or hung out like the others with you, but we asked Luke if we could come with to say happy birthday. Happy birthday." Amber said sheepishly.

"More like harassed," Luke muttered under his breath.

"And we bare gifts!" Angela said, motioning for Drake and Blake to move.

The twins behind her suddenly moved away from each other showing an impressive cart full of presents. My eyes widened at the sight of the colorful display. I counted them and then the people in the room.

"I know I'm bad at math but there are a lot more presents then there are people in the room," I stated.

" Those are just from us," Mila said with a smirk, there was a glint in her eye that said there were more to come.

I was grateful for the presents but I was so not going to open them in front of everyone. It was a bit awkward trying to show the right appreciation and excitement.

"We'll leave you to get ready. Happy birthday Luna!" Cort yelled out, shoving everyone out. There were some grumbles but out they went.

"Thank you everyone!" I yelled out.

Joshula paused at the door. "Happiest of wishes for you today Vivian, may your wildest dreams come true." He said mendaciously before leaving with a nod.

That was . . . nice of him. I think.

Hannah stopped at the door.

"We're not leaving, we're having breakfast here courtesy of your very nice mate." She batted her eyes at me, her only warning. " I know birthday sex is popular today, but please refrain from having me explain to your kids why they were born nine months after their mother's birthday!" She slammed the door behind her while I was left gaping at her with an open mouth and a flamed face.

Behind me Zaliver's soft growl filled my ears.

"Birthday sex . . ." he whispered softly behind me, his tone sinfully seductive. "Sounds much more exciting than breakfast right now, don't you think?" he asked, skimming his nose down the side of my face.

" I think," I hopped up and turned around to face him. "that I need a shower—*what are you wearing?*" My voice had gone undoubtedly deeper when I realized that Zaliver wasn't wearing his pj's. He was already showered and dressed.

Oh my.

Zaliver stood up to his full height before me, letting my eyes skim over the perfection that stood in front of me.

547

He wore white converse on his feet, his long legs were covered in soft washed gray pants that were tight at the ankles but stretched to accommodate his muscular thighs, neither tight nor loose. A white-collar shirt peeked out from mocha colored cardigan that stuck to his wide chest, on top he wore a dark coffee-colored long coat that stopped right above his knees. All but one shiny black hair strand was combed back, dark blue eyes framed by long black lashes watched me intensely.

I had forgotten how to breathe, blink and function entirely at this point. And I'm sure my wolf had fainted stiff, tongue out and everything.

I suddenly understood why Zaliver dressed in mostly casual black attire. It was because his dress code was in between sophisticated, casual, professional and a whole lot of sexy.

The man didn't care what he looked like before and now seeing what he looked like when he actually tried left me in a devastating situation. I was suddenly very much aware of the male in the room with me, as if I wasn't before.

The smirk on his face let me know that he knew the effect he had on me. And probably all of the women on the planet, there was no way a lesbian woman and straight man wouldn't want to tap him.

"You did say you wanted me to dress myself better, will this do?" he asked coyly.

Without really answering him and skimming my eyes over him again I took the bottom of my shirt and lifted it over my head leaving me in just my bra and pj pants.

"Birthday sex . . . Yeah that sounds good," I said half distracted.

It was a good day, most definitely.

Zaliver threw his head back and let out a laugh that warmed me to the core, it was nice seeing him laughing. Now if only he would only take everything off, I thought dryly.

"Oh no." He shook his head at me. "you wanted to go shower. So go." He shooed me away mockingly in the direction of the bathroom. Eying him I pulled out the card every girl in my position would use.

"It's my birthday, aren't you supposed to give me what I want today?" I asked him, taking steps towards him.

He surprised me by jumping and rolling over the bed, putting space between us. I narrowed my eyes on him and then realized that his own eyes, now a midnight blue were flickering from my face to my chest and back. I smirked and reached for my bra strap, seeing what I was doing a panicked look entered his eyes, he lifted both hands.

548

"You know I do that everyday anyway, besides, you have impatient guest downstairs eating the breakfast I prepared and if you don't hurry they might eat it all, he pointed out.

I gave him a sultry smile, tilting my head to the side and letting all of my hair fall away from my shoulder, baring his mark at him. I saw his jaw clench.

"They can eat it all, " I whispered breathlessly and went again for the clasp.

"How about this?" he said. I narrowed my eyes at him but stopped. I was slightly curious as to why he'd refuse sex, besides the fact that there were people downstairs.

"I'm listening." I dropped my hands to my sides.

"While you're okay with missing your breakfast, I am not. I cannot allow my mate to skip a meal, especially in our home. While I would love to drop everything and give you want you right now that would put us behind the schedule I spent so much time planning for today. So I say we postpone this for later tonight," He bargained. After a second he gave me full mouthed grin, showing off his pearly whites. "and when the night finally comes you can release all the sexual tension you have and ravish me to your heart's desires. I'll be all yours for the taking," he whispered persuasively.

I bit my bottom lip and pondered over it, I knew that if I got my bra off he'd be a goner but he obviously wanted to spend the day in a certain order and it'd be rude of me to ignore all his hard work or whatever. While I thought out my decision his panicked dark blue eyes just darkened even more as he skimmed over my chest.

"Fine. You win." I pouted, crossing my arms under my chest, partly to taunt him. He made sure to keep his eyes on my own as he walked around the bed and in front of me. He leaned down and kissed my forehead.

"Good girl."

He spun me around and pushed me in the direction of the bathroom. "Now go shower before they devour everything on the table."

"You're mine tonight," I grumbled.

"Forever and always." I could hear the smile in his words.

I entered the bathroom without turning around to look at him.

"Now for a cold shower." His laugh echoed in the bathroom even after I shut the door.

I quickly showered, brushed my teeth and dried off, when I came out of the shower Zaliver was no longer in the room. Smart man.

I decided to wear a thin but multi layered lavender dress that stopped a bit before my knees. It had short sleeves but my favorite part about the dress was that as it ended the lavender started turning darker

549

shades of purple. Even though the dress was short and I'd have to be careful bending down I boldly decided not to wear tights or leggings underneath, although because the dress was so light I had to go for the lightest undergarments I had. I accompanied the dress with knee-high black heeled boots.

I quickly blow dried my hair and pulled back only the front. I only put on eyeliner and lipstick, chose small diamond earrings and two black bracelets. I didn't really have any rings to match the dress so I didn't put any on. Looking in the mirror I realized that I looked more mature and happier than I had probably ever been. As well as sexy.

Hell, if Zaliver wouldn't let me jump him then I'd have to get him to jump me.

Opening the door the first thing I realized was that the hallway was very colorful and super crowded. By large and carefully wrapped presents.

From what I could see there were more than hundreds in the hall and as I made my way down the stairs and saw more stacked on top of each other on the steps I came to the living room and gasped. If I thought the hall and stairs were bad, I couldn't even see my living room anymore.

"I do not know this many people." I snorted, amusement and excitement filling me. This was most definitely going to be the best birthday ever.

I had asked Zaliver not to throw me a not so surprised birthday party, balls I could stand, meetings were okay, reunions ah, but a birthday party were everyone sings and you're left in front of cake like 'okay' until they're done is just so baaaad. He didn't need much persuasion, I really just preferred to spend the day with him. It was our first birthday together.

I walked into the kitchen expecting to see everyone. I quickly realized that because of the amount of people that they probably all wouldn't fit on the kitchen counter and so I walked to the unused dining room.

Hannah was of course the first to see me, letting out a whistle that made everyone turn to look at her and then follow her eyes which then led to me turning scarlet.

"Wow, nice."

"You look lovely Luna."

"Vivian. . ." That had been Joshula.

"Killer heels."

"So pretty!" I got a lot of compliments from everyone which made me smile in return.

"Pass me that bagel," Johnson said, eyeing a bagel wantonly in front of an unamused Mila.

"Damn girl! Someone remind me why I'm not tapping that?" Hannah asked pointing her fork at me. Beside her Mark rolled his eyes.

"How about me and the child you're carrying, mine by the way, too." He said stuffing pancakes int his mouth.

"Right, right." She smiled.

I shook my head at her and looked for Zaliver to find that he was already looking at me. Sometimes no words have to be spoken for a message to be received. My legs shook a little as I made my way to the empty seat beside him, as expected he sat as the head of the table.

My plate was already filled to the brim with cut pancakes, fruit salad, french bread and bacon. I didn't need to guess to know Zaliver had done it himself. I poured myself a glass of orange juice.

"Thank you," I said. He took the hand closest to him and brought it to his lips, kissing my knuckles, making sure to have my attention. Somehow that action alone was better than a complement.

It wasn't until I began eating that he said something through the mind link.

Are you wearing shorts under that dress? he asked with a dark edge to his voice.

Instead of answering him, I turned to quickly wink at him. His shocked expression made me hold in a giggle.

Half through breakfast and conversation the twins Drake and Blake who sat next to each other had started sharing one of their birthday experiences. Both brown-haired and eyes brothers were strikingly similar if one didn't notice that one had higher cheekbones and the other a stronger jaw definition. It also helped that Drake had on a blue sweater and Blake a green one.

"But mom had wanted us to share a cake and since we had already ate into the second one we ended up agreeing," Blake said.

"Wait, which birthday was this one?" Amber asked.

"The transformers one," Blake said. His amber eyes widened before she busted out laughing as if remembering something, beside her Angela giggled, even Luke snorted and shook his head. I had a feeling the twins were about to explain.

"We were big on pranks at that time," Drake said looking over in my direction.

"No, you were big on pranks. I usually just got hurt," Blake pointed out, his brother waved him off as if it weren't true. "And so when it was time to sing happy birthday, you know when everyone's like 'Bite the cake! Bite it!' ?" Drake asked, I nodded, everyone knew the custom.

"Well our mom made us do it and so when they put me and Blake side by side we had to wrap our arms around each other to get

551

both of us in. Of course when the time came I would push my brothers face in the cake." Drake said.

"And for once I wanted to retaliate and do the same to my brother for all the pranks he did. Except. . ." Blake trailed off with a grin on his face while beside his Drake looked at his brother dryly.

"Go on, tell them what you did," Drake grumbled. Amber shook with silent laughter.

"I miscalculated," Blake said sheepishly.

"And while I pushed his face into the cake, he slammed my face against the table," Drake muttered.

I busted out laughing, not one of those lady like, adorable laughs, more like the ones you do when your best friend does something stupid and you laugh because you knew it would happen and yet it came out better than expected.

"Blood, tears, picture and a whole lot of 'sorry' and it turned out Blake broken my nose."

"I remember that, it was the funniest thing I've ever seen in my life. Blake looked as if he had just won a battle and then he realized only his face was in the cake, saw your face and began bawling as if you had done it to him!" Amber roared.

"Remind me to push all the kids away from ours at birthday parties." I heard Mark say to Hannah who had a pained smile on her face, she nodded. This made me laugh even harder.

Wiping all of the tears away I turned to Zaliver who was looking at me softly with adoring eyes. I grinned at him.

"Has anyone ever done that to you?" I asked, everyone looked at Zaliver curiously. I noted how they spoke about him and yet even with him in the room didn't directly speak to him. He still intimidated everyone, maybe except for Hannah but then again those could be the hormones talking for her.

"Slam my face on a table or into a cake?" he asked, lifting a dark brow at me.

"Cake." I clarified, I knew my mate and his behavior, I'm sure someone had already tried the first one.

"Albericus tried and paid the price for it," he said mysteriously.

"Okaaay," I said. Now he really scared everyone.

When everyone finished up their food and began cleaning I heard something that caught my interest.

"drowning in homework. I have a life outside of school you know? It's not my fault Ms.Andres isn't getting any dick in her life," Leslie muttered to Angela, not knowing that Zaliver could hear, but Luke did.

"Leslie!" he whispered harshly in warning, she flushed in embarrassment at her brother hearing her. He motioned towards me and Zaliver with his head without actually looking but she did.

I wasn't surprised to see her lose color when she meet my eyes which to her were probably knowing. I caught Zaliver out of the side of my eye, he looked elsewhere, not caring for her words even though he could hear them.

I however did care, not about her expression, I had used that at one point in my life.

Leslie and her friends were around my age and maybe the twins a bit older but I knew they weren't in high school which made me think they were in college.

"You're in College Leslie?" I asked her, some of the conversations quieted. I began to notice that happened whenever Zaliver or I had to say something. She nodded quickly.

"We go to Golden Lupus, art, architecture, merchandise, acting, network production, marketing and business," she explained.

"Where do you guys go to?" I asked the twins.

"I go to Red Lupus, english, writing, languages, culture study, cooking, dance, poetry, psychology, social and economic studies," Drake responded, naming everything with a thoughtful look while using his fingers as if he had been counting.

"Silver Lupus, mathematics, science exploration, history, environmental studies, beauty production and the experimental division," Blake said. I guess the confusion was clear on my face because he explained on the names.

"On this side of the island there aren't any colleges per say, after high school you apply to the careers and classes you want after an application process and then you get sectioned into your house. Gold is for the creatives, Red for the self knowledgeable and study, Silver for the book nerds and curious one and so many other houses.

It's way faster than the human college because you go straight to the classes that will help you, thus faster graduation. And it's basically free, the only payment accepted is that once you get a job you help improve the island with your knowledge and if you're the top of the field you may get repositioned out of the island and somewhere between the humans for power positions to help Alpha," he explained.

By the end of his explanation I was awed and suddenly filled with the need to find out more about this place. I would have already been in college by now if not for the abrupt kidnapping and all. I opened my mouth to ask something when a strong but subtle emotion flared through the bond.

I turned to look at Zaliver who seemed beyond tense and quiet. He knew I was looking at him and yet had his eyes focused ahead

553

of him. The emotion through the bond almost felt like. . .displeasure or—

"Are you interested in going Vivian?" someone asked.

I turned to find the voice, across the table, towards the end Joshula was looking at me with intent. Everyone at the table hadn't asked or had been given an explanation as to whom he was but the resemblance to Zaliver was self-explanatory. The question caught me off guard because I myself wasn't sure anymore.

"I don't know, perhaps," I said truthfully.

My ears caught the faint sound of something like metal reforming under pressure. Joshula wasn't done asking his question though, so I couldn't turn to look at Zaliver and ask if he was okay.

"Aren't you around the same age as they are. Referring to my knowledge, don't most high school student apply after? Were you not accepted?" he asked.

Those are fightin' words. My wolf growled.

The table went silent as everyone eyes Joshula with surprise and uncomfortable fidgets. I felt a small wave of anger come from Zaliver as well as guilt. I myself felt unease,but for a completely different reason. My wolf was grumbling something about throwing my unfinished toast at his face.

"I was, actually," I said calmly. "But you know how it is, life happens. Besides, I have a lot of time to decide when I do go." I answered nonchalantly. My tone and body language seemed to calm everyone but Zaliver.

"Hmm." Joshula said nodding. "So what would your classes be? What do you like?" he asked.

"English, psychology, art," I said naming the top three from my mind. A grin made its way across his face. It was the look on his face, the teasing gleam, the way he held his head, that made his words and expression seem wrong.

"So you'd be in Red Lupus, perhaps Drake." I suddenly got where he was headed and a cool anger came over me. "Could show you around sometime. Show you what you've been missing all this time."

Drake paled at the mention of his name, he looked as if he suddenly wanted the ground to swallow him. Beside me Zaliver's side of the bond went cold and not because he had shut me out. It was one thing to poke at me and not get a reaction.

It was a completely different thing to poke at my alpha mate,poke me in the process and make speculation that would then piss off that very possessive and jealous alpha mate.

The room suddenly felt very chilly to how it had been a few minutes ago. As if without needing to he told everyone looked down and bared their neck in submissive to Zaliver who suddenly seemed very much like a pissed off alpha. He had let go and was letting his presence fill every inch of the room. Fierce icy blue eyes looked across the table to the only person who was not showing submission. His very own brother. No alpha would take a jab and disrespect at the table and not say shit about it.

Great.

"Joshula," Zaliver said threateningly, pronouncing every letter. I hadn't seen him like this in a long time.

Joshula didn't answer, all ready I could see that it pained him to look at his brother, the wolf in his knew his place and yet something in him fought.

"You are to go back to your room and not to leave for anything until tomorrow morning at sunrise. Go," he ordered. It was a bit frightening to be honest because instead of yelling out the order he said it calmly, as if he hadn't basically just grounded his brother.

Joshula didn't have much room to argue, as soon as Zaliver said 'go' his legs made him follow the order. When he left the room Zaliver closed his eyes took a breath and sighed.

Immediately the air became less tense and everyone looked up as if dazed. Had he taken their hearing? Probably.

I reached over and took one of his hands squeezing it. He gave a small smile, it didn't quite reach his eyes however. Before I could open my mouth to say something Algebra walked in with a wrapped blue gift.

His green eyes swept across everyone and everything and then he shook a finger at me and Zaliver.

"Oh yeah, don't invite the beta, send him on errands instead, make him get the—" Zaliver threw him a withering look that had him clamping his mouth shut. I cocked my head to the side in confusion and suspicion.

"What—" I tried asking but Algebra tossed the gift in the air, automatically I reached out to catch it.

Something clicked in the box, changing my train of thought. What's in here?

"Happy birthday! I don't care what you get or say my gift is the best," he said almost defensively.

"Thank you Algebra." His green cat-like eyes rolled at the name. "If this box explodes all over me, I hope you know I'm setting your ass on fire."

Surprised gasps filled the table, I'm sure they weren't use to seeing their Luna, Alpha and Beta together or being threatened. Algebra made an offended gesture.

555

"Honey, you can't set what's already hot on fire, you'll only add to my charm." He licked his pointer finger and put it on his forearm, making a sizzling sound. I laughed at the motion.

"Zaliver says you tried to cake him once," I said, at first he looked confused and then he looked horrified. Zaliver laughed at his expressions making Algebra look pained.

"Do not ever do that. Death by cake is possible. He almost suffocated me with his own cake. I think it was his what? Six hundredth . . . There is something seriously wrong with you man, you almost killed your own beta for getting you cake, is that what my life is worth to you? Cake?" Algebra said dramatically, while picking up the bacon plate and munching off of it.

"You're still alive aren't you? Is it done?" Zaliver asked, pushing back and standing up.

"Yeah, but when you do the—"

"I know, I'll keep it in mind."

"Aurora said to tell her about the—"

"Does she really need it?"

"She's gonna—"

"Fine. I know."

"Do you have—"

"Yeah."

"Okay."

"Okay."

"What the hell was that?" I mumbled to myself. Zaliver and Algebra just finished a conversation that wasn't really a conversation faster in the weirdest of ways. Algebra grinned at me.

"Years of knowing someone's train of thought will do that," he said.

"We're twins and we aren't even that good," Drake said, pointing to him and Blake who looked honestly bewildered. Zalivers voice went a bit more serious for the next part.

"Albericus I want you to talk to Hogan and figure out what Joshula speaks to him about," he ordered, the others pretended not to listen.

Algebra nodded, for some reason I thought it looked like he wanted to say something, but when our eyes met he cleared his expression and made way for a grin.

As soon as Zaliver began cleaning away at his plate everyone else stood up and did the same, Hannah came around and put her hands on my shoulder and turned me to Zaliver.

"Don't worry Alpha, we've got this. You two go have fun," she said.

Zaliver looked down at her sceptical for a moment before, nodding.

"Thank you everyone," he said. Typical of him. No 'Make yourselves feel at home'.

"Thanks for coming and the presents!" I said grateful to everyone. I mean sure breakfast got a bit weird but it still went great.

No blood, no foul.

Zaliver took hold of my hand and looked at me. "You ready?" he asked. I looked at him in slight confusion.

"Where are we going?" I asked. He hadn't mentioned anything about going out but his wardrobe did point out to outdoors.

A devilish smile was the only answer he gave me before he lead me out of the dining room, everyone called out goodbyes and waved at us. Algebra grinned at me as I passed him, a knowing glint in his eyes.

Before we left the house Zaliver ran upstairs for some things, the house phone rang so I picked it up. I wasn't all to surprised to know it was my parents wishing me a happy birthday and wanted me to know that as soon as they could they'd come to visit. For some reason they sounded even more emotionally charged than usual when it was my birthday and when I asked they just blamed it on realizing that 'their baby was actually an adult and going on to make adult decisions that would alter her life.'

I had to remind them that I was turning nineteen, not eighteen, the age where that was considered entering adulthood. They actually snorted at me. When Zaliver came down he had in one hand a black long coat that I recognized as mine and a backpack over his shoulder. He handed me the coat which I put on.

"What's with the backpack?" I asked him.

"A surprise," he said, checking me out with his eyes, which lingered a lot on my boots and where both them and the dress ended. I made a face at him.

"I don't like surprises and speaking about them. Where did all of these presents come from? I know for a fact this is more than my Facebook friends and I don't even really know some of them," I pointed behind me to the overcrowded living room and put my hands on my hips to look up at him. His eyes casually looked over my shoulder and then back at me.

" As Luna of all wolves it's only normal for you to get gifts," he said a bit too nonchalantly.

I narrowed my eyes in suspicion at his tone.

"Normal? Or Expected?" I asked him.

He took my hand, grabbed the car keys from the door side table and pulled me out.

557

"A bit of both," he answered. I rolled my eyes behind his back.

"Oh what am I going to do with you?" I muttered mostly to myself, under my breath.

As he opened the door to his car for me to get into,he leaned down to answer.

"You already know what you're going to do with me tonight. Buckle up." He promptly closed the door on my astonished face.

As he walked around with grace and wicked confidence to his side of the car, I had to get myself to stop squeezing my legs together. Damn him and his hotness.

When he got into the car it took him less than a second to smell my arousal in the confided car. His jaw clenched as he gripped the wheel hard enough that I heard a faint shifting.

"Damn it. Didn't think about this," he said before starting the car and rolling down every window in the car. This made me laugh.

"How's the growing sexual tension working out for you?" I asked his mockingly and then gasped when black eyes turned to look at me with strong focus.

"Just great," he said roughly, turning back to the road.

Hot. My wolf panted.

This was going be a long day.

CHAPTER 41

VIVIAN GREY

As Zaliver drove out of the driveway, I began to wonder where we could be going. So I began noting down things mentally. We had already eaten so that cancelled out anything with food.

We're both dressed nice, one more so than the other, I'm also wearing heels and the fact that he didn't tell me to change means no walking or hikes. He had a black backpack in the back seat.

What does that all lead up to?

It was quiet in my head.

Yeah that's what I thought too, what is he up to? Eyeing him I gave up and turned the radio on, he glanced over but didn't say anything.

"Hey!" I exclaimed excited as I realized what song was playing.

"Understand me, just simply do the things I say."

Give into me by Michael Jackson. A devious plan began to form in my mind.

I started off by softly swaying side to side and tapping my fingers on the car door. I waited a few seconds before humming along to the song and then I began moving my feet to the rhythm. From the corner of my eyes I could see Zaliver smile.

Mwahahaha, enjoy the show.

Then I began rocking my hips and moving my arms slowly in the air in a swaying way, over my head and holding onto the back of the head rest. I turned my body slightly towards him.

He was no longer smiling, or he was, but it was a painful, 'why are you doing this to me' smile. I hummed along to the song softly, noting how his eyes flickered from me to the road. We were approaching a red light.

Here comes my que. Even with all the windows rolled down I could smell his arousal in the car, it didn't help that he was beside me. I pushed wanting thoughts and emotions through the bond. Let's see him resist this.

"Love is a feeling, quench my desire, give it when I want it, taking me higher, love is a woman, I don't want to hear it, give into me. . ." I sang softly, smiling.

I put my hands on the bottom of my dress and making it seem a part of my car dance I slowly inched it up slower and slower, this time when I moved my hips I let my legs follow. A small rumbled began from Zaliver's chest, his body turned in my direction now, almost subconsciously.

No doubt he would get a good glimpse of what was under the dress if I inches another bit.

He quickly reached for my hands, yanked down on them, bringing my dress back over my thighs and almost destroyed the radio when he turned it off. Turning back to face the front his chest raised up and down with quick movements. I could hear his heart pounding in his chest, he peaked over to me. I pouted at him which he quickly looked away from.

This time when the light turned green he slammed his foot on the gas, driving faster than before.

With the way he was driving we reached whatever destination he had in mind because he suddenly pulled the car at a stop in front of a tattoo shop.

Wait, what?

I got out without waiting for Zaliver to come around like usual, he made a face at me but I was so busy looking at the store in confusion and uncertainty. It was a small store beside many ,but by the decorating and exhibiting art in the window I could tell that it was a good one. The store looked old and like it had seen better days but somehow it also looked new with dark brown wooden walls, black framed windows and an odd entrench door that resembled that of a heavy church door, with the engraved detailed drawings and everything. The only thing missing was the door knob.

Zaliver took hold of my hand firmly and began walking to the shop.

"Umm Zaliver, what's going on?" I asked, waking reluctantly with him.

Me and needles were a no. I looked around to see if there were any other stores where we could be heading into knitting, pet store, candy shop, medical pharmacy.

"What do you think?" he asked without looking back. I quickly thought if reasons for him to bring me here.

"You finally decided to take up knitting but don't want to do it alone because people may laugh at you?" My answer came out high-pitched and full of utter panic.

560

He stopped and turned to look down at me with a raised brow, blue eyes full of amusement as if to say 'Even if it were true, people making fun of me? Let them try to see if they live'.

"So no to knitting?" I questioned.

"No to knitting," he clarified. "And relax," he added, squeezing my hand in his. I took in a breath. He stopped in front of the tattoo shop door.

"How are we even going to—Oh," I said when he released my hand and crouched down and took hold of a handle I didn't notice. Instead of the door opening sideways he pulled it up with him as he stood and raised it above our heads, he motioned for me to step in.

I looked at him for a moment before stepping in hesitantly and stopping in the middle of the room, music was playing on low. It was the waiting room, each wall was painted a different dark color blue, green, yellow and purple. There was a dark-skinned man with tattoo sleeves and a piercing on his nose, he had a long beard that I wanted to ask how long it took him to grow since he looked to be in his mid thirties.

I could hear buzzing and smell ink in the air, metal, cleaning supplies and blood. I felt sick for a moment but then pushed my sense back. There were a handful of wolves in the store, a few sitting down and reading magazines. They looked up and blinked in surprise to see us, I smiled at them. There were doors leading to private work rooms I imagine.

I felt Zaliver's chest meet my back as he put his hands on my shoulders and pushed us forward to the man at the desk. The man smiled and stood up to greet us.

"Apha nice to see you again, hello and happy birthday Luna." The man said, going the whole man hand thing with Zaliver.

"Hello Mero," Zaliver asked stepping back.

"Hi, thanks," I said, sort of surprised he knew, but then again I'm guessing he sent a present. Wonder what it is? Piercings? Tattoo designs? I was suddenly really curious.

Some of the wolves in the room watched on like we were buzzard beings. Which to them I guess we were. Would I ever get use to the way people stared?

"Eddie's ready for you if you want to go now," Mero said and then backed away to his desk when Zaliver gave a curt nod.

I turned to look at Zaliver with horrified realization. I knew for a fact that I wasn't getting anything done to me but him? He was unpredictable?

"Zaliver—"

"Come on," he said, not letting me finish and dragging me off with him to a black door to our left.

561

Entering the room the first thing that caught my eyes was the long white bed like chair seen in dentist or in this case tattoo shops. The second thing that caught my eyes were the neatly arranged needles.

I felt myself pale. They were so sharp. I heard someone rummaging in what must have been this room's bathroom, Eddie I assume.

There was a chair, a normal one, a bit off to the side with a perfect angle to see just the artist at work but not the actual design. Zaliver pushed me down to sit in the chair. I stood back up.

He sighed and began taking off his coat and then the one underneath, passing them to me to hold which I folded neatly and put over my arm. I wasn't going to stop the show just yet. He wore a white collared button down shirt that clung deliciously to his muscular build. I didn't allow myself to stay distracted for long.

"I can't believe you're getting a tattoo," I began.

"I'm not," he said distracted with his shirt. That made me stop for a moment.

"You're not?" And after a moment asked. "Don't tell me you're getting your nipples pierced?"

He took off his shirt with a raised brow.

"No, but would you like me to?" he asked.

Yes!! My wolf hissed.

"No!!" I hissed at the same time. A smirk made its way over his face.

"Are you sure?" he murmured jokingly, passing his shirt to me.

Don't look down, don't look down, don't look down, don't look down, don't look down-

"Zaliver," I said seriously.

"Fine, I'm not getting a tattoo. I'm getting *tattoos*," he said smarty.

He went over to the bed like chair and laid down and boy what a sight that was alone. He was the perfect sculpture, the perfect male and he wanted to mark his body.

"Where the hell did this come from? You haven't, not once, mentioned wanting to get tattoos." I snapped, walking over to him and leaning over him. He frowned at my expression and cupped my face in his hands.

"You're really worked up about this aren't you?" He sighed. Of course I am.

"Wouldn't you if I suddenly decided to do something permanent to my body without telling you?" I asked annoyed.

I was more angry over the fact that he was about to mark his perfect body with God knows what nonsense. Like what if he decided to

562

get an image done on him and the artist turned out to be crappy? Or sneezed mid artwork?

Zaliver gazed into my eyes for a long time and then without warning brought my face down to kiss me sensual kiss that made me put my hand on his bare chest to stop me from falling due to weak knees. He nipped at my top lip and then with the tip of his tongue went over my bottom lip. With one last kiss he pulled me back.

I was gasping for breath even though the kiss lasted less than a minute. My thoughts scrambled and seemingly unimportant now.

"So. . .the tattoos?" He asked softly, stroking my face with his thumbs. I blinked a bit dazed, knowing I was getting played but not really caring as long as he fished what he started.

"Fine, fine. Just don't complain about them to me in a few years saying how bad it was and why I didn't stop you." I said with narrowed eyes but a goofy grin.

"What are you getting anyway? Bird? Tree of life? Howling wolf?" I asked him, causing him to roll his eyes at me.

"Maybe, it's a surprise." He said. I huffed.

"This is why I don't like surprises." I pointed out to him. And then in that moment Eddie walked out of the bathroom and stopped for a moment to look at us.

I looked from Eddie to the shirtless Zaliver, when I looked back at Zaliver my eyes flashed silver.

No. I snarled through the link. Zaliver gave a mental groan.

I'm sad to say that after a rather awkward and stiff greeting, mostly from my part, Zaliver finally convinced me to let Eddie work on his shirtless figure.

Eddie being a five foot eight, slim yet curvy figure with beautiful caramel eyes and purple dyed hair with blue ends, one side of her head was partly shaved leaving what looked like music notes in its place.

She'd have known what he wanted, he must have come in before which pissed me off even more, because other than greeting us she didn't say much. That made me dislike her a little less.

I was letting this punk rock chick lean over my mate and touch his skin and mark it, I don't care if she had gloves on. Although from where I was sitting I couldn't see what she was doing to Zaliver, due to the angle of the chair, I knew that she could both feel my unhappy gaze on her and that Zaliver could feel the uncontrollable anger and possessiveness coming from me. And I could feel his amusement and pleasure.

I did not like the thought of her touching my male, my mate. And I wasn't the only one.

I say we make her sing for us since she likes touching what isn't her. My wolf said maliciously.

Zaliver suddenly cleared his throat loudly while the Eddie wiped at his chest. I held back a snarl that wanted to come out of my mouth. My gums were aching to release my canines.

Or we break those pretty little artistic fingers of hers. Gets the message and job done a lot faster. My beast snarled.

Hmmm.

When the buzzing began and Eddie eyes focused, I knew she had begun.

Twenty minutes in and I was going crazy with the sound of the buzzing, the smell of ink and the fact that she was marking my mate. During the whole time I noted how not once Zaliver tensed or even gave off the impression that the sensation hurt of getting a tattoo.

"I can't believe you're doing this. These things last forever." I mumbled knowing he could hear me over the maddening buzzing.

"It's not my first actually and not forever," he said casually.

"What? Bull." I said, ranking my memory of every inch of his skin, trying to not squirm at the images, knowing not once had I seen a tattoo or even the image of the removal of one.

"They don't last long on us," Lycans he meant. "after a few decades they begin fading, I'll have to keep coming back." He cleared up.

"Great," I muttered. Well at least now I had a chance of getting him not to come back. And if he did, I'd make sure it would be a man doing the touch ups, always.

After fifteen minutes, I could no longer take the buzzing, my ears were hearing it but my mind was no longer sure if it was still going on or if it was my imagination.

I stood up and neatly placed his cloths on the chair. Who knew how long he'd be in here and I knew for sure I wouldn't be able to take the buzzing any longer. I didn't like the thought of leaving him with her, but if she tried anything I'd choke her with her own purple hair. Hearing me stand and guessing my need to leave he spoke.

"Don't leave the shop. I'll be out quickly," he said seriously.

Not answering him I stepped out of the room and instead of slamming the door like I was tempted too, I closed it softly. I decided to look at some of the art work on the walls, wondering if any were the ones that Zaliver choose to get.

There were fewer people in the waiting room now, I'm guessing they were like me, waiting for whoever they came with to come out. Mero was still in the front,but this time he was drawing. I'm guessing his wolf told him his Luna was looking at him because his expression went from focused to confused and then he looked up. I waved.

Walking over to his desk, my boots made a slight clicking sound on the marble floor. I sat down in front of him, he seemed slightly surprised but excited to see me.

"Hello Luna, can I help you?" he asked.

"I'm fine, just waiting for him to finish." I didn't have to say who. Quickly looking down at his work I gasped. "Wow, that's awesome, what is it?" I asked him.

On his paper were different colorful patterns coming together to form one shape, but it was unfinished so I wasn't sure what it was yet. Mero actually seemed embarrassed at the compliment.

"I was doodling," he confessed after a moment, sheepishly rubbing the back of his head. I snorted.

"Well shit, I wish I could doodle like that." I said, laughing afterwards, he joined after a moment.

"Thank you Luna, coming from you it's the best compliment I've ever received." He said happily. It sort of brightened my mood to know that was the way he saw it.

"Do you mind if I join you in your doodles?" I asked him.

"Not at all, here you go." He handed me a stack of paper and pushed his container full of different colors in the middle of us.

"Thanks," I said and began to ponder over what I should draw first.

Reaching for a colored pencil I let my mind wander.

"Do you draw a lot?" I heard Mero ask me.

"Sometimes, I use to want to be an artist but I couldn't decide which type of art I liked more." I said distracted, moving my hand quickly over the paper.

I liked neat and perfect art lines, but I mostly prefered messy yet organized art, the one where you could see where the artist went a bit too far and yet somehow made it work with the art.

Zaliver was in the room for a lot longer than thirty minutes before he came out, but I was so distracted between drawing and talking to Mero that I didn't notice my mate was standing a few inches away from me with both a look of surprise at my art since he'd never actually seen my work and a mixture of annoyance at being ignored by me for another male and newfound dislike for the male of my attention, poor Mero.

"Your mermaid looks like it came to land just to go shopping, nice touch with the scales. How'd you get them to shimmer on paper?" Mero asked with awe, turning his head to look at the paper.

"I used your silver marker and then played around with the white, green, blue and baby blues. Turns out this is some thick paper," I joked, if it weren't for the stack underneath I probably would have gone straight through paper, past the desk and onto the floor. This was some serious ink the man had.

Over all I had drawn a shopaholic mermaid with shimmering scales, big hair and shopping bags in one. On others I had drawn landscapes, starfishes, sketches of a medieval ballerina, jellyfish, a nerdy looking guitarist with hearts around him, blooming roses and a shadow hunter lurking in the forest. Mero said the last one was his favorite.

Out of habit I signed all of them so when Mero asked if he could keep them I hesitated, but decided there was no harm. Besides, he'd probably just redraw them, better than I had. At the moment we were looking over our, mostly my sketches. A cleared throat made me jump a bit, turning around I saw Zaliver standing behind me with a strained smile. I stood up quickly. He was already dressed.

"Ready?" he said with a hint of petulance which made my eyebrows raise in question at his sudden tense mood. And here I thought I wanted to hurt Eddie.

"Uh yeah," I said, pushing my chair in. Mero stood quietly, collecting the scattered drawings.

"Good. Mero," Zaliver said curtly, they did the hand thing guys do but I had a feeling Zaliver put a little too much force into it because Mero winced at some point.

Zaliver took my hand and began walking out, pulling the door up quickly and motioned for me step out. Ignoring him I turned and waved to Mero with a happy grin, he waved back with a grin on his own. I turned and stepped out.

Once in the car Zaliver sprang on me, I got out a small squeak out before his mouth was over mine in a dominating and demanding kiss. It was like he was both apologizing and demanding an apology in one kiss. I kissed his back just as fiercely.

When we pulled back we were both panting and had stupid grins on our faces. Ah, the power of love. Buckling up he started the car and began to drive down the street.

"I didn't even get to see your tattoos," I mentioned breathlessly.

He grinned at me and took hold of the closet hand to him, bringing it to kiss lips to kiss my knuckles.

"You'll see them tonight," he promised in between kisses. I felt my heart flutter at the romantic gesture.

"Don't you need to keep them covered or whatever for twenty-four hours?" I asked him. Just because I didn't like him getting a tattoo in the first place, meant that I was going to allow him to not take care of them.

"They're healing as we speak, by tonight they'll be fully healed," he said, winking at meA few minutes into the drive we had gone under a large bridge, we've never gone under a bridge.

"Where are we going now?" I asked him, looking out of the window at the new scenery. After thinking about it I added hurriedly. "And if you say 'surprise', I will punch you in the face. I swear I will." He laughed at my threat.

He thinks we're playing. I thought.

Let him, it'll be all more unexpected when we do. My wolf grumbled.

"Fine, fine. I won't tell you where we're going, but I will give you clues. How about that?" he asked me.

I perked up at the idea of a guessing game and only because I was really bad at them, I seemed to frustrate the people whom I played with. I didn't tell Zaliver this, but he seemed to pick up on my glee.

"Okay, go." I turned to face him and clasped my hands together.

"We've been together how long?"

Fuck, a number question. Think fast, pick a number, mutt! 3! Not weeks and not years.

"A-Around three months?" I stuttered, damn it, I'm bad at this all ready.

Zaliver eyed me for a second and that second was the longest of my life. He nodded. Oh mighty jeezus, I can't breath! Dear lord, let me just thank you, I promise to go to church next sun-

"What do we own, together?" he asked. My brows furrowed at the question. Owned.

Does he mean as a couple, together?

"A house?" I began, seeing his nod of approval I continued. " Cars, an island, I'm gonna say a plane, money, Netflix account, Hulu account, a shit load of granola bars and gatorade." I gave him a pointed look to which he ignored.

"What else?" he asked.

"Well what do you mean?"

"What do we own that is living?" I glared at him.

"If you mean the wolves, you're really messed up." I said a bit bothered.

"Well, technically—"

"Zaliver—"

"Fine, nothing. We own nothing living," he said, raising a hand in defense.

"So?" I asked, still not seeing where he was going.

Until he pulled into a parking lot. Of a pet store. He turned to smile at me.

I think I might have screamed a little, I'm not really sure with all the jumping, running and skipping I did once I was out of the car. Zaliver, of course, chased after me when he saw that I'd bolted for the store doors before he could take hold of my hand so we could walk in together. They were automatic doors so he caught up quickly, taking my hand in his firmly he leaned down to whisper in my ear.

"Don't run off without me, you could get hurt!"

I didn't pay all that much attention to him because as soon as the doors opened enough for me to squeeze through I did, pulling Zaliver behind me. Upon entrance there a large desk in the center if the store with a few people positioned in every direction. I could and smell the animals. A a teenaged blonde girl caught sight of us and grinned largely, on her blue vest the name Amy was printed on.

"Hi! How can I help you?" she said, by the lack of title I already knew she wasn't are of who we were, by the slight pause on Zaliver's part so was he.

"Hello, I've made a payment to buy a pet and whatever comes with it. We're under Azrala." Zaliver said calmly, tightening his hold on my hand when I pulled away to go look at an animal.

I saw a lot of pretty fish, but fish die fast if you don't know how to take care of them and then there was the cleaning the tank business. Dog and cats were cute but I didn't want the general house pet, maybe a turtle?

"Just a moment." Amy looked down and began typing something into the computer in front of her, when she looked up she looked genuinely surprised and a bit mortified.

"Alpha, Luna right this way to the pets." She walked around the counter and began walking to the large wall with all types of pets.

Somewhere outside in a little play section, with workers watching over them. Others were sleeping in their cages or behind plastic walls. The fish section was across the room. There were some birds perched high in the store, playing or sitting on a fake tree that seemed to come out from the walls.

"What do you want?" I asked Zaliver, looking around for an animal that caught my attention. He shrugged.

"I don't really care as long as you like it and it doesn't shit all over the place." He responded, this made me snort. Amy, hearing the last part, timidly answered.

"Most of the animals here are trained, unless they have a condition, are rescued animals and are really stubborn. Like this cat, Sabrina." She gestured to a white cat with light green eyes which watched us with bored interest, her tail flickering behind her.

Amy showed us cats, dogs, fish and even turtles. I got to pet some of them and no matter how cute they were I couldn't seem to see

568

myself taking one of them home. Zaliver had stayed by my side and asked Amy about how the animals would respond to the owner if I seemed to really like a specific pet.

It wasn't until I waked by a plastic little square box that slight movement caught my eye. Without a doubt it was love at first sight, I kept that part to myself since I was sure Zaliver would have never let me take it home had he knew. I let go of Zaliver to his surprise and practically ran and pressed my face against the plastic with a stupid grin on my face.

The little fellow slowly looked up and wiggled it nose at me, I fell in love with the fierceness in its black cuddly eyes. He shuffled to the plastic and then balled up.

He's kinda cute. My wolf piped. Even my beast tilted her head in maternal curiosity.

I turned around to see a scowling Zaliver already making his way to me, when he saw my grin his expression softened.

"This one." I pointed to the cute ball of adorableness.

Zaliver's eyes went from me to the animal inside, surprise at my choice showing in the way his brows lifted.

"That one? You're sure?" He asked stepping closer, he pointed at the plastic box with scepticism.

"Frank." I said firmly, naming my pet.

"Frank?" Zaliver repeated slowly.

"Frank." I confirmed, crossing my arms over my chest.

"Frank the hedgehog?" He asked, amusement clear in his voice as the corners of his mouth twitched up.

Frank had unrolled showing his bottom white fur, he had black eyes and a black nose that wiggled as if he was unhappy with his situation. At the moment the little brown and white spikes on his back were flat and down. He was a bit smaller than my palm, a baby really. I saw fierceness flash in those black eyes.

Amy had joined us and realized that were talking about Frank. She asked me if I wanted to try to pet him. I said yes, Zaliver of course asked how safe it was. Amy made me go wash my hands which I did quickly.

"Oh stop it, look at him, what's he gonna do?" I smacked his arm and wiggled my fingers when Amy picked him up.

When Frank saw what was happening he curled up into a small ball and let his spikes out, Amy must have been used to this because didn't even flinch so I didn't when she set him down gently in my hands. Zaliver was having a fit. Which I ignored.

After a few minutes of me staring and holding still Frank finally seemed to trust me enough to uncurl and slowly lower his spikes, but they were still slightly raised in case of an attack. He sniffed around my hands, wiggling his cute little nose.

Shifting his weight to one hand I began to pet him with the other causing him to spike up again but after another few minutes he relaxed enough for me to pet him. I brought my index finger to his nose and tapped it lightly.

He bit my finger.

I think Zaliver was ready to have a stroke by now, he loomed over me as if ready to snatched Frank away for my safety. Ignoring him I brought Frank closer to my face, eye level and pulled my finger out of his vicious hold.

"I like you, you've got fire in your heart." I said, black rebellious eyes blinked at me as he wiggled his nose.

"This one." I said turning to look at Zaliver who did not look happy about Frank.

"You sure you don't want the little poodle?" He asked me hopefully.

"She keeps shaking like an earthquake every time you or I try to pet her. No. Frank." I said firmly. He pursed his lips but nodded at Amy.

She put him back in his little cage and began telling us how to take care of him, bath him, what to feed him and the do's and don'ts of owning a hedgehog. Although Zaliver didn't seem to agree on my choice I saw attentiveness and seriousness as he listened to Amy. I had a feeling that although I'd be listed as Franks owner, he'd be the one double checking to make sure Frank didn't die on me.

When Amy mentioned the hedgehog shop section they had I didn't have to say anything for Zaliver to pull me over to it. I went a little crazy getting Frank hats. I got him a fancy tall hat, a war helmet, a baseball hat, a clown hat, sombrero, party hat, knitted hat, Dracula cape, Christmas hat, chief hat, kings crown, batman ears and even a superman cape.

"Awe I bet he'll look all handsome with the bow tie." I gushed, playing around with it. It wasn't until I looked up to see Zaliver looking down at me with adoration and fondness that I began blush. With the differ shades of color he was wearing, the blue in his eyes and the black of his hair really popped out. It was mesmerizing combination.

He cupped my face in his hands and kissed my forehead and pulled me close. The hats now forgotten,I slipped my arms under his top coat and wrapped them around his solid frame.

"God I love you, you're adorable you know that?" He asked me with a hint of hopelessness, as if he knew he was forever stuck with me and was accepting his fate.

Good, because he was.

"Yes, because going on and ranting about hats for a hedgehog is cute." I mumbled into his chest, he shook from silent laughter but I felt as if he was laughing at something else entirely.

"You'd be surprised by what you learn about someone who rants about buying hats for a hedgehog." He murmured into my hair.

"Like what?" I asked pulling back to look up at him. He grinned at me, I knew that grin.

"It's a surprise."

So Frank was to come home the next day with us, the store would deliver him and all of the things we brought for him, including the huge cage, playing toys, bathing and food supplies and hats.

It was a little after one and the day was nice and clear. When we got back into the car Zaliver began driving again, I came to the conclusion that he truly did have places to take me.

"Where to next?" I asked him buckling up and turned to him.

"A quick stop and then lunch. What does the birthday girl feel like eating?" He asked me.

"Pasta!"

"I should have known." He mused.

We chatted about small things until he pulled up to an Electronics/Music store, the amount of money they must make by that combination had me chuckling.

Entering the store Zaliver went off to talk to someone, the sound of music was all over the place but there was another song playing and the sound of rapid footsteps had my heels clicking on the floor to find where it was coming from.

A small group of teenagers stood around a flat screen TV which showed two dancing figures, looking closer I realized that the group surrounded two teens dancing in the middle with something attached to their wrists. I joined the group and moved my head to the music as the two danced off and their friends cheered them on.

Both of the dancers on the stage were fairly good, the guy more so but the girl fought back with cool twists of her own and precision that earned her good points. At the end the guy won but you could clearly tell they were doing it for the fun. When they ended I joined in on the clapping and was getting ready to go when one of the kids noticed me, or more so what I was wearing.

"Wow, looking good." One of the guys whistled. I could tell from their ages that not all of them were in touch with their wolves, as my own snickered with those who were. Some of the kids decided to keep their mouths shut and let their friends continue to talk without knowing I was their Luna. For all they knew their Luna was a chick in her thirties with a wart.

"Thanks. Nice moves." I called out to the dancers they grinned.

"Want a go?" The girl asked me, I shook my head.

"Oh come on, I'm sure you've got some moves!" Someone called out, I'm sure the guys in the group mostly wanted me to shake my ass but I was sort of curious about the game.

I hadn't competed in a dancing game in a while and there was really no harm. Besides, it was my birthday! Bring the music!

"Fine!" I said, making it look like I was giving in, I pulled off my coat, I'd just get in the way. I ignored the cat calls and stood beside the first guy I saw dance, he passed me the white bracket that went around my wrist, monitoring my movements, he extended a hand.

"James." I extended mine and put on the bracelet thing, covering my thinner black one.

"Vivian."

The screen showed gave the decision of whether we wanted to follow the dancing direction or go solo. My hand reached over and tapped the S on the band. The screen cut in half so that James side had the directions and mine just showed how many points I would get for each monitored move.

"Oh shit, we got a pro over here!" Someone called out behind me making me grin. Seeming to like the challenge James clicked on his S as well.

The screen read Move Your Body by Sia. I loved this song, as the beat softly floated to my ears I began softly rocking.

I found a rhythm and just moved my body to it, waiting for the music to really start before I started moving around. I let my shoulders go up and down, moving my body in the opposite, shifting side to side and moving my hips.

I began adding on a little shuffling and when the I felt like it, went back, forward and then raised my arms above me. Feeling the music, I glided to the sides and put a foot forward and then stepped out. Beside me it seemed as if James had caught my pattern was mimicking it to his own.

We even sort of looked like dance partners, if I do say so myself.

Throughout the song at some point I began laughing as my adrenaline jumped, it felt like all of the hairs on my arms and neck were on end, I could feel a predatory gaze on me. There were only one pair of eyes which would give me a reaction like that.

During one of the dance moves I turned my head slightly, looking over my shoulder. It was just for a moment but that was enough to have me feeling hot, bothered and thoroughly appreciative of all the witness here today.

I couldn't tell if Zaliver was happy, hungry or wanted to murder who I'm guessing are some of the guys in the ever-growing crowd.

When the song ended I wasn't sweaty, thank god, but I did have a certain flush to me. Thanking everyone for the fun I made it out quickly, trying to not pity the disappointing expression on the guys which quickly morphed once they made eye contact with the direction I was headed to.

Putting my coat back on I stopped in front of him with a half guilty half shy look on my face. Through the bond I could accurately guess why he was looking at me the way he was.

"Did you have fun?" He asked calmly, but with burning blue eyes.

"Mhmm." I nodded.

Clenching his jaw and briefly looking over my shoulder he grabbed my hand gently in his and began walking out of the store.

"Well I'm glad, but can you do me a favor?" He asked, his tone arduous.

"What?" I asked carefully, for all I knew he'd ask me to wait in the car while he came back to kill everyone. He turned to looked down at me.

"Please refrain from becoming the wet dreams of hormonal male pups, if you are ever in the need to dance as you did back there or more please do in front of one person only." He said seriously.

"And who would that person be, if I may be so bold as to ask?"

"Me, always." He answered without a moment's hesitation, a sly grin made its way across my face. "And what would I get in return?" I asked stepping closer to him and wrapping my arms around his waist, under his top coat.

He looked down at me with calculating eyes.

"What do you want?" He asked, caution in his voice. I thought about it and held in my laugh, this was the only way.

"One of these days I'm going to hand you something and I want you to wear it, no arguments." I said, choosing my words carefully.

Worry and curiosity flickered in those blue eyes of his, but as if remembering my little show they darkened.

"Fine."

"Deal."

Walking to the car I couldn't help but notice that Zaliver didn't have anything on him for a guy who just went into the store to buy something.

"What did you get?" I asked, buckling my seat belt.

" Just wanted to check on something."

573

"Like what?"

"Stuff."

"Stuff, right." I wasn't going to force it out of him, I was lucky this was all the reaction he was giving to me basically shaking my rump in front of as he called them 'Hormonal male pups'.

He was being very calm today. Happy birthday to me.

~•~

For lunch Zaliver took me to a fancy but not too fancy Italian restaurant he said made the best healthy pizza he knew, I asked if they had handmade limonene and when he said yes that was good enough for me.

The food was, to his word, the best and to my surprise the lights dimmed and a birthday cake was wheeled out a large red velvet cake. Of course Zaliver would also make sure to have everyone in the restaurant then sing me happy birthday in a suspiciously perfect harmony. The cake wasn't to sweet and the dough to hard, it was the perfect balance.

I was almost sad when I got full, everyone in the restaurant enjoyed free cake that day. And Zaliver received a very grateful kiss which made him walk out with confident strides.

Throughout the day Zaliver took me on what felt like was a mini road trip. We went to the park to, as corny as it sounds, feed the ducks which was actually harder than it seemed because Zaliver kept scaring them away so it made it look like he was chasing them.

Look at him chasing all those D's. My wolf tsked. Which made me laugh until tears streamed down my face.

He took me shopping in this sketchy antique store that made me feel jumpy, but once we got in he had to force me out after an hour of me becoming more and more obsessed over hair clips. They were all so pretty and shiny, ironically it turned out that Zaliver was the stores most gracious donor of antiquities. I had snorted and then pointed to him.

"So how much would I get if I put him on the black market?" I had asked the old wolf who owned the store.

Zaliver did not find that funny, thus the abrupt leave.

We then went to a bookstore where we both went our own ways and then came back with heaping piles of books. After that we went for ice cream, we swayed to a live performance outside by a beautiful water fountain, walked through little booths until I got tired and made him carry me (bridal style because he was afraid I'd flash someone) to a bench where he placed me on his lap snuggly.

The sun had begun to set a few hours ago and twilight washed over the sky like a painting. I sighed content in Zaliver's lap.

"Happy?" He murmured, his hand rubbing at my back soothingly.

"Mhmm, thank you for today Undoubtedly the best birthday I've ever had." I said, liking how warm and sturdy he felt against me.

"Well the day isn't over yet, we still have one more thing to do." He said so softly I missed the waver in his voice.

"Really, what else? I can't possibly see how this day can get any better. You know, this means I'm going to have to start planning for your birthday starting now if I want to top this." I muttered contemplative, I still had a good handful of months left.

His laugher moved me along with him, when he abruptly stood I clung to his neck, knowing he wouldn't let me fall but not liking his lack of warning.

"You can plan all you want but I already have all of my birthday wishes and then some." He said.

"I bet I can beat that." No I can't.

"I bet you could." It was nice knowing he thought so.

Once in the car I tried not to fall asleep, but the day's high was hitting me pretty hard. Somewhere between oblivion and awareness I noted that the road he was taking was lonelier, buildings no longer surrounded us. In fact, I could see civilization getting farther and farther away.

"We're not going home?" I asked sleepily.

"No, not yet. It's okay, go to sleep, it's a long drive." He softly in the dark of the car, I felt his hand on my face, pushing locks of fallen hair behind my ear.

"Oh-kay." I said in a breath and dozed off to sleep.

I'm not sure how long I fell asleep for but when I came to it Zaliver was leaning over me with an unreadable expression on his face,but warmth in his eyes. He was shaking me gently.

"Hey, come here." I blinked away the sleep and let him help me out of the car.

All around it was dark, the sun had long ago set and in its place was a full moon. I took in a deep breath was startled fully awake at the fresh and raw scent of sea and sand. Usually I could hear the faint sound of waves crashing and dragging sand but now it was closer, in person. I could see water all around from where I stood, we were parked in a small hill, the ground slanted which had probably stopped the car from going any further.

I turned to look at Zaliver, baffled by what I saw.

"What—"

"It's a surprise, don't make that face, I promise you'll like it." He said.

"Fine." I huffed reluctantly with him.

575

Taking my hand in his he guided me over the rough ground and down the small hill, these boots were so not for climbing. I made the comment out loud.

"They're just boots-"

"Tell that to Vera Wang." I grumbled.

He groaned and turned around, picking me up effortlessly and making his way down faster than before.

"See if you would have just done that in the beginning. . ." I began.

"I would have saved myself what exactly?" He asked grinning down at me. In this dark light his electric blue seemed to glow brilliantly. They captivated me for a moment.

"Uh. . ." He smiled.

As he walked I realized he was wearing the black backpack over one shoulder, eyeing it with suspicion I spoke again.

"You're not going to dump my body at the bottom of the ocean floor and weigh it down with rocks over some Vera Wang's right?" I asked. His eyes narrowed on me.

"You are the most logical and illogical female I've come to know, no I will not drop you to the bottom of the ocean floor with weights over some Vera Wang's." He snapped.

"So what's in the bag?" I asked, motioning to it with my chin.

Instead of answering me he turned me around, all of the talking had made me ignore my surroundings. I couldn't now. Setting me on my feet Zaliver stood behind me in silence as I took the scenery in.

Smooth stone tiles made a long trail ahead of me, on either side they were surrounded by small candles. At the end of the trail was a small and simple house. The outside was painted a dark pale blue, outlined by black, the door faced in my direction allowing me to see that it and the roof were the same dark wood. All in all the house was simple, small and yet it somehow seemed to command the air around it in a lonely yet strong sense.

"I use to come here when I wanted to get away from everyone and everything. Being Alpha can get a bit tiring you know." Zaliver joked softly.

"And now?" I whispered, staring at the house in front of us. Why did this house seem to mean so much more than what he was letting on? Why was I suddenly so. . .nervous?

"And now, I don't know. Why don't you tell me?" he asked, putting his hand firmly on my back he gave me a gentle nudge to get me to start walking.

When we got to the front door Zaliver moved a hand from behind me and twisted the doorknob open. As his chest pressed against

576

my back I could feel how hard his heart was pounding, fluttering about in his chest like the wings of a hummingbird.

Opening the door I stepped inside, Zaliver followed closely and shut the door casting us in darkness. I had expected him to turn the lights on but he surprised me when instead something on the roof began to lift and the stars and sky illuminated the room in their own light. I heard something get dropped onto the floor and some shuffling but I was too busy looking up at the stars. This close to the beach and at this time, the sky was at its most beautiful point.

I looked around to see that the house was indeed small as I had thought, the living room and the kitchen were combined and around a sticking wall I imagined that it must have had the bed. There were bookshelves, a couch, a desk some tables and necessities any house would have, but there were no electronics, no tv, no speakers and no distractions. Just us and quiet.

I turned around to ask Zaliver something but all that came out of my mouth was a shaky breath.

Before me Zaliver, on one knee.

My being wasn't ready for this, hell I wasn't ready for this and yet somehow I could not allow myself to move. Strong emotions coursed through me and some I was sure, we're even mine. I didn't know what to do with my hands, I wanted to cover my mouth, clutch my hair, clap, do something but they just stayed at my sides.

His eyes, oh how I loved those blue eyes, were a force to behold as he pinned them on me with such intensity that if I weren't for the moment I'd surely faint.

"Vivian Grey, I know that the journey we have taken to get to where we are now hasn't been easy, mostly because of me, but I'd go through everything again if it meant being with you. You are without a doubt the most stubborn, fierce, humorously inappropriate and bizarre female I have ever met, but you're my female and I have fallen in love with all of that and the beauty you carry both inwardly and physically. Your caring and loving nature and witty comebacks.

All my life I've known nothing but darkness, death and evil and yet somehow being with you I've never felt happiest, whole and alive and I would give anything to keep you with me for all eternity. I'm a selfish man Vivian, everyone knows that, I've stolen, taken and conquered but I'm here on one knee today to ask you something.

Will you become mine in all ways possible, allow me to introduce you to those not just as my mate but my wife, the future mother of my children, the only woman whom I could love and live with forever?

Will you marry me?"

I'd be a rotten liar if I said I wasn't crying my soul out of my eyes. I had tried wiping at my eyes with the back of my hand but the tears just kept coming. They say you know when someone was speaking from the heart, Zaliver was doing so much more as he looked up with anxious eyes, he showed his vulnerability in this moment, the fear of rejection, the hope of acceptance and the uncertainty of a future. He spoke from his soul.

"Y-Yes," I managed to say through a watery smile and a shaky breath.

I was awarded with a heart breaking and soul twisting smile. He popped open the box.

Bah- My wolf sniffed.

Inside had to be what I knew was the most beautiful and unique ring ever made. The band was a smooth silver that came together like a hundred little intertwining vines, poking out were the smallest of colored diamonds, they almost looked like flecks because of their size, they were euclase, alexandrite, taffelit and heliodor. As the vines got closer to the top they morphed into small claws on either side of the diamond in the middle, those claws held a dazzling and mystifying blue that oddly resembled that of Zaliver's eyes. But the diamond in the middle, that was the one that captivated something in me. The longer I looked at it, the longer it took me to decide what color it was, the size was no doubt attention grabbing itself, but their was almost something magical about the way the gem glowed and changed. I'd never seen anything like it in my life.

Zaliver took the ring out and grabbed my hand and slipped the not surprising heavy ring onto my left hand on that very important finger. He looked at my hand for a long moment and then brought it to his lips, he looked up. I felt my insides tighten at the all consuming possessiveness and loving gleam swirling and turning those blue eyes darker by the second. Those were dangerous combinations.

I looked down at the ring and was once more sucked in by the utter beauty of it, as if understanding Zaliver spoke.

"Only the best for my woman," he said huskily, standing up.

Looming over me Zaliver appeared every inch of the dominant, possessive and strong alpha male that I knew he was. My heart began beating quickly in my chest, each step that brought him closer to me brought me closer to the realization that although he had said I would have the night to take him as I pleased, that by the look in his eyes he won't be too far behind.

"Vivian . . ." he whispered into the dark of the night.

"Huh?" I breathed out roughly, feeling as if I were about to fall over and die from possible overload.

"Your heart's beating like crazy." He cupped my face in his hands and leaned down, skimming his lips over mine in the lightest of touches to whisper one word. "Breathe

Lord have mercy.

I reached up and gripped one side of his sweater while with the other I gripped at his shoulder. He trailed small kisses down my face and then down my neck, leaving me in a mind buzzing state of nerves and emotions.

"My mate, my fiancée, soon to be my wife." He groaned, deeply from his chest and his arm suddenly wrapped around my waist, pressing me to his body. " I like how that sounds." He growled out. I reached up and grabbed a handful of his hair and pulling his face to mine.

"I love you," I whispered softly.

Some of the intensity left his eyes as it was replaced by softness and love.

"I love you too," he said before leaning down to kiss me in what started to be a gentle and loving kiss but quickly turned hot and heavy, fire starting and life consuming.

When we pulled back we were both panting and at the same high as the other. I gripped at his coat and began tugging it off of him, he released me and in a flash he had it on the ground. Doing the same to mine, he leaned down so that I could wrap my arms over his neck and tangle it in his hair as I kissed down the side of his neck, planting open-mouthed kisses.

He ran his hands up my legs until they were under my ass and lifted me up, making me by instinct wrap my legs around his waist. I let out a pleasurable moan from the sensation that move alone gave me because of the very noticeable bulge coming from his pants.

Zaliver tilted his head to the side, allowing me more room to kiss his neck as he began walking to what I assume was the bed. Zaliver shifted a bit for a moment, side to side before I landed on a soft surface with him over me, a wicked smirk in place. I tightened my legs on him.

He straightened up and lifted the mocha colored sweater over his build, because if the white of his shirt I could see two thick white long bandages on his body. The tattoos.

I sat up and began unbuttoning his shirt, wanting to see the tattoos now that I had the chance.

What had he gotten?

When I finally got the shirt off of him I looked up, sort of asking for permission and not wanting to peel the bandages off of him incase they hurt. He surprised me by reaching for the one on his chest and just yanking it off, then for the other and to my surprise reaching behind him and over his shoulder. A total of three tattoos.

He sat very still as I leaned in closer, but his eyes, as ever were vigilant. Over his peck, above his heart I read the clear and neat writing.

Vivian, my life, my lover, my love. The only being in existence to control the heart of this beast.

This time I did cover my mouth as a fresh new round of tears made its way to my eyes. I looked up at him with amazement.

"I told you it would be a good surprise," he said huffing.

I leaned forward and kissed his cheek, I leaned back and looked onto the next. My eyes narrowed as I went for the next tattoo, having to unbutton and unbuckle his pants for me to fully read it. Just above the 'V' he had and on his right hip I read the same neat writing.

When even the moon is abandoned by the stars and endless darkness lurks around, only my cloud will give me the strength to make it home.

As touching and heartwarming as it was I still looked up at him with hard eyes. A devious smile was already in place, he knew what I was churning about.

"You let her unbuckle you?" I hissed at him. The animal in me didn't like the thought of another female getting this close to what was mine.

"Of course not, I did that myself." I growled at him. Hopping off the bed I went to see the last tattoo on his back.

On his back, instead of a quote or a poem of his there was a drawing no bigger than the size of my palm. It was a shockingly detailed drawing of a moon with a lone cloud floating in front. Somehow Eddie had managed to seemed to make the cloud glow brighter than the moon.

I kissed Zaliver's shoulder before using my strength to throw him down and flip him over, I straddled him as he placed his hands on my thighs and inched them behind me. He gripped at my hips firmly. I leaned down over him, placing a hand behind his head and the other on his chest.

"You're mine." I growled out, not happy that no matter how sweet and romantic the gesture, he had to unbuckle his pants. Above the waist Eddie was fine. Below? The bitch was dead.

He gave out a dark laugh, eyes glowing in uncontrolled glee and suddenly flipped us over, him on top while he pinned both of my hands above my head with one of his.

"Yes and now everyone will see it. I like it when you get all possessive, really works for me." He wiggled his eyebrows at me, I huffed and lifted my head to kiss him.

Pulling my hands free from his, we both managed to get undressed, thankfully without any clothes ripping. My Vera Wang's hit the floor with a thud as I threw them somewhere. Managing to somehow get under the blankets, Zaliver gazed into my eyes with tender love, carnal desire and a raw wanting desire that I shook under his gaze.

With my hand on his back I could feel the weight of the ring, the band of it pushing against his flesh.

I gasped when he entered me in a fast and fulfilling thrust. Capturing my cry in a scorching kiss he moved his body in a soul playing way, morphing and using my body to his will and I happily obliged.

Reaching down with one hand he played with my breasts, kneading them and putting pressure on my nipples until I had to let out a moan. When he began to move against my lower half in an almost punishing way I began to shake as I felt myself come close.

And then he stopped. My eyes sprang open to see him grinning down at me.

"Remember what I told you?" he said through clenched teeth, grinding his lower half into me. I raised my hips to the movement, squeezing his biceps.

"Huh?" I could barely remember my name, how the hell did he want me to remember something he said?

I whimpered when he leaned down and nibbled directly on his mark, the action shooting down straight to my core.

"In the closet, Vivian," he whispered softly. Tracing an unfamiliar pattern on my skin with the tip of his tongue.

A fuzzy memory slowly made its way to mind, making me giggle. He pulled back and gave me a mocking disapproving look which quickly turned to hunger. Moving his hips slowly, oh so slowly I tried to move faster but he held my hips down.

"Oh no baby."

"You're so mean," I whispered achingly.

He kept this up for torturous minutes until he had he had me high and twisted up inside. He took my hands in his and kissed me quickly.

Just when I thought I couldn't take it he pulled back and rammed in hard and then pulled out, repeating the same motion only speeding up the more he did it making me scream his name repeatedly. When he felt my muscles tighten on him and I began to see stars behind my eyes we both reached the ultimate high with a lovers kiss.

He rolled over and pulled me on top of him, keeping me firmly on his chest, the hand with the ring gleamed in the moonlight, reminding me that I was now engaged. Looking at the tattoo on his chest I lean over to kiss it and then trailed then hand on his chest lower, to softly rub my hand over the second one. I liked the way the bottom of his abdomen tensed and tightened every few seconds.

I looked up to see Zaliver already gazing down at me, no hint of tiredness or even strain. This was going to be a long night.

He leaned down to kiss me gently, pouring all of his love and hopes into that kiss.

"Happy birthday, Vivian."

CHAPTER 42

ZALIVER AZRALA

I glanced beside me to watch Vivian, a smile making its way onto my face. She had her hand raised up in front of her, studying the ring like an astonished scientist at a new discovery that would bring new things into the world.

"It's so pretty. . ." she murmured to herself, probably forgetting I was even in the car sitting beside her because she was lost in her own little world.

I was alright with that because I was the cause of the twinkle in her eyes, the happiness seeping out of her every pore and the constant leap and spark of her soul. My chest puffed out, I lifted my head a bit higher with pride at how happy I had made my mate, my wife to be. My little cloud.

I was reluctant to leave the small beach house so early in the morning, but Vivian was determined to be productive today. I had a feeling it was more of her wanting to open her presents than anything, but not wanting to deny her something, or anything, I played along.

Being confined in this car with her was a lot harder than it had ever been so, for many reasons. The first and obvious would be that she was my mate and wife to be, the second being that even after a long night of libidinous activities with her I knew that I was nowhere near done or satisfied. The third being more from my beast than me, his ever-growing fanatical need to have her wrapped around us.

Not that I disagreed. I shifted a bit in my seat and briefly glanced down at my crotch, mentally cursing at how much lack of control I had over my body when my mate was involved.

Coming to a stop at red light I looked at her, the breath in my throat catching. Even she hadn't been able to run anything other than her fingers through her hair, my own urged me to play with the thick dark strands. The corners of her lips were turned up as if she was fighting and happily failing to hide a smile, her usually pale complexion had a healthy warm glow, as if the sun was rising with her.

From where I was sitting I could see the smoothness of her skin, I could remember how it felt to have that same skin under my lips, remember how it felt to cup her face in between my hands. Long dark lashes that casted a second shadow over warm brown eyes that seemed to captivate me for reasons unknown.

But besides Vivian's obvious outside beauty, I was just as enthralled with her mentality and soul. Something I never knew I could love about someone was how unguarded they could be.

I hadn't realized it before but when Vivian was with me she never raised her mental barriers or tried to guard her thoughts to me, even when she was trying to be sneaky, she was just so open that it was honestly frightening just how much. It frightened me because it showed the utmost intimacy trust another being could give, it showed how much faith she had in me and it demonstrated more than trust, confidentiality or faith.

Her one-act showed me that she accepted me as I was, monster, Alpha and lover. And that she trusted me with herself.

Through everything we had been through I would have more than understood if she had her mental shield around me, if she had rejected my marriage proposal because deep down there was still a piece of me tha had waited to be rejected. That part had died the moment she said yes.

It still shook my to my core to think about what her simple answer indicated. Before the light turned green I snuck one more look.

Lovely brown eyes blinked up at me with an eager expression over her face. A dull moment would never happen with Vivian by my side, of that I was more than sure.

"Wow, we're going to get married. I almost can't believe it," she gushed out happily, turning to face me.

"Well it's happening and now that you said yes, there's no going back. None," I said, partly joking. She'd be in for a surprise if she thought there were any take backs on this deal.

I'd get her drunk and drive to Las Vegas to get a shady priest if I had to. She'd get over it after she beat the crap out of me, eventually.

"Yeah yeah,there's so much to do, so much to plan. When do you wanna do it?" she asked, tapping her fingers quickly against her bare thigh, momentarily distracting me.

"Whenever you want." I turned in the direction of our house.

"So in a year or two then?" I had to stop myself from slamming into the break and instead calmly turned to look at her with a raised brow.

"Why so long?" I asked. Red lights flashed in my mind at the time period in which she thought I could wait.

I wanted her to be legally recognized as mine as soon as possible, I needed to hear her new name. I had forever to make her mine in all ways and although that was a long time, I felt a pressing need not to take my time. Not with her.

She tilted her head to the side, her brows furrowed in confusion, he lips parting a bit as brown eyes blinked at me.

"Well don't most couples stay engaged for a year or two to make sure that they don't ," I narrowed my eyes. "never mind then." She quickly fixed her answer.

"You and I are forever, there is no need to wait for anything," I said firmly, looking directly into her eyes to remind her. I felt the bond vibrate strongly as her face flushed enticingly, lashes batting at me under a shy smile.

Fuck.

I gripped the steering wheel a bit harder, turning to focus on the road ahead of me, trying to focus on the green scenery passing by me instead of the welcoming flush that I knew would cause me to pull over if I didn't look away.

A sudden thought, reminder filled my mind.

"Ah yes, I forgot to tell you that I had Aurora spell the ring so don't worry about it breaking or any stones falling off on you. The ring is spelled to withstand anything," I informed her, mentally thanking Albericus for not being able to keep a secret and his mate mentioning a woman's paranoia of losing a stone.

"Oh that's good, wouldn't want to break it super punching someone. That'd be bad.," she muttered the last part with displeasure.

And then of course there's that. My mate had a temper.

"And who exactly would you be super punching? If I may be so bold as to ask," I said seriously, but not being able to hold back my grin.

She slumped in her seat and dramatically looked to the ceiling of the car with a hand over her forehead.

"You, Algebra, anyone who stands in between me and my food or lemonade and people who judge books by their crappy movies. Like, shut your face or I'll do it for you." Through the bond I felt anger spike from her, warning me how very serious and how close she was on ranting about the last one. It both thrilled and impressed me.

"I'm going to acknowledge the fact that I accept my name as well as Albericus on that list. May you have mercy on the other two." She shook her head before the same breathtaking smile made its way over her face, doing exactly so.

"On a serious note, it's good to know the ring won't break on me, it would be a shame." I pulled up in front of the house, my mood

585

momentarily darkening at the remembrance of the talk I was to have with my brother.

Before I could fully stop the car Vivian was out and speedily walking to the front door and hopping on the front porch, waving me over to hurry. I chuckled at the booming energy I could feel her channeling, she was on a high at the moment and I knew that the moment she crashed I'd have to scoop her up from where ever she fell asleep at.

I waited for the annoyance at the realization, but the only thing that spread through me was warmth. I looked forward to taking care of her. I was whipped and I was proud, there was no shame in showing that I loved my woman.

Calmly walking to the front door I opened it and let her pass, immediately she went into the living room and the sound of shredding and a phone call being made met my ears. I leaned against the living room entrance and watched Vivian go through the presents like a kid on Christmas morning. She was talking to someone, making them guess her good news.

Feeling only positive emotions coming from her and seeing her jump and squeal at every little thing that she liked warmed my heart, it provided more entertainment I ever thought possible. I had gone my entire existence with hole in my heart that I had never thought I had. She was slowly filling them.

Leaving her in the living room I made my way upstairs to talk to my brother. I took a breath before knocking and opening the door. The first thing I realized was the darkness and I wasn't talking about the shut curtains, absent lights or mess throughout the room.

Two vivid yellow eyes centered themselves on me from within the dark room.

The hairs on my arms stood on end, my stomach muscles tightened in an uneasy way that I knew wasn't going to go away from experience. Yellow eyes were not normal in the werewolf or lycan community, it was an odd factor. He blinked once and familiar blue-green eyes looked at me.

"Zaliver," he said, looking submissive as he stood straight with his hands behind his back. Although his build was smaller than mine, it caught my attention how subdued.

I took a step forward, careful not to step on the broken glass by the door. I did not question the room, for many times I had seen this in the rooms of angered wolves. And he had been angry.

"Joshula, there's no need to be so formal," I said, pausing in front of him, he nodded once, my voice hardened. "There was also no need for what you said yesterday morning," I stated, the pent back emotions from yesterday arose in me once more.

586

His head tilted to the side as if confused before a reserved look entered his eyes, body language suggesting defence, something which alarmed the alpha in me instantly.

"I don't know what it is that you speak of—"

"You and I both know I'm not talking about the comments you were making during breakfast was the problem." I took a step forward, something snapping under my weight. " I'm talking about the vexatious thoughts you were projecting. I do not like what you insinuated and I dislike it even more knowing that it was done with a purpose."

The room chilled for a moment before Joshua sighed, I tensed, wanting to know what was going on through his mind. His answer was very important, my brother was playing a dangerous game.

"You're correct, I . . . behaved not like myself," he said slowly, his brows furrowed in genuine confusion. "I wish to apologize with you for the . . .unpleasant happenings of yesterday morning. With Vivian as well at some point," he said seriously, looking at me.

I gave a slight nod with my head, I knew from memory that Joshula wouldn't apologize for something of which he didn't feel the need to, but I also knew my brother worked in organized and intentional way that no other could do. I knew because that was how we took down others when we fought side by side, he was the plan and I was the action that followed.

"But why, is what I want to know," I pointed out his lack of answer. My eyes took in my brother in the darkened room. It was almost unnaturally dark, a disturbing realization. Even the sun which I knew was out seemed to overlook this room.

"I must say that it was probably due to the unfamiliar presence at the time or even my dislike for social engagement with people of whom I do not wish to befriend," he answered bluntly, a hint of hostility in his voice.

His answer neither surprised me nor put me on edge, all it did was piss me off. I knew better than anyone in this world what avoidance looked like and that was exactly what my brother was doing. I did not like repeating myself twice.

"You are yet to explaining to me why I shouldn't treat you as an Alpha would do to any pack member who insinuates, insults and tries to belittle his Luna. If you have a problem Joshula, be it with Vivian or myself you can talk to me about it, privately. I will not tolerate you, brother or not, disrespecting Vivian in her home, in front of her friends on an important day for her," I said colder than I had ever spoken to him before.

His face hid any thought he had on my verbal attack but I felt there was rigidity to his movement, a tension that wasn't there before.

587

He looked off to the side for a moment before seemingly nodding about something. Something in my mind gave off a warning, something about his last action sent a red spark off.

There was something off-

"I can say to you that I will not repeat my mistake, I did not question my action before and perhaps I do have a problem. There is perhaps a bitterness in me. You were not the one to die," My flinch was spontaneous. "you prospered and now look at all that you have. It is hard for me not to come into something that reminds me of this," he said calmly.

Guilt ate at me, pushing back any and all previous thoughts I had come into this room with.

He was right, I had taken his chance to make something of himself in the world and brought him into a place where he'd be reminded of history's past mistakes and my victory. I'd be bitter as well.

"Joshula I apologize, I did not think of your emotional state." My voice came out gruffly, my own emotions choking me.

Guilt. Shame. Sorrow. Hope. More guilt.

"Oh it is fine brother, I'm sure that in time all will be well and that I will have what I need," he responded monotonously, I frowned at the vagueness of his words but nodded.

"I'm sure you will, just better." I ran my fingers through my hair and thought about something. "Look, I know I've been busy and that it probably the last thing you needed but how about we hang out and do something, catch up on missed time?" I asked, hoping he'd say yes but knowing he had every right to reject my proposition.

He regarded me with familiar eyes, for the briefest of moments his face tightened before relaxing.

"Sure, I don't see why not."

"Great, how does tomorrow sound, I've got to take care of some things today—"

"It would be fine." I pursed my lips at his interruption but didn't say anything.

"Well, alright," I said nodding at him and began to turn around when I remembered something. "And before you hear this from someone else, I proposed to Vivian and she said yes. We're getting married." I said, my tone conveying my pleasure in the situation.

Surprise filled his eyes and as he blinked it away something else took its place.

"You love her enough to follow through even the human rituals?" he asked, curiosity clear in his voice.

"Yes," I answered without hesitation.

"Huh. Well congratulations then. May you and her get the life you both deserve," he murmured.

588

Unease filled me with the way he said it, but I pushed it away. His formality and rigid way of expression could sometimes come out awkwardly, this was it.

"Thank you."

Without another world I left him in his dark room, standing by the window with an odd expression over his face. Walking to my bedroom I wasn't aware of the frown over my face.

It was clear to me that both he and I were completely different individuals from when we were younger and human. Even though he was younger he was used to bossing everyone around and I, the brash and careless one didn't care much for order. But it should have been beyond clear to him that I was not the same, I was Alpha to all alphas and wolves.

Perhaps this new adjustment to my personality was the cause for his own misplacement, I couldn't imagine how hard it was for him to adjust to new people and a new environment when he was still in the same mindset. I hoped that time with me would help us not only bond but help him find his own path.

Entering the room I sat down on the bed and put my head in my hands. I was very confused and I did not like it, my beast wasn't contributing with his own emotions. Because I had gotten him only after Joshula's. . .vacation, my beast hadn't gotten around to meeting or knowing Joshula so at the mention he was mistrustful of him. Sometimes I'd try to remind the beast that it was my brother so in short his brother, but the animal was stubborn and didn't like the other male in the house, be it my brother or not.

I had been so wrapped up in my thoughts that I hadn't noticed how quiet it had gotten downstairs, so when the room door slowly opened I looked up as a head poked in. I had to hold in my laughter at the sight of her.

"What on earth do you have on-Oh god." I lost it as she pushed the door open and stepped into the room.

It was clear to me that Vivian indeed loved all of her presents and had made it a personal goal to try wear/carry as many she could. She had at least four hats on, five shoulder bags on and three across her chest, shoes poked out of some of the bags, something that resembled a dress and coat was thrown over her shoulder while her arms were covered in different types of bracelets.

She struggled to cross her arms over her chest, but she still narrowed her eyes at me.

"What? How do I know all of my presents won't be gone if I leave them for a second? So, I took the ones I liked the most with me," she defended herself. I felt her actual panic at the thought through the bond.

589

"Where do you even get all of these ideas from? No one would dare steal any of your presents, you know that and it's not like you wouldn't be able to stop them" I said surprised by her, as ever.

Her mind was both a wonder and odd place to be in, but it was all so intriguing.

"It's called thinking outside of the box and then thinking outside of the outside of the box. Get with the program," she said walking over and setting some of her carry on the bed behind me. I noted how she took off all but one filled bag. I chuckled.

"Oh yes, I see that now." I pulled her on my lap and wrapped my arms around her, feeling her soothed me. She wrapped her own arms around me and stroked at my hair, causing me to purr into her neck.

"You seemed off so I came up here, you okay?" she asked softly, more serious.

"I'm good, I just went to talk to Joshula." There was no jump, no sudden movement from her but the moment I said his name she tensed. I said nothing but I stored this to memory, Vivian's reactions, even the small ones, we're of great importance. Because she usually had a reason.

"Oh, well how did that go?" she asked me, twisting a strand of hair around. At some point she had removed her knee-length boots and so I was rewarded with the sight of her soft legs. Absent-mindedly I began to run my hands down her legs.

"We're going to take some time to bond tomorrow, catch up. I hadn't realized how hard this situation was for him, I hadn't thought about him as much as I should have." My words were full of

guilt and negligence on my part.

I was no doubt the world's worst brother, first I killed him and then I ignore him when he miraculously returns? No wonder he was bitter.

Perhaps feeling my sinking mood, Vivian stood up in front of me and took my hands and began to pull me up, I allowed her to.

"No," She stomped on the ground, determination brightening her eyes as I looked down at her. "Absolutely no sulking, crying or mental breakdowns a day after proposing to me. I will not allow it!" she yelled.

I just wanted to smother her in kisses but I comforted myself by cupping her face in my hands as she looked up with her big brown eyes and kissed her forehead. She was adorable when she thought she was taller than her normal height.

The sound of two cars pulling into the driveway meet our ears. Both Vivian and I made our way down stairs (she still had the bag with her), I saw that all of the gift wrapping paper was gone and that her presents were organized in a peculiar way. I went to go open the door at the sound of a door opening. By the mental range I was getting I knew one of our guest was Albericus, opening the door I caught sight of a large van with a familiar logo on it.

Vivian standing behind me squealed when she caught sight of the van and literally, shoved me, the woman *shoved* me, out of her way and ran out of the house barefooted.

"Vivi—"

"Frank!!" I snapped my mouth shut with an audible snap.

Albericus got out of the car and looked from me to the van where Vivian was chatting excitedly with a happy looking wolf whom made her way to the back of the van. Closing his door Albericus walked over to stand next to me, watching with curiosity what would make my mate shove me. He smelled of Aurora, but this time her scent was more as it had been in the past. Light, happy and healthy, yet there was still the scent of darkness and pain.

"Hey man. Who's Frank?" he asked.

"Her new pet," I muttered under my breath, crossing my arms over my chest. He eyed me and the van.

"Right. Since you're not in tears and she's not patting your back, I take it she said yes?" he asked with a mocking grin. I turned to glare at him with annoyance.

"Of course she said yes and I wouldn't have cried," I stated.

He nodded in agreement so I turned back to watch my barefooted mate.

"No you're right. You would have gone on a rampage, killed thousands and then bawled your eyes out all while standing in silence in a very manly way. That's more your style." He rationalized to himself.

"I'd hate to make you look for your own replacement beta—"

"You wouldn't be so cruel—"

"Yes I would," I said cutting him off, he gave out a mocking gasp. I fought off the smile that wanted to take place on my face at his idiocy.

"After I have done nothing but been loyal to you, faithful to you, gave you my heart after all these years? You men, you go and you get a good soul and what do you do? You use us to your pleasure and toss us out once you're done," he said dramatically, fanning his face with his hand as he pretended to slump down.

I blinked at him.

"Are you done? Is it out of your system?" I asked. I rue the day I decided Albericus Wilt, a drama student of the late 80s made a good beta. I mean I wasn't wrong, but I probably shouldn't have pulled him out of school so young either.

He stood up straight and a pensive expression crossed his face before he answered seriously, green eyes full of mirth.

591

"No, I think I still have a few left in me."

"What a joy," I said sarcastically.

"Should I leave you two to settle this on your own or should I sign you up for couples therapy?" An amused feminine voice called out making me look frown.

Vivian had a large cage in one hand full of everything the hedgehog would need, three large bags sat on the ground beside her for the animal to eat and in the other she held the curled up ball of spikes. Beside me Albericus answered.

"It really depends on the price, some therapist are expensive and crappy and then some are cheap and crappy while others are-"

"Shut your face Albericus." I growled out, he pouted like a petulant child but remained quiet. Until he was what was in Vivian hands.

"You bought her a rat!" He scrunched up his face in disgusted fascination. My mate did not like his comment. She looked up and glared warningly at my beta.

"I will subtract your ass from this conversation, you're on my punching list, don't think I won't." She threatened, beside me my beta nodded almost frantically but with confusion.

Note to self, don't call it a rat.

"Oh, she got math jokes now," he muttered under his breath, we both ignored him.

Walking over to Vivian I took the cage from her. The store van had pulled out and was driving off with a final wave. Looking at her hand and eyeing the animal I began to wonder if my choice of buying her it was a smart move.

"Is this all?" I asked her.

"Yeah. Come on Frank, let me show you your new home," she murmured to the ball of spikes, walking past me without another word.

Albericus came over and picked up the bags and watched with me as Vivian stopped at the doorway and took a breath and then stepped in. . .and started to tear up.

I felt alarmed at the sudden change, it was spontaneous. Before I could asked what was wrong she began talk to the ball of spikes.

"You're in Frank, aw don't be scared, come on now." She set him down gently by the doorway and sat on her knees staring intensely as he curled up even tighter.

"I thought you said no tears or mental breakdowns after your proposal?" I teased. She huffed and looked up momentarily.

"Of course I'm the only exception, it was my proposal, I can cry all I want. When someone proposes to you I'll let you bawl all you want the next day," she responded snippy. I raised my brows in surprise but couldn't keep my comment back.

"Are you saying you're going to propose back or should I go fetch tissues for you?" She gave me a reluctant smile and then shook her head and went back to staring at the ball of spikes.

"I'd pay some good hooker money to see someone drop on a knee for you," Albericus muttered, nodding to himself with a disturbing smile on his face. I had no comment for that.

It took a few moments but it uncurled itself and slowly began moving around, it's nose wiggling as it sniffed around. Because Vivian was by the open door, I wasn't surprise when it made a run for it.

"No, wrong way Frank," she admonished, picking him up quickly and turning him around. But he just kept going for the door.

"Stop it Frank, can you guys come in before he tries to run away?" she asked us, not looking up due to her picking the ball of spikes up and resetting him on the ground again.

We both carefully stepped inside, trying not to step on the ball of spikes. Albericus didn't even look down which earned him a growl from Vivian, which then caused the little animal to ball up.

Rolling my eyes I began looking for a place to put the cage, there was no way in hell that thing was going to stay in our room. Placing it down momentarily, I motioned for Albericus to do the same to the bags but in the kitchen. Knowing without a doubt that my mates attention was solely focused on her new pet I walked into the kitchen to talk to Albericus.

What did you get? I asked through the pack link. Thanks to years of working with each other he didn't need clarification.

Hogan says that the only times he's spoken to your brother were brief and inconsequential.

Albericus looked at me with seriousness but as Alpha I could feel uncertainty coming from him, crossing his arms over his chest he leaned back against the counter.

But? I asked, knowing when my beta was keeping something to himself. He looked away briefly.

Nothing that I can prove, but Hogan's been acting weird.

Weird how? I asked, my interest peaked.

I had little contact with my third in command only when I needed files or important documents. I wouldn't consider him a friend or acquaintance, more like a very useful member. I've worked with him for the last twenty years and not once had I ever seen him with any friends, family or even love interests.

Thinking about it, why would my brother go to my third in command when he could just speak to me or Albericus?

I'm not sure how to explain it yet so I'll tell you when I have solid proof, but he gives me an odd feeling everyone he's around. Has your brother been off lately? Albericus asked cautiously.

I went to my brothers defense at once, knowing that I owed it to him.

Of course not, he's just been trying to adjust to his new settings. If anything he's entitled to any reactions he's been showing. I spoke harshly into his mind.

Albericus looked at me for a moment before nodding slowly, but I knew he was hiding his true reaction and thoughts. Before I could force them out of him Vivian walked in with a panicked expression.

"I lost Frank!" she whisper-shouted in panic, eyes flickering all over the place.

This halted both Albericus and I, disbelief clear on our faces. She threw her hands up in the air.

"Don't just stand there help me!"

"How the hell do you lose a ra-Frank?" Albericus choked out, scratching the back of his head in confusion, barely catching his slip up.

"I looked away for like a minute, I swear, I wanted to put a hat on him and when I came back he was gone." She gestured back at the living room.

"Did you follow his scent?" I asked knowing fully well that she had completely forgotten that she was not human and had instead panicked.

My theory was proven correct when she froze and straightened up. Without saying another world she walked out of the kitchen.

You dumbass, why didn't you do that before going into the kitchen? I heard the faint voice of Vivians wolf grumble.

Oh I'm the dumbass? That's funny, seeing as how I didn't hear you offering any ideas when we realized he was missing.

Don't blame this on me!

I shook my head as they bickered back and forth between one another, a few moments later she called out.

"Found him! Naughty Frank." Both Albericus and I looked at each other before chuckling.

We decided, or more so I decided, to leave the previous topic alone for the moment. Albericus and I discussed upcoming business trips and work related issues I'd have to take care of soon, Vivian had gone up to shower but not without tying her cellphone to Frank, muttering on about "gps" and "failed escapes."

Not completely understanding my mate's logic but getting her reason, I picked up her pet which instantly curled up in a ball of spikes and placed him in his cage, untying her phone from him which he clearly could not drag around. I made sure to fill and stock his cage full of water and food.

When she came down she wore a navy blue shirt tucked into white jeans and her normal black converse, it honestly didn't matter what she wore, she still managed to look spectacular in everything to me. I wordlessly handed her phone to her and watched her kneel beside the cage and poke at Frank through the bars with a carrot from his food tray.

I wasn't sure, but I think he was glaring at her. Could hedgehogs glare? Because it sure looked like he was.

Albericus went to the couch and sat down, he too then began to poke at the animal. I rolled my eyes at the two.

"Did you like my present? Why am I asking, of course you did," Albericus said, answering his own question.

"Actually," Vivian said standing up. "I haven't opened it yet, I wanted to do it when you were around so that if anything popped out I could hit you on the spot." She walked over to her stacked presents and pulled out the box he had given her.

I myself was curious as to see what he had given her, all of her other presents I had checked to make sure they were safe. I was overprotective to the extreme, I'd been trying to tone it down.

"There will be no punching, especially not to this face, my parents worked too hard to finally get the perfect child. Now open it." Albericus laughed, shaking his head.

Eyeing him suspiciously and then the box she opened it and gasped. Setting the box down carefully she launched herself at Albericus who faltered at the sudden hug, but returned it nonetheless.

I couldn't help the immediate dislike I suddenly felt for my beta, but knowing it was the bond I let out an unhappy grunt. My mate didn't even turn around to comfort me which made me give out another unhappy grunt.

"I do believe the saying is 'Something old, something new, something borrowed , something blue'. Do you like? I went for something new," he said smiling fondly.

"I love it! Thank you, and to think I was going to super punch you." Vivian joked, pulling away at last. She picked up the box and turned towards me, a knowing glint in her eyes as she took in my tensed stance.

She reached in and took it out to show me, immediately all ill feelings I had gotten a moment ago disappeared and I looked over to my grinning beta.

"You like it don't yah?" I couldn't hold back the grin that came over my face. I was a possessive knave and he knew it

"I'm impressed," I acknowledged, Vivian rolled her eyes but I felt her own different type of glee at the present. At the end we were both pleased with it, just for different reasons.

"To the future Mrs. Azrala," Albericus cheered.

In her hand Vivian held a golden bracelet with light feminine designs, in an elegant, deep and silver-colored markings the name ' Mrs.Vivian Azrala' stood boldly. My beta knew me well, I'd give him that much.

"You cavemen and your claims, I'm letting it go because it's actually cute and totally a great accessory." Vivian scolded us both with a reluctant smile. "Oh, speaking of great accessories, the ring. How is your mate?" she asked.

" Oh uh, she's doing better now. Thank you for asking," Albericus said momentarily surprised with her question. I took the opportunity now that Vivian was standing close and pulled her onto me by the back of her jeans.

I enjoyed having her in my embrace, she was so small and fit well with the hard planes of my body. Having her like this gave me a brief moment of peace to all of the activities going on in my mind, so many wolves to keep watch of, so much work. She made it easier, removing the strains I'd long ago gotten used to carrying with me.

"her in person."

"I don't think that's a good idea." Because of his panic-stricken tone, I snapped out of my mind and back into the conversation just in time to catch my betas frantic green eyes meet my own.

From the little I gathered I figured my mate was on a mission that involved in getting to meet Aurora. I briefly wondered how both women would behave like in each other's presence. Would they be friends? Auroras state changed from kind and caring to snarky and dark, Vivian was headstrong and sarcastic. Huh.

"But didn't you just say she was doing better?" Vivian's voice came out skeptical.

"Well yeah—"

"So can I go see her?" She interrupted him, not giving Albericus a chance to explain anything.

So he turned with pleading eyes to look at me for help. Which in cause made her look up as well, deep brown eyes looked at me pleadingly, but looking deeper I saw a spark of determination. I looked back at Albericus and pursed my lips.

"Is she still attacking you at random?" I asked grimly, his shoulders slumped in defeat.

"No, but she's mean as heck," he muttered, covering his face with his hands.

"Just take her man, before she ends up stalking your car," I joked, but knowing by the way Vivian tensed in my arms that, that had been her plan. Albericus parted his fingers momentarily to show wide green eyes.

"Wait, you mean you're not coming with?" he cried out. I shook my head.

Vivian jumped in my arms and spun around, taking my face in her hands she yanked me down to plant a firm kiss. I was pulling her closer when she pulled back with a smile.

"Thank you," She turned and went to grab Albericus, grabbing his wrist and yanking him to the front door. "come on Algebra, we're gonna go see your mate. Cheer up." His pleading expression was met by my mocking one.

"By Zaliver," she called out, opening the front door. "take care of Frank for me, love you!"

"I love you too, have fun. Take care of her," I ordered Albericus.

"Forget her, who's going to take care of me? Those two are going to rip into me." my beta said before my mate yanked him out of the door.

"Oh don't be so dramatic Algebra!" I heard her call out to him.

"Me dramatic? She tried to kill me last time, hell, she dragged my ass—" he exclaimed, the sound of doors opening met my ears.

"Oh I'm sure she did," she responded sarcastically, not believing him whatsoever.

I heard Albericus mutter something unintelligible under his breath and then the car pulled away from the house. Sighing I looked down and got down on one knee to look into the cage. Two black eyes looked back at me.

"You're staying in the cage." I pointed at it and stood up. For a moment I thought I heard it make a sound of protest but shook my head.

Since my beta was probably going to be out for the day I'd go to the office today to finish and check some things out, but first. . .

In less than five minutes I had all of Vivian's presents in our room and organized in the same order she had them but this time on her side of the closet. I knew that if I didn't bring them up that she never would have done it herself, this made setting Frank's cage in the living room easier. She was lazier than she liked to admit, but I was fine with it since I liked to know where everything was.

While I hopped into the shower I caught the sound of Joshula leaving the house which made me acknowledge something. How was he getting around? I hadn't given him a car and I was pretty sure he didn't

597

know how to drive an automobile yet, so just how was my brother getting around? I would have known the moment he shifted, it would have made his silver lining stronger in my mind and yet since he got here he hadn't express his need to shift.

In fact, in my mind his silver lining was perhaps the dullest and weakest of all, it was almost as if he were. . .no, I shook my head at the absurdity of it.

My brother was obviously alive, his wolf was probably just weaker than most since he was neither born nor bitten but made into a werewolf.

Remembering Vivian's new dressing code I wore black jeans with a black and white striped shirt with a denim jacket on top. I ran a hand through my still wet hair and decided to just let it air dry and went to go put on my black boots. It was sunny today so I got some shades out, grabbed my keys and headed to my car.

I spent the morning going around the island and checking up on certain wolves and businesses, going to the main office I wasn't surprised to see Hogan in here but my betas words rang through my head and like the alpha I am it made my beast grow distrustful of him.

"Hello Hogan," I said, ignoring my office and entering his for once. Startled he looked up and stared at me for a moment.

"A-Alpha, hello. Was I supposed to prepare something for you? Albericus didn't say-" I shook my head and watched him from behind my shades.

Hogan wore a black button down shirt with a white tie today,his usually brown curls were cut shorter. He regarded me with expectant, he too watched me with an odd but not alarming look in his eyes. His office was clean and ordered, files and documents in place, he had four computers spread around him. Both windows in his office were open, filling the room with a soft breeze.

"No, I just wanted to see how you were. I've come to realize that in the time we've worked together I haven't gotten to know you all that well. You're always behind that desk aren't you?" I asked, leaning against the door frame.He leaned back in his chair and nodded slowly.

"Not by choice I assure you sir, but if I can help you in any way then with pleasure,' he answered lowly, eyes trying to see mine through the shades.

"I'm glad to know have such a dedicated and loyal person working for me." I slowly, looking for any type of indication of something. " But you're right, it's not very fair to have you behind the desk days and nights. Why don't you take the rest of today and tomorrow off?"

He looked surprised and confused at my suggestion but also interested.

598

"And do what?" he asked me.

I grinned largely at him, deciding not to note the quickening his heart suddenly did.

"Rest, party, meet someone, the usual things people do when they're given the day off," I pointed out to him standing up straight.

A crossed expression made its way on his face when I mentioned meeting someone. Was my third in command seeing someone? Interesting. Seeing that I didn't sense anything off about him I turned to leave when the wind outside gave a strong gust and a scent so faint a werewolf would never have caught it, hit me. I froze, the inside of my body chilled.

Without turning around I spoke, a plan automatically forming in my mind to solve my sudden unanswered questions.

"Hogan?"

"Yes?" he asked, confused and half excited, for what?

"You haven't met my mate have you?"

There was a short pause before his disappointed and somewhat disgruntled voice answered me.

"No, I haven't had the pleasure."

"Hhm, come over to my house sometime this week for dinner then. I'm sure she'll be delighted to meet you," I said, leaving no room for a denial.

"Oh. . .sure. Can't wait."

Walking out of his office I walked into mine and softly closed the door behind me. I walked over to my desk and dug my claws into my desk.

I could feel my canines pushing out, I could feel my eyes slowly becoming darker. I was careful to close my side of the bond as to not alarm Vivian, the last thing I wanted to do was ruin her day. Taking a breathe didn't help, a darkness that I hadn't felt in a very long time began to awaken once more in my beast as he snarled around my mind.

The scent I had caught in Hogan's office had shocked me to my core, it was a scent that was familiar and most importantly, a scent that should not have been anywhere near this island.

I had but the faintest whiff of it, but that was all it took for a lycan to remember a scent. A unique scent, a scent that was two in one. Two of the most impossible beings together. Unique, but not indistinguishable to me.

Especially when you not only grew up with one but was around the other for a very, very long time.

One scent brought in a series of emotions that I'd wished not to recognize, but by nature had to face, to make sense of my new situation.

And the other?

The other brought old emotions back to the surface, emotions that poked and prodded at the stirring darkness within me.

One was meant to be looking for a new start and the other was supposed to be withering in the darkest parts of their mind. They were not supposed to be together.

What the hell was going on my island?

CHAPTER 43

VIVIAN GREY

"I can't believe you haven't let her out, I mean so what? Maybe she threw a little dirt at you and tossed you around like her bitch."

"Are you serious right now? I just told you that she tried to kill me and this is what you tell me?"

"But did you die though?"

"No but—"

"So that's it then," I stated in triumph, getting ready to settle back into my seat. Algebra turned to look at me as if I was crazy, he held up a hand with his pointer finger in the air.

"Uh no, no, no. That's not it. Are you just going to ignore the fact that she not only tried to stab me in the eye with her fork, but then strangled me with her scarf?!" he exclaimed.

He makes a good point. My wolf nodded in agreement.

"She wouldn't have been able to stab you if you hadn't given her the fork and as for the scarf you should be happy. Not a lot of people go out in style," I joked. He opened his mouth but then reluctantly chuckled.

"That last one was kind of good," he grumbled, turning left onto a bumpy road.

"I know." Algebra shook his head, his stubborn look returning. As soon as we had gotten into the car he had tried to convince me this was a very bad idea, apparently he thought telling me all the things she had done to him would scare me off. If anything, it only intrigued me to meet the woman. She sounded so nice.

"I'm begging you to reconsider coming, she'd probably prefer if someone new saw her only at her best and right now that's not it," Algebra said with worry in his voice.

" I'll go, but only if she says so. How am I supposed to ignore her after hearing how you've kept her locked away from civilization-"

"For everyone's safety—"

"And have probably had your wicked ways with the poor girl." He snorted.

"If I'd had my wicked ways with her, you and I wouldn't be speaking now. I wouldn't even be in this car, hell, Zaliver would have had to find a new beta already," he grumbled grumpy.

I felt a bit bad for the mopy wolf, I knew he was probably just worried about her but in a sense I didn't want to let him feel as if he had to do it alone. . .then there was the fact that it was just plain unacceptable that I haven't met my mates female beta. Like, come on.

"Oh don't mope, I'm sure your chance will come. Now, any warnings?" He gave me a long withered look.

"You mean besides every other warning I've given you which you've ignored and will probably continue to do so? No, you're good," he answered sarcastically. I tsked at his pessimistic mood.

"It will all turn out okay, stop stressing out so much." Seriously, I worried for the men's health.

When he pulled up in front of a small but homey looking cabin I knew immediately she was here and it wasn't just because of the bars on the windows or Algebra's mumblings, it was the odd scent of pure earth with sunlight but the smallest edge of something negative that left me slightly on edge. It was almost metallic and yet bitter-sweet. Magic.

I'd never been in such close proximity to a witch, but it'd be a lie if I didn't say I was both nervous and excited.

At first, I was afraid, I was petrified but then I- I cut my wolf's singing off.

I don't care how long or what I have to do but I will find a way to punch you without hurting myself in the process. I hissed. She grumbled something to herself and laid on her belly, ears perked up.

Be careful. My beast said seriously Witches are not within our control.

Hearing my beast made me become a bit more guarded, I trusted Algebra to keep me safe but if it came down between his Luna and mate I wouldn't fault the guy for picking the later. I'd just have to be cautious and slow on my advance, if I got the hint of anything that could possibly end up wrong I'd hightail it out of here. It would be foolish of me to put Algebra in a sticky situation, and that alone was coming from myself. Better safe than sorry.

The sound of a door softly closing behind me and the soft steps alerted me of Algebra's slow approach. My ears perked up at the moment now coming from inside. She must have sensed her mate near. I wasn't completely sure how mating worked with mixed pairs and in this case a witch and a werewolf, so I was genuinely curious to see how this worked. I also had to keep in mind the fact that Aurora was a bit. . .off, so whatever I saw might not be completely right.

Well. . .this ought to be good.

Stepping in front of me, Algebra opened the door and treaded carefully and called out, sparing me one last warning look.

"You've brought friends," A low female voice purred, almost bored, from somewhere inside.

Peaking around Algebra's figure I couldn't help it when my mouth dropped at the sight of the woman sitting on the couch.

Wavy long dark hair that seemed to turn black at the end, a tall slender figure that could easily be guessed even when sitting down with an elegant leg crossed over the other, a heart-shaped feminine face with sharp features and black eyes blinked, unnaturally alert at me. The woman was unnervingly beautiful. And also very mischievous from the sudden tilt of her head and the tapping of her fingers.

"Or one."

She hummed and narrowed her eyes at me suddenly, looking over at Algebra from a moment I caught a faint change in her body. It was faint but it seemed as if her eyes lightened a shade to a cool brown instead of black, her posture which I had assumed relax, deflated a bit and she blinked a bit as if startled.

"Uh hi," I said with uneasy, but still wanting to know her. She intrigued me. "I'm—"

"What he holds close to his heart," she whispered softly, a new tone in her voice. She squinted at me as if she were trying to see me through thick glass, or as if she were standing miles away instead of inches.

"Vivian." I finished, confused by what she had said. I felt my beast push forward a bit, looking at her through my eyes but not trying to take over so I let her.

"Ah yes, Vivian. Zaliver's mate." She uncrossed her legs and stood up showing me just how tall she was.

She wore a long navy dress which ended in different lengths towards the ends but that opened up at her knees to show her long legs, two thin strap held it around her neck showing off her pale shoulders and neck. She was barefooted, the only other piece of clothing she wore was a thin lace and teared up cloth thrown over her figure, lazily, for cover. On her figures she wore many rings of different sizes and shapes, yet nothing around her neck.

Her attire screamed witch. In fact, everything about her screamed witch, it was very. . .odd yet something about her wanted you to get closer.

Beside me Algebra tensed at his mates movement and from where I stood behind him I could sense the dilemma he was facing on what he should do, or better yet whom he should protect.

To make it easier from him I spoke, wanting to say what I needed to just in case something went wrong. . . and also to win her over to my side. There was nothing wrong with making someone who could possibly toss your ass around like a doll-like you. Call it strategy.

"I want to thank you." I blurted out quickly, making her stop. I continued, seeing the momentary confusion on her face. I lifted up my hand to show her the engagement ring.

"Ahh." She nodded in understanding, but also seemed to be slightly trying to focus herself.

"Yeah, I now don't have to worry about it falling apart on me or a rock falling off, so thanks for that." I really did mean it, I would have been devastated if it had fallen apart for punching a hoe.

"Well, now that we've said our 'hellos' and 'thanks' we should—" Aurora cut Algebra off with a grimace of a smile.

"Calm yourself Berry, I'm in control most of the time now. While it would have been better to meet her when I was," Her eyes briefly meet my own with an apologetic look. "better, it's fine. I'm not going to do anything stupid."

It was dumb, but the only thing I heard was 'Berry'. Aww, Algebra's got another nickname.

Hahaha, no one remembers his name but our mate. My wolf snickered.

I looked up at Algebra to catch the vulnerable look on his face, green eyes pained at her words. His lips opened as if he were going to say something but closed a second later and nodded his head at her, taking a step away from me she showed he trusted his mates words.

I was glad he did so, because it seemed as if his action removed something off of her, as her eyes took on another lighter brown shade and she rolled her shoulders back as if getting rid of a heavy burden. She still seemed to have a sort of darkness around her persona, but there was a crack in place and somehow innocent seemed to spill from it.

Walking towards me, her steps were both confident and yet shy, I couldn't quite describe it.

"It's a pleasure to meet you Vivian, I've heard much about you. I'd wished it only to have been under better circumstances," She murmured softly, standing in front of me. The woman was several inches taller than me, Algebra's height actually, and yet she seemed to try to make herself small.

Where all witch's like this? Probably not.

"It's nice to meet you too, I agree but it's fine with me, Algebra's been keeping you to himself I see."

"Who?" She asked looking at me in bewilderment. Oh right.

"That's his nickname for me, Albericus is a mouth full and—" A large grin, for once not looking strained nor distant, made its way onto her face. She jumped up once and capped with almost restrained joy.

"Right! Why did you pick a math term for a name?" She looked at me eagerly, expectant and almost hopeful.

"Uh," Her sudden burst of joy caught me off guard but I was quick to follow. " because Albericus, Algebraic, Algebra. He hates it, but since he responds to it, it's stayed. Had he not I would have called him by his real name, but it's too late. Besides I'm his Luna, not my problem," I said smugly.

"Wait-what?" Came a horrified voice behind us. We both ignored him.

"Oh I think I'm going to like you," Aurora said with narrowed criteria that seemed to be going in a good direction. It seemed I was on the witches good side. A faint 'ahh shit ' came from behind us, we ignored that too and went to go sit on the couch together.

This could be the start, of something new-

I officially blocked my wolf out, but sadly enough I could still hear a faint humming in the back of my mind and the feeling of smugness coming from the wolf. My beast pulled away from my mind and simply watched now, her feelings that of cautionary trust and slight understanding that the witch was slightly in her right mind. My beast was giving her the benefit of the doubt. That was good enough for me.

"Berry's a nice nickname too. Makes me wonder if I should give Zaliver one." I had just come to the realization that not once had I given Zaliver a nickname.

Was that odd? I didn't think it was, I just really liked his name. . .even if it was his name of choice. That last thought came with a bit of annoyance. Zalvius, huh.

"I'll tell you one thing,"Algebra added himself into the conversation and took a seat on across from us, putting his feet on the table. And then quickly taking them off at Aurora's glare. " he hates it when you call him Z-ster, Count Zalcula, Zal, ZZ, Lil Z, Z-bag, Alpha Z, X-Y-Z and whatever you do don't call him Zalvius the great. It's not even worth it. Apparently Alexander the great wasn't so great in person. His words, not mine."

I stared at Algebra in both amusement and amazement.

"You called him some of those and lived?" I raised a brow at him. Aurora snorted, I turned to look away from a sullen Algebra.

"No, he called him some of those and healed. Sometimes he'd come home and depending on where he was hurt, I could tell he'd made

605

up a new name. Zaliver had a knack for knowing where it would take Berry longer to heal," Aurora explained, shaking her head, she tucked some of her hair behind her ear and grinned at me.

"Yeah, that sounds like something Zaliver would do." In the past, I added silently. Looking over at Algebra I noted that he to was looking at me with a raised brows as if he had thought the same thing. He gave me a discreet nod.

Trending onto a different and not heavy conversation with Aurora I came to the conclusion that she was like me in many ways, but most of all I came to see her as a nice person under dark times. Every once in a while she would snap at me or Algebra with a harsh comment or look, but after a quick pause she'd apologize to which I explained that I took no offense.

I was surprised to have noted how she called me by my direct name and although she was, oddly enough, technically in my pack, I'm guessing titles didn't matter much to witches and so the offense as it could have been coming from another wolf, was nothing at all to me.

My beast had shocked me by showing me the aura that connected both her and Algebra after her second odd reaction, I had seen that their vibrant green, that connected them both to each other was tainted in an odd way with darkness. It was like looking at water and oil, but in this case the oil clung to Aurora in a desperate kind of way, it hissed and coiled around Aurora in an unnatural way with sharp edges and bubbling heat.

I wasn't going to lie. That scared the shit out of me when I saw it.

If it weren't for the fact that I wasn't one for showing much weakness during first impressions and the fact that I didn't want to startle her, I probably would have cut the meeting short. But one thing was disturbingly real, whatever magic the witch had used was indeed dark if it could live and fight inside of her to the point of controlling her enough to make her disregard her mating bond.

Unlike Algebra's playful banter and sometimes beta like behavior, from the little I got from what I'm guessing is her true personality, she was a kind yet serious and borderline mischievous as a person. For a moment I wondered if Algebra's playfulness was really his coping mechanism to keep his mates past behavior alive, that perhaps she was the playful one in the relationship before. As she was talking to me, from the corner of my eye I could see the love and patience in Algebra's eyes as he looked at her. It saddened me to think that the two had to go through such pain and struggle to get back to any form of normality.

Fate was cruel to those who didn't deserve it sometimes.

Aurora moved her hands a lot when she talked, so I was bound to see one of her rings catch the light from outside and want to see what had caught my eyes.

"I love your rings, they're very pretty,

"I mentioned, to which she had faced me with her palms flat down so that I could get a closer look.

Reaching out I played with the large oval gem, painted and decorated in gold, now barrier free my wolf nodded in agreement. I hadn't noticed her go stiff at contact with me.

"Berry can you get me some lemonade?" Aurora asked, her voice soft yet tight. I looked up at the mention of it.

"I love lemonade," I muttered more to myself, happy to know there was some around. She gave a small smile.

"I know." She turned to look at Algebra who still hadn't gotten up.

Wait what? How did she know? Did everyone know I loved lemonade?

"We don't have lemonade?" His brows furrowed as he looked at her and them me, he made the statement come out as a question. I deflated a bit at that.

"There's a lemon tree outside, go get some lemons." Aurora said abruptly. At that Algebra frowned in confusion and uncertainty.

"There is?" he asked looking at his mate suspiciously.

"There is now. Go." She snapped. He looked like he was going to argue but then shook his head and looked at me, I nodded showing that I was fine and with that he stood up but not before muttering 'witches' under his breath.

Aurora stared after him until the door closed softly and then she turned to look at me,and odd glint in her eyes.

And suddenly lemonades not worth dying for. Bring the beta back and tell him his mates crazy. Pretty, but crazy. My wolf grumbled.

I pulled back a bit at my wolf comment, agreeing that Aurora's staring was making me uncomfortable. Her hands suddenly reached out and clasped my own, I let out a small nervous laugh. Ah shit, why didn't I take Algebra's warnings from before serious, now I was going to get thrown around like her bitch.

"Not all witches are born the same, some are born to cast spells, do dark magic, create a strong coven, heal, become an earth witch or know things that others do not," She began talking quickly, my eyes widened at her sudden explanation.

Did you sign up for Witch 101? My wolf asked.

No.

You sure? Cause she seems pretty damn focused on teaching you the ways of her people. You sure you didn't sign one of those online weavers? My wolf asked skeptically.

Yeah.

"Very few are born with more than one gift, I am," She grimaced. " was one of those, but because of what I did I lost the connect I had, but over the last few days I've been getting a glimpse of things, feelings and control of my previous powers. I had the power to heal and manipulate all of earth's elements to my desire-thus why that idiot is out there looking for a lemon tree." She smirked in amusement and I couldn't help but to chuckle.

"I also had the gift of knowing things others would not know by touch, but witches with that power are just as clueless to the message as the receiver. Do you know how hard it is to tell someone something important, but not be able to because you yourself don't know what the answer to their questions are? Goddamn hard," she muttered.

"Why are you telling me this?" I asked seriously, I knew by experience that no one told a stranger their powers and bindings from 'the unknown' at first greetings.

It was like a date, you gotta wait until date number four to throw yourselves at each other. You could do it on the third, but it showed self-restraint to make it to the fourth.

She opened her mouth to speak but seemed to be choking on something, she squeezed my hands and then closer her mouth. An annoyed yet calculating expression came upon her, her brows furrowed as she bit her lip.

"Whatever I saw can be interpreted in many ways, sometimes even I don't know what I know, so please do forgive me if all I do is give you a headache," she apologize.

"It's fine." At the moment I was more concerned about her falling over with how hard she was thinking, then her actually telling me anything at all.

Like, Algebra would walk in with a whole lot of lemons and find his mate on the ground trying to say something. For all he knew, I'd punched her in the throat and she was trying to tell him that exactly. God, it would be horrible. And I wouldn't even get my lemonade.

She made sure to have my attention and then spoke in an ominous voice. Her face became dazed as if under a spell, ironic, right?

"*Wherever you go, you will carry light from now on, but you will be followed by night and night will take over to snuff your light out. Those whom failed to see the connection will pay the price in blood and those who do not play by the rules of their agreement shall face the fury of the heartbroken. There will be pain, no cure and no salvation, only death. If your light goes out. . .so will you.*"

I blinked at her af her.

608

"You know. . .if you were a Psychic, I would so have demanded my money back," I joked weakly, not wanting to show her how much her words, even if she didn't remember them, bothered me.

If I had been standing I would have needed to sit down. . .or a nap. A nap sounds good too.

"Did it make any sense to you whatsoever? What does it mean to you?"

"Something along the lines of me possibly dying if I'm not careful with my electricity and whatnot." I removed my hands from her and waved them around. She frowned at me and put her hand on her chest.

"That's odd, whatever I said came with a really bad," At that moment Algebra came back with a shit load of lemons through the door, but I was no longer thirsty. . .or hungry. Quite frankly I was shaken.

"Oh no, don't stop talking on my account. By the way, when you send a man to get some lemons from a fucking magical lemon tree, maybe you should warn him about how if you pick one-" He walked over to the kitchen and dropped them all simultaneously on the counter, not caring for the ones that rolled away and fell. " they all fucking fall." He glared at his mate, who smiled innocently at him.

"When life gives you lemons, what do you do?" she asked slyly.

He picked one up and pointed it at her.

"You fucking throw it back until she gives you some water, sugar, a cup, and a knife because last time I checked a lemon wasn't the only ingredient in that bitch." He snapped sassily.

No matter what had gone through Aurora's mind, or my own we both had to laugh at his response. And as for the moment, I pushed back her odd words because for that time being, everything was okay.

Algebra and I didn't leave until much later, we had already had lunch by that point and ignoring Auroras odd words, she was alright. Promising to come back as soon as possible me and Algebra made our way to the car as she watched on from the window, staring at me with those oddly alert and knowing eyes.

One word. Witches.

"It's okay, it took me a while to get use to her eyes too. It's a witch thing. Apparently the concept of 'Staring is rude' means nothing to them," Algebra said once in the car.

"Oh yeah, I'm sure all witches stare," I said, putting my seatbelt on.

"I'm serious, dinner with her family the first time was so awkward, I thought I had food all over my face. Don't even get me started on how Zaliver had to keep reminding himself that she wasn't trying to intimidate him. Now that, was funny." He shook his head and sighed happily, running his fingers through a mass of curly brown hair.

"You seem happy," I pointed out with a raised brow at him.

"Thank you

"For what?" I asked confused, had I said his name at some point of the day?

"For talking to her even through her relapse. She might not say it, but I know she's been lonely both here and before she got here, she knows that for everyone's and her own safety she has to focus on herself before she can go out, but you coming today even though I insisted you didn't-"

"And you did that a lot." He rolled his eyes at me.

"Yes, I know. It means a lot to me and I know to her as well that she got to talk to you today. You're the first person she's actually talk to and hasn't tried to kill or manipulate onto letting her go since she's got here. She was smiling and laughing and . . . Thank you Vivian." He turned to look at me with a sincere smile that quickly morphed into confusion.

"Why are your eyes all shimmery?" he asked in a worried tone.

"Because that was so sweet and sappy and you love her so much and I'm getting married!" I wailed in an excited shriek.

"Oh my god, I did not sign up for this," he muttered under his breath, suddenly picking up the car's speed.

"I'm getting married, Jeezus Christ, what the hell?!" I exclaimed surprised and panicked.

That moment when it finally hits you. My wolf muttered.

"Shut the hell up!" I snapped at her, out loud, which made Algebra look at me like I was crazy, which I probably was at the moment.

I've never planned a wedding, what do I even want? Where? When? Great, I was having a mini break down in my mates betas car and he was possibly freaking out more than I was. That thought made me laugh, like giggle-wheeze, laugh.

After about a good minute I was done and calm in my seat, a one hundred percent freaked out beta sitting frozen stiff beside me, probably going over the speed limit like as if he were a race car driver.

"Ahh, I needed that. Too much pent-up energy and excitement, you know?" I asked turning to look at him.

"Yup," he answered quickly, high-pitched.

"You know if Zaliver hears that you drove above the speed limit with me in the car, he'll kill you right?" I asked after a moment of silence.

I wasn't sure what was going through his head when he realized that too, but I'm pretty sure he regretted slamming on the brakes more than I regretted not taking that lemonade earlier.

"You're a hand full, you know that?" he asked once the car had stopped, turning to look at me with a pained grimace as he rubbed where the belt had probably cut into his neck. Sucks for him, I had braced for it.

"Yup and you know what?" I asked cheerfully.

"What?" He asked starting the car at a slower speed than before.

"You still adore me. Admit it," I stated playfully. It was a moment before a soft expression crossed his face, green eyes shining in a tender way that had me questioning if I had gotten in the car with the right beta.

"Yeah, I guess I do." He reached over and ruffed up my hair.

"Aw—"

"I mean you're a pain in the ass, have hurtful comebacks and you also gave me that awful nickname-"

"Hey!"

"But you're like one of the many sisters I have but never wanted but would be okay with having." He sighed.

I narrowed my eyes at him and bared my teeth, to which he ignored.

"I'm honored." Sarcasm left a familiar taste on my tongue.

" As I knew you would be," he replied smartly.

For once, I didn't have a comeback.

It must have been his luck day.

~•~

"Hannah, you can't get on a diet now."

"Why not?"

"You haven't even popped the baby out!"

"Do you know how long it takes to get rid of baby fat, if I'm going to be your maid of honor, I'm gonna look good."

"You'll look better than good, you'll look fabulous, so don't worry now. Besides, we haven't even picked out a date so relax."

Mark placed his hand on a pregnant, extremely determined and extremely disgruntled Hannah, he rubbed her belly slowly to try to calm her down. Doing so, she stopped trying to do crunches on the couch and just leaned back against him. . .and didn't try to get back up to touch her toes.

"I guess," she muttered, unhappily.

611

I smiled at my friends dedication to a wedding that wasn't even picked out yet. As soon as I had told and asked Hannah about the wedding and to be my maid of honor she had tried to do some crunches.

Johnson, the ever encouraging big brother that he was counted her off much to Mark's annoyance. She got to three before she started wheezing. That baby was going to come out this week, I had a strong feeling about that.

After asking Algebra to drop me off at Hannah's house, I wasn't surprised to see my guards show up a few minutes later. It was amusing to see Johnson welcome everyone and try to get Mila to kiss him to come in. She kicked him in the shin, pushed him out her way and strolled in with an annoyed look on her face which grew as a grinning Johnson followed closely behind with his eyes on her behind. Those two. . .were something else.

I didn't do much after that, I did stop around a few places with wolves that were giving off some really strong distress signals to which I couldn't ignore, turns out ones of those was from a guy in this thirties stuck under the frame of his home improvement project. Who knew ignoring instructions could be so deadly? That last thought came with sarcasm.

When I returned home it was later than I usually did, apparently that guy was dead set on proving to his wife that he could get out without our help, trying to be polite, I watched him squirm for thirty minutes before he called it quits. The expression on his face when I single-handedly lifted the wood,metal frame and rubble off of him was worth the wait.

I could sense Zaliver in my room, who I couldn't sense was Joshula, which lead me to understand that this was another night out for him. I didn't like this, him going in and out all the time without warning or saying where. Maybe it was the Luna in me wanting to know everything, maybe it was just plain old me not liking the feeling I was being walked around instead of approached, but either which I didn't like it.

That boy was either out there partying like an animal, in a band, hanging with some friends or doing some really shady shit. Somehow, I didn't picture him as the party type, I doubted his years as a dead body healing taught him how to play an instrument and I don't think he's been here long enough to have found the group of friends that made him feel whole and accept. That left me with the last one. And the thought of him going for a booty call, I decided not to focus on that.

. . .he was an odd child that one. I really hope my gut was wrong because if we get a call in the middle of the night about someone needing bail money, my ass would declare bankruptcy. At least until morning.

Going up to the room I opened the doors and was surprised to see that they were off when I could clearly sense Zaliver in the room. Looking around I found him sitting on his side of the bed, facing the side. I closed the door behind me.

"No Zaliver, it's not creepy at all to sit in the dark for who knows how long in silence," I started, walking towards him.

When he said nothing I cocked my head to the side and forced myself to focus only to realize that at some point in the day he had closed himself off. He was getting good at shutting me out without me realizing it. I didn't know if I should be happy about that.

The only thing that was going through my mind was 'cold feet'. My chest felt tight.

I hope he knows he ain't gettin' the ring back. My wolf snarled at the thought of him regretting the proposal.

The only acknowledgement he made to my wolf's thought has the tilt of his head and a sigh. Pushing my, probably illogical, doubt aside, I walked to him until I saw seated beside him.

"What's wrong?" I asked, my voice coming out not louder than my pounding heart.

"Vivian?" His voice came out cold, distant. After a long pause from me I spoke, filled with uneasy, the bottom of stomach churning with a bad feeling.

"Yes?" I asked softly. I was afraid of what he might ask.

" How much do you trust Joshula?"

The question took me off guard, but only because it nothing compared to what he could have asked me, what my mind had come up with. Thousands of questions, with thousands of outcomes, but all ending in pain in heartache. Now thinking about his question I pursed my lips.

"Honestly?" I asked. I could tell him what he wanted to hear, I could lie to him, but I knew Zaliver and I also knew that he valued an honest opinion and response from me above all.

I felt as if whatever was going on with him was not some small commotion, but a deep wave which he had ignored at first and was now forced to deal with the chaos of his decision. My mate was in mental turmoil.

He still didn't look at me, but I felt, more than saw his hesitation.

"Honestly."

I took a breath and sighed, putting my head on his bicep provided me with a small comfort to his distant mind. He might not have known, or even acknowledged it, but his tense form relaxed the slightest. I thought to the first time I saw Joshula, to the moment I had contact with his skin, the dark and mysterious feeling that had come over me. I thought of his watchful eyes, the pretense calm and watchfulness he gave off, his odd words and phrases. But I also thought of his shaken form and the night of his nightmare, of how he must have felt as he heard the world advance without him and lastly I thought of his yellow eyes which were bizarre and unheard of.

"Your brothers weird and I mean that in a 'I'll be watching your every move so that if opportunity strikes I'm stabbing you in the back the first chance I get because you killed me' kind of way. No offense, he seems like under all that creepiness he'd be a great guy. So how much do I trust him? Not at all." I was tense, waiting for him to jump up and defend his brother. His humorless chuckle was what greeted my ears. Somehow, it was worse.

Turning around to face me, which made me lift my head, electric blue eyes glowed in the dark and pinned me to my spot. I held still as he lifted a hand to my face and took my jaw in his hold in a firm but soft grip, tilting my head a bit. The corners of his mouth lifted up in an empty smile that didn't reach his eye.

"It would appear so, mate, that I have ignored the wolf in sheep's clothing in our home. Shall I butcher it once more, my love?" he asked in a sickly soft and sweet voice that sent shivers down my back, for the threat was not for me and yet I still felt the danger behind them.

Even my sarcastic, quick-witted brain shut down at the question because it was moments like these where I was once again reminded that Zaliver was feared and respected for many reason, for he was not a man to be messed with. He was Alpha of all Alphas, the Lupus Deus of werewolf horror stories that I still wasn't sure if they were just stories.

And at this moment I wasn't sure if this was a trick question or if he really was asking me if he should murder his brother. . .again.

Seeming to sense my dilemma, he leaned down and pecked the side of my mouth on each side before kissing me briefly on the lips and pulling back. Faster than my shocked mind could comprehend, my back was against his front as I sat in between his legs, both of his arms wrapped around me securely.

He buried his face on the side of my neck with his mark on it, kissing around it he pulled back a little to whisper in my ear in coldest of voices, in the calmest of ways.

"They will not hurt you, over my dead, resurrecting body. I can swear to you that."

They?

For some reason Aurora's words from earlier in the day came to mind and with them the feeling of something big coming.

"What are you saying Zaliver?" I asked hesitantly, my body stiff in his arms.

614

"Don't worry about it Vivian, he spoke relaxed and began trailing kisses down my neck.

What are my choices? I asked my wolf, whom cleared her throat.

A)Ignore him and whatever's going on in his head.

B)Ask what's bothering him and clarify whatever he just said.

C)Talk about something else, like what flavor the cake should be. Personally cheesecake sounds delicious.

Fuck. Cheesecake did sound delicious though.

"Zaliver." My voice came out strained but not for the obvious reasons.

"I know of the best recipes for cheesecake if you'd like-"

"Zaliver," I repeated, slower this time.

"Leave it."

"It's sort of hard to ignore you mentioning killing your brother, especially when it's the second time. Now please explain," I said firmly, standing up and out of his arms. Turning around to face him.

Zaliver's head was down, black hair covering his expression from me, but the way he sat up rigidly, the clenched fists and shaking chest with every breath did nothing but worry me even more so.

"Zaliver, don't keep whatever it is, inside of you, it's not good. Trust me, you know you can." I placed my hands on his hair and softly strokes the silky strands.

In the dark and silent room, it was almost a little overwhelming, heightening the bond between us even with him closing himself off. It tore at my heart and mind, this odd behavior of his. Wasn't he happy with his brothers return? I mean, I know they probably aren't as close as they were before and maybe things do seem to be a little odd when they're in the same room together, but to kill him over so awkward air? That didn't seem like Zaliver at all. He was usually all 'there's a reason for most things I do and if not, there shall be'.

"Do you. . .do you remember what I told you I did to Fate?" he asked gruffly.

I felt myself pale. Oh. Whatever was going on was suddenly much more frightening than I realized.

"Yeah," I responded in a hoarse whisper.

It took some time and a few days and a lot of pestering from me, but I finally got Zaliver to tell me exactly what went down on the day that he left. It didn't take long into the story from me to regret asking him, but I was never one to interrupt a story, sadly.

I didn't know what to think when he told me he'd trapped Fate, a god of choice and mystery to my mind, in his own body to be tormented and tortured until every one of his sins and cruel choices drove him crazed.

"I caught his scent on the island today."

Cold. The air traveling in my body was very cold. I pulled my hands away from his hair, but shock froze the moment halfway.

"W-Wha—"

"Along with Joshula's scent."

"Wait, I don't-"

"Neither do I, but I know one thing," he said ominously, waves of pushed back anger coming forward. Luckily I didn't have to ask for him to answer.

"My brother died a very long time ago, whoever is in our home, in his body, is not Joshula." He growled out, his head snapping up to show pitch black eyes.

"What are you going to do?" My throat felt as if an imaginary hand was squeezing tight, as if air was not making its way into my nose and to my lungs. My stomach filled with dread and threatened to make me throw up the little I had in it.

But it was fear that clogged my veins. Fear for my mate and what all this would do to him.

And yet it was something else that filled my heart. Something that I could not name, but that left the taste of bliss and death on my tongue. Zaliver blinked at me once and answered.

"I will do what I do best and teach whoever it is playing, that the game begins and ends when I say it does."

With another blink his eyes went back to normal but I remained the same. Zaliver looked down and his face hardened. Reaching for my hands he took them into his own.

"You're shaking," he said angrily, but not at me.

I looked down and saw he was right, I hadn't noticed how badly my hands-no, my body shook.

"I-I hadn't re-realized." Damn it. If anything, my broken sentence only seemed to worsen Zaliver's mood.

"I shouldn't have told you. I shouldn't have had to tell you because this shouldn't have happened. I'm going to make someone's ending very painful." He snarled infuriated, standing up he wrapped his arms around my shaking form once more and pulled me close.

Inhaling his scent soothed me enough to stop shaking and to come to grips with what he'd just told me. I hadn't met Fate in person, but from how Zaliver described him, Fate was a bitch.

But what the hell were we going to do about Joshula? I voiced the question. He pulled away from me to look me in the eyes, searching for something. I wasn't completely in control of myself, so I didn't know what my expression resembled but whatever it was made

616

the corner of his lips curve upward into a smile that promised chaos, fun, danger and something that made my stomach tug as if a pull to him had established itself like never before.

"How do you feel about playing my version of I Spy?"

~•~

Hot, so very hot and humid.

When I opened my eyes I had to blink a bit to adjust, the room was still dark but I was a bit groggy. A bit of moonlight spilled into the room and made an eerie picture.

I was sweating and very tired and yet not so in the sense that made sense. I turned slowly to look at Zaliver who was thrown over me, one arm wrapped around my waist while the other laid beside my head thrown over my chest, our legs intertwined. With his eyes closed and body relaxed he looked at peace and not at all angry like he was before. Black hair spilled wildly over him making him look younger.

This would have been romantic if he his build wasn't currently suffocating me with his heat.

It wasn't only his heat, the blankets or even myself that had woken me, I was. . .hungry.

I think.

I wasn't sure, I was partly mad that I had been awaken from precious sleep for food, but eh, it was food so I guess that was an okay reason.

Perhaps it wasn't even hunger that had woken me, but the still overwhelming and worrisome information Zaliver had told me before bed. I guess my mind was still in whirl about what to think and decided my ass needed more time to think and process, even if it meant a cranky Vivian in the middle of the night.

Now all I had to do was get from out and under Zaliver without waking him up. Should be easy right, not like he had super senses at all. No. Not at all.

Let me. My beast said softly. My wolf was silent, perhaps still slumbering. It was a good thing because if she had been awake her conscious would have probably woken Zaliver up.

I relinquished myself to her and let her control my body for the moment, she'd probably do this swift and with a whole lot less stiffness that I would have done.

I don't know if Zaliver was a deep sleeper of if my beast was a ninja in her other life but instead of carefully picking up one lb at a time and untangling ourselves, she simply pushed our body closer to Zaliver's until we pushed his back and rolled over him, his body following subconsciously, quickly taking hold of my pillow she placed it in his outreached arms. I watched him cuddle my pillow.

It's a shame I didn't want to risk waking him up for a picture. Maybe later, if he was still asleep.

Getting to the door and opening it was a piece of cake, going down the stairs I passed a glaring Frank halfway down.

He was curled up right smack in the middle of the stairs with his sleeping hat on him. I stopped to pet him and went to the kitchen, leaving the lights off since I didn't really need light to see. Once there I looked around.

What did I want? Looking at the clock over the stove I saw that it was a quarter to three.

Nothing to heavy, cold or sweet. Did I feel like chewing? Nope. I felt like tea. Green tea to be exact.

Not wanting to use the microwave for heating the water I just boiled it instead. Taking out a tea bag I watched the water carefully. My cooking skills also included boiling. When I figured it was good enough, by my standards, I removed the water. As I sat on the kitchen counter I looked outside the window, the night sky was beautiful tonight. Moving the bag around in my cup I got lost in my thoughts.

What exactly did it mean to have Fate as an enemy? Did it mean that even as he was he could make something horrible happen and we would be powerless to do anything to stop him because it just had to happen? What about the real Joshula? Was he truly gone and dead? Who the hell was in his place, in our home instead then?

How would Zaliver deal with having to end his brother-sort of-person-thingy? I didn't want to watch him torture himself over this or fear that he may close himself off. With startling realization the thought came to me.

What if I had to end Joshula's life? What if he attacked me and I had not choice but to end him, in front of Zaliver?

The thought alone shook me. How would I looked Zaliver in the eyes? What if-what if he was so angry he decided he could no longer be with me? I mean, it would be really hard to stand at the altar and stare into the eyes of the person who you love knowing they killed your only blood relative.

And what if Aurora's words?

Wherever you go, you will carry light from now on, but you will be followed by night and night will take over to snuff your light out. Those whom failed to see the connection will pay the price in blood and those who do not play by the rules of their agreement shall face the fury of the heartbroken. There will be pain, no cure and no salvation, only death. If your light goes out. . .so will you.

What did that even mean? God I hated puzzles.

I should probably tell Zaliver this, he's known Aurora for a longer time and at some must have received one of her cryptic messages. Maybe he knew what to make of it.

If your light goes out. . .so will you.'

Her words floated in my mind, leaving behind a feeling of dread and unease that pooled in the pit of my stomach.

I picked up my cup to drink from it when the hairs on my arms stood up. I don't know what made me do it but I turned to look over my right shoulder, down the hall that lead to the rest of the house. Everything seemed normal in the dark of the house. Until I spotted a shadowed figure.

And it began walking towards me.

Fear, adrenaline, confusion and did I mention fear kicked up in me, but also the strange urge to protect. But what? Myself?

I was about to throw my hot tea at the shadowed freak and introduce him to my newly engaged fists when it's scent meet my nose.

"Joshula," I whispered softly. It all happened very quickly, but I was still half-frozen in the same position that I had been in when I first seen him, so it looked as if I were about to put my cup to my lips.

He stepped out from the shadows of the hall and into the kitchen with an eerily calm smile, green and blue eyes suddenly looking too big for his face, pale and deadened looking face. It was almost as if the edge of his eyes were being tainted by a murky yellow I now recognized as his wolf's eyes. Purple shadows seemed to cover his face like bruises.

I blinked and whatever I had just seen was . . . gone. He stood straight with his hands behind his back and a half surprised, half glad expression making its way to his face. He had with him a bag behind his back.

This was not my region of expertise, this was some different shit. My heart began to pound in my chest.

"Vivian? What are you doing up?" he asked quietly, cocking his head to the side in an alarmingly alert and curious way. My chest felt tight. I felt sweat begin to form on my skin. Setting the hot cup down I was glad it didn't shake, not like I was on the inside. Damn it, why was I always the one stuck with creeps, it didn't help that Zaliver's words played in my mind with big red lights.

"I decided for a night cup of tea." Now I wanted to throw up. "You?" I asked, keeping my eyes on my cup which reflected the moon back at me.

"I was just returning from somewhere," he said casually.

Returning? I frowned. There was something about this. . .

"Oh." Was all I said instead, feeling his eyes on my figure. Time to go. "Well-"

619

"You glow in the light of the moon., he said huskily.

Oh. Hell. No.

"It's my new night cream, I read it works wonders for the skin. I could lend you some if you want?" I spurted randomly, making the lie on the spot. I did not like the tone in which he spoke. And even if I did have night cream, like hell I'd share with him.

Looking over at him briefly I realized that he had an intensity to his eyes that the rest of his body did not show.

"I don't think so," he replied hauntingly, taking a step towards me.

A hand landed on my shoulder.

I felt like I could cry on the spot from relief.

"It seems I wasn't invited to this night party," Zaliver's voice came out playfully hurt, but through the bond I felt cold, unbidden anger and past whispers of panic unfurl from within him, mixed in with a dark edge that he must have held in. I let out a small shaky breath and laughed softly.

"Don't be silly, you're invited to all of the parties I throw, even the ones I don't know I'm throwing. Like this one." Taking hold of the hand on my shoulder I squeezed hard,but short enough not to alert Joshula of anything.

Why is it that a girl can't come down for a cup of tea in her own house without starting a brother stare down? Before anything could happen between the cool demented brothers I stood up and pulled on Zaliver.

"How about we all get to bed, sun's going to come up in a few hours and I don't know about you but I'd rather not have to deal with a cranky Vivian. I know first hand what a bitch she can be." I tugged again at Zaliver, a sort of desperation to get away from here starting from my stomach and into my veins.

Joshula looked away from Zaliver and looked over at me making Zaliver tense besides me, narrowing his eyes briefly before a chilling smile graced his face.

At this Zaliver was the one tugging on me as we turned to go to our room. I knew that turning around from what we both knew must have been a silent challenge to his alpha was hard, but it needed be done. At least for now.

"Vivian?" Both Zaliver and I stopped at the kitchen doorway, I half turned to look behind me to see Joshula holding my cup of tea in his hands.

"I think you forgot something." The gleam in his green-blue eyes made my beast growl in warning in my mind, I had to hold my own back.

"No, I'm all good," I responded tensely, forcing a small smile on my face. Beside me Zaliver's hand in my own began to shake and I knew it wasn't from fear.

"Hm." With a smile he brought it up to his lips, taking a drink from my cup while keeping eye contact. I was glad Zaliver didn't see the way his tongue went over his bottom lip.

I turned my back to hide my flinch, but I had one more question.

"Hey Joshula?" I asked, I stroked Zaliver's hand with my thumb. It was a good thing his back was to Joshula or else he would have seen the cold murderous expression on Zaliver's face, along with the sharp canines and black eyes.

"Hmm?" Did that sound like repressed humor in his tone?

"If you're returning, why use the back door instead of the front?"

That had been bothering me, as soon as I realized it was him coming from the shadows of the hall which lead to the rest of the house, why use the back when the front was closer? It was a moment before he responded.

"Old habits die-hard, don't they brother?" Was his only response.

Zaliver clenched his jaw and made a nose that to Joshula might have sounded like a chuckle but to me sounded like him trying to convince himself he was choking.

Without another word Zaliver pulled me up the stairs, with quick moment I picked up a stilled Frank. I was so not leaving him out with that creep lingering around.

Entering our room I sat in the bed as Zaliver closed the door softly. He was beyond infuriated and this time I could tell some of that anger was for me.

He turned around to face me and walk over until he loomed over me, crossing his arms over his chest, standing with parted legs. His jaw was clenched and blue eyes livid, his pupils expanded and retracted as he tried to control himself. He took a breathe.

Are you hurt?

I was surprised to hear his voice in my mind and hear him so calmly. But a part of me recognized that this was smart of him, using the mind link just in case had ears in us.

No.

Vivian, My only warning. what were you doing down there with him!? What if he had done something to you while I was asleep? And why didn't you fucking wake me up if you wanted something instead of sneak off into the night?

You want to know what was scarier than an enraged and screaming Zaliver? An enraged and screaming Zaliver that stared at you calmly and coldly while he did so screaming in your mind.

I grimaced but let him vent, knowing that he was more worried about me then angry.

If I hadn't felt your fear who knows what would have happened? What if he had done something to you?! His chest lifted rapidly, hands fisting and then releasing.

And how dare he, I'm going to rip his head off of his shoulders, the way he acted and spoke—

Okay maybe letting him rant wasn't such a good idea.

Hey, hey. I said as soothingly as I could. Standing up I placed Frank on the bed.

And that damn hedgehog! You brought it into our room again, you know he likes to come in between us and stab me!

Oh don't be so dramatic, it was one—

Three times. I'm sorry I didn't wake you up before, but I thought he wasn't home so I went down. I'm okay though, see? I placed my hands on his tense and coiled shoulders. Small growls were threatening to come out from his throat.

Breathe Zaliver, look at me and breathe. I took his face in my hands and made sure to look him in the eyes,my expression serious.

If you growl now, he'll probably hear and I doubt he's an idiot who will assume we're fighting. He'll know you were angry about me being alone with him meaning he'll know you're onto him, so breathe.

After a moment, that had me thinking he didn't hear me after all, his arms dropped from in front of his chest, he opened his mouth at first I thought to growl but instead he took a breath.I relaxed a bit.

Taking a step towards me Zaliver dropped us on the bed, thankfully not hard enough to bounce Frank off but enough to make him go running straight for Zaliver's pillow. Above me Zaliver grumbled his distaste about getting a handful of hedgehog when he reached under his pillow in the middle of the night. Refocusing on me he placed both arms on either side of me, keeping a portion of his body on top of mine but not completely.

Don't scare me like that, if you want something next time, even if I'm in a coma and bleeding to death, just—

Try and wake you up to get me a cup of green tea? I asked with a slight disapproving look. He responded with a crooked grin.

Yeah, even then, for a cup of green tea.

Okay.

You don't usually get up in the middle of the night. His words came out worried but all I did was shrug in response, it wasn't that odd really.

After a bit more of us discussing mentally, I couldn't help but ask him one more question.

What did he mean by what he said, that old habits die-hard?

Wrapped around me, Zaliver tensed, but I looked up to see him staring at nothing.

Back when we use to . . . conquer land or objects, if the plan required two, then he would have to come along even though fighting was not his specialty. But if he did, our favorite approach was me coming in through the front, the obvious threat, while he came in through the back. . .

Unexpected. I finished.

That explanation was a bit disturbing. Especially now. Before I fell asleep, one last realization entered my mind, a frightening one.

Joshula didn't speak like he usually did tonight, his words were much more casual.

It was like he was a different person.

~•~

Running down the stairs early in the morning, still in my pjs, I stopped at the bottom to greet Frank and to spin him in the direction of the kitchen instead of the door which he'd headed for every morning. Today he wore a sombrero.

Zaliver followed quickly behind and like the other two days halted roughly and cursed.

"Every goddamn morning, always in my fucking way." I heard him hiss under his breath as he stepped around Frank and then stomp his way into the kitchen. I said nothing and sipped my orange juice.

He narrowed his eyes at me as he sat across and drank from his coffee. I smiled because I knew that if I could hear the tapping of Franks movements then so could he. Standing up for a moment I picked up Frank and made cooing noises at him. When I went to look at Zaliver his frosty glare made me pause.

"What?"

"Nothing," He grumbled, standing up and moving around the kitchen to make breakfast. Maybe I should learn how to cook? While he did that I had fun spinning Frank in a circle a few times until he bit me and wiggled his nose at me in what appeared to be indignation. Funny little thing, he was.

I was sidetracked when a heaping plate of eggs, bacon, an omelet and a bowl of fruit were placed in front of me. It was more than my usual so I turned around to ask why, but let out small startled shout when I was picked up from my seat and discreetly placed on a lap. Zaliver's lap to be exact. Turning to face him I raised a brow in surprise.

"What, I can't feed my mate?" he challenged, narrowing his eyes once more are me. I lifted my hands in mock defense.

"Processed."

"Goo," he said seriously, tightening his hold on my waist and bringing me closer. Do you ever notice how thin pj bottoms are? Because I certainly have.

It was only after I had ignored the fork to playfully tap Frank on the nose that it happen. Mid chew, Frank, who had been by Zaliver's elbow, flew away and off of the counter table as if hit with enough force to push him off. A small thud meet my ears.

I almost choked on my eggs and would have went to catch him if Zaliver hadn't tightened his hold that exact same second. I swear my heart stopped, until I heard the quick tapping of Franks movement and then saw his small body run out of the kitchen and to the door where I could then hear him try to claw his way out.

"What the hell Zaliver?!" I tried to jump off of his lap but his hold wouldn't let me.

"Open." He held the fork up, ready with more eggs.

"No."

"Open."

"No."

"Please open."

"No."

"Why not?"

"You elbowed my hedgehog off the table!"

"It was an accident."

"Then why didn't you catch him?"

"It happened too fast." His answer was ridiculous because we both knew his reflexes were beyond perfect but from his smug expression, he didn't care.

"You rotten liar, you elbowed him on purpose. Why?" I demanded, poor Frank.

Zaliver put the fork down, seeing as how I was no longer hungry. He wrapped his other arm around me and tried to bring me into his chest.

"Oh no, you're not cuddling this one away." I put my hands on his firm chest and pushed away enough so that he couldn't keep me there. He pouted. Fuck.

I closed my eyes and turned away but the urge to bit his bottom lip didn't go away, I squirmed on his lap and then stopped at the feeling of what was now under me.

"What do you want for Christmas?" He suddenly asked, trying to distract me.

"For you to tell me why you elbowed my damn hedgehog?" I grumbled. He chuckled, the small movement making me shift slightly on his lap. That halted him, he gave out a soft growl.

"Forget about the hedgehog," he murmured into my ear, my breaths came shallow and harder as every second passed, my body suddenly feeling as if I were in flames and he was the only thing able to sooth me.

I must have surprised Zaliver when I spun around to straddle him and planted my lips on his, but he was always quick to react, except when Frank was involved apparently. With his own, he parted my lips and began kissing me fiercely. I wasted no time in tugging harshly on his hair, which just seemed to please him as his hands on my waist pulled me closer.

I nipped at his bottom lip with my teeth, earning a snarl from him which I just loved. And then the sound of a door opening above us made us freeze.

Pulling away from one another with heated eyes, we knew Joshula was awake. I felt mild annoyance and frustration at the fact that we had to stop because there was a bloody fool in our house, but fine, fine, I'll play along.

My wolf growled in annoyance while my beast sharpened her claws at the menace living in our home. No one had forgotten the tea incident. I had to throw away a good mug.

Nodding once at me Zaliver took a breath and sighed, seemingly distancing himself from the mood we had just reached. Lucky him, because my body was not agreeing.

Jumping off of him and quickly getting a panicked Frank I sat in my chair quickly, just in time to see a smiley faced Joshula walk in.

"Good morning," he said, polite as always.

Zaliver, master of calm and collectiveness, responded with a nod and cool eyes.

"Morning Joshula, sleep well?" I asked throwing in a quick smile and then looking down at Frank to make sure nothing important was broken or hurt. I'd get Zaliver for this. I shall avenge my hedgehog!!

"Pleasant as always, I see the . . . house pet, will be joining us." He eyed Frank with concealed distaste.

I want to claw his eyes out. My wolf growled.

Patience.

I must have forgotten to mention Joshula's obvious but horribly hidden dislike for Frank over the last two days. I didn't even hold back on my glare, but looked away when I felt a nudge from Zaliver through the mating bond. Right.

625

"Yup." I turned Frank on his back and stroked his tummy, liking how adorable he looked, as if his life was complete. Casually I spoke, "So, what are you doing today?"

Joshula hesitated when he reached for the eggs, but didn't turn to face us when he answered.

"Nothing much, I've thought of going hunting later on, would you like to join me?"

"What type of hunting?" I asked cautiously, but made sure my tone came out innocent enough.

"I've always wanted to fire an arm the way the humans have. You could be my look out if you wish not to deal with the weapons."

And get shot? No thanks. My wolf grumbled.

If I hadn't seen Zaliver's eyes flash black I wouldn't have known to put my hand on his arm and held him still. It seems him and my wolf were on the same page.

"Thanks, but I think I'll pass on the offer."

"Alright. Zaliver——"

"No." I squeezed his arm.

"But I'm going to ask you to return on time for dinner tonight," he added swiftly, almost making it seem as if he didn't just outright reject his brothers offer at hanging out.

Joshula walked over with very little food on his plate and sat across from us, his face scrunching up in confusion. The expression would have been seen as innocent confusion if one didn't pay attention to the scheming distrust going on in his eyes.

"Why's that?" he asked Zaliver, even I turned a little to look at my mate. Yeah, why?

"We're going to be having a small dinner gathering tonight and I'd like you to go."

"I'd hate to be a burden during such important matters that you must discuss-"

"Not at all, in fact it's not a social gathering. I've even invited a friend of yours." Zaliver drank from his coffee, eyes solely focused on the stiff Joshula. "Hogan."

I looked from one brother to the other in annoyance and frustration. As well as curiosity and intrigue.

"O-Oh well. . .in that case. . .I must go. What time?" I've never seen a pale and panicked yet calm Joshula. What was wrong with him?

Better yet, what was up Zaliver's sleeve and why the heck was I being told about dinner plans right now?

"Eight thirty sharp, don't be late or we may be forced to start without you," Zaliver joked, partly, watching Joshula squirm on his chair.

Noting that he was being watched Joshula's face darkened, hostility rolling off of him like fresh pizza next to a fan. It was coming in waves and hard to ignore.

"I wouldn't want that would I," Joshula replied.

"Would you?" Zaliver just couldn't help himself, leaning back into his chair he looked at his brother-sort of-person-thingy. There was a tense pause, one even I wasn't stepping over.

It's like poking a hibernating bear and waiting for him to spring on you. My wolf muttered.

Yup, but I don't think this bears hibernating anymore.

Joshula suddenly stood with loud moments.

"I shall see you at eight then." And turned to leave without a goodbye. Hell, now I couldn't help myself.

"I think you forgot something!" I called out, my tone slightly mocking as held up his plate of food. He stopped at the kitchen doorway.

"I find I no longer hold appetite. Do with it as you wish." And left the house with a slam.

I dropped the plate noisily and turned to glare at Zaliver.

"What is this about dinner? And why am I being told just now?" If I had stood I would have had my hands on my hips. The man had the gals to look sheepish.

"I might have forgotten to mention it to you."

"You don't say?"

"But I've invited my third in command, whom I think is involved with Joshula seeing as how it was in his office that I caught Fate and Joshula's scent." My mouth parted to form a small 'o' as I guessed where this was heading for. He nodded and took my hands in his, kissing each knuckle until he got to the engagement ring and looked up with dark eyes.

"I was hoping that by having them together in the same space with us, that one of them, probably Hogan, is bound to make a mistake and reveal something on accident. There's a reason I've had him behind a desk doing paperwork instead of out in the field."

"Smart, but that still doesn't explain why you didn't tell me earlier?"

"Slipped my mind love."

"Right, we'll I want to invite Aurora and Algebra then, before it slips my mind." He gave me an uncertain look.

"Are you sure, she's-"

"Okay, the woman needs social contact besides Algebra, even if it is with betraying psychopaths." My okay as in 'I have enough hope

627

that she won't throw me around like a rag doll but I'm not promising anything else for you or anyone else', okay.

"Alright, your call." He leaned down to kiss my cheek.

"It'll be great, with her unwavering stare she'll probably get everyone to confess their deepest secrets and with Algebra's and your constant pestering they're bound to mess up somewhere," I pointed out. He lifted a dark brow at me.

"And what will you be doing?" he questioned.

"Making sure everything goes according to plan and that any and all fights leave no blood stains on my carpet floor." He rewarded me with a proud grin that left my blood pumping quickly through my body again. My wolf's sudden burst of humor took me off guard.

What? I asked as she laughed away.

You're the Blair to his Chuck.

That thought alone had me laughing as well, it would seem so I guess.

"What?" he asked, not getting it.

What does that make Fate and Joshula? I asked her, knowing her response would make me laugh.

Fucking Dan Humphrey and Little J.

I lost it.

"What?" Zaliver asked, looking even more puzzled.

"Oh, tonight is going to be awesome."

CHAPTER 44

VIVIAN GREY

There are perks that come with being a werewolf, then there are perks of being a Luna and then there's being the Luna of all Lunas. But my overall favorite perk? The mind link, I mean, do you know how much you save on phone bills alone? A ton of money that's what.

You can talk to anyone from anyplace in the world with a perfect connection, sort of. Then there's the whole, hands free situation going on, which is a huge positive. So imagine my disappointment when I realized, after trying for six minutes, that while a certain witch was most definitely in my pack, she lacked a certain mind link. Thus my knocking on a certain witch's door.

I really hope that coming to give a person invitation doesn't get me killed . . . or tossed around like a salad. I really like how nice my hair looks today.

My ears perked up at the sound of barefooted movement until Aurora opened the door and stood over me in all her glory. Unblinking black eyes gazed at me, a certain tilt to her head making her long hair sway a bit. She wore the same dress style as before, but the shade was a lavender one with violet ends. She seemed calm.

"Hello Vivian." She purred, nodding at me as if in confirmation.

While a part of me felt very. . .exposed with her, another part of me felt almost at peace, as if I were in a clearing in wolf form under the sun's shade. She made me feel complex, but it was a welcome feeling. I smiled up at her.

"Hey Aurora, mind if I come in?" The sentence wasn't even out of my mouth before she was walking away from the door and back to the living room where she ignored the couch and sat on the floor with her long legs tucked underneath her.

"Okay then," I mumbled, closing the door behind me.

She could sit on the ground all she wanted, but I knew that if I sat down with her, if I even struggled getting back up that I'd give up. It

629

was just too much effort really. I took the seat closest to her on the couch, she gave a closed lipped smile.

"So how are you today? Still being held captive by Algebra?" I asked leaning back against the couch.

"I'm . . . adjusting once more to being in better control of myself and no, not being held captive, just, looked after." Her dark eyes grew lighter for a moment as she looked away from me and off to the side. "I realize that now."

I was very curious as to know what was going on in her head, but I knew first hand how annoying it was to be asked something I didn't want to share.

"People really should give you more credit, young Luna," Aurora murmured softly, closing her eyes and tilting her head back as if completely relaxed and tranquil. I frowned.

"And why is that?" I asked curiously.

"Because, a good Luna asks questions, but a wise Luna knows that the answers will come to her in time. You wish to know and yet hold your tongue, even some of the oldest Lunas command or demand to know and yet seem to never realize that it's best to wait for a full meal then a partial meal."

"Thanks." I think. Almost as if hearing the hesitation in my answer her eyes open, an odd glint in her eyes.

"So what time's dinner?" she asked.

"Oh, it's at eight thirty sharp-wait . . . I didn't mention a dinner. Damn, is it a witch thing to know everything or are you just really good?" I asked both surprised and suspicious. She'd be great to have on a gaming team.

"The world may never know," she said ominously. Well then.

"So are you in?" I asked her. The corner of her mouth lifted up.

"Do I have a choice?" Smart witch.

"Not really. I refuse to have you being left out when all the players will be sat at the table," I stated.

She lifted a brow at me and half turned her body to face me. "And is that all?"

"Well . . . it doesn't hurt to have a witch who can toss people around like rag dolls at the table," I said smugly.

"I've known you for less than a day and I've already seen the effect Zaliver has had on you, you will grow to be a Luna these wolves need. I'd be honored to help. It's been awhile since I've played, by my rules." Aurora's voice faded as she finished her once intrigued sentence. I felt more than saw her sadness and regret.

There was also grief within her, but I had the feeling that this was a healthier emotion, softer and more controlled than at some other point in her life. She didn't speak for a few minutes and neither did I, giving her the time to collect her thoughts but when she spoke I was momentarily caught off guard.

"Andrew was six when he . . . died."

The air was sucked from within me and I wasn't prepared for the stinging of unsheathed tears that appeared in my eyes. Outside, the windows were covered by sudden dark clouds. Aurora looked out of the window, a blank expression on her face.

"He was always so energetic, so happy, there wasn't a morning where he wasn't bouncing around. I think he got that from Berry, that and his hair, he got my eyes. But every now and then they'd go green." She gave a small smile. " He was always attached to me at the hip, wherever I went, there he was trying to help. I think he would have grown to be a great healer." She took a shaky breath.

I could see it, a child of six running into his parents room where Algebra and Aurora sleep, dark brown curls bouncing with every small step, large brown eyes lighting up and a small toothed grin. The joy and expectant look already on his parents faces when he jumped on them, their acted out surprised yells and the child's roar of triumph.

I could imagine it and it hurt.

"He even had Zaliver wrapped around his finger, I've never even seen him sit down to rest, but from the stories Andrew told me your mate would always play a game with him and lose with grace. That was kind of him.

Had I known, I would have kept a closer eye on him. Did you know that a child of two different origins has a fifty out of fifty chance of either getting their powers from inheritance early or late? Andrew's came early. . .too early. He was just sitting under a tree one day, studying herbs and then he was gone. Too much power can drain the body, but rest can replenish it. His little heart couldn't take it and since his werewolf genes hadn't kicked in yet...my poor boy. My little Andrew."

How do you-what do you say to a mother who lost a child? To a mother whom had to live with the knowledge that her child left the world before her? I was finding it difficult to focus on anything as she talked, all I could feel was the heaviness of my own body, the crushing and heartbreaking fear of being I'm her position. I didn't even want to imagine losing my pups. I clenched my hands.

"I didn't exactly help Berry at the time, so full of despair and anger, I was-am a witch of light, but how I loathed my power then. What good could a witch of light do? I screamed, I pleaded, I begged and yet my coven could do nothing. . .I could do nothing. When a witch enters the own darkness in her heart, it's much easier for outside forces to morph and capture the mind. But you're always aware, you know what's going on and how to stop it. But I didn't want to, I had to try everything within my power, be it good or not, to try to . . .

I know now that I was blinded by grief and perhaps my own guilt at not knowing this would happen to Andrew, it wasn't until many years later that it clicked. By then it was too late, I was far away from here, from Andrew and Berry. Oh Berry, he looked everywhere for me the first few years, I could still feel him every once in a while. He pleaded me to come back, but I was so buried I just couldn't.

I think the guilt of what I was doing to him was another excuse I made to stay away. Yet, when I look into his eyes I see no anger, no hatred or resentment at what I did." She turned from the window to look at me, I almost wanted to look away from her gaze. Her eyes were a window to grief and years beyond what was seen. "Why? I left him to deal with everything, I basically abandoned him. I ran."

I knew that there was no correct answer I could give her, but I still had to try. From beyond what my eyes could see, I could feel one last strand of darkness trying to cling to her, I could feel her trying to get rid of the darkness that she had let take hold of her for so long, I could see her need to be freed and her want to be who she was once more.

She wanted a hand to reach out and help her back into the light.

Perhaps the reason for why she didn't take her fears to Algebra was because he was the last restraint holding her back, from herself. Whatever he said, she would have believed but a part of her would have always questioned.

Why? I reached down and took hold of her hand, feeling older than I've ever felt in my life. My eyes gazed back at her, I didn't try to hide the tears that had been streaming down my face silently.

"You went as far as you could get and he respected that, but he also wanted to be there for you, even if you didn't think you wanted him there at that moment. I'm sure that you know that he loves you beyond himself and the reason that you see no anger or resentment in his eyes when you look is because he doesn't see a woman who ran from everyone who loved her, but a mother who didn't just lose her child but herself.

I think that when you look in his eyes and wait for anger and resentment that he's also waiting to see the same thing in your eyes directed at him because just maybe, he thinks he could have done something too. Everyone grieves differently Aurora and I might not have known Andrew but from how you speak of him it seems like he would have made the world a better place and it's a loss the world will miss but I'm sure that wherever he is, he's made a change for the better."

"Do you really think so?" she asked, he voice small and shaky. I squeezed her hands.

"What do you think?" I asked her. She froze before slowly turning her head to look out of the cloudy windows.

"I think that you're right. I think that Andrew would have wanted his family to stay together and smile and live." Her voice was softer than I've ever heard before.

She lifted her free hand as if she were reaching for something, in the direction of the window.

"I-I think it's time for a change."

From outside, sunlight peeked through the dark clouds.

Aurora let out a shaky breath as if a weight had been lifted off of her thin shoulders. It might have been my imagination but I thought I heard a shriek of enragement before the thread of darkness that surrounded her disappeared.

Aurora turned to look at me with a gentle smile, she blinked those large black eyes at me and I watched as they lighted until they remained a lovely shade of brown.

They didn't change back.

~•~

I can't cook.

I know that, I think the whole world knows that actually.

Haha, so what am I supposed to do about dinner then?

What makes you think you have to worry about dinner?

Well you're busy right now.

That doesn't make dinner your problem though.

So you're saying you're cooking then?

No.

I let out an annoyed breath, shifting my weight to my left foot and adjusting the things under my arms. I felt his side of the bond flare up in amusement at me.

So if you're not cooking and I'm not cooking then what the heck are we going to feed everyone tonight?

I've already ordered take out for tonight, so there's no need to worry about it.

Oh.

Realizing that dinner was taken care of, I looked down at the things in my arms and frowned, but looking to my right, I caught sight of an empty cart and walked out of the line and dumped everything in there. I faintly wondered if whatever he'd order would have pot stickers. I wanted some.

"Right." I patted the cart awkwardly before looking up and catching the eyes of fellow shoppers, smiling I began to back up.

Well okay then.

Were you just grocery shopping? There was a teasing note to his voice. I froze at the side of my car door and looked around in suspicion.

No.

You sure?

Yeah.

Really?

Yup.

Okay.

Feeling smug at myself, I got into the car and was about to pull out of the grocery store when he asked.

So your guards really are there with you and not working out in the pack house?

Okay, okay, I might have forgotten about them when I ran out of the house this morning.

I drove with my shoulders hunched, I felt like I could feel his disapproving blue eyes on me. I played the radio, drumming my fingers to the catchy beat.

You forgot about the four guards, wolves, whom have been with you every time you've gone out, almost since the day you got here?

I turned the music to the radio up.

Sorry, I can't hear you over the music.

What—

What?

Vivian—

I closed my mind to him, biting my lip.

I don't know why I'm feeling all rebellious. I knew it was dumb to go out without the guards, especially with what he'd just told me about Fate and Joshula but there was just something.

I felt like I was forgetting something important or like there was something I had to do. Shrugging off the invisible irritation around me, I focused on my new location, knowing Zaliver was bound to be grouchy when I'd see him later. Oh well.

Could you imagine how mad he would be if we drove to the beat of the music. My wolf snickered.

What do you mean? I asked.

Like, for every high beat or picked up pace you swerve to the right and for every low or slow beat you—

Do you want to crash this car?

Of course not.

I think she's lying. My beast muttered, edging away from my wolf as if cautious.

634

Am not, it would just be interesting. My wolf defended.

When's the last time I let you out for a run? You seem crazier than usual.

I think if my wolf could have given me the middle finger, she would have. Chuckling at the set of words she dedicated to me for the next few minutes, I quickly apologized for doubting her state of mind...sort of.

It felt kind of nice to be by myself, no need for conversation or fussing over me. Maybe that's why I went out today and chose to drive my own car instead of waiting to be picked up and driven around. It's nice to be independent every once in a while. I think the last time I was actually by myself was a few months ago, that's a pretty long time. I think that today I had subconsciously decided that today was going to be a 'Vivian catches up with the world' day.

I drove for a long time before I reached my destination. I took the small bag from the back seat and smiled to myself as I began my hike.

When I finally got to the top I cursed and put my hand on my knees. All this power and I still hated hikes. It was pitiful, really.

"All these new goddamn touch screen phones that all look the damn same and," I wheezed for a breath. "Still no damn escalators in the mountains. I mean, what the heck is that shit?"

Huffing, I straightened myself up. Taking a few steps I had to catch my breath again, but not because of the hike, but for the view. I was back on the mountain ledge Zaliver took me for our first date, the one that over looked a little lake and the rest of the forest that meet the rest of the ocean.

Sitting down close to the edge, but not too close to the edge because I was a land creature and I knew that no amount of wishing could help me grow wings if I fell off the edge, I crossed my legs and gazed out. I pulled the small bag closely to my side and unzipped it, pulling out the bag of caramel popcorn I began to munch on it.

It was nice out here, not to hot and not to cold, windy but not the kind that made you squint to keep out random shit from flying in. Just right.

Lifting my left hand up I looked my hand, I was already settled with me now being engaged. But would anything change? What type of wife would I be?

Probably the same, I mean marriage in human terms didn't change much for wolves. There was so much plans and scheduling to be done and I had started on exactly. . .nothing. Yup. I chuckled to myself, humored by exactly how odd I was. I think I was more excited about being engaged then probably the actual wedding day.

Then there was the whole Joshula deal. The thought made me lower my hand and put a handful of popcorn in my mouth.

Deep down I think that's what had me more worried, but not so much about myself. I was worried about the effects of what tonight's dinner or the next few days might have on Zaliver. He'd already lost his brother by his own hand, even if by force, the guilt of that alone was what had brought me to him.

What would happen if Zaliver killed Joshula with Fate around? If it had been Fate that brought me to Zaliver, could it be Fate that would take me away from him? The thought chilled me to the core, but it was a possibility I couldn't just ignore.

I brought my knees to my chest and hugged myself, not liking now I felt. Zaliver would be so..sad and angry. I knew that without a doubt and didn't like it. But would happen to me? A worse thought crossed my mind?

What if it was Zaliver who was taken from me?

My hand fisted around the bag of popcorn so tightly I might have turned a few into dust. I pushed away the dark and malicious thoughts that came with the idea of being separated away from him.

I'd burn the world's food supply and starve the world as I'd be starved of my mate

I put another hand full of popcorn in my mouth to distract myself. There was no reason to plan for something that could potentially not happen, Zaliver had remained top Alpha, the feared and my serious Lupus Deus for a reason. He could take on anything, I knew it. Could I?

I've never really been put in a kill or be killed position, but I guess I already had luck on my side if I couldn't be killed. But there were things worse than death in this world. What was Joshula up to? Fate? What game or end point did they want? Hurting Zaliver had to be on their list. What were they waiting for? Him to be weak? I don't think I've ever even seen Zaliver bleed. He was immortal, he healed faster than he could be hurt, he was a skilled warrior and mastermind.

So what? What wait so long? What else was not being said or overlooked?

I snarled in annoyance. There wasn't much I could do right now and it sucked, I almost felt useless but I knew that I wasn't. I had to a role to play too and I'd be damned if I didn't get an imaginary Grammy, I had to make sure that tonight's dinner gave Zaliver what he needed without putting himself in danger or giving away anything.

Joshula would be put to the test tonight, but it was as much his as it was mine. Tonight would be the test to see who was the most cunning, the most observant and who would lead to the next level.

I was usually all humor and sharp wit and I knew that I would remain so, but I would need more than that tonight. I could play the carefree young Luna everyone probably thought me to be, the she-wolf who was dragged and mated to the big bad wolf with a shit load of problems she had no idea how to solve or I could be the future Vivian Azrala.

Luna of all Lunas, the heart and kindness to an alpha known for cruelty and viciousness, but who could turn that kindness and that heart into a heart of steel and stealth when the wrong buttons were pushed.

I wasn't an idiot, I knew that there were things I was supposed to be doing in the island and perhaps outside of the island as Luna, I knew that Zaliver had no problem dealing with things most Alphas didn't deal with because he was so used to doing it alone for so long. But he wasn't alone anyone.

Stretching my legs out I put my hands behind me to lean back, I played with the long strands of grass under me and sighed. If you're up their moon goddess, help a girl out.

Today had started a bit heavier than I would have expected, but I guess that's to be expected when life is going to good. I felt both sorrow and happiness that change had finally entered Aurora, though such sad circumstances but, that was life. I hoped that Algebra and her find the peace and happily ever after their due.

I stood up with abruptness, determination and not hope but perhaps change in me. I was sick of the people around me being played by Fate's cruel strings, of life snatching away loved ones and negativity clouding the sight of those who lived too long in the shadows. I want to be a Luna who's known for brings happiness and change to the wolves of not just this island but also outside of it.

Stretching my things off of the ground I stalked back into the forest with change in my heart.

Back in the car I gulped down the water before getting into the car, I looked back at the faint trail I took.

"Nah, still don't like hikes."

I pulled out of there and drove down the empty road. I must have driven no less than thirty minutes when there was a sort of . . . snap but not in my mind. It was odd, it felt like something had just unlinked itself but was still in there. Pulling over to the side quickly I closed my eyes and focused on what had just happened.

Then I realized it wasn't a snap, but more of an unlinking. A silver lining that had been already in my mind, forming a bond of its own individuality. The original silver lining was Hannah's.

I grinned. I was right before.

I quickly got back on the road.

Hannah's water had just broken.

~•~

"Let me push!"

"Miss, you have to wait until you're-"

"I'm wide open, trust me, I'm wide open, let me push!"

"Honey, just breathe—"

"This is your fault, weak ass pull out ga—"

"Hey, it's not just him. Takes two to tango you know." I butted in, beside a sweaty and grimacing as well as raging Hannah. But she had a nice look to her with her blond hair pulled messily on top of her head and the baby pink hospital dress on.

If contractions had her like this, I'm sure birth would be beautiful.

I can't tell if that's sarcasm. My wolf said blankly, fascinated with what was going on. Hannah to be exact.

She looked over at me and bared her canines at me. The Luna in me wasn't even offended, shit, it wasn't even an option. She could leap off this bed and sit on me and I'd be the one apologizing. The woman was about to give birth.

"And it takes exactly one foot up your ass to—"

"Okay!" I said. lifting my hands in surrender. Luckily for me, unluckily for her, another contraction hit.

We'd been in the hospital for about five hours and let me tell you nothing got boring when you have a protective male wolf whose extremely pregnant mate is about to give birth,a nurse who looks as if she's been through it all and seems to be thinking of letting Hannah have her way and a very amused Luna sitting beside that very pregnant mate.

Not to mention that very pregnant mates brother who could still he heard grumbling about how 'unfair it is not to be the one to pull the baby out', I don't think I've ever seen Hannah pale so

fast and flush red at the same time.

Her exact words had been: You are going nowhere near my body and you are most definitely not pulling anything that's been growing in me for nine months just so you can decide how ugly the kid is.

Most definitely the best five hours of my life. I even got to meet Johnson and Hannah's parents. No words for the blonde folk who walked through the hospital doors. No words. But I had to give Johnson and Hannah points for surviving those two, because they were mini replicas if their parents. Geneve and Andy. Holy cow. Those two had not only energy but a whole lot arguments in them about which grandparent would be holding the baby first.

638

"Oh god, what did I do to deserve this? You couldn't have just shipped the baby like Amazon? Or via email? With like a live printer? Oh god!!"

Mark gave the calm nurse a frantic look and then glanced down at the hand Hannah was gripping onto with a look of surprise and fear. I had a feeling he was going to be thanking werewolf healing in a day or two.

~•~

I had no choice but to leave a few hours later to prepare for dinner, but I think Hannah was sort of relieved. I know I wouldn't want people looking at me if I were in her state too. Besides, it was a special moment for the pair.

I promised to be back the next morning, I'd probably be in time for the birth, deepening on how much more the baby felt like playing 'I paid the rent, it's mine' with Hannah's body.

Opening the door I was startled when Frank made a mad dash down the steps and across the front yard. Holy shit, he was fast!

Speeding over to him in less time than it took him to run I picked him up and put him at eye level. Took the poor guy a second to realize he wasn't going anywhere because his body was still moving as if he were running, I could have sworn I saw smugness in those little black eyes before horror took over as they met mine.

"You rat! I should have known you'd leave me at the first chance." He made a noise that faintly reminded me of a high-pitched "well duh." He tried curling up.

"Oh, you're going to pull that one? Go ahead, I haven't played baseball in a long time, I fucking dare you." I hissed at him.

As if understanding he slowly uncurled and then sort of. . .went limp.

What the-

"Frank?" I asked softly. Did he pass out. Guilt began to eat at me. "Frank?"

"Aw, come on, you know I didn't mean it. Come on buddy wake-you bitch!" The rat had played me, he played dead and then bit my finger in attempt at taking me by surprise and probably drop him.

Tough luck.

"Oh, you're so grounded." I stalked back into the house. A rebellious Frank in hand.

Once I took care of Frank I went up stairs and began looking for what to wear tonight. Dinner was in a two hours and I did not feel like wearing heels. I didn't want to break a heel if I end up kicking anyone in the face.

Feeling that the house was far too quiet I walked over to my laptop which I was sure I had put under the bed instead of on the room desk I turned it on. I had a nagging suspicion that Zaliver was responsible for the cleanses of our room. . .hell, the house. Hitting shuffle on my music I walked back into the closet and went over my choices.

Finally content with an outfit I walked over to the bathroom with a groan. I had already showered before but being in the hospital just made me feel like I'd come home with some disease or bacteria. I was about to enter the bathroom when Zaliver walked into the room, stopping at the doorway.

I paused at the sight of his hesitant form by the door, both hands in the front pocket of his jeans and his face that of worry. I smiled faintly at the unsure giant at the door.

"Hey," he said softly after a long wait.

"Hey," I said, just as softly.

"You okay?"

"Why wouldn't I be?" I cocked my head to the side, momentarily confused.

"I'm not sure, you just. . ." He trailed off, looking at me with a mild yet accusatory look in his eyes.

"Oh, yeah, sorry about earlier. I guess you could say I just needed the day to myself." It then hit me that I had kept Zaliver out of my mind and quickly opened my mind to him, the effect was immediate.

His form relaxed, muscles uncoiling and a tenseness that I hadn't realized was on his face disappearing. He took his hands out of his pockets and ran them down his face. I walked over to him and held his face between my hands.

"Yourself?" he repeated in a tired voice. There was tension in the room from both of us, but it wasn't directed at one another, it was a form of worry for the situation we were in.

"Just to sort things out in my head, that's all," I said, trying to make him open his eyes but they remained shut, my thumbs rubbed at his jaw, feeling the little stubble that he'd not removed this morning.

"Like what?"

"Like how weird I am, or wedding preparations or even how it would be nice if Fate and Joshula would just tell us what they want instead of playing around." He opened his eyes at the last part.

"I doubt revealing your plans of mass destruction and conquering have 'reveal my plans at some point' in the guidelines." He lifted a brow and narrowed his eyes down at me. I pouted.

"Maybe, but it would make life easier if they did." He chuckled at me.

"Yes, it would." He tilted his head to the side. "Is that all you were thinking about?"

"Mostly yeah, but . . ." I trailed off.

"But?" He pushed.

The corner of my lips twitched, I moved from in front of him and before he could turn around I stood behind him and wrapped my hands around his middle. I felt his muscles tense under my hands and smiled into his shirt. Trailing my hands down, very slowly, I reached for the button of his jeans, enjoying the way his breath hitched.

"But now I think that you should join me for a shower." I unbuttoned his pants and was about to reach for the zipper when he took hold of my hand and maneuvered himself in a way where I was once again in front of him, as graceful and fluent as only he knew how to move.

I looked up at darkening blue eyes, his tongue poked out to lick at his bottom lip, I subconsciously did the same thing.

"Do you now?" he asked huskily.

"Yeah, I do." And with that I tangled my hand in his hair and roughly yanked him down to me. He wrapped an arm around my waist and fisted a hand full of my hair with the other

This kiss was filled with all the worry and tension that we both carried, every nip and rough tug was not how we showed one another we were there for the other and how we fueled each other. He thrust his tongue into my mouth, letting a taste of euphoria explode and takeover my sense, all I could taste was him and it was all I wanted to taste. When we pulled away our breath was labored and harsh, we took deep breaths.

Zaliver frowned for a moment and pulled me closer, I didn't resist when the hand in my hair pulled to bare my neck to him. He pushed his face into the crook of my neck and inhaled deeply. He did this over and over again until pulling back with a confused look on his face.

"What?" I asked, he was sniffing the air now.

"Where have you been?" he asked me instead.

"I went to the place you took me for our date, the one where I had to hike. Oh, then I went to the hospital. Hannah's having her baby!" I said, excited. He nodded faintly, but every once in a while would sniff. "Why are you sniffing me? Do I smell that bad?" I asked, sniffing at myself but catching only traces of woods and muted chemicals.

"I'm not sure, there's something there but it's faint, barely there." He pushed his head back into the crook of my neck, ticking me with his breath so I pushed him away laughing.

"It's probably just from the hospital, now stop sniffing me and join me in the shower." At that, whatever had bothered him slipped out of his mind as he got a cheeky grin on his face.

"Now we're talking." I rolled my eyes and turned around and began walking to the bathroom, a happy Zaliver in tow.

After a shower that lasted longer than it should have, I was slipping on my light brown flats when I felt Zaliver come up behind me. Standing up I looked over my shoulder in question. Like always, my heart speed up at the sight of him.

I wore a tight one sleeved white shirt that bared one shoulder and ended with pale flowered patterns and a cotton candy pink skirt that clung to my form. In my ears I wore turquoise teardrop shaped earrings and matching bracelets. I pulled only half of my hair up and did my makeup like usual, light.

Zaliver wore light washed blue jeans with a white V neck shirt, on top a black blazer, he accompanied it by his white converse. Freshly shaved and slightly damp hair which I could see he had run his hands through my mate was looking hot. By the devilish grin and gaze in his eyes he knew it as well.

He lifted his fingers to show something dangling from them, a long chain with something on the bottom. Before I could look closer at it he was putting it around my neck and positioning it in between my breasts with his fingers, he placed his hand on my bare shoulder. Looking down I saw that it was a flower, a bit bigger than my thumbnail. It reflected color whenever my chest rose, every petal a diamond of a different color. The part I liked was how it seemed to have vines made up of different shades of green reaching out and twisting at the ends.

"I've wanted to see you wear that for some time now," he murmured behind me, but I was a bit distracted by the way his hand was rubbing up and down at my bare arm.

"Hmm, is this from one of my presents?"

"Yes, from one of the Western Lunas I believe. They have good taste." He leaned down and placed a kiss on my shoulder and after a pause sniffed.

"Okay, that's it, stop sniffing me. Now you seem like a dog." I shook my head and walked out of his reach. He bared his teeth and snarled softly, not liking the comparison.

"I think you still have that smell, but I can't tell—"

"Maybe it's you," I pointed out, putting a hand on my hip.

"It's not."

"Right."

For some reason we were both smiling at each other like idiots, as if the funniest joke had been told and we were resisting laughter. Feeling only slightly foolish, I stuck my tongue out at him and decided to go down stairs. We had at least another twenty minutes before anyone got here, but the food wasn't even here.

I was hungry though.

I went to go sit in the living room and turn on the TV to a random channel, realizing that we never use the tv. Zaliver sat himself down beside me and put his arm around my shoulders.

"So, what exactly did you order?" I asked after turning the tv off after watching a commercial about some medication that would probably kill me faster than it would heal me.

"I didn't order per say, I about just told the pack house chef to cook a variety of things," he answered absent-minded, playing with the back of my hair.

"So a buffet. And when will this buffet get here?"

"Why? Hungry?" He was teasing me.

"Yes, very actually." After a pause I couldn't help but ask, more out of curiosity than anything. "Does it bother you that I can't cook?"

He pulled back a little away from me to look at me, his eyes looking over me as if looking for whatever had prompted the question.

"No, not at all. Where did this come from? You're usually all 'I can't cook, suck it'-" I busted out laughing.

"I-I do-don't-" I couldn't even speak correctly from all of my laughing, I felt tears form at the corner of my eyes. "say th-that!!"

"Well that's what I get from you," he said, smiling at me. "And just to settle it, I'll have you know that I actually like the fact that you can't cook because that just means that you'll have to depend on me for a home cooked meal." He cupped my face and ran his thumb over my bottom lip. "I like taking care of you."

Any other time I would have leaned forward to kiss him for being so cheesy yet adorable, but I was hungry. So no.

"So where are we going to be placing everyone because I doubt this is gonna go down as a 'pick a partner-pick a place'." He tapped my bottom lip twice before removing his hands and seemingly keeping them to himself.

"I'll be at the head-" Of course." with you on my left, Aurora can sit next to you and Albericus can sit at the end of the table. Hogan and Joshula can pick their seats but wherever it is, they'll still be next to each other," he spoke with such confidence and assurance that I had to look over his seating arrangement in my head.

I knew we weren't going to eat in the little counter like usual so that left the actual dining hall, but recalling the largeness of the table left the odd arrangement. . .odd.

"Did you switch out our table for a smaller one to make sure that they'd have no other choice but be by one another?" I asked, fully turning to look at him suspiciously.

He smirked at me.

"Don't worry, it'll be back by morning." I was going to ask him where the hell he put my table but the sound of a large vehicle made my ears twitch.

"Foods here." Zaliver stood up and walked over to the door and opened it.

Just as I was standing the smell of food hit me and catching me by surprise, I swooned a little. Balancing myself I frowned. I must have been hungrier than I thought, hospital food wasn't that filling.

There were wolves dressed in white walking around my house, down the hall and setting up. Each carried at least two or three large dishes of different types of food that almost had been on my knees begging them to let me taste before it got to the table. Why beg? Because the pack chef was four-foot three and had eyes that scanned each and every dish like he was picking out the juiciest lambs to sacrifice if anything looked even a little out-of-place.

I'd decided just to stand next to Zaliver who looked over the food with judgment only an alpha could muster. God I was starving. As I too scanned over the food as well I couldn't help but frown. They didn't have it.

They didn't have pot stickers. I felt oddly deflated and sad at this.

When all of the wolves were leaving I side stepped away from Zaliver and moved as quickly as I could while he talked to one of the carriers. I walked over to the short woman before she could get into her car.

Turns out I wanted pot stickers more than I cared about how unrealistically scary the woman seemed.

Feeling satisfied with myself I walked back into the house to see Zaliver still standing over the food. As if sensing me he turned around and shook his head.

"This will have to do," he said dismissively, as once more, only alphas knew how to do.

"Are you kidding, I hope everyone knows they're taking food home, that includes Joshula. I don't care if he lives here, we'll section off his food. We've got enough for weeks." I began picking out what I would count as mine off of the table, I'd have to make sure that they didn't eat too much of the deep-fried shrimp.

Did I mention how hungry I was? Walking over to the shrimp I told myself that I was only grabbing one and that it didn't hurt anyone if I lingered near the plate. I didn't hold back on the moan when the crunchy goodness met my taste buds.

"I'm in love," I mumbled, knowing I had to have another one.

Tossing all care I turned around and reached for another one. It's not like anyone knew we even had deep-fried shrimp on the table-

644

someone cleared their throat- except for Zaliver, but he'd keep his mouth shut if he knew what was good for him.

Again, someone cleared their throat. Louder this time. Unhappy. Impatient. A flare of jealousy. Oh right.

I picked one more off of the plate before turning to find my mate. I blinked. Had he been standing this close the whole time? Why was he looking at me like that? With panic I thought that maybe he wanted one of the fried shrimps.

"They're not that great. You don't want one." I took a protective step in front of the shrimp. A whisper of amusement and suspicion shone in his blue eyes.

"Really?" he asked, looking over my shoulder.

I nodded and without thinking lifted the shrimp in question to my mouth and ate it. His eyes followed the movement of my tongue when I went to lick at what remained.

"Yeah," I said firmly.

He nodded and then stood up straighter, looming over me entirely. He crossed his arms over his large chest.

"Vivian?"

"Yeah?"

"Did you eat lunch today?" Blue eyes turned into slits as he scanned me over as if he were waiting for a shameful confession.

"I did, hospital food just isn't as extensive or good or colorful or, " My stomach made the noise of a wounded warrior. "filling."

He was about to open his mouth to probably say something about making packed lunches when he stiffened, when his head turned an inch of the direction if the door, I could tell by the expression on his face that we had guest arriving. Soon.

Turning back to me he looked at me seriously before leaning down to whisper in my ear, when he pulled back I looked at him wide-eyed but nodded.

Standing up straighter and pushing my ever-growing hunger down, I swear it's like I was a black hole from outer space, I stepped into my Luna role and plastered a charming yet easy-going smile on my face. Right on time because not a moment later the front door opened and Joshula walked into the dining room.

Dressed in a button down black shirt and matching black pants he strolled in, his dark hair in disarray, giving him a wild look that emphasized his green-blue eyes. He looked as good as he looked crazed and cornered. It was even more eerie when he moved and spoke calmly.

"Good evening, it seems dinner's ready." He stopped a few inches away from Zaliver, whom discreetly moved to stand barely in front of me.

"It is." Was all Zaliver said curtly. Not stepping away from Zaliver but leaning slightly to look at Joshula I gave him a cheeky smile.

"Right on time, a man of your word,huh?" He looked me over before nodding at me.

"So where are our guests?" he asked no one in particular.

Fortunately at that moment the front door was knocked so I, like the kind person I am, went to go open the door with a warning tap on Zaliver's back not to kill his brother while I was gone. Besides, if we both went, who knew if Joshula would try to poison everyone.

Opening the door my phony smile turned real at the sight of Aurora and Algebra at the door, both with large grins on their faces. Aurora had kept the dress she had in earlier but had pulled her long hair up into a ponytail and actually had sandals on her feet, she wasn't barefoot for once. Instead of his usual get up, Algebra had on a tight long sleeve black shirt with a well fitted gray dress vest on top, white jeans and dress shoes. I couldn't help but smile even more at sight of the black headband pushing his curls back.

"Look who I found outside walking around in a nervous circle," Algebra said a twisted sense of humor, he turned around to clasp a hand on a man's shoulder.

Blinking I realized that there was someone standing behind the two giants. In a full meeting suit the color of a dark red apple with delicate and patterned embroidery that made me feel underdressed. Underneath the suit he wore a black shirt and a silver gray tie. Rich brown hair the color of redwood bark was cbed back forcefully but I could see waves in his roots. A long yet squared face with with deep brown eyes, a long but not sharp nose and a stern expression made this man seem like the ultimate test of life.

"Hello there."

However, as well dressed and stern looking as he appeared there are just somethings you couldn't look past. Like the hunched frame, the shuffle from one foot to the other, how his eyes focused more on my outfit than me, the lip biting and the really cute teddy bear to which he clung onto like it was his lifeline. The stud in his left ear also caught my eyes. Pretty.

"Hogan here is third in command. Right?" Algebra asked the giant muscle of a man.

"Yeah, nice meeting you L-Luna," he said lowly, not meeting my gaze then he reached out to hand me the teddy bear, a bit reluctantly if I do say so myself. Well then, if you didn't want to give me the bear you shouldn't have bought it. I thought, but still grabbed it with a smile.

It's okay, he must have known we needed a chew toy. My wolf grumbled.

You've been quiet today.

What, you can have a day to reflect but I can't?

Touché.

"Nice to see all of you, please come in, foods ready," I said, stepping to the side to let them in.

Yes, please come in so that I can start eating without looking rude. My wolf muttered, I resisted the urge to roll my eyes of agree.

"Nice headband," I muttered to Algebra, green eyes lit up as he grabbed his head band and snapped it.

"Keeps the curls back but still free. Best invention ever." Aurora rolled her eyes at him but smiled fondly.

Zaliver and Joshula were still where I'd left them, both back straight and staring at each other with calm expressions, Joshula looking a little to innocent and Zaliver looking a little too calm to be good.

As soon as we all walked Zaliver half turned to face us, enough to keep him in sight out if his side vision. Him and Algebra did the whole 'bro half hug-hand clasp thing', Me and Aurora shared a knowing look. I was partly surprised to that Zaliver looked over at Hogan and only give the man a nod.

I was even more surprised to see his stern expression turned grim as soon as Zaliver looked away. I almost missed the way his eyes flickered over to Joshula who paid him no mind whatsoever. Sensing that he was being looked at Hogan looked over until his eyes caught mine, I smiled innocently, his expression went back to stern.

"So do you all want to eat now or are we waiting for someone else?" I asked no one in particular.

"I say we eat all that delicious food," Algebra muttered, looking like the wolf he was, a hungered animal who'd found his sheep.

His sheep of large variety and whom had been slayed and perfectly set on plates with the perfect dipping sauce and condiments beside it. There was a pause in my mind.

Damn, that was beautiful. You are hungry, aren't you? My wolf piped up.

"Of course you do, you practically raced here," Aurora murmured beside him, shaking her head in amusement as her rocked back and forth on the balls of his feet

"Then let's eat," Zaliver said, then throwing me a look. "Before anyone faints." I resisted the urge to stick my tongue out, but I did feel my face heat up.

As if Aurora and Algebra knew of the seating arrangement they sat exactly where they were supposed to. Zaliver pulled my chair

647

out before taking his own. This made a very robotic Joshula sit down and the stern Hogan seemed a little paler in his fresh suit.

I didn't need to be told twice to begin eating and probably piled my plate higher than Zaliver's, but seeing as how everyone but Aurora had the appetite of an animal, we all ate food that could have lasted weeks. But I hadn't forgotten the reason for the dinner, while I ate I also observed.

Hogan while a wolf, ate perhaps less than he should have. I didn't know whether to blame it on his nerves or if that's how he usually ate.

Joshula fared alright, eating the right amount just as the others. He ate slowly and without a fuss. He kept his eyes on his own plate, but everyone once in a while would look up and scan the table.

Aurora ate less than anyone at the table, understandable, witches don't usually have to eat as much as wolves do. Hogan had at some point made eye contact with her and must have realized how

Algebra . . . well, safe to say it was a tie between us both. Zaliver was the perfect image of calm, graceful and the perfect host.

As for me?

"So as Third in command, what's it like Hogan? Must be quite busy if I've come to meet you until now." I wiped my mouth with my napkin.

Hogan coughed in his water but took control quickly and looked up at me. Almost without meaning to, his eyes went to Zaliver, but my mate paid him no mind. After all, it was a harmless question.

"I organize pack documentation that could be ID, bills, property or pack transfers of new installments, requests of entrance—"

"He does a shit load of paperwork, that's why he's so pale." Algebra snickered. Aurora threw him a look.

Hogan closed his mouth with a grimace, but his hand fisted around his fork. I didn't need to check in on his emotions to know that Algebra's comment on his job were frequent and very, very unwelcome. Again, Hogan's eyes went to Zaliver's as if waiting for something, when whatever he was waiting for didn't happen his shoulders dropped a bit. I felt almost bad but then-

"And what do you do again Beta? I've forgotten," Joshula said without looking at Algebra.

"Of course you have," Algebra muttered lowly under his breath. " Second in command of the seconds so I basically do all the things our lovely alpha over there doesn't want to do. Telling everyone what to do, making sure they follow through and kicking some ass every once in a while," he said with a hint of pride.

"And let's not forget popping up unexpected and torturing people with your math like name. Beta by day, probably math teacher by night." That soured his expression entirely, he pointed at me with a french fry and a devious look on his face.

"Pass me the shrimp you've been guarding." I sucked in a breath.

"That's right, hand them over-"

"I love your suit Hogan, was it specially made?" I asked, ignoring Algebra, I caught the twitch that Zaliver's lips made.

Hogan looked from me to the beta at the end of the table.

"You can ignore me as long as you pass-"

"Oh leave her alone Berry."

"No, I want the shrimp." Aurora sighed.

"You're allergic to shrimp."

"I don't care, she has them so I want them."

I looked on at Hogan, ignoring the two bickering at the table.

"Custom made Luna," Hogan said after an awkward pause. I smiled at him, I couldn't tell if he was shy or just reserved.

"Well it's nice."

"Thank you."

"So what do you like to do in your free time, seems like I have a lot of that. Any good ideas?" I asked, picking at an odd-looking thing on my plate. Not eating that.

"I wouldn't know much about that since I work around the clock Luna, but I'm sure you'll be able to find something to busy yourself with," he said seriously.

I sighed sadly.

"That seems unfair Zaliver, you should give Hogan more time off." I said half turning my head to look at Zaliver with a pout.

He leaned back against his chair as if he had no cares, he looked at me for a long time before answering.

"But then who would do the paperwork? Albericus-"

"No," Algebra said from the end of the table.

"Wwouldn't do nearly good of a job as Hogan does," he said. I sighed dramatic and turned to look at Hogan with apologetic eyes.

"I tried." He gave me a stiff nod, but I think there was color in his cheeks.

Hm.

"Heaven forbid I be in charge of the paperwork." Algebra said, Zaliver nodded in agreement.

I finished chewing what was in my mouth before slyly glancing at Joshula. He'd remained mostly quiet, smart move for anyone hiding something, but also a normal trait of his.

"Why so serious Joshula? You know, you and Hogan seem like you need a good party or something. Good thing the holidays are coming up." Joshula raised a brow at me.

"You do seem like the type of person who would enjoy, what you call them, holidays," he said, playing with his fork.

"Well who wouldn't, free presents, free food and the perfect excuse to do something rash and blame it on excitement or alcohol-" I glanced at Zaliver. "not that I've had any, of course." But let's say if I had, he wouldn't need to know.

Algebra scoffed.

"I don't think it's getting a free present when you have to give one back, that's basically trading. I give you something, you give me something back and if I don't like it I rip the name tag of and switch it with someone else's. It's seasonal trading, that's what it is," he declared.

"Right," I muttered before eating. "I swear, Algebra."

Thankfully Aurora decided to start a harmless conversation between Hogan, Algebra and herself. She did know Hogan longer than I did, even with her, abscess, they were acquaintances.

I keep waiting for someone to jump on the table and pull a knife or something. I said to Zaliver through the bond.

His expression and body language remained the same as if I hadn't said a word but he answered me with a grim tone.

I hate it when we have to fish for information, I'd be happier to stab him here and now just for dropping something off of his plate.

Hogan seems nice, are you sure Fate/Joshula wasn't just in his office when he wasn't. Even secretaries have to use the bathroom you know.

Do they open up their windows to fan out scents and pale every time you get near them, even though you're their boss?

You are intimidating. As for the windows, I open them every time it gets hot, does that make me a suspect?

I heard his fork scrape harshly against the plate and looked over to see him stiff. Zaliver didn't like me questioning his judgment, or better yet, was hurt that I was defending his supposed enemy.

This isn't me doubting you Zaliver, this is me making sure you don't accuse your third in command who from what I can tell from sitting here with him, has worked extremely hard to be acknowledged and befriend by his Alpha and crush.

The fork full of food Zaliver brought up to his mouth halted mid way, his mouth open and everything. Blue eyes wide and blinking repeatedly he clamped his mouth shut with an audible 'snap' and put it down on his plate and then reached for his water only to take gulps of it. Then very calmly he asked me.

I'm sorry, could you repeat that last part?

My wolf snickered in my head while my beast eyed Hogan with narrowed eyes.

650

"I haven't gone to see her yet, but maybe next time I'm in the area," Aurora said.

"I can't stand her," Algebra grumbled like a petulant child, Hogan rolled his eyes, more relaxed. Beside him Joshula looked back and forth at the banter. Seeming both entertained and annoyed.

"She does have a knack for annoying anyone in the room with her," Hogan agreed reluctantly. "At least she's nicer when her mother's around."

"I can't stand that old raisin either-"

"You can't stand many people." Aurora butted in.

Don't tell me you haven't seen the way your third looks at you? Or has been point-blank, glaring at me when he thinks no one's looking. I may be wrong but believe you have a fan at the table. Looking down, I smiled to myself.

Through the bond I felt an odd emotion, something I've never felt from Zaliver that had me wanting to laugh. I knew that if I looked over at him I'd laugh. What was Zaliver feeling at the moment?

Dumb.

Purely and simply dumb. The man wasn't even thinking, I should know, I've been in his multitasking, overpowered, strong hold of a mind. A mind that was blank now. After a few seconds he snapped back, but a last-minute, frantic sense of denial was there.

No, no way. He would have told me, I would have known.

I held in my snort at the table, my grin making it hard to eat.

You act as if tall, dark and sexy isn't attractive. All, by the way, which you are. He growled in my head, mumbling to himself about clues and not being possible. My wolf couldn't help but pitch in.

And wait, there's more. Just for a total of forty-nine, ninety-nine every month for the rest of your immortal life, you too can be granted the highest of positions in society where everyone becomes your bitch and have access to his deep and never ending money. We'll even throw in long and hot nights of passionate and wild sex. Shipping and handling sold separately.

Oh god.

I mean look at that suit, he'd be delighted to not only have his bank account but his fine ass too, liter- Thankfully my beast put a sharp claw over my wolf's snout.

I don't know who was dying more on the inside, me from laughter or Zaliver from. . .well. I was shaking from how hard I was holding it in, it was very obvious from the looks I was receiving from everyone.

"Are you okay Vivian?" Aurora asked, reaching out as if she were going to put a hand on my shoulder.

"Mhmm," I said in a high-pitched and shaky voice. She gave me a disbelieving look but turned back to the conversation that had been going on.

"So you're not seeing what's his-"

"No."

There was a brief pause.

No. Just no. Zaliver said, looking over at him I bit my lip to stop the bubbling laughter that wanted out. His expression seemed to be stuck between a grimace and that of someone who's just eaten something sour.

"That's a shame, you two looked so cute together."

"You think everyone looks cute together."

"Shut up and eat your taco Berry." There was a crunch a few seconds later.

I bet you if I asked about his love life he'd look at you at least once.

No he won't, because you're wrong, I've known him half his life Vivian he could never-

"Are you seeing anyone now Hogan?"

No, wait! Zaliver stilled in his chair but, his blue eyes meet mine with admonishment.

What? It's an innocent question? I blinked innocently at him and turned back to a flustered Hogan.

"No, no I am not," he said casually.

See! Zaliver exclaimed in triumph and a bit of relief.

"But, do you like anyone?"

I could hear Zaliver groan in the back of my mind.

Hogan seemed to hesitate for a moment, Zaliver must have taken that hesitation as him being uncomfortable or perhaps even surprised at my brashness and relaxed into his chair. And then tensed when Hogan's eyes met his in a moment's flicker. I roared my triumph through the bond.

"Well I, um . . ." Hogan seemed a bit disoriented, but his jaw was clenched and his hold on his fork kept readjusting. In a blink my eyes unfocused from looking right at him to looking around him. His aura had flared enough to catch my attention.

It was a puzzling one.

A mixture of a warm brown seeming to be mixing in with a vibrant green, but the way it moved around him was unusual. More than just mixing it seemed around if the two colored were clashing, as if indecisive or. . .

He took a breath, snapping me out of my little moment, he seemed more focused, serious and almost delirious with the way he suddenly seemed to change in that one breath. Throughout all of dinner and even just meeting him, he'd kept his eyes away from mine and seemed almost too shy in on himself, but the drastic change was unnerving. Brown eyes suddenly meet mine full force, unblinking, he seems to straighten just a bit in his chair and the tilt was small but the corner of his lips seemed to resist an expression of what I presume could have been smugness with the way his brow lifted in the way that left the impression of knowing something no one else did.

The change was small, small enough that no one else seemed alarmed or bothered to note. I had even though I'd imagine the change in the man but then I realized that I was wrong.

Joshula's lips were pressed tightly against one another, his expression remained the same, his head tilted slightly to the side but not enough that it looked like we was invested in the conversation. But his eyes. His eyes held a sign of a clear warning. A warning to keep his mouth shut.

Joshula had seen the slight change the third in command had and he did not like it apparently.

"Well, I can honestly say that it's been a very long time since I've been in a serious relationship with anyone," he spoke louder than his usual mumbles, his words clear and filled with confidence that made his deep voice sound silk smooth. Our eyes were locked on one another. There was something in his stare that made the hair on my arms stand in their ends. My beast was tense as she sensed something unpleasant.

"But that's the thing about life, it's kind to those who deserve what they want and work hard. I have a feeling that life will bring me own happy ending soon. Don't you agree Luna? Life does have a funny way of making things...come together," he said seriously, his gaze not wavering from mine while he spoke. Somehow, I felt as if he was teasing me by calling me Luna.

"Right," I answered softly, moving my mouth but not completely there with my response.

His words although, not a threat and not a complete declaration of war, chilled me to the core. His words were spoken with a soft touch of satisfaction, as if the end was in sight and he liked what he saw. He suddenly blinked as if startled and then snapped his head over to Joshula and as if realizing what he'd done quickly looked away.

"Don't tell me you're the type to sit back and wait for life to come to you?" Algebra asked, undisturbed and unaware of what had just happened.

"What's wrong with that?" Hogan asked softly, back to his shy and in turned state. He didn't even look in my direction.

653

"Nothing, but there's no fun in sitting around and waiting for your prince charming. I mean, for all you know he's waiting for you," Algebra pointed out.

"Very well said," Aurora agreed with a displeased expression her face, her brows furrowed as she scanned my face. I gave her a small smile.

I glanced over at Zaliver was looking down the table, a pensive look on his face, his eyes looked over at me and before he could say anything the door rang. Thank god. I felt like I needed a second.

"Are we expecting anyone?" Joshula voiced the thought in the room, I stood up and pushed my chair back.

"Not you, just me," I said before walking out if the dining room and into the hallway.

Now that no was looking, I removed the smile off my face, my cheeks hurting a bit. I slowed my steps, enjoying this small moment to myself that would end as soon as I got back to the table. Hogan's words left me wanting out of my skin and into my fur. There was just something very wrong and unpleasant about all of this, I felt like we were all wearing masks and waiting for the first one to fall to point and attack.

As a kid I use to envy people with colored eyes, I use to think brown was boring but as I grew I slowly began to appreciate having brown eyes. Because they were mine. But tonight? Looking into Hogan's eyes I felt a flicker of apprehension. Why? Because for once, I wasn't sure if I had looked into brown or black eyes.

Dinner was barely starting and I already wanted it to end. I hope not all of the Alpha dinner's were like this because if they were I knew I was going to be beyond grouchy and probably end up telling everyone that they had to declare what they wanted before they could get through any door. No one has time nor patience for fake pleasantries. At least, not me.

Taking a breath I shook my shoulders and walked over to the door and for the first time in the night, smiled for real. After sorting out my appreciation and gratitude I began making my way back but as I passed the living room I caught sight of a small movement and grinned.

Walking back into dinner everyone's eyes were on me or more specifically, my hands. In one I had a foil covered platter of pot stickers and in the other-

"Why is the ra- I mean, what's his name? Frod? Fred-"

"Frank," I clarified. Algebra snapped his fingers and pointed at me.

"Right, right. Why is Frank on a leash and is that a bow tie?" he asked amused.

"Because he's grounded for trying to run away and as punishment he has to sit through dinner aware of the fact that he's a spectacle," I explained, sitting down and tying the leash around my wrist and then setting him down on the ground. I wasn't going to set him on the table, I'm not that rude.

Immediately he started heading for the door but could only get so far, he tugged and the sound of his small feet could be heard pawing at the ground with all his might.

"You're talking about him as if he understandings," Algebra said disbelieving. I shrugged, I'd look crazy but I knew my hedgehog. Aurora peaked down at Frank with a smile.

"He's cute."

"Thanks."

"Is it safe to eat with that thing in here?" I looked over to see Hogan squinting at Frank like he was ready to march over and step on him with his shoes- wait no, I feel like he'd get them to dirty. He'd probably ask someone else to do it.

"He's clean." I resisted the urge to roll my eyes or throttle him.

"Why is he grounded?" Zaliver asked, eyeing the plate of pot stickers I sat down in front of my plate and began unwrapping with a look of disbelief.

In his defense, we were wolves and we were known for eating crazy amounts of food, like the one still on my plate, but I was putting every male to shame at this table with the amount I was eating.

"I opened the door to get in and you know what that little rat does? He bolts right past me, down the stairs and makes it halfway across the grass before I get him." I looked down at Frank who's still pulling at his leash, I feel every tug. "And here I was thinking he liked me." As if feeling my glare he stops pulling and just lays limply on the ground with his eyes closed.

"Did he just—" Algebra looked shocked as he looked down at Frank's small body.

I snorted and pulled softly on the leash, dragging his body on the ground for a few seconds before he gets to his paws and try to run. Idiot still has the leash on.

"Not falling for that one anytime soon buddy." I dug into my plate as everyone looks between me and Frank in a mixture of shock, amusement, wonder, and curiosity.

We continue eating for a while until I get back into my role of the night. I had a job to do.

"You know, we've spoken about everyone's love life except yours." I said casually, everyone stopped and looked over to where my eyes were.

Joshula cleaned his mouth with a napkin but didn't respond back. This guy's like a damn rock, silent but there and deadly when thrown hard enough to the back of the skull.

"So, anyone who's fancied your heart? Who's the lucky girl? Or gal if you swing for that team too." I winked at the last part, ignoring the way his eyes narrowed. No answer.

"Oh don't be shy. Unless-" I gave a loud gasp. "You're a player aren't you? You probably don't want to tell us because we know them or are there so many you don't even know their names?! Joshula, I never knew you'd be the type. I hope you wrap it before you tap it because I know some guys on the run because of child support and let me just say-"

"No! It's nothing like that!" he exclaimed quickly, his face scrunching up in distaste and repulsion. Algebra was dying at the end of the table while Aurora and Zaliver chuckled under their breaths, Hogan had a reluctant smile on his face. I blinked innocently at him.

"Are you sure? Because I know some really good bridges you could hide under-"

"No thank you, it's not like that, at all." His face was tight as he took in deep breaths, jaw clenching and relaxing over and over again. I could hear his teeth grinding together.

"Really?" I asked in a disbelieving tone, reaching for my cup, eyeing him suspiciously. He gave me a strained smile.

"I have no care for frivolous relationships or people. I have no interest in love or anything to do with the matter," he responded forcefully, as if trying to get me to understand.

Oh, I understood. I brought the cup up to my mouth and then paused,looking at him from over the rim of my cup.

"So if you're not sneaking back into the house in the middle of the night from tapping it, what are you doing?" I took a sip of my lemonade.

Joshula paled.

Technically I'd asked him an innocent question, an innocent man who had nothing to hide would answer right away but a guilty man wouldn't answer. I'd backed him into a corner. He had to give me an answer either way and he could either lie about it and then make up more lies to cover that up, where I'd just fish and fish until he messed up or. . . He could tell a half truth where no matter what he said, he's still be revealing something and I'd get a chance to twist his words. Rocks don't talk. He was not a rock. He was a dead man.

I felt a surge of pride and possession from Zaliver directed towards me, as well as astonishment and a hint of something I couldn't name.

I could kiss you right now. He growled in my head.

You can do that later.

I looked at Joshula with expectancy but also a normal amount of curiosity. In a way I was curious, but the longer he took to answer the more time I had to make more questions. His blue-green eyes flickered around the table, his window for giving an innocent answer was closing and he knew it. If he didn't respond now then I wouldn't even have to ask him what was taking so long, it looked like Algebra was getting ready to do that on his own.

Beside him Hogan flinched and I mean that in a way that it wasn't a voluntary flinch, but more like a 'someone is squeezing my balls under the table and they don't mean to play with them' kind of way.

"I, uh, like to go out for strolls or just prowl the forest at night. You know, it's good for the wolves." Hmm, half truth it is then.

I picked up a pot sticker and smiled.

"So where do you usually go, do you have a path you stick to or is it random? Maybe I'll join you one night, I bet it's just beautiful." I bit into my potsticker. Damn this is good.

Joshula looked like he wanted to leap across the table and punch me. I almost wished he would, that would be enough for Zaliver to kill him without looking completely psycho and sane to everyone.

But he didn't.

Booo. My wolf grumbled.

I don't care how many good answers Joshula had, because I would have a question for everything. Honestly, he should confess to everything now while he had the chance. He could either tell us that he had a path he travel and then Zaliver would probably go around sniffing for a repetitive trail or he could deny it to which Zaliver would still do the later. There was no correct answer. Just a whole lot of lies.

"It varies," he said.

"Hmm," I responded. I continued to eat, as did he but his moment was tense and strained.

At this moment he was probably thinking about whatever plan he had going on, so he'd think of answers to possible questions I'd ask. I guess in a way it was sort of a Fate thing, he would try to control the situation with his answers and probably ask me some stuff in return. I'd let him plan, no matter how many answers someone had and no matter how good they were, a liar had weaknesses and I knew which ones to poke at. In fact I had three.

No matter how good a liar is, there are only so many lies you can keep track of without having to forget a few to make room for more.

A liar's brain and mouth move at the same phase because they know the goals, but the body always takes a second to catch up. Sticks

657

and stones break bones, words and lies break lives but your body will betray you.

And last but not least.

There's only so much bullshit you can talk before you get called out on it.

While I ate, Frank had changed his plan from crawling away to trying to chew through the leash, damn rat looked adorable while doing it too. From the end of the table Algebra couldn't help but comment.

"Does anyone know the number for animal abuse?"

And neither could I.

"You mean animal control? What, you finally gonna turn yourself in?" I responded without looking at him.

In front of me Hogan choked on his water. I chuckled at my own joke, beside me Aurora didn't even hold her laughter in.

"You're not suppose to laugh at me woman, you're suppose to back me up, the Internet says those are the steps to be 'goals.' "Algebra quoted and then turned his narrowed green eyes at me. "And you, it's on!"

"The fact that I'm winning proves it's been on for a while. And I'm in the lead." He pouted dramatically and leaned back into his chair.

"Why are you so mean to me?" he asked.

"Why do you make it so easy for her?" Zaliver asked, his mouth turned up in the faintest of smiles.

"You're supposed to have my back man, that's how friendship works," Algebra accused, Zaliver rolled his eyes.

"I do have your back. . .when it's not against someone who slays you in her mind. You think that was bad? I bet you didn't know that half of the things that come out of her mouth when directed at you are the result of her dimming them down so that they're less insulting," Zaliver declared, reaching out to put his hand on my forearm and squeeze. I smiled. Algebra looked horrified.

"Dimmed. . .down?" I nodded.

His look of horror turned into one of awe and then excitement. Oh oh.

"Show me. Let me have it," he said leaning forward.

"Careful Berry, I don't have the strength to carry you into the house because you can't feel your legs from the burn." Aurora said, amused. I high-fived her.

"Oh, you too?" he asked, playing offended. She shook her head and lifted her hands.

"Well, come on Luna, let me feel the full extent of your fire," Algebra asked, seeming to doubt Zaliver now.

"We'll okay, throw some shade my way." I leaned back against my chair and looked over at Algebra, he had full attention, slightly. I think even Frank stopped his chewing.

"Hm, okay." He seems to think about something before a large grin took over his face.

"You ready?"

"Yeah, go for it."

"I don't know, you might get crazy and I don't want Zaliver to punch me."

"I promise he won't punch you, but I'd be lying if I said I wouldn't go crazy since I already am." My response seems to make Algebra hesitate, my grin didn't seem to help. I felt my wolf inch forward, responses already in her head.

"So, have you picked out a wedding dress yet?" he asked.

He better not say anything about us looking fat on our wedding day. My wolf grumbled, eyeing him.

"No, not yet,

"I answered truthfully. What was his goal?He smirked at me.

"I don't see what's taking so long, I mean, you'll probably end up looking like Casper the ghost anyway," he said playfully, beside me Aurora gasped, I tilted my head to the side.

Roast this bitch. My wolf growled.

"Fashion advice? From you? I've ever only seen you in like three outfits. What advice could you possibly tell? How to style my bed sheets? Looks like your own aren't even being shook."

The table was quiet for a moment before one look at Algebra's face had everyone laughing.

"Wait, if that was the full on Vivian response, what would the dimmed down one be then?" Aurora asked after everyone had calmed down.

"I probably would have said something along the lines of 'Thanks, I've always wanted advice from some who shops in Zaliver's closet from two months ago'".

"Hey!" Zaliver exclaimed, still chucking a bit.

"I love you, but it's true. It's was like you had a full black color chart, I'm not saying you don't look nice in it, but a girl's gotta have some spice in her life." I shrugged at his incredulous look.

"You know," Algebra said, putting a hand on his chest. "I'm not gonna lie, I'm a little hurt."

"Aw. If it makes you feel better it was a comment more than it was an honest opinion," I said with a small smile at his offended look, green eyes wide and slow blinking.

"No, still offended. Give me a moment to rethink life," he said, acting as if he were about to stand up.

"Oh please, she's practically right, I think you only have like nine-"

"Who are you mated to!?"

"Oh come on!"

"It's me or her!"

I gave a very unladylike snort and ignored the bickering couple. The rest of the dinner went without a hitch but I had two more things to do before I could have a good enough excuse to kick everyone out. Unsurprisingly, most of the food was gone. Not sure if that was mainly my doing or Algebra's, but it was quick going. At one point Zaliver's hand had reached out for a potsticker, but one look from me had him reaching for a shrimp instead, begrudgingly I let him have one. He'd been eyeing them for a long time.

There's a moment where everyone finishes their food and sort of just stay at the table, realizing how full they are and regretting the last bite, in that moment short conversations or long ones, are made. We were at that moment. But unlike everyone else I was sort of chewing on random stuff. I think Zaliver was beginning to think I had missed meals instead of just one. I'd probably die of a food coma but it was great being immortal.

"Joshula?" I asked, munching on fries. I was surprises Algebra hadn't eaten them all.

At the sound of his name he tensed and then looked over at me with a forced smile. He totally hates me.

I bet if he had a knife for every time you annoyed him, he'd use them all to stab you. My wolf whispered, feeling the food comma herself.

I didn't doubt it.

"Yes?"

"Earlier you said that you didn't have any interest in love, so I can't help but wonder, what are you interested in?"

What person comes back from the dead and basically says 'fuck love, even though I probably didn't have it before, nah, I'm going avenge my death with doing shady shit that will probably get me killed again'? I mean really, it's just not right.

He must have sat through dinner planning answers to so many questions and here I'd just asked him one. One question he must have overlooked due to the look on his face. He raised his hand and ran it through his hair, adding a crazed look to his already wild hair.

"I've grown intrigued in many things, this word is vast and full of things that still surprise me at every turn," he answered vaguely.

"Like what?"

660

"The home people have built for themselves, to shelter them from nature. As you said before, the clothing and the importance of it. The human society and their rules. I've gotten to know a lot of things that still surprise me." He spit out through a forced smile. I myself, resisted the urge to frown and just nodded.

Was it me, or did those seem like things he hated? I asked Zaliver.

No. Was all he said.

When we began cleaning up I instructed the guys to bring in all the full or half full plates into the kitchen where they set them down on the counter.

"I hope you know you're taking some of this home?" I said to Aurora and Hogan, I heard Algebra let out a 'yay' from the dining room. Without another word I began pulling out containers and pulled out a two knives to part and cut sections, when Joshula walked in to throw something away I grabbed the second knife I hadn't used and walked over to Aurora who was standing by dining room entrance, putting her containers of food on top of the knife and handing them to her.

"Oh, thank you. I guess now we don't have to worry about food for the next two days, or one, deepening on how hungry he gets," Aurora muttered the last part to herself, I laughed, but didn't lose focus.

Calculating carefully, I waited to turn the exact moment I felt Joshula come up behind me and try to go around. He must have thought the containers of food was all I had because he didn't even dodge the knife until it was too late.

"Ah!!" He looked down in surprise and rage, I let out a believable scream and pulled back the bloodied knife. I hadn't gone too deep or it would have looked like I mean to stab him, I just grazed deep enough to go through his shirt and leave a gash about three inches long.

"I'm sorry. I'm so sorry. Jeezus Christ that's a lot of blood, oh my god I'm so sorry!"

Jumping back I began apologizing quickly, my voice coming out shaky and high-pitched as I moved around to get a towel and hand it to him, keeping the knife as far away from him as possible. The guys, hearing my scream and probably scenting blood came rushing in and then took sight of a bleeding and glaring Joshula and my panicked and guilt ridden face.

"It was an accident, I swear!"

Zaliver walked over to me and put his hands on my shoulders, a calm look on his face but a different look in his eyes.

"Alright, out of the kitchen. It's official, you are banned from trying to cook or cut anything in the kitchen ever again," he said, starting to push me out into the direction of the dining room.

"I'm really sorry Joshula!!"

"Holy shit, remind me not to let her into our kitchen." I rolled my eyes.

We moved past the dining room and straight for his office, we would have a few seconds while they fussed over Joshula. Because while they fussed over him, I got out with the bloodied knife. Turning around to face me Zaliver grinned.

"Is this enough?" I asked, handing him the knife. He carefully took it from my hands and looked it over.

"This will be more than enough, good job baby," he praised, taking the knife and setting down into the prepared container that he then put under lock in his desk. He'd have to wait until everyone left drop that off at the lab.

I had been surprised when Zaliver had leaned into me earlier and asked me to find a way to make Joshula bleed without it being suspicious. But it had quickly clicked, my man and his blood tests. Zaliver handed me the disinfectant and bandages that were ready on his desk. I looked down at my white shirt and made a whining noise.

"He got blood on my shirt!" Does he know how hard it is to get blood off of white shirts? Because I honestly don't, but I imagine it's not that hard. Zaliver smiled down at me in raw amusement, a full smile making its way onto his face for the first time since dinner. I liked his smile.

"I believe it was you, who got blood on your shirt, after you cut him." He pointed out.

"Boo hoo, at least he will heal," I said before walking out of his office and back to where everyone was. I made sure to look super distressed and guilty.

"I'm really sorry. Here, this should help." I handed him the disinfectant, even though the knife was damn new, and the bandages.

"It's fine, accidents will happen," he said looking at me with cool anger. I frowned.

"You mean 'accidents *do* happen?'" Algebra asked. Correcting the odd arrangement of words.

"Yes, of course. That's what I meant," he said after an unforgettable pause, a lazy grin making its way onto his face. I however, felt that he meant what he said.

Just what, would that blood sample cause us?

~•~

After getting everyone to leave with a heaping pile of food and Joshula doing his 'nightly stroll', Zaliver and I went upstairs after putting

662

an irritated Frank down in his cage. He usually slept wherever he wanted but he was grounded.

"I feel like this went on forever," I said, sitting on the bed and taking my shoes off, next came the jewelry. Zaliver walked over to his side of the stand and placed his phone and things on it.

"That's only because you did most of the talking." He walked over to me until he stood in front and squatted down to get to my eye level. "I never realized how good you were at cornering people, perhaps I should get you to do the interrogating my little Luna." He took hold of my chin and tilted my head down to kiss him softly.

"I've never tortured before, but if you say so," I said jokingly, he rolled his eyes and stood up.

"So what do you think about what he said?" Zaliver asked me after a moment, removing his blazer and setting it down on the bed, he walked over to the couch and sat down.

Removing my hair tie, I ran my fingers through my hair and felt it fall around my face messy but I didn't care, the lack of pressure felt great. And besides, it gave me a moment to look over tonight's answers.

Although I could have just kept asking and asking Hogan and Joshula questions, it would have looked odd if I just kept going, but I feel like the few questions I asked were important.

"Hogan seems very reserved and pulled in but towards the end of dinner I felt as if he knew something that made him feel as if he were going to win a prize we don't know about. I do believe that there's something going on between him and Joshula since at some point it looked like he was being squeezed under the table and I'm sure you weren't playing footsie with him. No matter how much he probably wanted it." Zaliver glared at me, but didn't deny it. So it was Joshula then.

"I still can't believe I didn't realize that he. . .is attracted to me. I've never even seen sensed it from him, the man's remained either afraid or serious whenever I've been near him. I've never even gotten a hint," Zaliver mumbled bewildered.

"His fear of you was probably due to you being completely terrifying sometimes and then of you finding out. The smell of fear is a good cover for desire." I sang the last word playfully.

"What about Joshula?" he asked, that made me frown.

"Quiet as a rock during dinner but I still think you should have sent someone to follow him after dinner," I said, he shook his head.

"I know his mind. He probably didn't even head in his normal path out of suspicion that we'd do exactly that, he's changing his course, covering up his scent," he explained.

I begrudgingly did because if I was Joshula, I would have done it too. I groaned.

"Why can't you just do that thing you did to me when we met and just get into his head?" It would solve our problems so much faster. Zaliver smiled at me and ran his fingers through his hair

"Because if I did, if Joshula really is working with Fate, it would be a move they'd already plan for. How do I know that as soon as I get into his mind, I won't be locked in and my body will be as defenseless as a vegetable?" He lifted a brow at me in question, waiting for a response.

"He could do that?" I asked instead, surprised and horrified of the thought of Zaliver stuck in that guy's head all while his body would be defenseless and an easy target. I would undoubtedly protect it, but still.

"The mind is a complex thing, capable of unimaginable things when pushed beyond its normal capacity. If Fate indeed trained Joshula and taught him all he knows today, then he would undoubtedly know how to close his mental shields around me. Keeping me in, instead of out. There's always a danger of that happening when I do that, which is why I prefer to do it under my own conditions." Zaliver explained, his face softened as the look on my face turned from worry to horror.

"But you did it on me?"

"Perhaps deep down I already knew I could trust you," he answered without hesitation. I took a minute to process.

"Whatever Joshula's planning has to be somewhere secluded and away from the people of the island, he must know that if any suspicious activity was going on he'd be reported. So, he's definitely doing something shady in the forest, you just have to look for the closest forest away from as many wolves and inhabits as possible and perhaps an hour or two away from the house if that's the reason he comes back so late," I said, looking towards the ground as if more answers could be given. My brain was fired up and processing and breaking down whatever clues I had like crazy.

"How'd you get that?" Zaliver asked, I answered without looking up.

"Well, he said he was taking a random path now and then to which I call bullshit, but to say you're taking a random path indicates that the forest he goes to has to be big enough to even have random paths. It's survival instincts not to get caught when you're doing something shady and to not get caught you have to stay away from people, so the forest it is. Since he always comes back late and you haven't even mentioned feeling Fate's presence the whole time Joshula's been here, perhaps they've been meeting somewhere far away from the house and then even farther as precaution. If you can smell Fate's scent but not sense him then it must be a place where Joshula can wash up. So maybe a river? Or a lake? But-"

Zaliver's lips cut me off, surprised it took me a moment to respond back but I did so. He pulled back I gaze down at me with awed and hooded eyes.

"Did I mention how much I love your mind?" he asked huskily. I shook my head, huffing a bit.

"Well I do. Continue," he said walking back over to his place on the couch and sitting down as if he hadn't just done that.

"U-Uh, W-Well, I'm a bit confused as to where homes, fashion and society play their part in this. He said he was interested by it but they sounded more like complaints to me. You don't think he's trying to take over the world and remake fashion do you?" I asked half jokingly, but Zaliver seemed to take it serious.

"I wouldn't put it past him to plan world domination, but perhaps he'd be pleased with just this island. Go big or go home, I believe is the saying?"

"Yup, that's the one."

"I've had the nagging feeling that there's something I'm missing, overlooking somehow. What's their end goal, kill me? I'm immortal. Control all wolves? Good luck. I'm sure they're not stupid enough to go after you, that would be beyond suicide. What do they want? And how do they get it?" Zaliver spoke mostly to himself, but I agreed with him.

"Why don't we look at this piece by piece? Break down the bonds and everyone involved," I suggested.

"Well for starters, what would Hogan gain in working with Joshula and Fate?"

"You mean besides you?" I asked him, irritated at the thought, but it came mainly from my beast.

"Not funny."

"Not joking."

He sighed and nodded reluctantly, like a person trying to shrug off an unwanted love confession. Careful Zaliver, love can cause people to dangerous things. The thought came with a dark edge.

"You're right, but even if Fate did promise him that, I'm happily mated to you and Hogan must know that his feelings are one-sided. How would-no, it could never happen, no matter what Fate promises or does."

I stood up and shamelessly began to undress, feeling his eyes run over me, by not paying any attention the tingles and heat that spread over my skin.

"My usual inclination would be to go confront him about his feelings but that may just cause more problems, right now his role in this

665

could be minimal but if you crush whatever hopes he had then we might have a vengeful 'not even' ex on our path. Those might just be the worst enemy's." I shook my head and picked up my clothes off the ground, standing in just undergarments.

"So what do you have in mind then?" he asked me, looking over at him I had to lift a brow at the glazed look over his darkening eyes.

Not what you have in mind, that's for sure. My wolf laughed.

Zaliver's eyes focused and then he cleared his throat as if he hadn't just been checking me out.

"Well, let him keep his fantasy and see what's off about his work. Someone keeping a double life as a loyal worker and a spy has to mess up on something small, paper work, filing, forgetting to do the smallest of things. Catch him there and asks what's on his mind. And as much as you may dislike it, flirting would really win you some points-"

"I will not flirt. I'm happily mated and soon to be married." He was firm on this.

"Oh come on, I know that, you know that, he knows that, but it doesn't mean he cares. Just bat those baby blues and you'll have him like salt, falling everywhere," I pointed out. I think I would have won him over if my wolf hadn't made a comment.

More like falling on his hands and knees.

Zaliver's eyes went hard on me and he shook his head, his jaw tightening.

"No." He snarled quietly.

"I didn't even make the comment, don't look at me like that!" I snarled back, ignoring his growl I went to the closet and was about to reach for my pj's when I caught sight of a wrapped box. Oh yeah.

"I'm going to go drop the knife off, stay inside and lock the door," Zaliver said, cranky.

"Wait!" I called out, reaching for the box. I knew he listened when I didn't hear the door open. Walking out I walked over to him and pushed the box into his hands. His face went from annoyed to confused.

"What's this?" he asked, shaking the box for sound, when nothing rattled his frown deepened. I grinned at him.

"Remember when I told you that you would have to put something on for me, no questions asked?" I asked sweetly, his face paled. I wanted to roll my eyes, it's not like it was a thong, though I guess I could still change my mind. I pointed to the bathroom. "Go change."

His eyes looked down to his hands, me, the bathroom and then back at me.

"But I have to go deliver the knife—" he whispered.\

"You can do that after you go change." I smiled and moved to the side to let him walk over to the bathroom.

He dragged his feet, but finally made it there and closed the door. I held in my chuckles, this was partly for me and in making him go dressed like this to the lab was for Frank. He's lucky I didn't make him wear it in the morning.

Walking into the closet I pulled out my own little present and got dressed, I felt the exact moment he realized what I wanted him to put on. His mood was all over the place, from mortification, to annoyance and rebellious, then to acceptance and mild amusement.

I stepped out of the closet and a few inches away from the bathroom door, camera in hand and ready for as soon as he stepped out. As soon as the door opened the flash went off and he froze with a murderous look on his face that would have made me reconsider my position but I just couldn't take him serious and instead squealed. I heard the door knob reform to his will.

While I had on a loose white with pink spots unicorn onesie, Zaliver had on a full batman body onesie. He even had the hood up so there were ears on his head.

"Delete that."

"No, it's going to be my screensaver." I didn't even look up as I did exactly as I said. When I was done I put my phone in my pocket. I smiled at his grimace.

I got the largest one they had but it was too short, so I went with the longest one they had and well, I wasn't regretting my decision. It was his height alright, but not exactly his fit. Just like the real batman he filled out the suit and even more as the material strained to keep together on his muscular form. It honestly did his body justice, with the outlines of his abs and strong legs. The suit was all black except for the outlined yellow bat logo on his chest and the utility belt around that sexy ass waist of his.

"I knew this would look good on you," I mumbled, I must have had a dreamy look on my face because I felt and saw his murderous look change into one of complacency. After me staring like an idiot he sighed and walked over to me.

"I guess it's not that bad." He tapped the horn on my head. "I can't stay annoyed at you when you look this adorable. So I'll wait until you take it off." He smiled down at me. I half turned with excitement.

"Look! I have wings too!!" I began jumping up and down as if the movement would make them flutter on their own.

"I see." And then he frowned. "Do I have to wear this to go drop this off at the lab? I mean I can change and then—" I narrowed my eyes at him and poked his firm chest.

667

"It was Batman or Winnie the Pooh. I still got the receipt, don't make me go back for that bright ass yellow bear!" I threatened. Zaliver rolled his eyes and leaned down to kiss my forehead.

"I should be back in five minutes, mind link me if you need anything. Be careful." He made his way to the door. **Damn that's a fine ass.** My wolf appreciated with her own sigh. He stumbled a bit on his way out. I threw my head back and laughed.

When I heard the front door close I decided to go down stairs to check on Frank, maybe the rat had reconsidered how to appreciate freedom. Nope.

Just by leaning over, he scrunched up his face and bared his sharp little teeth at me so I bared mine back, letting them out. Little shit hissed at me, that actually made me laugh. Brave and feisty, I liked him.

Making sure that all the food was away and perhaps taking a one more shrimp for myself, I returned to the room. I really shouldn't have eaten that shrimp, I knew I was full, but by God I didn't know I was that full. I was on halfway through a song when I felt my dinner coming back up, thank god for super speed, although that might have made it worse. Alarm went through the bond and in an instant Zaliver's voice rang in my head.

Vivian! What's wrong?! he asked, so concerned and worried he was screaming down the link, making me wince.

I closed the lid and flushed the toilet. Ugh. There goes dinner. Damn, not as delicious going out, no matter how.

Don't worry, note to self, don't ignore the feeling of fullness in stomach and definitely don't eat cold shrimp. I felt him relaxed, even if just a bit.

Okay, hang tight, I'll be there in a few more minutes.

No problem, hanging on tight to the toilet. I can do that. I smiled, god, I was on a roll tonight. I froze for a second and blinked. Okay, maybe I needed some rest.

Brushing my teeth and positive that I wouldn't be throwing up again I made my way to the bed and laid down and bundled up.

It didn't take Zaliver long to get back, he opened the door and was in bed in the next second. Blue eyes bright with worry, his onesie was damp, was it sprinkling? He laid next to me and leaned over, cupping my cheek.

"You okay?" he asked softly.

"Yup. Shrimp one, Vivian done." I turned around to snuggle into his chest. "You turn it in okay?"

"No problems. I'm taking you to the doctor tomorrow," he said suddenly. I pulled back a little to look at him in bemusement.

"Why? I'll be fine in the morning."

"It'll soothe both my beast and me. Better safe than sorry, but I'd feel better knowing it was just the cold shrimp and nothing more." He leaned down and rubbed his nose against mine. He did this a few times, but I really liked it when he did.

"Okay, but no needles." He chuckled deep from his chest.

"You'll have to get over your fear of needles eventually," he murmured.

"Well not tomorrow." I warned.

"Okay, not tomorrow." He pulled me closer to his body, throwing his leg over mine.

"Aurora told me about Andrew," I said after a beat, he stilled and then relaxed, sadness coming off of him. " And how you were with him. I wish could have met him." Zaliver didn't respond instantly, as if revisiting memories. I didn't bother him.

"I wish you had met him too, I have a feeling he would have had you wrapped around his finger like he had the rest of the pack. It's a shame he had to leave us so early," he said gruffly, emotion thick in his voice. I squeezed him tightly.

"I'm sure we're ever he is, he appreciates you for letting him win," I said softly. Zaliver's laughter made my whole frame shake.

"I had my doubts about him being Albericus's kid at first, he was to kind and caring, even with his father's looks. But as soon as he won it was like a miniature Alberícus, bragging, declaring victory and rubbing it in my face." Zaliver let out another laugh, but it ended on a sadder pitch.

"I'm glad she told me, it seems like she needed to get it off her chest."

"You surprise me every single day, you know that," Zaliver said honestly.

"Really?"

"Yes, my little cloud, saving the day and interrogating with stealth," he joked. I lowered my hand and pinched his butt. He growled into my ear, but I left my hand where it was.

"Fine." He lowered his hand and pinched my butt, I let out a small noise, but didn't oppose to his hand on my tush.

"You have to turn the lights off," I told him.

"Why me?"

"Because I'm under the blanket, you're just on top," I said smugly.

"Ugh."

He had the lights off and was back in bed but this time under the covers and in the same potion in less than a second.

"I don't see why you complained," I said with a tired giggle.

Now that all the nights were off I felt as if all the days events and the heavy thinking was just hitting me.

"Hmm, you must be rubbing off on me."

"I could rub—"

He growled, warning me. Haha, I felt something poke at my lower stomach. To late.

"Must you tease me?"

"Must you make it so easy?" He didn't respond. But then he pinched my butt and not to softly either.

"I'll have you explain that to the doctor." This time his growl was anything but playful.

"He's not going anywhere near your ass."

"Right." I stretched out my toes. He inhaled deeply and then with hesitation sniffed me. I pinched his butt super hard.

"Stop sniffing me you damn dog or you can go sleep with the rat downstairs." I hissed, opening my eyes to glare at his batman chest.

"Don't call me a dog." He growled, peeved.

"Then don't sniff me like one. I smell nice."

I couldn't help the yawn that came out of my mouth and the little noises I made after. Zaliver relaxed against me.

"Go to sleep."

"No, really? I was going to throw a party!" My sarcasm came on thick.

"You really are tired aren't you?" he asked amused.

"Yeah," I muttered, nuzzling his neck until I got comfortable.

"Then sleep, you can throw your party tomorrow."

"Okay, don't forget though, you're the main guest," I whispered, feeling sleep pulling me deep.

"I'd never miss your parties." His voice was softer, lulling me to sleep.

"I'd know, they're the bomb."

I was close to sleep when I remembered something.

"Hey Zaliver?" I muttered, probably incoherent.

"Yeah baby?"

"You make a hot batman."

I sensed his smile in the dark.

CHAPTER 45

VIVIAN GREY

"Honestly, I feel fine."

"Then there shouldn't be any problems when the doctor checks you."

"He shouldn't have to check me because I feel fine."

"Win-win either way. Besides, Hannah's in the same hospital so—"

"Two birds, one stone. I know." I crossed my arms over my chest and sighed. Honestly, I felt fine.

"Okay then. I'll get the car." A moment later Zaliver was walking out of the front door. I sighed as I went to the kitchen.

Today was a sweats day for me. Loose gray sweats with a long-sleeved black tight-fitting shirt and my hair just piled around my shoulders. I frowned down at some of my strands, my hair was almost close to passing my breasts. I think it was time for a haircut.

Passing by Frank, I decided to switch the Superman cape I had put on him earlier for a green war helmet, he struggled at first like always but let me put it on him. I patted his helmet and sat him on the floor again. I sighed.

Rummaging around the fridge I couldn't find what I wanted, which I myself didn't know, but I just knew I wanted to chew on something. Going to the cabinets next I stared and examined, eyeing my pop tarts and fruit snacks I knew I didn't want sweets, but there was something that caught my eyes.

Reaching in I took hold of it and made my way to the front, making sure to grab my keys and both of our phones. Guy leaves it everywhere, I swear. Guess he loved the pack link more than he loved his phone. Pocketing my items I locked the door and didn't have to wait long for Zaliver sleek black car to pull up. When I got into the car I handed him his phone and buckled up.

When he remained still for the next few seconds I looked away from my snack to look at him. His eyes were locked on my hands, brows furrowed and lips slightly opened, he had a slight frown on his face.

"Are those my granola bars?" he asked after a long wait in silence. His tone made something in me flare up in defense.

"I thought they were *our* granola bars?" I asked with narrow eyes, tightening my hold on the bar just slightly. His eyes and ears didn't miss anything.

"That's not what you said when I bought it," he pointed out, leaning in towards me. Keeping one hand on the wheel, with the other he put it on my forehead.

"You feel fine," he muttered to himself, I resisted the urge to roll my eyes at him and instead softly smacked his hand away.

"Because I am fine. What is so weird about me eating a granola bar? I've never seen you eat cereal, do you see me making faces anytime you're near milk or a box of coco puffs? No." I snapped at him turned to look forward.

I could feel him gazing at me and through the bond he felt worried and confused as to why I was in such a bad mood. With a clenched jaw and another look my way he started the car. He wasn't the only one wondering.

I woke up this morning and immediately knew, it would not be a good day. Like, you open your eyes and even though your gorgeous soul mate is slumbering besides you, you just know shit isn't going to work out today for you. It's like I woke up with a dark cloud over my head. It didn't help that it was beyond an unholy hour, since I didn't want to miss Hannah giving birth and since Zaliver had no problem with going to the doctor early, it was freaking six in the goddamn morning.

I felt bad for snapping at Zaliver when all he was doing was trying to help but that didn't motivate me enough to open my mouth and apologies to him. I'll just make it up to him tonight or later or when I didn't feel like I wanted to punch everything that moved.

Half way through the drive I realized something and thoughtlessly began smacking Zaliver's nearest arm, catching him by surprise and causing him to swerve a little.

"What the f—"

"Stop! Go to the mall or the store-no! Babies R-Us! We have to get the baby a present." I exclaimed panicked, I can't believe we almost went into the hospital empty-handed. Do you know how bad that would have looked?!

Zaliver growled under his breath but changed course. I think, perhaps, my bad mood was contagious.

"Was the smacking necessary?" he asked, raising an amused brow at me.

"Love taps, darling, think of them as love taps."

"I know a smack when I get one," he muttered. A few minutes later we were pulling into the almost empty store parking lot. I haven't been to baby stores often, if at all really.

Even in a bad mood Zaliver was still courteous, he went over to my door and opened it for me, taking my arm and looping it up with his. Feeling calmer I snuggled to his side, he must have felt my shift in mood and did looked down at me and sighed.

"I like your outfit today. Very sexy in a lumberjack kind of way," I muttered into his bicep.

He did remind me of a lumberjack today though, he even had a little scruff on him and his hair was the perfect balance of 'windswept' and 'just rolled out of bed'. He had on dark washed jeans and a white shirt under oath, on top of that he had a red flannel and a light jean jacket with a dark cotton hood attached which he had over his head. I really liked how he tucked his white shirt into his pants, it made the shirt cling on even more to the front of him and outlined his abdomen. A very sexy lumberjack indeed.

"Well don't expect me to go cutting down trees anytime soon.This lumberjack is taking you straight to the doctor after this," he said seriously. I smiled faintly at him, we were nearing the entrance.

"And then you'll cut down some trees?"

"Do you want to see me cut down trees that badly?" He went to grab a cart and was back quickly. I shrugged and looked around.

"It's more of the muscle flexing that I'd look forward to," I confessed distracted. "Wow,they had a lot of baby things in here. It's kinda scary." We were just at the entrance and I could already feel how large and versatile the store was.

"It's called Babies R-Us for a reason," Zaliver said, but by the look on his face he was just as bewildered as I was. "I take it you don't come here often?" I joked, he let out a deep chuckle and shook his head.

"My type of store sells either work out cloths or the latest weapons technology. I don't exactly have motive to come into a baby themed store."

"Point taken."

I just wandered around and Zaliver followed behind, commenting on something that would catch his eyes every once in a while. While I would point out decorations or something cool, he would contrast it with safety standards and persuade me to something better.

"Well she's having a girl, so we can either get her clothing which is what everyone usually goes for or-"

"We can get her something useful that will actually last," Zaliver muttered, squatting down to examine a stroller, a serious and thoughtful look on his face.

"That's what I was thinking."

673

So far we had just grabbed random things and put them into the cart. By random I mean some toys, blankets, dresses, shirts, onesie's, bibs, hats, mittens, a shit load of diapers, a lot of baby health kits and some baby formula. Zaliver had actually added most of the things, including a back up baby monitor with its own monitoring setup system, just in case theirs broke down, a lot of cute headbands, a teddy bear that had me wanting one and for Hannah and Mark he got them both a three-year free diaper hook up. That would probably top it all.

"I don't like this stroller," Zaliver muttered, standing up and looking at it as if it had offended him.

I peeked over his shoulder, I didn't see anything wrong with the dark purple stroller, it had black handles and a dark blue seat for the kid. Looked kinda cute.

"Why? It looks fine to me." I looked it over again, trying to see what the problem was.

"See how the chairs pulled in tightly to the back again and how the straps are? When strapped in-" He effortlessly spun the stroller on one wheel so that the back faced us. "The pole would dig into the child's spine and after a while, I'm guessing this would cause some serious growth problems."

I blinked at Zaliver as he studied the stroller. My mate was full of surprises. A young man with a name tag was passing by when Zaliver called out to him, the guy turned around and did a double take when he saw us.

"Oh, Al—

"Get rid of all strollers like this. Do you guys not check the manufacturing or seating placement? Who the hell authorized this to be sold here? How many parents gave bought this model?" Zaliver didn't even let the poor guy get a word out as he began lecturing, quite harshly, the importance of the safety of the pups being born into our world.

"Y-Yes sir-Alpha s-sir." The kid stuttered.

Luckily, the model was from a new company that after today I'm sure would be going out after Zaliver got a hold of the company's name. Zaliver got the worker to get rid of the stroller and contract the two parents who had bought it, making sure to let them know they could trade them for any stroller of their choice from any price and that it would be on the store.

"Do they just put this crap up without checking the safety standards?" He snarled, a dark look on his face. I patted him on the back.

"At least we know that now all stores will probably be double checking the items they sell out of fear of you going raging alpha on them." I stopped petting him when I caught sight of a cute pair of shoes someone had put beside a crib.

674

"Aw look at these! How long do you think it'll take for her to grow into them?" I said turning around and showing Zaliver, unsurprisingly, he inspected the shoes too. He nodded his approval.

"Maybe a few months, pups grow fast," he commented, looking at the crib beside us. Maybe I should pull him away now before he starts pointing out the flaws of everything in the store and parents get forced to teach the kids how to live in bubble wrap from an early age.

"You said they had a crib right?" he asked me.

"Yup."

"Shame, this one's kinda nice." He tapped it twice and went to stand behind me, putting his hands on my waist. I could tell he did it without thought because he was still looking at the golden painted crib with an interested look. I smiled.

"Hello, do you guys need any help-wow." Both Zaliver and I turned simultaneously to the voice of bright-eyed girl.

She's one of those. My wolf grumbled out, half awake half asleep.

One of what?

The "I can actually function hella early" one. The ones that have no problem rolling out of bed, that only need one alarm to get up. She's one of them. She ranted softly and then sort of lost conscious. She was sleep again.

Well okay.

Bright blue hair pulled into a ponytail and a sweet looking face looked wide-eyed at me and Zaliver, her mouth parted in surprise and a look of excitement.

"Oh, hello," I said, behind me Zaliver nodded at her and looked back at the crib. He sure did like that one.

"Alpha, Luna, it's a pleasure to have you here. So, um-" I frowned at her flushed face and eager as well as curious look.

And then she looked down at where Zaliver's hands were and point-blank stared at my stomach like she trying to call up her x-ray vision.

Oh.

"Oh no, nothing like that. We're here for a friend." I couldn't help the flush that came over my face, behind me Zaliver leaned in and looked from the girl and to me with a curious look. He had missed her look, but he hadn't missed my reaction. He narrowed his eyes in question but I turned away and walked up to the girl.

"So we've bought some things for a newborn baby, but what do you think is the ultimate gift we can give, besides free diapers?" I asked her, crossing my arms over my chest.

The girl looked momentarily disappointed and then surprised as she blinked at me.

"You're asking me? For my opinion?" she whispered. The Luna in me couldn't help but see the aura of bright yellow and green around her. Yup, she was one of those.

"Well yeah, you do work here right?" I smiled softly at her, amused.

"Yes! I totally do, we'll okay, I see you guys have bought a lot of the essentials and the good stuff. My friend recently had her baby and I was surprised to see that a lot of parents don't know that they can buy pup insurance here instead of waiting until they come of shifting age—"

"I'm sorry but did you just say that you can get insurance for your pups?" I asked bewildered.

"Yes?" she asked unsure of my reaction.

"I made a policy where you can get your house ensured from all damage done by young pups from ages twelve and up. Kids have nasty tempers and bad control, I got sick of the amount of repairs having to be sent over to the pack house for that. This is faster and efficient. Not to mention, parents don't throw big fits over how much money that have to spend on repairing and instead can focus on teaching the pups control," Zaliver explained, looking away from the crib and around us.

"Oh, that does sound good. Wish my parents knew about this, would have saved me from being grounded as a kid." I shook my head, Zaliver grinned at me and looked down, pullin gbn out his phone. I turned to look at the girl- Bridget, that's what her name tag said.

"So can we get that for them as a surprise now or do they have to sign some legal documents? Because then it wouldn't be very surprise-y," I asked.

"Well, I mean, the standards are that the parents have to come register and bring some papers," I deflated a bit, she picked up her talking when she saw this, lifting up her hands. "but since you guys are, well, *you*, you don't have too! I'll go get the papers, I'll be right back." She legit, sprinted out of sight and was gone.

I turned around, he had moved off to the side, speedily typing on his for a moment.

"That's really smart, I would have never thought of that," I murmured, walking over to Zaliver. He looked up and put his phone in his jacket pocket and shrugged, pulling me into his chest and wrapping his arms around me. I hadn't noticed how cold this store was until wrapped in his toasty warmth.

"Just doing my job and making life easier," he said humbly, burying his nose in the crook of my neck. I snaked my arms under his jacket and around his waist.

"You're a good Alpha, you know that?"

"I try."

676

"And you succeed."

"Not always," he whispered sadly. That didn't sit right with me.

"Nobody's perfect, I gotta work it, again and again 'till I get it right-"

"I should have seen something like that coming." I nodded.

"You really should have." I grinned against his chest, being in his arms made me feel a bit sleepy.

We stood there for a few seconds in each other's company, in the middle of Babies R-Us until I shivered. And it wasn't a small one either. Although the gasp that left me was mainly one of surprise, it sounded way worse than it was. Zaliver pulled back to look at me with a wild and panicked look on his face, looking me over for any visible injuries.

"What's wrong? Vivian? Tell me what hurts?" he repeatedly asked, his hands going up and down, over my body as if making sure I was still in piece. I shook my head.

"No, I'm fine-"

"You are not fine," he said in a flat tone.

"I am, I must just be colder than I thought, but seriously, I'm good."

"We're going to the hospital. Now." He was already beginning to pull me away from our shopping cart, but I grabbed it and pulled it along.

"We have to pay for this first and then wait for the papers," I reminded him.

"I'll have someone take care of it, we're going." I dug my heels into the floor, he probably could have just pulled me along with him but I doubt he wanted to just in case he thought my arm would pop off or something.

"Vivian, you obviously aren't well-"

"We were going to the hospital anyway. A few more minutes won't hurt anyone and I think we should let the doctor decide if I'm well or not. But personally I feel okay," I pointed out to him.

I readjusted my hold on the cart. I'd run out with it if it meant I could take it to the hospital, but I'd be damned if I showed up empty-handed and with a cute little baby to stare at me with eyes that would one day ask "so what did you get me aunt Viv?"—yes I know where not related by blood but I've claimed that kid already.

Zaliver looked down at me with a storm of blue in those eyes that showed every emotion his face wouldn't. It would just be a few more minutes, I tried to plead with my eyes. His face went soft as he cupped my face, I grabbed onto his wrist with my free hand, he brought out foreheads together. We didn't close our eyes.

I can't lose you. he said though the link, his words catching me off guard.

You won't.

How do you know? he asked, a certain vulnerability in his words that made me tighten the hold I had on his wrist. I smiled up at him with all the love I had.

I can only be lost if I'm not with you.

"*Five minutes, no more than that.*"

While he drove to the hospital with glances my way every few seconds, I tried to fit as many items into the present bags be bought. Some things were just not going to fit though. So I put a bow on those bitches.

"There, all done," I said in triumph. He didn't even have to look at me to ask me.

" Did you put who it's to and who it's from?"

"Fuck. Pen? Pen? Where's a pen? Gotta find a pen." I started looking around the car as if a pen would magically appear. Zaliver must have been made up of magic because he pulled one out of nowhere.

"Thanks."

"No problem."

When we pulled up into the hospital, I wasn't surprised to see Luke and Country outside for us to help with the bags. Mila and Johnson were probably inside. I was getting ready to turn left with them when Zaliver grabbed my upper arm and pulled me to the right.

"What are you doing, they're going that way!?" I knew myself, I wouldn't be able to remember the way to her room and even with their scents, trying to track them in a hospital would be a pain with all the chemicals. Hospitals were the worst place to track someone and the best place to lose someone.

"Did you forget?" he asked me disapprovingly.

"No, but I want to be there when the baby's born."

"You would be in the waiting room with the rest of them."

"I know, but it's the waiting part that's the best in situations like this. Everyone is all 'Is it out yet?!' I like it." I pouted.

"They're getting her ready right now, so if we hurry it up, you'll probably be in there, waiting with the rest of them in no time," he reasoned.

"Fine. Let's go see the good doctor." I groaned and let him lead me to the room.

We were in a standard room with plain walls and a paper covered bed. Nothing fancy. There was only a nurse in the room when we arrived, she did the usual things; took my pressure, weight- way nicer than the last time my weight was taken. When Dr. Leandro walked in he took one look at Zaliver's impatient face, said hello and got straight to it.

"What seems to be the problem?"

"There is no problem, I feel fine-"

"She threw up last night. She says it might have been because of cold food, but I'd like to be sure that was all." Zaliver interrupted. I sighed.

"Was that the first time you've thrown up Luna, or has this happened before in the last couple of weeks?"

"First time and probably last time, I've learned my lesson. Heat it, then eat it." I nodded, Dr.Leandro tried to stifle his smile when he looked back at his clipboard.

"Uhh, have your menstruation cycles been on time?" he asked a bit awkwardly.

"They've been on time," I answered quickly, move on, move on! Wait.When was the last time-

"Any allergies?" he asked without missing a beat.

"Kiwii, but I haven't been in contact with any," I stated.

From my side vision I saw Zaliver shift a bit on his feet.

"Have you been on any medication or a specialized food program?" I shook my head.

"Hmm." He frowned at me. "From your previous doctors notes it mentions your metabolism being slower than a normal werewolves but is it safe to assume after your shift, that it has changed?" At the mention of that my face soured but I nodded.

Dr. Leandro wrote something down on his clipboard and put it down on the chair behind him. And motioned for me to step forward.

"Can you sit on the bed please."

With heavy feet I walked over and did as he asked, ignoring as he fussed over me and just looked straight at Zaliver who watched the good doctor with careful eyes. His eyes lingered where the docs hands touched bare skin, which he had to do to take my pulse.

Under the hood, the blueness of his eyes stood out a lot. I studied his profile, how wide his shoulders were and how his jacket was a size bigger fitting him nicely. If I wore it, I would without a doubt, wear it as a blanket. My eyes lingered on the sharp edges of his jaw and the way he stood. His stance was firm and masculine, very militant. Both of his hands were in the pockets of his jacket. When my eyes went back to his, I realized he was focused on me this time. I gave him a lopsided smile. He didn't return it.

Hmm, he was really worried.

"Well-" I looked back to Dr.Leandro who was putting away his light after nearly blinding me with it in the eyes. "Your pulse seems a little accelerated, but other than that you seem fine-"

"Ha! I knew it!" I said victoriously, getting ready to hop off of the bed.

"But I'd like to be absolutely sure so . . ."

We probably would have left a little faster if he hadn't pulled out some needles.

"You just said I was fine!" I cried out. Dr.Leandro gave me a worried look, brown eyes flickering behind me to where Zaliver stood, blocking the door.

"Luna, I promise to be quick about it, but this is just a last-minute test to make sure everything is absolutely fine," he responded quickly, needle in hand.

I didn't just hate needles, they made a sense of dread and unease fill me. The thought of something poking through my skin and taking blood out was just, wrong. I looked over at Zaliver with big eyes. He bit his bottom lip before answering my plea.

"It's going to be fine." He walked towards me and took my hands in his. I resisted the urge to punch him in the face and run to the door. He'd probably find me in the waiting room anyway. "I'll be right here, you know the pain is mainly in your head," he said.

"Fine, fine," I mumbled, taking my hands out of his and rolling up my sleeves.

Three minutes later I was humming happily.

"That wasn't so bad," I confessed. Dr. Leander smiled down at me as he closed the little blood bottles.

"I'm glad you think so Luna, we should have the results in an hour or two."

"Good. I want a personal report from you, if we're no longer here, call my personal number." Zaliver ordered, doc nodded and grabbed his clipboard before leaving.

"Come on! Let's go." I took Zaliver's hand and pulled his out of the room, passing the startled doctor and going the hall where we split up with Luke and Court and then realizing I didn't actually know where they were. I looked around.

Zaliver caught me off guard when he leaned down to kiss my forehead and took the lead, he must have known where they were at.

"I have to be somewhere-" He pulled out his phone and checked his phone. "in half an hour, but I'll try to stick around as long as I can."

"Got a meeting or something?" I asked looking up at his back.

"There's been a disturbance in some of the packs, I've tried contacting the alphas but I can't seem to get a hold of them," he said seriously, looking over his shoulder down at me. I frowned.

"Has that happened before? I mean it's not like they can just block you like a phone call right?"

"No, they can't."

That didn't seem good.

"I hate to be that one person that points the blame for everything at your brother but the timing seems a little suspicious to me. You don't think him and Fate have something to do with this?"

"I haven't ruled it out yet. I'm having Albericus deal with it for the time being but even he's out of his depth. The betas in the other packs seem to have no knowledge as to where their alphas are." By his tone he was not happy about this and would have a serious punishment for them when he got a hold of them.

Rogue alphas? That was not a good thing, this could lead to pack chaos and wild wolves were dangerous wolves.

"What will you do?" I asked. He ran a hand down his face and let out a breath of frustration.

"Whatever I have to do," he answered ominously.

Before I could say or even ask him anything we turned the corner and found Luke, Mila, Court, Johnson and his parents in the waiting room, pacing. When they caught sight of us they rushed over and informed us of the progress.

"She's been in there forever, how long does it take to-"

"Johnson, not one more complaint from you. Your sisters giving birth, be happy I gave birth to you. Big headed baby." His mother shushed him. Johnson shut his mouth and reached for his hair to pull on a blond curl.

"Not that big," he muttered before taking a seat, Mila rolled her eyes and went to go sit with him, holding each other's hands and whispering among one another.

"We've put the presents in Hannah's room for when she gets out." Luke informed us. He wore a light blue shirt and black pants, looking like an average wolf instead of the serious guard that I've seen. The others also wore normal clothing. After a while Luke's sister Leslie, the twins Drake and Blake showed up with backpacks and panting.

"We came as soon as we were released from class, Angela is still trapped but she said she'll come as soon as she can. Has she had the baby yet?" Leslie asked around.

"Nope, still inside," Court answered, me and Zaliver were standing a little away from everyone, he had his arms wrapped around me while my back to his chest. Although he was quiet, I could almost feel that mind of his plotting and communicating with wolves around the world, so I stayed quiet and let him be.

I'm not sure how long we waited for, time seemed to slow and then speed up randomly and during the most mind breaking moments. I wasn't the only one growing impatient, but I was apparently the only one hiding it. Zaliver must have felt me fidgeting because he mindlessly calmed me down as he traced random patterns on my lower stomach.

Babies were so cute, it was hard not to be impatient when you just wanted to hold one and watch it look around in wonder and curiosity. That reminded me.

"Have Hannah and Mark picked out a name yet?" I asked, breaking the silence. Hannah's mom looked up with a watery smile.

"They decided on Jayda. That was my mother's name," she said, I smiled.

That's a nice name. Zaliver said in my mind, startling me a bit because I thought he wasn't paying attention. I should know better by now, he's always paying attention.

It is. Jayda. I repeated the name.

I couldn't have held in the shiver that came over me even if I knew that it was coming. Zaliver pulled away and removed his jacket and had me put it on. I was right in guessing that I would wear it like a blanket, I had pull the sleeves us multiple times. He turned me around and put loose strands behind my ears. I'm drowning. I joked, but my joke seemed to have fallen on deaf ears.

I can't wait until we get those results around see what's going in with you.

I wrapped my arms around his neck and pulled him down to kissed his nose.

If you keep worrying you're going to get stress lines and I don't want to have to give you age remover creams for another few years.

His lips thinned as his eyes narrowed unhappily.

I'm serious, Vivian.

I am too, I'll love you stress lines and all but still, if I can prevent it I will. I gave him a goofy grin that I knew he wouldn't be able to resist. I knew it was the right thing to do when he rolled his eyes and kissed my nose.

We don't age so no age marks.

Good to know.

It seems to take forever but the doors finally opened and out walked out a tear-stained Mark, a smile that reached his eyes and spoke more words than anything. Seeing his face must have triggered something in all of the girls because we all busted out crying tears of joy.

"She's alright, they're both alright." he said, his words thick.

Cheers and joyous exclamations were heard in the room as everyone jumped and down and hugged one another in happiness.

"I'm an uncle!"

"We're grandparents!"

"She's the cutest thing I've ever seen, she has my eyes!"

Hiccups left my mouth as I thought of the cute little green-eyed baby girl snuggling in her blankets.

682

"Congratulations to both you and Hannah, we wish you the best of luck on your long journey." Zaliver said behind me, rubbing at my back to calm me down"

"Mhmm w-what he s-said," I managed to say through blubbering lips and blurry eyes"

"Thank you." Someone said, not sure who because I wasn't really paying attention anymore.

I wondered when we could see the baby. It seems I wasn't the only one with the thought because Hannah's dad asked, his voice a little deeper with emotion.

"So when can we see her?"

"In a few minutes, they're transferring Hannah to her room and checking Jayda," Mark answered, his expression entirely ecstatic when he said his daughter's name.

Babies, they bring us all together. My wolf wailed, my beast patting her and wiping at her own eyes with her other paw.

It was a comical sight to see once we knew we could see Hannah and Jayda, everyone filled the once large room. Hannah's face was tired but radiating joy at the little bundle in her arms wrapped in pink. Everyone was fussing over the two of them, commenting and asking if they could get them anything.

When the baby was in Johnson's arms it was pretty comical. He got all teary-eyed.

"Are those tears big brother?" Hannah asked with a fond yet teasing smile. He looked up from Jayda.

"Ugh no, I think I'm allergic to your baby sis, that's it." Contrary to his words he was making faces at the baby and kissing over her face. Mila stood besides him, cooing quietly.

"Really, you're blaming this on allergies?" Mark asked him, shaking his head in disbelief, holding Hannah's hand. I noted that his other hand was in a bandage. Ha.

"Really. I'm sure the Luna will agree with me. Here, you'll probably-"

"Wait—"

"be as allergic as I am."

And then the baby was in my arms.

I've never really held a baby so I was scared I might over do it with my strength when Johnson put her in my arms, but it was as if I had done it thousands of times. She was a good weight and seemingly asleep, but her mouth was slightly parted and making little huffing noises. She had an odd combination of Mark and Hannah's hair, not completely dark but not completely light. It had to be the prettiest of browns. I could feel myself softening as I held her.

"No, I don't think she's allergic," someone said.

When I looked up I meet with deep and never-ending blue. I smiled at him. He looked down and with a finger, carefully stroked the baby's face, with a look of wonder and curiosity.

We both held our breath as the baby's eyes fluttered open, definitely Mark's eyes. She blinked a couple of times, making a face before I saw one of her small arms reach out, her tiny hand wrapped around Zaliver finger and grasped firmly. It was heartwarming.

"Well hello there," he whispered, low enough that even Johnson and Court who were the closest nearby probably didn't hear. "I'm Zaliver. It's nice to officially meet you Jayda."

I gazed up at him as he gazed at her and I found that the sight before me and the feeling of the moment moved something within me.

Have you ever lived in the moment? Like actually lived in the moment and knew you were experiencing something that you'd relive in your memories because that moment. . .that moment meant something beyond words or your own comprehension? That's what this moment felt like for me.

But all moment have to end at some point and time and mine ended a few minutes later, bursting my bubble. Zaliver was in the middle of a conversation with Hannah's dad when his frame tensed, his eyes got a glossy look and just as fast as it came it was gone, but in its place was a dark look that had everyone who heard his sudden cut off, step back.

"Excuse me," he said flatly, quickly walking to the door, he looked at me as he passed. "I'll talk to you later."

I wanted to stop him and ask what had happened but now was not the time, I wouldn't ruin this happy moment so I just nodded and gave an apologetic smile to the others. Knowing that Zaliver was running around trying to solve a problem that wasn't even on this island gave me a bad feeling with even worse thoughts. It was a bit harder to go back to the mood of earlier, the happier, light and cheerful mood and it seemed the other knew that because I felt as if I held baby Jayda the most. Bless them, they were too kind.

Rather than staying in the hospital all day with the close family, I decided thirty minutes after Zaliver left to also leave. I did try to sneak out of the room, but Luke caught sight and offered or more so, demanded I let him take me home, so with a quick goodbye to everyone and giving both baby Jayda and Hannah a quick peck on the cheek I left.

"Sorry I had to pull you out," I apologized.

"It's no bother to help you Luna, it would be shameful of me to allow you to find your own means of transportation," Luke said seriously, but a spark appearing in his usually serious eyes. I guess babies really do bring out different sides of people.

When Luke drives me around we usually have a large, black SUV, but I was pleasantly surprised to see that his personal car was actually a blue truck that showed years of usage. Like the gentleman that he is he opened the door for me and then went around.

"Where to Luna?" he asked me, pulling out of the parking lot.

I wanted to go home, but at the same time I didn't. I just felt like I needed to be somewhere. What an odd feeling. It probably had more to do with me wanting to be more of assistance to Zaliver but not really knowing how to help.

"I'm not exactly sure," I said truthfully. He looked at me from the corner if his eye, a look of concern for whatever he saw on my face but made no comment.

Luke was always like that, while the others soon learned that I didn't care if they voiced their opinions, Luke was a bit more conservative and cautious. It made me wonder if he disapproved of me somehow or if that was just the type of person he was. I mean, he was respectful and all- don't get me wrong, but lately I've questioned how I've spent my time and I guess an outside opinion from someone who's been around me and seen me here could shine some light.

"Hey Luke, do mind if I ask you something. You don't have to answer if you don't want to."

He frowned but didn't say anything, waiting for me to speak. He wasn't heading towards the house, just driving around until I tell him where to go. I thought of a good question that could represent or at least get a satisfying answer, but let's be honest. Most question never fully get answered because most answers are never the ones people truly want to hear.

"What do you think a Luna represents?" I asked slowly.

"I am correct to guess that this is a self-evaluation question?" he asked without missing a beat. I smiled faintly, feeling my face warm but nodding either way.

"Well that's a hard question to answer-"

"Because I'm your Luna?" He chuckled and shrugged his shoulders.

"There's that, but no. The thing is, all Lunas bring something different to the table because, I guess you can say they're all eating a different meal in different places. Just like one can bring a fork, another can bring a knife or a spoon," he said, his brows furrowed in concentration as he stared ahead. His metaphors were very intriguing and yet easily comprehensible.

"Is someone hungry?" I teased. He flushed but continued his explanation.

" What I mean is that just like a mating bond there's a certain type of balance needed between the two partners. While some people might say that Luna's bring peace and hope to a pack others might say that they bring strength and a strong will to succeed. There is no wrong or right answer as to what Lunas bring, there is only the hope that it's what the pack needs the most."

I sat back in my seat and pondered over his words, letting them sink in.

"What do you think I bring then?" I asked without looking at him. He hesitated for a moment but then sighed.

"I'm not sure yet and it's not exactly my place to say, but just like all good things, it takes time to know one's self-worth and limits. But I'm sure that whatever you bring, will be what the pack needs, not wants." I felt the clear honesty of his words fill the car and swirl around me peacefully.

So just like all good things I had to wait and see what exactly I could bring to the table. His words seemed to settle in right with me, this was a good place to start, I knew that. Before I could go around making promises or voicing anything, I needed to know what my limits and ideals were. I felt as if a little of the self-doubt and fog I carried around with me fade, there's a difference between being confident and showing confidence.

What type of Luna did I want to be recognized for? As Luna of all Lunas I had a lot of eyes waiting for me to mess up, but also to see just what I was made up. I took a breath.

"Thanks Luke, I think I needed to hear that." I had to hold in laughter when I caught sight of his shoulders relaxing, the grip I hadn't noticed he had on the steering wheel loosening.

"As long as I was helpful and didn't step over the line."

"Don't worry about it. Life might be hard but it would be a lot easier with blunt truthfulness and an open mind." The words came out of my mouth before I even fully comprehended the thought. But then I really thought about them.

"I think I'm ready to go home now Luke, if you don't mind."

"No problem Luna. No probe at all." He made a sharp left turn and began driving to the house.

I thought about my words thought out the ride home.

Blunt truth and an open mind.

Huh.

~•~

I had Zaliver's phone. Or better phrased, I had his jacket where he had placed his phone in.

I didn't realize it until I was already inside the house and looking for my keys. Stepping through the open door, I took the phone out of the pocket and was about to mind link him when I was startled by said device. It was ringing.

686

Looking at the screen I read the collar ID. Dr.Leandro. My results were ready, even though I already knew what the doctor was going to say, 'perfectly fine, nothing to worry about, your mate was overreacting, here a cookie'- maybe not the last part.

"Hello?" I answered quickly, before he thought there would be no answer.

"Hello Al-oh. Luna? Hello," he quickly corrected himself. I hooked my keys on the wall and took off Zaliver's jacket, setting it down carelessly on the couch like a huge blanket.

"Yeah, he's not around at the moment. Are you calling about my results?" I asked opening the fridge, in search of something to drink. My tone came off partly smug, ready to be proven right.

"Yes actually—" The doctor's voice took on a certain tone that made me straighten up. Did he sound excited? Was he also happy that I was right? "About your test results, I'm pleased to announce that you aren't sick at all—"

"I freaking knew it," I muttered under my breath, accidentally cutting him off.

"Well yes, what, we'll the thing is Luna that after looking at your results I can see that you-"

There was a beeping sound coming from the phone, blocking out whatever Dr.Leandro had just said. I frowned.

"I'm sorry can to repeat that? I didn't hear you," I asked, pulling out a soda.

There was a pause before he seemed to start talking but the same beeping interrupted him. Confused I pulled the phone away from my face and saw I- Zaliver had an incoming call.

"I'm sorry Dr.Leandro, but can you give me a moment. I'll be right with you." Without waiting for his reply, I answered the incoming call.

"Hello Alpha, I'm here to inform you of the blood results from the knife you gave us." A females came through, she sounded a bit frantic.

Today must be result day. My wolf said factually. Both her and my beast probably felt as curious as I did about what would show up.

"So what did you get?"

"Hello?" I asked after a way too long pregnant pause.

"Luna?" The woman asked almost uncertainty. I felt annoyance and something unpleasant build up at that. What other female would answer the phone for Zaliver? Not wanting to blow up on the woman for no reason other than my own unjustified thought, I inhaled through my nose.

"Yes," I confirmed through clenched teeth. A sharp and stinging sensation in my left hand informed me that I had squeezed the

687

soda can so hard it had cut and spilled over my hand. I released the reshaped material and shook my hand of the sticky substance.

"Oh I'm sorry Luna. I-I . . . is the Alpha around you somewhere, I had to report something to him immediately. " From her tone it was urgent.

"No he isn't." I walked over to the sink and turned the water on, washing my hand and then turning it off and drying. "But I am."

By her silence I could tell she didn't want to tell me, I proven right when she next spoke.

"I can call back later—"

"Or you could tell me."

"Luna, I'm not sure if I'm allowed to—"

"I'm the one who stabbed the man. You won't get in trouble for telling me. Now talk," I said, pushing all the authority I could into my voice without sounding straight up rude. I quickly cleaned my mess up and began heading up the stairs, passing Frank who was just making his way down the stairs with a soft "thump" every time he landed.

"Alright, I'm sorry. After receiving the knife and analyzing the blood we've come to a rather disturbing findings," the woman whispered, her voice shaking only slightly. Something disturbing? About Joshula? Why am I not surprised?

"Disturbing how, exactly?" I asked, opening the door to the room and closing it behind me. No one but me was home, so I didn't have to worry about Joshula hearing what he probably already knew. That nobody trusted him in this house. I was removing my shoe when she informed, exactly how disturbing.

I barely made it to the bathroom to throw up.

When I was partly done I put the phone back to my ear, wincing at the sound of the woman's frantic pleads for me to answer. I felt Zaliver's attention about to focus on me but I knew he didn't need this, not this moment so I threw my shield up as quickly as possible.

"I'm sorry, he's doing what?" I whispered, feeling as if my stomach was about to force everything or the little I ate back up.

"Luna, perhaps it wasn't such a-"

"I'm fine, but what do you mean?" The tone in my voice was firm enough that she knew I wouldn't let this go, but if she had known what I looked like, pale faces, a thin sheet of sweat dampening my skin, brown eyes wide and watery, she would have put her foot down so firmly on me not knowing that I wouldn't have tried to argue as hard. She sighed before repeating what had disturbed me so greatly.

"We found the trace of twelve diseased wolves in his DNA, all twelve on file of dying of natural causes but of not being claimed by family or friends. Upon a closer inspection, I realized that there was something abnormally wrong about the blood sample. No cells were functioning and we're all dead or disintegrating, normally they would be normal as we regenerate, but in this case the cells would die and remain without growing new ones."

I shut my eyes and scrunched my face, feeling an oncoming headache from the back. This put on a new meaning of dead man walking.

"So let me see if I have this correctly. There's a...man, possibly going around eating the remains of dead wolves, who are decomposing on the inside?" I asked in all one breath.

"Yes, pretty much," she confirmed nervously.

"Well, thank you for the information. I'll pass it to the alpha as soon as possible. Have a good day." And then hung up on her and emptied the remainder of my food into the toilet. When I was done I leaned my back against the cold stone wall and looked and the ceiling.

"A cannibal. He's a werewolf cannibal. You couldn't have made his ass vegan or something?" I choked out.

Well, I guess this explained a lot. The lack of appetite, his late nights out was probably him grave digging or in this case feasting. I guess you really couldn't bring back the dead, you could raise them and bring the consensus back but- something, a question struck me. How was it exactly that Zaliver and I got to be immortal then? Why wasn't the same magic used on Joshula? Or was it?

That moment when you realize you should have asked way more questions in the beginning. My wolf tsked, but it lacked her humor as she realized the very bad situation we were in.

Zaliver had said I would become immortal as soon as he turned me and seeing as how I survived death by tree branch, he was right. But I didn't come back starving for dead things. Did Fate give Joshula a beast? I hadn't noted, but my frame shook on the hard floor, with weak legs I pulled myself up to stand. Mother Luna would have had to help him, but would she be apart of something so twisted? Would she subject her wolves to be disrespected and degraded even in their death's? As Luna I knew that I would do everything in my power not to let anything happen to the grave sight of a fallen wolf, even in death they were still part of the pack, so I seriously doubted Mother Luna would care less than I.

Quickly brushing my teeth and splashing cold water on my face in the hopes of regaining color-nope, I bent down to pick of Zaliver's phone when I remembered it had not only hung up on the girl from the lab but also on Dr. Leandro.

"Shit." I debated on whether I should call him back or not, he had said I was fine but it seems like he wanted to add more. I quickly called back but it seemed destiny was not on the man's side because as soon as he picked up Zaliver's phone died.

"Great. Freaking great." Grumbling, I looked around the room.I shook my head and went to go look for the man's charger. He never charges it. Ever.

At the moment ,I knew that I needed to get the information I had just gotten to Zaliver and while I could do that by mind link, I didn't feel like being alone with the knowledge and possibility of Joshula coming back. It was one thing knowing too lived with a crazy possessed man, it was another knowing you lived with a crazy possessed man who ate your people.

Rushing down the stairs I took them two at a time and was putting on Zaliver's jacket when I whirled around at the sound of moment. Think of running from the devil and he shall appear.

That's not how it goes. My wolf gulped, eyeing Joshula, ears flattened against her head but canines ready.

Joshula stood behind me with the calmness of still winds, but the eyes of a cold killer. I couldn't hide the sudden skip my heart did but I could hide how much it truly terrified me to be in the same room as him. I didn't stop putting the jacket on, but my movements were to tense, to stiff to play off. I also knew that I didn't exactly look happy to see him, or happy in general. I couldn't explain the need in me, growing and begging to leave. Fight or flight. I wasn't going to ignore my instincts.

"Hey," I whispered, clearing my sore throat. Green-blue eyes took me in, there was a slight movement but enough that I involuntarily flinched. He saw that and narrowed his eyes on me with suspicion and something else that had the blood in me cooling.

"You don't look so good Vivian," he stated clearly, taking a small step toward me as if to check on my temper. I held my ground and shrugged.

We probably look damn delicious to him right now. My wolf growled.

Now was not the time, I ignored her.

"I'm fine. I'm going to the store, want anything?" I lied. The only thing I was gonna bring back for him was my mate.

"No thank you. Are you going accompanied?" he asked, casually leaning on the sofa beside us so that it brought him closer to me. I put my hands in my pocket. They were shaking. I had not force my breaths to look calm and not as if I were running out of air.

"I'm meeting my guards later on. Why?" Stepping back, I took one hand out to quickly reach for the keys but also kept my eye on Joshula. I was very close to the door, but I needed a few more inches to get to it and I couldn't just sprint off. He'd know something was off and would no doubt chase me. After all, whatever percentage wolf he had, we always chased.

690

There was gleam to his eyes that reminded me that of an indecisive animal that didn't know if it wanted to continue to play with its meal, or tear it to shreds already. I hoped he was ready for a brawl, because that's what he would get it if he tried anything with me.

"Well, have fun," he encouraged, his eyes boring into mine. I turned to leave.

"And Vivian?" I felt the hairs on my neck rise as if his words had been spoken beside my ear. I felt a shiver make its way my spine. I quickly looked behind me to see him in the exact same place, but the corners of his mouth were lifted a bit.

"Yes?" I asked stiffly.

"Say 'hi' to Zaliver for me. I felt as if we haven't seen one another in a very, very long time."

"I will."

He stood up and with a grace of years of practice he stood up and seemingly made his ways up the stairs slowly, his arms behind his back and he whistled a tune that made everything in my body scream out 'wrong',there was something very, very wrong here. As he moved up the stairs my eyes seemed glued to his back, for a moment my vision swayed and I saw double but when something sharp bit me I looked down.

Frank. He had bit me. Not thinking twice about it, I picked him up, put him into Zaliver's front chest pocket and ran like I've never ran before. Away, I just had to get far, far away from that house, where he was.

He knew.

There was no way he didn't know.

He knew.

And suddenly I didn't care anymore what Zaliver was waiting for, a signal, a threat, but Joshula or Fate or whatever they wanted to be called knew. And I wanted this whole mess done. This was no longer just a game to me, whoever is in our house was no longer just a theoretical threat.

He was a threat and I wanted him and this whole mess done with. I could feel it in my body, the wrongness of his presence, the iciness of death surrounding him and the way he seemed so happy to play a part that no longer fit him.

I was done.

I didn't know where I was running, but I just knew I had to put some distance between me and the house. I clung on tightly onto the front of the jacket, I could feel Franks little claws digging into the material of the jacket as his heart speed up. He didn't have to see to know I was going way too fast, but I couldn't just leave him there.

I had to find Zaliver.

I'd never been to his office-office. The one where he does his personal training or meets up with his advisers or what not. He also has three offices. The one in the pack house, the one at home and the one I was running towards at full speed. The one that looked like a very large cave with armed wolves patrolling and with cameras positioned everywhere.

There were a few surprised shouts as I blurred past all of them and straight into the cave, following Zaliver scent, I came to a shaky stop in front of two large wooden doors. Panting a bit I looked around and leaned against the harsh cavern wall, with shaky hands I took Frank out of my pocket. I would have set him down if I wasn't afraid of him getting lost, so I just held him to my quick beating chest. Zaliver must have not only heard of my arrival but also sensed me because not even a full two second later the large brown doors burst open and he came out, worried and confused. Seeing me by the wall he rushed over and took sight of me, he kneeled down in front of me and put my face in his hands.

"What—"

"Eating them, dead people,already in the ground. It sick, we can't just- I can't. Zaliver- please we have to—" I couldn't form proper sentences, my words were coming out to fast and my throat was to sore, my voice was breaking with every word.

I was breaking with every word. Tears were making everything blurry, so I blinked them away but more would come out, they streamed down my face as I shook him his hands. There was an odd noise echoing in the cave, it sounded wounded and frightened and scared.

"Hey, hey Vivian. Look at me. Breathe."

Zaliver's words were commanding. It didn't affect me right away, but my wolf listened and that was what got me to realize that those broken and fearful echos were mine.

Through my tears and blurred vision all I managed to see were his eyes, focused on mine. As I was submerged in my fears and worries, all I felt was his warmth and comfort. It took a few minutes but after a while my breathing slowed and so did my tears. He wiped at the remaining ones and stared at me with anguish and worry, but also relief and a desperation that showed how deeply disturbed he was at my pain.

"What is it?" he asked.

"The results—" And so I told him about what I was informed, about my theory on Joshula having some type of beast, of how he acted when I left and I watched the emotions come over his face like a flooding lake. Shock. Abhorrence. Shame. Hurt. Numbness.

Anger. Fear. So many emotions and yet it was the last one that made me shake in his arms as they tightened on my shoulders.

As the blood rushed to his face in anger he took a shaky breath which showed me exactly how his canines just pushed from out his gums in a way that looked excruciating, but that he showed no sign of pain. His lips pulled back slightly as he bared those canines. The blue in his eyes didn't even darken, in a blink they went from blue to complete black, expanding over his pupil and over his iris. His expression had lost whatever softness or warmth I had grown to love and recognized.

It was like he was a completely different. Zaliver and I didn't know how to deal with him.

"Zaliver?" I whispered.

There was no answer. My heart seemed to slow, I felt Frank push himself further down into my chest as if he felt the change in the atmosphere. It was as if he were frozen. He didn't move. He didn't blink and he wasn't even breathing.

"Za—" My surprised scream was drowned down by his roar of anger. Both of us jumped back from one another for different reasons.

I jumped back because he was scaring the hell out of me and he jumped back because he was losing what little self-control he had over his shifting.

Zaliver dropped to the ground harshly, landing on his hands and knees but repeatedly hitting the dirt ground with his fists so many times that it quickly became stained with his own blood. He let out roars that shook the cave, that made the wolves nearby retreat and that made me put a hand over my mouth in surprise or fear, I wasn't sure. His whole body shook violently, tremors taking over his body as his muscles rippled an tensed in preparation to something he must have fought.

He didn't want to shift, but he was so overcome with emotions that his body didn't want to handle them. He was overwhelmed. My heart reached out to him, but my body was frozen. My mind wanted to help, but my feet could not move. How? How could I help him when I was so afraid to go near him? But why was I afraid? I knew he wouldn't hurt me. At least not intentionally. I was his Luna. He was my Alpha.

A memory. A solution. I was remembering how this all started, in the tunnels with my cousin Lily. Her Luna had given a command. A command that had over ruled her Alphas. The command of a Luna, not a request, but a command, could over power her alphas.

I could do that. I had to at least try. But what would I say? What could I do to make his pain go away? I swallowed hard and lowered my hand as watched the love of my life twist around the ground in fury and the agony of a forced shift. His face although the perfect mask of maliciousness and murder, could not hide his ever-growing sadness and shame. Zaliver wasn't a bad guy. He just had a really bad start in life that had gotten him into positions where he had to do what he had to, to survive and this was one of the cases.

For no matter what my mate said or promised, it still twisted his soul to know that once again he would put down his brother, even if it truly was not his brother. Because just like everyone else, Zaliver had a dream. And all he wished was for his own family, to be able to have his past and his future to coexist together. And right now, it was crushing him, knowing that he would never have that dream.

I lowered myself to my knees, letting Frank run far away with the knowledge that I would have to look for him later and slowly made my way over to him, flinching every time his growl sounded particularly nasty. A thin layer of black fur had started spreading over his smooth skin, his nails had grown look get and sharper as like the wolf men from movies, he clawed at his chest, bringing forth blood. I felt sick but inched closer. Not like I had anything left to puke.

When I was close enough to him I reached out and then had to stop as one of his clawed hand wrapped itself around my wrist. It was neither painful nor pleasant.

"No! No!" He spit out through clenched teeth, roughly pushing my hand away. I knew he probably did it to protect me, but the small act of rejection hurt, but I pushed through. I'll be damned if I let him go though his pain alone.

I had to be careful with my words. I could either help him or make it worse. Here goes everything.

"Zaliver. I know it hurts, it's okay, I'm right here for you. You don't have to hold your pain in anymore baby, you can let it out."

I knew he could hear me, but I needed to know if it was working so I hesitantly reached out. He snarled, but didn't push my hand away from his damp locks. He was burning up.

"I'm not going to say I understand what you're going through, so I'll tell you how you might have lost one brother a long time ago but you gained another through Algebra. You might be his Alpha and he might be your beta, but I've been in your head, I know how much you care about him, even if you don't say or show it. You might not be related by blood, but blood doesn't always make someone your family.

"I know you're sad about being the last of your family, but hey, we can make our own family one day and since we last forever, we can even have our own little fan club. I say fan club and not soccer team because those are a lot of players. I'm so sorry you have to go through this again Zaliver, so sorry you can't just have everything you want and have everyone not think of you a some over power alpha when all you do is care about people and their well-being. They've never really seen your self-worth, but I have and I'll be damned if I don't get everyone to see that. "

It was safe to say I was crying again, but this time they were silent tears. Zaliver had calmed down thankfully, but his body still shook. I added as much power as I could to my next words. My command. " I need you to let yourself feel without holding it in, there's always going to be pain and I don't want you to go through even more just because you bottled it all up. You need to go into this with a clear head and heart because . . . I couldn't function if you get hurt Zaliver. I won't. Just let yourself feel it."

And he did.

He didn't cry. He didn't shout out his pain for the world to hear. He also didn't maul at himself to let it out though physical pain.

No, that wasn't my Zaliver.

He stilled on the ground, my hand pushing his damp locks away from his forehead as I let him work through whatever he was feeling. After a moment he sat up,making my hand drop onto my lap. Shirt torn and bloodied, eyes slowly retreating and fading back to blue, fur disappearing and claws retracting along with his canines, he sat up and stared at me with vacant eyes. I stared back with worried eyes. Brown and blue. And then I was in his arms.

No words were exchanged. They weren't needed. He had none to say and I had no more to give. We were just Zaliver and Vivian. One for the other and the other for one.

~•~

Venom looked odd on-screen. That's what I had first thought when I stared at the pale man on the screen. He also looked uncomfortable. Was my second one.

It was more of a "I hate technology. Let it burn to the ground" kind of look.

Really? I thought it was more of a "I hate whoever invented technology because back in my day" sort of look. My wolf argued looking at the golden eyed man. I squinted and after a moment had to agree.

After both Zaliver and I had calmed down he took my into the room he had left so suddenly from, turns out he was in a meeting.

A meeting with some nice look men. My wolf added not so silently. I noted Zaliver's brow twitch just slightly. He definitely heard that.

There were three guys on three very large screens. There was a dark-skinned Asian werewolf with dark eyes and awesome hair called Fern, Venom of course looking good in white as always and a chocolate-colored man with one gold eye and one black eye who I was told was called Lexero the lion. Mhhhhm, my man had some nice friends. I felt Zaliver's eyes on me.

Without looking at him I snuggled deeper into his jacket/blanket in his chair.

I'm skimming the menu, not ordering.

He glowered at me. His friends had all been really friendly when we were introduced and then got really serious when Zaliver growled, except for Lexero. Yeah, he would smile at me every once in a while he would wink a golden eye whenever Zaliver scowled at him. It was nice to know Zaliver had more friends, even if it peeved him to know that they were eye candy. Like I said, there's nothing wrong with skimming the menu as long as you don't actually order.

Algebra was actually on call, Zaliver had sent him to the nearest pack with a missing alpha, wanting to know what was going on. So far Algebra had one confused seventeen year old alpha kid, a suspicions beta, one uninformed pack and a missing power couple. Yup. Both the Luna and the alpha were missing.

Zaliver said he could feel them but not pinpoint their location or even communicate, which was the biggest problem here. We didn't know if it was a case of bailing, fleeing, quitting or just a tired couple saying 'fuck it' and taking a vacation. Zaliver was royally pissed and for the sake of the couple, I kinda hope they had a good reason as to why they don't deserve to die together.

"It makes no sense, they left all of their clothes home, no suitcases are missing, they didn't withdraw large amounts of money and they were last seen taking a stroll. That doesn't exactly scream 'were going away, see you soon', now does it?" Algebra's voice filled the dark room which was only illuminated by the screens.

It was interesting how each screen background for every one sort of expressed them. For example, Lexero definitely had a roof over his head, but not walls. Around him all I could spot was vast land of brown, oranges and dark shaded greens. Fern...I didn't know if he was in a dark club or if his room had some weird flickering light because every so often a shadow would move behind him, he appeared aware undisturbed by this so I didn't mention anything. Venom however. His was a bit tougher. I didn't know if I was staring at a really white wall or if everything behind him was just so clean it shined. The man was a fan of clean and clear, that was for sure.

"Perhaps they borrowed money from someone so that they wouldn't be traced by their own money," Lexero theorized, looking behind his screen at something that made his eyes narrow in warning, a child's squeal was heard before he looked back, a smugness in his eyes and posture.

696

"No, I've checked all bank account of everyone in this pack, so many goddamn papers, and not one person checked out a suspicious amount of money that would alert any red flags. Unless you count a Mr.Midson, but I honestly just think he's bribing his daughter's teachers not to say anything about her being the one who set fire to the gym, but in her defense I would be mad to if I had to wear those ugly ass uniforms—"

"Albericus." Zaliver snapped, his eyes closed as he took a calming breath.

"Right. So other than that, no over the top withdrawals or loans that would last for two high-class werewolves," Algebra ended seriously.

"Would you like for me to dig deeper into the matter Alpha?" My eyes went to the dark computer screen, Fern had offered his mysterious services. From what I had been gathering the last hour is that he was who Zaliver went to when he wanted answers, be they real answers or action. He was that one shady friend who had questionable hook ups that you took advantage of when offered but didn't really want to know how it really went down.

Zaliver cupped his jaw and stayed quiet, thinking for a moment before shaking his head.

"No, I have something else for you. I'm going to send you a list of names, I want you to go through their lives for the last six months and find any connections that they might have with one another. If you find nothing, then feel free to send me anything that's corrupt or good enough for blackmail. I don't care what you have to do, but find a way to locate the missing Alphas and Luna's on the list, use our satellites if you have to," Zaliver ordered.

Fern nodded once in understanding. That's a lot of work for one guy. I almost felt bad but there was just something about Fern that made you feel as if none of your secrets were protected, especially if they were online. Black eyes gazed over me for a moment, I think he tried to smile, I gave my own small smile back.

"Lexero, when you have time, I'd like you to—"

"Let me guess, track the rogues in my area to see if they've been up to anything suspicious like say, kidnapping alphas?"

Zaliver glared at being interrupted but nodded anyway. Lexero's eyes gleamed in excitement and mischievousness.

"Anything for a friend." He saluted. Zaliver turned to look at Venom screen. Venom as always was silent and as still as a statue.

"Venom." Zaliver said in a quiet voice.

"I know." A hissed response that made me believe there was something up Zaliver's sleeve. Venom computer screen flickered and then went dark. Very ominous.

697

"I've fished up here, what do you want me to do next Alpha? Go to the next pack? Check out their situation?" Algebra asked through the phone. This time his voice had lost the humorous edge, he was a lot more serious. I looked over at Zaliver who was reading something, a type of book. He was flipping through the pages quickly and looked to be searching for something in specific.

"No, I want you to head for the following packs; Morsto, Aleinta, Krezo, Quzun and Sofro . Those are my main concerns right now, their packs have a tendency to be wild and chaotic even with their alphas. If we don't find their alphas in the next twelve hours I want you to initiate Beta Control and rerank them."

Wait. He didn't mean . . .

Algebra went quiet. "Are you sure?" Zaliver didn't even blink at the question, focused on whatever he was reading.

"My job is not to locate and keep watch over pups I've ranked as Alphas, if they are not found within the next twelve hours they will be stripped of their ranks and then sentenced for a punishment fit for those who bale on the job." His words came out in a snarl, displeasure coming off of him in waves.

"But what if the reason they've disappeared was not by choice? Something out of their control?" I asked him. He didn't disappoint, looking up there was a feral look in his eyes, not directed at me but just in general.

"If they can prove it, they can have their rank back. If they deserve it. But if they can't and don't ..." He sneered and shook his head, letting his words trail off in a clear statement.

I shuddered. Zaliver was not to be messed with today. In all of history, *all* Alphas had never been stripped of their rank at the same time, but then again they all haven't gone missing.

"Keep this in the dark until further notice, I don't want pack revolts or brawls breaking out. The last thing I need is everyone fighting it out in hopes of becoming the next Alpha, they would kill one another. I want to remind you of Beta Jaredson, Albericus." Zaliver said looking over at the phone, as if knowing that the growl was coming. Which it did.

"Please tell me you're replacing that bastard and not making him alpha."Algebra growled darkly. My brows raised at this, I've never actually heard of Algebra growl at another person that wasn't playful.

"Unfortunately for you, no. However, you know you still outrank him so don't let him pick a fight, I need you working, not fighting. I don't care who throws the first punch. Inform him-get out. That's it. Do I make myself clear?"

"So just to be clear, you don't care who throws the first—"

"Do I make myself clear?" Zaliver's voice rang through the room, and I saw Fern flinch a little while Lexero looked around as if pretending not to listen.

"Yes, Alpha. Anything else?"

"No, I'll be telling all Betas to keep the packs under lockdown and monitoring, that should help somehow." Zaliver said that last part to himself.

It was interesting to see what Zaliver was like when it came to being Alpha, since I was never fully around, it helped me know what he was mostly responsible or in this case, what concerned him as Alpha. It sort of made figuring out what as a Luna I should be worried about. And at the moment I knew what I was worried about.

"What about the Alpha children? The ones old enough to talk- will and what about the younger ones? Someone's bound to notice a the lack of parenting. You also can't just strip their titles. They didn't do anything." I pointed out. Zaliver blinked at me as if remembering that some wolves actually had children and that they also needed to be taken care of.

"Right," he said after a moment and then looked at me seriously. "What do you want to do about them?" he asked me, catching me off guard. I didn't actually think he would ask, I just wanted to remind him of the kids.

"Well . . . they are the kids of the missing Alphas. Someone should question them to see if anything seemed off about their parents lately. Kids are bound to notice when mom and dad are breaking normal routine, they might have seen something that everyone else overlooked. No one really pays attention to kids because no one thinks they're paying attention. You might learn something you may not get off of a computer or bank records." I said quickly.

Zaliver looked at me approvingly before turning back to the phone.

"Did you get that?" he asked Algebra.

"Got it. Looks like I've got to step up my game, good thinking Luna." He complimented me, I was glad he wasn't here to see my face turn red or I would never had heard the last of it.

"I'll make sure to get someone to talk to and take care of the kids, they've probably already noticed their parents disappearance so I'll get right to it."

He hung up without another word, but since Zaliver didn't say anything I'm guessing he was also done with Algebra. Zaliver looked over at me for a moment before sighing.

"Fern, I want you to also look over any cameras where the missing wolves were last seen, look for any cars or vans with out-of-state licensing, that could be false or stolen. Check out warehouses, abandoned buildings or run down homes that have suddenly had their water or electricity turned on or have been reported to the police of having recent activity in the area," Zaliver said all of this while looking at me.

Fern voiced his understanding and his screen flickered. He probably left before Zaliver could give him anymore work.

"I take it, you'll actually be trying to find them this time, instead of just locating them?" Lexero's voice made us both turn to look at him. He had a slight smile on his face, there was a small figure running around behind him, being chased by what looked- wait, was that a lion?

"Yes. I guess it wouldn't hurt anyone if I started looking instead of just turning a blind eye and moving on with life," Zaliver said through a frown. "You are aware of the fact that your oldest is chasing your youngest?" Zaliver asked. Lexero frowned and turned around before whispering under his breath something that had me blinking in shock. Well then, not all parents disapproved of being chased by a lion it seemed. He turned back to the screen.

"Savanna says 'hi' and that you're expected to bring Vivian so she can meet her godchildren." My head tilted slightly, looking back and forth between Lexero and Zaliver, who nodded discreetly.

"Well alright, I'll leave you two love wolves alone now." The screen flickered, but not before we heard his scream. " Spit your sister out! Spit her out or I will chase you up a tree where you will sleep for the night!" And then an unhappy snarl before the screen officially went dark.

I wonder if they spit her out? My wolf asked, curious. I had to admit that so was I. Wolves usually stayed together and away from different types of shifters or supernatural beings, but when we meet one, we were quickly intrigued.

"You never did tell me how you ended up with the lab results," Zaliver asked me, I looked over at him. He stood across the dark room, seeming to pull at the dark shadows of the room towards him, as if they feed off of his dark mood.

I lifted one jacket covered sleeve at him and let it flop around as I waved it at him.

"You left your phone in the jacket and then you left from the hospital without your jacket," I reminded him. The corners of his mouth turned down, he straightened up and patted himself down as if he would magically find his phone and when he didn't he shook his head.

"It's not like me to forget my things." And then recalling earlier he sprang up. "Did Dr. Leandro call?"

"He did." I held in my smile and looked at him gravely, he must have sensed my lie because his eyes narrowed on me. I rolled my eyes and let my smile show. "He said I was fine." He eyed me uncertainty, I almost felt offended that he didn't believe me.

700

"You're fine? That's all he said? Nothing else?" He didn't seem to believe that I was fine as he looked me over, I resisted the urge to squirm under his probing eyes.

"Yes, that's all he said." Before I accidentally made him wait and then hanged up on him. Twice. I'd call him later on or just go find him at the hospital when I went to go see Hannah tomorrow.

"Hhmm," he said. Uncertainty and doubt filled his side of the bond, directed at me this time

"Look if you don't believe me, you call the guy," I said snappily.

"Fine, hand me my phone." I froze and gave him a sheepish look.

"What?"

"Look, all I knew was that I had to get the hell out of the house and that your phone needed charging so I left it charging on your nightstand," I said sweetly. He sighed and then looked at me worriedly.

"You left it in our room with Joshula in the house?" He seemed as if he were getting ready to bolt but I shook my head.

"Don't worry, I doubt he'd be able to crack the password." I frowned at the thought of him being in our room, he would have to know we'd be able to smell him, it would be stupid of his part to go in.

"What password? I don't have a password," Zaliver asked confused.

"I know, even though you don't have pictures or top-secret messages—" I would know, I looked for them. "I thought you would need one so that you'd remember to at least charge your phone." I declared, crossing my arms over my chest.

"What's my new password then?"

"You'll never guess it," I said smugly. Blue eyes looked at me for a while, I even felt his mind slowly make its way to mine, as if trying to seduce it out of me. I gave his mind a smack.

"Something along the lines of 'I-love-Vivian-for-charging-my-phone-when-I-don't-PS-What-are-you-getting-me-4-christmas' Am I right?" he said, this time he was the smug one.

"Mind seduction, not fair."

"Not my problem, I've got a new password. A long one," he said with a shudder. Ha, all that typing. Took me a while when I had to confirm it.

Zaliver chuckled before his mood from earlier returned. We could only joke around for so long. It worried me that their were wolves out there that we couldn't find. What if they were hurt? Or worse? What if they needed help and were waiting for help? Our help? I didn't want any child to have to be told that their parents would never come home again.

"Good thinking, with the kids." Zaliver's voice brought me back. If I had to say it, he seemed a bit disoriented. I could feel his stress through the bond and while I would comfort him and try to easy it, I would go nowhere near it. He had too many things in his mind and then some. I'd already had my break downs of the day. I was good.

"Why do you think they've all disappeared so suddenly?" I asked him, standing up from his desk chair.

He was leaning over a large table with a map with what to me seemed random pins stuck in but that must have had some type meaning to him. "I don't know." It pained him to say that. He always liked knowing or being able to control the situation and this was not one of those moments. "What really pisses me off is the fact that I can feel them but I can't communicate with them. Every time I try, it's like there's a wall or something," he said through clenched teeth.

"You said this has never happened before. Is it's possible that there are Alpha's and Luna's being kidnapped world-wide, does that mean there's a possibility that there is someone out there blocking you off from reaching them?" My brows furrowed at the possibility, it scared me that it was possible. Who could come in between an Alpha and his wolves?

"And then we have the whole, your brothers feasting on corpses thing. Where would he even find unclaimed bodies from?"

"Do you remember the temple you were taken to when you first were introduced to the pack? Lupus Temple? We bury some of the dead there, mostly the unclaimed," he said blankly. That just made the whole situation a bit more sickening. He didn't even respect sacred grounds.

Zaliver's silence wasn't doing anything to help my every growing questions. As he stared down at the map in thought, I jumped when he suddenly punched a hole in that same map.

"It has to be him. It has to be. But why? What does he get from this?" Zaliver spoke to himself, pacing the floor back and forth, putting his fingers into his hair and pulling on it harshly. I didn't interrupt him, in case he got something, some answer.

From his words alone I knew that he must have talked about Fate.

But how? I'm so sick of so many unanswered questions, remind me why we haven't just confronted the bastard? My wolf piped.

Zaliver stopped his pacing and turned to face me. His face showing an inner struggle, he seemed torn up about something. When at least, he had whatever sorted he walked up to me and took my hands.

"You're right."

I frowned in confusion. "About what?"

702

"I've been waiting for him to do something, a sign. No more. For all I know this is his sign, I won't wait for him to do anything else. To possibly hurt you next. No more." Zaliver said looking down at me, he cupped the side of my face, his hand firm. Bending down he captured my lips with his in a frightening kiss.

It was frightening because it was so full of despair, worry, fear and anger. Of adrenaline, fight and power. This kiss was not a hello, but a promise of a possible goodbye. I responded without thought, but I tried to push as much love and hope as I could into him. He pulled away far too quickly for me. Putting both hands on my shoulders he promised

"I'm going to end him. This ends today." And began pulling away.

There was something wrong. Deeply wrong with this. I entwined our hands, making him stop to look down.

"Last time you did this alone, it didn't work out as well. He came to our home. We're doing this together." My voice came out stronger than I felt, but I let him know how serious I was through my eyes.

He looked at me. Truly looked at me. I could see so many emotions coming through his eyes, could see so any scenarios playing through his mind and so many outcomes. He wanted to protect me as much as I wanted to protect him and he knew that if he left me here, possibly locked up, I'd find a way to him.

Finally, he decided.

"Okay, let's go." He gave my hand an encouraging squeeze and pulled me out of the dark office.

I was surprised to see Frank huddled close to the door when we walked out, I bent down to scoop him up and put him in the same pocket. He didn't put up much of a fuss. His war helmet was very fitting for today it seemed.

I looked over at Zaliver who was already gazing down at me with a worried expression on his face. To make him feel at least a little better I smiled at him assuring him as much as I could. He smiled back but it didn't quite reach his beautiful blue eyes.

~•~

Somewhere deep within the cave, the lights flickered. And then went out.

CHAPTER 46

VIVIAN GREY

As soon as we took off from the cave, we began planning and preparing for anything that Joshula might throw our way. Yet the creeping sensation of missing something vital, as if we were rushing right into something beyond our control never left me. Even the forest seemed darker than before, as if filled with an ominous agenda. So many emotions, so little time and not enough words to express what be needed.

There was something mesmerizing about the way Zaliver was moving, perhaps even my own movement in the moment seemed so to him. Maybe it was the knowledge of what we were running towards. Around us it was just a blur of nature's creation. We were truly one as we ran together in human form, each step one took, it went in time with the others. His eyes stood out the most in this dark and twisted time. A fierce and ever darkening blue. His face was set to stone with determination and calculation. He would not lose, but what would be counted as a loss?

He couldn't afford to. Neither of us could. While we couldn't be killed, it didn't mean that there weren't things worse than death. Besides, death couldn't be completely be ruled out, not with Fate involved and Joshula . . . well, being Joshula.

"Shouldn't we call in backup?" I asked, lunging over a log.

"No. Involving anyone might mean sentencing them to death. Only you and I can handle him."

There was a mental pause from him.

Or at least I hope so. Looking over at him briefly, I saw him grimace before his eyes focused again. "We can't afford to use a surprise attack, I can't leave you with him without the possibility of him attacking you, and you don't have the training to know how to work in a team yet." He was clearly unhappy with that, but I wasn't prideful enough to tell him he was wrong.

It was one thing when I fought Venom alone, and with pure instinct, I knew I didn't know how to fight with someone, especially someone trained. I'd be fighting blind and wildly, I could possibly hurt him more than Joshula. We had to go into the house with a clear, unclouded and well-thought-out plan. Nothing would be overlooked.

"So what do you suggest we do? Head on attack?" I rephrase my question. "Are we aiming to hurt, maim, or kill?" His response didn't take as long as I thought it would.

"The objective is to kill," he said, his sounding detached. I kinda felt bad for asking, but I still had to.

"Are you sure you're going to be—"

"It's us or him. I chose us. I'll alway choose us," he said firmly. Alright then.

"So what's the plan?"

"Keeping him inside and ending him quickly is going to be the problem. If he gets out of the house, he could go on a killing spree before we get to him. I know you said that we're in this together, but I don't know who will be in the house or in his body. It could be Joshula or Fate. Leave him to me, but if you see an opening, go for it." His last words came out tense, as if all of his instincts told him to keep me away from any possible danger.

"So stay clear and far, but if I see an easy kill, go for it?"

"Yes. Under no circumstances are you to shift into your lycan form with him near," he said harshly, trying to make his statement clear. I didn't answer. "If you're right about him being able to shift into his own then I want you to get out of range if you're going to shift first—"

"But—"

"I'd rather him rip out my lungs if it gives you the chance to shift undisturbed. You're at your most vulnerable when you shift. If he gets to you—" He cut himself off with a snarl.

My eyes narrowed as I caught sight of the house ahead of us, we had run as slow as we could while also keeping a good speed, but we were getting close. We slowed down.

"Fine, but don't expect me to just sit back if he starts kicking your ass." He looked over at me with a grin in place.

"I don't dream awake, love."

I would be lying if I said I wasn't afraid or that my heart wasn't pounding in my chest. I could only clench my hands to stop them from shaking, if Zaliver saw, he didn't mention it. As much as Joshula might have deserved what was coming for him, it was against every value as Luna to kill a wolf, even one as twisted as him. But under the circumstances, I didn't have much of a choice. How exactly do you live with ending someone? I could practically imagine me staring out of a window in the near future, just replaying what was going to happen today. Now.

A life. We were still going to take a life, but what would we have to give in return?

"Are you sure about this?" Zaliver's voice brought me out of my daze. I gave him a grim nod.

He studied me, looking over my face for something. I knew my face showed exactly what I felt, it would make no sense to hide what I was feeling from him when he could feel it though the bond anyway. I had no training, no battle skills and absolutely no experience with ending someone's life. Shit.

Thinking about it now, I wouldn't be that pissed if he knocked my ass out with a rock and locked me away somewhere.

But I was hoping my godly strength, wit, quick-thinking and instincts would help. There was also my warrior-trained, killer instinctive, dead set, skill set mate. Yeah . . . he had to be good for something in this. The corner of my lips twitched, making him raise a brow as if he could tell I had just made a joke about him.

"Here's the plan . . ."

It was wild, stretchy and dangerous, but then again, so was what we were doing. Before we got to close to the house he took my hand firmly into his.

"You can still back out now." I shook my head, this time, I was the one to squeeze his hand.

"It's okay to admit you're nervous." I half joked, well aware of the fact that the only nervous one was me. He leaned down and pecked me on the lips far to quickly, shaking his head at my poor choice of words.

"Love you too, baby."

With one last glance of one another, we went home and towards   the   monster   hiding   in   it.

~•~

It's funny, life, I mean.

You can go your whole life not realizing that you might not truly be living to your full potential. Perhaps you've felt as if you were, you had the perfect job, house, car or even family . . . but at the end of the day, just as the moon starts rising and you watch it with an ever-deepening malachy, you might soon see that having a perfect life means having a safe life. No one ever knows who they are when they live in a bubble. Sometimes it's better to pop it yourself, then to let someone else do it for you. After all, it's your life, not theirs.

When I think of everything that I've been through the last few months I can honestly say that they have probably been the best months of my life. Hectic? Definitely. But I would do it all again. I've gained

706

more in these past months then my life before, I don't know where I would have been if I hadn't been taken months back. Would I have been happy? Bored? Looking for a meaningful purpose in life? Working with a forced smile at an everyday job I hated? I'm sure that whatever I would have done wouldn't have brought me what I had today.

Friends. Family. Adventure. Memories. Love.

Sometimes when life gives you lemons, it doesn't want you to make lemonade. As a friend once pointed out, it takes more than just a lemon to make lemonade. Maybe, just maybe, when life gives you lemons, it simply wants you to hold it and appreciate it.

No one appreciates lemons, until they're drinking lemonade.

~•~

Sometimes I really, really hate planning.

Why? Because there's always that person that cancels last-minute and fucks everything up for everyone.

This was one of those moments.

As soon as Zaliver and I walked in through the front door, we knew Joshula wasn't home. The house was empty. Vaquent. Lonely. Call it what you wanted, but he was nowhere in it. As soon as Zaliver realized that he let go of my hand and with a wall-shaking growl began running all over the place like a madman. He knew he wasn't here but I guess it wouldn't hurt to check.

I stood in the living room entrance for a moment, ignoring the sounds of furniture and glass shattering under Zaliver's hands. When something began moving under my hand I carefully took Frank out and set him down, thinking he was going to scurry off like usual but was surprised when he actually climbed on top of my shoe and stayed there. I picked him up again and brought him up to my eye level.

"Now you wanna cuddle and be friends, huh?" I said, lightly patting his nose. He made a sound that sounded a lot like a 'so.' I rolled my eyes, his little nose wiggled around as if he caught scent of something distasteful, big eyes gazed at me unhappily.

"I'm gonna put you in your cage, not because you're in trouble, but because if Joshula's around, I don't want him swallowing you whole, okay?" I wasn't sure but I think my hedgehog nodded. After putting him in his cage and then relocating the cage somewhere, Joshula would never think to look under the dinner table, which by the way, was partly destroyed from one side.

After taking a breath, I put my hands on my hips and looked up at the ceiling. If Joshula wasn't here then he was outside, roaming, a danger to the innocent wolves unaware of the cannibalistic werewolf, possibly lycan, going around. I really hope Joshula was one of those

707

killers that only killed those on his list and didn't just randomly go killing left and right. Since I haven't felt any death's on my end of the pack link, so far so good. It was a help to know he only ate the dead, everyone was safe for now.

Until he starts snapping necks and munching on the dead like people on Black Fridays when they realize everything is cheaper if you get to it first. My wolf said dryly.

I shook my head but acknowledged her reasoning.

Just because he eats the already dead, doesn't mean he couldn't decide on fresh dead meals. I shivered in disgust. Then I stopped. The house had gotten too quiet. Searching around, I found Zaliver in our room with a note in his hand. Sniffing around I caught scent of Joshula.

The positive thing in this? He hadn't messed up or seemed to take anything. Creepy? Yes. Wrong and disturbing? On so many levels. The negative? There was a big shiny sword laying in the middle of our bed. There was some serious dry blood on it too. Just from first glance you could tell that this sword was neither fake or to be played with. The thing had some serious edges.

Pure silver and engraved with detailed markings that I had never seen before, as if carved in old age. The handle seemed sturdy, it had none of the markings on it as the rest of the sword did, but it had one eye-catching adornment that was perhaps more of choice than need. A small stone the color of a familiar blue shade that I would recognize anywhere.

It was small, but it was visible and it left no doubt as to who the owner was. There were no metal frames or bars sticking out around the handle, just the handle. But from then on the handle was the thinnest and smallest thing on that blade, not even the dullest as it had a sharp edge that made the bottom because from the handle and up it just grew out into a monstrosity, longer than my arm, growing wider towards the tip, there were out curved and jagged edges on it. I knew for certain that if that thing got into someone's body and Zaliver yanked it out . . . it would be pulling out a lot more than just flesh.

Ain't no band-aid big enough for that. My wolf whistled.

I don't know what it was about the sword that left a bad taste on my tongue and an uneasy sensation running through my body. That thing was bad news. Focusing my eyes elsewhere helped, so I looked specifically at the note he held in his hands. Zaliver's face which had been flushed with anger before was now paler than normal, yet he wore no expression on his face. Wordlessly, he handed me the paper before I even asked and then looked down at the sword, blue eyes glazed as if he were recalling some memory. It didn't take a genius to guess why there was dried blood on the blade, it was old enough that no scent clung to it to identify the owner, but just by being here I could guess. I read the note.

Neither elegant nor messy, the writing was clear but jagged, as if a pen had not been used, but something with darker ink. I made sure not to touch the actual writing. I wasn't trying to bring a whole new definition to ink poisoning.

> *This game has gone on long enough, Zalivus. Let's end the charade. As you can see I've left a present for you, forgive the mess, but I believe it adds to your character. Would you not agree? Does it please you, the sight of your brothers blood on your precious blade? Does the sight of it open the door of the many memories of the souls that screamed mercy to the mindless beast who slaughtered them? If not . . . I presume it does now.*
>
> *Meet me at the temple. Bring Vivian or I will gladly behead the visitors and any roaming this night and then go look for her myself. If you choose to oppose my wishes then do as you please, but keep in mind that you cannot stop what must happen, my word is law and you are nothing more than the subject of my doing. There is no contingency plan that will save you from what I have already set into motion.*
>
> *It is time we ended this. Fate will not be on your side this time. We shall test that immortality you seem so fond of.*
>
> *Your executor,*
>
> *F or J ? I'll leave the choice to you.*

I reread the note more than twice, not quite believing what I was reading. Be it Fate or Joshula who wrote this, or both, they sure were cocky that they would win at the end of the night. I don't think I liked that. What had Fate done that had already been set to stone? I looked over at the bloodied sword, no doubt placed there to torture Zaliver by the mere sight of it, but did Fate really intend to make him fight with the weapon that had previously ended his brother's life before? That really was fucked up. I felt a growing disdain and hatred grow for the God of Fate. Looking up at Zaliver, I already caught him looking at me with a bleak,almost desolate expression on his face. I walked over to him, placing an arm on his back and gave him a half forced smile.

"Zaliver?" I asked, honestly curious as to what was going through his head. It seemed that no matter what went on tonight, my mate was bound to end up hurt. Be it physically or emotionally, his jaw clenched before he answered, forehead furrowed in concentration.

"This was my pride and precious blade, and with it I took not only my brother's life, but many more before him. How very cruel of Fate to make me end his existence with the same blade, but then again . . . who am I to deny a dying man's wish?" Zaliver turned away from me and started pacing, running his fingers through his hair roughly. My arm dropped to my side.

Looking down at the bloodied and truthfully frightening blade, I could now understand exactly why it took Fate so long to put Joshula's body back together. I had thought it was a jab of the sword, a beheading that did the job. As much as I wanted to completely comfort Zaliver, we just didn't have the time. The fact was that time was not on our sides and people were still roaming around him without the slightest idea that there was a monster loose on the streets.

"Well what's the new plan then?" I prompted, this seemed to have snapped Zaliver out of whatever mindset he was in because he stood tall, brows furrowed as a he began calculating the new situation. Remembering the note still in my hands I quickly added.

"And don't even try excluding me out of it." I waved the note at him.

"Wouldn't dream of it, babe, you're staying with me. He's got something up his sleeve," he said distracted but firmly. Good, something we both can agree on.

It could seem idiotic to do what Fate wants us to do, to go together, but what if by doing the opposite was doing exactly what he wanted? There were too many variables that could make us fall into whatever plan he wanted, why not just go with one and make it the best option?

The only reason for having me tag along that made sense was that Fate would without a doubt try to hurt me just to get at Zaliver, but he said he'd come after me if I wasn't there so there was no point in running, he could hurt anyone around me. Besides, two is better than one in this situation. If Fate wanted to have his ass handed to him then I'd gladly step up for the offer.

"Albericus is out, he's not on the island. Aurora however—"

"Barely stable." I crossed my arms over my chest, fixing a hard look on my face. We weren't putting her at risk, Algebra would never forgive us if she went 'dark side' again. And neither would I if she got injured. Or worse. Zaliver stilled for a moment before nodding in agreement, but I could tell that he didn't like our odds without the witches help.

"What about Venom?" I asked, during the meeting I never did figure out what Venom's job was. Zaliver halted in his steps before frowning, looking torn before turning to look at me. The expression on his face had me feeling as if I too should be conflicted about involving him.

"What exactly did you ask Venom to do for you, anyway?" My eyes narrowed on him.

"With so many Alpha pairs disappearing, I needed someone who would be able to make sure the wrong people wouldn't looking into their disappearances," he confessed, his tone made me feel a bit uneasy. It was a bit too carefree. I blinked a couple of times, waiting for him to finish. When he didn't I pushed myself to ask.

"What do you mean 'the wrong people'?" I asked, not quite understanding. Did he mean the members of the pack?

"Werewolves might function in packs the way they are supposed to, but even we have to play along with human rules. Jobs, school, ID's, social security. If so many people go missing, and these people happen to be part of the small percentage that live in private property which is suspiciously far from civilization? The wrong people start to get nosy. Humans tend to get nosy. Venom has a talent for making sure that doesn't happen," Zaliver explained. I started at him in surprise, my beast was impressed.

Damn . . . our mate has a clean up crew. Made up of one. My wolf choked out. Zaliver nodded. Shaking my head, I focused back on the problem at hand.

"You mean you just ask Venom to make disappearances . . . go away? Unnoticed?" He made an odd expression which had me thinking there was more to it.

"Something like that." I decided to leave it be, I'd be asking about that later if we made it out alive. Or maybe not. I'd plead the fifth if ever asked by official government.

"So will he be able to help or not? Won't we have to get going soon, you know, to prevent neck snapping and stuff?" I said anxiously. I'm so sick of this situation, all this tip toeing. It didn't help that my beast wanted a good swipe or two at Fate or Joshula for hurting my mate.

Feeling a little blood thirsty, are we? my wolf asked, licking her muzzle with her tongue, baring her canines.

I'd be a liar if I said I wasn't.

"I'll call him even though I doubt he'll be able to make it on time, but we still have to get ready. So who knows. If this bastard wants to fight, then I'll give him his fight." Zaliver's eyes darkened to an ominous sea blue, fiercely looking at me before his eyes flicked onto the bed. "And then I'll rip his head off his body without that damn thing." For a flash of a moment, his features turned animalistic.

His words spoke volume about what he wanted to do, but through the bond, I felt his emotions and they were rocky. I think the sword threw him off and probably would continue to do so. I turned to look at it and then back at him.

"You don't need to fight him with it, you don't have to do anything he wants if you can prevent it," I pointed out. He was the

711

strongest man I had ever met and that excluded his lycan form. Hell, if he wanted to he could probably beat Joshula with a bat if he didn't have Fate on his side.

He breathed in deeply before slowly walking past me and to the bed where he reached out with his right hand and hovered over the handle. I watched as the muscles on his back strained, shoulders tense.

"I'm bothered by something," he whispered, the honesty in his words shocking me more so then the words themselves. I felt my heart tighten. Zaliver rarely confesses when something had him off balance, at least, not without me probing first.

"I'd be bothered if you weren't." Outside the wind blew strong, like a ghosts cry against invisible hands holding it down. Zaliver sighed before continuing to talk.

"I'm not scared or disturbed by what I have to do, Vivian," he said solemn, dropping his hand before he turned to look at me.

I frowned not understanding, wasn't that what had him worried? The reason behind his internal dilemma, the remainder of his past actions?

"When you spoke of us back there, of how I had lost a brother years ago and gained another, how we were to be a family in the future, I think you set the piece that hadn't forgiven me about what I had done to bed. You made me realize that I did lose a brother and that I had mourned him already, I had moved on, even when I brought him home. Shouldn't I have tried harder to befriend him? To spend more time with the brother whom I thought I lost? Perhaps I'd known all along that he was not truly my brother, I don't know, but what I do know is that I'm not scared of what I have to do. The killing doesn't scare me."

I went blank for a moment, in all aspects and senses.

"Then what are you scared of?"

"I've come to grips with what I have done years ago, I've come to terms with who I am. But the mere thought of having you there, to see me be the monster I was, it scares me. The thought of scaring you." Lacking humor, Zaliver chuckled before shaking his head, causing dark locks of black hair to fall forward. He looked sad.

"It scares me to know that he's the reason you are in my life and that he can take you away. It scares me to be powerless to protect you, to not be able to control the situation and make sure that no matter what the outcome is you'll be safe. But most of all, I'm scared of going back to everyday life without your love in every little thing I come in contact with."

He turned to face me, bringing his hands to hold my face in an unbreakable hold that was as soft as it was firm. His eyes that so mere moments ago was sad had gained a crazed look as if he were unraveling at the mere thought, it was borderline obsessive and desperate. But most of all it was intense as those eyes seemed to flow impossibly brighter in the dark room. I was as if he were trying to reach into my soul with his gaze and keep me where I was. Beside him. With him.

"For however selfish and cruel I've been in the past, you are the one who brings joy to my old tortured soul. I've been living for far longer than I deserve, but it wasn't until you that I realized that I was not truly living. Even now, I do not exist. Fate says he is the reason you exist. I believe you exist to bring light to this world for which I have filled with so much pain. I am a monster. A man. But for you I wish to only be able to stand beside you and show the world why you are the reason for my existing. I feel as if I'd go back to being the mindless beast, selfish and inconsiderate without you to put me in my place. I don't want to.

I wanted to wake up every morning and remember how cranky you'd be if you actually had to make your own breakfast. To look around any room and know that you'd find a way to make it messy without trying. To take you to the best restaurant and know that you'll always order lemonade to drink because you want to find who makes it the best. I want you to be there with me when I go to talk to some asshole to watch you say something witty to put them in their place. I can't live without you. Not anymore. I wouldn't be able to." He leaned down to place his lips on my forehead, pausing to inhale my scent before pulling away and dropping his hands from my face.

It was quiet as his eyes slowly lost their blinding glow as the silence grew. He scanned my face.

"Say something, you're usually quick to say something," he said, worry slipping through his tone.

"Give a girl a minute to restart her heart will you, damn." I put my head down on his chest and burrowed my head. I hope he wasn't looking for a romantic confession for me back, most of my mind was a little mushy at the moment. "Acting like you didn't just swoon me but knowing you did. I'm yours, I said yes to you. No take backs, no matter what. I promise to love you even if you do end up going rabid dog on him and try to pee on every tree on our way back to stake your claim," I mumbled into his shirt. I felt his arms wrapped around me, holding me close to him.

"I'm glad to hear that, I really am," he said, his tone half dry yet relieved before giving me a squeeze and releasing. Took me a little longer then I thought to pull my emotions in. All this was getting to me and we hadn't even done anything for the night yet. I was going to take a long a nap after this.

I was surprised to see Zaliver turn around and casually pick up the sword. He gripped it tightly in his fist before throwing it up and catching it in his other hand. There was a sound as he spun it in a half circle and then suddenly cut straight. It was what I thought death sounded as he cut the ties between life and death.

"Well, now that you have your life saber, the sword of death and are in a good mood, what do you say we go kick some ass?" I asked sarcastically. That sword gave me the heebie-jeebies. I was gonna sell that thing on eBay as soon as he cleaned it later.

"Not yet, first I have to get you battle ready. If I'm going to take you to a death match, I want to make sure you're deathmatch ready," he said seriously, eyeing the sword he pointed it down at the ground as if to be safe. Yeah, not like the other edges were gonna stop anyone from impaling themselves if they bumped into Zaliver.

Do I feel a slay suit on its way? My wolf cried out excitedly. Zaliver's serious mood cracked a bit as he let a small smile grace his face.

"Yes, there is. I hope you're not hoping for a cape though." He raised a brow at me, from the expression on his face he totally expected me to ask for one. He knew me well.

"A girl can dream."

There was something nagging in the back of mind about all of this. Or better yet, someone.

"Wait, Zaliver, what about Hogan?" Zaliver's whole expression changed, something like delight crossed his face.

"Oh yes, Hogan," he said in a pleasingly calm voice, something which I've learned to recognize as his 'I have something up my sleeve' voice. "How do you feel about putting those interrogation skills to the test." My beast perked up at the sound of this.

"You want me to question your third in command?" I asked, amused. Oh, this was gold. Me and Hogan in a room together, no holding back?

You've trained for this, all those TV crime marathons, all those missed assignments to catch up on episodes. This is your moment! My wolf yelled, cheering me on.

Zaliver rolled his eyes, but held still, focusing on something. Then he refocused on me.

"At the moment, Hogan is at the office. My question is why isn't he with Joshula? Want to know why? Because Fate is done with him, he's put him to usage and no longer needs him. I'd interrogation him myself but, I'm sure I'll kill him before I get anything out of him and even if I want to I still need him alive long enough to tell the next wolf who'll replace him the way he's run everything. "I felt a sense of betrayal and anger come from him, but also a small amount of sadness.

My instincts flared at this, Hogan betrayed my mate, someone who I think he obviously liked more than just what he showed, but the million dollar question was why? What motive?

714

"Fine, I'll have a go at him." I rubbed my hands together and wiggled my brow. Zaliver growled.

"I know he's gay, but I still don't like the sound of you 'going at', another man." He snarled at whatever image passed through his mind. I raised a brow at him.

"Even if said man, probably beats it off thinking about your anatomy way more than mine?" I questioned innocently.

I've never seen a grown man flush so fast before. Clearing his throat and turning away he quickly grabbed my hand with his free one and began pulling me down the stairs.

"Where are we going?"

"To get your slay suit."

Less than five minutes later, I was dressed in some skin-tight suit made of whatever metal Zaliver wore when he came home after the fight. We were quite the pair, him in his tight suit, me in mine, but of course I wasn't not walking out without a little extra, no, I'm not talking about the cape. Apparently my mate was the one to go to for any type of fully stocked closet. Armor? He had it. Fashionable clothes? He had it. Fully stocked weapons? He had it.

"What website do you shop at? GotItAll.com?" I murmured under my breath, adjusting the sturdy light polymer vest. Bring a bullet proof vest to a sword fight, I had a few questions. I braided my hair back away from my face and changed into some boots like Zaliver's. When I asked him why the suit fit me perfectly he simply said, "better safe than sorry." I was impressed and curious. How blood thirsty did my mate think I was if he got me a war suit? I only snapped his neck once. That didn't mean anything.

"Your suit will morph with you if you have to take your other form, there is absolutely no reason as to why you should be stabbed, but if you are and if he is wielding the weapon I think he is . . . then the suit will take a few blows before you'll actually feel anything on flesh," Zaliver explained unhappily before muttering quietly under his breath. "Thank god for lycan healing."

I looked over at Zaliver, who was sharpening what apparently had been a very 'dull' sword. If I thought the sword was sharp before, now it was something else entirely.

"I told Hogan to come down to the base levels of the pack house." He turned to look at me with those striking blue eyes, hair slicked back and out of his way, sword gripped loosely. "Do you remember your, umm, interrogation room?" I felt a flicker of annoyance.

"You mean the room where my mind was torn apart by yours so you could get information you could have just asked me for?" I said snippy. He pursed his lips.

I know what else he tore apart— My wolf whispered suggestively before I cut her off. The smirk that grew on Zalivers face was enough to make me bare my teeth at him. He made the motion of biting me with his own.

"He's headed here now, so we should meet him halfway. Incase he tries to run." I nodded and motioned for him to lead the way. As we walked down halls, around corners and after various passwords, I couldn't help but notice something.

"Indulge me, but why put your . . . questioning room, arsenal and protective closest under the pack house?" We made a sharp right, the cement walls beginning to look somewhat familiar.

"Soundproof building, large amount of space included in the blueprints and tons of witnesses incase anyone ever tries to get past the basement. Besides, people always assume that anything dangerous is kept away from large family areas, so they tend to stay away from large family areas and go look for the building that looks top secretive and well guarded from the outside. The pack house in general is exactly that, but beyond their basement you would need more than brute force or smarts to get in here, it's guarded by the best technology and wolves."

"So what you're saying is, after everything was built you said fuck it and put everything under the pack house because there was extra room? Because that's what I'm getting." He gave me an unhappy sounding grunt as a response. The corner of my mouth twitched.

Zaliver soon stopped at an annoyingly familiar metal door. My ears picked up on light footsteps getting closer and closer. Hogan was going to be here in three, two . . .

Speak of Prada and the devil shall appear. My wolf said in disdain.

We weren't speaking about Prada. I pointed out.

We are now. Coincidence? I think not.

Even for a backstabbing third in command, Hogan was impeccably dressed for what he didn't know what probably his hearing with the lovely judge Future Mrs. Azrala. Soft lilac-colored dress pants that seemed to made of something closely related to silk covered his long legs, black dress shoes with what looked like a silver-covered front tip, a long dark violet sleeved collared shirt which was well put together with a fine fitted grey vest that had frond patterns on it, just a shade lighter than the vest to match. And it wouldn't be completed without the diamond stud in his ear.

Although I was there I'm sure Zaliver hadn't mentioned that when he called him down here, thus his hard to contain eager expression, brown eyes wide and bright, mouth grand and pulled up to show those pearly whites, slipped right off his face as soon as those eyes detached themselves from my mates form to meet mine. He was a moment too late into hiding his total and obviously abhor about me, something which Zaliver did not miss. I felt a spike in the bond from him as well as saw him take a step forward, I grabbed onto his clenched fist before he did something that would make things harder from me.

Nah let him go, I wanna see him backhand Hogan. My wolf growled, my beast pushed forward her agreement.

If he does then he'll be crushed because the guy he likes just backhanded him, and who wants to talk about betrayal when their heart was just broken? I know I wouldn't. I'd close up and mourn my imaginary loss.

I find that I dislike it when your logic gets into the way of my blood lust. My beast informed me politely.

I do too, but when it's time I'll let you out. I promised her.

Hogan, catching our little moment, looked over to Zaliver, whom I know for sure wasn't concealing whatever he was feeling because Hogan's steps slowed and an uneasy expression crossed his face as he tried to give us a sure smile that looked all too strained and out-of-place.

"Alpha, Luna how may I be of service to you?" he asked, notably a few feet from us. Sucker was gonna make a run for it if he had too.

"I find that if I try to speak I might kill him. This is your interrogation my dear, you take the lead," Zaliver said. I squeezed his hand in understanding. I squared my shoulders as I looked at Hogan directly in the eyes.

"I like to think I'm a fair person, so instead of simply calling you a backstabbing third in command," Which I've technically already done. "I'm going to give you a chance to explain anything you want," I said cheerfully.

The forced smile fell from his face as a blank look took over, but the blood loss to his face, the sudden intake of breath or the calculated panic that flashed through his darkening eyes couldn't be hidden.

"Luna, I honestly have no idea as to what you speak of, I would never betray my Alpha." His words came out stiff yet forceful as if he were trying to make me believe it, he glanced over at Zaliver but didn't ask him to clear his name. And wouldn't a guilt free employee ask his boss for clearance? It was only logical.

I shrugged. "Well then as a show of good faith in the justice system and to prove your innocence I guess you'll have no problem stepping into this room." I motioned towards the silver door which Zaliver opened silently. "Your cooperation would be highly noted. I promise." I couldn't quite hide the smugness in my voice.

Hogan stared at the door with genuine fear on his face, his muscular frame seemingly trembling. He lifted his left leg up slowly as if to take a step forward-turned . . . and then ran for it.

717

I let out a 'humph' as I dropped my arms, Zaliver's blue eyes turned livid as the pounding heavy footsteps of Hogan echoed in the cement walls.

"Capture. Not kill," I reminded him before we ran off after him.

Hogan was fast, but so were we and he should have known that. Zalivers furious hulking form appear a few feet in front of Hogan, causing him to come to a sudden stop which almost caused him to lose his balance, I appeared in behind him, I crossed my arms over I've my chest and shook my head.

"I'll take that as a no for cooperating then." I tsked, disappointed.

Hogan half turned to face me with a mixture of emotions that ran from anger, hatred to panic and disbelief. He made sure his back was to the left wall, so he could see if either one of us tried anything. Not that it would matter if he did, I doubt he'd be able to stop it. He was cornered and he knew it. Hogan's eyed me before he began shaking, as if he were about to transform into his wolf. Eyes pinned on me. I raised my brow back at him.

"Hogan." Zalivers voice was so bone chillingly cold and yet field with so much calm rage that even I looked at him when Hogan froze and stopped shaking, he slowly turned to look at Zaliver.

Zaliver's face had gone from furious to something I had no words for, his facial features becoming more pronounced making him look as much beautiful as he did frightening. Blue eyes a shade so intense that looked as if he could kill on the spot, the eyes of a storm. His body which had shaken with anger before had stilled. I'm not sure that was a good thing.

"Your Luna asked something of you, yet instead you run," he said softly yet there was no emotion in his voice. Hogan seemed to want to disappear and yet unable to look away from Zaliver at the same time, as if he were enchanted.

"I-I was . . . I—"

"You were what? Going to shift to attack your Luna?" Zaliver took a step forward, Hogan's heart could be heard pounding against his rib cage, he could have been a professional drummer if he tried. He whimpered and looked down, baring his neck in submission to my mate.

Pitiful this wolf is. Betrays his Alpha and yet can not face him and explain why. My wolf muttered unhappily.

"Now, Hogan," I said, making him lift his face slowly to look at me, making sure his face only faced me he glared but didn't move. "This isn't an execution." Yet.

Hogan's eyes narrowed on me before scanning my body in an obviously way to point out what I was wearing before turning to look at

Zaliver in the same, taking much longer than appropriate, lingering on the monstrous sword strapped to Zaliver's back and then turning back to me to raise and perfectly trimmed brow.

"Not your execution at least." With that I flashed over to one side and grabbed onto his arm and before he could do or say anything, ran us into the room with the silver door and threw him in, locking the door before Zaliver could come in.

I felt his uneasy and unhappiness with that but also his trust and understanding and that was all I needed.

"I'm going to give out orders to clear the streets tonight. Try to be quick about this," Zaliver said, briefing me.

"Now, take a seat or I'll rip your legs off and you won't have much of a choice," I said calmly as if I hadn't just threatened him.

He was a bit disoriented due to the speed I used to get us in here or maybe it was my not so gentle toss, but he found the lone silver chair that sat in the middle of the room on a small platform and took it with unease.

"So that's the deal, he's gone and you're finally showing your true colors," Hogan spat out, both hands gripping the armrests. I remained by the door but stayed quietly and watched him.

"Well, what do you want, me out of the way so you can keep him? Are you going to torture me now? You can try but I have nothing to say. I've done nothing." Although his words conveyed strength, he seemed anything but. To be be honest he looked like a sacred man. No sign of wolf in him whatsoever.

"No. Torture isn't my thing," I said truthfully.

Me on the other paw. My wolf piped up. I held in a chuckle.

"Oh please, everyone in this world is capable of torture. And I doubt you're such a saint, you don't have me fooled."

"Hogan?"

"What?

"Why betray Zaliver if you like him? And before you deny it, don't, I don't care. I'm just curious as to what would be tempting enough." I mean, have you seen the man? He was sex on legs.

Hogan looked away, glaring at the wall in silence. I narrowed my eyes at him, I didn't have time for his silence, but I wasn't going to torture him for him to answer either. At least not physically. Time to put all those crime TV marathons into use.

"I don't think you know how . . . torn up inside you've made Zaliver feel Hogan," I said, pushing sadness into my voice and sighed as if tired of this whole thing, which might have been more true than false.

Hogan didn't turn to face me but I caught the twitch in his eyebrows and the way he leaned his body a bit closer as if saying 'go on'.

719

Everyone who's ever had a crush on anyone can not deny that there's a type of pleasure you get about hearing someone speak about how you impact the life of the person you have a crush on, it's like a sign that they care about you to the point that you impact their everyday life. Like you were meant to be in it. To be with them. I was going to use that against him. Cruel but necessary.

"He hasn't been the same Hogan, you've . . . I don't know, shifted things between us." I began pacing, but made sure to stay a few inches away from him, but I felt his eyes on me as I rambled on. " He doesn't even want to kill you for what you've done, which I don't understand why." Frustration thick in my voice, I turned to look at him with a fixed glare on my face. "It doesn't make sense, you betrayed him, you shouldn't get to live." The last statement came out with a whine.

"Really . . ." he whispered, his voice conveying pleasure at what he was hearing but still suspicious of my words. Good.

"Do I look like I've prepared the room for torturing? Look around you. He wouldn't even give me safety scissors." I made a look around notion to which he hesitantly did. The room was empty.

"You could claw me up without anything—"

"And yet here I stand, blood stain free. Like I told you. This isn't an execution."

Already affected by what he was hearing and seeing, Hogan was less frightened and more sure of himself, his back which had began to slouch was straightening, head lifted higher and instead of clutching onto the armrest he was subconsciously softly tapping on it as he pondered over my words.

I'd turn the chair he thought he would die on, into his throne. In his eyes I was no doubt, losing control of my bond with Zaliver and it was all due to him. The illusion of love could be beautiful but it could always be turned against you. Been there. I hated middle school kids sometimes. Meanest fuckers you'll ever meet.

"You're lying, he seemed as if he was going to hurt me just now." He disagreed but not whole-hearted, he wanted me to reassure him of his imaginary grip on Zaliver. The only grip Zaliver wanted to have on Hogan was by the neck.

He wasn't going to hurt him . . . he was gonna kill him. Small difference really. Not that he has to know. My wolf added hastily.

I crossed my arms over my chest and snorted at him as if thinking him a fool for even thinking Zaliver could hurt him. "He was angry alright, but more so hurt at what you did. He even admitted that he needed you, that you were valuable to him," I gave out a huff, "that he wouldn't be where he is today without all your hard work. As if." I gave him a one over and rolled my eyes. "Anyone can do paperwork, so what if you know the way he likes it." Let him think of an innuendo for that last one.

Technically I wasn't lying, Zaliver did need him for his valuable hard work....but only so he could pass it down to the next person who would replace him. After that, was a whole different matter. Hogan fully turned to look at me, eyeing me with distrust and anger. But there was a hesitant cockiness he couldn't hide. He crossed his arms over his chest, at the same time crossing one ankle over the other.

"And I guess you just expect me to believe everything you say. How do I know you aren't just say this so that I feel confident and just start babbling away?" He raised a finely trimmed brow at me.

Sucker's smarter than he looks.

It makes sense if he's working for Zaliver, you'd need a lot of brains to manage all that man's paperwork.

I did the opposite of his body language and opened myself up for his expectation. Widening my stance and lifting my arms to hold my palms up in a 'what' motion that pointed towards him, scrunching up my face in a look of confusion and opened my mouth a little.

"What . . . oh wait, you mean like tell you what you want to hear to get you to start talking? Isn't that reverse physiology?" I asked cocking my head to the side as if that plan would be a brilliant plan.

Isn't that what we're doing?

Taking in my expression, Hogan turned his head and whispered under his breath, aware of the fact that I could hear him.

"Gave this bitch way more credit than she deserved." I couldn't stop the scowl that appeared in my face but quickly recovered when he turned back around.

"Sure I did, because everyone likes admitting that someone out of their relationship has a much larger impact on their mate then they do," I said with a sarcastic edge.

"That's like me admitting to Zaliver that if I had to choose between having dinner with him or watching Frank make a run for it, I'd chose the hedgehog. Zaliver doesn't wanna hear that shit.

He'd step on Frank if he knew."

These walls are soundproof right? My wolf asked nervously.

Because if they're not, there's a good chance Frank is already under Zaliver's army boots... She trailed off, but not before sending me a vivid picture of what that image would look like.

Taking heed to my words I let Hogan regard them. Zaliver's voice came into mind.

"Whatever you're doing, you're going to have to speed it up," was all he said, his voice not giving anything away.

"Well...I can't do anything about that, if Zaliver believes in...me, then it's with good reason. I've worked for him for many years, loyally, I haven't betrayed him," Hogan said contemptuously after a minute with his own thoughts before allowing a mocking smile to grace his face. As if angered by the taunt I growled softly.

"But you and I both know you betrayed him."

"I did no such thing, you ignorant brat."

Ohh, he's got insults now. A voice growled in my head, I ignored her.

"So what do you call fraternizing and working with Joshula or do you know about Fate too?" I took a step forward and pointed an accusatory finger at him, I made sure to slowly pronounce each negative word I threw at him. "You betrayed Zaliver, you lied and stabbed him in the back, breaking his trust in you—"

"I'M SAVING HIM!" He roared out, but I had already caught him by the tail and I wasn't letting go anytime soon.

"From what?! What could you possibly save him from, a paper cut?" I returned.

"I'm saving him from you! Ever since you've come into our lives, he hasn't been the same. Always rushing to get things done in the office. That was my time to spend with him and now all I have time to spend with is his paper." He snarled out leaning forward as if wanting to pounce on me but still aware that it wouldn't work out for him. But I'm sure that he'd forget that in blinding rage.

"So what, did Fate promise you to erase me off the map and paint a clear road for you?" I asked sarcastically, turning to look away from him.

"Yes."

Well that was both expected and unexpected. My wolf muttered. I turned back to look at him with narrowed eyes

"What do you mean 'yes'? Even if I were gone do you honestly think Zaliver would joyfully go to you, after being a part that played in my death?" My beast was beyond angered at what she was hearing so pushing her back was getting a little hard seeing as how I myself was angry at it too.

"I'd make him forget all about you. As if you were never even there," he said seriously. I stared at him, expecting him to take it back. When he didn't I had to blink a couple of times. Wow, this dudes not joking.

"Sorry to crush your dream but I'm immortal, Zaliver made me immortal. I can't die. He can't die. But you can, that wouldn't work even—"

"That's not what Fate said," Hogan taunted. I stilled at his words, alarm going through me.

"I'm sure that whatever Fate said was a lie, I've died, Zaliver's died. We're still here," I pointed out slowly. I snapped his neck myself.

722

Hogan sat back and shrugged, I didn't like that.

"What did Fate say, Hogan?" I asked wearily.

Hogan turned to look at me as if I were less than trash to step on. I had to resist hurting him a lot more than I thought, but I couldn't stop my eyes from glowing silver in the room. Hogan looked away quickly, but didn't respond. Taking a deep breath I thought of something. Whatever Fate had told Hogan was now top priority because if Zaliver and I went to Fate without clue what he had then we might actually not walk out of there alive.

"Fine." I made it seem as if I were going to walk out before I stopped in front of the door. " but if Zaliver dies it's on you. At least I'll still be with him." Nothing riles up haters more than the thought of you still winning at the end. Before my hand touched the doorknob he spoke.

"What do you mean if Zaliver dies?" I turned to stare at him with a hardened expression.

"What did Joshula promise you? Because I'm imaging that if Fate promised you something, then Joshula had to do it as well. I mean, it is his body that is being used to presumably kill me." Hogan frowned as he listened to me.

"I've only ever dealt with Fate, what does it matter if Joshula promised me something or not? " Interesting, so was Joshula aware of Fate in his body or was he just a passenger, creepy, but innocent of Fates plans? Could we save him? Could we actually save Joshula?

Fuck no, give him the stick. My wolf said quickly.

That is our mate's brother, no matter how creepy.

I know, we'll wear black to his funeral and buy him the best coffin we find. I promise to even shed some tears. She said sassily.

Snapping back, I answered Hogan. Honestly how did he not see it?

"Fate might have promised you my death, but I can promise you Zaliver's death because Joshula will kill him if he has the chance too. He hates Zaliver for killing him, why would he let him live when he has the chance to level the field?" I could see the realization hit him as he inhaled sharply. This dumb ass. How did he not see this?

"But they're brothers—"

"And do you think Zaliver would just let his brother walk away from killing his mate? I mean what do you think we're going to do once we find him, talk about the election?" I huffed, outraged.

Hogan's body began to curl in up on itself as his eyes became distant and glossy. He was going into his own little world. "What have I done? I don't want his to die, I can still save him..." He began talking to himself. That's really too bad, but I didn't have time for his melodrama.

"What did Fate tell you Hogan, you can still save Zaliver if you tell me?" I asked walking over to him, there was no aggression in his body, only shock, fear, sadness and hope.

"You mean, save *you*?" He sneered bitterly.

"Yes, me and him. Because your reality is that you can either damn me and he dies too, or you can save him and accept that it means saving me too," I answered truthfully. "Now tell me what you know." He didn't hesitate to answer this time.

"All he said was that for however many times you died didn't matter if you weren't killed properly. He mentioned something about blood but nothing else." Blood? Whose blood?

"What else, you have to remember something. A specific weapon? A place? Something to—"

"He didn't say anything else, alright! It was just a random comment he said, he was talking to himself more than he was me." He exclaimed, frustrated and panicked. I stood there watching him trying to go over every conversation he probably had with Fate, watched the way his knuckles paled as he gripped the very chair he had feared, listened to the whimpers that soon started to come out of his mouth and watched as his form began to shake.

I think we're done here. I sent to Zaliver.

Come out. If I go in I'll have to kill him.

I turned to the door but not before I said one last thing to Hogan. His eyes snapped up to meet mine and fury took over his desolate expression. I got out and slammed the door at the same time that a full thud was heard as his body slammed against it. Zaliver was waiting for me a few inches away from the door, his eyes narrowed behind me before looking down at me.

"What did you learn?" We started walking, making our way out from there.

"Not much, but apparently Fate was the one Hogan was in contact with, there's a possibility that Fate found a way to actually kill us, I'm a pretty good integrator is if I do say-"

"Fate found a way to kill us?" Zaliver grabbed my arm forcing me to stop and turn to look at him. I grimaced and shrugged.

"Caught that part too huh." He glared at me. "Hogan didn't seem to completely know what Fate meant, but apparently he said something about 'blood' and having a 'proper death'. I'm guessing Fates found a loophole to the whole immortality thing." I rambled. "I mean it makes sense. If you can't die what's the point of fighting. All you two would be doing would be blowing off steam. No one likes a repetitive process."

"I don't like this. In all my years I've had all kinds of deaths. There is no such thing as a proper death, but knowing Fate he has

724

something already planned. Something that makes him think he has the upper hand." Zaliver began walking again, this time his steps were quicker. He was agitated. I tried to think over our situation. Just because I didn't have the fighting skills didn't mean I didn't have the paranoid skills. In an event like this anything was possible.

"Lets see. He wants both of us there with him, he's given you back your sword, he spent a shit load of years putting your brother back together and at the moment there in some freaky fusion with him and Joshula sharing the same body." I counted them off with my fingers. " Didn't you say that you trapped Fate in his own body with some dark mumbo jumbo trick, because you can't actually kill Fate because he's....well Fate? So how did he get into Joshula?" I pondered. I wasn't there so I wouldn't know exactly what happened between Zaliver and Fate.

"It wasn't mumbo jumbo. In a way, the bastard had a part in creating my lycan form even if it was with the help of Luna, he ultimately was the one in charge so I answered to him. In the beginning I was, as he put it a 'mindless beast' because it was hard to think about anything other than slaughtering, winning and whatever else he told me to do." His voice darkened as he continued, I could feel his reluctance at telling me about his first years. "I couldn't control myself but he could."

"I'm going to go on a whim and say that it wasn't a leash that he used on you?" I coughed at the look he threw my way. "So what was it then? Mind control? And don't get offended, house training?"

"No offense taken. It was a bit of everything, but it was more of the awakening that did it. Just like I was the only person around you when you transformed, he made sure he was the only person around me. After a few years my beast learned to follow his orders. Took me a century to stop." I wanted to pat his back but wasn't sure that would be appreciated at the moment. My face scrunched up in confusion.

"That still doesn't explain the whole body sharing thing and what happened to Fates body." I pointed out.

Zaliver and I had made our way out of the pack house, I could immediately tell that while I was with Hogan he really had evacuated everyone away from public areas. It was silent. The whole island was silent. It were as if everyone had gone home and gone to sleep. Eyeing Zaliver I wouldn't have put it past him to give a command like that. To put everyone in a deep sleep. Or on mute at least. He led us into the forest which I would guess would lead to a path to the temple. I felt a sense of worry for anyone who might have been around the temple while with Joshula. Just because I hadn't felt any lost pack links didn't mean it couldn't have happened.

"Fate is the god chance and destiny. You can not simply kill him, for the world would not work. Something the smug bastard knows.

You can however, reset his clock. Every Fate will be the same man, but every Fate born can be raised differently and thus give the man different personalities. This one knew this and has made sure to keep himself from being set for a long time now. It's why I didn't do it myself. Why kill the man who put you through hell and punish his new form? I trapped this Fate's mind in his body to make him relive the sins of this life, I wanted him to boil in his own despicable self. He would have broken after a few years and probably reset his own clock himself. My mistake. This time I'll do it."

"So he basically reincarnates every time he dies and is reborn?"

"Yes, he'll just pop back up in his domain, whichever one he avoided in this life."

Instead of exiting through the front of the pack house like when we came in we ended up in the pack garage where the Camaro was parked.

"What are we doing in here?" I asked but Zaliver ignored me and made his way past the car and toward the back wall. I was about to ask him once more when he lifted his hand, formed a fist and punched right through the wall. Wall plaster, dust, and debris covered Zaliver's arm up to the elbow but he didn't seem to care as he yanked his hand out.

He's hidden something inside of the wall. My beast said, fascinated and curious as to what it could be.

Or maybe he just really wanted to punch the shit out of the wall. I've heard it's something people do to relieve stress or when they're really pissed. My wolf said in a voice that sounded very teacher like.

Yeah, I don't think that's why he did it. I responded half distracted as I watched my mate obliterate the wall before him. She bared her teeth at me in an attempted smile.

It could be. You tried to punch Jorge junior year, missed and punched the wall instead. My wolf brought up before I could stop her. Immediately Zaliver stopped what he was doing and looked over his shoulder.

That was a whole different situation. I added quickly.

"Who's Jorge?" The question came out calmly, not curious. As if he knew he would know soon enough. A nervous laugh made its way out from within me before I could stop it, my eyes zeroed in however, in what Zaliver clutched in his left fist.

"What's in your hand?" I pointed with a finger. He narrowed his eyes and grunted at my change of conversation but answered anyway. Holding out his fist toward me, fingers relaxing to show a...test tube?

Not completely trusting my eyes I walked closer and peered down to get a closer look. It was a test tube. Covered in dust and what

726

appeared to be splotches of dried blood, smaller than Zaliver's palm but as long as my middle finger. Zaliver grabbed it with his other hand and held it up between his thumb and pointer finger, moving it around lightly like he was stirring something.

"Right before I separated myself from Fate I took something of his."

I leaned closer to squint at the tube in his hand. My lips pressed together tightly before I opened them and then closed them. I took a step the left to change the angle at which I was looking at it. After a moment o

looking I had to comment.

"You took his . . . dust?" I guessed. His jaw clenched as he passed his tongue over his top teeth, his chest rising as he took a slow breath. I felt a hint defensive at his reaction.

Well what the hell was it suppose to be? It was a dusty tube that looked to be filled with more—

"Oh, you took his past lives ashes?" At his short nod I leaned back. That thing must have been in the wall for years, it was making my nose twitch and I wasn't usually this sensitive to smells.

"How is that possible? Your holding the ashes of his body, that isn't the one that's still-I'm guessing, intact today. Is he like a Phoenix, born from his own ashes?" I questioned, he maneuvered himself in a way that guided me away from the crumbled wall and towards the exit of the garage with one hand at my back and the other holding the tube.

"In a way, his last death was caused by fire and so his ash was all that remained. If he had died of let's say a broken neck, then his bones would have worked just as well. I could have stabbed him with his own bone but ash will work just as well." I opened my mouth but he cut me off.

"And no, I'm not going to blow it on him like pixie dust."

My mouth shut with an audible snap.

"The downside to this is that the ashes will only work with a fatal blow. His heart or head has to go. Otherwise he might just heal through it. On the bright side a fatal blow will take care of Joshula. Two birds—

"One ashy blade," I muttered.

Zaliver stopped me once we began getting closer to the beginning of the forest. His expression was grim.

"Last chance to—"

"Nope."

A rueful smile graced his face as he shook his head, I smiled up at him and leaned up on the tips of my toes. I wanted to grab him by the front of his suit but because it was molded into his body so tightly I settled by reaching around him, grabbing a fist full of hair and pulling him down to me.

Sound did not fade, it was turned up and explosive around us. I could hear everything, from the distilling of leaves to the quick beating of both of our hearts and better yet, I could hear the way the material that separated our body's were pushed against one another. I did not breathe because I could taste all I needed on my tongue. Passion and love could not be measured but I could trace them with the tip of my tongue. My eyes were clenched so tight that I could see color, but I must have imagined the various shades that all seemed to blend into a familiar blue. Silk in my hands and warmth in my heart, against my body and surrounding me. I made a sound. Or maybe he did. I'm not sure but we both smiled before we pulled away.

Blue eyes glazed and almost hypnotizing, I peeked down to look at his lips and felt a sense of pride to see thin bite marks. Those same lips turned up to a smirk, forcing me to look into the eyes of the owner.

"And what shall I label that as?" His voice came out softer than a whisper, but no less thicker than a growl. I pondered over it for a moment before answering.

"You can call it, 'To be continued in the wake of winning.' Yup, I like that name." I nodded up at him. He pulled me closer to him before kissing the top of my forehead. "This is in no way the ending of us my little cloud."

"Then let us continue on to the hardest chapter then."

Taking my hand in his and giving me one last lingering look we raced into the forest to go kill family and foe.

~•~

It was as if the closer the we got to the temple the more uneasy I started to feel. It wasn't as if I myself was starting to feel physically sick, but as if the air and earth around the temple itself was just out-of-place.

"Do you—"

"I sense it too."

So it wasn't just me, if Zaliver was sensing this then there really was something wrong with this area. That led me to a thought.

"Do you think this is where he came every time he wasn't home?" It took Zaliver a second before responding.

How didn't I think of that before. Or course the bastard would go to a temple dedicated to someone other than himself and then use it to his pleasure. If Zaliver didn't have so much control over himself I'm sure he would have been a large snarling beast by now. But I could

728

see why it would take him this long to figure it out. People don't usually go to sacred places and disrespect them. It's just something most people don't do.

Normal people don't. Vengeful brothers who are being possessed by a vengeful god do. My wolf pointed out.

True.

I hate to admit that there's something to appreciate in the way they planned this. My beast murmured. Her confession almost made me stop running but thankfully I didn't end up tripping over my feet.

What the hell do you mean? I asked disturbed.

They infiltrated our den as a wolf in sheep's clothing, now we learn that they lure us like the prey, which we are not, into their den. A den which we own but do not dwell into because of what it represents. The enemy has mocked and now is ready to release the joke onto us. We are going to be attacked. I do not know by what or who, but this enemy has the courage to dine with us and the cowardice to attack behind or back. They will tire us out before we truly fight.

I didn't have time to feel the horrified realization that she was right. I quickly conveyed the message my beast gave me to Zaliver. It was his response that bothered me perhaps more than the first.

"I've noticed," he said calmly.

Great, apparently I'm the only one not informed. I've got to start reading more. Preferably with 'How to trap a bitch with her own help 101 for dummies' book. We slowed when the first sound of gravel under our boots could be heard. The temple was just as eerily beautiful with its dark and crumbled walls in rusted with sparkling jewels. Whatever remnants of the sun was setting, leaving only a trace of a fading dark magenta that would soon be replaced by true night. Already I could feel my eyes adjusting. It was a shame that all of this beauty was now giving off a sickening feeling.

All of my senses become heightened as my beast and wolf edged closer to my conscience, I scanned in front of me for not only Joshula but anyone else who wasn't him. Dead or alive. The bright side of the temple not being complete was the fact that from where we were standing we could peek into it. From what I could see it looked completely empty, so where was Joshula? Or Fate?

Zaliver's hand tightened on mine, answering my question. I turned my eyes to where his were and felt my lips curl over my teeth in a quiet snarl. I don't know how I had thought they could have been identical before, the only similarity between these two was the fact that they had a sword with them. Where before Joshula had tried to seem quiet and polite, although he was doing so creepily, he was the complete and total opposite. He wore no shoes, no shirt and no pants.

729

No shoes, no shirt, no service. Sorry, just had to put that out there. Ignore me. My wolf said quickly. I ignored her.

Instead he wore some sort of wrap around his lower waist that while it seems sturdy, did not seem to be something he would care very much if it was torn into shreds. As if he wouldn't mind if shifting would destroy it. Chest bare and on display as he breathed, his muscular build was similar to Zaliver, if only by a miniature comparison. An arrogant and wild expression was formed on his face as if he couldn't resist showing his true nature. His lips were twisted in smile that left me uneasy but not as much as his eyes. I had once thought I saw a flash of something in those blue green eyes once. Now, they were in full display. The murky yellow of a calculating coward in full bloom. Hanging almost lazily from his right hand was a sword that could have been identical to Zalivers if not for the face that it was not one bit two swords made to look as one. But I could see from out of all of those sharp edges, where there should have been one there were two ends. It was as if his had been cut in half, where Zalivers had been whole.

He took a step forward and pointed in our direction with his left hand. The sword dragged behind him, giving a brief but clear sound that echoed through the air. If Zalivers gave off the sound of death, then Joshula was the sound of the screams that followed.

"And here we are. The beast, his prize, his executioner and the judge." There was a sadness to me when I heard him speak. Because it was not a voice that belonged to that twisted expression. Smooth enough to lure anyone near Joshula when he spoke softly and yet hate filled and wise in a way that reminds me of elderly people when they gave advice.

When Joshula spoke, he did not do so alone. And that's what had saddened me. If it had been only Fates voice then that would have meant that Joshula was simply a pawn. But if I had made a distinction between the two voices, then that meat that I couldn't be the only one.

Zaliver an only response was to release my hand and pull his sword from his back in a swift motion, his head tilting to the side very slowly.

"Oh come now, Zalivius, you use to be one to boast before doing the hard work. Or not so hard, since you did seem to enjoy it," Joshua taunted, raising a dark brow as his grin grew larger. Murky eyes flickered over to me. I couldn't tell if he was speaking to me or simply doing so because he knew it would bother Zaliver. Which it did. It was like the mirror effect.

When Joshula's eyes roamed over me, I saw Zaliver do a small motion. Whatever I would have missed standing at his side was graciously shown to me as Joshula committed the same motion. At the same time. Twisting and flickering his wrist, the sword spun vertically

730

around quickly until it landed in his tight grip. The two-bladed sword pointing up instead of down like it had been before.

His gaze moved back to Zaliver's, the grin which I thought could not grow, doing so, to the point where it arranged his features to look Jokerish. He hummed for a moment before talking.

"Now, how did I know you were going to do that?" he asked no one in particular. "Could it be because we're 'brothers? No, that can't be. How about because I taught it to you? Hmm, could be. Or could it simply be because I know everything?" Just as fast as the grin was there to bother anyone who looked upon it, it was gone. An equally disturbing sight. "What does it matter how, at the end all that matters is that I did. Just like how I know I will-"

"Are you done with your villainous speech or shall I get a chair and wait until you're ready?"

My brows lifted as Zaliver interrupted Joshula. If anything I was more surprised by the comment because it's something I would have said. Matter fact I was probably thinking it. I guess hanging around someone long enough does leave habits. The corners of my mouth involuntarily turned upward as I fought back a smile.

But it appeared I was the only one who found that comment amusing. Clenching his jaw so tightly I could think I heard a snap Joshula, glared over at my mate.

"What? Not a fan of speeches? Alright. How about the one you gave your mine, before you gutted me

"This time the voice was strongly Joshula. This was actually him speaking now.

"I am getting sick of this. It is not as if you did not fight back," Zaliver said in a cold tone, calmly.

"It is not as if you held back either," Joshula spat out in a growl. Zaliver chuckled. Both Joshula and I stilled. The air grew colder and the wind suddenly picked up, brushing against my flushed skin. I felt anxious for what I knew was about to happen.

"But I did," Zaliver said.

Something in his tone had me turning to look at him, apparently Joshula caught onto it too because he bent his knees as his eyes narrowed. Oh shit. I made sure to move back from Zaliver as he fully turned towards his brother. It's was as if the man I had gotten to met all these past few months disappeared and in his place was someone-something else. This was what Zaliver had feared me seeing. The wild and calculated coldness in his eyes. The way his muscles strained to keep still. Him.

"Oh? Did you now?" Joshula murmured. His eyes tracking Zaliver.

A vicious grin spread over my mates face.

"I left your head."

The roar that followed boomed through the island as the brothers charged for one another.

Right before they were inches from one another Zaliver reached up and smacked his sword, no he didn't smack it. He smashed something onto it. The test tube. The ashes would now cover the blade.

The sound of their blades clashing met my ears the ground shook on the very impact of it. While my legs almost buckled from beneath me, it was as if they had no realization of the impact they had around them. Because they did have an impact. If it weren't for the fact that both my wolf and beast were keeping me completely aware then there was a tremendous possibility just my beast's eyes would have missed the two at the blinding speed at which they worked. A lot of people say watching professionals do their thing is mesmerizing and it's not until now that I understand where they come from. Because that is what Zaliver is. A professional warrior down to his core. But I knew that, that wasn't the only thing that made him.

I didn't know where to keep my eyes focused on or who to keep them focused on. Where one attacked the other blocked, when one advanced the other pushed back. If Zaliver took a step forward Joshula followed with the opposite foot but I didn't need to watch to know that Zaliver wouldn't let Joshula stand between us. I hadn't seen Zaliver fight with a sword during practice but watching him now left me without words. Fate had clearly not been lying before when he said he trained Zaliver. It was as if they were dancing to music only they heard. Joshula ducked, kicked his leg out and spun all in the same breath, trying to swipe Zalivers feet from under him but he easily flipped into the air a few feet away from him.

I had been right. I would have missed the fight completely with just my beast. My eyes still weren't fast enough or trained enough to know what to look for. Now that they were a few feet away from one another I was seeing things I hadn't during the fight. Both of them were covered in cuts, so many in fact that someone of them seemed to have already healed and all that remained was the trickling blood. I scanned Zaliver to see if anything was amiss but he gave off no indication of being wounded.

"We are a bit rusty aren't we brother?" As Joshula spoke his left eye started healing from what looked could have been a nasty black eye. Like before Zaliver did not respond to his chattering. For all of the quick moves and jabs that they did both seemed as if that were nothing else but a warm up. Joshula sighed as if disappointed to the lack of response and then turned to me a sly look which quickly became creepy. We both ignored Zalivers soft snarls. The only warning I got as to who I

732

would be speaking to was the tilt to his chin, the arrogance which over passed the wildness to those murky eyes.

"Vivian. Created solely for bargain. Did you know that when I thought of you we were in a meeting watching as Zalivius tore into people and colored the ground red?" I wanted to take a page out of Zaliver's book and stay silent but that wouldn't be much like me.

After all, no one does petty as nice as I do.

"It's nice to know I had bitches coming together before I was born." I bared my sharpened canines in a smile.

That comment did two things:

turned Zaliver's soft snarls into full-blown laughter,

and made Fate glare at me with unequivocal repugnance.

"Perhaps I was wrong to choose backbone over submissiveness," he said as if his opinion really mattered to me that he was disappointed in how I came out. He waved a dismissive hand in my direction. "None the less your services are no longer needed."

I know I should have been more alarmed by his words but my wolf shoved forward and took over my mouth before I could stop her. My voice deepened and my worlds while harder to pronounce had a sharper edge . . .

"Services? Who the fuck are you calling a hoe—"

"Such disgusting words from a—"

"Try me, you molding piece of shit."

I let her have the last comment before I shoved her out and took my mouth back. I wasn't even annoyed. From the corner of my eye I saw Zaliver eye Joshula. I had a feeling that if he were one-hundred percent sure that throwing his sword would end this and hit Joshula that he would, but if it didn't then we would be at a disadvantage if he did.

"Enough!" Both Fate and Joshula snapped at me. I must have really pissed both of them off because his body trembled just slightly.

"I've got something for you." I positioned my body in a way that felt natural to me, both legs shoulder length apart and knees slightly bent so that I could move quick enough to move if he came at me. Hopefully.

I tensed when all he did was turn to look at Zaliver, expecting him to do something. Zaliver must have had the same thought because he slowly made his way in front of me, even several feet away.

Calm yourself, Zalivius, we have more urgent matters at hand then a foul-mouthed wench. My wolf snarled out the words 'try me' very softly, licking her muzzle as her claws grew out. *After all, you failed to make the connection between me and your missing Alphas.*

We were watching Fate and Joshula carefully. While Zaliver hadn't expressed a deep concern about the missing Alphas I knew that he cared about their whereabouts, they were still parents and had loved one's.

"Oh, I've got your attention now, don't I!" Fate threw his head back and gave out a laugh. And while my wolf sent me the image of decapitation I reminded her that information was first and that was second.

"Unfortunately to keep the flesh on this body together I had to heal and a dead werewolf doesn't exactly have those capabilities now does he? No, he doesn't. And since we don't all start off as cannibals, I had to start off small." A crazed grin made its way to his face as he brought his arms together towards his chest as if he were holding something. I didn't get what he meant until he started rocking his arms. "Well, dead and small that is."

My mind went blank.

Then all I could feel was anguish.

Some part of me knew that he had told us this to distract us, to bring emotions fore front and cause us to react but another part of me knew that right now that could end very badly for us. I looked over at Zaliver for a brief moment. He was a still as stone, but his grip on the swords handle had turned his knuckles bone white. My stomach turned as I looked back at the monster before us. I resisted many urges at that moment, held back the shiver that made the hair on my body raise and left behind a void.

"As my . . . appetite grew I had to switch to bigger meals. And then mhmmm." He let out a pleasurable moan that did nothing but make it harder from me to breathe. "Warmer meals. But not just any old wolves would do since I needed quick healing. And who has the best healing capabilities? Besides you of course. Alphas."

How did we live with this in our home? How did we sleep with this....thing just a few doors down? He ate from our utensils. We could have used the same fork! I had the sudden urge to clean everything. And then do it again.

I felt as if breathing was a robotically thing, but also as if the air had thickened with whatever was in the air.

"You use to be better at hiding your emotions Zalivius. I can see your hatred on your face. It's quite pleasing actually." While I hated the fact that he was looking at Zaliver, I was relieved he wasn't looking at me. I knew I would have thrown up on the spot if his eyes turned to look at me. "I hope you don't mind that I had a few of them, I needed a booster."

The air. It wasn't just my imagination. It was thick. As thick as it would be if a scent was in the air. But . . . there was no scent. My eyes widened as I looked around me. Where was the air thickest? Why couldn't I smell anything? My beasts words made their way into my mind as I scanned around me.

"Where. Are. They?" Zaliver barked out with an edge of a man barely hanging on to restraint. Joshula smiled and the peaked over Zaliver shoulder at me.

"You know, don't you, Vivian?" My heart was beating rapidly in my chest, I didn't think about it, I simply let what was natural come to me. So when my hands morphed to claws and my face felt slightly morphed I didn't say anything. I don't think I could have as I whipped around trying to find where the air was thickest.

It couldn't be. We had been here long enough to know. It couldn't be, could it?

"Where the fuck are they?" Zaliver repeated.

I looked over at Joshula who already had his eyes on me. I could imagine what I looked like, half morphed with round not completely human eyes filled with disbelief and panic. Fate lifted a hand and then as quickly as it came it was gone. A blinding light that once gone, took away the barrier that hid them from all senses.

We were surrounded. And when I say surrounded I wish I could say by what.

Some what in human form with what appeared to be chunks of flesh missing from them, blood slowly dripping out from wounds that looked like canines much larger than a wolf. Others passed the color of deathly white and were moving into various shades of decomposition greens and purples. Some faces were severely destroyed. Chunks of flesh hanging loose and some just hanging from faith that they could be pushed back in. Even hair color was hard to distinguish with all the matted blood and gunk, clothing just as covered. Very few were in wolf form, but those that were fortunately did not look ill or dead. Banged up and bleeding but not dead. Unfortunately once the barrier was gone, so was whatever was holding back the smell of decaying and dying flesh. The stench was strong enough to force the bile I was trying hold onto earlier to come out now.

I turned to the side and threw up to my heart's content, thankfully not as painful as before. I had nothing to give so that was a plus. I hated throwing up alone so doing so with an audience pissed me off enough to get over it. Straightening out I turned back to my original position and then scanned, which made me realize there were twenty or so surrounding us. I couldn't completely turn my back towards Joshula for fear of getting stabbed but I also couldn't just stand with my back to all of the....I'm not even sure what to call them.

Some of them looked alive. Others were definitely not and yet they still stood and stared with dark and graying eyes. If they had eyes.

Well this explains why Zaliver couldn't tell if the Alphas were alive or dead. There wasn't really a 'dead but still walking' feeling he could go on. But how could Fate hide them on the island without us knowing? "I hope you don't mind. I have a terrible habit of playing with my food."

"You sick fuck!" Zaliver snarled out furiously, taking a step backward to get closer to me, but stopping when Joshula took two steps forward.

"Careful there, brother."

"Stand down!" Zaliver yelled out, using the full force of his Alpha voice. I waited for them all to drop, or at least most of them.

Nothing. It was as if their blank faces heard nothing, saw nothing. Were nothing. Zaliver tried again and when it didn't work he let out a warning growl. Some responded with their own. Others simply stared.

"Side note, just like they respond to you, they respond to me. And being dead makes them more mine than yours. Don't you agree mutt?" As if to exact his point Joshula walked over to the one closest to him, a blank eyes female who wore a bloody bed dress, snatched her hand roughly and bit into it. Then tore her hand off and dropped it by her feet. "It's great. They don't even scream. It's like after the first bite they just stop reacting." Chunks of flesh and blood flew out of his mouth and onto the ground. Blood covered his lips, trailing down in a thick dark trail onto his chest as he bared stained canines.

I felt my legs start to shake. At least she hadn't screamed. She didn't even look to know what was going on. My beast and wolf were oddly silent, but I knew they were watching and waiting.

Zaliver went pale. I thought I knew why. We were surrounded by werewolf-Zombies and his Lupus-Zombie-God possessed brother. I'm sure I looked like a goddamn ghost at this point. It wasn't until Joshula spoke that a bit of information from long ago stirred in my mind.

"Vivian—"

"You can fight me. Or you can fight them. You can't do both," Joshula taunted with a pleased tone.

Somewhere in the back of my mind I remembered an argument some kids at school had over Zombies. Some kid asking why Zombies, if they were just humans who had been turned ,could suddenly do things they couldn't before. Like get shot multiple times yet not be bothered by it and the pain shitting death grips they suddenly gained on their preys. And I suddenly understood why Zaliver paled. The undead were immune to pain because their pain sensors were dead. And when you had no pain sensors to warn you that you would get hurt, were in danger or could die, then you were immune and you would go at

736

something even if you ended up ripping your arms off. Not that you would feel it.

And since Zaliver had to focus on fighting Joshula or he and then most definitely I would end up with that fucked up sword in the gut, then that meant I had to fight all the pain sensorless Zombies who, since they were previous werewolves, already had superhuman strength.

"Ahh shit."

"Vivian, he's right. I can't fight them with him still here." He didn't even try to hide the panic or worry in his voice, but I knew that if I looked over at him that Zaliver's eyes would be cold and wholly focused on Joshula.

"I know. It's okay, I'll deal with the ...are we calling them Undead-Wolves? Zombie-Wolves?"

Right now was probably not the time to be giving them labels.

"If I take him out, his control over them should end. If not then just try not to get bitten or scratched by them. He's started some fucking disease for wolves."

"Trust me, you don't have to mention that part."

"I've given my orders. Proceed." Fates voice rang out, seemingly to be the only thing that caught the attention of the Undead-Wolves that surrounded us. At once their gazes brightened a bit, the ears of the wolves twitching to the sound of his voice and their bodies crouching low to the ground with their paws spread out evenly in front of them. Like when they were preparing for an attack.

My eyes flickered to the left of me to see that my suspicions were true when the ones that had surrounded Joshula slowly began to prowl past Zaliver which was giving off an oddly sort of infuriated growl mixed with a snarl and tried to surround me in a tight circle. Like hell I would allow myself to be surrounded.

"How long do you think you'll last Vivian? They have orders to—" Whatever Joshula was going to say was cut off when that same ground shaking echo of two blades crossing met my ears. Joshula's booming laughter filled the air but was quickly cut off by what sounded like flesh hitting flesh and his grunt.

Before they completely close off a circle around me and hoping that the only thing they gained was just strength I ran past the first opening I saw, flashing myself outside of the circle and further, backing away. Contrary to what most TV shows say, the undead were not stupid slow. Or stupid. Some form of tacit must have still been working in their minds because those who were dead had no problems turning around and coming after me. The wolves both undead and alive worked like a pack, forming a line that was going to spread around me in a U shape until they completed a circle around me again. They were trying to surround me again.

"Are you going to shift?" asked Zaliver, his words coming out rushed yet soft. He truly was fearful for me

I fought the urge to look over at him. Walking backwards quickly but turning to look behind my me I caught sight of the crumbling temple and knew that I would need to go inside for higher ground. Not getting one last peak at the two brothers I turned and ran for the temple entrance. Once gravel turned into uneven ground of stone I raced up the steps, taking two stairs at a time and crashed through the doors and ran for the center of the largely crumbled building. I began looking around while I had time.

I thought about Zaliver question for a moment before shaking my head and then remembered that he couldn't see me.

In Beast form, I would be stronger them all of them and just as fast as Zaliver now, but I would also be larger and easier to grab onto by multiple attackers. In wolf form I'd be smaller and would be able to take on human forms faster but I'd have to actually battle out other wolves. Right now I'd have two feet allowing me quick movement and claws and sharper teeth as well as a smaller form. This form was better.

"No."

"Alright. Be careful Vivian."

"Just do me a favor and rip his head off before I end up becoming one of them. I don't think a white dress would look good with pasty undead green skin." My attempt at joking probably would have worked if my mental voice hadn't of sounded so fearful and shaky.

I peeked out through the doors and saw the small undead army walking towards me. They made almost no sound except for the dragging motion of their feet on the ground. Expressions blank and dead but eyes focused on one thing. Me. I took in a breath.

"Will do." There was a determination in his voice that gave me the push to be strong as well.

He couldn't do everything. As his Luna it was my job to dispatch the threat laid out before me and I would do exactly that. Feeling my own cold resolve I looked around me instead of closing the doors behind me like I wanted to. It would do me no good to be a princess locked in a tower.

I needed to get to higher ground. The wolves wouldn't come up here, at least I hoped that the instinct of keeping to the ground was strong enough in all of them that they would linger close enough. The ones of two legs however, those would most definitely follow. As night officially fell and the moon illuminated through the cracks in the walls, jewels of different color bounced the light off and gave off an odd look to the walls that wanted to mess with my eyes. It immediately went away when the silver tint covered my eyes, turning the world into cooler tones now that my beast was analyzing everything around us. There were half crumbled stairways that looked as if the slightest pressure would cause the stone to crumble. There were floors above me half reaching and supported by wooden beams to keep them from collapsing. A few lanterns attached to the walls, ropes that seems to have been attached to something but now only dangled from the walls. The more I took in, the faster my beast and wolf came up with ideas and plans. I was running out of time so with a quick prayer to whoever was listening that quick steps meant lighter steps I made my way to the closest stairway.

Higher ground. Had to get to higher ground now. I could hear the wolves forming a circle around the temple and I knew that they wouldn't stay outside for long. Already I could hear the dragging motion of feet as the ones on two legs began walking towards the open doors. Thankfully as soon as my foot touched the first step it didn't crumble so with not much of a choice I raced upwards, making sure to widen my steps in case that caused a direct crumble before me. The stairway led upward but the higher I got the more the sound of dust and creaking could be heard directly under me.

But that wasn't the only thing I could hear. I didn't need to turn around to know that they were inside now. And I think so were some wolves. I had about three more stairs ahead of me.I doubted I had enough time to stand on the last one, the sound of multiple feet hitting the bottom of the stairs and continuing forward at a much faster pace made me scramble upward.

If they all come up together we'll all collapse and be buried by rubble. Best not linger. My beast pointed out to me. While we would survive that, being buried by rubble also meant being easier to grab.

As I scrambled upward I couldn't ignore the height we were climbing up to. Or the fact that there were no handles or bars to prevent anyone from falling to the side. A blur of brown and black caught my attention. Across from me two wolves were racing up the stone steps, jumping from ledges to ledge. They had to slow when they did but they were sure-footed. They were trying to cut me off.

Above me by roughly one meter there was a piece of stone floor supported by wooden beams, but most import was that a few inches away from it was a ledge that looked sturdy enough that I would be able to pull myself onto it and move on. Just barely.

Before I got to the last step I took a breath and exhaled before bending my knees and pushing off and leaping into the air in the direction of the beam, both arms extended out above me. My push-off of the stairway and the additional weight of the undead wolves climbing the stairs had the desired effect, as spot that I was just standing on crumbled beneath my feet with a domino effect that went in their direction, collapsing under their weight. Stone hitting flesh and bone breaking meet my ears but no screams.

While the force of my jump had aided me in that aspect, I over did the force behind it. I flew upward and crashed onto the wooden beam with a grunt as the side of my face and upper chest took impact. There was a small tremor from the wall that left me feeling uneasy about the hold of the structure but I dug my claws into the beam and held on for dear life, even if it did mash the wood to my body uncomfortably.

Check your one o'clock. My wolf growled. Loosening my hold enough to turn my head I cursed when I saw how close the other two wolves had gotten in the time it took me to reach the stairs.

They had split up so that the lighter colored wolf would be directly under my hanging legs, enough so that a lunge would be enough to bite me. The darker colored one was climbing higher. It was going towards the ledge I would need to get too.

I liked it better when Zombies were slow and dumb. My wolf surmised, licking her nose with her tongue.

First things first. Tightening my hold on the beam with one hand the other reached out to the stone above my head, reaching for the edge to pull myself up. When I had a good enough grip I tried to pull myself up and gave out a small yelp when it disintegrated under my hand, almost dropping me with it if I hadn't kept my hold on the beam. Looking ahead of me I knew I was going to have to play monkey bars with the beams to reach the edge. I was going to have to do this quickly. The open gripped hold I would have to take would have to be sturdy.

And my palms were fucking sweaty.

Swinging my body and counting to three I stretched out my right hand and when my lower body rocked forward again I tightened my hold while swinging my left hand forward. I did this two more times, clenching my teeth together as the motion jerked my claws in and out of wood in a painful yank. Once I made it to the last one with both hands on the beam I began to pull myself up like a chin up but this time I swung my legs closer to my chest and wrapped them as best I could to the beam. I wouldn't need to stand on all of the crumbled stone, just the part that was supported by the beam I was clinging too.

As I reached upward I knew that the parts that weren't supported would crumbled so I closed my eyes and punched through the stone. That sent dust and debris onto my face in sharp chunks but I didn't have time to dwell on it as I kicked my right leg up and hoisted myself onto a straddling position. Once up I spit the dust out of my mouth and shook my face. Like hell would I reach up to remove it from my face and the tip over. Squeezing my thighs tightly and intertwining my legs behind one another I scooted back to the wall so that I would have something to lean against. This left me in a good potion to see what was going on down below me.

I thought the best advice always said not to look below? My wolf asked.

I don't have that luxury, I responded half heartedly. Once I felt my back touch the stone I peeked down below me and felt something twitch in my stomach.

I told you not to look. My wolf barked out.

Below me there were some wolves staring upward at me, pacing around in wait around one another. But that wasn't what made me wish I had just kept my gaze upward. Some of the undead wolves that had crumbled under the stone were up, torn and bloody but up. A few of them remained down. Actually the ones with crushed skulls remained down. The others however. They were no longer going for the stairs. They were now just climbing the walls bare handed. Slow and steady. Spider Man style.

Okay, time to go.

Bracing both hands behind me and easing myself up shakily by placing one leg in front of me until the forced friction picked me up. Now standing I could see the pale wolf under me and the dark-haired one edging closer, almost standing directly above me. Turning around quickly and reaching up on the tips of my toes I reached the ledge and gave a silent prayer when it felt sturdy under my hands. Pushing up just slightly I got to place both elbows onto the ledge and felt my arms shake slightly as I eased myself up. I swung a leg up, over and rolled. I laid there for no less than a second when the wolf that had been above me lunged for me with effort for the first time.

Muzzle open to show off the sharp teeth and forepaws extended to me, it leapt at me with a snarl of rage and nothingness in its eyes.

With my beast in forefront I swiped at it with a clawed hand and slapped it away from me, it flew into the air with the force of my hit, through the wall which gave a shudder before falling back because of the impact of the blow.

Hey that reminded me of the time you smacked that one chick. My wolf yipped.

I was momentarily rocked because of the force of my own arm and almost rolled off but I lifted my leg and pushed down to quickly fix myself. If I had stood there when I pulled myself up, he would have taken me down with him. I tried not to think about what that would have meant and stood up. It was easy enough to walk on. Just as I was about to take a step a pale limb flashed by my foot. I didn't have to think twice about what I did next

As soon as I made eye contact with black eyes, I swung my boot clad foot and with all the force mustered in me I kicked its head clean off its shoulders. An explosion of pink, dark red and whites flew into the air as the body lost its grip and slid down the wall. I would mourn what I did later but for now I had to get to the top. Right now I was just grateful for two things. The first, that Venom made me work out with him, making me work on those obstacle courses. And the second, that I had decided to go with this form rather than my beast.

Quick footing to the edge I jumped off and landed softly onto a platform that was connected to three stairs, also though one lead directly to a wall with a lantern. Before I could choose which way to go, three bodies lunged off of walls and fell in front of me. Standing up somewhat sluggishly. I was surrounded by two females and a large male who I automatically knew I could not let touch me. Because I would not be able to break out of his hold.

Crouching low and turning so that all three stood next to each other I decided how to best deal with them. Both females suddenly reached for me while the male struck low as if to tackled my waist. Dropping lower than him I slid down between his legs and turned to slide onto my stomach until I stopped. The force he went to tackle me at sent him flying into one of the stairs which crumbled under his weight and took him down with it. The two females spun around and stepped to surround me on both sides. Behind me was the stairway that led to the wall.

And the lantern.

Standing up and flashing over to the wall, I didn't even bother with trying to detach the lantern. Fuck it. I took it and all the wall attached to it.

Before the closest female to me could turn I swung it at her, glass and flame quickly attaching themselves to her hair, partially impaling her with the end of the lantern and some wall. Yanking it out I was relieved to see her stay down.

But now that the other female saw what I had done some form of hesitation seemed to come off of her. And I realized she wasn't giving off the dead stench and was actually just covered in blood, but it didn't seem to actually be hers. This one was alive. With a grin that was probably more frightening than I meant it to be I swung the lantern at her with less force and pulled back as soon as I felt it make contact with her skull, knocking her out. I was about to move on when I realize the other chick was on fire. With a quick apology I rolled her off the plate form and sent her down, hopping some of the wolves directly under us would catch fire.

At the sound of sizzling fur and the stench of burnt flesh I took that as a positive.

"Whoops."

The higher I got, the more open it felt, with walls missing from some areas, allowing for the cool night air to be better felt. I had to pause for a moment when I saw Zaliver and Joshula. I felt my pulse pick up when I saw that at some point Joshula had separated his blades and was now fighting with both. Zaliver was quick, but how much energy would you have to be fighting one blade and attacking the other? Giving one last worried glance at him I jumped to a ledge beside an open wall that looked towards outside.

My momentary distract cost me. Something rocked me off of my feet and I flew into open air with something attached to me.

Claws dug into my sides and I think its jaw was in my shoulder. I say think because I couldn't feel it through the suit. All I felt was a sharp discomfort where it's claws dug into me. I'd crash to the ground if I didn't get this thing off of me. Quickly reaching behind me I dug my claws into its neck and ripped it off of me. Jolting with enough force I righted myself and not a moment to soon as I landed roughly on my feet. I bit my bottom lip enough to draw blood when I felt something snap in my foot. And then re-snap when it healed.

Looking around I realized I landed somewhere in the back of the church, on a ledge that wouldn't hold me for- I leaped off as soon as I heard it crumble. And directly in front of four wolves.

Allow me to Handle this. My beast purred. I didn't have enough time when they all lunged at me. My beast shot forward like a bat out of hell.

I might have been in human form but my mind was that of a beast, I crouched down on all fours and gave out a viscous and loud snarl that left no doubt that I would be victorious in my conquest for blood. I felt my lips grow into a deranged grin that could have competed with the one Joshula had given earlier. I felt my canines sharpen if possible. I didn't let them make the first move.

Lunging forward as if I would take out the one in front of me I somersaulted onto my back and spun on my back with my right arm stretched out and plunge my hand through its neck and grabbed onto its spine. I paid no attention to the horrid stench its dead body gave off and with my body rolled under it at the same time that I swung it in front of me, knocking two wolves down. I released it when I heard the snap of its neck and left the limp body.

The wolf in front of me snarled, its frame larger than the others. My ears twitched at the sound of the two the two wolves I knocked out. They were giving off small wines. Like they were snapping out of something.

Lunging at me with bared teeth I punched my hand as if to hit it, but aimed under its jaw and then swung upward hitting its jaw with

743

the force of a bullet. The force knocked its lower jaw into its upper mouth and sent it flying backward only to hit the ground and stay down.

With those wolves down my beast retreated slightly enough to give me reign again. I stood up and scanned around me. Creepy enough, pale limbs and bodies started peaking through the holes in the walls and started to crawl out. Two full-out ran out at me, both males quicker than the others I had seen. One dead the other under what I assumed was in a trance. As horrible as it would sound, it was easier when all I had to do was kill some of them. With one I had to use restraint while with the other I had to kill quickly without getting bitten or scratched. It was a large help that my beast could take over for most of those times.

When both guys reached me the undead one made a swipe at me that made me take a step back to avoid being scratched, but in order to avoid the scratch I had to take the swinging fist of the one in the trance. I turned my head in the direction of his fist to reduce the force of the hit. I couldn't help the air that escaped my mouth at impact, I had blink a couple of times before I found my footing again. Quicker than him, I swung my own fist at the guy, feeling satisfied at the feel of his nose crunching under my fist as he crumpled to the ground.

Turning over to the other I did the same, but he didn't seem to feel the blood trickling down his nose. From behind his shoulder I could see wolves running at full speed toward us. Not good. When he went to grab for my face I sent both hands for his throat but when he smacked my hands away with enough strength that they stung. He wrapped his hands around my throats and began to squeeze.

My eyes widened not because of the lack of oxygen that was supposed to make its way to my body but because he was squeezing so hard with a force that it was abnormal. It felt like he was going to snap my neck and I couldn't afford to heal that. By the time I would heal and I'd wake up the wolves would already would be feasting on my intestines.

Sending my fingers into his eyes I plunged my fingers in what felt like pudding and took hold of his eye sockets and pulled in opposite directions until I heard a crack and felt the front of my face get splattered with blood and facial tissue.

As soon as he dropped to the ground I inhaled loudly as oxygen filled my lungs. Oxegen had never felt better. Bringing my hand to my throat I rubbed at the slowly healing flesh. I coughed a couple of times as my throat returned to normal. I had to blink a couple of times to get the moisture out of my eyes. I inhaled a couple of times to make sure I didn't go light-headed.

I think you should avoid their hands. My wolf suggested.

You don't say! I snapped back, rubbing at my throat. Taking a step back, I was surprised when I wobbled a bit, but ran towards the upcoming wolves anyway.

I was finding it harder to maneuver being surrounded by so many wolves. My original plan had been to fight them one on one, but that plan was out.

Two wolves lunged at my sides, so sending a quick kick to the ribs of one I sent both of them flying into the closest tree. Turning back to face the remaining wolves I cursed when I realized I would soon be joined by two-legged attackers.

There are less of them now. My beast asserted quietly.

It was true, now that she mentioned it I realized that the majority of the wolves I had fought I had to knock out rather than kill. My first scan through the crowd had led me to believe that they were all dead, but they were actually just gravely wounded and covered in gore of other dead wolves. As expected of alpha pairs, fights to the death. Joshula had said he played with his food, but perhaps his food had played with him as well.

Instead of facing them I turned and ran to the side of the temple, towards the front. I had to take down a few wolves in the process but as soon as I made it to the front I knew that I would be faced with more two legged wolves and that was my plan. During all of my fighting I had noticed that wolves attacked with only wolves and the two-legged wolves only attacked with other two legs. They would get in each other's way trying to get me.

Slowing down just enough so that the wolves were on my heel and watching for the pale limbs I timed it and then speed up. The sound of crashing bodies was like a melody to my ears. Not wasting the opportunity, I turned and ran back to the tangled wolves who had crashed into four dead wolves. I had the pleasure of removing the head of the nearest one with my boot, picking up the paw of one wolf and throwing him against the temples wall and repeating my finger pudding episode with another. I was covered in gore and smelted awful but I couldn't stop, some of them were starting to stand up.

Right as I began to swing my leg out for another decapitation I heard a terrified scream that bounced around my mind in a paralyzing effect.

Suddenly my eyes were not my own as I watched from another.

My arms swung forward with a familiarly heavy object in them, but were pushed back with an echoing movement that tried to push me back with equal strength that pissed me off immensely. With another hand he swung towards my neck forcing me to jump out of reach. I felt a gash by my face start to heal at the same time that my opponents began to bleed. Murky yellow eyes winked at me in a wild savagery sort of pleasure.

Our blades pushed at one another, unrelenting. I kicked upwards with my right foot for momentum and then made to kick the bastard in the ribs with the heel of my left foot when he half spun to the right and threw his left sword in the direction he was facing. I knew he had turned back to face me but I followed the trajectory of his blade.

Directly in line of Vivian who was about to kick someone's head off.

"VIVIAN!"

My name snapped me back into my body, I dropped to the ground faster than republicans dropping healthcare bills.

But not fast enough.

Something passed through the back of my suit, and sliced at my back. I cried out at the feel of jagged edges and felt like something that felt oddly like flesh was hanging, while something wet and warm trailed down my back. Pain made me shudder and shake, but the familiar heat of my skin knitting itself back together was a comfort. That's when I remembered that in my haze to avoid getting gutted I threw myself down to the ground.

Right next to the dude I was supposed to decapitate.

"Hmm, missed." I didn't need to know who said that, nor did I need to look to know that Zaliver must have managed a hit if the sound of blood splattering the ground met my ears.

Ignoring the painful tingles that followed, I rolled over to see someone's foot coming towards me at full speed. All I had time to do was curled up.

Pain exploded up along my left arm as I slid back and was forcibly stopped by the wall that greeted my bare back. Rugged stone cut into my tender back as I groaned at the feel of it. There was something wrong with my left arm. I could feel it trying to heal but-ah shit. Standing up on wobbly feet and forcing myself not to look down I took hold of my curled up arm and yanked it straight. Something popped and lowered into place, I placed a hand on my lower hip as a sudden jabbing pain flared up and disappeared.

I shook my head to clear myself and turned to the left where a slightly blood coated sword was sticking out of the wall. Taking hold of it with both hands, I yanked it out.

I spun back around to face the asshole who kicked me and my lips curled over my teeth and my tongue passed over them. I tasted blood in my mouth. My own. He lunged at me. He wasn't the only one, a second wolf also did. But the idiots didn't seem to realize that I had a sword in my hand. You don't need to know how to use a sword to know how to swing one like a bat.

746

Sliding my left foot forward and bending my knees I held the sword by right ear and waited. When they were close enough I swung out twice. Once in front of me to the left and then tucked my left elbow in to swing at an angle to the right.

The second head hit the ground before the first one.

I was off the stairs and swinging away before both of their bodies had hit the stone steps. I was tired, snore, a bit dizzy and a whole lot pissed off. Pausing momentarily to scan the temple and the area around it I was momentarily proud to have taken care of everyone by myself, but also saddened by what I had to do.

Those who survive are usually left with guilt for it while those who were not there are usually filled with accusations. But at the end of the day those who perished are usually at peace that they no longer have to fight. Do not blame yourself for others doing. My beast said doleful.

Agreeing with her, I quickly made my way back to the fight where I was greeted with both brothers still going at it. I hadn't wanted to carry the sword around with me because it was Joshula's but reason won over want when I recalled movie scenes where people drop their weapons only to have them used against them, so, I kept it with me. Knowing that my wolf couldn't help her comment the closer we got I watched on.

You've got a sword. Maybe you should go end this. She hinted out.

I watched as Zaliver lifted his blade and used the bottom of the handle to hit Joshula in the left temple which seems to freeze him enough for Zaliver to flip the blade and stab him in the calf. Joshula roared out but didn't stop because of that, instead he let the blade cut through his leg as he yanked it backward. Torn ligament and muscle just hanging everywhere, blood gushed out of his leg and quickly muddied the ground. Swinging his sword sideways and then switching his blade vertically, Zaliver was fast enough to miss being skinned but he still got a slice on his forehead that would give out more blood before it healed properly. They were both covered in blood.

I pursed my lips at the sight, frowned and shook my head.

Nah . . . he-he. Looks like he's got this.

But then Zaliver's words came back to haunt me. "If you see a chance take it." I'm pretty sure he said that to make me feel better, because I doubt I'd get a punch in before Joshula removed that vary same arm and beat me with it. But that didn't mean I couldn't return his possession.

Stopping at a safe distance, I picked up the sword and held the handle like a spear.

"I'm going to throw his sword at him," I told Zaliver, knowing he would take the opportunity to get Joshula

"Do it." And then as if the thought occurred to him he added briskly. "Aim at him, not me."

I kept my comment to myself.

Lifting the sword, I took aim and fired, perhaps it was the strength behind the thrust but it flew in the air steady and fast. At the same moment that it flew at him he took a step to the side and it almost passed him but with his left hand he reached across his chest to catch the handle. At that exact moment Zaliver aimed his sword for his heart, but since he had reached across his chest to catch the handle. The fucker took a sword to the shoulder to catch it.

Ah shit. Pulling his blade out Zaliver had to quickly spin it to block both blades. I wanted to murmur a sorry, but I think he already knew. That and I didn't want to chance distracting him.

I rubbed at my left arm, it was still aching from being kicked. I still felt whole and okay. A little beat up and tired but alright. Man, I needed to work on my stamina.

Joshula suddenly laughed, making me focus back on the fight. I took an unconscious step forward when I saw Zaliver half bent and with an arm at his lower abdomen. He was bleeding badly. Even though I knew he would heal, didn't mean I liked the sight of him bleeding everywhere.

"Finally. Guess I was the only rusty one." Joshula shook his head in disappointment, but then looked over at me. "Oh, good. You're done. You look a little tired there. That means I can now-" He ducked his head as Zaliver swung out wide.

The bastard was happy that I got rid off all of his minions, our own wolves. He really didn't care who he used as long as he got what he wanted.

Jabbing forward and then aiming for Zaliver's side, Joshula suddenly dropped to the ground low, while Zaliver deflected the blows, meaning he couldn't predict Joshula kicking his leg out swiping his own from under him. Before Zaliver could right himself Joshula plunged his sword into Zaliver's chest.

"No!"

Zaliver let out a pained sound as Joshula dug in deeper with the sword, pushing it further into Zaliver. Blood. All I could smell now was Zaliver's blood. My body began to tremble as I felt the shift want to come over me.

Joshula stood up quickly and looked down at the blade in Zaliver hand. If he tried to take it from Zaliver then there was a high chance he would die. He knew that. So with an annoyed huff he looked up and began to walk over to me, twirling and spinning his blade as he did so.

"Johsula." Zaliver coughed out in the ground, blood leaking from the corner of his mouth as he reached for the blade that pinned him to the ground. "Don't fucking touch her!" He snarled savagely as he broke the top part of the sword in half, tossing away from him and began to slowly pull the sword out of himself.

More than just blood was coming out now. A sound came from my chest. It sounded strained and anxious.

The corners of Joshula's mouth began to curl upward in sick amusement as he made his way to me. Looking at Zaliver I made to go around Joshula as we walked over to me to get closer to Zaliver but if he knew what I wanted to do, then he was doing a splendid job of blocking me.

What are my options here? I urged my wolf.

A) Fight the fucker.

B) Run from the fucker.

And C?

Hopes he trips on a pebble on his way over? she said hesitantly.

The closer he got the more I began to feel fear claw up my chest and tighten the air passages of my throat. Feeling cornered in an open field I bared my teeth at him in warning but all he did was laugh as if I amused him. The hairs on my arms began to stand in the wake of danger, loose strands of hair were tossed around as the wind began to blow in the vacant sky.

"I won't touch her brother," Joshula murmured as he stopped a few steps from me. Those words did nothing to calm me.

Behind him Zaliver gave out a weak grunt as he finally pulled the sword out of him, he tried to roll over and stand but the sickening sound of something that didn't sound like flesh, but something else hitting the ground with a wet splash. Pain screamed out at me from his side of the bond, he was in too much pain to fully keep his shield up correctly. He hadn't healed yet. I knew for a fact that he needed a few more minutes to do so. He needed time.

I would buy him time.

Taking a step back, I gave Joshula a look. Perhaps Joshula wouldn't touch me, but Fate hadn't been in on that promise. And while one brother seemed to fight for revenge and honor the other seemed to do so out of ego and pride. I just had to hope that the villain in one of them still loved to chat.

"Why Hogan?" I blurted out. It took the desired effect as Joshula hesitated before he took on a much more arrogant stance. "What would he have to offer a god that supposedly knows all?"

"That love-sick mutt? A means to an end, he had the exact numbers and locations of all of the delicious Alpha snacks. It helped that he was easily swayed with words of love when it came to your so-called mate." He rolled his eyes. "When it comes to making decisions, love should not be involved. It's such a stupidity."

Spoken like someone who has never known it. My wolf said dryly.

Agreed.

"Alright, but how would that matter? How did you even get them here unnoticed?" I asked, both to buy more time and genuinely curious. I dared to look over at Zaliver who while still an alarming pale shade was now beginning to stand slowly as to not gain attention.

"As you said I am all-knowing. I know the melody of chance and the calls of occurrence. I do not need to be a god of fate to know that your mate would choose vengeance and punishment over forgiveness. In doing so he would find a prize." He gestured to himself. "Who he would then take as a sign of self forgiveness and bring home with him forgetting." He took a step closer to me. "to close the doors which bind this world and those beyond it."

I didn't need to look over to know Zaliver must have beaten himself over that small mistake. I could feel it through the bond.

"So you used the door that he used to get to you, to transport back and forth with the...alphas. But that doesn't explain how you kept them hidden," I pointed out. Murky eyes narrowed in annoyance as he glared at me. I wanted to ask about what Hogan had said, I wanted to know if he really did know of a way to actually kill Zaliver but I wasn't going to be the one to remind him of that. Nope. Not me.

"You are not listening. I am a god of Fate and chance. I can do things beyond you and that mutt." A sudden gleam entered his eyes. "Like striking a tree." The air grew tense as he leaned forward, as if to share a secret. "Which you might have been standing under. After that, it was easy enough to catch your little wolves and plant them at the most convenient places for me to nab them."

The truth behind his confession was like a physical blow itself, the inside of my head feeling like it was suddenly filled with static electricity that wanted a way out, a flashing pain that left as soon as it came. His words reminding me of how it had felt moments before my skull had met ground and was then forcibly crushed by the horrendously heavy tree. I couldn't help but flinch at the memory.

"Y-You did that?" I couldn't help the way I stumbled over the first word, my tongue feeling heavy. A sense of boiling rage went through me, an emotion that I knew wasn't my own.

All the creep did was smile.

He was responsible for that. How was that even possible? How could he have forced nature to do his bidding? Knowing that he had powers beyond what I believed didn't make me want to stand any closer than I was now, in fact, it just made me want to get as far away from him as possible. The hackles on my wolf were lifted.

He took a breath. "Now, are you done trying to buy time for him to heal?"

"I don't know. Am I?" I whispered.

He smiled.

"Yes."

"Then I guess I am." My words made me sound relaxed and calm, the complete opposite.

I couldn't have dodged even if tried. And I tried. As on as he lifted his blade I held out my clawed hands as if to push it out-of-the-way or take it from his grasp. Not flinching from my rough reach for him Fate brought his blade right through my right hand. I felt a sharp sting before I felt as if my skin was begging peeled off with the muscles still attached, stretching them beyond normalcy. He continued to push forward, ignoring my gurgling scream. Out of instinct to lessen the pain I bent my right arm, following his projection. Something sharp impaled my right shoulder. The tip of his monstrous blade. I cried out as my blood dropped down onto the blade.

Joshula looked down with keen focus as he held still and watched me bleed out around the blade. I couldn't smell anything other than blood, my nose filled with so much blood that I felt nauseous and dizzy, almost sagging against his blade but the smallest movement knocked that to the back of my mind. I opened my mouth in a silent scream, knowing that if I forced air out of my mouth my chest would be forced to comply to the appropriate movement.

The only warning I got was the looming shadow that sent Fate flying into the air, the sound of stone walls breaking as a body flew through it hitting my ears. Without him holding the blade up I was forced to the ground with the blade when it began to drop. I clenched my teeth, feeling sweat trail down my face as I looked up into eyes so black that it numbed my pain for a moment. Zaliver's beast stood before me, perhaps larger than I had ever seen him. His form was so colossal that it blocked out the moonlight and bathed me in his darkness. It was as if his muscles and claws had grown twice their normal size, filled with hatred and anger so vehement that it filled him. Those familiar sharp teeth gleaming with his blood lust.

I knew that he was going to ask about me, but I need him focused so I interrupted his questioning with a firm voice.

Just kill him already. I kept the rest of what I was going to say to myself. Something along the lines of 'before he turns me into a pincushion'. I doubted he wanted to hear that at the moment.

He hesitated for only a second, and then I was standing alone again. Turning to follow the sound of quick steps I saw only a shadow covering ground in the direction of a slowly standing Joshula. Zaliver had hit him so hard he had flown right into the temple, I shouldn't have been as shocked to see that he had taken half of the temple with him. Dust,rubble and stones falling off of him as he stood up almost shakily. Blood trailed down his face and flesh slowly mended itself back together. A pained grimace on his face as yellow eyes flared with anger.

"And the beast is out. If you wish to play before your death then I will grant you that much," Joshula said, stepping out of the ruin around him and began to pick up speed towards Zaliver's form.

It was like each step not only brought him closer, but also changed him as his form began to lengthen, sharpen, stretch, deform and reshape until his physical form began to morph into a form that would watch the one he was about to take on. I let out a shaky breath, perhaps from pain, or unease at the confirmation of the shape.

Joshula could shift into a beast as well.

When both forms met one another, the distinction between the brothers was tremendously different and if just a little, easing me. While the might have matched in height, claws and teeth that was as far as similarities because where Zaliver's fur was a glossy black, Joshula's were varying shades of discolored gray that covered him in patches. As I had noticed before, Zaliver's form larger than before whereas Joshula managed to take a form that was terrifying and monstrous and managed to make it look no less but also starved and sickly. His form was muscular but not enough to hide the sharp protruding ribs and outlines of his bones.

Even as Joshula threw himself at Zaliver his own force was rickashaded backwards from the pure impact of my mates body. Flying straight into his previous landing he rolled through the rubble, a clawed hand reaching out to dig into the ground to stop himself in time to have Zaliver dig his claws into his form and claw downwards. Skin came apart like paper under claws. Trying to dislodge Zaliver's claws from his back Joshula opened his jaw to take a bite out of the nearest thing to him, Zalivers neck and would have if my mate hadn't released him.

Dropping to all fours, Joshula swiped a clawed hand from Zaliver's chest and upward to his muzzle while the other went for the wound that I knew was still healing, trying to reopen it with an L shaped attack. From where I was I could see pink streaks from the claw marks, but there had been more blood flowing from Joshula then Zaliver. For a moment I worried that Joshula's thinner form would be advantageous to Zaliver's larger one, but the more I watched the prouder I felt to realize that Zaliver had more years of experience with his beast form and was there for the better fighter, while Joshula just seemed to go for the first chances he got.

Taking a moment to look away from them I looked down to see how my own situation was going. My vision went double sided as I realized just how much blood was coming out from the still open wound.

I don't usually say this, but get that shit out! My wolf howled. She didn't have to tell me twice.

I shook and shuddered violently with pain, my skin aflame which only seemed to grow within the second as I knew what I would have to do. Even if it was only the tip it was causing inscrutable amount of pain. All I had to do was get it out. With an agonized cry I yank my shoulder back. Huffing heavily as I felt it leave my flesh. The blade fell to the blood coated ground. I pushed at my shoulder, feeling faint at the pain but needing it to heal quickly. Blood loss could still kill someone.

A a gleaming object caught my gaze,I turned to look and saw Zaliver's sword laying on the ground. Son of a bitch, he wouldn't be able to kill Fate without out it. I turned back to look at the fight that would go on forever if Zaliver didn't snap out of his rage induced state.

I was just about to tell him when I heard him give out a snarl so loud it sounded painful, I turned in time to see how he held one of Joshula's arms under his lower body, ignoring as claws dug into his back and scraped at him. Bared teeth opened and closed in an attempt to bite at anything, his large head jerking side to side in trying to get loose. One of Zaliver's clawed hand-held down Joshula from the neck while the other held his right hand up before him.

Seeing the hold he had on Joshula I began going for the sword thinking he would ask me to bring it over.

But I had to stop at the sight of my mates jaw widening enough to see the way saliva made them gleam right before he closed his mouth over Joshula's jerking shoulder and with a merciless yank, rip his arm out of his socket.

Joshula's pained howl reverted through the sky, but not louder than the words Zaliver said to me as he spit out a hand that slowly began to mold of its fur and shrink until flesh began to slip from it as if no longer being held by stitches. Bones hit the ground with a clatter.

"For you, my love," he said with a perverse joy that sounded borderline fiendish and inhumane.

"How romantic of you," I responded stiffly. "But we both know that won't kill him."

Before he could reply he was thrown off as Joshula's body jerked, perhaps from the pain of losing a limb or out of anger, forcing Zaliver to release him. Instead of blood gushing out like I'd seen in movies, his fell to the ground in thick and slow drops that made me want to gag with disgust as the stench reached my nose. It smelled like he was rotten from the inside. Perhaps this bony and wild creature was Joshula's true form. Him. It was a good enough representation if you ask me.

I think we were both shocked when Joshula turned and began to run from Zaliver, who didn't hesitate to chase. Realizing he was heading towards me, I didn't take very long to put a pep to my step.

Realizing too late to turn around, I remembered the sword. Not hearing him behind me I turned to see him hesitate by Zaliver's sword before tuning straight to his own which I had left on the ground. When he was close enough he quickly shifted back, nude and bloody, he turned and pointed the sword in Zaliver's direction. His arm trembled and shook only slightly, but his direction held firm. His whole arm was missing from his human form.

"You'll have to shift back if you want a chance to finish me. Do it!" Joshula snarled out, spit flying out of his mouth with the force of his words. "I'll fucking kill you for everything you have done," he continued.

I went rigid at his threat.

Zaliver's form stopped before his sword, his frame as still as the shadows that he casted on the ground. His suit was torn and bloodied but it still managed to stay true to its purpose as it clung to him. It was a moment before his fame began to reduce and shrink, but even when beast became man I could still see the signs of his beast. It was like he couldn't complete finish the transformation. He was to fueled with rage,I realized. Dark fur matted his skin in a thin layer, hands were still curled into claws, teeth more animal than man as he bared them in a frightening smirk. It reminded me a little of how he was in the beginning.

"You sure you can kill me? One handed and all?" Zaliver taunted in a voice that strained to pronounce human language, a slight growl behind his words. He bent to pick his weapon. "It took both hands to keep me down and look where that got you."

Joshula was in front of Zaliver no sooner after the words left his mouth, proving that even one-handed he was sufficiently enough trained to do so. Without missing a beat the brothers were back to fighting, but there was an urgency in both of them now that hadn't been before. Blows were thrown with less precision on Joshula's part, his body moving as if he still thought he had his right arm. Zaliver did not try to hide his goal when he attacked, going for his opponent's heart and when that failed he tried to decapitate him.

My wound was starting to heal enough that I no longer had to put pressure to hold the tissues and muscles together. Looking down at my hands I grimaced at the blood that coated them, I even had blood under my nails. I must have morphed them back at some point. A fading pink ragged line marked both sides of my hand where the blade had gone through.

I mentally cursed Joshula when I realized my hands were so bloody that I couldn't even see my ring. I could feel it, I just couldn't see through all the blood. I was that dirty, dried blood meshed with fresh creating a pasty texture. It was gross.

"You will die tonight, Zalivius, by my hand. I made you, raised you and gave you everything you have now!" Fate screamed. All his words managed to do was piss off Zaliver. Spinning just out of reach Zaliver's sword went through the air, had Joshula's shoulder been in place he would have caught it.

Before Zaliver could pull back his extended arm, a blood coated sword impaled him through the shoulder. Joshula didn't give him a chance to pull back before he twisted the blade, yanked it out and jumped out of reach. Zaliver brought his hand to his shoulder in a soft grunt, pushing at the wound. Blood seemed to leave his face as he looked down at his shoulder with wide eyes filled with confusion. Shaking his head he stepped forward toward Joshula.

Fate gave out a wicked laugh.

As Zaliver walked forward, I noted the blood that still gushed from his wounded shoulder. With every step he took blood dropped drop his elbow as blood trailed down his arm, seeming to grow instead of lessen. Fate lunged at Zaliver with exuberance, sliding his blade down Zaliver's and flipping it so that the bottom of the handle faced opposite of him before he dug back in the wound he had given Zaliver.

The sound Zaliver made was different from the ones he had given before. Joshula yanked his handle out roughly. Zaliver gave out a shaky exhale and blinked quickly. Fate stilled and tilted his head before chuckling.

"Feels different, doesn't it?" he asked Zaliver, aiming to stab him in the other shoulder which would force Zaliver use his wounded one with force. "I bet it's starting to really hurt."

Zaliver's arms were shaking. He looked strained. Something was wrong, but I couldn't- and then Fate whispered something in a sickeningly soft voice that could have been the lyrics to a song. But that made my heart skip a beat.

"You're not healing anymore. Are you, Zalivius?"

What? How could he not be healing? What is happening? Fate had stabbed Zaliver before and he had healed, I hadn't seen him do anything different. But Hogan had said Fate figured out a way to kill Zaliver. And Zaliver need to heal if he was going to make it out of this.

If Zaliver couldn't heal... he would bleed out from his wounds and die. And if not, then Joshula would do it. He would kill him.

True and unrivaled fear that made every inch of my body feel cold and unbearably warm filled me. Just the thought of Zaliver truly dying, cold and unmoving broke something in me that I could not put back together.

Fate made to slice at Zaliver but he blocked at the last-minute. Pushing onto him Fate forced one of the bloodied edges of his blade closer to Zaliver's face, cutting above his right eyebrow and pushing forward to lean down on the blade, forcing it to trail down into Zaliver's skin. He got past his eyebrow before Zaliver pushed him off with a rough grunt. Blood dripped down his eye, he had to wipe it off to not hinder his sight.

Because he wasn't healing.

"What did you do?" Zaliver asked between clenched teeth. I'm not sure if it was pain that drove him now, but Zaliver was being more cautious now. He watched Fate carefully.

"Isn't it obvious?" Fate responded. The began to circle around one another. "Think boy, I stabbed you before and you healed. I stabbed you now and you no longer heal. Do I have to give you a clue?" He barked out, amusement thick in his voice.

I could see the calculations and playback going through Zaliver's mind as he worked out Fate's words, but I didn't need to think about what he had done. Instead, Aurora seemed to say something that seemed to repeat itself over and over again in my mind: *Those whom fail to see the connection will pay with blood. Pay with blood.*

My blood hadn't been on the blade before but now that it was, Zaliver wasn't healing.

"My blood," I whispered, horrified. Knowing that I could be the reason for my mate dying made me feel as if the very existence of my soul was being torn to shreds. Seeming to hear me Fate whistled.

"Smart girl. Bet you didn't think of that, Zalivius, you were so worried of her before that once you knew you she was no longer a threat, you forgot to check on the 'after'." Practically glowing with mirth Fate's shoulders shook with contained laughter. "Her blood will be your undoing. Her. The one you love. How does that make you feel?" Fate asked.

From where I was, I couldn't see the reaction the words had on Zaliver, who had been so cautious, so paranoid in the beginning. I knew it wasn't my fault, I didn't know, but a small stream of guilt began to pool in the bottom of my stomach. Zaliver had been cold and indifferent to me when we first met to prevent this. A weakness. Each word made his face harden until I could no longer tell what he was thinking. Feeling. I didn't know if I wanted him to look my way or not.

Was he angry? Did he regret loving me? I clenched my hands, digging my nails into my palm to keep the pain for front instead of my wild thoughts.

"So this was your plan," Zaliver said through clenched teeth. Either with anger or pain. "While I applaud you for the plan you've made an error." Fate stopped and lowered his blade, disbelief flashing through his face.

"Have I really? And what would that be?" he questioned, but from his arrogant tone I could tell that he didn't believe anything that came from Zaliver's mouth could be even true.

"You did not hand me a weakness, you gave me a different type of strength. Something which I won't waste my breath explaining because it's obvious that it is something that an all-knowing god such as yourself has never known in this life." Zaliver's eyes grew brighter with every word, my hands unclenched and hung by my sides as his words soothed me.

Fate said nothing as he threw daggers with his eyes, rage turning his skin red, veins pulsing around his neck as he clenched his jaw.

"That feeling in your chest, the void emptiness that you think is hatred for me is nothing else but your very own weakness. I should know, I was once a reflection of you before. This could be the moment where I say something along the lines of 'I pity you', but that would be a lie. And my mate has taught me better than to lie to the less fortunate." Fate opens his mouth to say something and then closed it.

"Be it brother or god," Zaliver let his gaze run over Fate/Joshula and shook his head. "You are nothing but a pest."

Damn. My wolf whistled. *If that didn't kill him just a little . . .* she trailed off.

"You should have killed her when you first saw her," Fate snarled out, behaving like the animal he hadn't before. "Now you will die because of her blood."

Joshula and Fate must have both agreed to work together this time, running across the space that separated them from Zaliver before a heartbeat, not completing swings and jabs before they switched into new positions to attack. Zaliver has the advantage of still having his arm, throwing the blade into one hand he used the now free one to swipe at Joshula's face while he managed to jab the blade into his upper thigh. Swinging blindly as blood covered his sight Joshula's hand almost slit Zaliver's throat in a savage scream that ripped its way out of his throat.

Kicking out faster than I've ever seen, Zaliver sent Joshula flying, jumping into the air after him he punched down, sending the body straight down. My balance was rocked when Joshula's body made impact.

Using gravity, Zaliver positioned his blade to point down with both hands as he landed on top of Joshula, ready to plunge his sword into his heart.

I felt a breath leave my body as Zaliver stood and stumbled backwards. Clutching his side. They say it hurts less the second time around. They lied. Faster than Zaliver could block or dodge, Fate had also plunged his blade into Zaliver as fast as he took it out. Zaliver fell to a knee as he began to cough out blood and wheeze, surprise mixed in with pain. I was already moving towards him before I knew it. Instinct taking over.

A sudden ear-piercing scream made both Zaliver and I go to cover our ears. I looked over to see Joshula yank the blade out of his chest, taking with it his heart which suddenly began to crumble like sand—no, like ash. A blurry figure loomed over the ashes, almost reaching out before vanishing. A shuddering breath made look over to Zaliver who was covering his side as blood seeped around his fingers.

He still wasn't healing.

Before I could take another step in his direction Joshula rose and with him the scent of decay, skin going from pasty white to a slowly darkening yellow-green. The musky yellow in his eyes clearing as his soft blue-green eyes glared at Zaliver.

"You might have gotten rid of him, but if I go, I'm taking her with me." Joshula turned towards me with the bloody blade.

"And you know what the best part about this is? Your little blood bond?" He waved the blade at me. The closer he got the stronger the stench of decay. The gaping hole in his chest began to peel away at the skin, flesh seeming to drop with every step. He was dying. Or at least his body was.

Behind him Zaliver's eyes widened with realization of what Joshula intended and it was like he forgot about his own wounds even if his body hadn't because he stood up and ran towards Joshula, stumbling slightly as more blood poured from out of him.

I began to scramble backwards, if I turned to run he'd just stab me in the back. He was in front of me before I could start my backwards jog, kicking my legs from under me so hard that it felt as if they had gotten hit from the side by a car. I hit the ground with a thud, putting my hands behind me to crawl away even if just with my arms.

"Don't—" Zaliver bellowed, it almost sounded like a broken plea.

"It works both ways." Joshula revealed casually. The soft wind being enough to push some of the now green flesh from his face. It fell next to my fingers. He smiled down at me, crazed joy in his eyes.

Before sinking the full blade straight into my chest, still hot with Zaliver's blood. The force of it going through my chest jerking me, the sound of the blade end hitting the ground defending.

758

Something hot clawed at my throat and forced itself out, twice I jerked as it left my mouth. There was a horrible rasping sound. It sounded like a choked breath.

There was a fire in my chest that would not allow my heart to beat. It burned at everything I was. Something sharp was scraping against my heart, tearing apart every time it beat. My heart beat was killing me. I didn't want the last eyes I looked into to be his.

So I looked beyond him and instead gazed at the sea that filled my days with warmth and the joy of love.

I looked into the sky that kept watch over me no matter where I went.

I ventured into an electric storm of thunder and lightning that filled my world with sounds of happiness and roars of unimaginable wonders that would be only ours.

Something wet trailed down my face as I looked at him.

I opened my mouth. I don't know what I wanted to say. I don't know what I would have said.

He opened his mouth as well. Perhaps he said something. I'm not sure. Maybe he said nothing, like I did. But he was so beautiful. So blue. In all of the senses.

I wanted to look into those eyes forever.

But I felt my body begin to shut down as my eyes left his and rolled up to see the light of the bright moon.

And then it was all gone.

And I was nothing.

There was nothing to me.

Because I was gone.

CHAPTER 47

There was something touching my face.

It was a light touch, warm.

I sighed in content, whatever I was on was hard and tickled, but not in a bad way.

Whatever was touching my face stopped when I sighed. But it hovered, I could tell. Curiosity got the best of me and I peeked open my eyes.

Open sky greeted me, but it wasn't it blue per say. More like the color of a pearl. White and yet still not white, I hadn't known there could be so many different shades in one. But that didn't catch my attention for long. No, that wasn't what I wanted to see. Something else.

I raised my head a little off the ground and looked over to my left.

I was in a garden, or the section of a garden but overall it was a forest. All healthy green trees surrounded me. But the vibrancy of the different plants that surrounded me caught my attention. They weren't planted perfectly or in order of color or even height, the were random and spread out or bunched together. It was a relaxing sight. It was wild and true at heart. But still taken care of as if someone was in charge of it. If only for a moment, I forgot why I had opened my eyes.

But something small was peeking down at me.

It was a boy.

He looked hesitant enough to be talking to me but stubborn enough to look like he wasn't comfortable with not talking to me. It made the corners of my mouth lift up in amusement. What mixed emotions he must have been feeling.

"Why are you in my garden?" he questioned softly. His hands, covered in dirt fisted up and then relaxed. He repeated this many times. I think I made him nervous.

I looked around and scrunched my face in confusion. Why was I in his garden? I turned back to look at him uncertain.

"I'm not sure." Looking him over and seeing the dirt that seemed to be imprinted into his knees I looked back up at him. "But your garden is very pretty."

His face flushed at the compliment, eyes lighting up as he too looked around. "Thank you! I like working with plants. Did you know that they all have different uses and that you can use them in different ways for the same thing?"

"I think I do, but I don't know much about plants." I sat up slowly, looking down at myself.

I was laying down on a grassy section of his garden, a light summer plum dress covering me. I was barefooted.

"Yeah, you look like you don't know much about plants." I turned to look over at the boy with an open mouth, he had a cheeky little smile on his face.

"And what do I look like then?" I asked raising a brow. His cheeky smile dropped and a sudden seriousness took over him, something I wouldn't have s expected from one who looked so young.

"You look like you shouldn't be here," was all he said before standing up and holding a hand out to me.

What?

I took his hand and stood up, following quietly when he guided me away from the garden. I wanted to stay.

There was something soothing about it.

"What do you mean?"

When he stayed silent so did I. I looked around as we moved, there were things flying around that were larger than life and looked like enchanted or extinct creatures. Some peered down at me with large eyes that made me stop and want to walk over to investigate their curious little smile. The boy would take a look at what caught my attention, wave and then pull me along.

"Where are we going?" I asked after a while.

He turned to look at me and shook his head, brown curls bouncing around when he did that. I went to tug at one when his small hand pushed mine away. Like he knew I was going to do it. Like it was normal for people to d

that to his hair. It made me smile.

"Where you were probably meant to go," he muttered with a hint of petulance.

Something about him made me chuckle, I'm not sure what.

"And where's that?"

"You'll know soon enough lady." A tone of exasperation grew in his voice.

"Well then why didn't I wake up there first?" I asked pointedly. He tugged at me to walk faster when I began to slow down.

"I dunno. Maybe you're lost?" He paused. "A lot of people get lost here."

"And where is here?" I asked. All he did was shrug, but I think he knew and didn't want to tell.

The trees began to lessen around us the more we walked, instead the dirt gave way to long and rough stones under my feet. They didn't hurt, but they weren't smooth either. I could feel the temperature get a little colder, my dress not doing much to warm me. I stopped and tugged at the boy's hand. I didn't want to go any further.

"It's okay, it's a pond. See?" the boy said, taking in my hesitation. "The water is really pretty and clear." Taking a few more steps forward I saw what he meant.

Below us, at the edge of the rocks was a pond so clear I could see through it. But I could not name what I saw. I did not know what was at the bottom of the pond. There were so many things, it was as if the pond was indecisive as to what to choose to show me. It was like nothing I had ever seen before. We were walking down the stones, which surrounded the pound like stairs. I was mesmerized by it, no longer needing the boy to lead me forward, it was like I was being called to it.

But the warmth of his hand made me turn to look down at him as we got closer. He wore light brown pants marked with dirt at his knees and since he gardened I knew why, even his plain white shirt was covered, but there were little grass stains on his back leaving the impression that he like to nap on the grass like I had been doing earlier. Feeling my eyes on him he turned to look at me, lifting a bushy little brow. Something in his expression seemed teasingly familiar.

He had soft brown curly hair that couldn't seem to pick between a dark or light shade of brown, his curls just as indecisive as to which direction to point. He had a dark complexion, be it from being in the sun or naturally, but his skin was sun-kissed. His nose, cute little thing was small and well-rounded giving him a humble yet stubborn appearance. He couldn't be younger than four but no older than seven. It was like the harder I looked the more I recognized facial features. But it was the eyes that made me remember his name.

"Andrew?" He stopped and peered up at me.

"Yeah?"

He gave out a little squeak as I took him into my arms and hugged him to me. After a few seconds he shrugged and wrapped his arms around me and with all the force his little body could muster and squeezed me back. A choked laugh escaped my throat.

"Oh Andrew." I pulled back to look at him. He held still and peered up at me curiously.

Aurora hadn't been lying when she said he had gotten her eyes, large and light, brown eyes looked back at me.

"How do you know my name?" he asked.

"Your mom and dad—" He jumped up and grinned.

"You know them? How are they?" he asked immediately.

He knew. I don't know why that realization broke my heart.

"They're pretty sad buddy." He nodded as if he wasn't surprised.

"I don't want them to be sad. I'm okay, I have my garden and all the plants in the world. It takes time to grow them so I have to watch over them carefully. Besides, I'm not alone," he said quickly, as if trying to convince me, he jumped a few steps ahead of me.

"You're not? Well that's good to know. I'm sure they wouldn't want you to be. And I know they would be proud if they could see the garden you have. I know I am." He turned to smile shyly at me.

When we made it to the last stone, the pond right at the edge of it, Andrew stopped and peered up at me, something like indecision in his eyes.

"What's wrong?" I asked, crouching to his level. He bit his lip before squaring his shoulders.

"I'm happy, I have a garden and I'm not alone. I want them both to be happy and not to worry about me," he stated.

I nodded slowly, not understanding.

"Remember that, okay?" he asked, looking into my eyes seriously.

"Okay," I promised, not sure why.

"Good." He sighed before smiling up at me, the look reminding me of his father suddenly. There was a twinkle in his eyes.

He placed his hands on my shoulders and squeezed, I placed my hands on his and squeezed back. Leaning forward I kissed his cheek. His cheeks flushed a deep red.

And then he pushed me back with a lot more strength then I thought he had.

I went flying off of the stone, flinging my arms in the air as I tried to grasp onto something. Eyes widened I looked over at him, he was waving with a cheeky grin on his face.

"Bye, bye plum girl!"

I hit cold water a second later.

~•~

I was on the floor again.

Except this time it was much more cold and much less comfortable.

I sat up and looked down at what I wore now. I was wearing white dress pants and a gray shirt. I raised a brow, I didn't look that bad. But I was still barefooted.

Standing up I noted a slight discomfort in my chest, it didn't hurt but it wasn't very comfortable. I rubbed at it with my hand as I looked around me.

Beneath my feet white marble shone clean and polished, I was in a large building. I knew it because of the silence it had. Only a building so large could give off a silence so intimidating. Whatever room I was in was filled with a lot of pale shades of gray, silver and creams. The walls went up to the highest roof I had ever saw, if I was even looking at it. It felt like the roof was never-ending. There was a tinkling sound from behind me.

On a large white couch a beautiful woman sat with her legs crossed, pale white robes of silk and lace that looked see through in some parts covered her body, but it still felt as if it was not clothing on her. Her long silver hair was not pulled up nor was it fully lose, it was half pinned up by what appeared to be wooden twigs. Pale limbs moved gracefully as she moved her cup around in front of her, not sloshing it out of her cup. Her gaze remained down, but her perfectly framed white brows were furrowed as if she were unhappy.

I glanced sideways before taking a step forward, as if to announce myself. Even though she was in the room as well, I felt very lonely. Perhaps it was her presence, or the lack of it. She was here and yet I did not feel her here. There was something about her that made it seem as if the room could not hold her.

763

"Welcome back, Vivian," a voice soft as silk said quietly, her voice made me relax but when she looked up I realized I shouldn't have.

Those eyes. There was something animalistic lurking behind those black eyes. Something with teeth and claws.

Then her words registered into my mind. She called my name.

"How do you know me? Where are we?" I asked, moving from one foot to the other. Not sure what to do.

She took a sip out of her cup, gaze unwavering from me as she did. She was very....intimidating and yet, I didn't feel threatened by her. I tilted my head in wonder. She almost felt familiar to me.

"You don't remember your first visit here?" she asked softly.

"Should I?"

Before the words had fully left my mouth I was suddenly seeing images before my eyes. Me under a tree, lightning and pain. But after the pain I remember silky silver strands and someone holding my hand, whispering comforting words and calming my wolf.

'Awaken my child. I shall see you soon enough.'

That had been the first thing I heard when I woke up at the hospital.

I couldn't feel my wolf.

The realization made me feel sad and odd. Like there was something missing from within me. I was missing a lot more than just her. I felt less than half complete.

She must have seen something go off in my eyes because she let out a soft sound.

"Luna?" I asked, stepping forward. She nodded and then patted the empty space beside her. Now that I was feeling a bit more trusting and still just as lonely, I walked over.

My feet didn't make a sound on the marble floor as I moved across it.

Setting her cup down she turned to me and smiled softly, reaching forward with her hand, her nails long and sharp but all she did was tuck my hair behind my ear and tapped my chin before sighing.

"I had to do it," she said after a moment. I frowned, not comprehending her until she explained. "Nothing in this world can truly be immortal, to live forever. Not even I." Her words brought on more images before my eyes. Zaliver. Joshula. A blade and me on the ground beneath it. I rubbed at my chest. Even though I knew that I should probably feel something by those images I couldn't. I felt oddly at ease.

"Oh," was all that left my mouth as a response.

"Everything has a weakness," She turned to smile at me. "even if it is just a small one. Although you are peculiar . . ."

"Maybe, but that doesn't mean that those weaknesses will help prevent so many lives from being ruined," I said without much thought. It was what I felt I should say. It was small, but she flinched.

"So many lives. So many . . ." she trailed off, looking up at the ceiling again. This time I looked up with her.

764

I gasped as the moon peered down at us, it's glow soft and so lovely. It made me want to reach up and try to touch it even though I knew I wouldn't be able to reach.

"Even those in high places can do nothing but to look down and wish they weren't so high." I was too focused on the moon to look at her but she knew I was still listening. "I can not change the paths that were meant to happen. But I do what I can, why is it that the paths to the end are what matter more than the end?" Her voice lowered, a tremor barely making it through. But there was fury in there as well.

"Perhaps because that is what allows us to know that we have come to the end?" I asked. She moved, but I did not turn to look at her yet.

"If that is true then how cruel the world can be. It takes and takes and gives only to take again. The forest provides, yet it still gets taken from. The future will not stand for this much longer," she murmured cryptically, almost as if she had forgotten I was there.

I turned to look at her.

"So many things could have been avoided, so many lives could have still been. Now every path has been altered." She glanced at me. "But not all things are meant to be."

"Why not?"

"Some howls are louder than others, some quieter. Some howls are heard while others are drowned out. Which howl would you rather have?" she asked me curiously.

I thought about it for a moment before answering.

"The quiet howl."

"And why is that?"

"So I could hear the drowned out howls. That way they would know someone was listening." I nodded my head as I spoke, feeling pleased with my answer. She looked at me for a moment before nodding with me.

"What now?" I wondered.

She looked up towards the ceiling as if it would answer the question. The moon looked back.

"What now indeed?" She mused to herself.

Looking in front of me I felt my heart skip a beat when I saw a clear pond surrounded by stones right where I had woken up. Something pulled at me to get closer so I did. The pond before was different from the other. This one had a clear image at the bottom of the pond while the other had been indecisive. Perhaps it had finally made up its mind.

Stepping up on the rough stones I peeked down as water splashed around harmlessly. It was an image of me under a blade and Joshula standing above me. But what caught my eyes was what was behind us. Zaliver.

I had never seen such pain on someone's face. It was not a pain that was caused by physical wounds, though he was hurt, but one by the soul crying out from the body, of the spirit within someone breaking. In his eyes I saw broken dreams and *unfinished stories, quiet rooms and dark rooms, long roads and the sea. Vast and yet so empty that he seemed to sink to a never-ending bottom. A gasp for air that would never come, in those eyes I saw rage that would grow and never find an outlet. Rage born of loneliness that would burn him from the inside out until it took the world and everyone with it.*

I had to look away from those eyes.

I hadn't heard her get up and yet I wasn't surprised to see her next to me. Peering in as well

"He will be lonely," she murmured. That made me sad.

Silence surrounded us.

"Does he have to be?" I questioned quietly.

She turned to look at me for so long I thought she hadn't heard me. I felt water lap at my feet and looked down to see water from the pond come up again to wet my feet. I wiggled my toes, feeling woeful at the moment.

The moon was looking upon me and all I could do was bask in its glow. It filled me with nothing but gave everything. There was peace here and yet I did not feel at peace.

Why was that? I rubbed at my chest again, feeling a different sort of pain then the one from earlier. Lost. Something was lost within me.

"No." I looked up at her voice. "No, he doesn't."

She had a smile on her face, I responded with a smaller one. She reached for my hands and held both of my palms out towards her before kissing them, filling my body with a sense of something beyond my understanding. As she did that it was as if the light from the moon above us had grown brighter, the water in the pond beginning to splash and become almost violent, bubbling and becoming bluer as the darkest parts of the ocean. I could no longer see the image.

Looking up I, black eyes peered at me with fondness. She opened her mouth and spoke. When she was done I was left opened mouthed and shocked. She laughed at my expression. Her laughter the sounds of wolves hiding in wait, of leaves brushing up against bark in heavy wind and of howls that traveled far and wide.

And that's how she left me when she pushed me into the pond.

~•~

VIVIAN GREY

I was laying down.

I was on the ground again , but this time there was a god damn blade sticking through my chest.

It was like I hadn't gone anywhere, hadn't died and come back. But I knew I had. I just knew it.

It was like I had a few seconds before time resumed. Joshula was still looking down at me with twisted triumph as his body slowly fell apart, a hand still holding onto the blade in my chest. Zaliver still stood behind him a few steps to far but looking tortured in the worst of ways.

And the blade in my chest still fucking hurt. I tried not breath, no point in wiggling the fucker.

With one last look up at the moon I gave a wink.

Joshula blinked and I knew time had continued, I gave the fucker a second before changing my pained expression to a glare.

His grin dropped from his face in angered confusion.

"You done?" I asked sarcastically.

Behind him I heard Zaliver's sharp inhale.

"W-What—" Joshula spluttered out, blue-green eyes widening. His face was rapidly thinning, his hair beginning to fall from his head.

I reached up with one hand, as soon as the palm of my hand made contact with the blade it turned to a cold mist that sprayed my face and chest. I felt my wound begin heal. Slower than usual but enough to strengthen me. I stood up, forcing him to back up.

"B-But how!? I stabbed—"

"The only thing you're taking down with you, is the realization that even with help, you still aren't worth shit." I lifted my hands and shoved him back with all the strength I had left in me.

It was enough to send him directly into Zaliver's open arms.

Joshula looked from me to his brother, opening his mouth.

"No! Wait—"

Zaliver snarled in face as he shoved his fingers into his brothers open mouth and ripped his jaw open so wide he separated his head from his mandible. He tossed it onto the ground and stepped on it multiple times, the bones shattering after the first kick. Something popped. He then went to the body and tore it to shreds with his claws. Not that there was much to shred. When he was done he spat on it.

Zaliver quickly looked up at me, anger dissolving into an emotion so strong I could pick a name. He took a shaky step towards me and almost collapsed, but even then he kept going forward.

"Vivian . . ." My name came out of his mouth like a prayer. Or perhaps like a plea. Whatever it was I would give it to him.

Right before he made it to my arms he fell to his hands and knees, coughing out blood. I raced over to him. He kept going for me, crawling over to me. I fell to my knees just as roughly, not caring about the slight sting as I wrapped my hands around him. His hold on me was weak but I knew that he was putting all of his strength towards hold me to him.

"Vivian." He managed to say shakily before a choked sound left him. I knew what was going through his mind, what he saw and how he felt.

"I know, it okay. We're gonna be okay," I whispered, kissing his head. His hold was loosening.

He's not. Not if he keeps bleeding out into your loving arms. My wolf reminded me.

He gave out a strained chuckle and then groaned.

She was right, looking towards his wound I reached out with the hand I hadn't used to grasp the sword and put it on his wound. It covered my hand in more blood but I didn't care. He hissed before his body became noticeably less tense and strained. I removed my hand when I felt his skin began to heat up. Checking it I saw that the wound was still open, but was no longer bleeding like it use to, the skin was starting to heal itself slowly. Perhaps slower than I was healing.

"H-How?" he asked, pulling away enough to look at me.

How beautiful his eyes were. So blue and nothing like they had been before, moments ago. And quickly closing.

I didn't even get to warn him when he slumped over me, his familiar weight forcing me to lay down with him on top. I held him tight as he lost consciousness. Peering up into the sky I whispered a 'thank you' to the moon.

Giving a sigh I did what Luna's did best and went to clean up the mess only my Alpha mate could make.

~•~

I had to override Zaliver's sleeping order which took me a while because I had to figure out what exactly he had commanded. First I woke Luke and told him what had happened, or some of it. He didn't need much to get me what I needed.

But by him going around to do what was needed he needed to talk to people and I knew word spread around the island as soon as I heard the howls of the wolves. They had all shifted. Some gave the howl for mourning of the alphas lost, some battle cries and other victory cries. I strained my ears and smiled when I heard the faint howls of wolves who simply howled to say 'we are here.'

A clean up crew arrived before I had finished counting to sixty. Trucks with wolves who jumped out with clean up suits on and tools. It was almost comical how they reacted to not the sight of all the blood shed or bodies or even the distraction of the temple but to the sight of their Luna pinned under their unconscious Alpha's weight. I would have poked fun at them if I hadn't been so bone tired.

When Luke arrived, Johnson jumped out of the car with him. I wasn't surprised to see that he slept with a nightcap on. Really. I wasn't. I knew those curls were too perfect in the morning.

They quickly got him into the car, laying him down gently, something which I appreciated. Johnson even scooped me up and walked me over to the car. I shook my head but didn't complain.

When we made it home, I wasn't surprised to see the lights on, Courtney and Mila stood at the doorway holding a blanket and cup of something that smelled like green tea. I'm not saying I snatched it out of her hands but I'm not saying I didn't.

I asked the guys to take Zaliver up stairs to our bedroom where the doctor was waiting anxiously. When he looked at me he immediately started talking rapidly, explaining. After a very long conversation to get him to calm down I let him check me over. All the while keeping my eyes on Zaliver's chest, making sure it rose and fell steadily. If I was tired he must have been exhausted.

Once the doctor was done with me I had him immediately check on Zaliver. I wanted to shower and change but I couldn't. Not until I knew Zaliver was fine. I took hold of one of his hands as the doctor began stitching at the wound in his shoulder which hadn't begun to heal. After checking that one the doctor was surprised to tell me that he would be healing at a human speed but that there wouldn't be any permanent damage, besides the scars, that is. The wound on his side also needed stitches and a wrap.

He was lucky. So *damn* lucky. I brought his hand to my lips and kissed it.

In total he would have three noticeable scars on his body. One on his side, the other on his shoulder and the one that now ran down his face, where Joshula had tried to peel his skin off. I think it added character, but I would have to wait to hear what he had to say. Zaliver had never had scars before, or at least none that I noticed. I would have a scar too. A vertical, ragged and un-patterned line where the blade had went through my chest. But I wasn't bothered much by it.

It was a reminder that nothing could live forever. Somehow that made life feel so much more important.

I had the doctor stay over, in case anything came up. Thankfully all Zaliver needed was rest and nothing straining when he woke up. Because he would, when he was ready.

Before going to shower I removed the bloody and ruined suit off of Zaliver, taking a wet cloth I cleaned him as best as I could, combed his hair and wrapped him up in cleaner blankets. He already looked much more comfortable, I kissed his forehead before I went into the shower.

Blood and grime washed off of my body, tears mixed in with the water after a while. I'm not sure how long I stood under the water, but when I got out I felt much better. Changing into some sweats I checked on Zaliver one last time before telling Luke to stand watch. I had things to do before I could sleep. While Zaliver was out I had to make sure things went back to normal, or as normal as they could get before sun up.

I mind linked Albericus and informed him of the basics of what happened. He was serious and helpful when I asked him to do something for me, but over all listened. Through the pack link I could feel his worry and need to get back, but he didn't sound it when he responded to me.

I'll be back soon, okay? Just hang in there. He said softly, as if not to startle me. I smiled. Alright. We'll be waiting.

I went down stairs where Mila and Courtney stood up immediately upon seeing me, they tried to hide their worry but it didn't matter if I still could feel it. I gave them a small nod and went free Frank from his cage. I laughed quietly when instead of running past me he nudged my closest hand until I picked him up. Reaching into his cage I put on the hat I had saved for him for this moment. He looked really handsome in his party hat.

Turning around I walked out the door and looked for Johnson who had given himself the duty to guard the house from the outside. I smiled every time I saw his nightcap. I don't even think he knew he still had it on.

I didn't have enough knowledge to pack link anyone who was working at the temple to clean up but I knew that Johnson probably did so I spoke to him about what I needed to be done. He pulled out his phone and began making out calls as soon as I was done.

Zaliver had said that my guards were more for detail and company once and maybe he was right, but they sure did get things done. They were the best.

Nobody seemed to be surprised to see me stay up for the majority of the night, but they didn't seem to happy about it either. When I did finally go back into the room Luke gave me a look that I was too tired to look into before leaving me alone with Zaliver.

Rather than bother him on the bed I went over to the window and sat there. At some point falling asleep.

The next day, Zaliver was still sleeping away with no hint of waking up. His sleep was so deep that I was sure that at any point he would start snoring.

Algebra had also come back at some time during the afternoon. I knew because my front door exploded off the hinges. I had sent everyone away, which they did so rather reluctantly, I was extremely grateful at that moment for that choice. They would have jumped on him and I would have hated to see just who won from that scrape.

"What the fuck, I can't leave for one freaking week without you two doing something I would have loved to be involved in! It's like you don't care about me!" he yelled, stepping on my door as he made his way in.

He came in barging in with a gift basket, goody bags, two teddy bears, a bouquet of beautiful flowers, a suitcase and a notebook. He dumped them all on my couch without a care, took a look at me, shook his head and wrapped me up in a hug.

I think this is the only time I can say I love Algebra. My wolf wailed.

"Know that I'm moving in and you two can't do that anymore," he murmured into my hair. My eyes widened.

I spoke too soon. My wolf muttered, shaking her big head.

He'll interrupt every time we try to have sex. Get him out now before it's too late. My beast growled.

"Who the hell invited you—"

"I did."

"Well, don't—"

"Stop being mean—"

"Suck my imaginary—"

"Hey, now—"

"Barry, we're here to comfort not smother. Put her down before you choke her." I heard Aurora say behind him. If possible Algebra's arms tightened around me. "I will light your ass on fire, you know I will."

I was lucky my feet landed on the ground before the rest of me did. I grabbed onto the couch before I fell. Algebra reached out to steady me, worried green eyes looking me over from head to toe in a frown.

"I mean this with total offense. You look like shit," he said seriously.

"Thanks for not holding back." I said dryly. He nodded.

Walking around the couch, I picked up the flowers and set them aside separately so that they wouldn't get crushed. I went through everything else with ease until I got to the notebook. I looked up at him with a questioning look on my face to which he nodded. I sighed but didn't say anything else on the matter.

Looking at both of them I waved them over to have a seat. Aurora and Algebra took the couch while I made my way and sat on the line chair so that I could face them.

"I died," I blurted out.

Both of their eyes widened in surprise at my words, or perhaps the randomness of them. Before they could say anything else I explained to them how Fate had found a way to kill Zaliver and I using or blood against one another. Perhaps Zaliver wanted to keep this a secret between the two of us, I wasn't sure, but I knew that it would be best to have someone else know in case anything in the nearby future were to happen. They listened with incredulous expressions, fascinated in some parts and concerned in others. I tried to keep my explanation short. This wasn't why I was telling them. Not completely.

"Real actual Zombies? Hmmm, somehow I'm more disappointed that you took the chance to fight them from me, then surprised that they actually exist," Algebra murmured, bringing his hand up to his chin.

"I didn't take anything from you. You just weren't here," I pointed out with an eye roll.

"Must be the fact that you're a werewolf, anything else that isn't human isn't that much shocking." I agreed with Aurora there. As long as you weren't human, anything past that was almost normal.

"Even so, she gets to cross off 'fought off zombies' from her list." He accused. My mouth fell open.

"I'd have to have a list—"

"Do you?"

"Maybe."

"See!"

"Oh shut up!" I leaned back against the chair. " Where was I?" I asked no one in particular. "Something about—"

"Um, you were . . . stabbed. In the chest. Dying," Aurora said unsure.

"I'm not sure how but after he stabbed me I woke up in a garden." I took a pause and then smiled. "It was beautiful, there were all kinds of plants and flowers everywhere." They were silent, still waiting for me to explain or get to my point.

"When I looked over my shoulder I noticed a little boy." Aurora inhaled sharply, her expression becoming understanding. Albericus tensed and then leaned up slowly. "He had these beautiful little curls that he wouldn't let me touch and brown eyes, the cutest little nose," I said fondly.

"You saw Andrew," Aurora whispered, shakily her hands went to her throats and chest as if she couldn't breath or wasn't sure how to. Albericus didn't move, his green eyes staring intensely at something on the ground before he cleared his throat, his voice strained and wavering.

"How was he?" he asked. His hands gripped at the cushion under him, knuckles turning pale. "Was he happy?"

"He told me to tell you that he was because he had his own garden." Aurora gave out a weak laugh, tears trailing down her face. "And he isn't alone, he also said he wanted you two to be happy and not worry about him." I gave them a sad smile, his shy smile forever ingrained into my mind.

Albericus brought his hands to his face for a moment before reaching over to Aurora and pulling her into his chest. She went in willingly, laying her head on his shoulder, her long locks blocking her expression but by the shakes of her shoulder I could tell she was silently crying. I just didn't know if it was from happiness or not. Albericus whispered something into her ear and she nodded, squeezing him tightly.

It was a sad but welcoming sight. I knew that they still had some healing to do and other things to go through, but felt like they could finally start now. Everyone always wonders about the after if death, now we all knew that there was something. And wherever I went for that moment be it heaven or some supernatural soul catcher, all that mattered was that Andrew was happy wherever he was. And that's all they could ask for in their position.

Looking away to give them their privacy I looked away but the looked towards the bottom of the couch they were sitting on when something small caught my eye. Behind them, inching towards the door that still laid broken on the ground, was Frank.

As if feeling a predator's gaze on him he stopped, his little black nose wiggled in the air as he sniffed the air, he turned his body to look around the room. Black eyes meeting my glare.

"Don't you dare!" I mouthed at him.

He made a small sound that could have been a 'fuck' in hedgehog language. He remained there for a moment before shuffling his small body around and quickly made his way down the hall.

As long as he was in the house I didn't care where he went.

I turned back to find Aurora and Algebra staring at me with amusement. I made and awkward sound that sounded between a sheepish laugh and a high-pitched sigh. Both of their eyes were a bit red but other than that they looked calmer if possible. A they were still hugging. Algebra's arm was over her shoulders, his hand playing with a lock of her hair as she had an arm wrapped around his waist.

"You still aren't moving in," I said, giving Algebra a pointed look.

"Fine, but not because you asked." He sniffed, acting snobbish.

"Oh I'm so grateful, thank you oh wise calculator," I said mockingly, raising both arms over my head and made a bowing motion from my chair. Aurora laughed as he flipped imaginary hair over his shoulder.

"Yes, well, you'll be missing all this glory every morning," He said off-hand.

"What glory? You look like all your allergies activated at the same time the morning. Face all swollen," Algebra gaped at his mate, jaw slack, "and eyes looking like green grapes that are about to go bad. Don't even get me started on the nest-"

"You said you loved the way I looked in the morning," he accused softly, pouting. She looked up at him and smiled.

"You are pretty in the morning . . . from the back." Maniacal laughter exploded out of me, filling the room. "Especially when your back is to me. Best view in the morning."

Algebra glared at his mate, teeth bared in a feral grin. He turned to look back at me, becoming serious.

"How is he?"

I turned to look up the stairs as if that would call him down, but even while talking to both of them I has still been checking up on Zaliver's breathing. Not much had changed. Overnight he had broken out in a cold sweat, but thankfully that hadn't lasted long. I think healing at human speed was at odds with his body and he was focusing on healing himself, even if he himself didn't know that.

"He's still sleeping. Doctor said some of his wounds would be healing at human pace-" I nodded at his shocked exclamation. "but that overall he just needs rest and recovery should follow. The only thing new would be some scars." I grimaced at that last part.

I still didn't know how he would take that. I knew he wasn't very vain, but he would have to look at the scars and think of his brother. I wouldn't be happy about that in his position. It was like a never-ending reminder.

"Has he made any progress?"

"Not much, but I checked his bandages in the morning and the wounds seems to be...okay. I'm not sure how human healing works, but I've been told it's slow." I was startled to feel a hand on my shoulder, Algebra had reached over, squeezing in a comforting gesture.

"I can help in that department," Aurora said happily. "Witches don't get the ' heal as fast as you bleed' thing. If you want I can check up on him, see if his healing is going in the right direction." A strain that I hadn't known I was carrying left as I nodded, grateful to have her around.

Both of us stood up and began making our ways to the stairs when Algebra stood up with both hands on his hips and looked at us with exasperation.

"Hello? Are you forgetting something?

"You're completely right. How could I have forgotten the most important thing here." I thumped my head. He smiled and began to speak but I cut him off.

"Fix my door." I pointed to it and then him. "Or I'll be demoting you from Beta to doorman." We went upstairs to the discouraged grumbled of an unhappy working wolf.

We were quiet when we walked in, not that it made much of a difference. Pointing out his wounds and holding his hand as she went to wash her hands I watched as she inspected him. Reaching up to comb his hair back even though it was already neat I played with his locks. When Aurora caught sight of his tattoo she made a small sound.

"Nice tats." And then got back to checking Zaliver over.

I thought she was going to say nice t-

I know what you thought she was going to say.

The scar on his face hadn't been that deep, but I didn't like to see him hurt. I ran my hand down the side of his face feeling his stubble. He had told me once that he had considered letting it grow out, but he didn't have the patience to let it grow out without getting annoyed at the feel of it on his face. The thought made me smile.

"Thank you." I looked over at Aurora who already had her eyes on me.

"Shouldn't I be the one saying that?" She chuckled and shook her head.

"You forget, it's my job to aid and help my Luna. I do so with pride." She took a breath. "But that's not what—"

"You don't have to thank me for anything," I said seriously. After a moment, a look passed between us.

I do believe we just had a moment. My wolf said, sticking her rear in the air as her tail moved from side to side.

Yeah, we did.

They didn't stay for much longer, perhaps because Algebra knew that I wanted to be alone for the rest of the day. I did have a lot of things to do, some which had me appreciating Zaliver's job as Alpha more. The dude never complained. Much. On the bright side Algebra had managed to fix the door. And when I say fixed I mean he had someone stop by to fix it. I rolled my eyes at that one.

The only surprise that came through the day was the amount of visits I kept getting. Each time I went to close the door I could sense someone near the border, on their way or I would hear a car come up the driveway. Pack members came in groups with things tied to their bodies if they came in wolf form or they would pull out gift baskets and get well cards. It warmed my heart and made me really happy to know that even before I was on the island Zaliver was still cared for.

Perhaps the best part of all of the visits was the fact that I didn't even have to cook. There was so much food being sent from the pack house chef that I had enough food that I was beginning to consider buying another fridge. After packing all the food away I had to make many trips up and down the stairs as I brought flowers I got the room. It gave the air a flowery smell. At some point I think I saw Zaliver's nose twitch. I took that as a sign that either the room was way to floral or that he was about to wake up soon.

When the sun began to set I turned all of the lights off and brought two plates stacked all the way to the top after my wolf began to whimper about 'midnight snacks and how rolling over and reaching was so much more convenient than getting up'. I had to agree with her there. That and Zaliver would be hungry when he woke up. Yup, that was the main reason. Nothing more.

I was going up the stairs, trying not to drop the asses of water balanced close to my chest when I heard a small sound and looked down.

"Whoops." I moved my foot to the side. "Almost crushed you there. Well, that would have been a bit traumatizing." I not sure if he scoffed or screamed in his own way.

Frank scrambled from under my frame and instead of heading down the stairs started to make his way back up. Either he was running from me or he was declaring where he was staying for the night. Giving him enough room I made my way up.

"Do they make glow vests for hedgehogs? They should," I muttered under my breath.]Entering the room I placed the food on his desk and panicked a bit when I noticed the stains on the laptop.

"What the hell, I didn't even touch you!" I whisper shouted, glaring at the smudged contraption. Shoving it to the side gently I made more room for the food. I placed both cups away from the edge but also away from the laptop. I'd take a smudge over spilled water anyway.

I turned back around and went to close the door when I caught side of a Frank, struggling to pull himself up on the last step. I hear my wolf and beast give a mental 'aww'. When he finally managed it he immediately came over to the door, I welcomed him in and shut it behind him. He went directly for the bed. It would take him a while to reach his goal, Zaliver's face. I would remove him before he did.

I went back to my original spot of the night before and looked out the window as the sun went and the moon slowly rose. I was munching on some chips when I heard a sharp inhale. I spun around and placed my plate down hastily, Zaliver had his eyes shut tightly before he opened them, immediately looking towards the door with a fearfully desperate look in his eyes but his movements were jerky like he couldn't quite control his muscles.

"Vivian?" he yelled out, beginning to untangle himself from the blankets, I briefly heard a muffled high pitch noise.

"I'm over here," I said walking over to him before he could tear anything.

His head turned over to look at me so fast his hair which had been brushed so nicely, flew all over the place. Blue eyes widened as he

776

took me in, it was like seeing me only lit a fire in him because he was out of the

bed and stumbling to me with more desperation. When I reached him his arms engulfed me, pulling me tightly to his chest. I hugged him back carefully, not trying to agitate the wounds I knew he would feel in a few seconds. He was whispering my name repeatedly, over and over.

"It's okay Zaliver, I'm right here. We're gonna be okay." I felt him take in deep breaths, inhaling my scent and clinging to me tighter.

One of his hands came up to cup the back of my neck, his hand forming a fist in my hair as soft growls vibrated through his chest. The grip wasn't painful but I knew that he wasn't in complete control at the moment. He tilted my head, baring the side of my neck with his mark. He leaned down and just skimmed the top of his teeth over it. I jerked, my knees suddenly feeling shaky under me.

"Y-You-" It was like he had just finished running a marathon, his breaths coming out harshly. "I saw his stab you. I felt- gone, you were gone," he said pulling away from me to look down as he towered over me.

His face was so close to my own, strands of black hair barely skimming got my forehead. If it hadn't been for the window behind us, it would have been hard to see the way the blue in his eyes swirled in different shades as he fought to control himself from doing whatever it was he wanted to. I had a basic idea. I'm sure it involved a lot of teeth marks on my flesh, but he had just seen something that meant he also didn't want to hurt me. Even if just a little. His side of the bond was screaming from his end, it was like his soul was just holding on tighter to mine, it was like he was slowly ingraining himself until nothing separated us. Not even the bond that tied us together. It was intense.

"But I'm not. And neither are you. Something we can thank Luna about," I said softly. Swallowing heavily, he didn't say anything, just gazed down at me, checking my face all over for something.

"I'm going to want a run down later about what exactly that means, but right now all I can think about right now is never letting you out of my sight," he said seriously.

"And how do you think I felt? You fainted on me," I said, my words only coming out harshly from sound, but though the bond I pushed all the love and warmth I had for him.

"I'm sorry, but out of both of us you gave me the bigger scare. I fainted, you died," he said just as harshly, but he returned my affection. "As your Alpha I find that the suitable punishment for that is forever at my side." He declared. I heard no amusement in his voice. He was really ordering me to be by his side forever. I bared my teeth at him, he did the same.

After a moment I felt his hold on my hair loosen until he let it go and brought it to my face to hold it. He leaned his forehead down to mine. I closed my eyes and let the calmness of the moment wash over us.Opening my eyes again I pulled away, or tried to, his growl made me stop. He shook his head and brought my head down to his chest.

"No, you're never leaving my arms," he murmured, I let out a small laugh. I rubbed my hand on his lower back.

"Not that I want to, but you're going to have to relax if you don't want to tear at your stitches." I began.

"Stitches?" he asked momentarily perplexed. When I felt him tense I knew the pain was starting through get through to his instincts.

"Yeah, stitches." I tried to lead him to the bed to sit down, but he shook his head and instead pulled me to the bathroom. It was a slow walk, but I didn't mind.

"I've never had stitches before," he said looking down at himself. He raised a hand to poke at his side wrap and hissed when he did. The skin was red and pinkish when I had checked earlier. Aurora said it was healing faster than a human but slower than a wolf.

You look down too. My wolf said enthusiastically. I rolled my eyes.

Zaliver threw his head back and began to laugh and then groaned half way.

"I'm not going to last with them long with that smart mouth of yours and your wolf trying to heat things up between us every chance she gets," he said shaking his head and looking down at me.

Is it working? My wolf asked shamelessly. Zaliver grinned down at me.

When we made it into the bathroom I figured he was going to go into the shower but was surprised when he turned and lifted me up and placed me on the edge of the sink.

"What the hell, you're not suppose to over work yourself Zaliver! You just woke up, you can't just lift me up," I growled out at him, checking to see if any blood had seeped through his wraps. Ignoring me, he began to lift his sweater off of me. Letting him I glared. When he began to lift up my shirt I huffed but lifted my arms again.

"I'm suppose to be taking care of you." I pouted, annoyed. He leaned down and nuzzled his nose with mine.

"You did. You still are." He pulled away. "Now it's my turn. Where are you—" He froze.

I softened, knowing he was looking at the scar on my chest. His jaw clenched as he lifted his hand and traced it softly with the tips of his fingers. I made sure not to squirm. Rage and a darkness began to taint the calm mood he had just been in. I tried to calm him before he exploded a blood vessel.

778

"It's—"

"Don't say it," he said through clenched teeth, his eyes snapping up to look at me. He dropped his hands on either side of me, something began to bend in his hold. This was what I was afraid of happening. Closing his eyes he took a deep breath, his chest lifting as he did so.

"At least we'll have matching scars....sort of." I joked softly, easing my hands through his hair to massage his scalp in hopes that it would distract him. It did. He leaned further into my touch, tension leaving him slowly. He raised his head and looked over my shoulder before leaning forward.

He'd seen the scar over his face. I held still while inspected it. Turning his face to the side. He didn't say anything for so long I was beginning to get nervous until his eyes flickered over my face.

"Does it bother you?" he asked, his voice coming out blankly.

"No. Why?"

"No reason." He began to lean away from me when I took his face in my hands and pulled him back.

"I think you look handsome and dangerous." I kissed over his eyebrow and pulled back. "It will add a whole new section to those bad ass stories that will spread about you."

"You alway have to look at the bright side of things, don't you?" he murmured with a shy smile.

"If I didn't, then you'd be in trouble," I pointed out. He shrugged and stepped back. When he began patting me down and trying to rip my sweats off, I poked him.

"Quit it."

He gave up once he was done with his search and saw that my next approach was aimed between his uncovered legs. He turned around to start the shower and then began to stepped in.

"I'm pretty sure you're not suppose to get those wet," I said jumping down carefully. I began to remove the rest of my clothes.

He turned to look at me from over his shoulder, his eyes roaming over me in a way that wasn't the same as he had been earlier.

"How sure is pretty sure?"

I made a face. How the hell did humans heal with that thing on? Did they wrap plastic around themselves

"Just . . ." I began to worry when he reached over and pulled me to him.

"How about this, we do one limb at a time?" he asked, raising both brows for approval.

Just limbs? My wolf asked perversely.

"Has she always been like this?" I asked out loud, trying to shush her.

"You mean have you always been like this? Don't forget, she just voices what you really think."

I had no response to that so instead I just grabbed a sponge and helped him shower. Doing as he had asked me before, I told him what had happened when Joshula had stabbed me. He was quiet through it all, sometimes he would stop and look down at me as if he couldn't believe I was there, when he did that he would bring me closer to him. He only interrupted once when I mentioned Andrew.

"I'm glad he's happy," he said his voice sounding amazed and a tad bit sad.

By the time I finished telling him everything he was as clean as he could be. I had to make him sit on the ground to clean his hair, but I don't think he minded all that much, wrapping his arms around my legs he leaned his head back with closed eyes, but he would trail his hands up and down or he'd draw patterns on my skin. It was maddening. We were quiet while I rinsed his hair, him thinking and me enjoying how heavy his dark locks left when wet, they were silky.

"I'm going to start to use your shampoo if my hair starts looking like this," I muttered, lifting a strand and watching it slip between my fingers. He smiled and then opened his eyes. Small droplets of water clung to his dark lashes, the clearness of them contrasting against his vivid blue.

I leaned down and kissed him. Immediately I felt his arms detangle themselves from around him and go to my shoulders, trying to push me down. I smiled against his lips.

"I believe you owe me a continuation kiss." His voice came out deeper, longing and want burning thick.

"And I believe the doctor said recover and no strain."

"The only—"

"I will bite you if you make a dick joke."

"Is that suppose to be a bad thing?" he asked flirtatiously, winking at me.

"Up, clearly you need food." He pouted but did as I told him.

Grabbing two towels he threw one around his waist and then began to pat me down, we tugged for the towel when he realized I wasn't going to let him bend down with his stitches. A whine came from the back of his throat, I ignored it and took the towel from around his waist, knowing he would just run the towel down without caution. I bundled it and softly dried around the bandages carefully, I didn't need to see his expression to know that even if it wasn't on the wound directly it was tender skin.

When we were all patted down and we went into the closet to change. I decided to go with just one of his shirts, I picked out one of his button down burgundy shirts and slipped on some underwear. He

780

picked out his normal sleeping bottoms and a loose black sleeved shirt. When he I walked over to him he smiled at my choice of sleepwear, he planted both hands on my waist.

Lifting his shirt I gently patted at his bandages, staying away from his wound. I grimaced at the feel of his bandages. We might as well just got them wet with how damp they were. At least the one around his shoulder we seemed to have been able to avoid wetting besides the few drops that landed. But the one around his waist? Not a chance. When I told Zaliver he shrugged, turned his nails to claws, lifted his loose black long sleeve and ripped the bandages clean off and threw it in the direction of his towel. I groaned in disapproval, but also agreeing that wet bandages were probably a bad thing.

"Don't worry, I'm going to put another bandage on it," he said letting his shirt drop. He reached for the towel around my head and began to dry my hair messy. I looked up at him with disbelief.

"You're going to put twelve bandages on twelve stitches? Really?" Now he was the one who rolled his eyes at me as if I were being absurd. I could tell that his method of drying was creating a mess on my head as I saw strands stick up in all sorts of directions but I paid that no mind. I'd make him brush it out later.

"Yes Vivian, I'm going to put twelve annoyingly small damages on each stitch individually. You caught me." A reluctant smile forced its way into my face. Seeing that Zaliver smirked at me. I stuck my tongue out at him. He gave me a look that warned me of what he would do if I did that again.

Stepping back I motioned for him to go put his bandages on, I took over the drying of my nest of a hair. When I was done I walked over to the bed and fixed the sheets. I also discreetly looked for a missing hedgehog. When I couldn't find him I walked over to the plate I had left by the window and continued where I had left off.

A few minutes later I heard Zaliver make his way out from the bathroom. I turned and motioned to the food on the table but he ignored me and just placed his hands on my hips and brought me back until my back touched his chest. Once it did he let out a content breath and put his chin on top of my head.

"You need to eat—"

"I will. I just want to hold you first," he said, his thumbs rubbing soothing circles on my hips.

I wasn't going to shove food down his mouth so I let it be, once I was done with my own I set it down and drank some water, all the while Zaliver clung to me.

"How are you?"

"Hmm?"

"You know, after everything. How are you emotionally?" It took him a second to respond but I sensed only the truth when he spoke.

"Relieved. Like we can finally move on with our lives without shadows lurking from the past."

"And you?" he asked me, squeezing me gently. He didn't have to ask twice I knew what he really meant.

"I'm saddened by what had to be done, but I also know that it had to be so I feel guilty to think like that. I didn't want to kill them, but they were already dead." I didn't know if I made sense but he seemed to have understood me. I'm guess I got that with his experience, he must have been through tons of battles and deaths.

Did he feel so . . . tired afterwards? So tired that he couldn't sleep because he was in some kind of numb fatigue? I felt as if I could sleep for days but I didn't want to close my eyes, I was scared of what I might see. Their faces. What I would hear.

"You did what you had to and there's nothing to feel guilty about. They took their lives from them, their loved ones, their bodies and he used them for their own sick pleasure. If anything Vivian, you liberated the ones you could from his hold. Anything else is coming from your heart baby. Your such a good person, that you can't help but to feel it all."

I didn't have anything to say to his response because I didn't know what to say. I let him hold me to his chest, content to feel his heart beating. Alive. I nodded in agreement and felt like that should be the last time we touched the subject. At least for now. We didn't have to rush.

When he did finally start eating it was only in small bites before his brows furrowed and he stared at the food and then raised a brow at me.

"Where'd you get the food?" he asked, finishing his water.

"I could have made it." I crossing my arms over my chest. He waited silently.

"Yeah okay, I didn't make it," I admitted sheepishly. He chuckled and kissed my cheek. "But I could have!"

"And I'm sure I would have loved it," he said nicely. I snorted as soon as he finished.

"A lot of pack members stopped off today with food and presents." I gestured around the room to all of the flowers. He frowned and followed my movement, his eyes widening slightly as he looked around.

"Huh, hadn't noticed." He turned back towards me.

"How do you not notice all of these flowers?"

"I only had my eyes on you," he said simply. I felt my insides warm at his words. He wasn't even trying. He was quiet after that, a pensive look on his face. I had a guess as to where his thoughts where.

"You're going to relax and do absolutely nothing tomorrow. I don't care if Algebra comes in screaming about how humans have discovered wolves." I poked at his chest. He glanced down at my finger. "You're going to rest." He shook his head at me, his eyes glowing with amusement and fondness.

"I love that you want me to rest—"

"Because you will."

"But there are so many things-"

"That are already taken care of." That shut him up. For a moment. He gave me a look that read between 'what exactly have I missed' and 'am I out of a job' with a pinch of 'I don't know if I should feel proud or worried'.

"Bodies?"

"The dead were tagged with names and sent off to their family after they were medically cleared. Those who were left alive were tended to and some are still under surveillance to see if whatever Joshula did to them have any side effects beside the obvious," I said calmly. He raised a brow.

"Temple?"

"Under cleaning and reconstruction. A temporary area was set up close by, where here's an easy access to it for everyone from all ages and not far away that anyone who gets lost won't wander off a cliff." A challenging look entered his eyes and I held back a smile.

"Pack?"

"Accounted for and checked. No one was bitten or scratched while Fate hid the alphas here. They haven't asked for an explanation, all they seem to know is that they were put to sleep for their safety."

"Weapons?"

"Weapon. Cleaned and ready for your disposal if ever needed." By the look that flashes over his face I doubted that blade would last another day on the island.

"Traitorous brother?"

"Smashed to pieces. Burned. Burned again. Burned one more time. Mixed his ashes with salt to keep him salty in the afterlife. Put in a jar which was placed in a box which was then labeled 'You open, you die' and placed in your man cave." I saw his lips twitch.

"Hogan?"

"Probably dehydrated in that room we left him."

"Door?"

"Algebra said he'd handle that."

"Venom?"

"Checked in and apologized for not being able to come, but that he'd be here in a week's time."

"Numbers?" I didn't need to ask to know what he meant.

"Out of the mated alpha pairs, five gone, seven mateless and two completely fine, the others are in different states of wounded. Total death count up to eleven. Not including the alphas that are still...unaccounted for." He flinched at the numbers. There had been a few more bodies found near the temple.

"Alphas?"

"Put together based on pairs, those who still have them." I took a breath. "Family members have been informed of their whereabouts and their losses. I took care of calling personally."

It was the least I could do. That's what the note-book had been filled with, phone numbers and addresses of deceased and family members of the alphas. I spent the majority of the afternoon hearing people cry over the phone and having to explain things as the best way that I could without giving too much away. I still wasn't sure how much information was too much.

Putting his cup down he fully turned towards me, cupping my face in his hands he ran his thumbs under my eyes. Pride shined in his face before worry over rode it.

"You haven't slept much have you?" he whispered, his face worried. I shook my head.

Did I really look that tired?

"How could I? I knew as soon as you woke up you'd start running around the place and I think after everything we've been through we could use a day or two of relaxation." I sniffed, feeling my eyes get watery. "So I took care of it."

"I'm so proud of you." He pulled me into a hug. "My brave and strong Luna. So, so proud." I took a shaky breath, his clean and strong scent calming me.

He walked forward, making me sit down on the window seat. It wasn't long before he sat by the window as well, picking me up until I sat on his lap. I leaned back against him as he brought me close.

"We'll rest for however long you want." He promised me. "Albericus can do all the work." We both laughed softly at that.

Something small ran across the floor and disappeared as quickly as it appeared. I felt Zaliver tense behind me.

"Was that a rat?" I pinched his forearm. His growl rumbled through his chest, shaking me.

"You know who that was."

"Yeah. A rat." I went to pinch him again when he nipped my shoulder. "Or it could have been Frank." I giggled at his grumble.

"So, what are we going to do about the blood thing? You know the whole reason for your stitches." I stretched the last words out, feeling awkward for some reason. Maybe it was because I could be used to kill my mate. But then again it worked both ways.

I felt Zaliver shrug from under me, no tension coming off of him. I turned to peer over my shoulder.

"What do you mean?" I shrugged, lifting my hands in question. He shrugged. Seeing my glare he sighed.

"I'm not worried because nothing like that will ever happen again. You won't be in the same place as me or another enemy. The possibility of getting stabbed with the same weapon, or even getting stabbed-"

"What if we invite someone over for dinner and they stab me and then come at you with the same knife?" I asked seriously.

"Like hell, they'll be lucky if I let them hold anything other than their plastic plates with you in the room," he snarled softly.

"Zaliver—"

"We'll take this as it goes, but now we know what to look for." I let his words settled over me,he was right. We couldn't predict the future but we could plan for it. Protect it.

"Alright."

I'm not sure how long we sat at the window for, but at some point I had turned my head to look out of the window. Perhaps we hadn't gone to bed because he had slept most of the time, I hadn't wanted to sleep yet or perhaps we simply wanted to enjoy each other's company after everything we had been through.

The moon was once more illuminating the sky with its glow. Seeing something move under it I opened the curtains, basking the room in a soft glow. Behind me Zaliver turned his head to look at what had caught my attention.Nearby the moon a large cloud was moving closer.

"Look, it's a cloud," he said, amusement lighting his voice. I smiled.

We stared up at the cloud as it slowly made its way underneath the moon. Both of us watching as slowly it moved until a small part began to detach itself from the larger cloud.

Taking my hands off of my lap I placed each hand on top of Zaliver's and dragged them across my body and under his shirt until they laid on top of my lower stomach and then pressed down softly. It took a moment but he froze underneath me. His chest no longer lifting for air.

"What shall we call the little one?" I mused out loud.

He still didn't move.

"To bad clouds don't show gender, that would be really helpful."

Slowly his hands spread over my stomach, the faintest amount of pressure.

"I'm hoping your genes are stronger, your eyes are really pretty."

Slowly he sat up, moving me gently down so that his nose was at the crook of my neck.

"I'm not saying that there's anything wrong with my genes but I'm just saying. I think we can all agree my wits can paralyze the faint hearted." I chuckled at my own joke.

His chest was rising rapidly, his breath tickling my shoulder. His body trembling.

"We'll probably have to move the wedding up so that my dad doesn't glare at you during dinners from now on."

He began to stand up, sliding me down his body until my butt landed back on the cushion. Looking up I tried to catch the expression on his face but he was looking down, his damp hair dangling over his face. His arms hung by his sides limply.

Maybe he didn't get it. My wolf wondered. He didn't twitch, only his chest lifting to show that he was breathing rapidly.

"You know," I started. "because I'm pregnant . . ." I trailed off.

Something that caught light in the moon's glow and was clear made its way down his face quickly. He was crying. Before I could say anything else he was on his knees in front of me, his head on my knees, his hands holding onto my waist. He was mumbling something over and over again into my legs, his lips speaking directly onto my thigh. I put a hand on his shoulder.

"What are you saying?" I asked. He spoke a little louder. My brows furrowed as I tried to understand him.

"What?" I asked again.

When he lifted his head to look up at me, taking a hand I brushed back his hair, watery blue eyes looked back at me.

"Family." He croaked out, his voice sounding overwhelmed. He smiled at me. "We're going to be a family," he whispered, his eyes filled with felicity, love, hope and future promises that I knew he would not break for anything in the world. I smiled down gently at him, leaning down to rest my forehead against his, feeling my own tears of happiness stream down my face.

"Yeah," I whispered. "We are."

He closed his eyes for a moment, pure bliss overcoming his features before he opened his eyes. As ever, their intensity pulled at me from the core.

"Our own family, Vivian," he said amazed. I laughed, understanding where he was coming from.

786

"I'm going to be a dad," he whispered to himself, his smile turning into a grin. He leaned down and stared at my stomach with wonder. "I'm going to be your dad."

I snorted.

"They can't hear you yet." His eyes snapped up to stare at mine.

"They?" he choked out, surprised.

"Luna mentioned something about a 'them', so I'm assuming twins run in the family." I shrugged. I was beyond blown away when she mentioned that to me before shoving me in the pond. But I'd keep what she said to myself. A girl's gotta keep somethings to herself.

"I'm going to be their dad," he said proudly. They hadn't even been born and the man was proud of them. He looked up. " I'm going to be your husband." I smiled.

"And I'm going to be your wife and their mom," I agreed.

"And we're going to be a family." He reached up and kissed me with so much tenderness that it brought more tears to my eyes. He kissed those away too.

"I'm in love with you, Zaliver."

"And I will love you forever, Vivian."

"Seeing how I'm going to have your kids, that's the only option left for you." He shook his head with a laugh, watery eyes gleaming like jewels.

"You think I'm joking."

"I'd love you even if you were."

"It's a good thing I'm not."

Here he was on his knees before me, tears streaming down his face without any sign of stopping, pure joy lighting up his face. The man who dominated and controlled all those who roamed with teeth and claws, the howlers of the moon. Feared, hated and loved by many.

My mate.

The Lupus Deus.

EPILOGUE

The sound of sound of a car pulling up to the driveway made me turn around and wave my arms around wildly. Heads turned in my direction and nodded quickly, everyone shushing immediately. Well, almost everyone.

Two sets of small feet ran towards the door quickly, stumbling over themselves but holding one another to make sure the other didn't fall. I smiled and walked to the front of the house.

You know I can hear everyone.

I don't care. Act surprised.

A car door slammed in front of the house and someone began walking up the steps. Two little bodies stood a few inches away from the door, their little heads lifted up expectantly. As soon as the door began to swing open they let out ear twitching screams and launched into the arms that already awaited their attack. I grinned and leaned against the back of the couch.

Zaliver picked both of them up and held them close to his chest as they squealed and squirmed in his arms, their little hands petting and pinching him roughly. He turned his head to give both of their cheeks loud kisses which caused them to giggle crazily.

"Hi Saby. Hi Seby." His amused voice said leaning down to put both of them back on their feet.

"Hi daddy!" Saby and Seby said in harmony, happily.

Saby's wide blue eyes outlined in silver gleaming while Seby's large brown eyes outlined in silver reflected joy.

"What are you two pups up to?" Zaliver asked playfully, looking back and forth between the two.

Their eyes widened at the same time at his question, both opening their mouths and then closing. They turned back to look at me and then took off running down the hall and to the back, all the while holding hands. I shook my head with a small laugh. Turning back around I found my mate already looking at me.

I clasped my hands behind my back and took a few steps forward until we stood front to front, I tilted my head to look up at him with a large grin on my face. I felt his arms slide around my waist and pull me closer to his firm body. An all to familiar feeling began to stir in me as I looked into a pair of darkening blue eyes that peered down at me with none of the innocence that they had a few seconds ago.

"Well hello, mate, welcome home," I said cheerfully. His eyes narrowed.

"What are you up to now?" Zaliver asked leaning down, his black locks falling freely now that he wasn't using any product to hold it back anymore.

"Nothing. Why do you ask, my love?"

He opened his mouth to say something when someone from outside sneezed followed by a smacking sound. Zaliver looked over my shoulder and then looked back at me with a raised brow. I blinked, keeping the smile on my face.

"You wouldn't be throwing me a birthday party now, would you?" he murmured softly, leaning closer to my ear and then kissing under it and pulling back to look at me.

"Of course I am." My innocent grin turned devious.

I leaned up to leave a quick kiss on his cheek but he turned his head and captured my lips with his own, biting my lower lip he tugged gently. I couldn't help but bring my hands around to his back and pull him closer. His chest vibrated with his soft growls. Three days without him and it was maddening to believe I let him get out of my sight. When he pulled back I knew I was a little less composed.

I could tell by the stupefied look I could feel on my face and the look of pride and carnal appreciation he looked at me with. Leaning down to my ear he whispered in a voice that was silk on my skin on this hot day.

"That's a shame." I felt him pick a lock of my waist length hair and twirl it around his finger. "Because I really wanted to spend it with you." He pulled back completely from my body, taking only my right hand and bringing it to his lips as he looked down. "Alone."

I couldn't help the shiver that overcame my body.

That's it. It's a wrap. Tell all of those fucker's they got to go. My wolf howled. Her tail was wagging and hitting the barrier of my mind so hard I could feel it.

Zaliver looked down at me wickedly. I narrowed my eyes at him. Taking the same hand he was holding I hoped him in his stupidly sturdy and rock hard chest. His eyes trailed down to look at my finger.

"Nuh uh, I know what you're trying to do. It's not going to work this year." It worked last year.

"Are you sure-""Hush up and look surprised," I said firmly. He threw his head back and groaned before standing up straight.

I glanced over his attire. Brown work boots, white jeans with only the front of a light blue sweater with a low neckline tucked in. I glared up at him. He blinked innocently. The sweater was the only thing he had over his chest. If you stared hard enough you could see through and see the outline, not that with the front tucked in, was hard to see.

"Not like you didn't know you were coming to a party." I shook my head and turned back to go down the hall when I felt his arms slide around me, his body following mine.

"An alpha is always ready," he said smugly behind me, I felt him plant a kiss on my hair.

"So that's why you fainted when-"

His body pushed mine to walk faster, almost tripping out of the back door and into the crowded backyard party.

"Happy birthday!" Everyone screamed.

I didn't turn around to see the expression on his face but I knew it must have been comical by the sight of everyone else's. He might have expected the party, but he hadn't expected this many people in our new and temporary backyard. In order to get as many people from the pack here I had the wooden fence taken down and brought in extra tables and chairs.

"Bet you didn't see that one coming," I said smugly.

"Nicely played, mate," he said a bit reluctant. I laughed at the tone in his voice and escaped his grasp and went to check on everyone. The man needed to mingle and enjoy his birthday.

Thankfully people had brought their own chairs and tables, some just chilling out in wolf form and watching over the swimming of pups playing around. Very few people had actually ever been into our house so only a handful of people were in the pool. Some adults, like Luke who was chatting with Courtney still lingered and eyed the kids who looked like they were getting ready to make a jump for it as soon as they saw the chance.

I caught sight of my parents talking with Hannah's, Hannah herself was bouncing a now five-year old Jayda in her lap. Walking around the pool I caught sight of a three-month pregnant Mila with her feet in the pool, Johnson with newly cut hair, between her legs leaning over to say something to her belly. I strained to hear what he was saying as I walked by them.

"All the hair she cut off. You'll do me proud little buddy."

I chuckled and moved on. When I was halfway to the back and near the second grill I made a quick stop by Mark to grab a burger, all this walking was burning carbs. I made little stops every once in a while to chat with some friends or to ask who someone was. There were so many people here that I was surprised the island hadn't tipped over with everyone on one side.

When I was making my round back to the house I caught sight of Algebra and Aurora under a tree, a blanket under them. In between them was three-month old Lily. Her giggles and childish sounds making both of her parents coo at her. She had a mess of brown hair and lovely green eyes. She was absolutely a delight to be around. I stopped for a moment and watched them, feeling satisfaction at their happiness. Behind them I caught sight of a flower bloom, the petals a plum color.

When I was back in the backyard I saw the most adorable thing. Well it was hot before it got adorable.

Zaliver was standing near the empty part of the pool, shoes and socks removed, he simply lifted his sweater and threw it on top of his shoes before jumping in, white jeans and all. When he resurfaced he tossed his hair out of his face and neared the edge with both arms held open.

Seby was in his black swimming shorts, blue arm floaties on each arm. He didn't hesitate before jumping into his dad's arms with a laugh. There was a small splash, Zaliver held him above water with one arm. Seby splashed in the water before turning back. He pushed his black hair out of his face before holding his arms out like Zaliver had before.

Near where Seby had stood, Saby now stood in her pink arm floaties and bathing suit, she even had her swimming goggles on her head, somewhat tangling her long brown hair. She twirled her hands near her chest nervously, she shakily dipped a foot into the water and whimpered. I didn't have to look away from her to know that the sound had caught everyone's attention. I neared the pool slowly. Not really worried.

"Come on Sabrina, you know I've got you," Zaliver said softly, motioning for her to come forward. She did so slowly. "Has daddy ever let you down before?" She shook her head. Zaliver turned to look down.

"Has daddy ever let you down Sebastian?" Zaliver asked, Seby shook his head quickly and turned to look at his sister with big honest eyes.

Seby's brown eyes outlined in silver began to turn into a familiar icy blue now outlined in silver.

"You can trust us Sabrina." He splashed the water and the. Held out both of his hands. "See? The waters okay."

Saby looked into her brothers blue eyes outlined in silver and her own began to turn brown with a silver outline. She took another peek down and then jumped into Zaliver and Seby's arms. Everyone cheered when she did. I felt my eyes water a little at the sight. All three of them played around in the water for a bit. Zaliver keeping a firm hold on both despite their pleads and promises to hold the edge.

"Good job, papa wolf," I praised.

791

"All in a day's work for father wolf," he answered proudly.

Catching sight of a white-haired and rather tall fellow I quickly squeezed passed a group of pack members and made my way to Venom. He stood a bit off to everyone else, looking out towards open sea and the slowly setting sun. He wore a thin white vest over a button down white shirt and white slacks and golden tipped white converse.

"Hey, Venom."

He turned and looked down at me with golden eyes. It was easier to read his facial expressions over the years. Every time he came around he brought presents for both of the kids and it was easy to tell when he was amused or happy. Right now he was peering down at me with amusement even if there was minimal change made to his face.

"Hello, Luna—"

"What did we say?" I cut him off with a playful scold, putting both hands on my hips. There was a small lift on the corner of his lips, I caught sight of a small fang.

"Hello, Vivian." It was easier now to repress the automatic step that most people took when they heard the slight hiss in his voice.

"There we go. So, what are you doing over here by your lonesome self?" He looked back out toward the sea.

"Simply gazing at the sea. It reminds me of home," he hissed softly.

I looked him over. All these years and yet no matter how many times I asked Zaliver he would never tell me how he met Venom. All he said was that Venom was and I quote 'someone much like myself and yet completely trapped in his past actions'. When I asked if he had also pissed off a god Zaliver had given me a dirty look.

"Hmm," was all I said to his home comment. I also didn't know where he really lived or why he came around when he did but I trusted Zaliver's judgment so I trusted Venom too. "So, when am I going to see you with a partner?" I asked.

Venom turned to look at me, black iris contracting vertically in his golden eyes. It almost made him look angry but I felt not aggression coming from him, it was actually quite the opposite.

"When I catch one I shall let you know." I laughed at his words and nodded.

"Just make sure you're the one to catch her. Not a friend of yours," I muttered that second part more to myself.

"I heard that!" I heard Algebra yell.

"No but seriously, once you catch her let her know you mean business," I said, looking up at Venom. "You're a good-looking extra tall snake man with good fashion taste. Any girl would be lucky to have you. I'm surprised you don't have a flock of heartbroken girls trailing after you." I teased.

Venom shook his head, his pale face sharpening as his lips curled up enough to catch the sight of two fangs. I smiled up at him.

"You are far too kind," he said softly.

I heard a lot of mumbling pick up after that line. I turned to glare behind me and it all stopped. A lot to the pack had caught me on some moody days. And some savage days. And on days where the sun was out.

When it was time to cut the cake I went into the kitchen to grab the cake, catching sight of me as I walked by the mirror in the hall. As well as the photos of everyone on the walls.

The wedding, ultrasound, the twins, baby finger prints, all four of us together, my parents, Algebra and Aurora with little Lily and then one of all of us together, even Frank had his picture up there. I hadn't changed much. Sure my hair was longer and I was a bit taller and leaner but that was about it. Same brow eyes and smart mouth. I smiled at myself, eyes flashing silver.

We will continue to be for a very long time. My beast said. I had to agree with her. I wasn't going anywhere.

When I brought the cake out I looked over at Algebra who had the camera ready. With the sun giving enough light and the backyard lights on it looked beautiful, especially with the blue glow the pool gave off. Seby and Saby both sat on Zaliver's lap, all three of them wrapped in a bundle of towels. I counted to three before lifting the top of the cake. It was a one time moment and yet there were thousands of flashes to catch it.

Both Algebra and I laughed at the look on Zaliver's face as he read the wording on the cake. Venom had a particular look on his face. Behind him I saw my mom shaking with laughter and my dad shook his head with amusement, some of the pack looked down slack-jawed while others had the same reaction as my parents.

Zaliver looked up at me with a mixture of expressions on his face, mainly amusement, but also a little annoyance mixed in with a glint in those eyes that had me closing my mouth but that didn't stop my shoulders from shaking. Perhaps it was because on the cake it read:

Happy Birthday to the island ancient one. May you forever be the oldest one in the room.

Making quick of the candles I motioned for everyone to sing and then went to stand behind him as he blew out the candles.

"Picture of the ancient ones family!" Algebra cried out in a croaky voice. Lily giggled making Aurora fake coughed to distract everyone.

I was going to stay where I was but in a maneuver I hadn't felt until I was already in place, Zaliver had me in between his legs and the twins on mine. I looked down to see both of their crooked grins directed

793

at me. I couldn't help but return it. A flash went off. When I looked up Algebra and Aurora were looking at the camera with smiles.

I went to stand up but felt Zaliver's hands tighten around my waist.

"The ancient one?" he said in a low voice.

I let out a wheezed and panicked laugh. When both Saby and Seby turned and then jumped from my lap at the same time I knew I was screwed. It was like everyone had been given, they probably were, an order to make way because I felt Zaliver stand and turn towards the now empty pool.

"No! Don't you dare!" I shrieked, digging my heels into the slippery ground. He laughed behind me, but didn't slow.

" Swimming!" I heard the twins scream excitedly.

"No! No swimming!"

"Swimming! Swimming!" they chanted.

"And here I was thinking my kids loved me," I muttered, trying to turn in Zaliver's arms to claw around him.

"Oh they do, so much that they want mommy to go swimming," Zaliver taunted.

"Zaliver—"

He picked me up and jumped into the pool with me clinging to him like a cat. When we made it to the bottom we swam up with me spitting out water and pulling my hair away from my face. Before I could splash him with water or better yet, drown him, I heard a pair of two little feet running around the wet ground. That had my instincts acting up, worried they would slip. Both of us turned in time to catch them as they flew at us. Seby landed in my arms while Saby landed in Zaliver's.

"Sebastian Vinnelo Azrala—"

"Sabrina Zendria Azrala—"

"Sorry!" both of them cried out at the same time, brown eyes turning blue and blue eyes turning brown. Both Zaliver and I looked at one another before turning back to them.\"As long as you know what you did wrong-" They both nodded their heads at us so hard their movements jerked us. It brought a reluctant smile to my face.

When they started motioning to one another and glancing at both of us I got the memo and looked away with a smile. Both Seby and Saby were always together, so I wasn't surprised to discover a few years ago that when they were both on the same mental frequency or emotional state that they connected to the point of, well, they had a bond that brought a whole new definition of twin connection. It was like they knew what the other was thinking before the other knew, themselves. It was hard to catch them ever angry at one another.

Zaliver kissed both of their cheeks before turning to face everyone.

"Feel free to eat the ancient ones cake," he said half sarcastically. When he turned back around I was looking down into the pool water with fascination.

"Ancient one? Really?"

I looked up and gave him an apologetic look. He rolled his eyes and discreetly looked down at the twins who were in some silent eye conversation, making funny faces at one another. Their eyes would slowly turn back to their normal color when they were done.

I held Seby securely and walked over to the edge of the pool to lean on it. When I felt a tug I saw Seby holding his sister's hand, tugging her so that Zaliver had to follow. He chuckled and did so. When he were both comfortably on the edge, both of them in our arms and kicking their feet in the water I leaned my head against Zaliver's shoulder.

"So what you wish for?"

When I heard his mouth open to speak I turned to give him an incredulous look.

"You can't just tell me what you wished for?" I said flabbergasted that he would just tell me.

"Why not? You asked me," He pointed out.

"So, you didn't have to tell me. What if it doesn't come true?" His face softened as he looked down at me. His blue eyes seemed to gleam off of the pool.

"It already has."

I felt myself soften to the core, love and so much more than I could hold with me flowing out. So much happiness filled our lives, I could understand why he couldn't wish for anything. We had everything already.

"Yeah, I guess it has." I smiled up at him. He leaned down and kissed my lips.

A small hand pushed him away. I looked down to see the twins making squishy faces. Looking over at Zaliver we both grinned and then began cooing, making kissy noises and kissing the twins as they shouted and began squirming.

It was a beautiful life.

I wouldn't wish for anything either.

Do you like werewolf stories?
Here's a sample of another story
you might enjoy!

ALPHA'S DIRTY LITTLE SECRET

SYMONE R.

CHAPTER I

AMIRA

Gazing at the several unknown faces, I began to feel as if I was living in the shadows once again. I was left bearing a secret that made me feel like I was living in a lie.

Innocent humans watched as our college professor continued to lecture about Accounting and Finance. I looked to my left; beside me was a girl. Her blonde hair was draped over her brown eyes as she continued to scribble insignificant pictures on her notebook. What amazed me the most was how unaware she was of the nonhuman creature seated only inches away from her.

She sighed. My useful heightened senses allowed me to listen to her heartbeat and breathing that would accelerate every time the professor searched for a student to answer a simple question. Her heart rate would regulate once the professor called someone else. She slouched in her chair, her eyes occasionally wandering off from her work to a boy sitting in the far corner of the room.

"Amira? Are you paying attention?" I looked to my right, finding the eyes of my friend, Eric.

Eric and I have been friends since we were thirteen. Six years later, we were still going strong. We had a lot of classes together over the years, so our friendship continued to grow. However, despite us being friends, I could never find it in myself to tell him who I really was. Or should I say, *what* I was.

"Yeah…no," I admitted before we both shared a low snicker.

"Eric, you know I got all of this stuff already," I reassured him, slouching down in my chair.

I was known to be very intelligent in school. Unlike most, it was very easy for me to remember and comprehend any given task. This skill has been very helpful to me.

"Well, then, if it's so damn easy for you, you can teach it all to me because I'm lost as hell." Eric sighed. His eyes narrowed in on the textbook in front of him as I chuckled at him.

"Okay, ladies and gentlemen, class dismissed," the teacher announced as she wrapped up her lecture. I stood from my desk.

Students began gathering their things before everyone scrambled out of the door.

"So, lunch on me today?" Eric offered.

"No, sorry. I have to help my mom prepare for this dinner we are having tomorrow. Just a few out-of-town guests." I sighed heavily.

"Okay, cool. Well, I'll text you tonight?"

"Sure."

*　　　*　　　*

The appetizing smell of food danced its way around me, clouding my nasal passages with the mouth-watering aroma of my mother's home-cooked meal.

I walked into the kitchen to see my mother running back and forth. She was cutting vegetables, stirring food in the pots, and measuring the temperature of whatever she was roasting in the oven.

"Mom, is it this serious?" She was acting as if the president was stopping by for dinner.

"Yes, sweetie. This is when you'll see your new alpha for the first time." My mother was more cheerful than the rest of us were.

It was amusing how my mother cared about the alpha's arrival more than the actual werewolves that lived here. I expected her to feel uncaring about his presence as if he was just another regular visitor, her being a human and all.

I guess being married to and being the mother of a werewolf really had her interested in the supernatural world. Unlike her, I couldn't care less about the werewolf society. I found human life to be much better. Accepting. I enjoyed not living under the command and authority of some male who was determined to show his dominance over everyone because of a title.

That was why I loved living in the city. Majority of our pack, including the alpha and beta, lived far out in the country somewhere.

Honestly, that's how I liked it. I loved being away from the group who allowed their title to get to their overgrown skull.

I preferred the distance. However, my father seemed to not feel the same way I do. Recently, he had invited the previous alpha and luna, and their son—the new alpha—over for dinner. Only my father could ruin such a beautiful thing.

"But Mom, they aren't coming until tomorrow," I reminded her again.

"I know, I know, but I prefer to get things done now."

I sighed. Looking over everything, I could see how she had handled things.

"You seem to have everything done." The chicken was roasting in the oven; the vegetables were boiling in the pots; and she seemed to be starting on dessert. "Call me if you need anything then."

I snatched up my bag from the kitchen counter. Reaching into the cupboard, I pulled a granola bar from the box before I left the kitchen.

I silently cursed my mother and father again. I don't even know why I have to be here. If I could, I would disappear before the guests even made it to town. Sadly, my father requested that I should be present for the attendees.

Why did I seem so against the presence of the new alpha? I would say our past was just a tiny piece of the reason that I wanted to disappear. Even though my mother said it's the first time meeting the new alpha, it's actually not. We had already met before he had taken over the title, alpha.

When I was about eight years old, my father and I would visit the main pack house for some business. Since my father was one of the strongest warriors of our pack, the previous alpha would need him by his side during decision-making.

That's when I had first met eleven-year-old Xavier, the soon-to-be alpha.

My father said—to keep us busy and out of their hair while he helped the alpha—Xavier and I should go play, and we did. Honestly, I thought Xavier was cute. I was actually very fond of him. Stupidly, I asked him if he felt the same way. Let's just say it was not the answer I hoped for.

To impress his friends, who were the children of other higher ranked members, he knocked me off the swing. I remembered crying on the ground as he and the other kids laughed before they left me soaking in my own tears.

That fucking bitch.

Yes, I knew that it happened many years ago, but for some reason, I just couldn't forget and forgive. I guess I just didn't take rejection or embarrassment too well. I still don't.

Luckily, after that, I never saw him again, and I was perfectly fine with it.

I quickly shook the thoughts off before I disappeared into the bathroom.

I stood in front of the mirror in my room after I finished taking a shower. I ran my hands down my hips as I stared at my reflection. I adored my frame. I didn't consider myself fit or slim like the other female werewolves I had encountered. Other she-wolves had a fit and athletic physique, the type of body that would look exceptional in anything. I, on the other hand, did not have that. I was a curvaceous woman—full breasts, thick hips and thighs without such a slim waist. I would always assure myself that I would soon diet. At least, after I finish off the pizza I was enjoying.

I began to smile. My full pink lips looked well with my silky smooth skin and brown eyes.

I pulled out my blow dryer and started drying my shoulder-length black hair. When my hair was already dry, I pinned it up and leaped into my bed. Turning my television on, I searched through various channels until I finally landed on a show I could finish my night with.

*   *   *

Wrapped up in my comforter, I felt at ease. No classes. No early morning wake-up calls. Just the perfect time to oversleep.

"Amira, wake up. Let's go the mall." I heard my mother's all too familiar voice as she pushed through my bedroom door.

"No, thank you," I rolled away from her. "It's too early."

"Too early? It's 12:30 in the afternoon. Now, get your butt up."

I turned to my mother and an annoyed snarl escaped me. She narrowed her eyes and shot me a warning glare before walking away. It was a warning, convincing me that her wrath was more powerful than my teeth.

"Make it an hour, or I'm coming back."

"Fine." I sighed.

I stayed in bed for another fifteen minutes; I just did not want to get up. Mustering up some energy, I swung my legs and sat up from the bed. Tired and drained, I dragged myself to my bathroom.

After finishing my routine, I picked up my bag and made my way downstairs.

"Hey, Dad," I greeted my father as I walked into the kitchen. He glanced up from his paper to meet my gaze.

"Hey, where are you two headed?"

"She's dragging me to the mall." I slipped into a chair beside him. I reached for his paper and pulled the comic section from the crumbled pile.

"Oh, good luck." I could sense the humor in his comment.

My father knew how things went when it involved accompanying my mother to the mall. He had found a way to get out of it. During their mall trips, he would make her shopping experience hell. He complained, dragged his feet, and gave opinions my mother found useless. Occasionally, he would become 'ill' during their mall runs.

I could only admire his tactics for escaping.

"Okay, sweetie, I'm ready."

"Okay." I sighed and stood up from my chair.

I followed my mother out to the car and got in. I slumped down in my seat as I listened to the vehicle's engine roar to life from under the hood. I slipped my earbuds on and drifted into my own thoughts the entire ride.

*   *   *

We roamed the mall for hours, not looking for a specific item. My mother just wanted to buy random things. With the help of my complaints, my mother wrapped up her shopping journey, and we finally left the mall.

"Sweetie, can you tell your father to come help with the bags?" I scowled at her. *What am I? A personal beeper?*

Reaching into our mind link, I urged for his assistance. A few seconds later, my father emerged from the front entrance. He grabbed my mother's bag, refusing to have her carry her own.

He should have joined us in our mall run then. With his petty whining, I would have been home already.

By the time we arrived home, I made my way to the kitchen and walked over to the refrigerator, pulling a bottle of water from the shelf. As I turned to leave, I witnessed my parents sharing an intimate kiss in the living room. "We all have rooms for that, people."

"Sorry, honey." My mother's cheeks flushed red as she pulled away from my father.

"You will understand once you find your mate," my father explained.

A mate. To us werewolves, our mate would be someone the moon goddess has blessed us with. A mate would be someone we plan to spend the rest of eternity with.

Love. A destined bond that was almost unavoidable and hard to break. My mother and father were mates. He shared his secret with her, and she accepted his life and him as well.

However, some weren't that blessed. Some were cursed. Some were given a mate who could be careless, cold-blooded, and downright disgraceful.

There could be some who don't want a mate. Some who would rather remain unrestricted than fall into the spell of the mate bond.

Rejection. Some would rather reject their mate; it's their way of freeing themselves from the world they consider a prison. However, it's not always accepted by the other. The rejected mate may not fully accept it, leaving them with a broken heart and the feeling of desertion. Some would begin to feel as though it's their own actions that caused the rejection, and feel self-loathe and hatred for their wolves. Finally, another dangerous aspect was pain, hatred, and even suicidal ideation.

Honestly, I didn't care about finding my mate. I didn't want to find some wolf who probably believed that I my only purpose was to bear his children and sleep with him. A man who would probably only use me as his chew toy. I couldn't allow someone to have so much control over me, so much power. And then give me so much heartache.

"No, thank you on the mate thing, Dad." A waved my hands frantically. I didn't want that curse.

"Honey, go, get dressed. Our guests should be arriving in about an hour." My mom pressed.

Shifting my eyes toward my father, I shot him a venomous glare once again.

"Oh, honey, you will love them. They are nice people, so relax."

Disagreeing with him, I picked up the small bags I had gotten from the mall and ran up to my room to prepare for an unwanted arrival.

If you enjoyed this sample, look for
Alpha's Dirty Little Secret
on Amazon.

AUTHOR'S NOTE

Thank you so much for reading *Lupus Deus*! I can't express how grateful I am for reading something that was once just a thought inside my head.

Please feel free to send me an email. Just know that my publisher filters these emails. Good news is always welcome. sophia_moore@awesomeauthors.org

I'd also love to hear your thoughts on the book. Please leave a review on Amazon or Goodreads because I just love reading your comments and getting to know you!

Can't wait to hear from you!

Sophia Moore

ABOUT THE AUTHOR

I'm a normal girl that daydreams about extraordinary things on a daily basis. My passion for reading began around middle school and became so much a part of me that I could not imagine a world without books. During my free time, when I'm not procrastinating, I like to play the piano, listen to music and find new worlds to jump into.

Printed in Great Britain
by Amazon